BERNARD MALAMUD

BERNARD MALAMUD

NOVELS AND STORIES OF THE 1960s

A New Life
The Fixer
Pictures of Fidelman: An Exhibition
Ten Stories

Philip Davis, *editor*

THE LIBRARY OF AMERICA

 See Note on the Texts on
page 889 for sources and acknowledgements.

The paper used in this publication meets the
minimum requirements of the American National Standard for
Information Sciences—Permanence of Paper for Printed
Library Materials, ANSI Z39.48—1984.

Distributed to the trade in the United States
by Penguin Group (USA) Inc.
and in Canada by Penguin Books Canada Ltd.

Library of Congress Control Number: 2013941527
ISBN 978-1-59853-293-7

First Printing
The Library of America—249

Manufactured in the United States of America

Contents

A NEW LIFE

For Alex
and Bernadette

Lo, levin leaping lightens
in eyeblink Ireland's westward welkin!

ULYSSES

S. LEVIN, formerly a drunkard, after a long and tiring transcontinental journey, got off the train at Marathon, Cascadia, toward evening of the last Sunday in August, 1950. Bearded, fatigued, lonely, Levin set down a valise and suitcase and looked around in a strange land for welcome. The small station area—like dozens he had seen en route—after a moment's activity, was as good as deserted, and Levin after searching around here and there, in disappointment was considering calling a taxi, when a man and woman in sports clothes appeared at the station. They stared at Levin—the man almost in alarm, the woman more mildly—and he gazed at them. As he grasped his bags and moved towards them they hurried to him. The man, in his forties, tall, energetic, with a rich head of red hair, strode forward with his hand outstretched.

"Sorry I'm late. My name's Dr. Gilley."

"S. Levin," Levin said, removing his black fedora, his teeth visible through his beard. "From the East."

"Good," beamed Gilley, his voice hearty. He indicated the tall, flat-chested woman in a white linen dress. "My wife."

"I'm pleased—" Levin said.

"I'm Pauline Gilley." She was like a lily on a long stalk.

"Let me help you with your bags," Gilley said.

"No, thanks, I—"

"No trouble at all."

He had grabbed both bags and now carried them around to his car, parked in front of the station, his wife and Levin hurrying after him. Unlocking the trunk, where two golf bags lay, one containing a brand new set of clubs, he deposited Levin's things.

Levin had opened the rear door but Pauline said there was room for all in front. He shyly got in and she sat between them.

"We were delayed at the golf course," she explained.

"Do you play?" Gilley asked Levin.

"Play?"

"Golf."

"Oh, no."

They drove a while in silence.

"I hope to learn some day," Levin said with a broken laugh.

"Good," said Gilley.

Levin relaxed and enjoyed the ride. They were driving along an almost deserted highway, in a broad farm-filled valley between distant mountain ranges laden with forests, the vast sky piled high with towering masses of golden clouds. The trees softly clustered on the river side of the road were for the most part deciduous; those crawling over the green hills to the south and west were spear-tipped fir.

My God, the West, Levin thought. He imagined the pioneers in covered wagons entering this valley for the first time, and found it a moving thought. Although he had lived little in nature Levin had always loved it, and the sense of having done the right thing in leaving New York was renewed in him. He shuddered at his good fortune.

"The mountains to the left are the Cascades," Pauline Gilley was saying. "On the right is the Coastal Range. They're relatively young mountains, whatever that means. The Pacific lies on the other side of them, about fifty miles."

"The Pacific Ocean?"

"Yes."

"Marvelous."

The Gilleys laughed. "We could drive over to the coast some time before Registration Week," Dr. Gilley said.

He went on amiably, "Seymour shortens to Sy—isn't that right?"

Levin nodded.

"My first name's Gerald and you already know Pauline's. People aren't too formal out this way. One of the things you'll notice about the West is its democracy."

"Very nice."

"And we're curious about everybody," Pauline said. "One can't help be in a small town. Have you any pictures of your family in your wallet? Or perhaps a sweetheart?" She laughed a little.

Levin blushed. "No pictures, no sweetheart."

He said after a minute, "No wallet."

They laughed, Pauline merrily, Gilley chuckling.

"Oh, look there!" She pointed toward the eastern mountains.

In the distance, a huge snow-capped peak rising above the rosy clouds reflecting the setting sun, floated over the darkish blue mountain range.

"Extraordinary," muttered Levin.

"Mt. Chief Joseph," Pauline said. "I knew you'd like it."

"Overwhelming. I—"

His heart was still racing from the sight when Pauline said, "We're almost in town. Would you like us to drive through the campus?"

"Tomorrow," Gilley said. He pointed under the setting sun. "That's Easchester we're coming to. The college is over there to the southwest. That tall building just over those trees is Chem Engineering. That one is the new Ag building. You can't see Humanities Hall, where we hang out, but it's in that direction there. We live about half a mile from the campus, about that way. You'll be living close in if you like Mrs. Beaty's house, about three blocks from the office, very convenient."

Levin murmured his thanks.

They were driving through downtown, and were, before he could get much of an impression, out of it and into a residential section of lovely tree-lined streets and attractive wooden houses. The many old trees and multitudes of green leaves excited Levin pleasantly. In a few minutes they had arrived in front of a two-story frame house, painted an agreeable brown, with a slender white birch on the lawn, its lacy branches moving in the summer breeze. What surprised Levin was the curb-strip planted thick with flowers the whole length of the house, asters, marigolds, chrysanthemums, he guessed; in his valise was a copy of *Western Birds, Trees and Flowers*, a fat volume recently purchased.

"This is our house," said Pauline, "although Gerald would prefer a ranch type."

"Someday we'll build," said Gerald. "She'd have a lot less housework," he said to Levin.

Though Levin liked the house, birch tree, and flowers, to enter a house after so long a time traveling slightly depressed him; he hid this as he followed Gilley along the flagstone path and through the door.

Pauline said she would whip up something for supper, nothing elaborate, as soon as the sitter had finished feeding the children in the kitchen.

"Care for a drink after your long journey?" Gilley asked Levin, winking.

Levin thanked him, no.

"Not even a short one?" he measured an inch with long thumb and forefinger.

"No, I really—"

"All right. Mind if I do?"

"Please, I—"

"How about beer?" Pauline asked. "Or if not that I can open an orange drink, or give you a glass of water?"

"Beer is fine," Levin said.

"I'd be just as happy to bring you water."

"I'll take the beer."

"There's a blue towel for you in the bathroom if you wish to wash."

She returned to the kitchen and Gilley drew the shade at the side window before he mixed martinis. Through the open blinds of the front window Levin admired a small purple-leaved tree in front of the house diagonally to the left across the wide street.

"Plum tree," Gilley said. "Pink flowers every spring."

"Beautiful." Levin, out of the corner of his eye, watched the man watching him.

When Pauline returned with the beer her husband raised his martini glass. "To a successful career for Sy."

"Cheers," said Pauline.

"Thank you." Levin's hand trembled as he held the glass aloft.

They drank, Levin drinking to himself before he knew he was doing it.

"Do you mind eating early?" Pauline asked. "It makes a longer evening. We've had to do that since the children."

"Please, as you desire."

He was sitting on the couch enjoying the beer and the room. It was a long room, tastefully furnished and curtained. On the wall hung a black and white print of a hunter shooting at a bird, and a Vermeer reproduction of a young woman. The shelved right wall was filled with books. On the kitchen side, the room was apparently for dining, and an old-fashioned round table stood there with three place settings and four chairs.

"TV?" Gilley asked. "The set's in my den."

"Later, Gerald," Pauline said. "I'm sure Mr. Levin has seen television."

"I didn't say he hadn't, but there won't be much time later. He's got to get settled."

"Don't have any worries on my account," Levin said.

"I'll drive you over to Mrs. Beaty's right after supper," Gilley said, pouring another martini. "She's got a good-sized room with a private entrance by way of the back yard. And there are kitchen privileges if you want them, Sy, damn convenient for eight o'clocks, which I can tell you you will have. She's a widow—nice woman, former grade-school teacher married to a carpenter; he died almost two years ago, I'd say—came from South Dakota, my native state. Funny thing, I spent my first week in this town, just eighteen years ago, in the same room she's offering you."

"You don't say," said Levin.

Gilley nodded.

"I'll be glad to have a look at it."

"If you don't like it you can come back here tonight," Pauline suggested.

Gilley seemed to be considering that but Levin hastily said, "That's so kind but I won't trouble you any more. The hotel is fine. You wrote me they have one here, as I remember?"

"Two—moderate prices."

"Fine," said Levin.

"Good. Let me freshen your beer."

"This is fine."

Pauline finished her drink and went into the kitchen.

"You're our twenty-first man, most we've ever had full-time in the department," Gilley said to Levin. "Professor Fairchild will meet you tomorrow afternoon at two. He's a fine gentleman and awfully considerate head of department, I'm sure you'll like him, Sy. He kept us going at full complement for years under tough budgetary conditions. Probably you've heard of his grammar text, *The Elements of Grammar*? God knows how many editions it's been through. The department's been growing again following the drop we took after the peak load of veterans, though we've still got plenty of them around. We put on three men last year and we plan another two or three, next. College registration is around forty-two hundred now, but we figure we'll double that before ten years."

He smiled happily at Levin and Levin smiled at him. Nice chap, very friendly. He put you at your ease.

"We've been hearing from people from every state in the Union. For next year I already have a pile of applications half a foot high."

"I'm grateful for—"

"You won't miss New York? This is a small town, Sy, ninety-seven hundred, and there isn't much doing unless you get outdoors or are interested in football and such. Season tickets for athletic events are modestly priced for faculty."

"No, I won't miss it," Levin said with a sigh.

"Pauline's been talking for years about visiting New York City."

"Yes?"

"I wouldn't want to stay too long. I don't take to cities well, I get jumpy after a while."

"I know what you mean."

"You seem pretty glad to leave?"

"I lived there all my life."

"I should say. Eight million people, that's seven more than we have in the whole state of Cascadia."

"Imagine," muttered Levin.

"We're growing, though, about three thousand a year."

Pauline set glasses on the table, then came out of the kitchen, carrying a casserole.

"Tuna fish and mashed potatoes," she said apologetically. "I hope you like it."

"Perfect," Levin said. He was abruptly very hungry. They sat down at the round table, for which he felt a surprising immediate affection. Pauline had forgotten the salad bowl and went in to get it. When she returned she served the casserole, standing. A child called from the kitchen. Distracted, she missed Levin's plate and dropped a hot gob of tuna fish and potato into his lap.

He rose with a cry.

"I'm so dreadfully sorry." She hastily wiped at his pants with a cloth but Levin grabbed it from her and did it himself. The operation left a large wet stain.

"I'd better change," he said, shaken. "My other suit is in my bag."

"I'll get it," Gilley said, his face flushed. "It's still in the trunk."

"Everything will get stone cold," Pauline said. "Gerald, why don't you lend Mr. Levin a pair of your slacks? That'll be quicker."

"I'd rather get my own," Levin said.

"Let him do what he wants," Gilley told his wife.

"There's no need for him to be uncomfortable till we get his suitcase in. Your gray slacks will go nicely with his jacket. They're hanging in your closet."

"Please—" Levin was perspiring.

"Maybe she's right," Gilley said. "It'd be quicker."

"I'll change in a minute once I have my suitcase."

"Gerald's pants will be less trouble."

"They won't fit. He's taller than I am."

"Roll up the cuffs. By the time you're ready to leave I'll have your trousers spot-cleaned and ironed. It was my fault and I'd feel much better if you both please let me work it out my own way."

Gilley shrugged and Levin gave up. He changed into Gerald's slacks in the bathroom.

While he was there Pauline tapped on the door.

"I forgot about your shorts, they must be damp. I have a clean pair of Gerald's here."

He groaned to himself, then said quietly, "I don't want them."

"Are you sure?"

"Positive."

Before leaving the bathroom Levin soaped his hands and face, dried them vigorously and combed his damp whiskers. When he came out he felt momentarily foolish in Gilley's baggy pants but the food, kept hot, was delicious, and he ate heartily.

My first night in the Northwest, Levin mused, sitting in an armchair after dinner. Who could guess I would ever in my life come so far out? He began to think about the past and had to press himself not to.

Gilley looks restless, he thought. I'd better give him back his pants and find some place to sleep.

"Stay a while," Pauline murmured. She was arranging red roses in a Chinese vase on the table.

"Yep," Gilley said. He was scanning the Sunday paper, one long leg resting on a hassock.

I could be wrong, Levin thought.

Pauline shut a window and rubbed her goose-fleshed arms. "Gerald, would you build a fire?"

"It feels like fall," she said to Levin.

Gilley, grunting, got up. He stuffed several balls of newspaper under the grate of the fireplace, crisscrossed kindling, and topped the pile with two wood chunks with thick mossy bark.

"Burns most of the evening that way," he said to Levin. "The heat of each oak piece keeps the other going. That's the secret of it."

He lit the paper and the blaze roared. The operation was interesting to Levin, even moving. He had rarely in his life stood at a fireplace, never before seen a fire made in one. If the room Gilley had mentioned had a fireplace he thought he would take it.

A door by the couch opened and two children who had come downstairs with the sitter entered the room. They had been bathed and pajamaed, and when the boy saw the fire he ran to it. He was a red-head with a pale face. The little girl, blondish like the mother, had sores on her arms and legs. Though she barely toddled she carried a kitten.

"This is Mr. Levin, Zenamae," Pauline said to the sitter. "He's the new English professor. Zenamae Sonderson, Mr. Levin."

Levin blushed. "Hardly a professor—" Pauline paid the girl and she left.

The boy, turning from the fire, took a good look at Levin and began to cry.

"Bet it's the beard," Gilley said.

Levin picked up a magazine and pretended to read. The child stopped crying. Pauline led him by the hand to the new instructor.

"Mr. Levin, this is Erik Gilley. Erik, Mr. Levin is a nice man all the way from New York City."

He was grateful to her.

The boy said something that sounded like "Tory?"

"No," said Levin in surprise, "I'm a liberal."

Pauline laughed. "He wants you to tell him a story."

Gilley grinned. "Gave yourself away that time, Sy."

Levin, smiling in embarrassment, offered to tell the boy a story.

"Me," said the little girl, letting the kitten go and coming closer.

"She's our baby, Mary," said Pauline. "Does she look like me, Mr. Levin?"

"Something like," he said. "I'm no judge."

She smiled and kissed the child.

"Better not bother with stories just right now," Gilley said. "We'll be leaving in five more minutes."

"You promised." Erik had climbed up on Levin's knees.

"What kind of story do you want?"

"Funny."

Levin tried to think what he knew that was funny. Pauline, with Mary on her lap, sat on the hassock, attentive. Gilley had drifted into his den and had the TV on.

Levin, scratching a hot right ear, began: "There was once a fox with a long white beard—"

Erik chuckled. In a minute he was laughing—to Levin's amazement—in shrieking peals. Levin snickered at his easy success, and as he did, felt something hot on his thigh. He rose in haste, holding the still wildly laughing child at arm's length as a jet of water shot out of the little penis that had slipped through his pajama fly.

Gilley came into the room. "Stop it, Erik!"

Pauline set Mary down, grabbed Erik and ran with him, his fountain streaming in a high graceful arc, into the bathroom.

Levin stood there in Gilley's pants, wet down his thigh, neither of them looking at the other. He felt desperate. I've got to get out before they hate me.

Pauline returned with wet mop and sponge.

"I guess you'd better change." She didn't look at him.

He nodded, depressed.

"I'll get your bag out of the car," Gilley said.

"There's no need to," said Pauline. "His trousers are dry.

You can change in the bathroom again, Mr. Levin. Just drop Gerald's slacks down the laundry chute. I'm awfully sorry."

"Nothing serious." Levin went to the bathroom and began to wash up.

Pauline tapped on the door. "I have a pair of Gerald's French-back shorts for you. Yours are probably damp. They ought to fit if you use the third button."

"I don't want them," he said.

"You'll be more comfortable."

"No."

She burst into tears. Levin opened the door and reached out his hand. He took from Pauline a pair of her husband's striped shorts.

When he left the bathroom, once more wearing his own pants, in a good mood and ready to go, the room was in order, high and dry, both kids upstairs in bed.

Pauline had pinned a rose on her white dress and was crocheting on the couch. Gilley was tying dry flies.

"Won't you have another cup of coffee, Mr. Levin?"

"Thanks, Mrs. Gilley, I'd better be off now."

"Please stay a little longer."

Levin glanced nervously at Gilley.

"Stay a while, Sy."

"If you say," he muttered. They were being polite out of embarrassment, he thought, and it annoyed him because he was worried about getting settled for the night.

But he stayed.

Erik wandered down the stairs and asked his father to go back up with him.

"All right," Gilley said to Levin. "And after that we'd better scoot over to Mrs. Beaty. She'll be wanting to get to bed."

"Agreed," said Levin.

Erik went to him and raised his arms.

"He wants to be picked up," Pauline said.

Levin, after hesitating, picked up the child.

Erik tugged at his beard. "Funny man."

"That's enough of that," said Pauline.

Gilley took Erik from Levin and carried him upstairs.

"There's no telling what next," she said.

"I had no objection."

She was silent. He inspected the book shelves and drew out a book.

She crocheted a while, then asked what he was looking at.

"*The American*, Henry James."

"Oh?" She got up, searched on the bottom book shelf, and came up with a reprint from an academic journal, which she handed Levin. Gilley's name was on the cover of a short article on Howells.

"He wrote it in graduate school," she said. "He was a teaching assistant and I was one of his students. Gerald was the only person of his year to have an article in *PMLA*, during his graduate career. I hoped he'd go on with scholarly papers but he says they're a bore."

"Is that so?"

She smiled almost sadly. "He's done a few textbook reviews here and there, but not much else. Gerald is an active type, too much so to write with patience. And there's no doubt he's lost some of his interest in literature. Nature here can be such an esthetic satisfaction that one slights others."

Levin instinctively shrugged.

"Life is so varied and what happens so often unexpected," Pauline said with a glance at him. "There's so much to do—to be done. I find myself—" She inspected the strip of lace she had crocheted, then went on, "If Gerald were among more people who were doing literary research and writing, I think he would too. Of course Dr. Fabrikant, in the department, is a scholar, but they don't take to each other for too many reasons to go into, and Gerald feels anyway that at Cascadia College—the kind of place this is—the emphasis should be on teaching. He's quite a popular lecturer."

"What kind of place—?"

"—He does many things and gets a lot of pleasure out of his life. He fishes—this is the country for it if you're interested; he's a wonderful dry fly fisherman, and I've seen other fishermen stop what they were doing to watch him. He also hunts pheasants and ducks and loves to watch athletic events. I never thought I would myself, but you'd be surprised how exciting these games can get. We generally have very good football and basketball teams, though not as high-powered as those in

California. And Gerald is also an excellent photographer. He's very talented at candid shots and has won all sorts of prizes in almost every category. Last year one of his pictures won a first prize at the State Fair. Let me show it to you."

She slid open a door at the bottom of a bookcase and got out a thick picture album which she brought to the sofa.

I'm in for it now, Levin thought.

Pauline turned to an enlarged photograph of an old farmhouse that looked like an upended shoe box. "'Pioneer Farmhouse,'" she read. "He's done a series of these all over the state. We go camping in summertime—I hate it but it's good for the kids—and he likes to hunt out these places and snap them. Gerald is in love with Americana. This is the sixth prize he's won with this particular subject."

"Very nice—"

She turned to the middle of the album. "Here he is with his sister when he was a boy in knickers in Abilene, South Dakota. Notice how alert he looks. Here's his father, a retired merchant. I take to the mother. They were here to see the children this summer."

She flipped back several pages, pausing at a portrait of a dignified-looking man with pince-nez and a grayish beard. "Papa," she said. "A wonderful man—very affectionate and maturely generous. He was a physician and literally lived the Hippocratic oath. Once when he was sick he got out of bed to attend a patient. The patient lived but poor Papa died. He was only fifty. It killed my mother."

"Ah—" said Levin.

"I lived afterwards with Papa's brother, in San Francisco. They're a wonderful family." She wiped one eye with a slender finger. He looked secretly but saw no dew.

On the next page, age twenty, she stood, in unearned innocence, on a hilly city street, shoulders touching a young man's with an expressionless face. She looked unhappy and wore a mousey fur coat and felt hat with an off-the-face brim.

"After your father died?" Levin asked.

"A year and a half. This was a boy I was engaged to for six months, before I married Gerald. He had won a Guggenheim and was off to Europe to study medieval history but I knew he was tired of me and I wouldn't see him again. I never did."

"He looks a little stupid to me."

"He was a nice boy. I guess I hadn't much to offer at that time. I'm one of those people who developed slowly."

She put the album aside, removed one shoe, then the other, and raising her legs drew them close to her body. She had pinned a rose to her poor chest. Why not two, he thought, one for each flat side? Was this why the medievalist had gone to Europe, to escape the American prairie? It did bother a bit, the observer conscious that nature had cheated where it hurt most. Yet she was attractive, he thought, with shapely legs if big feet, the long boats on the floor the indisputable evidence. And her face, compared to the girl's in the picture, was a mature improvement over age twenty. Studying her, though pretending not to, Levin thought her, despite her longness and lacks, an interesting-looking woman. She had large dark eyes in a small face, much helped by a frame of thickish straight blonde hair that touched her shoulders. The lips were well-formed, her nose, as if sniffing expectancy, touched on long and in flight. She was wearing pendant earrings; he realized she had put them on and changed her shoes, since coming home. Levin guessed she was for sure a good ten years younger than her husband. He had thought that when she told him she had been Gilley's student, but now the sense of her youth surprised him.

I was tired, he thought.

"And now that you know about me," she said, reaching for a cigarette, "what about you?"

Levin felt himself react against her question—had made no bargains. He was, besides, on edge to be settled and alone.

But her smile was innocent enough. "What I would like to know," she said, "is why have you come so far? Was it some special reason, or just that the job happened to be here?"

Resisting much there was to say, he replied truthfully. "When the offer came I was ready to go." Levin rubbed his hands with a handkerchief. "What's there to say that hasn't been said? One always hopes that a new place will inspire change—in one's life."

"Have you been to many places?"

"The opposite is true."

He cracked his knuckles as she fiddled with her rose.

He went on although advising himself not to. "My life, if I may say, has been without much purpose to speak of. Some blame the times for that, I blame myself. The times are bad but I've decided I'll have no other."

He laughed immoderately and stopped abruptly. After a minute's silence he went on, "In the past I cheated myself and killed my choices." Levin mopped his brow. "Now that I can—ah—move again I hope to make better use of—things.

"That sums me up." He got up and began to walk back and forth in the room.

"What better use?" she ultimately asked. Her voice seemed diminished.

"I've reclaimed an old ideal or two," Levin said awkwardly. "They give a man his value if he stands for them." He stopped pacing. "If you'll excuse me, that's about all I care to say on the subject. Too many abstract words make me self-conscious."

Pauline seemed to be listening to something going on in another part of the house. She asked, "How long have you been teaching?"

"Two years—in a high school," he confessed. "I was twenty-six when I realized I wanted to teach, a late insight. One day I thought, What you do for others you can do for yourself. Then I thought, I can do it teaching."

She yawned behind her fingers.

He was irritated by her long empty shoes on the floor.

"You remind me of somebody," she said.

Levin yawned too. "Excuse me—the long train ride. I didn't sleep so well."

"Gerald will be right down."

He nodded listlessly.

"I hope you won't be disappointed in us, Mr. Levin. In the College and the town. Easchester can be lonely for single people—I don't mean the college students, their world isn't real. Someone from a big city might be disappointed here. You have no idea how sheltered we are, landlocked, and bland."

"Not me, I've had too much—"

She put out her cigarette. "I had a terrible time my first few years here. We miss a lot through nobody's fault in particular. It's the communal sin of omission. People here are satisfied. I blame it on nature, prosperity, and some sort of laziness, mine too, but for God's sake please don't quote me. Otherwise it's a lovely town, good will abounds, and there are many advantages for family living." She smoothed her skirt. "But for someone without a wife and children, maybe you ought to try San Francisco or Seattle."

"I've had my fill of cities," Levin replied. "For a change I want the open sky on my head."

"And the gentle rain?"

"It rains here?"

"It does. It almost drove me mad at first but I've learned to live with it. The trick is no longer to love the sun. Didn't Gerald write you about the rain?"

"No."

"About our community?"

"No."

"About the College?"

"A few words."

"He ought to have. It rains, for instance, most of the fall and winter and much of spring. It's a spongy sky you'll be wearing on your head."

"You can't have everything."

"To be fair I must also tell you the sun may shine for days on end in winter if a freeze sets in. At the same time it's not like Eastern cold, and Gerald wears a trench coat all year round. Many Cascadians want rain and warmth rather than sunlight and cold. But our summers, except rarely, are practically flawless. Even Californians come here then. There are people here, originally from the Plains states or the Midwest, who swear Easchester is paradise. Gerald is one of them. Wherever he goes he wants to come home."

A mild heaviness had settled on Levin's spirit. He felt he had talked too much about himself and was worried what she might repeat to her husband. Who could guess what a stranger would make out of his unguarded remarks about his past; he might already have endangered his career.

"I really must go."

Gilley came downstairs, yawning, his red head lighting the apple-green wall, one side of his face creased.

"Fell asleep in Erik's room."

"What did he want?"

"Company—he was a little scared."

"Of the dark?"

"Ghosts," Gilley said.

"Ghosts? That's new," she said.

"I guess we ought to go," Levin suggested.

"Sure thing," said Gilley. "I'll get my keys."

"Oh, my heavens, I didn't notice how late it's gotten," said Pauline. "Won't Mrs. Beaty be sleeping now, Gerald?"

Gilley held up his wrist. "By George, you're right, it's past ten. We'll have to make it tomorrow instead, Sy. My fault, I'm sorry."

"I'll go to a hotel," Levin said. "I had planned to anyway."

"Why waste five dollars?" Pauline asked. "We have a spare room, and in the morning Gerald can run you over to Mrs. Beaty's."

"I wouldn't want to bother you."

"You're no bother, Mr. Levin. It'll just take a minute to put a blanket on the bed." She ran up the stairs in stocking feet.

"Please—" Levin called after her.

"Give up, Sy," advised Gilley. "A woman's will. Drink?" he asked.

"No."

"It'll relax you."

"I'm relaxed."

"Good. Professor Fairchild'll love you. He doesn't touch liquor himself. His wife is first vice-president of the Anti-Liquor League. Mrs. Feeney's president, that's the recently retired dean's wife. Mind if I do?"

"Please—"

Gilley poured some Scotch into a glass and went into the kitchen for water. "Sy," he said warmly when he returned, "I bet you'll like the department and I'm sure we'll like you. We're a pretty nice bunch of friendly people engaged in the common endeavor. You'll find the comp staff particularly is nice—no false pretenses or such. Comp, as I wrote you, will be your program, plus one remedial grammar course which Avis Fliss will give you the dope on when she gets back next month. I will say this, that if you stay on here comp is what you'll be teaching till you get your doctorate—that's your union card if you want to stay in college teaching. After that you'll be given a lit class or two."

"I had hoped to teach literature," Levin sighed.

"I personally prefer teaching comp to lit. More satisfaction, I've found. You can just see these kids improving their writing from one term to the next, and even from one paper to the next. It isn't easy to notice much of a development of literary taste in a year."

"I suppose not—"

"We feel we make progress in composition. Morale is high, everybody works together—a nice bunch. You should see how we function getting finals out of the way and grades in. No problem children, if you know what I mean."

Levin nodded.

"The one or two we have around are in lit. I was very glad to be appointed director of comp some years ago and focus my attention on it. It's been an invigorating experience." He paused, seemed about to say more, then took a drink. "You'll like us all."

"I'm sure," said Levin.

"Good."

"Bad," Pauline said, coming down the stairs.

"Who's that?" asked her husband.

"Why didn't you tell Mr. Levin about the rain? I'll bet he came without a raincoat."

"No, I have one," said Levin, "and an umbrella."

"We have no more rain than you have in New York State," Gilley said, "only it's distributed more evenly. Anyway, it keeps Cascadia green."

"It's green enough," Pauline said. She put her arm around Gilley. He looked at her with affection.

Nice people, Levin thought, a real home. I shouldn't regret having to spend the night here.

"We'll get your bags, Sy." Gilley, putting down his glass, noticed the picture album on the table. "What's this out for?"

"I wanted Mr. Levin to see your prize-winning picture at the State Fair."

"Oh, that," Gilley said. He seemed momentarily lost in thought, then cheered up. "Got it with my Leica on a moderately bright day. I used Plus X on f11 at one one-hundredth of a second. Care to see my cameras sometime, Sy? Pauline bought me a Polaroid for my birthday."

"I don't know anything about them."

"Photography's not hard to learn. It's a satisfying and useful hobby. Come on, let's get the bags."

Levin went outside with him and almost cried out. In the amazing night air he smelled the forest. Imagine getting this for nothing. He drew in a deep wavering breath as he gazed at the stars splashed over the immense dark sky.

"There's your Big Dipper," Gilley was saying, "and that's the North Star. That way is Seattle, British Columbia, Alaska, and then the North Pole."

"North," said Levin, with a throb in his throat. "What profound mystery. You go north till there are no men. Imagine the silence, the cold, the insult to the human heart."

"You're a bit of a poet, Sy. The other way is San Francisco, and if you're interested, L.A."

Gilley unlocked the car trunk and got out the suitcases and golf bags. "We'll take one of each." He shut the trunk, paused a minute, then said to Levin, "Just this small matter, Sy. Do you always wear that beard?"

Levin looked at him in embarrassment. "I have for the past year. It's—er—given me a different view of myself." He laughed a little.

"Then it's not permanent?"

"I can't say just yet. It depends on how things work out—"

"I'll tell you why I mentioned it. I respect beards but some of your students may think you're an oddball. It doesn't take much to set them against a teacher."

"Some of my best professors wore beards," said Levin. "Americans have often worn them."

"Yes, but not so much since the safety razor. This is a sort of beardless town. No one on the faculty wears one that I know of. The administration is clean shaven. It's usually the students who will grow them. A lot of sophomores encourage whiskers for their spring carnival and they're a raggy, tacky-looking lot."

"I have a picture of Abraham Lincoln I could hang up."

"Well, suit yourself. I just thought I ought to mention it to you. The president's wife was saying only the other day every time she lays eyes on a beard the thought of a radical pops up in her head."

Levin guffawed.

Gilley beamed.

The new instructor carried in his valise and Pauline's clubs; Gilley, the suitcase and his new clubs.

Imagine me carrying golf clubs, Levin thought. Already he had done things he had never before done in his life.

In his room he removed Gilley's striped shorts and in the upstairs bathroom searched for the laundry chute to dispose of them. He located it in the hall at the top of the stairs but the door was nailed fast, probably to keep the kids from falling in. In robe and slippers he went downstairs to the other bathroom and got rid of them there.

Levin brushed his teeth, took a quick bath, soaping himself thickly, and combed his beard to a fine point. On the stairs, through the slightly open bedroom door he caught a glimpse of the Gilleys, man and wife, embracing in their nightshirts.

Standing a moment later, at the curtained window of his room, Levin gazed at the moonlit mountains in the west, more frighteningly higher than he had remembered. In the back yard a birch tree leaned to the left, its symmetry spoiled by its bias. Levin was at first too excited to sleep, but even as he contemplated the possibilities of the future he fell into slumber. He heard Erik calling "Papa" and tried to rouse himself, but then he heard a woman's steps coming up the stairs. He dreamed he had caught an enormous salmon by the tail and was hanging on for dear life but the furious fish, threshing the bleeding water, broke free: "Levin, go home." He woke in a sweat.

"I can't," he whispered to himself. "I can't fail again."

On the point of sleep he had the odd feeling he was being covered with a second blanket. Or maybe that was what she was doing to the children across the hall.

"God save us all," he muttered through his beard.

LEVIN SAW himself fleeing with both heavy bags when he learned the next morning that Cascadia College wasn't a liberal arts college. Gerald Gilley gave him the news, one long leg, thick-ankled in home-knit argyle socks, amiably dangling over the arm of a chair in Levin's newly acquired room at Mrs. Beaty's, complete with fireplace and optional private entrance. The new instructor had waked at the Gilleys in despair, typical of him in a strange place (it often amazed Levin how past-drenched present time was), but when, as he was putting on his new-suit pants, he saw that last night's high-walled mountains had shrunk drastically—their vast height illusion, a trick of clouds massed above the peaks—his mood changed and he heartily enjoyed breakfast. "Come see us often," Pauline Gilley had waved, standing by the birch tree and lifting little Mary to wave as Levin and her husband drove off in his Buick. Afterwards Levin had liked the old landlady and the large light room she showed them, but Gilley's news disturbed him.

Though he tried to seem casual, Levin had risen from his chair. "Why I thought—I was positive—this was a liberal arts college."

"I guess you didn't stop to examine the catalogue I sent you," Gilley said.

"Did you? I never got—"

"That's too bad, probably reached you after you had left. I guess I sent it out late in the rush of summer school closing. Anyway, if you had read it you'd have understood, from the section in front about our history, that we are mostly a science and technology college. We were founded in 1876—next year we celebrate our 75th charter anniversary—as an agricultural and vocational community college, but after ten years the state took it over, and to the original schools of ag for men and home ec for women, added forestry, animal husbandry, every kind of engineering you can think of, and of course the pure sciences, and others. We also had the liberal arts here, beginning around 1880, but we lost them shortly after the First World War."

"Lost them?" Levin, feeling behind him, unsteadily resumed his seat.

"They were taken from us, Sy. I won't go into the whole long story but there's a history of some nasty pitched battles for funds between us and our sister institution, Cascadia University at Gettysburg. —That, if you have checked the map, is our capital city, a hundred miles north of here, where they still rib us as 'southerners,' to say nothing of 'aggies' and 'hay palace.' Politics get steaming hot every biennium when the state budget is in the works, and I guess some of our alumni took it into their heads that it might make things easier all around to bring CU right down here to Easchester—they're the younger institution, 1878, and we have a lot more land than they do—and incorporate us both into one big super-university with one physical plant, which would, of course, have saved the taxpayers lots of money in the long run. Well, for too many reasons to mention, the plan didn't come off. Their alumni in the legislature raised a stink—they've always had the law and journalism schools and as a result can influence public opinion almost any way they want—and they got their own bill through, separating CC and CU more than we were in the first place. There was talk—as I've many times heard the story—of removing *us* to the Gettysburg campus, but then they decided to settle for certain punitive measures, which in this case were nothing less than cutting out our upper-level courses in the liberal arts, which people here thought weren't so important anyway, so we'd be two absolutely different institutions and theoretically uncompetitive. To make it look fair, and at the insistence of some of our boys in the legislature and two or three influential lumbermen in town, they had to part with their upper-level science courses. Now the dirty part of the deal was that during World War II they got all their science back on the ground that it served the national interest, while we never did get back the liberal arts—"

"A dirty shame." Levin was on his feet again. "The liberal arts—as you know—since ancient times—have affirmed our rights and liberties. Socrates—"

"That's how these things go. It's best to be philosophical about it."

"Democracy owes its existence to the liberal arts. Shouldn't there be—er—some sort of protest?"

"I appreciate your attitude," Gilley said, "but there isn't much that can be done about it now. Due to the fact that our graduates land so many influential jobs in the state, and since our athletic teams are usually better than theirs, we have a larger student registration than the University, which annoys them no end. And they also haven't forgotten that during the Depression they lost a lot more staff positions than we did here, and we lost plenty, believe me. They still think of those days, though a lot of the old timers who have always hated us have died off. They're afraid if we keep on gaining at the rate we have since the end of the war, they'll lose out percentage-wise in funds for buildings and faculty salaries, so you can bet your bottom dollar that as soon as somebody starts talking about bringing liberal arts majors back here they get hopping sore and start telegraphing the legislature. Frankly, it's a bread and butter proposition and you can't really blame them. We'd do the same in their place."

"But that's fantastic," Levin said, "—ah—isn't it? How can we—if you'll excuse my making myself familiar—teach what the human spirit is, or may achieve, if a college limits itself to vocational and professional education? 'The liberal arts feed our hearts,' this old professor of mine used to say." Levin laughed self-consciously.

"Don't get me wrong," Gilley said patiently. "We do have lower-level liberal arts courses here, though not many or in much variety. Still and all, there are departments of English, art, religion, history, speech, philosophy, modern languages, et cetera, on the campus. I will have to admit that the great majority of our boys and girls don't seem to be much interested in these subjects and take only what they have to. If they insist on more, they have to transfer elsewhere, usually to Gettysburg—and we don't go out of our way to encourage that. We have to handle it that way because the Higher Education Committee of the legislature just won't recommend an investment in a double liberal arts program in the two big state institutions of higher learning."

"But didn't you just say that full schools of science exist in both places?" Levin asked.

"They do but pure science has always been considered part of the liberal arts, and besides that's 'necessary duplication' because we have the Russkies to think about. What are you still standing for, Sy?"

"Excuse me." Levin sank into his chair. "I was just going to say—if you'll pardon me, I realize I'm a stranger—but I don't see how this situation can go on without weakening us in the long run. Democracy is in trouble. How are our students supposed to—" His right ear, when he absently touched it, felt on fire. Levin ceased speaking and gnawed his beard at the lip.

Gilley, lifting his leg off the chair, sat back. "I like your enthusiasm, Sy, but I think you'll understand the situation better after you've been here a year or two. Frankly, though I agree with some of the things you just said, Cascadia is a conservative state, and we usually take a long look around before we commit ourselves to any important changes in our way of life. You might keep in mind that education for an agrarian society, which is what we are—the majority of our state legislators come from rural areas—is basically a 'how to work' education. And if you've been keeping up on your reading on the subject, more and more liberal arts colleges in America are going in for more and more vocational subjects."

"I think they're making a serious mistake—"

"That's not to say that we won't be making some changes here, but most of us at Cascadia agree there's no sense hurrying any faster than most people want to go. If you push too hard you arouse resentment and resistance, and the result is the changes you are pushing for are resisted too. We've seen that happen too often in the past. Also keep in mind that a lot of very fine upstanding people in this community don't give two hoots for the liberal arts."

The new instructor, though suspecting he ought to drop the subject, said, "Isn't that where—er—good leadership comes in?"

"I'd say we have just as good leadership here as you people have in the East."

Levin bit his tongue.

Gilley, after a moment, rose with a smile. "All I can say, Sy, is I hope you didn't write to the wrong place when you wrote us for a job. Some people get us mixed up with our Gettysburg adjunct, and vice versa."

Holy mackerel, Levin thought. He had written to both Cascadia colleges and had probably confused the other, which had turned him down, with this.

"I'm glad to be teaching here," he said.

"Good," said Gilley. "Don't forget Professor Fairchild expects you this afternoon."

They shook hands and Gilley left by the outside stairs.

Levin sat long in his chair, tormenting himself for being the man he was. Why am I always committing myself before I know what it's all about? What's my fantastic big hurry?

"Anyway," he muttered as he began to unpack his bags, "it's a start."

Considering that he had just got his M.A. at thirty, and had only high school teaching experience to offer, Levin felt it was the greatest good luck that he had landed an instructorship in any college. Here if he watched his step and picked up two years of experience—the director of the N.Y.U. employment office had advised—and a couple of good recommendations, he shouldn't find it too hard to move on to a department where he could teach some literature, particularly if he began his Ph.D. work next summer. Wondering what Gilley would say if he knew his newly hired hand had been turned down, not only by the University at Gettysburg, but by at least fifty other colleges across the country, Levin felt a surge of gratitude to him for having given him, after so many failures and frustrations, an opportunity to begin his chosen career.

After a pleasant hour of wandering on the campus, Levin located Humanities Hall across the street from the Student Union at the corner of the college quadrangle. H-H, as it was designated in the catalogue, was a large gray clapboard structure with a huge leafy maple tree on its north lawn; it had been a women's dormitory before World War I, then had been converted into a "Museum of Pioneer Artifacts." After World War II it had been cleared out and rebuilt and now housed the English, speech and philosophy departments; English on the second and half of the third floors, according to the catalogue. Shortly before two, Levin went up the bannistered steps of the small, pediment-roofed porch, and slowly up a flight of creaking inside stairs. He dreaded interviews.

The long-halled second floor was divided into classrooms on one side of the stairs, and facing rows of offices on the other. Levin found the secretary's office but she wasn't there although a cup of hot coffee steamed on her desk. He waited five impatient minutes, then looked around to see if he could find her. Diagonally across the hall, at the very end of the building, he peeked through an open door and discovered Gerald Gilley. The director of composition was sitting in shirt sleeves behind an enormous cluttered desk in the center of a large green room loaded with bookcases and filing cabinets. He was cutting pictures out of *Life* with a pair of shears with blades a foot long.

Gilley glanced up at Levin absent-mindedly, placed him, and said pleasantly, "Come for your appointment, Sy?"

"I was wondering whether to go right into Professor Fairchild's office? The secretary seems to have stepped out a minute."

Gilley clipped a picture from the magazine, snipped four sides, and filed it in a thick folder.

"Future book," he told Levin.

"Illustrations?"

"Picture book of American lit." He cut into another page. "Like the idea?"

"Fine," said Levin.

"I thought the students would want to see what some of our writers looked like, the houses they lived in and such. Most of them can't tell Herman Melville from the Smith Brothers on the cough drop box."

Levin smoothed his beard. "Great stuff."

"Milly probably went to the ladies' room. She's been having trouble with her kidney. Come on, I'll introduce you."

He started directly across the broad corridor but in midstream changed his mind and asked Levin to follow him. Gilley tapped lightly on a door a bit farther up the hall, waited thirty seconds, then shook his head. "Guess he's not back yet. I had an airmail letter saying he might make it today from Carmel. This is George Bullock's office. He's a very sociable chap, city type like you, only he was born in L.A. George makes things happen instead of waiting for them to. He also has private means, which does no harm if you can manage it. You'll like

Jeannette too, that's his wife, originally from Las Vegas, a real stunner. They give some lively parties."

He knocked again, to make sure.

"A dozen of our crew is up on the third floor," Gilley said, "instructors like yourself, most of them in their twenties. I like to keep them together because they have a lot in common, but everybody usually visits in the coffee room sometime during the day. Come on, I'll show you where it is."

They went across the hall to a doorless room that looked like a kitchen.

"Very convenient," Levin murmured.

In the open cupboard a long line of white coffee mugs hung from hooks, each cup with a name written on it in India ink.

"Sometime I'd like to put an espresso machine in here," Gilley mused.

Levin nodded, studying the man with interest.

"People drop in for coffee between classes, or when they're keeping office hours. It's just the thing when you need a break. Milly starts the pot boiling first thing in the morning. Professor Fairchild is a steady customer—comes in at ten, right after his Shakespeare, and again at three, after his nap."

"I prefer tea to coffee," Levin said.

"Let me show you where we keep the tea bags. Right here. Also cocoa. Milly collects a dollar and a half a month, and that's for doughnuts too. What beverage you drink makes no difference to us. Meeting here during the day gives us all a chance to visit informally and relax with each other. Now let me show you the comp room."

"Comp room?"

"That's right." This was, once more across the hall, a windowless cubicle lined with shelves divided into individual filing slots, each partly filled, Gilley showed Levin, with graded student themes.

"This was the boss's idea. Once we collect them, the students can't pass them around for their friends to copy. I suppose you've heard about fraternity files?"

"Couldn't they keep carbons of the compositions?"

"Most are too lazy to. Also, having this room, if you don't mind my saying so, sort of keeps the instructors on their toes, because they know Orville—that's Professor Fairchild—or I, can come in here and count the number of papers they've assigned. We ask for six the first term, and eight each, the second and third. We're on the quarter system here, three terms during the year and the fourth is summer school."

"What happens when the slots are full?"

"Milly clears them out just about this time every year, and Marv Beal burns 'em, then we're ready for fall term. Marv is janitor of this building and knows more about Cascadia's team performances than anyone around, including George or me. The only thing I'd warn you is he's very talky once he gets started."

Gilley pulled the door shut. "Opens with the common key. Remind me to give you one before you go. It works for all our offices on the second and third floors, with the exception of Orville's and mine." He glanced to the right, considered something, then said, "I guess you ought to meet Joe Bucket."

Gilley rapped on the door at the end of the hall before the stairs and listened.

"He was here about twenty minutes ago, picking up his mail. I guess he's gone home to his house."

"Excuse me?"

Gilley smiled. "He's been building it for years, a board here, a brick there. Makes you wonder if he'll ever get it done, or for that matter, his dissertation. That's come back three times so far for revisions, and he can't seem to get them right though he passed his orals first shot. Maybe it's his subject matter—Laurence Sterne." He shook his head. "They moved out of the shack they were in for years, camped in the basement of the new place another six months and now have the upstairs working, plus an additional bedroom because the kids keep coming—five, though they aren't Catholics. Anyway, the house is about done."

"That's surprising—an English professor building his own house."

"A lot do it here. Some of the married students start houses and never take their degrees. When they flunk out they sell the house and use the capital to start a business. Lucky for Joe he was one of Orville's good students, and Orville has sort of kept an eye on him. This past year he promoted him to assistant professor."

Levin sighed. "My two hands are practically useless."

"We'll get you doing things, Sy."

"Not a house. I wouldn't know where to begin."

"Maybe golf? We have a fine nine-hole course."

"Maybe fishing. I've enjoyed Izaak Walton."

"Good," said Gilley. "Let's go back to my office."

They walked down the hall and the director of composition hesitated at the office between Bullock's and his. "This is Dr. Fabrikant's. He's the senior man after me."

"The one who teaches the course in liberalism in American literature?"

"How'd you know that?"

"I looked at a copy of the catalogue in the library before I came up here."

Gilley knocked curtly and waited.

"Not in?" Levin whispered.

Gilley winked. "Hard to say," he whispered. "He's the department scholar. A bit of a hermit."

"Really?"

He knocked again. "He doesn't mingle much around the office. When he isn't taking notes or something, he's usually home riding his horse. Let's go."

Levin, concerned about the time, hoped they were going straight to Professor Fairchild's office, but the director of composition, without warning, reversed his field and walked quickly up the hall to a door opposite the comp room.

He fished a key out of his pants pocket. "We used this for storage last year but Marv has just cleared it and neatened it up."

The new instructor secretly looked at his watch as Gilley opened the door and snapped on the light. The office was a small one with a single window and was furnished with a new desk, file case, and two chairs. Through the window Levin caught a view of the long green quadrangle, and beyond that, above the fir trees at the edge of the campus were the western mountains.

"Beautiful."

"This is yours, Sy."

"Mine? Holy smoke, I—"

"Don't say a word," Gerald said. A muscle in the corner of his mouth flickered.

"Whoever expected anything so wonderful? I figured I would have to share a place with somebody."

"That's usually the case with a new man, but you're a lot more mature, especially with your beard, than some of our crewcut boys upstairs, so I thought I would keep you down here with us."

"That's very kind. I've dreamed for years of being a college professor. This is so—" He could say no more.

"Glad to help those dreams along."

Gilley remarked, after an emotional minute: "This office used to belong to someone by the name of Leo Duffy, and the less said the better, but you'll probably hear about him so I'll just say who he was. He was here for a year in '48–'49, a sort of disagreeable radical who made a lot of trouble. Among his wackinesses was the habit of breaking his window panes and I finally put one in of thicker glass which, you notice, he cracked anyway—don't ask me how or why. When he first came here, Orville took a shine to him and assigned him this office. He treated him like a son and for all his pains got headaches. I was more than thoughtful to him too." He had to work his throat clear of hoarseness. "After he left—by invitation, I should say—the only man this department has ever employed who got publicly disgraced, Orville had this office turned into a storage room, but he agreed to reconvert it when I told him how tight space was getting. Ferris Farper and someone else upstairs had their eye on it but I kept it for you." He handed Levin the key.

"I am most grateful."

"We want you to like it here."

"I know I will—"

"While we're at it," Gilley said, "your department assignment is you're chairman of the textbook committee. Bucket, Jones, Millard Scowers and Carson Fitch are on it too. I'll send you a memo next week."

"Me?" Levin said, uneasily. "Thanks very much but I—I really don't know the first thing about college textbooks. To perform—er—competently on this committee, I'll have to make a study of available texts in the field. Couldn't you for the time being make me just a regular member of the committee, and then after I get to know the books, why maybe then I could—"

"You're obviously conscientious," Gilley said, "and I wouldn't advise you to worry at all about the textbooks. You'll get to know them as you go along. The salesmen call and they'll send you what they hope you're looking for. What with *The Elements* and *Elements Workbooks*, Forms A, B, C, for regular, and D for remedial classes, in use, all we really have to worry about is a new freshman reader once in a while. We've kept *Science in Technology* as our reader for the last five years because it's been popular with the students. For the lit classes Orville usually picks the texts himself with an occasional assist by Bullock, Kuck, or Merdith Schultz—his is the office next door to yours, opposite Bucket's, but his wife has been seriously sick and he isn't around much more than he has to be. Anyway, if you take the time to examine the books that come in the mail—just thumb through them—you'll more than do your job."

"I will and thanks for everything." Levin looked at his watch. "Wow, it's ten after. My appointment was for two."

"Nothing to worry about," Gilley said calmly. "I told Orville I'd be showing you around first."

"I like to start out right." He tried not to laugh but did.

"You have. We'll go right away. Since talking with you I have confidence in your ability to do a good job. As I said, we're looking for people who can hold up their end of it and keep the department running smoothly. This is a fine place to start your college teaching, and if you're our type, it's a good place to stay. We don't pretend we're anything more than a typical American state college. The atmosphere is relaxed. There's no 'publish or perish' hanging over everybody's head. There are no geniuses around to make you uncomfortable. Life is peaceful here—people deserve that after all we've gone through in the last generation. We don't ask more than that a man does his work conscientiously—his share of it. What we don't want around are troublemakers. If someone is dissatisfied, if he doesn't like what we do, if he doesn't respect other people's intimate rights and peace of mind, the sooner he goes on his way the better. If he likes it here and wants to stay on, at the rate we're growing I'm sure we can keep him. We don't offer the best of salaries but we do advance people in not too long a time, and once you become an assistant professor you're on permanent tenure. If you're the type I think you are, Sy—and so, incidentally, does Pauline—you can be sure of a worthwhile career here. On the other hand, if you don't like the climate, let's say, and want to go elsewhere, the experience you get here will make it that much easier for you. That's up to you and all right with us."

He said in afterthought, observing his shoe, "We've got a new dean, the man who replaced Dean Feeney, and I guess he seems to want to make some changes here and there. Well, they may be good ones and they may not, but I've heard him say we'll need some first-class people for the responsible jobs."

Levin felt oddly wrung out. "Thanks, but could we go in now? I hate to be late—"

"Righto."

But in the hall, Gilley introduced him to a gray-haired man in coveralls, holding a broom. "This is Marv Beal. He'll be sweeping your office."

Levin shook hands with the janitor.

"He get his athletic season ticket yet?" Marv asked Gilley.

"No, not yet," Levin said hastily.

"He will, Marv."

To Levin, Gilley said, "I'll have a copy of *The Elements* and the workbooks for you when you come out. All you have to do is follow them more or less according to our syllabus, keeping an eye out for the d.o. That's the departmental objective final we always give the comp freshmen at the end of each term."

"STRANGERS ARE WELCOME HERE BECAUSE THERE IS ROOM FOR ALL OF THEM, AND THEREFORE THE OLD INHABITANTS ARE NOT JEALOUS OF THEM—" B. Franklin

The framed tapestried motto hung over Professor Orville Fairchild's head as Levin entered his many-windowed sunlit office, directly across the hall from Gilley's. Gerald had knocked and held the door open as Levin went in. The head of department laid down his galley proofs, fixed a cigarette in a yellowed ivory holder, lit it, and resting back in his flexible chair, examined Levin.

He was, secretly examined by the new man, an old one, meticulously dressed, with a flower in his button hole; he had a bit of a belly, bags under both eyes, and a halo of sunlight ensnared in his bushy gray hair.

He frowned as he puffed and Levin quickly warned himself not to let a foolish word pop out of his mouth.

The head of department shook out the lit match that had nipped his fingers, a gesture that eclipsed the flame. Snapping the burnt matchstick he dropped it into the metal wastebasket, at the same moment blowing a stream of smoke that partly hid a sigh.

Life, or my interruption? Levin wondered. In the direct path of the smoke, the new instructor discreetly coughed but did not avert his head, not to affront.

"Well," said Professor Fairchild, chuckling to himself, "how do you like the West?" A vibrant old man's voice filled space. With small blue eyes, when he looked it penetrated.

"What I've seen I like," Levin said. "I only got here yesterday."

"I myself am an anomaly here, an old man in a young country. What about you?"

Ancient, thought Levin. Not sure whether the question connected to the statement, he cagily answered nothing.

"What I meant to say, is what brought you out this way? We hear from all over, true, but rarely New York."

"I wanted a change—" Levin hesitated.

"From the city?—"

"That's right," he said with relief. "I'm grateful to you and Dr. Gilley for—"

"You've spoken to Gerald about the department, I take it? Our program and course offerings are limited. Have you examined the college catalogue?"

"I have, sir." He had discovered a glut of composition, bonehead grammar, and remedial reading, over about a dozen skimpy literature courses.

"What did he tell you?"

"He said the people around were nice to work with. He—er—also mentioned your grammar text."

"Did he say anything about the history and purposes of the department? We're pretty much service oriented. Our school, for example, is called The Liberal Arts Service Division. Did he go into that?"

"Not exactly, sir. But he told me about the liberal arts, that they were—"

"Our main function, as I always tell everyone we employ here, is to satisfy the needs of the professional schools on the campus with respect to written communication. In science and technology men must be taught to communicate with the strictest accuracy, therefore we teach more composition than anything else in this department. Our literature offerings aren't very diversified or extensive but they're adequate to our purpose."

"I was hoping to teach a lit course," Levin said, "—that is, if it were possible."

Professor Fairchild seemed not to have heard.

"There's talk, now that the new dean is on campus—his name is unfortunate, Seagram—that we may in the future be called on for something more than we're presently offering in the way of literature, perhaps even to produce English majors, but I've heard that false alarm several times in recent years and it hasn't come to a hill of beans. I don't put much stock in it, not because I don't want it to come to pass—I do—but because I know intimately and practically the needs of this community. Ours is a land economy based on forestry—the Douglas fir and ponderosa pine for the most part; and agriculture—grains, grasses, flowers and some fruit. Our fishing industry is important too. We need foresters, farmers, engineers, agronomists, fish-and-game people, and every sort of extension agent. We need them—let's be frank—more than we need English majors. You can't fell a tree, run a four-lane highway over a mountain, or build a dam with poetry."

He chuckled to himself, drawing on his cigarette holder. Levin bent to tighten a shoelace but the smoke blew in another direction.

"Certainly I'm for English majors—I was one myself—but there are other colleges in the state that do a good job of training them better than we can presently, with our orientation and limited resources. My own point of view is that we ought to take pride in doing well a task that has to be done, though I'm frank to confess there are one or two in the department who don't see it quite my way, but that's their problem."

He dipped the cigarette into an ash tray and left it smoking.

The halo in his hair had faded, a trick of some passing cloud. As if conscious of that he ran a lacking hand through his hair.

"What was I saying? Well, I've made my point."

Levin nodded.

The old man picked up a ball-point pen and ticked off something he had written on a pink pad. He nearsightedly scanned the paper.

"Oh, yes." He turned to Levin. "Now I hope it won't unsettle you if I offer you a word of advice or two as a young man about to embark on his first college teaching venture. A word now may prevent future misunderstanding."

"Of course—"

"This department won't ask much of you in the way of research and the publication of small papers on matters of varying degrees of useless information—that's the headache of the big universities, to what effect I haven't been able to determine—but we *do* ask you to teach conscientiously and well. Get to know *The Elements* and give your students plenty of wholesome, snappy drill. You know," he said, "I've often wondered what we can expect of our American college graduates when so many of them don't even know the rules of syntax of their own language."

Levin agreed.

The professor scanned his pad and leaned back in his chair. "There are two kinds of people I deplore in the teaching profession. One is the misfit who sneaks in to escape his inadequacy elsewhere and who ought to be booted out—and isn't very often; and the other is the aggressive pest whose one purpose is to upset other people's applecarts, and the more apples, the better. We've had both types here, to our sorrow, and what's worse, sometimes in one and the same person."

The old man spoke sadly. "Leo Duffy comes to mind, a man no longer with us. Did Gerald tell you?"

"He mentioned him."

"He was—God forgive me—a nuisance of the thirty-second degree, irresponsible and perverse. He came here just two years ago—no, three." He coughed. "Two is correct, in '48. It was when Henry Wallace was running for president, something that shouldn't have been allowed to happen. That was a disastrous year. I remember my wife's brother, poor fellow, broke both legs in a tumble off his roof when he was erecting a TV aerial, the first in Easchester."

Levin, slowly stroking his beard, listened intently.

"Duffy was an ex-Catholic or something of the sort, from the South Chicago area. He was a handsome man in his way, with a wild head of Irish hair, intense eyes and a prominent jaw. He gave the impression of being thin and loose-jointed, maybe he was. When he appeared in this office my first thought was, here's an odd one now, get rid of him quickly; but his Gaelic charm was effectual and I neglected my warning to myself and later had to pay for it. He came to us very well recommended. Either he had forged his credentials, or he broke down here for causes unknown. In a short time he became a serious menace."

His eyes examined Levin, who, though he itched, forced himself not to scratch.

"His first term here—a terrible reflection on his teaching ability—he failed more than fifty percent of his composition students, and it gave us all a pretty headache before we could get that mess cleaned up. Luckily, my secretary called my attention to what he had done before we submitted the grades to the registrar, who would have been fit to be tied. In the end, after much frantic work we managed to reduce his failures to less than half the original number, though a figure still much above the department average of from three to five percent. For the moment at least we had managed to prevent a scandal."

Levin leaned forward. "Was he fired?"

"Not quite. Another characteristic of Duffy's was that he was unable to fit himself to the most elementary demands of a schedule and was constantly late to class, conference, meeting—you name it. Regularity, with respect to time, meant nothing to him. He graded papers, accumulated in a pile on his desk all term long, in one mad week at the end of each quarter, staying up nights with the assistance of pills; then returning hundreds of themes and quizzes in ferocious batches a day or so before the d.o., having deprived his students of the benefit of learning from previous papers what errors to avoid on later ones. I subsequently learned that he threw away, ungraded and unrecorded, more than one set of themes, because his dachshund, which had been trained to react on paper, wet on them. He apparently did his grading on the floor."

"Tst-tst."

"Where do you grade your papers, Mr. Levin?"

"Strictly at my desk, sir."

"That's as it should be. He wasn't a bad sort in his way but he became a problem with his numerous complaints against what he called, as if it were a dirty word, 'the status quo.' He wanted to reform us all in the shortest possible time—I'd say a week. I can stand legitimate criticism; as a matter of fact I invite it every time I prepare a new edition of my grammar, but the criticism of a man who is against you every minute of the day, who challenges everything you do, your ability and sincerity, even your purpose in life, without considering his own, eventually grates on people's nerves. Gerald—" he paused—"well, Gerald hated him."

"Was that why he was fired—if I may ask?"

"It all added up. I had a good deal of patience with him. He had, as I say, a certain charm. Still, there was no slowing him down or changing his erratic course. You thought you had repaired some harm he had done, and he promised to be careful and considerate, then a new incident occurred. For example, during the spring term—I beg your pardon, it was the winter—no, I'm wrong, it was the spring—after campaigning for Wallace he embraced another lost cause; but that was after a period of radicalism during which he asked his freshmen to write on the Moscow Trials, Lenin and Trotsky, the Lysenko theory and other controversial subjects I'm sure they knew nothing about. Some of the students who complained about him said he encouraged discussions of Marxism in his classes. Now I would like you to know, Mr. Levin, that I have no objection to an honest discussion of these subjects, though they certainly don't relate to our *Science in Tech* reader, but I'm sure you'll agree Marxism is specialized subject matter that ought to be confined to mature history or political science courses and not be intruded into freshmen composition. To give you some idea how far astray he went, Mr. Gallegher, our bookstore manager, called me one morning to tell me that Duffy had placed an order for one hundred and twenty-five copies of *The Communist Manifesto* as supplementary reading matter. I can tell you we soon scotched that."

The professor's cigarette ash dropped on the desk blotter. He blew it away and Levin sneezed.

"Don't you smoke?" the old man inquired. "Would you care for a cigarette?"

"I gave it up." Levin blew his nose.

"That shows will power."

"Not much, sir."

"Nevertheless," said Professor Fairchild, "towards the end of the academic year he was engaged in collecting funds on the campus for some radical group or other, I think they were called 'The Committee of Anti-Fascist Scientists' or some such name. You may remember that group, or one with a similar-sounding name, is on the Attorney General's list of subversive organizations. In fairness to all, I'll say I proceeded in this matter with the patience of a saint, because Duffy sometimes seemed to me to be like an overgrown boy challenging authority—but finally my patience wore thin."

He rubbed out his cigarette, detached it from the holder, flipped it into the wastebasket and leaned back in his creaking chair. For a minute his eyes were shut.

Opening them, he said, "You'll have a good idea what I went through after I tell you the following incident, although it's embarrassing to me."

"Please don't, if—"

"One Sunday afternoon about a week before Commencement I was relaxing in my tub. My wife was entertaining Mrs. Feeney, our former dean's wife, at tea, when Leo Duffy rang the door bell and had the effrontery to solicit a contribution for his radical scientists' group, but of course Josephine refused. Apparently annoyed, he demanded to see me. She foolishly let him in. Spying Mrs. Feeney there, either out of perversity, or malice, he asked her for a contribution. Now this lady is nobody's fool. She was raised in New England and is head of our local Anti-Liquor League, where Josephine is the first vice-president. Mrs. Feeney told Duffy that if he tried to collect good American money for bad foreign causes he might soon find himself without a position at CC. This was nothing more than an informal warning; she obviously had no authority, either direct or indirect, since her husband was retiring, to cause him to be fired. Let's just say she was giving him a bit of motherly advice.

"But Duffy was infuriated. He said he wouldn't stand for that kind of talk from anybody. His gestures were violent, he was practically shouting. They were afraid he might physically attack them—that is to say, with his fists. Half asleep in my tub I was awakened by the commotion and thought the house was burning down—he was loudly repeating the word 'fired.' Naturally I jumped out of the tub, and before I had thought twice, ran out into the living room in my birthday suit—"

Professor Fairchild chuckled.

Levin brought out his nail file, wondered why, and quickly returned it to his pocket.

"Mrs. Feeney passed out. My wife, without thinking, threw a cup of tea at me, the tea not the cup, and Duffy went into a fit of maniacal laughter, the like of which I had never heard before. I then determined he would thereafter laugh out of the other side of his mouth.

"'Mr. Duffy,' I said as calmly as I could—I had by this time a bath towel around my middle, and Mrs. Feeney had been revived with Josephine's smelling salts—'I hereby give you notice that you will be asked to leave this college as soon as the Administrative Regulations permit.' Well, you should have seen his expression. I can't exactly describe it, though to this day I still clearly recollect it. It combined anger, haughtiness, and comprehension of defeat, although I will say he looked more deplorable a few days later when he was publicly discharged from his position by Dr. Marion Labhart, the president of this college."

Levin, on the edge of his seat, asked, "Because of the incident—?"

"That as well as others," said the old professor. "In the meantime he had apologized to me for these contretemps. I had reconsidered and wasn't going to report him, but Mrs. Feeney telephoned Leona Labhart, and she told the president what had happened at my house. Now Marion is a man with a temper—I've heard it blamed on his first name, but be that as it may he's a disciplinarian of the old school, and he immediately called me for a dossier on Duffy. I had Dr. Gilley compile it, and the very day he read it the president called a college-wide open meeting. The entire staff, more than five hundred strong, crowded into Sheffield Auditorium in the Dairy Building, and heard the president denounce Duffy as a fellow-traveling radical. He read aloud the long list of his indiscretions—which he had had mimeographed and passed out to the audience. It was a terrible indictment. After reading the document, Marion, whose brain literally seems to boil when he's angered, spoke directly to Duffy, who, although he had not been asked to, had risen from his seat as though hypnotized. The president told him in front of all that he was a disgrace to the institution and his contract would not be renewed. Duffy was, of course, on a yearly contract—so are you—all new people are; he made no attempt to reply, remained speechless, a broken man, the shadow of himself, quickly abandoned by all.

"After the president had stalked off the platform the audience dispersed, I one of the last to leave. Leo seemed physically exhausted; it was all he could do, after half an hour, to drag himself out of the building. Perhaps he had not foreseen this end for himself, although it is likely he may have, yet was thunderstruck by his fate. I felt sorry for him—the man was obviously a misfit—and I was afraid he would do himself some serious harm; his eyes were turned inward in a frightening way. Yet when I saw him the next afternoon he had recovered a bit of his brashness and even asked me for a letter of recommendation, which I could not bring myself to write, although I did offer some sound advice about the future which he preferred not to hear."

"So that's it," said Levin with a sigh. He had secretly loosened his necktie but the image persisted of Duffy standing alone in the auditorium, the weight of his disgrace on his cracked head.

"More or less. He afterwards raised a fuss in our local chapter of the American Association of Professors, and for a while Dr. Fabrikant, who was chairman of the Academic Freedom sub-committee that year, and a few others on the faculty, were defending him, but in the end they came to their senses and voted against submitting a complaint to the national AAP. Dean Feeney's last act in office was to write the letter notifying Duffy of his dismissal."

"Er—Was it true that he was a fellow traveler?" Levin asked.

"What would you say?" The professor looked with interest at the new instructor.

"It's hard to say from the evidence. As for myself," he went on hastily, "I am not now, nor have I ever been, a member of the Communist Party."

Levin laughed brokenly.

"Funny thing," Professor Fairchild went on, "despite all that had happened, the last time we met he begged me practically on his knees for a last chance—as if I could. He said he had learned from his errors, was a reformed man, had more reason than ever for wanting to stay on. I felt he had grown more attached to this place than he had realized and it was a bitter thing for him to leave. Or perhaps he sensed this was the end of his teaching career, as turned out to be the case. I had to tell him the matter was entirely out of my hands and advised him in that last emotional meeting that he wasn't truly meant to teach and we were doing him a favor to let him go so that he might find his true place in society. Yet for a while I felt as many fathers do after punishing their children. I had built up some affection for the poor devil, perhaps thinking of him as a sort of prodigal son, except that Leo Duffy never returned to the parental fold, nor was I, when all is said and done, his father. In the end he went his predestined way."

Levin drew a long breath.

"That's how these things go." Professor Fairchild gazed out of a window. "It surprises me how often an evil genius, in one guise or another, will raise his horns on a college campus."

He looked suddenly bored.

Levin rose to go, but the professor, glancing again at his pad, amiably remarked, "I think the administration would expect me to say something in passing on the subject of sex."

The new instructor sat down with a throbbing dry throat. "Did you say 'sex'?"

"Call it what you will. You're thirty, your application states. Without any intention to pry into your personal affairs, may I ask if you are presently considering marriage?"

"Only vaguely," Levin replied. "First I have certain plans I would like to carry—"

"Ultimately?"

"Absolutely, sir. I want a home and—"

"Some do, some don't. Too bad you aren't married now. Easchester can be hard on bachelors. If you intend to stay on here I recommend marriage. It would pay to keep your eyes open this fall. Occasionally an eligible woman or two join the staff, but they are usually quickly spoken for so you will have to hustle if someone strikes you as especially fair. My own wife was teaching clothing design in home economics when we first met. I took her out of the hands of a professor of dairy products to whom she was considering engaging herself. However, the point I must make is that we expect you strictly to refrain from dating students, no matter what the provocation."

"I understand—"

"Nor is prowling among faculty wives tolerated."

"Yes, sir—"

"You might guess that Duffy would not respect these suggestions."

"You don't say?" said Levin, but the professor let it go at that.

He said, after a minute of reflection, "We once had a sad case of a nineteen-year-old student who killed herself when she became pregnant by her instructor—"

"You mean Duffy, sir?"

"No, this was long before his time. He was a young speech instructor, and when he denied responsibility, the poor girl cut her throat under his bedroom window outside the house he roomed in, the room in which he had led her astray. This unhappy incident occurred during the very first year I was here, or perhaps it was the year after—I'm not sure whether I was already married, I believe I was. Yes, I was. People still talk of the tragedy."

Levin shivered under his new suit. The professor ticked off a last item on the pad. I can go now, Levin thought.

But the head of the English Department, swiveling around so that he looked full in the new instructor's face, with no transition other than the mark he had made on his pink pad, said, "I trust you don't drink, Mr. Levin?"

Levin, breaking out in a sweat, answered loudly, "No, sir." He had set himself for the question, but the shock of hearing it almost lifted him out of the chair. By an effort of the will he remained seated.

Good God, he thought, have I given myself away? He suspected his face looked ashen, black whiskers sprouting out of marble.

"I'm glad to hear that. You might keep in mind that this community—this part of the valley—was founded a hundred years ago by missionaries from the East, hard on the heels of the forty-niners; almost overnight they established temperance societies. I met Josephine at an Anti-Liquor League social."

To appear calm, Levin slowly stroked his beard.

"Mores are mores."

"Yes, sir."

"I bring this up," the professor said, lowering his voice, "because your appearance reminds me somewhat of Father's."

"Er—Whose father?"

"Mine. He wore whiskers remarkably like yours and had your color brown eyes. I have a photograph of him among my papers at home; and your beard, black and full, is the spit and image of his at about the time he was your age."

"Quite a coincidence, sir."

"Papa was a drinker."

Levin patted his brow with his handkerchief.

"Not that I am in any way implying that whiskers equate with drinking. One thinks of the Hebrew patriarchs and prophets. And we have our own abstemious Amish Mennonites in this country. All I'm saying is that you happen to remind me of my poor father, who at one time of his life—I make no secret of it—was an incurable drunkard."

Levin's handkerchief was by now moist.

"Papa was a harness-maker by trade. In those days we lived above his place of business in a rectangular frame house in Kansas City, Missouri. My sister was eleven and I nine—no, we were twelve and ten, I remember detesting my fifth-grade arithmetic teacher—when Papa began to drink heavily for no reason that my poor mother could understand.

"Mama—a pioneer type—stood it for several years. At length, realizing the situation was not improving, she decided to leave Papa and move to Moscow, in the Idaho panhandle, where her parents were living. Before going she spoke to him in our presence—I still recollect her words. 'John,' she said, 'I'm taking the children to my father's for reasons you well understand. Nevertheless, I don't want to cut you off from your family if we mean anything to you. Father sent me fifty dollars to leave with you. I give you my heartfelt invitation to join us as soon as you can. If you will stay sober long enough to locate us, I believe you can conquer drink, and we will all live together again.'

"I recall my father wept. He told Mama that he loved her and the children dearly and would follow us to Moscow as soon as he was thoroughly sober, 'dried out' was how he phrased it. When we left he drove us to the train in his horse and wagon. He was, I learned later, true to his word, stayed away from the bottle and wound up his affairs. He sold what was left of his business, put on his Sunday suit, packed a bag, and set out for the railroad station. But he had rarely ridden on trains, and through some unfortunate mixup, was already in Chicago before he, or anyone, discovered he had been going the wrong way. He was so terribly disappointed he made straight for a saloon."

Levin softly groaned.

"Some kind person put him on the right train and Papa was off again on his journey. He had vowed, I was told, not to touch another drop; however he made the acquaintance of a tipsy drummer aboard the train, who persistently offered him a bottle. Papa said no often enough, but the drummer would not accept his refusal, so when the bottle was down to a mouthful or so, he said yes, apparently thinking he would take a last swallow and be forever done with it. However, his strategy proved impracticable because the drummer had a half dozen more bottles stored in his suitcases full of samples of ladies' underthings. The two of them managed to get as far as Omaha, where, because of their carousing they were ejected from the train.

"A few days later, eluding the drummer, Papa got onto another train going west, but he soon discovered he had lost his billfold containing what was left of the money Mama had given him and the sum he had raised from the sale of his harness and leather goods store. Unable to stand his profound disappointment in himself, he left the train at Pocatello, and having sold his gold watch and suitcase for a song, used the money to get impossibly drunk. He stayed in Pocatello for the rest of his life, which was not destined to be long.

"Many years later—it was shortly after the birth of my eldest son—he's a mining engineer in New Mexico—I set out one summer in search of Papa. Employing a private detective, I traced him first to Omaha, then Pocatello, and a man we located there, a merchant who owned a feed and seed store where Papa was employed for a time, told me what had happened. Papa had in truth sworn off liquor not long after his arrival in Pocatello, but he was, as I understand it, ashamed to face us, penniless. The feed and seed merchant told me that each year of the four he lived in Idaho before he died, both at Christmastime, and in April, a few days before Mama's birthday, Papa made plans to go to Moscow, but for one reason or another he never got there. I presume he died trying. At any rate, none of us ever saw him again after the day we said goodbye in Kansas City. His life was wasted, but at least it taught me how to use mine."

Levin rose unsteadily. He got out, "I promise never to touch a"—before he clamped his jaws tight.

Professor Fairchild stood up and warmly shook his hand. "'I greet you at the beginning of a great career.'"

The sun flared in his hair and he looked like a saintly old man amid his books. Picking out a volume from one of the shelves, he handed it to Levin. "*The Elements of Grammar*, revised, thirteenth edition."

Levin at last relaxed. "Thank you. Dr. Gilley is giving me a copy."

"Keep both, should you lose one."

"I'm much obliged."

"Tell your students the book will be very useful to them. Funny thing," the professor chuckled, "they may hate it in the beginning but they'll love it in the end. More than one of my former students have returned to tell me that mastering English grammar was the turning point of their lives."

Levin held a nervous hand on the door knob but the old man was still talking.

"You'll like it here, Mr. Levin. This is wonderful country. If you don't mind the rain you'll like the climate. We have a friendly department—no strife to speak of, although there is sometimes an honest difference of opinion. Gerald Gilley is a good man in composition, you can learn a lot from him. The work is interesting, the students easy to deal with. It's a blessing to teach. I've been at it for nearly forty years and have never regretted my choice of profession. I'm nearing the end of my stewardship here and look back upon my work with satisfaction. I've fought the good fight. *The Elements* was born here. The department, in my time, grew from three to twenty-one. Yet the path was not always without thorns: We've had hard times, when the administration gave us almost nothing to live on. I scrimped to save. I had to pare down salaries, occasionally causing friction, I confess; still, what had to be done had to be done. The first duty of a good leader is to carry out orders. I did as I was ordered. At one time I ran about the cheapest department on the Coast, and frankly I was proud to help keep the college solvent and functioning during times of crisis. Dean Feeney felt as I did. He's also a careful man with a dollar. We have to be—we're not a rich state. The dean and I saw eye to eye. I have in my papers at home a letter from him commending me for my efforts in the college's behalf. I'm proud of it. I admit it troubled me to discover later that not every department head always followed the letter of the law. A few, during the Depression, had bought almost no supplies and kept salaries slightly higher—not by much—than some of us were paying. One man did his own secretarial work and divided the secretarial fund among his staff, but he had a very small staff. Maybe I should have tried something of the sort, but it didn't seem honest to me. At least I gave employment to another mouth. In general, when I think of what I would change if I had my life to live over, I doubt I would change much."

He was still talking, the light fading in his hair, as Levin left.

WHAT NEW with Levin in the September weeks before classes began?

His world—inside he was Levin, although the New Levin, man of purpose after largely wasted years. For Mrs. Beaty, an old widow alone with her roomer in a bulky two-story white frame house, he performed chores he hadn't conceived doing before, in exchange for something off the rent. Levin mowed lawns front and rear—the health of the grass was amazing, it sprouted overnight and every week he had to cut. On a shaky ladder that left him with nervous knees he gathered yellow pears, shying away from the bees sucking the sweet wounds of fruit. The cherry tree had yielded, thank God, at the end of June, and the walnut wasn't due till late October. The landlady had eight trees on her hundred by seventy-five, including an orange-berried mountain ash, new to his eye. Three weeks after he had arrived, after a night of rain Levin raked off the front lawn the first enormous leaves, fallen like wet rags from the sycamores in front of the old houses across the street; he had thought, until the old woman told him no, that they were from some Bunyanesque species of maple tree.

A truck dumped a backbreaking load of practically orange sawdust in the alley, and Levin slowly shoveled it through a window into the cellar—working up respect for the shovelers of the world—where it gave off a Christmas-tree fragrance that all but levitated the house. Mrs. Beaty demonstrated how to light the sawdust furnace and Levin agreed to keep it hot when the weather got cold, load the hopper twice a day, and every month vacuum the dust filters in the heat blower. He learned a sickle was not a scythe when he laboriously cut down and dug up a weedy flower garden she could no longer take care of, and discovered last season's walnuts and acorns, six varieties of worms, a soggy doll, and thickly-rusted screw driver from yesteryear. The past hides but is present. Watching a robin straining to snap a worm out of the earth Levin momentarily thought of himself as a latter-day Thoreau, but gave that up—he had come too late to nature. He whitewashed cellar walls until his beard dripped like the brush he was using; hosed the clapboard front of the house; again on a ladder, dug leaves out of rain gutters; changed washers in water taps; and though it worried him to work with electricity, even replaced wall switches where old ones were broken. Levin was surprised at all an inexperienced hand could do with only a slight loss of blood. He seriously considered taking up hunting and fishing, and planned to visit Seattle and San Francisco as soon as he had a few dollars in his pocket.

Mrs. Beaty lived and let live, a woman of sixty-nine, gone half deaf; she wore a gray comb in her gray hair and a hearing button in her left ear but rarely turned it on except to answer the phone when she "felt" it ringing, and to talk with Levin when he ate in the kitchen—this was their major involvement. Sometimes when he avoided her he realized she was avoiding him. She went to bed at eight each night, except on the rare nights she entertained; and early the next morning, wearing galoshes to protect her shoes from the wet grass, was already snipping flowers, or poking into the shrubbery around the house. She lived unself-consciously in the presence of her dead husband's cabinetry, rocking chair, pipes; his tools were still hanging above his workbench in the cellar. She had, she sometimes said, nothing against the world, and Levin envied her a little. She actively cleaned, baked, canned and sewed; she cooked well and was generous with food although careful with a dime. The cat got scraps. Levin did better; more than once she insisted on adding something to his inexpensive meals. And to make things livelier she promised another roomer soon, a graduate student from Syria. She took in only a gentleman or two, she said; ladies were too hard on hot water, the telephone, and the gentlemen. She said she was a minister's daughter and then remarked how nice it was to have a "scholar" in the house. For a full week she called him "Dr. Levin," but he denied it until she reverted to "mister." Once or twice, apropos of nothing, she said she knew Dr. Gilley quite well. Her husband had worked for him more than once and they had gone fishing together. She was not well acquainted with Mrs. Gilley but had heard about her from mutual friends.

Levin enjoyed the run of the house; never before had he lived where inside was so close to out. In a tenement, each descent to the street was an expedition through dank caves and dreary tunnels. He enjoyed the cherry tree reaching its knotty, mildewed branches to his back window. At the side he had a view of the wooded hills, changing shape and color as the clouds did. He could see the mountains from three windows. Not locking doors when he went out was new to him and he worried things might be stolen but soon stopped locking his doors. He noticed bicycles and toys left on lawns overnight and was pleased this could be done.

Levin's large room, next to the smaller one awaiting the Syrian student, was lit in sunlight during the afternoon. It grew hot for a while but sea breezes cooled it at four. At night he slept under two blankets, another kindness of nature. His white metal bed was an old-fashioned double—he suspected it had been Mrs. Beaty's marriage bed; he slept on its right side, on his right; he dreamed too often on his left. The desk he used was a good-sized walnut table built by the carpenter; it stood at the window with a view to the hills. Levin sat there often during the day writing in a thick hard-covered notebook he had used years ago as a commonplace book, and had recently revived. He wrote in it summaries of books he thought highly of, copying out passages. One section of the notebook was for "insights," and a few pages in the middle detailed "plans." He often read over sentences he had copied, such as "To change intention changes fortune"—Montaigne; "Important principles may and must be inflexible"—A. Lincoln, and was lately writing them into short essays he tried his hand at. Among Levin's "insights" were: "The new life hangs on an old soul," and "I am one who creates his own peril." Also, "The danger of the times is the betrayal of man"—S. Levin. He exhorted himself to "keep the circle broken." He was a conscientious becomer but worried that it had taken him so long to get started. The future burned in his head. Time not converted to good use tormented him; he liked having his new alarm clock around because it helped, in a primitive way, to organize him. Sleep loosened the nuts and bolts of his defenses, but time used to good purpose tightened them. Sitting at his desk, he studied *The Elements*, did the workbook exercises, and read all the essays in *Science in Technology*, taking notes from which to develop class lessons. He wished there were a poem or two in the book.

Levin warned himself to get out of the room more often.

The warning was urgent so he walked. The country was conveniently fifteen minutes in any direction; if through downtown, then across a white plank bridge over the Sacajawea River. He tramped for miles along dirt roads, wherever they led, usually from one farm to another. For weeks the blue sky was cloudless but lately huge white masses drifted in from the Pacific, floating toward the east. He wore his raincoat and carried a large umbrella; he did not like to be caught in a storm and soaked. A city boy let loose, Levin took in all the sights, stopping for five minutes at his first row of rural mailboxes. He enjoyed the variety of aging and ancient barns. In bright sunlight the stubble of grain- or grass-harvested fields looked like snow on the ground. One farm had a green scrub oak at its center that seemed to be growing in snow. The illusion created pleasure. He watched farmers burning the harvest stubble and afterward the fields were black, a sight he had never imagined. One day, as he walked past a black field, a visible funnel of wind whirled over it and headed for him. Levin wildly wondered whether to run, grab a fence post, or lie still in the road; then the little twister turned and blew another way. Within a week men on tractors were harrowing the burnt fields, and the rich brown earth looked newly combed and awaiting planting. The sight of the expectant earth raised a hunger in Levin's throat. He yearned for the return of spring, a terrifying habit he strongly resisted: the season was not yet officially autumn. He was now dead set against the destruction of unlived time. As he walked, he enjoyed surprises of landscape: the variety of green, yellow, brown, and black fields, compositions with distant trees, the poetry of perspective. Without investment to speak of he had become rich in sight of nature, a satisfying wealth. In the past he had had almost none of this, though in winter he had tenaciously watched the frozen city trees for the first signs of budding; observed with reluctance the growth of leaves; walked alone at night close to full-blown summer trees; and in autumn followed dead leaves to their graves. Now he took in miles of countryside—a marvelous invention. He had never seen so many horses, sheep, pigs across fences. The heavy Herefords (he had looked them up) turned white faces to the road as he went by. He had never seen one in the open before, or black Angus; they had never seen a Levin.

The image of autumn was already in his eye, but he did not compel it, as he had in the past compelled every flower and tree, to solace, or mourn with, his spirit. He saw almost the moment when strings of white birch leaves faded from green to yellow; and under the green skirts of maples, bunches of leaves flared gold. Except for a scarlet vine on a fence there were few reds—this into October, a green and yellow autumn, less poignant than his last year's. Except on warm days it took a sharp sniffer to unearth its bouquet, for an almost monotonous freshness of air dampened the effects of odor. He missed the smell of change and its associations, the sense of unwilled motion toward an inevitable end, of winter coming and what of one's life in a cold season? What most moved him was memory. Yet when the autumn day was momentarily cloudless, blue-skied, still to the point of a dog's bark miles away, it sometimes burdened the heart.

One afternoon after a long lonely walk, a mood induced, he thought, by the odor of wood smoke in the air, Levin stopped off at the Gilleys.

Pauline, coming to the door in tight violet toreador pants and a paint-smeared shirt, drew back when she saw him.

"Oh, you frightened me," she laughed in embarrassment, "I wasn't expecting anyone. That is, a guest."

"Excuse me," Levin said. "Is your husband home?"

"Why no," she said, controlled now. "He's downtown doing something at the bank. After that he was planning to go to the hardware store to buy a toilet seat for our split one in the upstairs bathroom—the kids slam them down so hard. Would you care to come in? The house is a mess, I've been painting chairs."

But he saw from her distraction she wished he wouldn't. Levin said thanks and moved away. He said he would see Gerald in the office. The screen door slammed behind her.

"'Come see us often,'" he mimicked her.

Unwilling to be enticed by old habits of loneness, in late September Levin went to call on Assistant Professor Joseph Bucket. On Gilley's advice he had previously telephoned George Bullock, but he and his family, after returning from Carmel, had taken off for the coast. Bucket already interested Levin because of what he had heard about him. Mrs. Beaty knew the mother, the widow of a logger killed in the woods when the son was fifteen. He had transferred, after two years at Cascadia College, to the University at Gettysburg, then had served a year in the army, been discharged for an asthmatic condition, and after three hand-to-mouth years at graduate school in Arizona, Bucket had returned as an instructor in English at the College, his Ph.D. uncompleted. He had come back with a pregnant wife and three children. Since they were too poor to buy a house, and to rent a decent place at that time was impossible, Bucket borrowed as much as he could and began to build. Besides teaching and working on his house, he carried on odd-jobs all over town. Now, four years, two more kids, and a promotion later, he was still building, and still writing his dissertation. There was about this man's experience, as Levin had heard it, a quality that made him think they could be friends.

Bucket lived on the worn side of town, just over a twisting fork of the Sacajawea, a narrow arm of the river at times laden with logs floating down from the hills to a lumber mill at the southeastern edge of Easchester. One afternoon, Levin, wandering past the squarish two-story gray house, sporting a porch much too large for it, discovered the assistant professor on his hands and knees on the steeply-pitched high gabled roof, hammering nails into loose shingles and replacing others.

"Excuse me," Levin called up, "Professor Bucket?"

"Speaking." Bucket glanced down to see who it was, then turned cautiously, supporting himself against one of the two-by-fours temporarily nailed down. He was a long skinny man, about thirty-five, with a narrow face and meaty ears, and he wore large horn-rimmed glasses.

"Maybe I came at the wrong time?" Levin apologized. "I'm the new instructor in the English department. I happened to be passing by and thought I'd say hello."

Bucket, in cement-stained Levi's, large army surplus shoes, and a loose, thick home-knit green sweater, rested his hammer and can of nails behind a two-by-four, and still on hands and knees, examined Levin.

"That's kind of you. Sorry I can't talk just now. I'm not inhospitable, I'd like you to know, but I have to settle a leak that's been plaguing us, before it gets too dark to work."

Levin remained stationary in disappointment.

"Registration Week begins Monday, and since, as I understand it, we have offices on the same floor, we'll not be without opportunity to converse."

"With pleasure," Levin replied. He had harbored a sneaking hope that once they had got started talking Bucket would invite him to come back that evening.

The assistant professor may have sensed some such thought. "You're not from the West, Mr. Levin?"

"From New York City."

"New York?" He slowly slid down the roof and set himself cross-legged a few feet from its edge, worrying Levin that he might fall.

"How has it been coming along—your house?" he asked.

"I gather you've heard?" Bucket said. "If it strikes you as nearing completion, that's an illusion. This house—and, I might add, my dissertation—are as long in the making as Tristram Shandy in being born, or mine Uncle Toby in curing his military wound, a blow from a stone at the siege of Namur. If you happened to glance over the laurel hedge as you turned the corner, no doubt you noticed, in what was at one time part of our back yard, a bedroom I added last year; now Algene and I have decided that a playroom for the children is a necessity if we are to preserve what we have already built. As Tristram puts it in another context, '. . . such a building do I foresee it will turn out, as never was planned, and as never was executed since Adam.' In the meantime there remains a good deal of interior woodwork finishing, and I've also had to install an additional half bathroom—we're eight in the house—my mother resides with us—and to reinforce the foundation at the rear. Sometimes I think my life follows that pattern of events Sterne calls the 'sad vicissitude of things.'" He laughed at that—it was almost a cackle, over in a minute yet exhaustive.

"Ah, too bad," Levin murmured. "Would you," he asked, "be interested in resting from your labors by going to the movies tonight as my guest? I understand the film they're showing is fairly good."

"Awfully nice of you," Bucket said. "A bit of entertainment is not uncalled for but most of my evenings are spent at the office. I referred to my dissertation a moment ago, 'Disorder and Sorrow in Sterne,' in reality a study of his humor. It has, unfortunately," he said without shame or bitterness, "come back to me for the third time, and I am presently engaged in a new rewriting. What I'm really doing, I shouldn't be too surprised, is waiting for the chairman of my committee either to retire or expire, although I would prefer retirement if only he'd hurry. Though, if pressed, he will not deny that my scholarship has merit, he doesn't seem to care for what he calls my presentation and style, and I haven't in any of my attempts been able to satisfy him. Although my own mentor, my sponsor on the committee, is loyally with me, the chairman is influential and the paper has come back each time with new criticisms and requests for additional alterations. I'm now sending it in chapter by chapter but haven't got past the second of eight. I've many times been tempted to abandon the project but mustn't or there'll be no advancement beyond my present rank and a salary I find it impossible to live on."

"Tst-tst."

"Had I the courage of my convictions I would twist my committee chairman's nose till he passed me, but I know it would end up with his twisting mine. As Sterne puts it, 'They order these things better in France.'"

"I wouldn't know," Levin murmured. "This is as far as I've been from where I was born."

"What brings you to this knot of the woods?"

"My fate, I suppose—"

Bucket cackled. He got up carefully on his hands and knees. "I mustn't delay any longer, if you'll pardon me."

"Have you got another hammer by chance? Maybe I could help you?" Levin said.

"My heartfelt thanks, but I don't carry liability insurance and the roof slopes somewhat too acutely."

Levin, reluctantly about to depart, thought of something. "I'm sort of curious about this Mr. Duffy you had around here the year before last. In short, could you tell me what he was like?"

Bucket looked down at Levin with new interest. "Who told you about him?"

"Who not? In particular Professor Fairchild."

"What, specifically, would you like to know?"

"I was told he was a radical of some sort, but I'm not clear what kind. That is, was he a crackpot or somebody with a liberal idea?"

The assistant professor contemplated Levin's beard.

"I can't say positively but there were elements of a philosophy that may be defined as liberalism."

"You're not using the word pejoratively?"

"Not I—personally."

"Was he a communist?"

"I strongly doubt it, although there were some who thought so."

"A fellow traveler?"

"I've heard that too."

"What did Dr. Gilley mean, could you tell me, when he characterized him as a 'disagreeable radical'? Was it the political connotation he had in mind or the oddball?" Levin hesitated. "I might have asked him, but being new I thought it best not to."

"I can understand your discretion."

Bucket continued to gaze down and Levin to crane until the back of his neck grew stiff.

"Nice people—the Gilleys," he said, to adjust a possibly wrong impression.

"Yes."

"Pauline—Mrs. Gilley, that is—they're both nice. Very hospitable. He has many interests. She showed me some pictures he—"

Bucket lost his hold on the roof and slid forward. Levin, fearing for the man's life, rushed toward the house to break his fall, but the assistant professor managed to dig his heels into the gutter, stopping himself from going off the roof.

"Holy cow!" He looked sick.

"My fault," Levin said, disturbed. "Sorry I bothered you. I'm on my way."

"My own inexcusable carelessness," Bucket gasped. "I should never come up here without crampons." He drew a deep breath, righted himself, and crawled back to the security of a two-by-four.

"I'll say goodbye." But Levin turned at the gate. "Excuse me," he called, "could you direct me to Dr. Fabrikant's house?"

"Fabrikant?"

Once more with the big eyes, Levin thought. What's so strange about every question I ask? "C. D. Fabrikant, in our department."

"I wanted to be sure you hadn't confused him with Carleton Fabricius in entomology. I once courted his daughter Imogene."

"Not that one."

Bucket pointed west with his hammer. "About half a mile past the college barns. His house is the first you'll come to."

Levin lifted his hat.

"Nice to meet you." Bucket crawled up the roof and was again banging nails into shingles.

Poor guy, Levin thought. "Sad vicissitude of things."

On his way along the county road the new instructor peeked through the door of the voluminous red college barn at the pedigreed black bulls in pens, marvelous beasts, but when they bellowed at the sight of him he quickly left.

Coming to Dr. Fabrikant's mailbox, under a chestnut tree, Levin followed a graveled driveway to an old blistered-green house, set back about a hundred feet from the road. The house was of wood with broad tower-like structures on both sides of the façade, not what Levin had expected to see. This seemed to have a New England quality, the little he knew of New England after a three-day pilgrimage wandering in the vicinity of Boston.

It was an odd place and creaked in the breeze, he thought, until he discovered a thin-faced woman watching him from her rocker on the porch. Lifting his startled hat, he went to her. She was shelling beans in a pot on her lap.

"Good evening," said Levin. It was still afternoon. She was straight-backed and meager, her black hair grizzled at the tight hairpinned bun.

"Looking for somebody?"

"Please," said Levin. "Is Dr. C. D. Fabrikant home?"

"You're not a student, are you? I don't see so well without my glasses."

"No, ma'am—a teacher, new instructor here. I don't want to bother him if he's busy. I was just out walking."

"He's not at his desk," she said, still rocking slowly. "I think he's out to the melon patch on Isobel—that's his mare. I'd go look for him but I just got over my sciatica, and the fields are more than is ripe for me just now."

"Don't think of it," Levin said. "I'll be glad to wait a bit if you don't mind." He sat down on the doorstep.

"Doorstep's dirty, why don't you take the chair there?"

The chair on the porch held books that Levin didn't want to disturb; he said he was all right on the step.

"You say you're at the college?" she asked. "Do I know you? Not that I get around so much but after a while you know names and such."

"No ma'am. I'm the new man in the English department."

"Oh? Where from?"

"New York City."

She placed the pot on the floor. "I'd better call CD. He'll want to meet you. He got his Ph.D. at Harvard, in the East."

"You don't say," said Levin. "Maybe I'd better not disturb him."

She walked to the far end of the long porch and searched the weedy field, her hand shading her eyes. Then she came back to the rocker.

"My father sent him East. It was before the Depression and he was having some good years. He was a farmer in Montana. There were six of us kids, I being the eldest and CD right after me. He was the smart one right off. Read him something out of a book, even when he was a shaver, and he would rattle it right back at you in the same words. After his A.B., CD got three or four years of business experience, but he didn't like any of it, so Father sent him to Harvard, and he had a fine career there in A grades and all sorts of honorable mention. This professor he had—he was sort of a world authority—said CD showed remarkable promise and would have a successful career. He would have had for sure if the Depression hadn't come along.

"I guess you heard how hard things were then? I remember seeing pictures of bread lines in New York, hungry men, some with coats, some without 'em or even a hat, standing in the snow for a doughnut and coffee. We didn't have it that bad but we had it bad enough, partly on account of the drought we had in the state at that same awful time. Wheat was fifty cents a bushel, if that, and you couldn't get enough to pay for fixing your machines to harvest it. One year Father put in a hundred acres of flax, but though the clouds stayed low there was no rain and he cut less than three, not enough to pay back the cost of the seed. We used to mill a little wheat for breakfast food and bread, and we had some stock so no one starved. But our clothes were shameful and would come apart if I rubbed too hard on the board. And to make things worse our poor mother died. She didn't say how sick she was, although the doctor would've come for nothing if she had called him a few months before. Anyway, after CD had graduated with his doctor's degree he taught for two years in a real old college in Maine, but then it had to close down and he was out of work. He came back to Montana and after about a year took the first job that opened to him, in a country school near Bozeman. I knew it was a terrible trial to him with all his education. He never said much—CD isn't that type—but you could tell by looking at him what it meant not to be doing what he was fit to."

She began shelling her beans again.

"After a year of that, there came this letter from CD's professor at Harvard—the one I told you about that liked him—that Professor Fairchild, out here, was short a man because somebody had died, and he advised CD to apply right away. To make the story shorter, CD did get the place, but as fate had it, Father took seriously sick and CD had to help me care for him because we were the only ones around by now, and I was already on and off with my sciatica. Well, that winter Father died. In the meantime, some lady teacher on the staff here got herself married and quit so there was another opening, for which Dr. Gilley was hired. He came in September, 1932, just before the winter CD could come, and so he beat CD in by three months and has had seniority over him ever since by that one term, although in some of the departments of the college, CD found out later, the man with the Ph.D. generally gets the seniority over the one who hasn't got it if they come in close together. Dr. Gilley got his degree years later but that didn't seem to make any difference to Professor Fairchild. Just by that one term, after the two or three older men had retired,

Dr. Gilley got his promotions and raises first, including his full professorship. CD is still an associate, though he had many times been promised his advancement. I admit my prejudices, but I have my own doubts that Dr. Gilley really deserved advancement over CD. He hasn't got CD's intellect or his list of publications, but that's Professor Fairchild for you.

"When my brother came here he was paid sixteen hundred dollars a year. Of course he's doing financially all right now, since he's single and has me to help him, or we couldn't have bought this property—the house and twenty acres—but to tell you the truth, though he doesn't complain about it, I'm sorry for all the years he has stuck it out here. I wish he had taken a chance to move to a university where a man of his background could have had the kind of authority and courses he was entitled to by his education and writing. He didn't want to move, because once he had his assistant professorship and we had bought this farm, he got attached to it—we're all close to the land—and he said he'd rather not move to any place that might turn out worse than this. Even now I still advise him to look around for a change to a better college where he could get the respect he deserves, but he's fifty now and hasn't got the energy for that kind of a move. Besides he's disgusted with what he's been through in his life, though I can't exactly say I blame him for that.

"Personally, I still wish he had gone back East sometime, he'd have been better off for opportunities. He's the only one of the whole department here who will take the trouble to read up on an idea and write it out. He's had more than twenty different articles and essays published and some day hopes to have them all in a book. He has long since deserved his advancement, but I told you about this seniority business, and besides, the old dean who has just retired, Dean Feeney, was a tight-fisted man, and so for that matter, though I'm not trying to prejudice you—he has his virtues but he has his faults—is Professor Fairchild. They could have advanced CD as far as he is entitled, but they said the department wasn't big enough to hold three full professors. CD says they don't like his plain talk is why they haven't given him his due. He's an outspoken man and isn't afraid to call a spade by name. Last June CD blew up when he didn't get his promotion, and he told Professor

Fairchild a thing or two. He promised to see what he could do this year. Please don't go around spreading that—it's nobody's business but CD's."

"No, ma'am, I won't."

"Well, he's promised before, but I guess Professor Fairchild feels it's no nails in his pants if CD doesn't get what he ought to. Which is worse than it sounds, because he's always had it good with those textbooks that CD wouldn't, as a scholar, lower himself to write. And there are others around here whose names I won't mention who are jealous of him. CD says they have average minds at best, and he tries to stay away from them so they don't waste his time. I've heard him wonder if some of the professors here have a college education themselves. Of course that really isn't so, but CD says there's an essay by William James—he's also from Harvard—and it's called, 'The Social Value of the College Bred.' The whole point to it is, if you have read it, that the reason for getting a college education in the first place is so you can tell a good man when you see him, and that's what nobody seems to be able to do around here."

Levin listened, holding his hat in his hands.

"You're getting impatient," she said. "I'll help you find CD."

"Kindly don't trouble yourself," he said, rising and dusting his raincoat. "Not after your sciatica. I'll look myself."

"Watch out for Lady Macbeth. She's our cow and has a frisky tail for strangers."

He followed her directions—going around the back of the house and across a weedy pasture. He crossed a dirt road he wasn't sure was part of Dr. Fabrikant's property—trespassing made him uneasy—went through a stand of poplars and as they thinned out, found himself confronting a hefty, big-uddered white cow, Lady Macbeth, without doubt, and God help him if her lord were around. Horrified by the immensity of the beast, he retreated, his hat slapped off by a poplar branch. As he tried to sneak up and snatch the hat from the ground, Levin stepped into a recently deposited cow pie. Cursing, he wiped his shoe on some dead leaves. Lady Macbeth approached, mooing. Levin grabbed up his hat and retreated through the trees. On the road he heard the sound of hoofbeats, and as he looked up, saw a horse galloping towards him. He jumped wildly aside. The startled rider managed to pull the animal to a halt; Levin knew at once he was Dr. Fabrikant.

Gripping the reins short as he calmed the frightened mare, Dr. Fabrikant, a cigar butt clamped between his teeth, the pupil of a gloomy left eye enlarged over that of a sober right, under heavy eyebrows examined the intruder. His sister had said he was fifty but the associate professor looked older, his face seamed by many lines; he sat stiff on his horse, giving an impression of unease. Stocky, short, on top of his small mount, wearing an old camping hat, he resembled U. S. Grant, but Grant lacking something, maybe his whiskey barrel. Though he looked like an outdoor type in khaki pants and jacket, with field boots laced to his knees, Dr. Fabrikant appeared to Levin, conscious of his prior knowledge of him, an inside man momentarily out.

"I'm terribly sorry," he explained. "I got lost looking for you."

"I don't permit salesmen on this property," said Dr. Fabrikant. "That's tacked up on a tree in front of the house."

"I'm not a salesman—not any more, a month finished that. S. Levin is my name—I'm sorry to disturb you. I was passing by and thought I'd say hello for a minute if I might. Your sister—Miss Fabrikant, told me you were out this way, and on account of her sciatica I went to look for you myself. I'm the new man here."

"What new man?"

"In the English department I should've said. I heard about you and came to pay my respects to a fellow liberal."

Dr. Fabrikant, shifting his weight on the horse, studied Levin.

"I also heard from more than one source that you're the leading scholar of the department."

The associate professor, removing his cigar, laughed in two short syllables—engine and caboose. "That's not saying much."

"I hope to read your articles sometime."

Dr. Fabrikant bowed, finally seemed pleased. "Nice of you to come."

"The reason I mentioned liberal is I happened to notice the

title of one of your courses in the college catalogue. I also heard you were an outspoken defender of—ah—Mr. Duffy."

The horseman's expression was at once wary. "What did you hear about that?"

"Not much, really, except you had been sympathetic to him—for a while at least."

"Duffy was a damn fool."

"You don't say? I'm sorry," Levin was disappointed. "I had hoped he was worth defending."

"He was—up to a point."

"He seemed to me, when I heard about him, like a sympathetic person."

"Did my sister tell you about him?"

"Oh no, sir. Some other people did, including Professors Fairchild, Gilley, and Bucket."

"You've met them all?"

"I've been here almost a month."

"Where are you from?"

"New York City—Manhattan, to be exact."

Dr. Fabrikant dismounted and they shook hands.

"What satirical wind blew you hither?"

"I came for the change you might say."

"It's more than change, it's transmogrification."

"I know I'll like it once I make a friend or two."

Fabrikant lit a match and sucked in the flame, at the same time continuing to look Levin over. He thrust the burnt match into his pants pocket. "Woods are very dry about now." He gazed at the trees, puffing his cigar.

"Well, I guess I ought to be going," Levin said. He had hoped to stir up an invitation to stay a while, but the associate professor extended none.

They walked together, Fabrikant leading his horse, till they reached the road that led to town.

"Enjoying a place depends a lot on the people you meet," Levin was saying. "I already like Mr.—Professor Bucket, and I'm fond of Dr. Gilley."

Fabrikant grunted. "If you're fond of him I don't think you'll care for me."

Levin, off balance, did not know what to say.

The associate professor mounted his horse, then came an

edict: "Gilley and I may be in a contest for department headship after Fairchild retires. If you're a liberal, you may be called on to prove it."

He galloped back in the direction he had come.

The Syrian graduate student Mrs. Beaty had been expecting turned out to be Mr. Sadek Abdul Meheen, from Damascus, and Levin made his acquaintance the day he arrived. He was a short young man with a fluff of curly black hair on a balding brown skull, and a delicate Semitic nose that sniffed in the direction of vagrant odors. His moist black eyes were gently popped. He was respectful of Levin as an instructor, and although he spoke English well, consulted him in matters of usage. Levin tried but was not much taken by the man, hidden as a person and fanatic about hygiene. The fumes of Lysol stank up the bathroom for a half hour after he had been in it; he rubbed everything he touched—before, not after—with his personal bottle. He was majoring in sanitary bacteriology and taking courses in rat control and the bacteriology of sewage. But he played chess better than Levin and talked entertainingly of the Middle East.

Although they were uneasy with each other the two men restlessly roamed the Easchester streets together. The town, though attractive, was much of sameness. It had grown in a semicircle around a bend in the Sacajawea and now extended thinly to the western and northern hills; surrounding the long rectangle of green campus and red-brick college buildings. Downtown was a treeless grid of boxlike store and small office buildings, unimaginative and verging on abstraction. The goods in store windows supplied its only color. Around the business district were many old-fashioned double-pediform houses, mainly carpenter-built on small plots of ground, squeezed together; some were redeemed by gardens, shrubbery and trees, whose apples, plums and walnuts often rotted on sidewalks as Levin walked, evoking in him guilt for the waste. Farther out, past the campus, appeared the modern ranch houses with picture windows; tilted roof types; and split-levels climbing the hills. The fraternity and sorority houses were the most magnificent of the community. During the day, Levin enjoyed the town though it seemed entirely contemporary, without visible or tangible connection with the past. Nature was the town's true history, the streets and park barren of fountain spray or sculpture to commemorate word or deed of any meaningful past event. Lewis and Clark had not slept here, nor Sitting Bull, Rutherford B. Hayes, nor Frank Lloyd Wright. After the covered wagons apparently little had happened that was worth public remembrance except a few serious fires and the expulsion, not hanging, of Leo Duffy. But what Easchester lacked in communal memory and imaginativeness, it made up in beauty of natural setting, trees and clouds, cleanliness and quiet. Roses and ivy grew up some of the phone poles; and automobiles by law stopped at street corners when pedestrians crossed. This was civilized. Not since New York had any harried driver called Levin dirty names as he hurriedly crossed the street. There were no harried drivers. The new instructor's spirit was eased. He did not mind the smallness of the town. Had not Concord been for Thoreau a sufficient miniature of the universe?

But at night remembrance of New York City struck him like a spear hurled across the continent, adding weight to his body and years to his age. He walked with the map of the city underfoot; sometimes he thought of it as a jeweled grave to fall into, or a wound at his side. At night he missed the movement and mystery of people in dark city streets. The anticipation of adventure next block—walk one more and meet your fate among strangers—a bag of thousand-dollar bills dropped at your feet, or a wise and beautiful woman waiting for you at the corner. In Easchester, an hour after supper, although lines of cars were parked tight along the downtown curbs, the streets were weirdly deserted. Sadek and Levin met almost no one unless they entered a beer tavern or movie; these were usually two-thirds empty, more lonely than the streets. Levin had heard that the fraternal lodges were crowded, but at ten P.M., the town, from river to hills, except for a few scattered lights signifying human existence, was dead. Still they wandered, Sadek regretting that "a poor scholarship student" could not afford a car, Levin, who couldn't drive, not planning to learn. For want of something more exciting to do they walked out into the country; nature, except for the luminous furniture in the sky, hiding in the dark. Peering into the night, Sadek restlessly sniffing, they sought something it never seemed to offer. They were, Levin knew, on the prowl for a woman, who if she miraculously appeared, would run if she saw them—the bug-eyed Syrian who had smelled her out with his conjuror's nose, and the black-hatted, bearded Levin, unwed instructor, famished for love and willing to marry.

Several days before registration the college students began to arrive in town. Levin, though excited by their coming, was a little afraid of them for their looks and youth, whereas he was old at thirty and knew too much they didn't. The girls were mildly attractive, often hefty, not many truly pretty ones but the few who were, could make him ache. More could than could not. On Friday night before Registration Week Levin sat with Sadek in a booth in a tavern they had taken to coming to at the end of the evening. The tavern was barnlike, with a short blunt bar at which a few men with inexpressive faces dawdled. They drank with little talk, or quietly played shuffleboard. It surprised the new instructor how vast yet still the place could be. Most of the students left before eleven except for a married couple or two who sat around till midnight. This night Sadek and Levin were sitting in the rear booth, close to where the waitress stationed herself when she had nothing to do. She was a big-boned girl with a thinly pretty face. Her frame lacked flesh but her legs were good and her small hard breasts tantalized Levin.

She had served beers in a booth up front and was presently leaning against the wall, Sadek engaged in wooing her in a manner that had caused Levin astonishment and embarrassment the night before, when the Syrian had first demonstrated his attack. His method—was *this* the lore of the Levant?—was to turn his face to the girl's hips, where she was standing at rest, lean forward and address an incantation directly to the confluence of her anatomy. He crooned in an unknown tongue, his sensitive nose not more than an inch from her body. The waitress, after an amazed stare, squirmed, but then found it funny and broke into a nervous giggle, although she blushed when her eye caught Levin's. When she left to take an order, Sadek, as if his performance were nothing out of the ordinary, pared his nails with a small penknife, unmoved by Levin's sharp warning to behave. After the girl returned and took up her relaxed position against the wall, he again directed his plaint, or crooning, to her midpart. This occurred once more before they left the tavern. Tonight, as the Syrian repeated the ritual—it took less than thirty seconds and no one but Levin seemed to notice—the girl looked into the far distance but her eyes were tender.

As her affection for Sadek visibly bloomed, Levin, although irritated by the odd lovemaking, fought a growing jealousy of him, for the Syrian had developed a system that the new instructor envied. When Sadek left the table to relieve himself in the back alley—the toilet facilities of the tavern horrified him and he preferred not to do a major Lysol job there—on these occasions Levin talked to the waitress and learned her name was Laverne. He had told her he was Levin but she showed no interest. He wished he had the nerve to move up close and attempt to deal directly with the consumer, but this flair, or means of incitement, was beyond his talent and timidity, although the torment of his unexpected desire for the girl was now something to contend with.

It grew late—towards one. The college students had gone; only two silent drinkers stood at the bar, the bartender-boss on a stool near the cash register, glasses on, scanning a newspaper. The booths, except for Sadek and Levin, were empty. Laverne, dreamy-eyed, hugged the wall close to where the Syrian sat. He spoke to all of her now and she responded with smiles and laughter. At midnight Sadek had turned to Levin and asked him to leave, but Levin coldly replied he ran his own business. He sat in the pale beyond their acceptance, greedy for the girl and contemptuous of himself because of her indifference. Sadek got up and they moved away from the booth. The Syrian spoke quietly, she answered in low tones. Levin, straining to hear, grew tense with frustrated desire. He struggled to free himself from this degrading emotion but sat as if will-less. Sadek returned to his seat, not glancing at Levin, his dark face serene as he fondled his beer glass. Levin considered dashing out of the place to gulp fresh air but couldn't move because something he had often wished might happen to him, had happened instead to this freak. He longed to know from Sadek if he had made a date with Laverne, thinking that if he had he would accept the inevitable and depart, but he could not bring himself to ask, because he knew the answer. Sadek impassively scraped his nails. At closing time the girl changed her shoes and put on her coat as the Syrian, having drained his beer glass, ducked through the back door into the alley for a quick one.

Ten minutes later, as the bartender was putting out the window lights and the girl was standing impatiently by a clothes tree near the phone booth, a young policeman entered the back door and seeing Levin, spoke to him.

"Say, are you a friend of Sadek A. Meheen?" He read the name from a small black notebook.

Levin cautiously admitted he had heard of him.

"If it's all the same to you," said the cop, "would you want to come around to the police station and talk to the assistant chief? We just caught this guy committing a nuisance in the alley behind here. He was pissing against the wall, and my buddy issued him a summons returnable in Municipal Court tomorrow morning, but then this guy, or whatever his name is, got sore and called us some pretty filthy names, so we drove him to the clink to cool his ass off. The assistant chief wanted to call the dean of men and tell him what happened, but he don't like to be waked up past eleven, so when this guy said a friend of his was here and you were a professor at the college, the assistant chief sent me over because your friend might throw a fit if somebody don't calm him down. I'm telling you because if he keeps on acting this way he might get himself bounced out of college. Also we are worried because he's a foreigner and everybody is touchy on that subject nowadays."

Excitement boiled up in Levin as he foresaw adventure, although he warned himself not to be tempted. The battle he fought was short, nor would he admit he had lost, for adventure was adventure and how much of it had he had in his life?

"I'll drop in if I can," he said.

The cop answered, "It's no hair off us if you don't. We wanted you to know where your buddy was, and what for."

"I'm much obliged."

The policeman left by the back door.

Laverne, who had been standing near the bar with the boss, both curiously looking on, approached Levin.

"What happened to your boy friend?" she asked.

Levin reached for his hat. "Let's talk outside." His throat was tight.

The girl followed him into the quiet street as her boss put out the last light and locked the door. Under a dim street lamp in front of the tavern Levin told Laverne that Sadek had got into trouble and was now in the police jail.

"What'd he do?" she asked sullenly, as if he were to blame.

"He committed a public nuisance."

"What's that?"

"Frankly, he urinated in the alley."

"What would he want to do that for? We have a gent's room."

"You know these foreigners." Levin shrugged.

"Are you American?"

"American citizen, born and bred in the U.S.A."

"How come you have that big beard?"

"Out of respect for the dead."

"Oh."

"Look, Laverne," he said thickly, "I like you a lot. It would give me great pleasure to be with you tonight. You're very attractive."

"I bet you say that to make me like you."

He admitted every man had his own language.

"I've never done it before with a guy with a beard."

"It won't bother you."

She tittered. "We were going to my brother-in-law's barn, three miles out on Route 5 by the river. Have you got your car?"

"No, but why don't we go to a hotel?"

"Have you got six bucks for a double?"

"Frankly no, now that I think of it. All I have on me is four dollars and change."

"They won't give you a room for that. Your friend was planning on a cab out to the barn."

"In that case let's do the same—but how will we get back?"

"I don't know for sure. We didn't talk about that."

"Could you call a cab from your brother-in-law's house?"

"No. He don't know I use his barn or he'd tell my sister. Anyway, they don't run cabs after half-past two. Have you got a friend of yours who could pick us up?"

"No." Levin looked at his watch. It was one-twenty. "What we could do is walk home," he suggested. "It shouldn't take us too long to walk three miles if you know the way."

"All right," Laverne said. She linked her arm with his and they went through the deserted streets. He tipped his hat as they passed the police station.

The taxi took them out to the country, to Levin the pitch-black middle of nowhere. Somewhere along a road with a wire fence on one side and bushes on the other, Laverne told the driver to stop. Levin paid the fare and the cab disappeared in the dark.

"Duck under this wire," she whispered, "and you better be quiet."

"Are there any dogs around?"

"Just one in the house but that's down a ways."

"Which is the barn?"

"Straight ahead. You'll see it when your eyes get used to the dark."

"I see it now."

He followed her over harvested ground. Laverne rolled open the barn door. She snapped on the overhead light, found an oil lamp, lit it and set it on the ground in an empty stall. She then switched off the overhead light. At the far side of the barn several cows were sleeping on straw. The warm, fecund odor of the animals and the sweet smell of the hay and grain stored in the barn, filled Levin with a sense of well-being. It was overwhelming how his life had changed in a month. You gave up the Metropolitan Museum of Art and got love in a haystack.

"My first barn," Levin murmured.

"I'll get the blanket and then we can lay down," Laverne said.

"In front of the cows?"

"They won't wake up."

"Why not in the hayloft? Nice and soft."

"The hay prickles my skin and makes me laugh in the wrong places. I'll be right back with Buster's blanket. You better be getting your pants off."

"Is Buster your brother-in-law?"

"No, his horse."

"There's no chance of anyone coming in on us?" Levin asked. "Farmers get up early."

"At four he gets up. We'll be home long before that." She found the blanket and returned. Levin was still waiting.

"Why don't you take your pants off?"

"It's cold here. Have you got a blanket to cover us?"

"No, just this one to lay on."

"In that case I'll keep my jacket on."

"But take your pants off or they'll get crinkled."

"Why can't we take one of the blankets off a cow?" Levin asked. "We'll put it back later."

"If you look good you'll see the cows don't sleep with blankets on them. They'd get sick if they did."

Laverne spread the horse blanket on the ground, and standing on it began to undress. She was neat with her clothes, folding each thing and putting it down on a hay bale nearby. Levin placed his hat, trousers, and shoes stuffed with socks and garters, next to her things. He kept his shorts on.

Watching the girl undress in the shadowy light of the lamp in the stall, Levin felt for her an irresistible desire. Ah, the miraculous beauty of women. He considered falling in love with her but gave up the idea. He embraced Laverne and they kissed passionately.

"Your breasts," he murmured, "smell like hay."

"I always wash well," she said.

"I mean it as a compliment."

"It ain't so bad here, is it now?" she said softly. "The cows make it warm."

She knelt on the blanket and Levin got down beside her.

"Blow out the light," she said.

He did and crawled back to the blanket.

In front of cows, he thought. Now I belong to the ages.

"Do you love me any?" Laverne whispered, lying beside him. "Your friend said he did."

"I love your body. I love your breasts and am grateful to be near them."

She laughed, seeking him with her hand.

"Now," she said languidly. Levin rose to his knees and was about to be in her when a noise stiffened him. The barn door rolled open and a light flashed on them. Laverne screamed. Levin rose in panic.

Someone entered the barn, snatched their clothes off the hay bale and ran out.

"Sadek," Levin called. "Come back, you bastard." He chased after him but the Syrian was faster. He popped through the wire fence, dropping something but escaping with most of the clothes. A taxi was waiting in the road. The door slammed and the car drove off. Levin furiously shook his fist.

At the fence he found one of Laverne's shoes and her brassiere. He found nothing else there but near the barn he stepped on cloth and was overjoyed to pick up his pants.

Laverne had the lamp lit and the horse blanket around her.

"Sadek," Levin said. "They let him go and he probably got the same cab we had to bring him out here. He grabbed everything except this couple of things of yours I found and my pants. Would there be something around to wear?"

"Not that I know," she said, "but let's finish what we were doing and maybe by then he'll bring our clothes back."

But Levin, afraid he had waked someone with his shout, wanted to leave. He worried how to get Laverne home with only a blanket around her, and himself without socks or shoes. If they escaped freezing to death, suppose a cop stopped them in town? He could then kiss goodbye to his unbegun college teaching career. The thought gripped him by the hair.

"He won't bring anything back," Levin said. "Couldn't you possibly borrow some clothes from your sister? We'll surely get picked up if a cop spots you in that horse blanket."

"No," she said sullenly.

"Look Laverne, I'm sorry about the way this has turned out. I didn't plan it this way, I assure you, but we'd better do something sensible or we'll both land in trouble. We'd better start out for town right now, before the moon comes up, if it's going to, or dawn begins to show. In the dark we have a chance."

"You sure are some fine flop," she said acidly. "It's what I get for picking you instead of waiting for the one with guts."

He felt bad but answered nothing. Levin got his pants on, and she fastened her brassiere and slipped on her shoe. When she had the blanket wrapped around her they left the barn and got through the fence. They followed a rutted road, then a graveled one that butchered Levin's feet. He picked his way along the road, each step painful. Laverne limped along on one shoe but after a while took it off and flung it into the bushes. Barefoot, she walked without trouble.

"How far to the highway?" he asked.

"About a mile."

In ten minutes her teeth began to chatter.

"Cold?"

"My ass is frozen."

Levin, after a minute, stopped and removed his trousers. He handed them to Laverne. She stepped into them without a word, knotted the belt around her waist and rolled up the cuffs. They trudged along the dirt road till they came to an asphalt highway. Laverne wanted to thumb a ride but Levin asked her not to. When a car or truck approached they hid behind trees or lay down in the open fields. Then they went on again, neither speaking.

Stars peppered the sky but Levin's astronomy was the astronomy of fear, in particular, of losing his job. If he could get rid of the girl and her horse blanket he might make it, with or without pants sneak into town and quickly be home. He saw himself noiselessly jogging through the streets, as if training for a long distance race. He could ask her to put his pants in a bag and he would pick them up at the beer tavern the next night.

A dog appeared from off the side of the road and began to follow them. Levin considered tossing a rock at it but didn't want to antagonize the animal. The dog came closer, its eyes glowing in the dark. Levin was thinking of shinnying up the next tree but what would Laverne do? She bent for a stick and flung it at the dog. It took off with a whimper.

A truck approached from the rear. "Come on," urged Levin and ducked behind a tree, but this time Laverne continued walking. As the headlights hit her, to Levin's dismay she was jerking her thumb for a ride. The truck slowed down, then someone pitched an empty beer can at her, hitting her with a pong on the rump. Levin found her crying.

"Don't cry, Laverne."

"Bullshit."

They walked on. Once Levin went off the road into icy water in a drainage ditch. And Laverne tripped over half a rubber tire and skinned her elbow. He tied it with his handkerchief.

It seemed to Levin they had walked half the night before they finally entered Easchester. Under the garish highway lamps he was at his most anxious, fearing the police prowl car, tempted every minute to say goodnight and sprint home.

But he couldn't leave her because he considered it partly his fault they were in this mess, and he felt for her a certain tenderness for having for a minute lain under him.

They passed the lumber mill and a few minutes later he recognized Bucket's house. Laverne led him into a long alley, across a bridge and through a small park, where the icy grass froze what was left of warmth in his blood. A milkman stared at them from his truck. Levin urged her to go faster but when they turned the next corner she said they were home.

He was immensely relieved, at the same time fatigued and chilled. Only his overworked nerves had kept from him how bad he had been feeling. But on the porch, as Laverne took off his pants, the sight of her body aroused his desire.

"I'm grateful to you in more ways than one, Laverne," he said haltingly. "Couldn't we meet sometime—under better circumstances, and—"

She kicked his pants off the porch. "No, you bastard, don't ever let me see you again in your whole goddamn life. Don't think those whiskers on your face hide that you ain't a man."

This broke Levin up.

LEVIN WOKE with a sob from a dream of wrestling Leo Duffy, who when last seen, riotously tarred and turkey-feathered, was riding a rail out of town. Et tu, Brute? He shook his bloody fist at the new instructor. Levin leaped out of bed, indignantly shook the alarm clock, a new piece of junk, and pitched it out of the window. He hopped into his pants, fumbled with shoe laces, hurried into shirt, tie, jacket—everything thoughtfully laid out last night. Thank God he didn't have to shave; the beard paid off. Holding to his inexpensive broad-brimmed new brown hat, he ran on an empty stomach in a drizzle from Mrs. Beaty's house to Humanities Hall. Although it was only five after eight on the first day of fall term, the quadrangle was deserted, not a solitary soul visible. His students were already in class but Levin wasn't so he galloped to get there, his first hard running in years, heart whamming, throat parched, rain-coattails flying in the breeze. Bounding up the steps into the old wooden building he went two at a time up the inside stairs. On the second floor he shot a glance down the office side of the hall—luckily all clear, every door shut. Sneaking into his office, Levin dropped his damp hat and raincoat on a chair and grabbed books and papers. He hastened to class, running a broken comb through his whiskers. When for some unexplained reason he looked back, Professor Fairchild and Dr. Gilley, huddled together near the water cooler at the far end of the hall, were watching his progress.

A hush rose like a noisy fog as Levin entered the classroom. Confronted by sixty eyes exploring from the upturned soles of his shoes to his hairy face, he was momentarily panicked, wanted to fly—flee across the continent and hide in someone's cellar. But he said to himself, For shame, kiddo, with your experience! So he sat at the desk calling the roll in last year's voice, ashamed to have been late to his first college class; and to tell the truth the students seemed embarrassed too. But Levin recalled how certain of his old profs had habitually been unable to be anywhere on time, for which nobody he knew blamed them, so why exaggerate molehills? Tomorrow he'd be punctual as usual and a bad beginning would be forgotten. If

Professor Fairchild came to work at seven-thirty A.M. he would see Levin long since at his desk.

Having finished with attendance, still wobbly within, as if he hadn't yet caught up with what time it was, or had forgotten something he shouldn't have, although he hoped not, Levin wrote out on the board his name and office number and considered saying a few words of welcome, he the host so to speak. But since he was carefully following the mimeographed instruction sheet, he listed, first, texts, then described the course this was, namely freshman composition via formal grammar, a study he commended after a moment of silence; it clarified writing, that of course was the big thing. "A man who can clearly write an idea is one who can invent one," was Levin's good word for the day. In ten minutes he had gone through the fifteen items on the sheet and was vaguely considering dismissing the class—what could he teach them the nervous first day?—when by luck his eye fell on a line at the bottom of the page: "N.B. DO *NOT* DISMISS YOUR CLASS BEFORE THE END OF THE HOUR, G.G., DIR. COMP." Sweating over the error he might have made (he pictured both of them in the hall waiting for his class to let out before the bell rang), Levin got up and demonstrated on the blackboard types of sentences, as the students, after a momentary restlessness, raptly watched his performance.

Silence thickened as he talked, the attentiveness of the class surprising him, although it was a college class—that made the difference. He had expected, to tell the truth, some boredom—the teacher pushing the tide; but everyone's eyes were fastened on him. Heartened by this, his shame at having been late all but evaporated, Levin, with a dozen minutes left to the hour, finally dropped grammar to say what was still on his mind: namely, welcome to Cascadia College. He was himself a stranger in the West but that didn't matter. By some miracle of movement and change, standing before them as their English instructor by virtue of his appointment, Levin welcomed them from wherever they came: the Northwest states, California, and a few from beyond the Rockies, a thrilling representation to a man who had in all his life never been west of Jersey City. If they worked conscientiously in college, he said, they would come in time to a better understanding of who they were and what their lives might yield, education being revelation. At this they laughed, though he wasn't sure why. Still if they could be so good-humored early in the morning it was all right with him. He noticed now that some of them turned in their seats to greet old friends; two shook hands as if to say this was the place to be. Levin grew eloquent. The men in the class—there were a few older students, veterans—listened with good-natured interest, and the girls gazed at the instructor with rosy-faced, shy affection. In his heart he thanked them, sensing he had created their welcome of him. They represented the America he had so often heard of, the fabulous friendly West. So what if he spoke with flat a's and they with rocky r's? Or he was dark and nervously animated, they blond, tending to impassive? Or if he had come from a vast metropolis of many-countried immigrants, they from towns and small cities where anyone was much like everyone? In Levin's classroom they shared ideals of seeking knowledge, one and indivisible. "This is the life for me," he admitted, and they broke into cheers, whistles, loud laughter. The bell rang and the class moved noisily into the hall, some nearly convulsed. As if inspired, Levin glanced down at his fly and it was, as it must be, all the way open.

Pauline Gilley had telephoned Levin to invite him to the department potluck, held customarily on the evening of the first day of classes, at the river park.

"I've heard 'potluck' before," Levin said, "and think I know what it means but I like to be sure."

Pauline said, "Don't tell me you've never been to a potluck picnic?"

"Not that I remember by that name, though we used to bring sandwiches to Van Cortlandt Park on P.S. 111 field day."

"Stop, Mr. Levin, you'll make me cry." Instead she laughed. "It's a picnic supper where everyone brings some dish or other to share. Gerald says it kept social life alive in Easchester during the Depression."

"I'll bring a bakery cake," Levin said.

"Just bring yourself, bachelors are privileged."

He thanked her warmly.

"How do you like our department?" Pauline asked.

"Fine," said Levin.

"I'm so glad."

So Levin arrived empty-handed at the river park at 3:30 P.M. on Monday, feeling shy, a useless emotion returned from childhood; also foolish in new suit and sweater, since most of the men were in slacks and sport shirts. The park, thick with fir and spruce, redwood picnic tables strewn among the trees, was damp from the morning drizzle but no one seemed to mind and Levin was glad he had resisted the impulse to bring along his hat and raincoat. The number of people present surprised him, including many kids who set the park in motion. As the wives unloaded cartons and picnic baskets and laid the food on the tables, the men who weren't making the fire swung swings, played catch, and two or three fished with some of the older boys on the riverbank.

Levin attached himself to the Buckets. Algene was an awkward, long-necked, pretty woman. The five little Buckets, serious children, stayed together, Joe carrying the youngest on his arm.

He never lets up, thought Levin.

"Joe never complains," Algene said. "His motto is 'Labor, sorrow, grief, sickness, want and woes are the sauces of life.'"

"Sources?"

"Sauces."

"From Sterne?" Levin asked.

"What else?"

Pauline, in skirt and sweater and wearing pendant earrings, found Levin and insisted on introducing him to the department wives. These ran from plain to healthfully pretty; several looked like girls, two pregnant, the wives of Ed Purtzer and Wayne Sprinkle, instructors on the third floor. The other women ranged from young middle-aged to Mrs. Fairchild, old. Pauline said that among them were ex-grade school teachers, librarians, a nurse or two and some former secretaries. Several, married in college, had supported their husbands through M.A. degrees. None was without a suggestion of experience in the world and glad to be done with it—whatever their experience had been, the world outside Easchester, the unmated life. "We've settled in, all family," Pauline said.

Levin said he envied them.

"Do you envy Bucket?"

"Him, no."

She disappeared to round up her children, then returned to finish introducing him. Like their crewcut husbands whom he had met during the last week, the wives were hospitable and friendly. Despite his worrisome clothes, and bushy beard, which some of them scrutinized with interest, and one woman apparently could not abide, among them Levin felt more or less at ease.

Pauline saw to it that he got plenty to eat, his appetite inspired by the variety of food, the fresh air, and piney fragrance of the park. He sampled at least a dozen dishes, then, uneasy at all he had put away while contributing nothing, wandered from the table while Pauline was getting coffee. He met Gilley roaming around with a Zeiss Ikon, and watched him snapping people at random, responding happily to requests to take more. Gerald measured with a light meter what was left of daylight, screwed his eye to the view finder, patiently adjusted subject with object, then signaled hold it, and popped the shutter. A memory was fixed forever on shiny paper. Pauline and both kids came out of the heavier woods surrounding the park, Erik sobbing, and Gilley, to divert the boy, handed Levin the camera and asked him to shoot one of the family. He had set the instrument, balanced one kid on each shoulder, and moved close to Pauline. Levin, enjoying the novelty, snapped. Gilley invited him to pose with his wife but Pauline said it was too dark.

After everyone had eaten and the tables were cleared, the fire in the pit was built up within a semicircle of benches, and Professor Fairchild, in mackinaw and old hat, rose and stood at the far side of the fire, facing the picnickers. His wife, the Anti-Liquor League V.P., a gray-haired lady with two chins and rimless eyeglasses reflecting firelight, sat nearby on a portable chair, bulkily bundled in cloth overcoat and fur cap. In the ordered silence that descended, the children miraculously restrained, the professor spoke:

"The president and new dean have formally welcomed you, and I know Dr. Gilley has for the department, but I usually reserve this informal occasion to say hello to you and your happy families at the beginning of the academic year, and to announce what is new with us. I greet you, refreshed, I trust, by the long and peaceful summer—a priceless time of relaxation and pleasure, and, I sincerely hope, of reflection and the gathering of resources. I have no doubt you are looking forward to the duties of the new term, and the enjoyment and rewards of teaching.

"Let us at this time welcome back Dr. Leopold and Mrs. Alma Kuck, recently returned from Leopold's sabbatical year and the successful completion of his doctoral work. Leopold is now, and has been since June, the possessor of a doctor's degree in English from the University of Wyoming—his native state. A copy of his dissertation on *Piers Plowman* is now on file in the college library, and I urge you all to have a look at it. A lot of work goes into these papers and we ought to do everything we can to keep them alive. Well done, Leopold, and I hope this will be an inspiration to some of you younger men to consider your professional advancement. The Ph.D. is our conditio sine qua non, and everyone who has not yet acquired the degree should be working for it, no matter how rigorous the course.

"Once he had been awarded his doctorate, Leopold, with Alma and their two children, Mickey and Joanne, embarked on a well-deserved six-week vacation tour of the British Isles. Leopold tells me he has returned with twelve-hundred color slides of literary and historic interest, to entertain us during the coming winter. At my request he is also preparing a ten-page summary of the high spots of their trip, which I shall have Milly mimeograph and place in your boxes next week. We can't all get out into the world and are gratified when some of you bring it to us.

"Dr. Kuck." He pointed across the fire that reddened his face, and a man with gaunt features and prematurely gray hair got up and nodded to a sprinkling of applause.

"We also welcome back Avis Fliss, after a spring-term leave of absence without pay to attend her ailing mother in Louisville, Kentucky. Mrs. Fliss has benefited from her daughter's care, and we hope she is well along on the road to recovery. We've missed you, Avis, nice to have you back again."

He pointed into the dark. Again handclapping. Levin looked around but no Miss Fliss evolved. Apparently she was shy and the professor did not urge her to stand.

"I would like now to announce that Dr. George Bullock has recently been notified of the acceptance, by Koch and McCook, publishers, of his anthology *American Short Stories for College Use*. No doubt we'll be adopting it here in the near future for our 'Survey of Literature' class. And while I'm on the subject just let me say to you men"—he peered across the fire—"that I hope some of you will look into opportunities for writing or editing textbooks. The rewards aren't stupendous, but I can tell you from my own experience that the satisfaction in ordering one's thoughts and committing them to paper is greater than some of you young people seem to realize. We ought all to be expanding our horizons. George, I congratulate you on your usual energy and initiative."

George Bullock, a sharp-faced handsome man with light hair plastered tight on a long skull, bowed amiably, sitting on his hands.

"The department of vital statistics," the professor went on with a chuckle, "has no engagements, weddings, or births to announce presently, but we have acquired a new bachelor, so that we may be said to retain a stake in the future."

He said, after the momentary laughter, "I now take the opportunity to welcome among us Mr. Seymour Levin, a native of New York City, New York; B.A. from New York University, New York, 1940; and M.A. from the same institution, 1950. He comes to us at Cascadia College as an instructor in composition. We are happy to welcome him and hope he will enrich us from his experience in the East. There he is sitting with the Gilleys. Would you mind standing, Mr. Levin?"

Levin stood limply, with a bob of the head acknowledging the polite applause.

"Hooray," piped Erik Gilley in the aftermath of silence, and everyone laughed. Levin quickly sat down. When his color diminished to cool he noticed that Pauline's face still retained an embarrassed glow.

When Levin tried to think across the continent to a New York autumn his rainy thoughts no longer let him. They stopped at the drenched mountainside forests of the Cascades. He had cut himself off, he had discovered, from longing for the East. Without regret. If Levin regretted anything it was not long ago having escaped the city. In Easchester he felt comparatively at peace with himself, more than for years. To stay at peace he let days go by without opening a newspaper or turning on a broadcast. He knew what the news was and preferred to forget it: The cold war blew on the world like an approaching glacier. The Korean War flamed hot, although less hopelessly for America. The country had become, in fear and self-accusation, a nation of spies and communists. Senator McCarthy held in his hairy fist every man's name. And there were rumors of further frightening intercourse between scientists and atomic things. America was in the best sense of a bad term, un-American. Levin was content to be hidden amid forests and mountains in an unknown town in the Far West.

His alarm clock, retrieved and repaired, woke him in the dark shortly after six. He dressed in the cold, his senses like lit candles, and went down to the cellar to load the sawdust hopper with six pailfuls. The heat blew up in minutes. He fed Mrs. Beaty's white cat, then himself. Levin ate leisurely, reflecting that much of his enjoyment of Easchester was relief in having escaped the city's nervous hurry. After washing his few dishes, when the sky brightened he snapped off the kitchen light and sat in the morning dark. Afterwards he read for fifteen or twenty minutes in the front room, looking up from time to time at the ticking clock on the mantel—he was, after all, Levin—and left the house at seven-twenty. He walked to work, the streets deserted; fifteen minutes later the flow of students on foot and in cars, began. At seven-twenty Levin could still be the first man abroad in the world, another refreshment.

If it was raining he went under his blooming black umbrella. Usually the morning was overcast between wettings, the moving sky continuously surprising. Overhead the clouds roiled dark; ahead thinning through shades of gray to an accident of gold. To the north above the dark green hills, a moody blue. In the west white steam shrouded the mountain tops. Depending on the direction he looked, above could be gold, black, silver, gray. He had never in his life gazed so long at sky, probed so often the places of light, threads bursting, spoonfuls burning, webs of glowing caught in trees. Around noon, if it was going to, the sun poked its steaming eye through the mist, and clouds broke into rivers and lakes, creating blue afternoons. Marvelous.

Teaching was itself sanctuary—to be enclosed in a warm four-walled classroom. Levin taught twelve hours a week, a thankful reduction of the more than twenty of his high school program. Bonehead grammar was all daily drill, *The Elements*, plus workbook D; but Comp 10, the regular freshman course, was a little more civilized. Although *The Elements* again prevailed, with workbook A constituting two-thirds of the instruction, here at least were six themes, based on *Science in Technology*. These, with frequent quizzes, produced a heady pile of paper which the instructor, with Duffy in mind, labored to stay abreast of. He was told that in English 11, next term, he would teach writing. "It's more a college course," Gilley said. "First we have to teach them what the high schools didn't." Though disappointed in the subject matter, Levin taught with passion although it came out grammar. But the students respected what mystified them, so he enjoyed teaching it.

He was independent—no supervision nor direct official inquiries, though Avis Fliss, Gilley's assistant in remedial courses, gave tactful advice here and there. She had materialized as a not-bad-looking woman of about thirty-five, with a breathy voice and fluttery eyelids, the one who had looked away from his beard when Pauline had introduced him. Her taut, flexible neck was a surprising instrument, it seemed to Levin she might see behind her if she tried. Among Avis' assets were a well-stacked bosom, and behind like a hard head of cabbage in a tight skirt. Her scent was a warm mixture of orange blossom toilet water and tobacco smoke; Levin found it interesting. For a while she was ill at ease with him, not knowing whether to confront his whiskers head on or peek around or under to uncover a fugitive from justice. Her eyelids fluttered as she spoke to his left shoulder. But he waited for her to come to grips with him and before long she did. Her flutterings diminished, the voice took heart, and though coy, she addressed him to his eye.

Between classes he appreciated his private office—*his*—the first he had ever had, an unbeatable institution for someone who lived much alone. During two daily office hours Levin saw his students and "counselees"—ten, whose programs and performance he had to keep an eye on—did what he could for them, and sent them on their way. Once his hours were over he kept his door shut and graded papers, or read, a privilege during the working day. Yet when someone knocked, his impulse was to hide the book. Some of the other men, Bucket for one, gave unlimited time to their freshmen, and Levin uneasily thought he might be cutting it too short but finally figured he taught conscientiously and was available when he was supposed to be. After that he had work of his own and wasn't, like some of the boys on the third floor, whose voices he heard in the hall as he passed their offices, interested in discussing at length the World Series or the latest football scores. Being new at the business he needed time to himself. Not that he used every minute earning his salary. Often he stood at the window—the cracked part resembling a tree in the glass—watching the clouds drifting eastward. He gazed at the green-lawned, thickly-treed quadrangle, liking its order and beauty as he recalled the stone skyscrapers in which he had gone to college. And he was fascinated by the casting classes across the street, men and women with fishing rods, flipping weighted lines at colored hoops in the grass, for two college credits. A new world, Levin.

People visited informally from office to office. His coffee mug preceded George Bullock through doors, then he emerged. Avis, wandering, loved to sit on people's desks; her legs were fair. Others Levin met in the men's room, but the crossroads of Humanities Hall was the coffee room. Before hurrying to the lavatory with her weak kidney, Milly Womack, the secretary, about twenty-five, with harlequin glasses, set the forty-cup percolator going for the first morning round. Soon Gerald's practiced ear picked up the sound of bubbling and he called down the hall, "Water's boiling." Then the daylong trek began. Whenever Levin came in for his daily cup or two of tea he was sure to meet someone, if not a crowd.

His colleagues, gathered for coffee, were amiable people, sociable, unpretentious, several well-educated but no one eager to show it. On a dark day one might be momentarily invisible against the wall. Every man, no matter his rank, was every man's assumed equal, very relaxing. Competitiveness, if it existed, was hidden: no visible back-biting or in-fighting, promotions came when they came and nothing could be done about it. No jackdaws crowed, though Bullock's wit produced a mild vaudeville, a Californian among Westerners. Despite their degrees or progress toward degrees, their pipes and casualness, the professors looked like the Rotarians downtown, with cheaper suits. But they wore their clothes without self-consciousness, and those whose haircuts were the work of wives with Sears Roebuck clippers, were proud of it. Saving money was a serious entertainment. The upstairs young men were of the same friendly breed, livelier, with more colorful jacket and slacks combinations. About five of the dozen were addicted to flattop crewcuts and occasional jive talk, though not much beyond conservative otherwise. They were, as Gerald put it, "very normal people," and Levin liked them, except Ferris Farper, a heavy-faced man with eyeglass frames too tight for his head, who glowered at him whenever they met until Levin grew uncomfortable. Farper would not forgive him for acquiring Duffy's office. Levin controlled his feelings until he discovered that Farper, after using the toilet for whatever purpose, did not wash his hands; he then returned him dislike for dislike. During October the instructor was invited home by Millard Scowers, O. E. Jones, and Dave Fitznogle, all from upstairs.

With the exception of Levin, CD Fabrikant, and Avis Fliss, everyone in the department was married. Some had been at fantastically young ages, and Levin envied them the years of loneliness they had escaped. There was much talk of domestic matters: kids, houses, the high cost of living. In self-defense a surprising number of men were expert at fixing any mechanical apparatus—cars, washing machines, flush toilets, hi-fi sets. Courtney Haddock, Maurice White and Gene McElfrish teamed up to clean a blocked sewer, pour two yards of concrete, and install a twenty-five foot television antenna. They discussed these jobs with theoretic and practical knowledge that made the instructor feel he had been born on another planet. Gardens were carefully kept up. Leaves were raked—speared almost as they fell—into piles on parking strips for the town truck to haul away. No wonder Levin missed the odor of burning autumn leaves—it wasn't allowed. Lawn mowing went on and on. Let the sun shine a minute and Ed Purtzer, whose house was two blocks to the college side of Mrs. Beaty's, changed into shorts and sweatshirt, rolled the mower out of the garage, oiled and adjusted it, then shaved his lawn, raked the cut grass, edged and combed the one-inch turf until it resembled his own stiff haircut. If a shampoo for grass were on the market he would have used it.

Most of them were specialists at saving money—of necessity on their salaries, although Levin felt one or two went above and beyond the call of duty. Dave Fitznogle could quote from memory the latest *Consumer Reports* ratings on anything from baby diapers to Piper Cubs. John Cutler, another upstairs man, was fanatic about auctions. He attended those in Marathon on Tuesday nights and bought things at bargain prices. One night he bid a dollar for a case of corn flakes and to his surprise, got it. Cutler couldn't stand cold cereal so he gave boxes of it away to colleagues and neighbors. Thanks to his generosity Levin enjoyed two weeks of inexpensive breakfasts.

During the fall the men in the coffee room talked about flying saucers, five percenters, TV, Ben Hogan's golf comeback last June, hunting, fishing, their army experiences, and the graduate school ratrace. There was talk about the weather; they congratulated themselves on its mildness. Although books were mentioned they were rarely discussed, and Levin continued to confide his thoughts of what he had read to his notebook. At ten and three, when Professor Fairchild appeared in the coffee room, there was standing room only. The old man, his cup in hand—he never seemed to drink—discoursed humorously on politics. His subject usually was creeping socialism, where it crept, the tyranny of the New Deal, which Easchester had four times voted against, and the evils of federal aid to education. No one questioned his argument or contradicted his facts. Even after he left, controversy did not begin. If there was a mild discussion it ended in agreement. The men or the times? Levin wondered. He had been told there had been "some hot arguments" when Duffy was around. If there was no visible fear in the department—no one spoke the word—Levin presumed an innocence or vacuum he did not inquire into. He was afraid to.

Gerald Gilley often sat alone in the coffee room. Levin, on his way to Milly's office or the water cooler, saw him on the bench, long legs comfortably crossed, his finger on the loop of a half-empty coffee mug dangling down his knee, eyes reflectively lit; or the cup full and thoughtfully rising to his puckered lips. Seeing the instructor going by, Gilley would lift his arm in greeting; most often he seemed not to know who was passing, involved with his coffee, the sipping so satisfying he smiled as if the brew were bewitched to some useful purpose. Levin envied him his particular cupful, the same brand he tried at night when he had a set or two of themes to knock off before tomorrow, only it didn't jazz up his dreams. If Gerald, examining the interior of his coffee mug, saw a vision of the future, it seemed to please him.

He was, as director of composition, cordial and generous. He never stopped giving Levin things, ordered for him a Webster's dictionary, S. LEVIN lettered in gold on the cover, brought in a flowered tin wastebasket, desk calendar, red-ink ballpoint pen, handy for grading; and he predicted the arrival of a foam rubber backrest for the instructor's chair, and a replacement, soon, of the cracked window that split the campus scene. "You're too kind," Levin said humbly, and Gilley blew his nose. It could truthfully be said he didn't know who next to give what. Levin wondered what the secret of his good nature was—constitution? the woman he had married? Maybe it was the years he had lived in small towns, his nervous system protected from city pressures, city grind? Maybe a combination of these things? Levin was curious about Gerald's experience—his life seemed to have gone along evenly—and he wondered if he had ever been ecstatic or miserable. And with wondering Levin wished him continued good fortune.

One morning Gerald knocked on his door. "Coffee, Sy? I mean tea? We could go across the street to the Student Union for a change?"

"Thanks, Gerald, I just had my cup." He nodded at the mug on his desk.

Gilley shut the door quietly and sat in the visitor's chair. "I've been thinking we could drive out to the coast tomorrow, if you're agreeable, and do some salmon fishing. There's a river I fish that gives up some good catches on eggs and flashbait. The fish are beginning to color—they get bruised up by this time of the year, but they're still in good condition. I've more than once taken Chinooks out of the water weighing thirty or forty pounds. What I do is bring my outboard motor and rent a boat. There'll be plenty of room for you, George, and me. I could lend you a spinner and a couple of lures. The regular license is five dollars but maybe we could get you a one-shot visitor's permit for a dollar, or skip it altogether. I haven't seen a warden all year."

"If we went I'd better pay," Levin said. "I get socked when I try to get away with something." He thanked him for the invitation. "I would like to go, Gerald, but frankly, I happen to be loaded down with papers just this week. Maybe we could make it some other time?"

"Sure," said Gilley, "we'll do it in the spring." He didn't seem too disappointed. Still it was nice of him to ask, Levin thought.

Gilley looked absently out of the cracked window, then at Levin. "How's it been coming, Sy? Your work and all that? Do you like it here?"

Levin said he did.

"Good deal."

Gerald after a minute asked, "I was wondering if you had heard of Professor Fairchild's impending retirement next summer?"

"Only that and no more."

"Orville's had a distinguished career here. He's known all over the state. Still," he said, "there's a lot to be done in the department." He had lowered his voice. "He's a little on the old-fashioned side and that's hindered us a bit. I say this loyally, you understand?"

"Yes, of course." Levin felt his throat tighten.

"I hear the new dean has a change or two in mind for us. The right sort of thing, I hope, because change just to change is senseless." He sounded moody. "Wouldn't you agree with that?"

"Sure," said Levin.

Gilley brightened. "If I were head here there are a few things I'd be inclined to start off with. First, I'd ask for at least five additional positions. Comp, as you know, is running thirty to a class, about five too many, ideally ten, but who has money for the ideal? And some of our lit sections go up as high as sixty. If I could bring them down to thirty–thirty-five, we might have some class discussions instead of concentrating on lecturing. This is confidential, Sy, but Orville's a little tight on budget matters. He prides himself on keeping costs down, and I'm for that myself, a hundred percent, but with a little more depth on the bench we'd be a better department."

Excited, Levin thought. This is his vision.

"Would you agree with that?"

"Certainly."

The director of composition wet his lips almost invisibly.

"If you happen to have any suggestions of your own for improving anything I'd be happy to hear them."

Good of him, Levin thought, but I'd better lay off.

"I'm really serious about that," Gilley said.

"In that case," Levin said with a thick tongue, "maybe I ought to say I think English 10 is a good place to begin teaching writing. I hate to mention this, Gerald, but some of the freshmen think a paragraph is a new invention. And I'm not against grammar but I'm against—I don't care for only grammar. For the boneheads it's torture."

"Bonehead is bonehead, Sy," said Gerald. "That's why they're there, to get the drill they didn't get before. As for paragraphing in English 10, that's an idea, but some of the men would shoot anyone who suggested more paper work in that course."

"The continuous workbook stuff is deadening."

"You've got your reader."

"We could stand one for the bonehead course, something with a little variety to it. I respect science and technology but it's not enough for growing boys and girls."

Gerald smiled. "I'll say this, I've thought of some of the things you're talking about, but frankly, Orville swears by the course as it's given. Still and all, whatever ideas you have for improving comp I'd be glad to listen to when the time comes. I like suggestions given in a friendly spirit by people who are aware of what the practical problems are and how long it took to build Rome."

Levin decided he had said all he was going to. He stroked his beard, twice yawning.

"Anyway," Gerald said, "I have no doubt that we see eye to eye on the important things."

Levin nodded.

"And I can count on your support?"

The instructor left off pacifying his whiskers. "Support?"

"What I have in mind," Gerald said, "is that I would like us all to work in harmony after Orville retires, to make this the kind of department it ought to be."

"I'm for that," said Levin.

"Good." Gerald extended his hand and Levin took it. "Every man counts."

The instructor, without knowing why, blushed.

Gilley, looking at his shoe, then at the mountains in the distance, said, "Maybe you've heard there might be some sort of contest between Fabrikant and me for the department headship? Have you talked to him yet?"

"A little, is about all I can say."

"He's a Harvard graduate and all that, good scholar but stiff as a board. I have seniority over him and I think Orville would like me in after him. That's just between us, please. It's not favoritism either. Years ago Orville offered CD the directorship of composition but he turned it down, so I got it. I've been doing the dirty work while CD has sat behind a locked door, writing his literary papers. That's why Orville favors me."

"In that case, why worry?"

"I'm really not, but we do have this new dean and, frankly, people in power are just plain unpredictable. If he starts calling department members into his office to consult them about a choice, I want them to know what I stand for, although I admit it's embarrassing going around talking to everyone. Pauline doesn't like it either."

Levin shrugged. "Practical politics."

"I'm glad you understand, Sy."

Gilley was getting up but sat down. "By the way, would you want a phone of your own put in here so you won't have to be running to Milly's office when she buzzes? I got George one two years ago."

"Who would I call?" Levin asked.

"That reminds me," Gilley said. "Pauline has been talking about having you over but there's been a million things and the kids already have colds. Erik starts off hacking and then little Mary picks it up."

"Spsssh," said Levin. "Plenty of time."

"I just want you to know we've been keeping you in mind. Pauline finds it a little hard to get started entertaining after the summer. She says the town is over-organized—just too many things for everybody to do and she's in a lot of it, though I've been begging her to cut down. Tires her out. She's on the Library Committee, the Community Chest, and the Women Voters—they're trying to do something about the sewage and she goes to more damn meetings till all hours. I try to get her to ease up but she says it's all worth while, so she wears herself out. We've been a little snowed under but we expect to see more of our friends soon."

Levin thanked him.

Gilley got up. "One last thing. One of the textbook salesmen is after me to do a freshman reader. Would you care to lend a hand? It'd be mostly finding suitable articles and writing up a few questions and notes. After paying off contributors we could expect a yearly five or six hundred apiece for about half a dozen years. After that we could revise without too much trouble and the thing could go on and on. Nobody gets rich—Orville's sales are unusual, but the money is nothing to sneeze at either."

"Thanks, again," Levin said, blowing his nose. "Maybe sometime, but you know how it is on a new job. You have to work at it for a while before you have any spare time on hand."

Gilley grinned. "I think you work too g.d. hard, Sy. You ought to have more fun. I'm getting worried about you."

Levin, on the verge of cracked laughter, peremptorily cut it out.

Over the weekend, in blasts of wind and rain, the walnuts began to fall in the backyard, plopping down on dead leaves and sopping grass. When Levin saw what was happening he ran out with Mrs. Beaty's big aluminum pot to collect them. The nuts were large, their shells glowing orange when they fell from the broken pods. He greedily cracked one open and tried eating it but the meat was rubbery. When he brought the loaded pot into the kitchen, the landlady set aside those with broken shells and scrubbed the others with a brush. She showed Levin where to put up an old window screen, on pipes above the furnace, for the walnuts to dry out on. All day Levin went often to his window and when he saw any nuts on the ground, ran down the stairs with the pot. In bed, for hours he heard the nuts socking the wet earth in the dark. At dawn he quickly gathered them up, not at peace until all the walnuts were in and drying, and the tree was bare.

Leaves fell in the rain in droves, multitudes, refugee millions —maple, oak, chestnut, walnut, pear, cherry, mountain ash, and the large alien sycamore leaves from across the street; like a soggy blanket they covered gutter, sidewalk, lawn, backyard, bushes and alley. Levin resisted raking them until he could no longer stand his resistance. One afternoon after class he began to work. He raked first the front lawn, then the sidewalk and swept it clean, carrying wet bunches of dripping leaves to the piles on the curb-strip. He raked under each shrub and hand-picked the bushes clean. Although it was soon dark and he was tired he continued to gather leaves. By the light of the street lamp he scraped up those along the curb, and then in the light from Mrs. Beaty's kitchen window, raked the backyard. He raked wearily, without thought, both palms blistered, arms and back aching. The landlady, through her window, begged him to stop but Levin raked to destroy all dead leaves. He went on in a misty drizzle, stacking the backyard leaves on the mulch pile behind the garage. When he was through, at an unknown hour, the grounds around the house were neat and clean yet he regretted not having got at the leaves in the gutter.

The instructor was thinking of going to Gilley to make it clear to him that he wasn't committing himself to anyone for head of department until he knew more than he did about both candidates. Instead, on impulse late one afternoon, Levin knocked on Dr. Fabrikant's door down the hall. Though he had passed the scholar in the hall more than once, his white socks visible as he walked, his bachelorhood unyielding, they had not talked since the time Levin had visited his farm.

He was in, Levin heard him cough. He waited until something that sounded like a bolt was withdrawn. Fabrikant stared out at him.

"Excuse me, I—"

But the scholar held the door open. "Come in." Off his horse he looked less formidable. And he turned out to be, without a hat, bald, yet in need of a haircut around the pelted head.

His office, as Levin had expected, was overrun by books, including loose-paged piles on the window sill, radiator, and spare desk in the corner of the room. On his desk he had laid out rows of note cards, thickly scribbled; these ran onto the floor. Levin, envying work in progress, would have liked to know what the scholar was doing, but he had heard from Bucket that he was secretive about his research. Feeling with both hands among the paraphernalia on his desk, Fabrikant located a cigar butt, lit up, shaking the match out over his head, then pointed with the smoking stick to a chair. Levin, after stepping gingerly over the cards, removed half a dozen books from the chair and seated himself.

"I would hate to interrupt something important."

Fabrikant puffed his cigar butt without comment. "How are you coming along?"

"I can't complain."

"I can and do." The scholar laughed his two syllable laugh. "Do you like the West?"

"Yes, I do. Everybody's friendly."

Fabrikant, regarding him, grunted. "I wouldn't live in the East again if they offered me the mint. I've often thought if the capital of the United States were located out here we'd have a lot more sanity in our national life."

"I left New York on my own accord—"

"It was sensible."

"—seeking, you might say, my manifest destiny."

"This corner of the country was come upon by explorers searching for the mythical Northwest Passage," Fabrikant said, "and it was opened by traders and trappers in their canoes trying to find the Great River of the West, the second Mississippi they had heard of. Then the settlers came, fighting the Indians, clearing the land, and building their homes out of their guts and bone."

"Marvelous," Levin murmured.

"'There were giants in those days,'" Fabrikant said moodily. "Their descendants are playing a defensive game. Their great fear is that tomorrow will be different from today. I've never seen so many pygmies in my life."

"That's very interesting," said Levin. "It reminds me what you said last time: that if I was a liberal I might be called on to prove it. Those were your words and would you care to elaborate a little?"

Though his butt had gone out, Fabrikant still puffed. He puffed and said nothing. Levin grew uncomfortable. In his mind he began to search for an exit.

"Did I say that?"

"Something of that nature."

"I was annoyed. Frankly, I didn't like the circumstances of your hiring."

"Me?" Levin had partially risen.

"Yes," said Fabrikant. "The arrangement is for the three senior members of the department—Fairchild, I, Gilley—to look over applications for positions and make a choice. I wrested this morsel of democratic procedure, together with a course or two, out of them some years ago, but in your case my approval was omitted."

"I'm very sorry."

"It's true that there was an emergency when the man we had hired in the spring reneged in summer and a new selection had to be made in a hurry. Fairchild was in Walla Walla at his daughter's, and Gilley, without consulting me, acted on his own. He later contended he had tried to get me on the phone at my house but couldn't. My answer to that was he ought to have driven over to the farm, because he knew my sister was in the hospital with her sciatica and I am usually on the premises. He didn't bother and made the selection alone. He hired you."

"Ah—I'm sorry."

"No fault of yours."

Levin felt low. Once in his life he hoped to be somebody's unchallenged first choice.

"After talking to you," Fabrikant said, "I was satisfied Gilley had blundered into a suitable appointment. Nevertheless, I have to insist on the few prerogatives I have here."

"I understand," Levin said. "What I was referring to before is that since there seems to be a contest of some kind developing, I thought I ought to inform myself what your ideas are for running the department, if I may ask."

Fabrikant was deathly silent.

My God, have I jumped the gun again? Levin asked himself. "I—er—hope the question is not out of order?"

"No," said Fabrikant, "but I'll answer only if it's understood I'm not politicking. I don't care for that."

"Of course."

"If I become head of this department," Fabrikant said, "I'll change plenty." He gazed gloomily at the book-lined wall. "But this is all premature. I don't know that I'm even remotely considered as a possibility. There's been talk that the new dean may want—but that could be no more than rumor. At any rate whoever they may or may not have in mind for the job, I'll say without false modesty that I am at all odds the logical choice. They can't match my educational background, nor my research and publications, granted that they mean something in this institution, which I won't grant."

"I have heard that you were being considered—"

"Possibly. This is strictly confidential, but the administration hasn't always been happy with me. I've espoused more than one unpopular cause in the past."

"Like Duffy, for instance?"

Fabrikant grimaced. "Let's forget him."

"Excuse me—"

"I've been too independent for them. I haven't made friends or influenced people. Gilley has made a career of that. He's always washed Fairchild's dirty drawers so the old man could be free to potter with his textbook. Such devotion is not for nothing."

"Does Mrs. Gilley approve of that?"

"I have no interest in Mrs. Gilley," Fabrikant said. "Since you've brought this matter up I'll tell you what I would try to accomplish in the department. First of all I'd ask this new dean to do something drastic about salaries. Fairchild is stingy, so was Dean Feeney, a conjunction of two constipated stars in the same constellation. For years they kept us dancing in our bare bones; as a result, this department is the lowest paid on the campus. If Fairchild had gone bellowing to the president that he employs human beings, Labhart might have done something more than throw the poor dog a bone."

"Tst-tst."

"Before I brought it to a stop Fairchild wasn't spending the pittance we were allowed for a library allotment and was turning part of the money back to Dean Feeney, who assigned it to those departments who were overdrawn on theirs."

"That's too bad—"

Fabrikant drew on his dead cigar. "By the way, what are we paying you?"

"Me? Three thousand a year."

"That's scandalous. You should be getting thirty-five hundred, at least."

"Without college teaching experience? I taught for two years in a high school."

"Even so you're ridiculously underpaid."

"Dr. Gilley said he would have given me more if I were married."

"What's that got to do with your ability to perform your task? I'm not married and proud of it."

"I'm just saying what he told me."

"We have a few good men here, most of whom I've insisted ought to be hired, but their efforts are frustrated by those who came to teaching to hide their ignorance. I'll name no names. I'd throw them out if I could and bury the rest in composition."

"Could I ask what you'd do in composition—to improve it?"

"I'd throw out *The Elements.*"

Levin gulped.

"He's got stinking rich out of that atrocity."

"Er—What is your position on the liberal arts issue? Would you try to bring back English majors?"

"One couldn't unilaterally," Fabrikant said. "That's a political football and would have to be worked out with our idealistic friends at Gettysburg. Of course I'd plug for the return of the whole liberal arts program, but keep in mind that this situation has existed for thirty years and nothing's going to change it overnight. I don't think the majority of this faculty is interested in a good liberal arts program."

"But some are?"

"Very few and that includes those in our own division. They've lived in the graveyard so long I doubt they'll ever come back to life. I'm frankly pessimistic and don't foresee any change in the situation during my lifetime. It takes fifty years to grow a tree and that sort of thing influences people's ideas around here."

"Shouldn't we start propagandizing—working, that is, for the idea, to recover what we once had? With the right leader we—"

"There's only one leader at Cascadia College and that's Marion Labhart. What he wants is what we get."

"Couldn't it be suggested to him?—"

"It has been, but it won't do any good until he falls over it himself. One has to be careful with that type."

Levin imagined the scholar hadn't been.

Fabrikant dropped the cigar stub into the wastebasket and rose. So did Levin.

The scholar fixed him with his gloomy eye—it was almost without iris. "I'll have to caution you again to be discreet about our talk. In my position a man has to think along more than one track. If Gilley should be chosen over me I'd still have to live with him."

"I won't say a word." Levin stepped over the note cards on the floor. "Thanks, I've—ah—learned a lot."

Fabrikant lifted his shoe to strike a match, then realized he had discarded the cigar butt. He shook out the match and tossed it into the wastebasket. In afterthought he poured half a glass of water into the basket.

Levin had the door open but shut it. "Do you happen to know how much Mr. Duffy was paid?"

"Thirty-seven hundred."

"I guess he had more experience?"

"He had never taught before."

"You don't say? Er—Would you know any special reason or circumstance why I was chosen over other applicants for the job? Was I the only one who was willing to take three thousand?"

"As I told you, Gilley didn't consult me."

"Thanks anyway." Levin left.

A minute later he was back. "Sorry to bother you again. This popped into my head but I forgot to ask you. They're showing a good film downtown tonight and I wondered if you'd be interested in seeing it? We could have some coffee after—that is, if the idea appeals to you?"

"Thank you, no," Fabrikant said. "I don't go to the movies, too darn much sex."

Levin guffawed.

The instructor had discovered a rich night life on the second floor of Humanities Hall. He found not only Bucket at his lamplit desk—door wide open for he felt it unnatural to work in silence after living with five kids—but also George Bullock, usually with a half dozen six-footers sitting around his desk; and Avis Fliss typing or mimeographing objective tests for her remedial classes. Levin heard from her that Gilley popped in once in a while, and it was rumored Merdith Schultz also came in but no one tried to prove it.

Levin had several times spoken with Bucket, but only in passing, for the assistant professor was one of the few genuinely busy men in the department. When not in class he had one or more students in his office, who came early and stayed late. At night Bucket banged away in a fast hunt-and-peck on the latest revision of his dissertation. He worked in the same cement-stained Levi's Levin had seen him in on the roof, and in socks, his army shoes on the floor. Since he was always so busy Levin preferred not to bother him, but one rainy night in early November, shortly after his talk with Fabrikant, after twice wandering past Bucket's open door without attracting his attention, the instructor knocked on the jamb.

Bucket hastily covered the papers on his desk with a folder and swiveled to face his visitor.

"Could I see you for a few minutes?" Levin asked.

"Please come in."

"I won't stay long. I know what your time means to you."

Bucket cackled. "I've meant to visit with you but you know my situation."

"Tst," said Levin.

"It could be worse."

"I admire your patience."

"'Tis known by the name of perseverance in a good cause,—and of obstinacy in a bad.'"

"Sterne?"

"Touché."

Leaning back in his chair Bucket rested his shoeless feet on the desk. He reconsidered and withdrew them.

Levin sat with his handkerchief in his hands.

Bucket glanced covertly at the typewriter but waited patiently.

Levin sighed. "I've been teaching here five weeks, half the term, without a feeling I'm accomplishing much. I'm up to par," he went on quickly, "according to the syllabus, but short on satisfaction. Maybe you can advise me?"

Bucket glanced out into the hall. "You might keep your voice down."

Levin peered through the door but saw no one. "If you'll pardon me for saying so, I'm so busy with *The Elements*, trying to cover what I have to for the departmental objective, that there's very little time for much else."

Bucket nodded.

"The themes I've been getting are short on ideas, and I've had to take time off in self-defense, though the syllabus doesn't call for it, to teach how to organize and develop a topic. I know they're supposed to know—"

Bucket nodded.

"Er—The *Science in Tech* essays, when we do get to them are something less than inspiring, for which I blame not the subject but the selection. I blamed myself until I read them again. Believe me, I can understand why Duffy ordered outside readings."

Bucket, poking his head into the hall, quietly shut the door. In afterthought he snapped the lock. Stepping into his shoes, he polished his glasses and sat back in the chair.

"The way the world is now," Levin said, "I sometimes feel I'm engaged in a great irrelevancy, teaching people how to write who don't know what to write. I can give them subjects but not subject matter. I worry I'm not teaching how to keep civilization from destroying itself." The instructor laughed embarrassedly. "Imagine that, Bucket, I know it sounds ridiculous, pretentious. I'm not particularly gifted—ordinary if the truth be told—with a not very talented intellect, and how much good would I do, if any? Still, I have the strongest urge to say they must understand what humanism means or they won't know when freedom no longer exists. And that they must either be the best—masters of ideas and of themselves—or choose the best to lead them; in either case democracy wins. I have the strongest compulsion to be involved with such thoughts in the classroom, if you know what I mean."

"I do," said Bucket, "but if we all did that who'd be teaching composition?"

"That's what I tell myself but it doesn't help much."

"Take my advice and don't introduce any extraneous text into the course without Professor Fairchild's express permission."

Someone knocked on the door.

When Levin realized he was looking for a place to hide, he composed himself by smoothing his beard.

Bucket, after a quick glance around, got up and turned the lock.

George Bullock was standing in the hall, blinking at the light, his hat and trench coat soaked. His sharp nose and narrow cleft chin inclined him to hatchet-faced.

"Raining," he said.

"So?" said Bucket.

"I heard voices. Thought Gerald might be here." His glance fell on Levin.

"Sorry," Bullock said to Bucket.

Bucket shut the door, he seemed uneasy.

"Was he listening?" Levin asked.

"Sh." The assistant professor kept his ear to the door until they heard footsteps going down the hall.

"Don't you like him?" Levin asked.

"That's a difficult question."

"Excuse me for asking."

"We're not friendly, a case of mutual disapprobation." He put his ear to the door again, then sat down.

"What does he do here at night?"

"He tutors athletes twice a week."

"Athletes?"

"Bullock seems genuinely concerned about them as underprivileged people. Sometimes he has more than a half dozen a night who are having trouble in composition or literature, or both."

"Is that an assignment?"

"As I understand it, no official source has commissioned this particular occupation. Bullock apparently thought up the idea on his own and no one opposes it. At first it was a completely voluntary, and, I suppose, generous act on his part, but then the Physical Education department heard about it and insisted on paying for his services. I've heard no complaints about it. I understand that Leroy Davis and someone else from upstairs, have pitched in now and then, at George's request, to help. He's a popular figure with the athletes. Last Christmas Eve the football and basketball squads serenaded him and Jeannette on their front lawn. They held white candles and sang carols."

"Why would a Ph.D. in English be so interested in athletes?"

"The breed has infinite varieties." Bucket cackled.

"Is that sort of thing cricket?"

"Some say no."

"Er—Shouldn't something be done about it?"

"Possibly—under the right circumstances."

Levin pondered his remark. "You mean if the right person gets to be head?"

"I'll say no more."

"I'll go now."

"You needn't rush."

"I've wasted your evening."

Bucket denied it. "I'll be revising this accursed paper forever."

"Then one more question: I've lately talked to Fabrikant and Gilley—I've heard that either one or the other may be the next head. They're different types, that's sure, but both very conscious of the limitations of whatever powers they might have in the future—in other words, what they can hope to accomplish here. I'm a little more favorable to Fabrikant, I like his point of view, but I like Gerald too, as a person. I have no illusions that my support, or the lack of it, will mean anything much to either of them but just so that I know what I'm doing, who's the better man if you don't mind saying?"

Levin put away his handkerchief and Bucket pulled his out and mopped his brow.

He said in a low voice, "My own considered preference is for CD over Gerald."

"Aha."

"That of course is strictly confidential."

"Of course."

"Gerald, in his way, can be an efficient administrator. He may someday be dean of something or other, but CD, in my opinion, is more truly interested in literature and literary scholarship and would be more effective in raising our standards. Although I agree with your observation that there'll be few daring innovations under either man, yet what comes with CD will come with increasing value."

"I didn't mean—"

"When I say 'raising our standards,'" Bucket hurried on, "I speak without disrespect for Professor Fairchild, an old and much-liked teacher of mine. I've often thought it a shame that he did not devote himself entirely to teaching. I'll testify he does it well."

"Does Fabrikant have a chance at the job?"

"Your guess is equal to mine. I understand the situation is fluid. No one I know quite understands the preference of the new dean in all this. One hears all sorts of rumors."

"Is Gilley at all liberal? His wife sounds as though she might be."

"I wouldn't judge him by her."

"He was dead set against Duffy?" Levin asked, one hand investigating his beard.

"That describes it."

"And Fabrikant defended him?"

"At the outset."

"Something happened between them? Was it some sort of fight?"

"I don't think I'd care to go into that."

"Were they ever friends?" Levin asked.

"I believe they respected each other but that's as far as it went. They were both very independent people and tended not to attract one another." Having said that, Bucket stepped out of his shoes.

"I'm leaving now," Levin said, "after this: When Fabrikant dropped Duffy's defense in the AAP, wasn't there anyone else to take it up?"

"He had become universally unpopular."

"Was he, with you?"

"I personally liked him, though I can't say I liked everything he did."

Levin rose at last. "Thanks for your time."

"Think nothing of it. I rely on your discretion." He said it with an inquiet laugh.

"Have no fear," said Levin.

He tried grading papers but could not keep his mind on it and left the office. Downstairs he waited on the porch for the pouring rain to let up, thinking of his talk with Bucket.

Whatever's happening here, he thought, I'd better not get involved.

The door behind him opened, George Bullock. "Want a ride?"

Levin looked at the night. "Thanks."

"Wait'll I get the wagon," Bullock said. "No use both of us drowning."

In a few minutes he drew up to the curb in a mauve station wagon and Levin ran down the steps and ducked in. He noticed at once a whiskey odor, and Bullock, as if sensing it, lit a cigarette. He was an intense man and drove with his head thrust forward, his sharp face like a ship's prow directed against the saturated night.

"I'll take the Bay Area winter fog to this soup anytime."

"Is that so?" said Levin. "I heard in the coffee room you had recently turned down an offer from a college in Frisco."

"Nobody but Easterners say Frisco."

"Excuse me, San Francisco."

"Your information was correct. My wife loves her mother. I figure better us alone in Cascadia dew than mama living with us in the California sunshine."

"Aha," said Levin.

"Now that we're sharing confessions, and without meaning to be personal, I didn't know you were palsy walsy with Bucket."

"Er—Shouldn't I be?"

"Who said so? I have nothing against the guy even if he does talk like the *New York Times*, but what makes me uncomfortable is the futility he gives off. Of all the people to write about: 'Laurence Sterne: a long digression.'"

"What's wrong with Sterne?"

"That immoral twerp."

"You don't say?"

"Have you read Thackeray on him?"

"No."

"You should." Bullock shook his head. "What were you two boys doing with your heads together? I bet Bucket played up CD Fabrikant for head of department?"

"His name was mentioned," the instructor said warily.

"Bucket overrates him, take my word. CD is a fair-enough scholar but starched like my granddaddy's collar."

"I hear he's had a hard life?"

"Who hasn't."

"You've had?" Levin asked.

"At fourteen I was crippled by polio. The doctor said I would never walk again."

"Tst-tst."

"So much for medical science. In college I ran a hundred yards in eleven seconds."

"Wonderful," Levin murmured.

"Have you read any of his stuff?" Bullock asked.

"Fabrikant's?"

"Yes."

"I expect to."

"Be sure to go over it with a vacuum cleaner."

"It's dusty?"

"You'll die sneezing."

"No good insights?"

"They were decrepit when he came on them."

"Ah, too bad," said Levin. "I like the thought of having a good scholar in the department."

"Goddamn, imagine bibliographing Civil War fiction." Bullock snickered.

"Is that what he's doing?"

"That's what he told Avis. She drops in to see him every once in a while and he looks at her legs. That's the only time he keeps his office door open, to show he's not seducing her. What kind of head of department would he make if you have to get to him with a crowbar?"

"More important," said Levin, "is does he have qualities of leadership?"

"Who leads behind a locked door?—unless it's Casanova, which he's not."

"Sometimes the door opens and out comes a man with a sword."

"If you think so he's your baby."

"I've heard some of the men speak of him with respect."

"Maybe so, but they know Gerald is the better choice. He gets along with everybody, and don't think that's so easy. He plays pinochle with Labhart and they golf together. When the chips are down I'll bet lox to bagels that Gerald will get more for the department than CD ever could with his history of antagonizing the administration."

"Are you referring to the Duffy case?"

"No, that time he was safe on base."

"When he dropped the AAP defense?"

"Yes."

"Would you happen to know why he did?"

"Didn't Bucket tell you?"

"No."

"Maybe Duffy pissed on one of Fabrikant's Persian melons. Or the old boy finally discovered what everybody else knew all along, that Leo was a fake. Up to then they had a sneaking admiration for each other as members of the maverick's union. What Fabrikant liked about Duffy was he did what *he* didn't dare to. Leo was the oddball's oddball, he hit the wall with his head. CD is a Milquetoast Quixote."

As they turned onto Levin's street, Bullock said, "I'll tell you what let's do. Let's shoot over to my joint and see how much comes out of the rum bottle when we squeeze. Jeannette's a sociable girl and would be happy to have you."

"Thanks," said Levin, "but I'm behind in themes."

Yet when the station wagon stopped in front of Mrs. Beaty's house, he lingered.

"What I don't understand," Levin said, "is why everybody is choosing sides. Will our advice be so important to whoever makes the choice?"

Bullock shot his cigarette out of a window he had lowered.

"It was an appointive job at one time but may not be now. Gerald was a shoo-in until they dug up Seagram from the cornfields of Iowa. This former buddy of mine who teaches where he did, wrote me the dean had done a study for some foundation or other on the new rage—departmental elections. Charlie says he's bugs on the subject. Well, whatever the method is, appointive or elective, I have my dough on Gerald. He's the logical choice."

"An election?" Levin felt excitement.

"Nobody knows for sure, but nobody's taking chances." He winked in the glass. "Realpolitik."

The instructor, with the door half open, had another thought. "Ah—when did Gerald first get wind there might be an election?"

"I told him last spring after I heard from Charlie that Seagram was coming here. Why?"

Levin shrugged. He pulled the door shut and went with Bullock.

ON DAYS the rain let up Levin still walked on country roads. Once he passed a barn where he thought he had been with Laverne. He thought of her with desire, up to when Sadek entered. After weeks of rain he thirsted for color, the eye seeking it in whatever light. White birches stood in baths of tiny yellow leaves. Elms had golden hair and naked black bodies. Chestnut trees in strong sunlight wore orange impasto. Vine maples, the only adventurers, flared yellow, red, and purple around green at the core. In the setting sun maples turned bronze, and oaks red. Toward Thanksgiving, except for willows, flaming vine maples, and a few tenacious birch and oak, most of the trees that had leaves to lose had lost them, bare except for patches of soggy brown rags and abandoned birds' nests.

It seemed to Levin that just when he was about to take the loss, the yearly symbolic death of nature, to heart, he discovered that many of the recently harrowed fields were touched with bright green grass that turned out to be winter wheat. Bread growing in the harvested field—this went against pathetic fallacy. One day as he was walking outside a forest trying to persuade himself (against the NO HUNTING, FISHING, TRESPASSING warning) to enter and explore, he heard strange noises in the sky, and looking up, beheld for the first time in his life a flight of geese. The fluttering, honking formation of birds was like a ship borne by the wind into the high invisible distance. Levin's ear burned all night, as if soaked in pitch and set on fire. He wondered what omen the flight held for him and hungered for a victory over nature.

Leaving Humanities Hall late one Friday afternoon, the instructor skidded on a wet leaf on the porch and his books and papers took to the air; he landed on the wet walk, whacking his head. Star clusters popped in his brain. For a second he thought he would remember everything in his life and braced himself not to. The rain drizzled on him but he was too hurt to move. He was vaguely conscious some students, possibly his own, were passing by, but either he was invisible or they were in a hurry. I am a man alone, thought Levin. It seemed a long year but only minutes had gone by before he dragged himself up, found his soiled new hat, collected wet books and papers, and hobbled home.

Levin lay on his bed with Mrs. Beaty's ice bag tucked under the egg at the back of his bruised and aching head. After twenty minutes' freezing his brain he got up and stared out the dark window. None but the lonely rain. The instructor riffled through a wet set of quizzes, then thrust them into a drawer where he kept his bird watcher's guide and a pair of cheap binoculars he had recently bought to follow things in flight. Supper, Levin? He had planned just a Swiss cheese sandwich and a cup of tea but decided he could not stand Mrs. Beaty's mental health in the kitchen tonight. Sadek, the clothes snatcher, was long since gone with his Lysol bottle, and the landlady, possibly because she realized she was ageing, had not attempted to rent his room; which suited Levin fine. But he longed for company tonight and considered calling Avis Fliss, though not with great enthusiasm. He was disappointed at how lonely he still was after almost three months in Easchester. Was the past, he asked himself, taking over in a new land? Had the new self failed? He had had invitations here and there, but as Pauline and others had told him, it was tough to be a bachelor in this town. Without a family you were almost always left out. Even Bucket had never invited him to his house. Levin wanted friendship and got friendliness; he wanted steak and they offered spam. Each day his past weighed more. He was, after all, thirty, and time moved on relentless roller skates. When, for God's sake, came love, marriage, children?

Opening a book, he looked down a page without reading, then tossed it aside. In the cellar he filled the sawdust hopper and left the house. Levin walked in the cold rain, the wettest, dreariest he had ever been in. The town was tight around his shoulders, the wet streets long and dark, street lights obscure at corners. A man could drown mid-block and nobody would know. It was after eight but half the houses he passed were totally dark. On rainy nights people went to bed; it was, after all, a diversion for the married; another was the small blue images of television he occasionally glimpsed through drawn curtains. Levin listened, as he walked, for a human sound and heard himself walking in the rain. He stood for five full minutes at the next street corner, not knowing which way to go, finally wandering toward the Gilleys.

Half heartedly he rang the bell. A light in a glass barrel went on over his head and Gerald opened the door. When he saw who it was he seemed embarrassed.

"I was passing by," Levin explained. "But if you're busy or otherwise occupied, I'll make it some other time."

"We're late getting the kids to bed," Gilley said. He glanced back into the house. "Come on in if you can stand the mess."

He spoke without welcome so Levin held back.

"I'll make it some other time."

"Was it department business?"

"No, I was just walking by—" He looked at the rain.

Gilley peered out. "Better come on in." He held the door open.

Levin, relieved, entered, and Gerald hung up his soaked raincoat and hat.

Pauline, in her violet pants, came out of the kitchen with an armful of diapers. Seeing who it was she let out a little shriek and darted up the stairs. Levin was nervously having a beer with Gilley when she reappeared in a green woolen dress. Five minutes ago in pants, uncombed hair, flat chest, she had all the appeal of a pine board. Now, with the same apparatus, the green dress, her hair brushed, she seemed to glow. She knew how to use what she had, not a bad talent.

"Excuse me for coming without phoning—"

"Excuse *me*, Mr. Levin. I hope I didn't scare you out of your normal growth but I hate to be seen in my pants."

She giggled at the way she had put it, Gilley mildly eyeing her.

"Gerald," Pauline said, "please stack the dishwasher while I get Erik out of the tub before he goes down the drain. Excuse me for one minute, Mr. Levin."

"I came at the wrong time," he called after them.

A few minutes later, Erik, in bunny pajamas, waddled in from the bathroom and went through Levin's beard with both hands.

"Any bugs in it?"

"Butterflies."

The boy tugged at the whiskers, then ran with a little cry to the kitchen. He pushed open the swing-door and Levin saw

Gerald and Pauline facing each other across a table loaded with dirty dishes.

"We've got to get started entertaining again," he was saying with emotion. "It's hurting me in the department."

She grabbed the butter dish and flung it at the wall. It hit the electric clock. The butter stuck to the face of the clock as the plate crashed to the floor.

Gilley yanked Erik into the kitchen and the door snapped shut.

Levin put down his beer and got into his wet raincoat and hat. He was headed for the front door when Pauline, flushed, entered the room.

"Oh, you're not leaving yet, Mr. Levin? We haven't exchanged a word."

"I've got this headache," he explained, removing his hat and showing her his bump. "I slipped on a leaf and hurt my head. Tell Gerald thanks for the beer."

She touched the bump gently with cold fingers, Levin conscious she smelled like a flower garden. "I'm awfully sorry, can't I get you some ice?"

"I've had some." He moved towards the door.

"Try us again soon," she called after him through the open door. "We'd honestly love to see you."

He hurried away.

The rain had thinned to mist, and a part-time moon wandered amid the broken pieces of sky. Walking on the campus, Levin was drawn to the Student Union by the sound of dance music. He watched a dance through the barred ballroom window. The girls were prettier than they had ever been, the men with more possibilities than that morning in class. He stood there for a half hour, envying them their looks, their youth, their future. His own was imprisoned in the old Levin. Where is my life? What has become of me? he asked himself. Ancient questions. Once more the music began, the same he had heard in another time, in another world. Though Levin made no sound, his shoulders shook.

My youth, my lost youth.

After recovering from Levin's beard Avis Fliss took to visiting him in his office to discuss the tactics of teaching remedial grammar, sometimes staying so long he grew restless. Her virtue was her unique fund of information concerning department and college routine; she always knew what was due when, and usually had it in first. And she seemed to know the activities and accomplishment of everyone in the department. On a more primitive level his eye was drawn to her bosom and ungirdled behind. Whenever in her presence he found himself thinking of her as a woman, he sensed a response but wasn't sure. What bothered him about Avis was that as soon as she came close to revealing something personal, her eyelids fluttered autonomously, her voice took flight, and when it returned she launched into a long digression addressed to his shoulder. He had, however, learned she had stopped off at Easchester several years ago, after a summer school vacation in Alaska, to surprise an old friend. The friend had been married and was gone, but Avis, possibly inspired by the event, had stayed on where it had taken place. Although she had only a bachelor's degree, she had taught in a well-known private girls' school, and Professor Fairchild, with Gilley's vote—despite Fabrikant's lack of enthusiasm, "though not against the lady personally although I don't like having too many around"—had put her on in the flourishing remedial program. Fairchild, therefore, was a "dear," and the director of composition, whose unofficial assistant she was, "tops." She praised him as an able man with a lovely little family, although she said once in passing that his wife was not entirely suited to him.

"Really?" said Levin. He asked her why she thought so.

"Well," she said, with a hesitant laugh, "she strikes me as the sort of person who can't always be depended on to strengthen a man's rear when he's on the march."

"On the march?"

"Advancing careerwise."

"His rear?"

"Figuratively speaking. Please don't misunderstand me, Seymour, I have nothing against Pauline. She's been nice to me, especially when I first came to Easchester, kind with invitations to their house, though I suspect Gerald had to ask her to ask me. What I have reference to is that she gives the impression of being dissatisfied in the midst of plenty, and I imagine some people wonder whose fault that is and unjustly blame

Gerald. She can also be absent-minded about her social responsibilities, which rather disturbs him."

"What do you mean 'in the midst of plenty'?"

"What any woman would consider herself lucky to have."

"To me they look like people who generally get along. I could be wrong."

"Oh, they do," Avis said. She seemed worried. "Please don't quote me."

One Saturday night, Levin, with nothing to do, drifted up to the office. Down the hall Avis' door was open but apparently no one else was around, Levin wondering if Bucket were sick. He began a letter to a second cousin, a lady in Cleveland who sometimes wrote to him, when Avis knocked. She was looking for a match, but when he had none, discovered a last one at the bottom of her purse. She stayed to smoke, resting one buttock on his desk. They talked of this and that, then books, then poetry, and were soon reading aloud to each other from an anthology. Levin read several stanzas from "The Eve of St. Agnes," and Avis read Tennyson's "Flower in the Crannied Wall." One poem led to another, and soon Levin, taking Avis' bashful hand, gently drew her down upon his lap. A blessed thing, poetry.

They kissed, Levin suffused in her orange blossom and tobacco aroma, then kissed again more deeply.

"Your whiskers tickle," she laughed, her bosom heaving. "You ought to cut them off."

"Never."

"For a person who isn't handsome, Seymour, you act as though you were."

"Ha ha," laughed Levin.

After another breathless kiss Avis suggested they go for a drive.

"Fine," he said. "Where's your car?"

"I was thinking of yours."

"I have none."

"Oh, too bad. Mine's in the garage having its valves ground."

"Tst-tst." To test what she had in mind, he said, "We could walk if you don't mind the rain."

She coughed bronchially.

He was considering his room. They could sneak up the back

stairs, only Mrs. Beaty was tonight entertaining some club ladies. If sex was approaching Levin wanted it without the worry of visitors.

"What about your place?" he asked.

"I daren't. The landlady's teen-age daughter sleeps in the next room to mine."

He was weighing other possibilities when Avis hopped quickly up out of his lap.

"What was that?" She listened tensely at the door. "I thought I heard footsteps."

He listened. "Nothing."

Levin was aroused. They kissed at the door. He felt for her nipple. Avis pushed his hand away.

An old maid, he thought, I'd better not.

"Would you rather go to a movie?"

"Would you?" Her eyelids moved like a bird's wings.

"Then let's be honest," Levin said. "Will you come with me to a hotel?"

"Not in town. We'd be recognized as faculty people. I know I would. So would you with your beard."

"We could take a cab to the one in Marathon. It wouldn't be too expensive."

"The night clerk in Marathon is one of my former Grammar Z students," Avis said. "Couldn't we stay here?"

"In the office?"

"Might we?"

Levin seized a practical suggestion. "Gladly. I'll spread my raincoat on the desk."

"The desk?" She hesitated. "It seems sacrilegious."

"I hate to mention the floor but what else is there?"

"I have a blanket I keep in my office for football games," Avis said.

"Marvelous. Shall I go get it?"

"You'll find it in my closet."

Levin went for the blanket. When he got back she had her dress and shoes off and was in brassiere and half slip. He folded the blanket lengthwise on the floor, then removed his jacket and tie.

As they were undressing they heard unmistakable footsteps coming up the stairs. Avis frantically stepped into her slippers and pulled on her dress. Levin got his shirt partly buttoned, and tie on, knotted badly. He helped her zip her dress.

A knock sounded on the door.

"Sy?" The voice was Gilley's.

Levin shuddered. The danger was if he said nothing Gerald might open the door with the common key.

Avis frantically gestured: answer.

"Here," Levin said. He said, "Avis is with me."

There was a pause. "Could I see you?"

"Why not?" He heaped the blanket and kicked it under the desk. Avis had seated herself and poked her dead nose into a grammar text. Her poor neck was rigid.

"I saw the light under your door," Gilley said. He had a mackinaw and boots, and was holding a hunting cap.

Avis smiled dimly. "Hello, Gerald." She looked a wreck.

Gilley's eyes roved uneasily but Levin's glance assured him the blanket was invisible.

"Avis has been helping me in Grammar Z. She says I'm trying to cover too much in an hour."

"Good," said Gilley. He said he had come up for a book for Pauline. "George and I are taking off for some early shooting. We usually snooze in his wagon and are right on the spot when the ducks fly in. Pauline hasn't been sleeping too well lately and she wants something by Hardy around. All we have home is *The Return of the Native*, which she reread recently. Have you got something by him in your bookcase, Sy, maybe *Far From the Madding Crowd*? Maybe you have, Avis?"

"No, Gerald, I don't care for Hardy."

Levin searched his shelves. "Here's *Under the Greenwood Tree* in paperback."

"I don't think she's read that. Could I give either or both of you a lift?"

"Not me, thanks," Levin said.

"Nor me," said Avis. "I promised to return a set of quizzes Monday. Now that Seymour has his lessons in shape I think I'll go back to my office and finish grading my tests. I hate to work on Sundays. Good night, gentlemen."

"Good night, Avis," Gerald said.

"Good night," said Levin.

She walked quickly down the hall.

"Thanks for the book," Gilley said. "Don't work too late, Sy."

"I'll quit soon." Levin yawned. "Got a letter to my cousin to finish up."

Gerald lingered. He doesn't believe me, Levin thought.

"Give my best to Pauline. I hope she sleeps tonight."

"She has these periods." He said after a minute, "I'll make a note to have this window Duffy cracked, replaced."

"I would appreciate it."

Gilley said, "Listen, Sy, you might as well know the boss is very strict about the separation of the sexes in offices. That's why he's never allowed a man and a woman to share one."

"You don't say?"

"I just want to give you an idea how he thinks."

"I'm much obliged."

Still Gilley stayed. "Avis is a very nice gal, but if I were you I'd keep in mind that women her age who aren't married can be upset pretty easily. Well, so long."

"Good night, Gerald. Tell Pauline I hope she sleeps well."

"She will. She has these periods on and off."

When Gilley had gone, Levin rested his head on his arms on the desk. His galloping heart slowed down to a fast trot. He finished his letter and was thinking of leaving.

But then Avis was back, freshly made up, her orange blossom renewed.

Her eyelids throbbed. "Shall we—go on?"

Levin peeled his jacket, snapped the lock, and again spread the blanket.

"This time we'd better put out the light," she said.

When her brassiere came off, her breasts, handsome under clothes, hung like water-filled balloons from her chest. Levin shivered a bit, that splendid bosom formless. Still, for a starving man—

Once more they embraced, Levin in white shorts, Avis in pink panties.

He snapped off the light. Again she stopped his hand when he touched her left breast. "Not that one, it hurts."

"Hurts?"

"Feel this." Her fingers guided his. He felt a long scar on the underside of her breast.

She said she had once had an operation. "It was a benign fibroma. Now I have another and the doctor says it's the same thing but I'll have to have it out anyway, I imagine during the Christmas vacation. Here's what hurts when you press."

He felt a hard spot under his fingers.

Levin snapped on the light.

"Why, what's the matter?" Avis asked.

"I'm sorry for your breast."

"Don't worry about it. You may fondle the other."

Poor dame, he thought. She has little, why should I make it less?

He wavered indecisively, then reached for his pants and drew them on.

"I don't understand," she faltered. "Aren't you—aren't we going on?"

"When we have a better place, when you feel better," Levin said. "I don't want to hurt you."

Avis dressed quickly, grabbed her football blanket and left furiously.

To escape occasionally from town and loneliness, Levin, after much debate with himself—having consulted Bucket and Courtney Haddock, who knew about second-hand cars, bought himself one. He had arranged with a student of his, Lyman Myler from Los Gatos, another expert, a former hot rodder now majoring in automotive engineering, to accompany him to a used-car lot. Almost every one of his freshmen could drive, and most of them owned cars, usually new, but not Levin. Lyman helped him settle on a 1946 Hudson, a brown, two-door, five-passenger sedan, which though it sagged a bit in the rear, was in decent shape; and Levin agreed to pay three hundred and fifty dollars, a sum it made him nervous to owe anybody. He later learned he had bought ex-Dean Feeney's trade-in for the latest model. The Hudson didn't look like something he had dreamed of, but at least it moved on wheels, and so might Levin. He knew the town and a mile or two beyond, but not much more. It was time to venture forth.

Lyman drove the Hudson home and parked it in Mrs. Beaty's garage. The next day he gave Levin his first driving lesson. The instructor fancied he would learn fairly quickly but found himself less apt than he had expected. He couldn't understand how it was possible to shift, accelerate, turn, while watching direction, signs, and traffic—a confusing task for a mind that was non-mechanical or had come too late to mechanics. At the same time he felt a useless anger against himself for not at once mastering this carapace of tin over box of oil-soaked nuts and bolts. Two weeks later he knew the operation of the car but still overshot corners and skidded against curbs when pulling to a stop. He was uneasy in traffic, especially when making left turns off busy streets. What bothered him most was that he was careless in ways he would not have predicted: momentarily lost in thought he could forget stop signs, and which was one way in a one-way street. Twice Lyman had to grab the wheel to prevent a mishap. As a result, Levin had his fears of the car and said so. Lyman said, "We all have to die sometime sooner or later."

"Better later," Levin muttered. "I have not yet begun to live."

Lyman said Levin would feel better once he had passed his test and driven a hundred miles alone. However, Levin seriously considered giving up the car and going back to walking. He was at best a bus and subway man. As for loneliness, better than a car was a girl; he would look actively now.

A few days later he failed his driver's test and went home humiliated, convinced he must part with the car. Lyman offered to see if one of his frat brothers was interested, and Levin agreed to sell for three hundred dollars. He was ashamed of himself and mildly depressed. But after supper that night he sneaked downstairs, and backing the Hudson out of the garage, took off alone, a feat to begin with. It was of course raining and he felt a throb of satisfaction when he turned on the windshield wiper and it worked. Levin drove slowly in the rain, his heart beating thickly over the illegal thing he was doing, at the same time thinking he had never before so clearly seen raindrops falling into light. He felt intensely the danger of the adventure, pictured himself blundering into accident, arrest, being forbidden to drive in Cascadia, possibly sent to jail. It would all get into the paper, and everybody, including his students, would know him for the fool and lawbreaker he, by nature, was.

Bent over the wheel, peering into the dewy gloom, he drove in the emptiest part of town, practicing turns from street to street, and later—heart high and dry—drove downtown. Almost at once he saw the police car coming his way and felt paralysis of arm and leg; but when the car with its spinning blinker passed him, neither of the cops giving him so much as a glance, Levin headed for the main highway out of Easchester. He drove for three miles at his fastest speed ever, a breakneck forty-five—then not to tempt fate, turned at a gas station and drove back. Behind him on the misty light-studded highway lay San Francisco, ahead Seattle, cities he longed to see. He pictured the U.S.A. as a structure of highways and freeways, Levin at the wheel, embarked on one leading to another, speeding up hill and down in his trusty Hudson, his lance at his side, driving through a series of amorous and philanthropic adventures. Home safely, though his legs trembled when he stepped out of the car, he was all in one piece and marvelously elated.

After passing his driver's test and getting his license, Levin was giving some thought to calling Avis Fliss, if at all feasible, when an attractive girl in one of his classes, Nadalee Hammerstad, began to haunt the surprised forefront of his mind. One day as they were sitting together in his office, discussing her latest theme—she had come in to ask about her grades—Nadalee, imperceptibly leaning forward, nuzzled her hard little breast against Levin's lonely elbow. He moved his arm as if bitten although somehow managing not to be abrupt, at the same time considering the touch unintentional—someone else wouldn't have noticed. He continued talking about her paragraphs, and although he could almost not believe it, the breast again caressed. To test whether this was his imagination overworking, Levin kept his arm where it had been, and the girl for the third time gave him this unmistakable sign of her favor as he droned on about her writing, his thoughts in the wild wind. Two minutes later she thanked him for his criticism and left with a happy smile, not the vaguest sign of a blush on her, although Levin glowed as with high fever.

He had noticed her more than once, a slim girl with short dark-brown hair, pretty, with greenish eyes, mature face, and shapely figure. Although her lower lip was thin and she used eyebrow pencil a bit smearily, she had a way with clothes. Whereas the other girls in her class were contented with skirts and sweaters of pastel shades, or blouses, Nadalee fitted into tight dresses and favored bright colors, a blessing on rainy days. The freshman girls smelled of body heat and talcum powder, but she wore a spicy perfume, which when it touched Levin's nostrils, never failed to interest him. When she slid into her seat in the second row he knew it without looking. There was about her a quality of having been and seen, that made the instructor feel he could talk to her. And she wrote well, sometimes imaginatively. He felt let down when she was absent. Still, he paid her no special attention, and had given her not much thought after class until her visit to his office. After that she was in his mind so tenaciously it wearied him.

Nadalee took on a private uniqueness, a nearness and dearness as though he were in love with her. Although he told himself he wasn't, she had in a sense offered love, and love was what Levin wanted. Though he tried diligently to cast her out of his thoughts, she sneaked back in with half her clothes off to incite him to undress the rest of her. He tried to figure out how to achieve an honorable relationship with the girl. If they were elsewhere in another season—if let's say, in the Catskills in July or August, he might with comparatively undisturbed conscience have taken a bite of what she offered. But here in Easchester, at Cascadia College, English 10, Section Y, 11 A.M. MWF, she was his student and he her instructor, in loco parentis, practically a sacred trust. Levin determined to forget the girl, but his determination was affected by hers. Nadalee appeared in class, the day after the time she had upset him in his office, in one of her prettiest dresses, a thickly petticoated affair, white with wine stripes encircling hips, belly and breasts. She crossed and uncrossed her slim young legs enhanced in nylon stockings. On her narrow feet she wore black ballet slippers in which, without much trouble, he could see her on her toes in *Swan Lake*, himself the evil magician. Surely, he thought, this dressing up isn't for me; and though he went on in class as if he knew what he was doing, he could not keep from desiring her—to consume and be consumed. Afterwards, alone in his office, his chest palpitating as though he were contemplating murder, or flying off on a roaring drunk, Levin reread her themes and in one came across a biographical bit he couldn't understand why he had forgotten. When she was eighteen she had spent a summer on her uncle's ranch in Northern California. In the afternoon when it was hot Nadalee rode her horse to a small lake surrounded by pine trees, tossed off shirt and bra, stepped out of Levi's and underpants, and dived into the cold blue water. Though Levin's legs cramped after a too hasty immersion in cold water, he jumped in after her and spent most of the night swimming with Nadalee.

The next day the sight of her skirt clinging to her thighs was enough to upset him. After once glancing at her, every line lovely, conscious of his relentless consciousness of her he vowed not to look again, and managed not to that morning, but it was worse later when he was alone. Desire butchered him. He beheld his slaughtered face in the mirror and stared at it, wretched. How escape the ferocious lust that enflamed and tormented his thoughts as it corroded his will? Why must Levin's unlived life put him always in peril? Why obsessively seek what was lost—unlived—in the past? He had no wish to be Faust, or Gatsby; or St. Anthony of Somewhere, who to conquer his torment, had nipped off his balls. Levin wanted to be himself, at peace in present time.

He tried various means of self-control: exhortation, rationalization, censorship, obfuscation. One trick was to think of the girl as his daughter. He was her old man and had watched her grow from a thing in dirty diapers. At twelve she was menstruating; on her eighteenth birthday Levin married her off to a successful lawyer, to whom she bore seven children in six years, all boys. Her father, ever a man to be tempted by every damned temptation—life had plugged him full of sockets and it took only a slight breeze to make a connection—was safe and sound in her invasive presence, until by a dirty stroke of fate (try as he would Levin-père could not reverse it) the lawyer expired of a heart attack from overwork. But Nadalee was financially provided for, so Levin went off to Europe to live, traveling from country to country this side of the iron curtain. It couldn't be said he didn't enjoy his life, though where exactly was home? Several years later, in Sevilla—he was then fifty-five going on fifty-six—half drunk on val de peñas one festival night before the corrida, he met this masked beauty at a costume ball. One tango led to another, the dance to a sense of fundamental intimacy—what, after all, is a dance? So, whispering together—Levin confessing most of his sins, including advancing age, the señorita saying nothing of importance—they left for his suite at the Hilton. First they ate. George, the fine waiter, served wild asparagus, a plate of cold meats, manchego cheese and some dry white capri, iced in buckets; after coffee a bottle of anis del mono, which tasted like licorice and warmed all the way. Then they made love. The masked beauty refused—despite the inconvenience, which she argued was tit for tat for his grizzled beard—to remove her disguise until it was unalterably too late. When he looked at her true face at dawn, he groaned at the misery he had committed. Levin thereupon put out both eyes and threw himself off a high cliff into the shark-infested sea.

He argued with himself: I have evil thoughts, expensive to my spirit; they represent my basest self. I must expunge them by will, no weak thing in man. I must live by responsibility, an invention of mine in me. The girl trusts me, I can't betray her. If I want sex I must be prepared to love, and love may mean marriage. (I live by my nature, not Casanova's.) If I'm not prepared to marry her I'd better stay away. He exhorted himself: teach her only grammar, the principal parts of verbs, spelling, punctuation—nothing not in the syllabus. He would not let the casual brush of a girl's breast against his sleeve seduce him into acting without honor. The self would behave as it must. She would not make a fool of him, much less a worm. He would, in denial, reveal the depth of his strongest, truest strength. Character over lust. By night, after these terrible exertions, including two cold showers, Levin's mind was comparatively calm—he had bludgeoned desire, and though exhausted, beaten half to death by the bloody club he carried against the self, felt more or less at peace.

About a week later, Levin encountered Nadalee, one morning, in the college bookstore. He had been wandering among the book tables and looked up, experiencing overwhelming relief to find her by his side, for he had at once seen her as she was—diminished from a temptress into a nice kid. Levin observed with interest the errors of her face and figure, the thin underlip, too heavily penciled brows; her legs less than slim although not actually skinny, and her childlike ballet-slippered feet. Objectivity, if it did less for her, did more for him. It was her youth that moved me, Levin thought. Also her unexpected favor. He desired those who found him desirable, a too easy response; he must watch this in himself.

Nadalee said she was looking for an entertaining novel and could he suggest one: "It's a gift—a birthday present for guess who?—me, I'm twenty today."

Levin congratulated her. "Twenty, did you say?"

She explained why she was two years older than most freshmen. "You see, I worked in a bank before coming here." But the bank had bored her, so she had quit and registered, with some financial assistance from her father, at Cascadia College. All this was news to Levin, though he tried to sidestep the impression it might be good news. Could good news be bad? Her age, perhaps, explained her maturity. Yet twenty was not too different from eighteen. Before he could decide how different, if different, or where or why different, he hastened to think: she's still too young—ten years between us—a kid. Just look at her feet. Besides I'm her teacher.

Levin found her a novel, tipped his hat, and left for lunch.

Later, to prove he trusted his strength he telephoned her to ask if she liked to walk. "Madly," Nadalee answered. Since she honestly interested him, he had made up his mind it would be better for his nerves if he saw her now and then, in a Platonic relationship. A walk, a bit of a drive here and there, at most a movie in a neighboring town. Company, talk—a blessing under the right circumstances.

They met in the park by the green river. She came in cardigan and skirt, carrying a poplin raincoat; Levin had his on. They wandered along the bank of the Sacajawea. The morning had been gray but this afternoon was blue, infused with light of the invisible sun.

"Don't you just love the day when it's like this?" Nadalee said.

"Very much."

"Look at those clouds in the west. How would you describe them?"

"Vaporous, toiling."

"Tempestuous, like some people's emotions?"

"Whose, for instance?"

"Yours."

"You are observant," he said with a sigh, "mature."

"I'm glad you finally noticed."

Levin bent for a stone to scale on the water but it sank with a plop.

"If you had any idea that I am a little-innocent," she said, watching the ripples in the water, "well, I'm not, if that's what you're worried about. I was once engaged to be married."

The wall he had so painfully built against her, against desire, fell on his head.

He asked in hidden anguish, "Why do you tell me that?"

"Because I am a woman and wish to be treated so."

"By me?"

"Yes, if you must know."

"But why me?" he asked.

"I guess you know I'm different than most of the other girls in your class? I'm tired of college boys. I want real companionship."

"But why me?" Levin said. "There are other men around, graduate students, instructors, some handsome."

"I bet you'd be better looking without your beard."

"No, I wouldn't."

"Anyway, the answer is you happen to appeal to me. I've always liked the intellectual type. I like the way you talk, it's very sincere."

He was humbly grateful to her. They were standing under a tree and impulsively kissed, her young breasts stabbing his chest. They kissed so hard his hat fell off.

Levin said, as they went on, hands locked, "I don't have to tell you Nadalee, the need for absolute secrecy? Many people would not understand or approve this. It could make trouble."

She said she had thought of that and had a scheme for them to spend some time together alone if he agreed. He agreed. Her aunt, Nadalee said, owned a little motel on the coast. She was planning to visit her daughter in Missoula next weekend, and whenever she left she closed up and lit the no-vacancy sign. There wasn't much business at this time of the year, only occasional tourists and some hunters or fishermen. Anyway, Nadalee had promised to look after the place and they could have it to themselves. "We could walk on the beach and the dunes, and picnic and ride around, and just sort of relax. My aunt won't get home till late on Sunday."

Levin resisted every sentence but his imagination was whipped to froth. Who could resist Eden?

Came Friday. He was resolved to go but not necessarily to collect. The fun was having a place to go, companionship, not something he could unfairly get from the girl. He was obliged to treat her responsibly. He would explain this when he got there—she had left by bus that morning but he had a one o'clock to teach; it had been decided they were not to go or come back together. Let's be friends, Levin planned to say. If we can honestly be, later we may think of sex. It will come more pleasurably to friends—a two-fold blessing. That he had reached this conclusion satisfied him. After trimming his beard a half-inch around he drove out of Easchester in a marvelous mood.

For the first time in his life Levin was on the road alone in a car—his own—carried along on his own power, so to say. Three cheers for the pioneers of the auto industry; they had put him on wheels to go where he pleased! He thought with pleasure of the many things he had learned to do in his few months here: had mowed frequent lawns, the grass still green and growing in December; raked a billion leaves, fifty percent from neighboring trees; gathered walnuts in October; picked yellow pears; regularly attended and even cleaned Mrs. B's rumbling sawdust furnace, and so on and what not. Last week he had washed and waxed his car. Levin the handy man; that is to say, man of hands. And here he was with both of them solidly on the wheel, miraculously in motion along the countryside, enjoying the compression of scenery. Heading towards unknown mountains in voyage to the Pacific Ocean, world's greatest. Imagine, Levin from Atlantic to Pacific—who would have thought so only a few years ago?—seeing up close sights he had never seen before: big stone mountains ahead, thick green forests, unexpected farms scattered over the hillsides, the ghostly remains of forest fire, black snags against the sky.

Something else new: a little too close for comfort he passed a log truck, surely half a block long, pyramided high with enormous tree trunks, heavily chained, thank God. Here and there millponds were afloat with brown logs, to be fished out and cut into boards. He whizzed past a smoldering, tree-tall furnace shaped like a shuttlecock, a black slash burner that consumed wood waste, its head ablaze at night. He was discovering in person the face of America.

And the weather was better than the newspaper had expected. For short intervals warm sunlight—through thick clouds breaking into sky streams—lit the fields; some harboring sheep, a few with starlings on their backs, picking a living out of the wool. At times the clouds massed darkly, yet the day managed to be cheery, and the bright green winter wheat yielded hidden light. Levin guessed the temperature was around fifty, and this they called onset of winter. It said so on the calendar, and Mrs. Beaty was airing her winter undies and talking of Christmas. Who immersed in Eastern snow and icy winds could guess at Cascadia's pleasant weather? Here, Bucket had told him, spring came sometimes in midwinter; autumn in the right mood might hang on till January, and at times spring lingered through summer. A season and a half they called it but Levin would not complain. Only a week ago he had caught the odor of a white rose in the best of health on somebody's front lawn. So what if they paid in wetness for the mild climate; the warmth made up for rain, and wasn't it wonderful to be riding to the beach in December? Who but a polar bear would indulge in the Bronx?

He saw stone ascending and discovered himself doing the same. "Holy Moses, I'm up a mountain." As the road turned, his startled sight beheld below a vast forest of pointed conifers, and as he emerged from a corkscrew curve, a mass of peaks—rocks and shadow—extended into the dim distance. "Alps on Alps arise." His heart leapt at the view but when he realized how narrow the ledge he was traveling on, how sheer the drop if he dropped, his heart settled with a wham and he found himself toiling at driving. WARNING, SHARP CURVES. He was sweating to master them as his tires screeched, rolling the wheel as if fighting a storm at sea; to stay on the road yet keep from hitting anything that might come zooming around the bend—ahead invisible till he got there; also to move fast enough to satisfy the irritable pest behind him, sprung up from nowhere and blasting his horn till Levin had a headache. He was doing twenty and considered crawling at ten but didn't dare with this madman behind him. He tried to signal the fiend to stop with the horn, or quell him with a dirty look in the mirror, but no signals worked and he had to keep his eyes glued ahead for fear of losing the slightest sight of the perilous, tortuous road. Another blast of the horn filled him with rage and dismay. He considered stopping and getting out to grapple with his nemesis, but luckily the road widened a few feet, and Levin pulled hard against the side of the cliff to let the monster pass. He furiously shook his fist as a dilapidated Chevy squeezed by, the pee-wee driver with a snip of black mustache, more Chaplin than Hitler, offering a thumbed nose. His dusty license plate read New Jersey—too small world. With no further stomach for tight curves, Levin considered giving his breath a rest, but since no one any longer fastened onto his tail he went his winding way, conscious of abysses deeper than those in dreams, worried that a momentary lapse of attention might send him hurtling into the murderous maw of the forest below, dead, destroyed, never to be seen again. Yet he negotiated each curve as it came, some bent into such unpredictable tormented arcs that it flashed on him he knew for the first time in his life what "straight" meant; and this insight carried him down the mountain onto a peaceful road.

Peaceful for a short happy while, then the grade rose again and his eyes widened in the dusty windshield. But Levin got used to it: Steeplechase, you did what the bear did. There were many mountains and you took them one by one, paying no attention to the rest of the family. Soon the worst seemed over. Descending, Levin was surprised to sail through a momentary hamlet, a cluster of jerry-built, long-unpainted houses around a general store with a dirty gas pump in front. Here too America; you learned as you lived, a refreshing change from books. Out of the townlet and embarked on a broadly winding level road, he hypnotically watched a puff of smoke float up from his radiator and evaporate, Levin at once apprehensive of trouble although he couldn't call it by name. He wondered whether to drive back to the gas pump, but the narrowness of the twisting road made a turn impossible. And he didn't like going back once the plan was to go forward. It was getting late, he was slow, Nadalee was waiting. He studied the hood at intervals, and seeing no more smoke, vowed not to stop until the first service station he hit. By the merest chance his eye caught the progress of the needle of the temperature gauge. It was flirting with HOT. "What'll I do now?" Levin asked himself, trying to recall what the manual that came with the car said, but remembering only confusion. So he drove on till he again spied smoke. The red needle had struck HOT. Fearing fire, he quickly brought the Hudson to a stop on the road and shut off the ignition. A cloud of steam rose from the radiator. Levin, agitated, lifted the hood. He burned his fingers trying to unscrew the water cap, then managed to turn it with a folded handkerchief. A hissing stream of steam and bubbling brown water spilled over, a pox on ex-Dean Feeney. Levin remembered having read about this under BOILING OVER.

Two hours later he was on his way again. The sun was sinking and he was very late. He had been pushed by a pickup truck to a small gas station in a logging village not too far away, whose owner-and-mechanic-on-duty had "gone home for half hour," it said on a stenciled strip of cardboard on the gas pump. Levin fretted as he waited, because he had only twenty dollars in his pocket and Friday was going fast. When at last the man had appeared, he recommended a reverse flush, and though this sounded like a bad poker hand it suited Levin if somebody who knew said so; but the operation took more than an hour, the man wandering off every so often to attend his pump or sell something. Levin walked down the road and sat on a rock watching time hurrying by and nothing he could do about it. He considered trying to call Nadalee to tell her what had happened but gave it up as too complicated. He had estimated—she had—that they would be together by four, but four had come and gone, and with it went some of the beauty of the day and the pleasure of anticipation, because he liked things to work out as planned, time and all. He seriously wondered whether to take this incident as a warning of sorts, yet cheered up when the car was ready, paid twelve dollars courageously, and was again en voyage with a full gas tank and recommended change of oil, although he had changed it last week. He warily watched the temperature gauge, suffering when the needle went up and rejoicing when it settled back. Since the coast was only thirty-five miles away, he gave himself at the very most an hour to get there, counseling calm, the fun was yet to be, Nadalee will wait for me. The road was presently good and he clocked five miles in six minutes. Although the sun had sunk, and shade arose in the fields, a golden-green glow hung in the sky. He enjoyed the stillness, each tree still, the timbered hills multiplying silence. With some misgiving he climbed a new rise. At the first turn of the road a log truck, like a fat worm pulling itself out of a hole in the earth, rumbled forth hauling the largest, most terrifying hunk of wood Levin had ever seen; it looked like a threat to humanity. He pulled the Hudson quickly to the shoulder of the road, holding his foot hard on the brake until the long truck puffed by. When Levin was ready to move he discovered he couldn't, his right rear wheel sunk in a ditch.

"I'll die," he muttered after twenty minutes of struggling to free the wheel. Not one car had come by. He pictured himself frozen to death in the Hudson during the night. In the morning they would haul off a stiff corpse; he had read of these things in the paper. Levin desperately figured he had to do something, but the right rear wheel had no respect for reason or will. He was wondering why he had come on this impossible journey when a tractor rattled around the bend and wobbled towards him. It was an old machine, the farmer driving it a wizened man with a small leathery face. He wore a wilted straw hat, and sat up on a high seat, swaying as he sat.

To Levin's astonishment the machine passed by, the farmer lost in thought; he had to yell to get his attention. With a clank the tractor came to a halt, the driver gazing back at Levin as though he couldn't understand where he had risen from.

"Excuse me for bothering you," Levin explained, "but I'm stuck in this ditch."

The farmer in silence got down from the seat, dug a length of rope out of his tool box and knotted it to Levin's front bumper. In less than a minute the Hudson was out of the ditch. It had happened so fast he could hardly believe it.

"Three cheers for the American Farmer!"

The farmer smiled wanly. "Say," he said, "could you give me a hand with some trouble I been havin' of my own?"

"Gladly," said Levin, "although I have an important engagement."

He stepped out of the car. The farmer fished in his tool box and came up with a pair of needle-nose pliers.

"Got an achin' tooth here at the back of my mouth. Could you give it a pull with these pliers?"

Levin's muscles tightened to the point of shivers. He saw himself trying to pull the tooth, breaking it, not being able to get it all out, as the man bled, and it ended by his having to drive him to the hospital. Yet he wanted to show his gratitude to the farmer for rescuing him from the ditch.

"Couldn't I drive you to a dentist?" he said. "I'm on my way to the coast."

"Can't stand 'em," the farmer said. "An' I got thirty head of Angus to look after. I'm alone by myself since the missus died."

Opening his mouth he touched a gnarled finger to the offending tooth, a discolored snag.

Levin tried several times to get the pliers gripping the tooth. "Is this it?"

"Feels like. I ain't sure."

He withdrew the pliers from the farmer's mouth and handed them to him. "I'd only hurt you without doing any good."

"Sure hurts anyway," the man said. He tossed the pliers into the tool box and climbed up on his high seat. The tractor rattled down the hill.

"God bless your tooth," Levin called after him. Failed again, he thought.

He started the Hudson and stepped on the gas. "Nadalee, I'm coming."

It was almost six. I've got to make time. He sped along the mountain road, wondering why it was so dark, then hurriedly switched on his lights, gasping as the beams flew forward and were trapped in pools of fog. A sense of doom infected him and he fell to brooding. Where is the fog, in or out? He had slowed to a crawl, every minute convinced he would the very next go shooting into space. Should he stay rooted? If he stopped where he was and escaped being smashed in the rear, he would have to stay put until the fog lifted, if it did, in the morning. If he went on how would he know if he was on the road or off—levitated in space before the ultimate crash, decapitation, dismemberment—what sort of terrible end for a man who had lived through so much in his life and had so many plans?

He drove on with droplets of mist in his beard, at ten miles an hour, and could see only as many feet ahead, frightened by awesome crags that loomed up before him and the fragments of bare rock over his head. Every few seconds he braked, sounding his horn like a wail as he went, by the greatest good luck skirting half-hidden boulders and grotesquely twisted tree trunks whose crowns were shrouded in fog. He had endless visions of disaster, monotonously called himself "idiot" for having invented this purgatorial journey. Levin promised himself he would celebrate if he got out alive.

It seemed to him, his nerves pricking through his skin, that he had journeyed for years on an abandoned road, had started as a child but was surely by now somebody's grandpa, his hair turned bone-white, although the face, when he caught a reflected glimpse of it, looked hauntingly dark. He felt he had crawled on for hours, without confidence that he knew which road was presently which, and after a while, with a sense of not much caring. He went where the road went, because it was there; where it ended he would.

He saw then, lit in his headlights, a horse—could it be?—No, this was a mule standing immobile in the road, gazing at something in the night. It slowly came to Levin, for he was worn out, that the mule was not a nightmare; it was real and he was staring at it from a distance of thirty feet; and that the fog had broken into moving patches; the sky glowing with stars, amid them the moon. Yet even as he sighed in unbelievable relief at the lifting of the fog, the mule, like a stone statue, stood broadside on the road, impassable at either end. Ten feet from the animal Levin stopped the car and got out to see what he could do about moving it, offering first a Life Saver, gingerly holding it a foot from the mule's nose, hoping it might mistake the candy for sugar, but its nostrils didn't even mildly twitch. Levin, walking down the road in the glare of his headlights, tore up some wet ferns. He tried holding out a handful but the salad did not tempt the animal. In exasperation he hunted for a rock to bounce off its bony back, but as he was looking, gave up the thought. In the car he cradled his head on his arms folded on the wheel. The horn blast startled the mule. It gave a frightened whinny and took off in an unknown direction.

The moonlit road stretched ahead for visible miles and Levin made fast time. But after he had traveled another twenty-five and still saw no end to his journey, continuing doubts tormented him. Was he on the right road or headed for Mexico or Canada? Would he get there tonight? Would she still be waiting? With these worries he drove through a covered bridge, and as he emerged, saw headlights rising in the distance. Levin pulled to a hasty stop several feet beyond the bridge. After two minutes a car approached. Stepping out of his Hudson, Levin waved both arms and succeeded in flagging down a Dodge of ancient vintage, the driver braking to a screeching stop.

"If you'll pardon me," Levin said, "I'm looking for the coast. How far to go would you say?"

The driver, an old man wearing a large hat and rimless glasses, peered at Levin's limp beard.

"You a Mormon or somethin'?"

"Just a citizen."

"Live in Cascadia?"

"Yes."

The man lifted his hat, and with a finger of the same hand, scratched his veinous bald cranium.

"Beats me," he muttered. "Ain't it t'other way?" He pointed back over Levin's shoulder.

A minute later his car disappeared into the covered bridge.

Levin, about to collapse, tried to figure where he had gone wrong. He guessed in the fog. Somewhere in it he had missed a turn and taken the wrong direction. It served him right for his evil intentions.

As he drove aimlessly on, in sadness contemplating all the failures of his life, the multifarious wrong ways he had gone, the waste of his going, he sniffed a sea smell. Whirling down the window, he smelled again and let out a cry.

The ocean! Either the old geezer hadn't understood his

question or was lost himself; maybe he had suspected Levin was a Russian spy.

He beheld in the distance a golden lace of moonlight on the dark bosom of the vast sea.

Ocean in view, oh the joy. “My God, the Pacific!”

He saw himself as stout Cortez—Balboa, that is—gazing down at the water in wild surmise, both eyes moist.

Some minutes later he asked at a service station the way to Nadalee’s aunt’s place. Though it was about nine when he got there, the motel was dark, no sign lit. But Levin knocked on each cabin door until a light went on in one, and the door fell open.

There stood Nadalee in a sheer nightie.

“Mr. Levin—I mean Seymour.”

“Nadalee—I got lost.” Before he could say where or why, she had shucked off her garment and her gloriously young body shed light as he hungrily embraced it.

IN THE past, Dr. Fabrikant had told Levin, Professor Fairchild, to uphold standards of efficiency and purity, had locked the composition instructors—mostly ladies then—in one lárge classroom as they collectively graded departmental objective exams. Although with advancing age he had changed some of his ways, under Gilley other curious customs prevailed, for instance the competition among instructors and those assistant professors who taught comp, to get done with d.o. finals on the very day they were given. Gerald said he did not encourage the race for itself, though he enjoyed races, but he liked to have comp grades in well ahead of the registrar's deadline, so he asked all possible speed in correcting papers, tallying scores, and submitting term grades. Though Levin functioned poorly in a rush, he feared being left out of things, so he raced along with the others for hours without pausing to drink or pass water.

Each exam paper consisted of two hundred short-answer questions on eight mimeographed pages, and the instructor had one hundred and fourteen students, including Grammar Z inmates, who had their own objective tests, made up by Avis. Levin hurriedly counted correct answers, making little red check marks down the margin of the page, later changing to economical dots. He totaled aloud, wrote the number of right answers at the bottom of the page and hastily flipped to the next sheet, once in a while taking a few seconds to work his fingers against cramp. He fidgeted and sweated when he heard people running up and down the stairs and hall, worrying that they might be turning in their scores while he sat with a great stack of uncorrected papers in front of him. Though the coffee room was open for business, and he thirsted for tea, he didn't dare go in, fearing to fall farther behind. Avis was the talented one at this game and usually led the pack; at the very worst she came in second to Bullock, another speedster. Her flushed joy in victory matched Gilley's beamish approval of her deed; he liked a winner.

Try as he would, Levin was no match for the professionals, although he began to like the competitive hurry and the pleasures of simple arithmetic; but he finished third from last. Gerald afterwards ribbed him and Farper, who had come in after him, for holding up the making of the departmental curve for an hour. This was the Bell graph of grade scores, which Gilley, according to set percentages, divided into letter grades. As each instructor had handed in his tally sheet, Gerald and Milly had transposed the figures to a master tally. When the statistics were in, the director of composition retired behind his locked office door and working with a slide rule he was fond of, carefully plotted the curve and divided it into segments, indicating the number of A's, B's, etc., that would be permitted. He hoped someday to have an IBM machine that would do the job, grading and all, in a jiffy. Milly then typed the statistics of the curve on a stencil, which she ran off like a newspaper extra. Gerald grabbed up these papers and strode down the hall, handing one to each man who taught comp. Ed Purtzer, formerly a track star, distributed a pile to his colleagues on the third floor.

With this latest information, the instructors were able to inscribe letter grades on each exam paper. Once they had this done, they arrived at term marks by averaging the d.o., with class quiz, and theme averages, the latter two having been figured out during the previous week by all but the hopelessly disorganized. Levin thought the competition would end at this point, since it was late in the day, dark outside, but many of the comp people returned after supper to complete grades and transcribe them on two sets of cards so they could hand them to Milly first thing in the morning. Once all grades were in, working again from the individual tally sheets, Gilley drew a bar graph in colors to show how each man had fared in d.o. results. Avis again excelled; she had the longest red bar, signifying highest number of A's, whereas Levin had a medium-size bar. Hers was twice as long as his, a fact that made him feel momentarily ashamed. He tried to find out who the man with the smallest red bar was, hoping to befriend him, but Gilley wouldn't say. Later Bucket confessed it was he.

"I never teach directly for the d.o.," he said. "These tests are distasteful to me."

"Aha," said Levin.

*

Levin found himself thinking about the girl Professor Fairchild had told him about during their meeting in August, the one who had cut her throat outside her instructor's bedroom window. She often popped into his mind as he was running the subtle course between encouraging Nadalee not to expect very much more of their lovemaking and pretending he wasn't. It had been a mostly happy weekend for Levin until he had left her; only then would he admit he had felt no true affection for the girl, and that was enough to undo in aftermath some of his pleasure. This reaction was an old stock-in-trade of his and did not help endear him to himself. Why he should feel no genuine affection for Nadalee after his previous hot desire for her, he blamed to some degree on the disappointment of his trip through the mountains, and also on the fact that he had perhaps too severely previously subdued his ardency for her; or if it wasn't exactly that, certainly affection had been overlaid with a fear that troubled him all along, not that she would slit her throat under the cherry tree in the backyard; but that if news of their affair leaked out, it would end his career at Cascadia with a backbreaking thump. Levin worried she might give them away by a changed attitude, or sign, however unconscious or unwilling, that the teacher-student relationship had shifted to something more personal. It turned out that for the remaining few days of the fall term there was no serious change in her, except that she pretended nothing had gone on between them, and Levin was afraid her pretense was visible. He also worried that someone might have seen them on the coast—Bullock and Gilley, after ducks—or that she might, humanly enough, say something to her roommate about her new boy friend—tickle me and I'll tell you his name—a bearded member of the English department, ravished by her charms. The roommate might, in moments of passion, carelessly blow about this information, till it landed in Professor Fairchild's lap, whose wrath Levin feared most. He wondered if the fun he had had was worth it.

But after not too long he convinced himself the girl could be discreet. She had her own reputation to protect; and suppose news of the non-paying guest got back to the aunt who owned the motel, an affront to business? Levin learned with relief that neither Gilley nor Bullock had been out for ducks that weekend. Gerald had been on a recruitment trip to high schools in North Cascadia, while the University at Gettysburg—it said in the newspaper—was working southern pastures, practically a lost cause, since most of the kids there patriotically favored the southern college. And George, according to Bucket, had been busy tutoring his athletes for the finals; he had had them working last year's d.o.'s. Yet when Nadalee, looking most attractive, appeared in the instructor's office one afternoon not long after their recent intimacy and suggested another fling before finals, Levin, clearing his throat, said he didn't think it would be a good idea until maybe the Christmas or Easter holidays. He also advised Nadalee to take next term's English 11 with another instructor, and she intelligently saw the point.

"But we will meet now and again, won't we, Seymour?"

"Now and then," Levin said. "We might go for walks along the river."

She looked at him curiously. "Is something wrong? Did I do something you didn't like?"

"Oh, no," he said, "nothing of the sort. It's just that we have to be very careful, I told you that."

"Then when during Christmas will we meet? I could find an excuse to stay on at the dorm and maybe we could go to your room sometime, or something like that if it could be arranged."

"That would be nice but I may be going to San Francisco during Christmas," Levin said.

"Oh, swell! Wouldn't it be nice if we could go together? I'd pay my own way, of course."

He said it would be except he had promised a colleague he might go along with him, in the other's car.

"Oh," said Nadalee.

Though they talked longer, she seemed, when she left, to have grown cool to him. He observed this with regret. He was treating her badly.

A week later, two days after the English 10 final, she was in his office again, upset, angry, on the verge of tears. It was a dark mid-December morning, the rain blurring the wet world. She was herself drenched, her raincoat and poplin hat thoroughly wet, and Levin had hung them above the radiator, to dry. She had on a pair of tight red culottes, a white sweater that cuddled her hard little breasts, and white fur-trimmed boots on her childlike feet. Levin had serious second thoughts about the wisdom of so soon having called it quits with her, and even assembled a temporary plan for reclaiming her friendship, but this, on reflection, he abandoned. Yet he felt regret for the reduction, for whatever reason, of his former interest in her, and her feeling for him. If I were only in love, he thought.

She had come, it turned out, to protest her English grade. At her request Levin had mailed Nadalee her mark ahead of the official transcript, and she was clearly unhappy with the C she had got. She said, with moist, hurt eyes, she surely deserved at least a B and accused the instructor of having leaned over backwards in grading her.

"What do you mean?"

Her voice broke. "Aren't you punishing me because you did something you shouldn't have?"

Levin went to the door and listened. He listened at the walls.

"Please, Nadalee, keep your voice down."

She tightened her trembling lips as he, after a minute, spoke. "This I'll say: your term mark had absolutely no connection—it wasn't in any way influenced by my conscience, or any other feeling relative to our relationship, which I look back on with gratitude to you—if that's what you mean."

He showed her how he had worked out her grade. "First of all, we're all directed to grade the same way in comp, one-third each for class quiz, and theme averages, plus d.o. Now, going into the final, you had B plus in themes and only C plus in quizzes. I was hoping you'd hit at least a B minus in the d.o.—I was hoping for more than that, but at least a B minus to give you a B minus average for the term, which the registrar records as a straight B because he doesn't—as I understand it—like to monkey with plus or minuses because that means more clerical help. Anyway, to my deep disappointment—and I'm very sincere about it—you pulled a D for some strange reason, and that made your average C plus for the term, which is what I gave you, and that was the reason for the registrar's C. I will also admit I considered raising you to a B anyway, because, as

I just said, I feel a lot of gratitude to you. But the truth of it is that what happened to us, as you must understand, has no connection with your grade and I can't give it any. I thought it wouldn't be fair to mark you on one standard and everyone else on another. Do you see what I mean, Nadalee?"

She gave up her struggle to conceal contempt. "I see there were things you could bring yourself to do when they suited you."

Levin was shaken. "If that's honestly so, and there was nothing more to it than that, then I regret it."

She began to cry. She sat in the visitor's chair and wept in her hands. He pulled a tissue out of his drawer but she wouldn't take it.

"I had the curse when I took that final. I never do well then."

"I'm sorry, Nadalee."

"You don't know how much this means to me. I was banking on at least a B."

After a while she dried her reddened eyes and renewed her lips. Though he was tempted to ask her not to say or do anything rash, he managed not to. When she left she had regained a certain composure, but not Levin.

He was uncomfortable for hours in bed that night, trying to decide what to do. Had he marked her fairly? Possibly he had gone off a bit in grading her work in class, yet that might have been to her advantage as well as not. On the other hand, since she was a better than average writer in a comp course, why not raise the C plus to a B minus and let it go at that? Damn the small difference. He would not swear in the light of eternity and/or Second Law of Thermodynamics that his B minus meant a better performance than his C plus. Who was Gilley with his iron law of grade averages, God almighty?

Bullock had once said in the coffee room that he tended to upgrade the work of girls with good figures. Levin, on his part, was inclined to favor a petitioner. A student could arouse his sympathy by saying, "Look, Mr. Levin, I'm working extra hard this term. I have reformed and hope you'll notice it." Or by telling him his father had recently died and the widowed mother was entirely dependent on the son's grades. If his "objectivity" had been influenced before, why not now for her who had slept with him? He owed her more than he had owed the others.

I can't, he thought, as he stared out into the wet night. It's the principle of it.

He had resolved nothing. When he managed to fall asleep he woke after an hour and thought of what he had thought before.

She appeared in his office again the next day. Her pale face was without lip rouge or eyebrow pencil; and without perfume her body odor was bittersweet. She looked, Levin clearly saw, like no one he particularly knew, which he blamed on himself.

"When I spoke to you before," she said, "I didn't tell you why I needed the B, because I was ashamed to. But I have to have it because I found out I have flunked my math. I need the B in English to keep from being put on probation. If that happens in my first term here, Daddy said he would make me leave and go back to the bank. He's very strict about everything, Mr. Levin."

Now she tells me.

"I can't do it," Levin sighed.

"Doesn't how close we once were mean anything at all to you?" Nadalee asked.

"It does, but not to make me dishonest."

She looked at him bitterly. "Weren't you dishonest in sleeping with me?"

"How so?"

"To your obligations?"

"Yes."

"Then would it make you any more so to raise my grade just a teeny, to a B minus?"

"Yes."

Her eyes brimmed. He found her a tissue but she flung it away, shot him a cold look, and left the office.

Levin was afraid of the worst: When her father yanked her out of college she would take him along for the ride—the end of his short careless career as a college instructor. Ah, if I could begin all over again, he thought.

That night he was back at his desk at the office, reading through Nadalee's d.o. Possibly in the mad rush he had made a mistake. Levin first went through her paper to see that he hadn't skipped a page or marked any right answers wrong. He hadn't. Then he checked the count on each page—correct—and totaled the eight page scores. He added them three times and got three different figures, one twenty-two points higher than that on her paper. He flung down his pencil.

He hurried across the hall to Bucket, who obliged by doing the addition on Milly's adding machine. It came out twenty-two points higher than the original score. Referring to the grade distribution sheet, Levin saw she would easily make a B minus, giving her the B she needed. He was elated yet irritated by his carelessness.

"Something wrong?" Bucket asked.

"What do you do if you've sent the registrar a wrong grade?"

"I suggest you ask the secretary for a 'change of grade card' and say a prayer."

"Really? What for?"

"The registrar doesn't like to change grades."

Levin, in his office, kicked himself for not having checked his additions. He took his pile of exams to Milly's desk and sat there re-adding scores on the machine. By one A.M. he had uncovered three more errors. One wasn't serious—did not affect the student's letter grade; but three of the four were. Nadalee must, of course, be raised. A veteran in her class had to go up from B to A minus; and a girl in another section had to have her grade lowered from B to straight C. The instructor held his head.

Early that morning, the Friday before the vacation began, he asked Milly for three "change of grade" cards. She handed them to him, concerned behind her harlequin glasses. "They're hardly ever used, Mr. Levin."

He filled them out on her desk, writing "error in addition" for "reason for change," and then took them across the hall for Gilley's signature.

Gerald's face slowly flushed.

"For Pete's sake, Sy, three? Why, the registrar will go right through the roof. You have no idea of all they have to do right now. They'll be working through Saturday and Sunday and all of next week while the rest of us are loafing on our vacations. Each of these cards means half a dozen different changes for each student. It's a mess of clerical work, and they just can't spare that much time. The worst of it is it's entirely possible this girl you want to drop to a C may already have her transcript. Now what do you think she's going to feel like to get notice of this change?"

Levin, his beard prickly, was apologetic. "I'm sorry, Gerald, but a mistake is a mistake."

Gilley studied the three cards. "I'll tell you what we could do. Why don't you just turn in the two grade raises and never mind the other one? The girl will have a fit if she finds out her mark has been reduced. She could make trouble not only for you but for the department. Her father or some relative might call the president's office and the next thing you'd be sweating on his carpet, and we'd be hearing about it."

Levin, mopping his face, answered, "I would show him the evidence."

"It would still reflect on our good name."

"Still," said Levin, "if two changes are going to be made, why not the third? It's only logical."

After reflecting another minute, Gilley, his face resembling a lightly boiled beet, glumly gave in.

"But for crying in the sink, be careful in the future."

Levin promised and hastily left. Later he telephoned Nadalee and told her about his error.

"You mean I had B minus all the while?"

He admitted it.

"Then thanks for nothing."

She hung up hard but he felt comparatively clear in conscience.

During the long winter vacation it rained continuously, the sky a low thick motionless raincloud, the warmish wet-cold season without dry corner. After daylong rain it rained all night, the dark, liquescent, dripping from trees. When he woke in the night to heft his life, he listened to the rain as natural history, the Pacific extending itself over the land. Huge sopping clouds floated over breakers threading the beaches and struck against mountainsides, rain pouring from an armada of smashed hulls, drenching the craggy crawling forests, drowning green hills black, soaking the grasslit fields. In the dark Levin remembered the rain of his childhood, blown in wind against the faces of tenements, engulfing the leafless backyard tree in foaming bursts; but when it had ended—after a day, three, a week—it had ended and enter light, the worshipful sun. Here was no sense of being between rains; it was a climate, a condition, the water burbling, thick, thin, fine, ubiquitous, continuous, monotonous, formless. Once in a while he saw two rainbows in the same sky but after rainbows it rained. Wherever Levin went he went in rubbers, raincoat, umbrella; the only other man he saw with an umbrella was Professor Fairchild. Students stood bareheaded in the pelting rain, talking leisurely, even opening a book to prove a point. Meanwhile Levin had grown neither fins nor duckfeathers; nor armorplate against loneliness.

Bullock had invited him to drive to San Francisco with him, Jeannette, and the kids, and Levin was willing, but at the last minute George had to change his plans. Levin considered attempting the drive—for experience—in his Hudson, but he had tormenting visions of boiling over on every mountain top, being stuck in innumerable ditches, breaking down in snow, having to be towed and repaired until he was bankrupt. So he stayed home without much to do, though there were one or two little invitations, and he was looking forward to Bullock's apparently annual New Year's Eve shindig that Gerald had been rubbing his hands over. He read a lot, sometimes putting down his book to think of Nadalee, often with desire. One night he went to the tavern to see if Laverne was there but she had quit. He thought of the barn with nostalgia. The new waitress did not interest him so he left after one beer. During the week he visited Millard Scowers and O. E. Jones, and on Christmas night saw four hundred of Dr. Kuck's color slides. All eight Buckets—he had phoned several times and knocked on their door twice—had apparently left town. Levin thought of telephoning Avis but remembered her operation. The town had little to offer of entertainment. One night the instructor drove ninety miles to see a foreign film. The next day he drove two hundred, coming and going, to inspect the University at Gettysburg. While in the art gallery there, he bowed his head for the return of the liberal arts to Cascadia College. In the evening he searched the pages of the Easchester *Commercial Budget* for some local cultural event to attend, but what were Zonta, Daughters of the Nile, Men's Loyalty Club? He was too young for Let's Be Forty but considered dropping in at a meeting of You and Me because he had heard boy met girl there. Before he could go, Levin was sick in bed.

He had caught a miserable cold. His throat burned, sour nose dripped, head ached, and he sneezed in bunches. Sleep was hard to come by; when he dozed, his raspy breathing woke him. Bullock called to say Jeannette had the flu and they were canceling out for New Year's. Levin felt himself grow depressed. He thought of Nadalee endlessly, had got her without deserving to—fruit for teacher—a mean way to win a lay. His escape to the West had thus far come to nothing, space corrupted by time, the past-contaminated self. Mold memories, bad habit, worse luck. He recalled in dirty detail each disgusting defeat from boyhood, his weaknesses, impoverishment, undiscipline—the limp self entangled in the fabric of a will-less life. A white-eyed hound bayed at him from the window—his classic fear, failure after grimy years to master himself. He lay in silence, solitude, and darkness. More than once he experienced crawling self-hatred. It left him frightened because he thought he had outdistanced it by three thousand miles. The future as new life was no longer predictable. That caused the floor to move under his bed.

Levin fell into sadness, an old kind; this lonely man remembering this lonely man in the dark of a dirty room. So it went for ages, too long to think about. After came apathy; a rock with a cold in the head lay in bed, his own monument. But apathy he bore on the edge of shrieking; in iron desperation he concentrated on the sad golden beauty of a fifth of whiskey. The vision made him terribly thirsty. He reached for a bottle and found himself staring into a pair of brown eyes. Levin shuddered, no one had entered, was he already drunk? Then he saw Pauline Gilley watching him through the glass top of the back door, something like pity in her eyes. When she knocked, he craftily kept his mouth shut, but she had turned the knob and was already breathlessly in the room, naming, as she placed them on the table, what she had brought him: "Nosedrops, anti-histamine, vitamin C, a lemon for your tea, and some oranges and cookies. Excuse me for coming in the back way, but Gerald said Mrs. Beaty naps in the afternoon, and I didn't want to ring the bell."

She had removed her coat and was unknotting the black scarf on her head. Talking all the while, she picked things up, hung up his clothes, straightened the papers on his desk, saying as though it mattered she would have come before but Gerald hadn't told her until today that Levin was sick. "I had asked about you and he said George had said you had a bad cold. I'm terribly sorry."

He answered nothing, beard clotted, hair matted with sweat, the sick waste of a man. Whatever she thought she must do, let her do it and go.

Then she was sitting in a chair by his bed, facing the mess he was, knitting an obscene gray sock. "I wish you had phoned me." Her voice was at times inaudible. It made no difference.

"There's no need for you to be alone when you're sick. My father used to say that did more harm than the illness. Would you like me to read to you? I've brought *The Woodlanders*, a book I like very much."

He waited with shut eyes for her to go. It was a matter of time. She had stopped talking. Now he heard, as he stared at the ceiling, the click of her knitting needles. When the sound was gone she would be. He waited for that so he could take up his thirst.

"The children aren't our own," she was saying. "We adopted little Mary last year and Erik the year before, after being childless since we were married."

Levin waited with cunning patience and after long silence she put away the needles and got up. The rain had stopped. Under golden clouds the setting sun flooded the room. In the light she was knotting her scarf and then he no longer saw her. Afterwards his nose bled and he could smell the lemon and oranges she had left.

Levin got up and dressed. He pulled on rubbers but omitted the umbrella. Going out the back way, he walked along wet streets, sunlight glistening on the branches of black-trunked trees, to where the houses ended and he could see the sunset over the fields. The sun had sunk behind the mountains but the sky flamed rose. Clouds in surprising shapes and colors floated over his head. One looked like a fat red salmon. Another was a purple flower. One was a golden-breasted torso out of Rubens. His thirst was gone; everything was wet, trees, puddled roads, the grassy evening earth. His misery had exhaled itself. He was once more the improved Levin.

It was that goddamned cold, he thought. If I had kept that in mind I could have saved myself pain. He regretted not having said a kind word to her; but he felt like a man entering a new life and entered.

He returned to class still dissatisfied with his teaching. English II, "more a college course," Gilley had described it, though an improvement over last term's course, still depended too heavily on *The Elements.* Sometimes Levin interrupted drill in Workbook Form B, to speak of a good novel or read aloud a poem, the only poem some of them would hear in college, possibly in their lives. Sometimes, between a comma and semicolon, he reformed the world. But since that was irrelevant to the subject matter of the curriculum, he felt uneasy. Who am I anyway, the fourth Isaiah? And he failed more papers than he had last term. He lectured his students for the thinness of their themes, for their pleasant good-natured selves without a critical attitude to life. Then he was conscience-stricken for not patiently teaching.

A few people disappeared from his classes. When he got their withdrawal slips he assumed they had dropped English or left college, until he learned they had been in to see Gilley, who had arranged their transfer to other comp courses. Gerald admitted this to Levin once when they were alone in the coffee room. "Better take it easy, Sy. These kids have every right to be treated with respect."

"That they have," said Levin, secretly incensed, "—to be respected as people. But don't they have to earn my respect for their work?"

"You can't go lecturing them like high school kids. That's why they wanted out."

"Wouldn't it—er—have been better if you had advised them to stay with me? Since the issue was the quality of their work, if you transfer them out of my classes, aren't you really kicking my standards in the pants? Maybe you should have asked them to talk to me first?"

Gilley rinsed his cup. "My experience is that once a student has no further use for his instructor the best thing is to separate them both."

Though Levin denied the worth of the tactic, the loss of his students confirmed his fear he wasn't teaching well.

One wet January day, with Professor Fairchild present, sucking his yellowed ivory cigarette holder, Gilley convened a meeting of the composition staff to discuss the increase in plagiarized papers. Since October, the director of composition said, Avis had turned in three clinkers, he had lit on one, Farper one, and now Jones thought he had another. Gilley was sure others, as yet undetected, were around. He advised stricter scrutiny of all compositions, and consultation with colleagues if any seemed suspect. Avis had a flair for spotting work that had been copied. "Try her, Dr. Kuck, or me," he said. "Though the comp room does a good job of holding down the number of cribbed papers, some do get by us. If you suspect a theme—if it hits your eye wrong—that's a sure sign to watch out. If you can't spot its source right off, as I say, bring it to one of us. I've nailed quite a few of these tin potatoes in my time and will be glad to help you."

Levin asked what happened to a student who got caught.

Professor Fairchild removed his cigarette holder to reply, but Gilley spoke first. "Once we have certain proof, or a confession, the student is brought before the Student Dishonesty Committee. His or her instructor and I are the complainants, and he or she is advised as to his or her rights by the dean of men or women. Usually he or she fails English and is suspended from college for the rest of the term. If the case is very serious—if we have proof and he or she won't confess—we may expel him or her."

Professor Fairchild, nodding between puffs, added, "That's right. And once you've got a clear-cut case of cribbing, don't take the responsibility on yourself for judging or not judging guilt. Avoid false pity and turn the guilty one in to either Dr. Gilley or me. Preferably Dr. Gilley. It's the only way to stamp out this thing."

"That's right," Gilley said, but the old professor, with a chuckle, had begun a story: "About a year after I'd come here"—he scratched his eyebrow with one finger—"I guess it was closer to five, but no matter. At any rate, I had in one of my classes a boy I rather liked. I thought he was a gentleman until he handed me a paper I recognized at once as part of a magazine article I had recently read. You know, I had a chat with this young fellow—he came from a good family and readily admitted his error. He said he had been loaded down with engineering studies and hadn't any time left to do his English.

"I said that I'd forgive him his first offense and not take any drastic measures if he would turn in a makeup paper that same day. He did, that afternoon. It was a good paper. The boy was a competent writer—I knew that from a previous theme he had written in class, and I think I gave his makeup paper a grade of B or B plus, most likely B. But something about it didn't quite sit right with me. I woke up out of a sound after-lunch nap and began to wonder about the second paper. Something smelled fishy in Denmark. I spoke to Dr. Femur, in political science—he retired after we lost liberal arts degrees—and after some research he located the contents of the composition in an address by Theodore Roosevelt. I immediately wrote the boy's father, a successful shoe merchant, who came from Portland, Oregon, to see me. We had what amounted to an emotional session. The young man, in tears, swore on my wife's Bible that it would never happen again. I took his word, and so, may I add, did his father.

"Well, the boy handed in a third paper, but I was forewarned, and forewarned is forearmed. I asked Dr. Fabrikant—I think it was Fabrikant—" he looked around the room but Dr. Fabrikant was not present—"to read it over. He gave me the clue I needed and I located most of the contents of the third paper in the writings of John Stuart Mill. Needless to say, the boy was expelled from college. As an amusing postscript, I will add that the father wrote me an angry letter, in which he doubted my competence as a professor because I had given Teddy Roosevelt a grade of only B, or B plus, whichever it was."

He laughed to himself. "I cite this little story to show how they will take advantage of your good will, Mr. Levin, if you aren't alert and on guard. I've been hard to fool since then."

The meeting broke up, Levin pleasantly excited.

With him, to name an evil was to encounter it. In a few days he read a theme he was suspicious of. His suspicions made him nervous because one of his own painful memories was of cheating on a math final in college; he had copied from a paper a friend had slipped him—at Levin's request. But the instructor felt he had the right to judge his own students' honesty. It was the way of society: the reformed judging the unreformed. Better that than the other way around.

He compared the paper to two others the boy had written, one in class at the start of the winter term. The theme in question was a four-hundred word essay he had entitled, "Build Your Own House and Like It." Levin found this paper to be without any of the writer's usual weaknesses of structure and content, and with a kind of humor he hadn't encountered in his previous work. As a matter of fact, it was unusually good. The author of the paper, Albert O. Birdless, nineteen, from Marathon, Cascadia, was majoring in vocational education. His build reminded Levin of a young tugboat. He was stocky, with a short neck, heavy shoulders and legs, and stubby feet in square-toed shoes. His longish crewcut appeared to have gone to seed. On his head he usually wore a freshman beanie. Birdless was the exception to the almost universal rule of cordiality on the campus; his eyes were blue unsmiling marbles. He was a writer of less than average skill who did not attempt to hide from Levin his opinion that composition was a waste of time.

Since he sat in the last row it may have seemed to him that Levin paid no attention to him, because he sometimes put back his head and sneaked off a quick catnap during the hour. Levin had by now got over feeling very much annoyed with those who fell asleep on him; yet he had once or twice with a look tried to get Albert to resist boredom, and Albert had flushed and turned away. As he began to snooze one morning after a poor recitation, Levin asked him to snap out of it. He was then annoyed by the boy's scowl as he shifted his shoulders and reluctantly sat up, but the instructor suppressed a wisecrack and the incident was over. Later, passing each other in the hall, they exchanged cold glances. To some extent this bothered Levin, for there was little enough good feeling in the world and he did not like to add to the bad. Yet it seemed to him that those you chose to dislike had by some rule of economy in nature chosen you, so that narrowed ill-feeling.

Albert's average was a solid D plus when he handed in his spectacular theme. Although Levin's suspicions were at once aroused, after reading the paper he considered giving it an A under a remark that the improvement was miraculous and would he do the same next time they were writing a theme in class. But he was angered at the boy for trying to pull this on him. O. E. Jones, who had given Albert a D last term, shook his head over this paper. After some hesitation, Levin handed it to Gilley, who took in page one in a swoop, and said with a throb in his voice, "No doubt about it, Sy, this is a professional job. You've caught a rat."

Levin's throat went dry. "Are you sure? Where would it be from?"

Gilley, leaning back in his chair, reflected, one eye aimed at the ceiling. "I guess some place like *Reader's Digest* or *Coronet.* Also try *American Home* and one or two of that kind. Just thumb through the back issues of the last couple of years. Freshmen, as a rule, are too lazy to go too far back, only so far that the instructor isn't likely to pick up that same issue in the dentist's office. I don't think you'll have much trouble locating it."

"Should I ask him about it first—if he did crib it?"

"I have no doubt he did but I leave that up to you. Some ask questions first. Some would rather not until they have the evidence. Avis has a knack of going straight to the *Readers' Guide*, looking over the titles of articles on the cribbed subject for a couple of years past or so, and just about right away putting her finger on the one she needs. Her last incident she had this student nailed dead to rights an hour and a half after she read his theme. We had him suspended by his dean and off the campus before five o'clock of the same day."

After class the next morning, Levin, still uneasy, asked Albert to drop into his office during the afternoon.

"What for?" he asked.

"We'll talk when you come in."

"Okay." He popped on his beanie and left.

He didn't show up till after five. Levin had his coat on but sat down.

"Anything wrong—sir?"

"Would you mind taking off your cap?"

"Yes, sir." He was able to look at Levin without meeting his eyes.

Levin asked him to have a seat. Albert, placing his books on the desk, sat on the edge of the chair. When he thought about it he sat back and crossed his well packed thighs.

"Could I smoke?"

"Yes."

But he was out of cigarettes and Levin had none to offer him.

"I'll make it short," he said. "This last theme you gave me—this on my desk—is a very skillful job. It's so much better than anything you've so far handed in that I have to ask you if it's your own work?"

Albert's unsmiling eyes were steady after a quick glance at his theme.

"You weren't helped by somebody, directly or indirectly?"

"Who says so?"

"Some students don't quite understand where citation ends and cribbing begins. Sometimes they will copy material from a magazine or book and forget to acknowledge the source. Did you happen to do something like that?"

"Every word on that paper came out of my own head," Albert said.

"Every word?"

"Some came out of the dictionary."

Levin nervously stroked his beard. "But how do you account for such an unusual improvement in your writing? Usually—you have to admit, and this holds for your last term's themes which I've also looked at—you have at least one sentence fragment in every paper. Your ideas are presented with difficulty and without humor, whereas in this everything is lucid and the humor is really funny. Your paragraphs, Albert, if you don't mind my saying so, are generally badly built. After a short elaboration you pay no attention to the topic sentence, in the rare cases where you have one. Your first two themes, with indulgence, came to D. This, though, is a first-rate A. Suppose you were the instructor, what would you think?"

"If you don't write so good, that doesn't mean you're a failure."

"I never said so. All I ask is how you can explain this practically flawless piece of work?" He handed Albert the paper.

The student opened his mouth to let in air. His voice was emotional. "I worked twelve hours on that one theme. Isn't a guy entitled to a good grade once in a while? It just so happens I know about house construction. This last summer I helped my uncle who's a builder. And if this one sounds so funny that's because there are some things that happen to be funny, so why shouldn't I write that way?"

He was staring with a wet-lipped grin at Levin's hot ear.

Levin stood up, buttoning his coat. "I guess that's all."

Albert was also on his feet. "I bet you don't believe me."

"In this case I frankly don't see how I can. This paper is the work of an educated man."

"There's more than one way to be educated."

"This is educated in only one way."

"So you think I'm lying?"

"I don't think you're telling the whole truth."

"That's what I thought," Albert said sullenly. "I know damn well you never did like me. I'm not the only one that has your number. There are a lot of other guys who don't like your class."

"You've taken a poll?" Levin inquired.

"I hear people talking. They say you never give anybody a break."

Levin denied it but Albert did not stay to hear.

The instructor could hardly wait to get to the library, after supper, to find the article Albert had copied from. His hand trembled as he thumbed through a volume of magazines. Finding nothing that night, he returned the next morning during a free hour. Albert sat at a nearby table, watching Levin over the top of an open book that covered his face to the eyes. Levin imagined a disembodied smirk hanging behind the book.

Once or twice his heart raced as he thought he had the article, but it turned out no. The third day, impatient to get the unpleasant job done with, he gave the whole afternoon to the search. Nothing doing. Every night that week he read in the main reading room, adding other periodicals to those Gilley had suggested. Albert was almost always present in the vicinity, sitting behind a stack of books around which he peered from time to time, a sight Levin, to his surprise, found mildly pleasurable. Yet he was annoyed at all the time this was taking, angered that Albert knew what he wanted to know and so far couldn't. Amazing how denial creates doubt. He was out to destroy that doubt.

Twice Gilley came over to lend a hand; and Avis, now wearing bangs, although still cold to Levin—he had heard from Gerald the poor breast had been successfully operated on—pitched in for a full evening, together with Dr. Kuck. Though there were occasions they all felt they were approaching a definitive find, nothing came of it. One night after closing, as Levin was going down the stone steps of the library, Albert, a few steps behind, made a noise that even in Cascadia sounded like a Bronx cheer. Levin ground his teeth.

He extended his efforts, despite papers to grade and his own reading piling up; giving every spare minute to the hunt, and some not so spare, devouring volumes of up to fifteen years ago. He read with murderous intent, to ensnare and expunge Albert O. Birdless. Levin saw himself as a man-eating shark cleaving with the speed of a locomotive through a thick sea of words, Albert, a tricky fat eel hidden among them, only his boiling blue eyes visible through the alphabet soup. Levin, in fast pursuit, caught nothing in his toothy mouth and began to doubt he would catch anything. But Gilley cheered him on, though by now Levin was playing with the idea that Albert's theme had been the work of a talented friend, although how he would rate such a friend was a question. Gerald pooh-poohed the possibility.

In class Levin had given up calling on Albert, even avoided looking in his direction. Then one morning, about ten days after Levin had read the allegedly plagiarized theme, happening to meet the boy's eyes, the instructor saw they were soiled with worry, and his face had taken on a yellowish cast. Levin felt bad: he had created a victim. Albert might be guilty; if so he had got to where his guilt, by some trick of human drama, rubbed off on his prosecutor. Levin hadn't the heart to go to the library that day.

He sat in his office trying to decide what to do. If Albert was guilty he ought to be punished, but Levin, though almost positive he hadn't written the theme, couldn't prove it. Not having been able to prove it in a reasonable time—reasonable defined by the state of Albert's sagging nervous system, not to mention ten wasted days for Levin—wasn't it better to drop the whole business? He could forever go on investigating and finding nothing, creating a perpetual indictment. I've got to be quick with a reasonable doubt. He wasn't excusing Albert but had to stop torturing him.

Levin decided to call it quits. He considered reducing the theme grade to C but couldn't logically. It was, as a paper, worth A, and once he dropped the matter, A is what it would get. Albert would recover his contentment, but it was his contentment.

Levin made up his mind over the weekend. On Monday he called the boy to his desk after class. Albert popped on his lid as he approached. He stood near the desk, dully, swaying the slightest bit, not looking at Levin. His breathing was heavy, his breath bad.

Levin spoke through a constricted throat. "Albert, I haven't been able to prove your composition was copied so I have to assume you're innocent. Still, if you're really not, maybe you ought to say so? If you admit it, I'll drop you from the course without a grade. If you don't I'm forgetting the matter anyway, and you can stay on in the class without prejudice. The theme will go down for an A."

Albert's eyes were lusterless, as a smirk, a skull and crossbones rising on a tugboat's halyard, by degrees took possession of his face.

"I have no confession at all to make," he said in a quavering voice. "You tried to make a damn fool out of me and made one out of yourself instead."

He was about to cry and turned not to be seen, but Levin, unable to confront his image in Albert's eyes, had turned from him.

That ended it, he thought, until Gilley, seeing him in the hall, called Levin into his office.

"How's it going, Sy?"

"What?"

"The paper Birdless cribbed. How are you coming along on that?"

"Oh that," Levin said, scratching his cheek through his whiskers, "I couldn't prove anything so I dropped it."

"What!" said Gilley. "Dropped it?"

"I couldn't prove anything," Levin explained. "The boy was punch-drunk and turning yellow—his skin, I mean. I thought I'd better drop it."

"If he looked guilty," Gilley fidgeted, "that's because he was. He should have been tracked down and exposed."

"I tried, you know I did. I neglected everything else."

"In that case, why don't you leave his paper with me and I'll give it some more attention in a day or two?"

"Thanks, Gerald," Levin said, "but the case is closed."

"What grade did you give him?"

"An A."

"Are you crazy?" Gilley stared at him sternly.

Levin was startled. Yet when he looked again, the director of composition was smiling.

"Sy, do you remember what Professor Fairchild told us all in the last monthly meeting? About the procedure to be followed in a case of this kind?"

"Wasn't it in a different context," Levin asked, "referring to what to do after guilt was proved? I didn't prove anything."

"He said to avoid false pity and stamp this thing out. You and I know that boy is guilty. He should have been nailed or he'll do it again. I wonder if you have any idea what we're up against in cheating these days? Not only cribbed papers but all kinds of cheating. Students break into offices for exams. They steal Milly's wastebasket regularly to see if there are any copies of tests she might have mimeographed; I've had to change her lock twice this year. They cheat by every means you can think of. Girls pin notes under their skirts which they modestly lower when a proctor comes along. They hide answers in their brassieres. Some of the boys come with sentences diagrammed on their palms and definitions printed all the way up their arms. They keep notes in their cuffs and socks. One kid even had a kind of invisible ink he used to write with on his shirt cuffs, and a pair of dark glasses he could see the writing with. It's a regular industry and the only way to lick it is to stamp it out without mercy wherever we find it."

Levin agreed. "Still, if you'll pardon my saying this, Gerald, isn't it—er—partly our fault? I've never heard so much talk about grades as I have around here—including the coffee room. It's as though grades is what everybody graduates to after batting averages."

"Oh, come off it, Sy. Let's not get into complaining about the grading system. We have to have standards. And I'll bet you'll find just as much cheating in the liberal arts colleges as we have here. Let's stick to Birdless' paper."

"When I saw how he was beginning to look," Levin said, "I said to myself a good teacher is a liberator."

"Sure, but let's be relevant. You can't liberate a thief. Once you do he'll steal again. That was pretty clear from the story Orville told us. That boy cribbed three times in a row. If they didn't throw him out he'd still be doing it."

"I said to myself, You can't indict without evidence, and you can't indict in perpetuity."

"You could have got the evidence."

"I tried very hard."

"All this disturbs me."

"It disturbs me too."

"Then why don't you let me take the paper over for a couple-three days and ask Avis to finish the job?"

"No, I couldn't do that." Levin excused himself and left.

An hour later he met Gilley, in good humor, in the men's room. "Sy," he said, "something a lot more pleasant. Pauline asked me to invite you to dinner for Friday night. Can you make it?"

Levin tried to think of a way out but couldn't and accepted.

"Fine, I'll tell her. By the way, I've transferred Birdless out of your class. Avis agreed to take him. You'll get the drop notice in a day or so."

Levin, shaking in his clothes, tried to steady his voice. "Did you—ah—transfer him to get at his theme?"

"No," said Gilley, rubbing his hands with a paper towel, "he came in and asked to be taken out of your class. I did it because, as I said before, there's no point in perpetuating bad feelings between students and instructors."

"Don't you see," Levin said, "you are destroying my authority?"

"Now take it easy, Sy. I've done nothing of the kind. I respect your point of view but it's psychologically a bad thing to have a kid in the class of an instructor he says he hates. The student shows his disrespect in his attitude. He might spread all kinds of rumors or lies about you and it would be bad for class morale. You're well rid of a troublemaker."

This man is my enemy, Levin thought.

He laughed brokenly.

At the Bullocks' for cocktails Levin wandered restlessly from one group to another. He listened for a minute with half an ear, then moved on, wondering what he thought he might find in one bunch that he wouldn't in the next. The house was a stylish split-level on a fashionable western hill, whose large wood-paneled living room could hold thirty without trying and did this Sunday evening in the middle of January. Despite the crowd, with the exception of Avis there wasn't an unmarried woman around, and Levin thought that grim fact accounted for his dullish mood. People were pairing him off with her, he had noticed, and this explained, he thought, his recent popularity, if not with Avis. The beard seemed to help, making him in some people's eyes a person he wasn't. They could have it.

After a short stretch in the garden at sunset, Levin, a mouthful of martini held aimlessly in his hand, sat on the sofa between Alma Kuck and Jeannette Bullock, Alma again going on about the British Isles, and Jeannette deathlessly attentive, that rare thing, a beautiful woman who managed to be uninteresting. Pauline said she had never got over the fact she hadn't been to college. Levin noticed that although her legs attracted wherever she sat, she spent five minutes trying to hide them under her skirts, a pity. But she had constructed a lovely garden amid the oaks and fir trees on their property and was said to send everyone a birthday card on his birthday. As Alma talked and Jeannette listened, Levin, escaping from a yawn, had both eyes on Pauline Gilley across the room, standing partly turned from him amid some of the younger wives. She was attractive in a tight black dress. A small veil floating before her eyes from a wisp of hat created a mystery where none had been before. Who was the masked lady? Amazing what entices, Levin thought. Yet when she happened to glance in his direction, her thin-stemmed martini glass like a flower in her fingers, he pretended to be inspecting his new brown shoes. Secretly he continued to watch her. Alma diverted him with a question, and when he got up a minute later and went to Pauline she was gone.

Bullock appeared with his flowing pitcher, dispensing a boffo with every shot. The contents looked like innocent water but packed a hard wallop. People at the party were gay, they enjoyed Bullock's daring pitcher, a departure from the town's mores. Some were beginning to dance, a rarity in faculty houses. To dance, Levin had been told, one usually joined a social dancing club. There were dances the last Friday of each month, with extras for holidays. If Professor Fairchild or ex-Dean Feeney was present at a party, soft drinks and sweet green punch prevailed, but none of the older people having been invited, the host freely poured firewater, an empty glass seeming to threaten his security. Surprising the instructor without a glass, Bullock handed him one and aimed the spout, but Levin, worried by the man's unthinking prodigality, said he had had enough.

"I thought this was a party," George said. When he was drinking he breathed through a half-open mouth, both eyes verging on vacant. But a sweetness descended on him, and he loved on Sundays those he tolerated weekdays. Levin felt that neither of them took to the other. Bullock invited him because he sensed Levin disliked him, and he came because he couldn't afford to turn down an invitation. He got none from Bucket or Fabrikant, whom he liked, nor were they ever present at Bullock's.

"It is," answered Levin, "but I've already had two."

"That was my last batch. This will dissolve the rust on your gonads, if not the gonads. Have three."

Figuring he would abandon the glass, Levin let him fill it.

"Nice party."

George blinked. "Think so? We were late getting off the ground this fall. By now we've usually had three or four big blasts, but Jeannette hasn't been up to it lately—flu plus miscarriage (keep it quiet) et cetera. I also blame the late god-awful football season, let it rest. There's nothing like a consistently losing team to put a damper on your entertaining instinct. It depressed Gerald too."

"Is that so?"

"Yep. Everybody expected a bang-up season. *Look* predicted a possible Rose Bowl for us, then the roof caved in. We won three out of ten with some of the best material on the coast.

The alumni are sore as hell at Lon Lewis, the head coach, and he'll probably be traded for somebody with a T-formation. I know most of the boys on the squad and I'll tell you it was no inspiration to see their hangdog pusses in class on Monday mornings."

"They're all in your classes?"

"Some are. They have their free choice of instructors."

"I didn't mean they didn't—"

"Anyway," Bullock said, "exit football, enter basketball. We've copped the first four games and look like a shoo-in to take the coast conference. Bought your season ticket?"

"No," said Levin.

"Tough titty. Keep it in mind for next year. Saves you thirty percent. To the future champs." He raised his right hand, crossing fingers.

Levin lifted his glass. Remembering the red bumper-strip on Bullock's station wagon: "Keep Basketball King at Cascadia College," he drank to a better world.

Like raw gin. He had visions of being picked up drunk in town and fined a hundred dollars and costs.

"Gerald is also affected by a losing team?" Levin asked.

"After some of the rough ones he can't talk for an hour."

"Really? Pauline too?"

"She has her moments. Jeannette gets listless."

"Is that why the Gilleys didn't entertain much this fall?"

"It wouldn't surprise me. They like to have people in after a game but didn't do any of that after the shellacking we got from Cal, right off. He's the fan, though she keeps him pretty steady company at the big games. Both she and Jeannette say sports take their minds off their worries, whatever the hell they are. Pauline can be a moody dame, and I suppose having two kids all of a sudden is no picnic. Gerald did some lousy duck shooting in December. I've never seen him so bad. He's been worn out."

"She wears him out?"

Bullock winked. "I didn't say so but she helps, though last year the kids' colds knocked them both for a loop. Erik gets everything in the book plus some unidentified bugs. That was on top of the fact that Gerald hadn't recovered from L'affaire Duffy, the year before."

"It was that bad?"

"He bore the brunt for more than one reason, one being that Orville folds up his tent and goes home at the first sniff of scandal."

"It was really a scandal?"

"It amounted to one. Excuse me," George said, "the place is going dry." He lifted the spout but Levin withdrew his glass.

"Before you go," he said to Bullock, "have you seen where Pauline went?"

George looked vacantly around. "Try the upstairs bedroom. When she gets high she sometimes lies down."

Levin searched the bedrooms and daylight basement but she wasn't there. Back in the party he saw Avis eyeing him. He headed for the kitchen, slipped behind some people, and sliding open the opaque glass door, walked down six steps to the patio.

Levin sighed at the stars and was at once unexpectedly emotional. An odor of flowers assailed him. Because of the season he thought it was pure imagination, the result of more liquor than he should have had. I'm back in summer, Levin thought, or that far forward, why nobody knows. But he knew that even if he were living in another time he would be wishing for another time. The view in the dark, stars through bare-branched oaks, and the lights of the town below affected him as though he were listening to music. For the first time in years he thirsted for a butt.

Smelling smoke, he looked abruptly around.

In the dim light reflected from the interior of the house he made out Pauline Gilley standing between fir trees with a cigarette in her hand.

"Did I frighten you, Mr. Levin?" She had been watching him.

He went across the lawn to her. "I was looking for you, Mrs. Gilley."

He told her he felt bad about that time she had come to see him. "Excuse me, I was sick."

"Don't you like me?" Pauline asked. Her scent in the cool air was warm. He wished he could see her eyes through the veil.

"On the contrary—"

She waited.

"—I like you," Levin said.

"Then why didn't you come to dinner Friday night?"

He nervously fingered his beard. "Would you—er—keep it confidential?"

"I'm awfully good at that."

"Gerald and I had a disagreement and, frankly, I didn't feel like accepting his hospitality just then."

"It was my hospitality too."

He admitted it.

"What were you annoyed with Gerald about?"

"I would rather not say, some department thing."

She dropped her cigarette in the grass, stepping on it. "That was a mistake. Now I'm dizzy again."

He was eager to help. "Can I do something for you?"

She said in a throaty voice, "I should never let George get near me when he's loose with that pitcher. I can't keep track of how many I've had because he refills after every mouthful."

"For the sport?"

She gazed at the house. "Doesn't it look like a ship from here, and here we are, you and I, on an island in the middle of the sea? Or am I high? Are you?"

"I'm not."

"Excuse me for mentioning it but have you graduated to cocktails? The night we met, you wouldn't have one."

"Just a sip or two for sociability. I'm always saying no."

"Why?"

"Habit."

"What do you do for sin, Mr. Levin?"

Levin guffawed but came to quickly.

Hugging her arms, Pauline looked down at the lights of Easchester. "I should be home now, little Mary was running a temperature when we left, and I know Erik will have something by tomorrow. Have you seen Gerald?"

"No," said Levin. "Why don't you stay a little longer?"

"Should I?"

"There's a bench in the rock garden."

"Just for a short while, I have to get back to my children. I told Zenamae to have them tucked in by seven-thirty but I know they won't be. Erik gets up after he's been put down and goes exploring."

He was surprised, as he followed her across the patio, at her figure from the rear, so much better than he had noticed. The tight dress helped. Her shoulders, long waist and can were very good. Although a bit unsteady she walked with grace.

Where were my eyes? Levin thought.

"Don't be surprised if I fall," said Pauline.

"Let me help you." Levin took her arm and led her to the wooden bench in the rock garden. They sat in the dark, tall trees behind them.

"You look cold." He offered his jacket.

"I'll get my coat."

"I'll get it," Levin said. "You stay here."

"You won't know where it is. I'll be right back, you won't lose me, Mr. Levin," Pauline laughed.

She walked across the grass as though concentrating on not falling.

Five minutes later Levin was certain she wouldn't return. He was staring glumly at the stars as she came across the lawn with a coat over her shoulders.

"I'd've brought yours if I knew where it was," she said. "Why don't you go in and get it? I wouldn't want you to catch another cold."

"I've had this winter's cold."

"Do you plan everything, Mr. Levin?"

"What I can, I plan."

"My plans come to not much."

"Is that so?"

She touched his beard. "Does it keep you warm?"

She's high for sure, Levin thought. The veil irritated him. It hid as much as it revealed.

"I did have another drink," Pauline said. "George sneaked up on me when I was inside. I was feeling better and my defenses were down. I hope I'm not really drunk, Mr. Levin, because when I am I get sick. I don't want to be sick, please."

"Sit here till you feel better."

"My impression of your whiskers that day we met—it was my fault we were late, I was trying to get up my nerve to meet somebody new, would you guess that?—was they were coal black. But they're really a dark shade of brown. Do you know that beards bring out the quality of a man's lips and eyes? You have sensitive lips and kind eyes, Mr. Levin."

"I grew it in a time of doubt," confessed Levin. "When I couldn't look myself in the face."

"Should I become a bearded lady? Unless this veil does the trick. Does it hide me? At least my beastly nose?"

"Ah, but you're a lovely woman."

"How sweet of you. I'm not really lovely but I grow on people. I'd be nicer if I were less superficial and more accomplished. Oh, there's Gerald."

The glass door had opened and Gilley appeared on the veranda above the patio. He stood there for a wavering minute, a red-headed owl peering into the dark.

Levin sat silent, on the verge of disappointment.

But Gilley, probably affected by Bullock's powerful pitcher, blinked without seeing them although staring in their direction. He disappeared into the house.

They were motionless until she spoke. "I'll have to go now. Gerald wants me." Pauline got up but unsteadily sat down. "I feel like hell."

"Sit till you feel better."

A light went on in an upstairs room. It went out, and on in another. They watched it until it was out.

"What did he do that you didn't like?" she asked.

"It wasn't important."

"I'll bet it was."

Levin shrugged.

She did not pursue it. After a while she said, "I remember your saying, the night we met, that you hoped to make better use of your life here. Have you?"

"It's what one always has to do."

"Tell me what you want from life?"

"Order, value, accomplishment, love," said Levin.

"Love last?"

"Love any time."

"Pardon me for asking, but are you unhappy, Mr. Levin?"

"Why that question?"

"That day I came to see you—"

"Not as I have in the past known unhappiness."

"I sensed that."

"What about you?"

Pauline smiled. "I too am conscious of the misuses of my life, how quickly it goes and how little I do. I want more from myself than I get, probably than I've got. Are we misfits, Mr. Levin?"

Looking at her veil he thought, Take it off.

"Gerald suffers from my nature," she said, "though he's a patient man. With a woman more satisfied with herself, less critical and more appreciative of his good qualities, maybe he would have been a different person." She went on half absently, "Through the years I've known him he's substituted a series of minor gratifications for serious substantial ones. He's partly affected by what he thinks people expect of him, and partly he's reacted as he has because I've urged the opposite. Lately he's developed an intense ambition to follow Orville in as head of the English department."

"Wasn't it always what he wanted?"

"Not so much until the last year or so."

"Ambition is no crime."

"Not if you're strong."

She quickly said, "I wouldn't want to leave the impression Gerald is weak. He isn't, Mr. Levin, I assure you. He's always been an excellent provider, wonderful to me and the children. If you knew him better I'm sure you'd like him."

"I don't dislike him."

Pauline yawned. "Excuse me, I had a restless night."

Levin rose. "Shall we go in?"

But she sat there. "If you're a married woman past thirty you have at that age pretty much what you're going to have. Still, I blame myself for my compromises, and I resist the homogenization of experience and—if I may call it such—intellect. I wish I could do more for myself, I really can't blame Gerald for not wanting to make a career of shoring up my lacks."

He listened with interest, finally sitting again.

"Poor Mr. Levin, you came out for a breath of air and I've told you all I know."

"We could all do with a cause."

Pauline said, "Leo Duffy used to say, 'A good cause is the highest excitement.'"

Levin copied it on a piece of paper and slipped it into his

pocket. "People talk about him but don't say much. Was he a friend of yours?"

He thought for a minute she would raise her veil but Pauline sat with quiet hands. "What have you heard?"

"Not much—that he livened things up."

"Yes, he did. Leo was different and not the slightest bit fake under any circumstances. He was serious about ideas and should have been given a fair chance to defend his. People were irritated with him because he challenged their premises."

"That I guessed."

"I had the highest regard for him."

"I have his office now."

"So I've heard."

She gasped as they were drenched in glaring light. Bullock's garden spotlights had been turned on.

"That's the end of the party. George flushes the garden with those lights." Pauline rose, swayed in her tracks, and again had to sit down, her face so white the veil looked blacker.

"I feel deathly sick. Please, Mr. Levin, call my husband before I pass out."

"Couldn't I get you some coffee?"

"Just get Gerald."

"Let me take you in where you can lie down."

"Tell Gerald to come take me home."

Levin hurried into the house. The party was over, the room deserted except for Leopold and Alma Kuck in overcoats, talking quietly to both Bullocks.

"Pauline isn't feeling so well," Levin said. "Where's Gerald?"

"He'll be down in a jiffy," George said.

"She's in the garden and wants to go home."

The Kucks left. Jeannette saw them to the door.

"The dope is," Bullock said to Levin, "Gerald's in the upstairs head. I understand they both ate something that didn't agree with them. Maybe I ought to drive her home?"

"You're in no condition to, George," Jeannette said. "I will."

"Don't bother," Levin said. "I will."

He asked George where the toilet was.

"First to the left upstairs. There's another down here if it's for your use."

"Not for mine," said Levin. He raced up the stairs and knocked on the bathroom door. “Gerald, this is Sy. Pauline doesn’t feel so well. She wants you to take her home. If you can’t, can I?”

Gilley, after a minute, tiredly spoke. “Why don’t you do that, Sy? This has caught me by surprise, but I’m sure it’s something we ate last night, some Italian stuff with red peppers and olive oil. Plus too much vino. We both got up queasy this morning. Tell her she can expect me soon.”

Levin hurried down, found his coat, and returned to the garden. George and Jeannette were there with Pauline.

“I’m awfully sorry,” she was saying.

“Some food she ate,” Levin said. He helped her to her feet. “Gerald asked me to drive you home.”

She felt his beard and giggled. “For a minute I thought you were somebody else.”

“Who, for instance?” George said.

“None of your business,” said Jeannette.

“I’m awfully sorry, Jeannette,” said Pauline.

“It’s not your fault.”

Levin threw Bullock a dirty look but missed. They left by way of the garden. He helped Pauline into his Hudson and quickly drove off.

She rested her head against his shoulder.

“How do you feel?” Levin asked.

“Awful, but sexy. Do you think George wants to seduce me, Mr. Levin? He pours me such big drinks.”

Levin laughed although he felt a headache coming on.

“My one talent,” she said, rubbing her head against him, “only lately developed, is that I know people. I know you, Mr. Levin.”

“What do you know?”

“Who you really are. And you know me, don’t you?”

“I’m not sure.”

She sat up. “I’ve told you about myself but not about my children.”

“Later,” said Levin.

“At first I didn’t want them because I was ashamed a big girl like me couldn’t have her own. When we were first married I had some menstrual trouble and the doctor noticed I had a tipped womb. All along I thought that was the reason why, but years later we were both examined and it turned out

Gerald had no seeds. He had had the mumps and enflamed testicles when he was twenty-two."

"I don't want to hear about his personal troubles."

"I know I'm drunk, it makes me talkative."

She fell asleep with her head on his shoulder and awoke when the car stopped in front of her house. Pauline sucked a mint before she got out. He attempted to hold her arm as they walked up the flagstone path to the door but she wouldn't let him. In the house while she was paying Zenamae she showed no signs of distress but when the girl was gone she collapsed on the sofa, her hat awry, the veil crawling up one eye.

"Stay with me and hold my hand."

Her dress had risen above her knees. The legs were exciting though the long black shoes were like stiff herrings aimed skyward. Her chest had the topography of an ironing board.

"I'm suddenly terribly hungry. Could you make me a scrambled egg, Mr. Levin?"

That goddamn veil, he thought. On impulse he tried to pluck her hat off but Pauline clasped both hands over her head. "Stop, it's my only defense."

I'd better not start anything, Levin thought.

Upstairs Mary cried. Erik called, "Mommy."

"Mr. Levin," said Pauline, "I entreat you to look after my poor babies." Her head touched the sofa and she sat bolt upright.

"I married a man with no seeds at all."

She fell asleep, her stomach gurgling.

Levin went upstairs to the little girl's room and turned on the light. She stopped crying and stared at him. Her bottle was in the crib so he fed her part of it.

In the next room, through the open door he saw Erik sitting up in his bed. "Who're you?"

"Mr. Levin—the funny man."

"I want a drink."

He went to the bathroom and got the water. Erik drank and lay back. As Levin was covering him the child raised his head and kissed him under the eye.

Mary was asleep. Levin put off the light and listened to the children sleeping. The poor orphans. He burst into tears.

*

A warm, sunlit day exhaling pure spring startled Levin at the end of January. He had been forewarned of this, but the long habit of Eastern winter kept him from believing the season could go without once punishing by blizzard or lacerating freeze every dweller in its domain. He felt unsettled for it seemed to him the unused winter must return to extract a measure of revenge for dying so young, so little of it had there been: a few months of darkish rain, a week of soft wet snow (crowning the mountains and drawing the hills closer), gone quickly to slush then gone forever; the returned rain broken by nine days of sunlit cold—never below twenty degrees, afternoons warming—which exhilarated Levin although his students complained. Maybe a reluctant icicle had hung for a day or two from the roof of Mrs. Beaty's porch. Having as a kid, nose and feet burning, waded many times through snowdrifts, and often worn an overcoat into mid-April, Levin felt now as though he had been reprieved by prestidigitation, not entirely trustworthy, from ice, snow, and wild wind. If winter were already dead it left him with some guilt, as though he had helped murder it, or got something for nothing when they read the will, rare in his life. Yet the thought remained that to be alive was a short season.

Pessimism was momentary. Better enjoy the changes that had taken place with or without his knowing. Primroses, Mrs. Beaty had showed him, were in flower, had been all winter. At Christmastime, as Levin lay gloomily in bed, daffodil shoots were a stiff two inches above the ground; crocus under January snow. On New Year's day naked jasmine in the backyard by the cherry tree touched the dark world with yellow light; forsythia performed the same feat a few weeks later. Camellias were budding in January; quince and heather in flower, petals touching the stillest air. After the snow Levin had come upon a cluster of violets behind the garage. Rain was lighter, moodier, giving way to broken sunlight. And he enjoyed the lengthened day, seven A.M. now six-thirty. There was as yet little of spring to smell, either because early spring odors were still too subtle for his city-built nose, or the Northwest cool cheated scent, the throb of emotion in the wake of warm fragrance. If this was spring, Levin knew it because he eternally hunted for it, was always nosing out the new season, the new life, "a new birth in freedom."

On this reasonable facsimile of a late March day, a Thursday when Levin had no afternoon classes, although he had planned to return to the office after lunch and grind away at technical reports, the weather tempted him to a country walk to see what nature across the bridge had been busy at without him; and to feel the sun's beneficent hand on his head. He got out of his bureau drawer, where they had lain all winter, his binoculars and *Western Birds, Trees and Flowers.* Since he had read in last night's paper it might rain, he carried his trusty umbrella; and with this armload, tramped to the distant wood rising to the hills. He went by a route he had not tried before, a country road lined with old pussy willow trees, their sticky budding branches massed against the sky. Although Levin rejoiced at the unexpected weather, his pleasure was tempered by a touch of habitual sadness at the relentless rhythm of nature; change ordained by a force that produced, whether he wanted it or not, today's spring, tomorrow's frost, age, death, yet no man's accomplishment; change that wasn't change, in cycles eternal sameness, a repetition he was part of, so how win freedom in and from self? Was this why his life, despite his determined effort to break away from what he had already lived, remained so much the same? And why, constituted as he was and living the experience he engendered, he had not won anything more than short periods of contentment, not decently prolonged to where he could stop asking himself whether he had it or not? If I could only live as I believe, Levin thought. How often have I told myself happiness is not something you flush out in a planned expedition, a hidden complicated grail all at once the beholder's; that it's rather grace settled on the spirit in desire of life. We're here for a short time, often under the worst circumstances—possible that man may someday be blown off the tips of Somebody's Fingers; the battle lost before we knew what we were about, yet how magnanimously beautiful even to have been is. I have many times in differing circumstances told myself this, so why can't I quit worrying if happiness comes and how long lasts, if it does either? Discontent brings neither cold cash nor true love, therefore why not enjoy this tender marvelous day instead of greeting it with news of everything I haven't got?

He was still a distance from the hills when he approached a large wood—call it a forest—that he had come upon before by other routes. On impulse Levin left the road, hopped over a ditch, and crossing a field, entered among the evergreens. Once in the wood he was not entirely at his ease because he was trespassing, and as he went quietly along he worried about possible bears or maybe a snarling cougar or two, though he had heard of none in the vicinity; if there were any he had only an umbrella to defend himself with. Mostly his uneasiness arose from the thought that his life had been lived largely without experience of very many trees, and among them he felt a little unacquainted. Yet to be alone in the forest, this far in, was already a feat for a born city boy who had never been a Boy Scout. Levin took heart. He walked on soft ground among dark conifers, giants and dwarfs, and a large scattering of leafless other trees; but now he recognized fir, cedars, in green skirts touching the ground, blue spruce, and even hemlock, the trees in profusion, their branches interlaced, the forest gloom broken by rays of sunlight dappling the ground. The wood, as he walked, pungent with levitating coolness, suggested endless distance and deepest depth. Levin began to be worried about getting lost if he wandered too far in, and to avoid circular confusion, considered marking his way with bits of torn paper. The mystery of the wood, the presence of unseen life in natural time, and the feeling that few men had been where he presently was (Levin, woodsman, explorer; he now understood the soul of Natty Bumppo, formerly paper; "Here, D. Boone CILLED A. BAR") caused him to nudge aside anxiety and continue to venture among the trees in shade and sunlight.

As he came out of the woods into a clearing, a yellow-green, rich grassy meadow sloping downward, a flock of robins—from Canada, he had been told, while the Cascadian species was vacationing in California; you were dealing with strangers who looked like friends—scattered noisily over his head. From the wood across the field a bird hidden in a tree screeched at the world. Levin's head was immersed in silence deepened by a drumming in the wood behind, a woody tattoo. After a short bafflement he located with his glasses a bird drilling away near the top of a dead fir. Hurriedly searching for his bird guide, he read with the greatest satisfaction that he had spotted a red-headed woodpecker, never before seen so clearly. The bird spied Levin and flew into the forest. A moment later he turned pages hastily to identify first a Seattle wren, then a very blue, graybellied blue jay, exciting color; and a chickadee, the first he remembered looking at and naming; also a yellow bird he couldn't identify, whose flight above the treeline Levin followed with pleasure until it disappeared into light like a light gone out. Who sees this in Manhattan Isle? None but the gifted. Here the common man rejoiced in what was naturally visible. But being where he was not supposed to be continued to trouble Levin; he turned as if forewarned someone was in the wood behind him; expecting, if not a boot in the pants, at least the forester's hard hand and gruff get the hell off private property. He would run like mad. Instead, he saw Pauline Gilley watching him from amid trees.

She looked like someone he had never expected to see again, or was the thought a trick on himself to protect what was left of unused virginity? Pauline approached as if unwilling, an expression he attributed to an embarrassment of remembrance; then as though she had made peace with herself in mid-voyage, she looked up, smiling at his astonishment. Her raincoat unbuttoned, he took in blouse, gray skirt, long blue socks and walking shoes. He also quickly calculated what she had on underneath, an innovation in their relationship.

Her hair shone in the sun. "I'm sorry I startled you, Mr. Levin. I'm just as surprised to see you."

Levin explained his umbrella; the paper said rain. She smiled at his armload. "Let me help you."

"It's nothing much." Her presence in the wood aroused a renewed momentary sadness, as if he had come too late to the right place, familiar situation of his dreams.

"The day turned out so springlike I left the children with a sitter so I could walk," Pauline said.

"You've been here before—in this wood?"

"Yes, haven't you?"

"No."

"I didn't know you watched birds."

"If you can call it that. Most get away before I know what I've seen."

"You were engrossed when I saw you."

"When I was a kid I used to look out of the window at sparrows on telegraph wires or hopping in the snow."

"I haven't seen you for weeks, Mr. Levin," Pauline said.

"About two, I'd say. Time flies."

"I talked so much at the Bullocks'. I don't think I've been that much affected by liquor in years."

"No need to worry, I've forgotten what you said."

"Please don't."

They weren't looking at each other. When their eyes met, although he obsessively expected a veil, there was none, and Levin beheld an expression of such hungry tenderness he could hardly believe it was addressed to him. Enduring many complicated doubts, he dropped his things in the grass. They moved toward each other, their bodies hitting as they embraced.

"Dear God," Pauline murmured. Her kiss buckled his knees. He had not expected wanting so much in so much giving.

Levin warned himself, Take off, kid, and in their deep kiss saw himself in flight, bearded bird, dream figure, but couldn't move.

They parted, breathing heavily, looked at each other as though seeing were drinking—he could have counted twenty—and after mutual hesitation to the point of pain, embraced.

"My darling."

"Pauline." He kept himself from crying love.

Levin clutched at her chest, and seizing nothing, ran his hand the other way. She gripped his fingers, then let go, embracing him tightly.

"Where shall we go?"

"Anywhere."

She took his hand and they went into the woods, Levin glancing back to see where his things were. "Here," she said in the green shade. The evergreens were thick, the ground damp but soft with fir needles and dead leaves.

"Spread your coat." She spread hers over his, then stepped out of her shoes. She removed a black undergarment, the mask unmasked. Lying on the coats, Pauline raised her hips and drew back her skirt, to Levin the most intimate and beautiful gesture ever made for him.

He hung his trousers over the branch of a fir. When he knelt she received him with outstretched arms, gently smoothed his beard, then embraced him with passion as she fixed her rhythm to his.

He was throughout conscious of the marvel of it—in the open forest, nothing less, what triumph!

As she was combing the needles out of her hair the woods turned dark and it began to rain. They waited under Levin's umbrella under an old lichenous elm. If he expected uneasiness after the fact, he felt none. When he searched her eyes for guilt he was distracted by their light and warmth. He held the umbrella over their heads, his arm around her waist. They were resting against the tree trunk, her head on his shoulder. He felt, in gratitude, peace, and tried not to think of what he didn't have to, namely the future.

When she spoke he wished she hadn't. "Please don't worry about anything."

"Worry?"

"I mean if you have any regrets you're not bound to me. There are no obligations. You can leave this minute if you wish."

Levin pictured himself leaving her under the tree in the rain. Later he returned to see if she were there.

"Why speak of regrets? I have none."

"Your eyes seem sad."

"The fix of habit. I'm happy."

"What were you thinking of just now?" she asked.

"Oh you, your quality. I never had it this way before."

"You haven't had many women, have you?"

"Not many."

"I know you've been in love."

"Often—with the wrong kind. One or two made hash of me."

"I'm so sorry."

"My own fault, but that's in the past."

"Poor boy, did you have to connive for sex?"

"Not connive but pleasure never came too easy."

She was silent a minute. "Did this?"

"This is good."

"You respect me?"

"Of course."

"Mrs. Gilley, mother of two?"

"I respect you, Pauline."

They kissed again. She rubbed her head against his. "I'm hungry to know everything about you."

"I've had my bad times."

"Tell me what happened."

Levin was reluctant to speak about the past.

"You never do. I won't ask again."

He said, thick-voiced, half his face crippled, "The emotion of my youth was humiliation. That wasn't only because we were poor. My father was continuously a thief. Always thieving, always caught, he finally died in prison. My mother went crazy and killed herself. One night I came home and found her sitting on the kitchen floor looking at a bloody bread knife."

Pauline leaned her face against him.

"I mourned them but it was a lie. I was in love with an unhappy, embittered woman who had just got rid of me. I mourned the loss of her more than I did them. I was mourning myself. I became a drunk, it was the only fate that satisfied me."

She moaned; Levin trembled.

"I drank, I stank. I was filthy, skin on bone, maybe a hundred ten pounds. My eyes looked as though they had been pissed on. I saw the world in yellow light."

"Please, that's all."

"For two years I lived in self-hatred, willing to part with life. I won't tell you what I had come to. But one morning in somebody's filthy cellar, I awoke under burlap bags and saw my rotting shoes on a broken chair. They were lit in dim sunlight from a shaft or window. I stared at the chair, it looked like a painting, a thing with a value of its own. I squeezed what was left of my brain to understand why this should move me so deeply, why I was crying. Then I thought, Levin, if you were dead there would be no light on your shoes in this cellar. I came to believe what I had often wanted to, that life is holy. I then became a man of principle."

"Oh, Lev," she said.

"That was the end of my drinking though not of unhappiness. Just when I thought I had discovered what would save me—when I believed it—my senses seemed to die, as though self-redemption wasn't possible because of what I was—my emptiness the sign of my worth. I denied the self for having denied life. I managed to get and hang onto a little job but as a person I was nothing. People speak of emptiness but it was a terrifying fullness, the soul has gas. It isn't exactly apathy, you have feeling but it's buried six feet. I couldn't respond to experience, the thought of love was unbearable. It was my largest and most hopeless loss of self before death."

Her eyes were shut.

"I felt I had come to something worse than drunkenness. This went on for how long I can't say. I lived in stone. My only occasional relief was in reading. I had a small dark room in a rooming house overrun by roaches and bugs. Once a week I burned the bedbugs with a candle through the bedsprings; they popped as they died. One Sunday night after a not otherwise memorable day, as I was reading in this room, I had the feeling I was about to remember everything I had read in my life. The book felt like a slab of marble in my hands. I strained to see if it could possibly be a compendium of every book ever written, describing all experience. I felt I had somewhere read something I must remember. Sensing an affirmation, I jumped up. That I was a free man lit in my mind even as I denied it. I suddenly knew, as though I were discovering it for the first time, that the source of freedom is the human spirit. This had been passed down to me but I had somehow forgotten. More than forgetting—I had lived away from it, had let it drift out of my consciousness. I thought I must get back what belongs to me; then I thought, 'This is how we invent it when it's gone.' Afterwards I experienced an emotion of well being so intense that I've lived on it ever since."

He said no more. Pauline rubbed her wet eyes against his shoulder. "I sensed it. I knew who you were."

"I felt a new identity."

"You became Levin with a beard."

"What was new were my plans for myself."

"I won't interfere with them," she said fervently. "We shan't meet again."

Pauline smoked as they watched the rain let up. "I'd better be getting back."

Levin, gathering up his things, tucked the umbrella under his arm, and they went through the wet woods. He called it a miraculous forest but she laughed and said it was the property of Cascadia College, where they trained foresters.

"Then it's no miracle you came here today?"

"I've often been, on picnics with forestry friends, and sometimes I come alone to walk in the woods."

It worried him they might have been seen, but she seemed unconcerned so he was content. Whosever forest it was, he had gone into it, met her, and they had made love in the open, marvel enough for Levin.

On the road to town, although the sun shone brightly through broken clouds, he opened the umbrella over their heads.

IN HIS room Levin laughed one minute and groaned the next. Breathing heavily, he paced back and forth for hours. Or he stared out of an open window, lost in profuse memory. Sometimes he silently celebrated his performance in the open—his first married woman, sex uncomplicated in a bed of leaves, short hours, good pay. He was invigorated by the experience, one he would not have predicted for himself. A few minutes later he was soberly conscious of this figure within—an old friend with a broken nose warning him against risking his new identity. The new life was very new. Yet he wondered what he could be with her. Could he, with Pauline, be more than he was? Levin thought in terms of experience with her, not necessarily commitment. Hadn't she herself denied he was obligated to her? This could only mean she wanted no serious tie to him. Yet he was glad he had told her about the past; it was a relief to share that with someone.

By night the forest had taken on a dreamlike quality. Was there such a forest? Were the trees still standing? Were they real? Was it Pauline he had met there? He asked himself, Who is she? Extraordinary thing to have been in a woman and not know her. Could he trust her? What did she want from him; why, for instance, Levin? Because her saintly papa had worn whiskers—beard as totem? Was there perhaps some design in her choice of him (Had she purposely followed him into the woods? Impossible!) or was their lovemaking the more or less accidental end of a discontented woman's desire? If not, if she had in one way or another sought him out, what could he offer her, a man at thirty still running after last year's train, far behind in the world? Nothing. To be involved with a married woman—danger by definition, whose behavior he had no way of predicting was no joke. Who could guess what grade *she* would want changed; or what she might whisper to her lawfully-wedded spouse in a moment of tenderness, or hurl at him in hatred. If she threw Levin up to Gilley, farewell Levin. He feared his fate in her hand. Yet if she were concealment itself he knew his relationship to Gilley was changed for all time. This bothered him. Since he disliked him he wanted it to be for a just cause, to wit, Gilley, not because Levin had stolen from him—the primal cheating, result, oppressor hating oppressed. The thought that haunted him most was that the slightest revelation of the act under the tree would mean the worst disaster he could think of: end of future.

During the week, though she was often in his mind, Levin felt he didn't miss her, and probably vice versa. She could never be interested in a man with his kind of past. As he mulled this, he could not be sure he was right—she had seemed more than sympathetic to him, had practically wept. Probably it was closer to truth to think she had wanted the distraction of an affair, had had it, and quits. Or maybe she's now ashamed of it. She's the one with a husband; thank God I have no wife. So fare thee well. Yet too bad, for what's good deserves repeating. He had been thinking it was impossible to live on memory of sexual pleasure, no matter how satisfying. The better the pleasure the more useless the memory.

This was his mood one rainy night, the week after the forest, as he sat in his room. The fire of unseasoned applewood had sizzled out after nine, and Levin, tired of reading, had rebuilt it. He went back to his book but found it hard to concentrate; had to nail down each sentence before he could move to the next. The alternative was to shut the book and think of her. Let me be honest with myself, he thought; if I have her again I must keep romance apart from convenience. Love goes with freedom in my book. He had less than a minute to test his reflection, for there was a sound on the back stairs, and through the blurred glass he saw Pauline about to tap with a key. He rose hastily, his impression that she had been observing him, questioning what—his existence? worth? good sense? Levin momentarily thought of disappearing, but went instead to open the door where she stood. Could a man do less on a rainy night?

Pauline entered quickly. "Did you want me to come?" Her eyes hid from his.

If he said no it wasn't yes, but Levin said yes. Still, it was yes without pain, unless pain could be present without one's knowing, an unlikely procedure.

They kissed and at once parted as if there was much to say, or at least get straight, before they could kiss again. Her face and hands were cold, she had shivered as he held her. Levin hung up her wet raincoat. Pauline stood before the fire in the green dress he remembered from the night he had banged his head. She wore pendant earrings.

"Just let me get my breath back."

But breath she had. What was missing he wasn't sure. She seemed troubled, said little. Levin guessed what it probably was—the difference between last time and this. Their meeting in the woods was accidental. Tonight she must have lied to Gilley when she left the house. There was, in any case, that house to leave and this to come to.

For a half hour they watched the fire. She offered no explanation for her mood and he made it a point not to ask. He had disappointing visions of a short sexless evening. At length Pauline sighed and gave him her hand.

She looked around. "Is there anyone else on this floor?"

"Nobody. Mrs. Beaty sleeps downstairs."

Pauline plucked off her earrings and dropped them into her purse. She stepped out of her shoes and began to undress. He did the same though nobody had asked him. The contract was in the prior act, there in the forest.

In her lace-bosomed slip reflecting the fire she looked at him with a half-sad smile.

"Do you like me in this?"

"It's a poetic garment."

"You've never seen me naked."

The fact surprised him.

She drew the slip over her head and was naked. Her hips were slim. She was long waisted, the legs and trunk gracefully proportioned, her arms and shoulders lovely. Naked, she looked unmarried.

But her chest was barren, the flowerlike nipples only slightly fleshy. He had almost looked away.

"Shall I keep my slip on? Would you like that better?"

"No." He had to watch himself with her.

She pressed down the mattress to see if the bed creaked.

"Are you afraid?" he asked her.

"Dreadfully. I'd die if anyone heard us."

He took her in his arms. "Don't be afraid. The landlady's deaf when she's asleep. She's asleep now."

She was suddenly passionate, bit his lip. In bed she met him with open mouth. He thought what he must do for her but there was hardly time. "Take me." She came quickly, at the end half singing out as she had in the woods, a sound that sang in him. At its onset he had taken it for sobbing—regret for what she was doing—but it was a halting cry of pleasure. She took him with her before he thought it time to go. He laughed at the ease of it.

Afterwards she asked, her face lit in the glow of a cigarette, "Does 'My young love's rip'ning breasts' mean so much? Does my flat bosom bother you?"

"If it did it doesn't."

"At least I have symmetry," she said. "My roommate in college had a bigger right breast than left."

He was for symmetry.

"And I've never worn falsies, would you want me to?"

"You're not the type."

"What type am I?"

"The type that doesn't wear them."

"Please always be honest with me," Pauline said.

He said he had to or got mangled.

She asked if he always taught himself lessons from experience.

"Almost always."

"My poor Levin."

"I don't like to make the mistakes I've made."

She said, after putting out her cigarette, "What will you teach yourself from us?"

"Something good, I think."

"Something lovely, perhaps enduring?"

He said he thought so.

"Do you think you could fall in love with a woman without breasts?"

"I've never tried."

She said, suddenly, "I shouldn't really be here."

Pauline was at once out of bed. "Gerald's in Marathon tonight. The children are alone because I couldn't get a sitter. I feel like a heel."

But she swept off the bedsheet and tightened it under him. Emptying the ashtray into the fireplace, Pauline aired the room, dressed, and left. Levin was at once asleep.

She visited him not often but often enough. One of her "meetings" was a good enough excuse for a night out. And Gilley assisted by teaching a winter-term weekly extension course for teachers, in Marathon. Usually Pauline walked the dozen blocks to Levin's. When she had the car she parked it about two blocks from the house. Gilley was home from Marathon by eleven. She had left Levin's room at ten-thirty, short but sweet. He could read afterwards without a stray thought, a great convenience. He envisioned a new Utopia, everyone over eighteen sexually satisfied, aggression reduced, peace in the world. Once she came for an hour after Gilley had fallen asleep, worrying Levin. She was no longer dreadfully afraid; the change in her had escaped him. She said she sometimes slept on a couch in Erik's room and Gilley was a heavy sleeper. In the unlikely event he awoke he would not miss her. But Levin asked her not to take chances. She promised, then went frankly on record in extenuation of the chances she took. "Gerald can sometimes be indifferent to me for weeks. He began to be after we found out the true reason why we couldn't have children, although I will admit there are times when it's my fault, when I just don't have the energy."

What a waste, he thought.

The next time they were in bed, after Levin had dozed and waked, she brought up Gerald. "Why don't you like him?"

"I never said I didn't."

"Tell me what happened in the department."

"I told you we didn't agree about some things."

"Be patient with him," she said. "He has good will towards you."

"Let's not talk about him," Levin said.

"He's really been very sweet to me. Sometimes I'm a moody bitch, but he's usually patient and I'd like to be grateful."

He said nothing.

"We weren't doing so badly at first," Pauline said, "then we began to have some nasty spells. He disappointed me in certain ways, some not his fault. I know I disappointed him. We had a very bad time just before we got Erik but it's really been better since the kids came. They've made me as nearly happy as I've been in recent years. Gerald does a lot for us. Lately I've been thinking I'd like to be in love with him again. It was very nice when we first were. Do you think anybody can bring past love alive or is it gone forever once it goes?"

"I don't know."

"Sometimes I've thought that if I were having an affair he might sense I'm being attractive to someone, and it might awaken more of his desire for me. If that happened maybe I would respond. Do you think that could happen?"

"I doubt it," he said.

"So do I," said Pauline.

He interpreted this to mean she wanted pleasure, solace, a momentary change, but no serious involvement with him. Her marriage, deficient as it seemed to him, apparently meant something to her. The situation suited him. If it made their relationship seem less consequential than it might be, on reflection so much the better. If his affair with Pauline inspired Gilley to respond to her, and she to love him for responding, so much the freer Levin's conscience. It wasn't easy to be helpful while enjoying the fruits of another man's wife.

He anticipated her visits, the tap of her key on the glass. They embraced ardently, her hand going for his fly. Levin guessed this was new for her, probably a new way she saw herself. It was new for him. Off came her earrings, then her clothes, without embarrassment. Breasts or none, her woman's wealth satisfied him. When he touched her nipples the effect was electric. She could be a little wild in bed. "Your fingers are fires." He enjoyed her long body, the cool flesh, sex smell, fragrant hair. He enjoyed the possession and adventure, her intensity with detachment. In bed he rarely thought of her as Gilley's wife. If he did he countered conscience with the thought he could break it off by spending the summer in San Francisco. In the fall he could find some excuse not to see her. He could say he had fallen in love and was thinking of getting married.

The forest had shrunk to a double bed. In bed they lived, in bed explored their bodies and history. She often asked him about his life, what he was like at ten, seventeen, twenty.

"A romantic," Levin said.

"That's still in you."

He shrugged. "Almost gone."

"Don't you like it?"

"I've lived too much on air."

"I like that in you."

Then she said, "Is love air?"

"Too often it was."

When he asked about her she asked: Did he find her attractive? Did he like her hair long? Did he like her legs? "I have such big feet." "I'm not pretty, am I?" She said once she didn't think she was interesting. "I've had so few experiences. My life was so prosaically different from yours. It's almost as though I wouldn't go the extra step to make something happen, and not much did."

"You are an interesting woman," Levin said.

"Do you mean as a person or sexually?"

"As a person with sex."

"Is that part of me strong, the sex?"

"Yes."

"I wish I had been more that way when I was young. If I had been confident of myself I might have had a lover or two."

"Didn't you?"

"I was a virgin when I was married."

"After that?"

"I was interested in men but I've never had the sort of relationship we're having."

A minute later she asked, "Tell me what you hear about me?"

"In what way?"

"Any way."

"Jeannette says you're a very fine person."

"She's a very fine person. What does George say?"

"Nothing I remember."

"Avis?"

"She thinks you could do more to help your husband."

"She's right," said Pauline. "Is that all she said?"

"Yes."

"She's had a crush on Gerald for years."

Levin said he had thought so.

He fell asleep. She woke him. "A woman my age is too old for a man yours. Wouldn't you really be better off with a girl of twenty-three or -four?"

His thoughts were scattered and he answered nothing.

She said wearily, "I'd be afraid of intense love now."

She dressed and went down the back stairs.

He expected her nightly all the next week but she didn't come. One day they met by chance on a downtown street.

"Did I say something wrong last time?" Levin asked.

"No, I haven't been myself."

"Not my fault?"

"I've been nervous, nothing new, an effect of periodicity."

"When can you come again?"

After a while she said she would soon.

Pauline reappeared the next night. Usually she was at once affectionate but tonight she sat at the fire, chain smoking. They talked but not about themselves. When he looked directly at her she seemed to look away. Levin assumed she felt guilty and foresaw the end of their affair.

"Suppose we were to break up?" she said.

"It would depend on you."

It grew late. Pauline got up and put on her coat. She looked lonely. Levin, exploring an insight, lifted her and carried her to the bed. She stiff armed him. "You don't dare." He pushed her down.

Afterwards she grabbed his frontispiece. "I'll never let you go, Mr. Micawber."

The next time after making love, Levin experienced a fiery pain in the butt. He broke into a cold sweat and lay apart from her, his body stiff, pretending to be asleep. He shoved his face into the pillow to keep from crying out. For ten brutal minutes he was in torment, then the pain gradually eased. He felt sickly limp but relieved, thankful for his good health. Less than a week later he felt the same agonizing, flaming pain. Though tensed to misery Levin managed to hide it from her although the torture was worse than any he remembered. It moved up the side, then to the scrotum, then back to the butt, a harrowing embarrassment after sex and shameful way to be vulnerable.

After another such spasm he began to dread going to bed with her. At the same time he was disgusted with himself—pure Levin reaction, for every pleasure, pain. He thought of telling Pauline what the trouble was, but for a lover it was a too vital weakness to confess, one which might, if it continued, waken contempt. When she appeared the next time he suggested going for a drive or maybe to a movie in another town. Pauline seemed touched by the suggestion, sweetly agreed, but in one womanly way and another—although he sensed her puzzlement—enticed him into a performance. Levin paid the price of emission, a fiery pain in the ass.

"Aren't you well?" she asked after minutes of silence.

He said he was.

"I feel you haven't been enjoying yourself lately, I can't quite describe it. Has my breath been bad?"

"No."

"Would you like me to come less often, or not at all?"

"No."

She left it at that, perhaps afraid to ask more, obviously worried. When the pain was gone, although they talked affectionately, he saw her watching him. Before she left she clung to him.

On the night of Gilley's next class in Marathon, Levin tried hiding from her. After supper he went to a movie and later drank beer until midnight. She had left a note: "Sorry I missed you." He slept badly, dreamed his whiskers were on fire. It seemed to him he had just fallen asleep when he was awakened by footsteps coming stealthily up the back stairs. These weren't her steps. Levin listened, nailed to the bed, his heart thundering. The steps stopped. He jumped up in wet sweat, fumbled for the light, fell over his shoes, sprang up and flung open the door. Nothing. Rain in swirling light. Someone wandered up the inside stairs. Levin hastily got into a robe before Mrs. Beaty knocked. She stood at the door in her flannel robe, her earpiece in, holding the battery box in her hand. He said he had had a nightmare and fallen out of bed. She said to be careful, she knew a man who had broken his back that way.

Fearing something serious—kidney, bladder, rectal—possibly cancer—and because he was making Pauline so jumpy she went two moody visits without looking at the bed, Levin decided to see a doctor. He had hoped the pain would go without treatment but it was as bad as ever when they went to bed again.

One afternoon he drove to Marathon to someone recommended by Joe Bucket; he didn't want anyone in Easchester to know his business. The doctor, an old man, examined him elaborately with every instrument he could think of except forceps. He made various tests, then pronounced his judgment.

"Tinsion is all I can find."

"My God, what's that?"

"Some sort of tinsion is causing rectal and other spasms, though possibly it's the prostate, but I can't find any evidence. Have you felt like going to the toilet when you have the pain?"

"I've gone."

"Does it help?"

"No."

"No relief or relaxation?"

"Isn't sex supposed to relax you?"

"It is and it isn't. It does and it doesn't." The doctor scratched behind his ear. "Is the lady your wife?"

"Yes," he lied.

"Are conditions favorable for intercourse?"

"Yes."

"You aren't worried about your business or any such worries?"

"No."

"Beats me, I'm afraid," said the doctor, "unless you don't like your wife."

Everyman's Freud, thought Levin.

"You might rest up a week."

"I've rested, it comes back."

The doctor wrote out a prescription. "Take one of the little green pills before intercourse. If that doesn't work, take the white pill afterward. The first is a relaxant for your tinsion, it's an anti-spasmodic. The other is a pain killer. If neither of them work come back and I'll give you an antibiotic."

In the street Levin tore up the prescription and scattered the pieces.

Levin afflicted by mystery: What was the painful egg the rooster was trying to lay? In the middle of driving home a thought he had had but never particularly valued, stalled the car. He was asking himself what he was hiding from: That he too clearly saw her shortcomings and other disadvantages, and was urgently urging himself to drop her before it was too late?

That he was tired of the uneasy life, fed up with assignations with the boss's wife, sick up to here with awareness of danger and fear of consequences? Here was truth yet not enough truth. After mulling these and related thoughts, Levin tracking an idea concerning Pauline, fell over one regarding himself: the dissatisfaction he had lately been hiding from, or feeling for an inadmissibly long time, was with him for withholding what he had to give. He then gave birth. Love ungiven had caused Levin's pain. To be unpained he must give what he unwillingly withheld. It was then he jumped up, stalling the car.

Once home, he didn't know what to do with himself. Run twice around the block? Stand on his ear? Dig hard head into concrete sidewalk? Kiss the mirror or hit it with a hammer for imaging the dark-bearded one who ever complicated the infernally complicated? And Einstein, it said in the papers, used the same cake of soap to shave and bathe. Levin sat in his chair, momentarily slept, started while dreaming, bounded up to spend hours staring out of the open window at nothing he particularly saw. He lay on the bed, then rose up as if the sheets were on fire. He left his room to hurry somewhere—anywhere—and awoke to find himself standing on the back stairs. Above the tops of budding trees he watched the flaring, setting sun, wanting to abolish thought, afraid to probe the complexion of the next minute lest it erupt in his face a fact that would alter his existence. But nature—was it?—a bull aiming at a red flag (Levin's vulnerability, the old self's hunger) charged from behind and the Manhattan matador, rarely in control of any contest, felt himself lifted high and plummeted over violet hills toward an unmapped abyss. Through fields of stars he fell in love.

. . . Love? Levin eventually sighed. Is it love or insufficient exercise? Escape, perhaps, or excitement born from the tension of secrecy, wrongdoing? Love? How at all possible if the proposed lover had such profound reservations concerning the game, rules, even players? Consider once more, for instance, her lank frame, comic big tootsies, nose flying, chest bereft of female flowers. He mourned that motherless breast, the lost softness over the heart to pillow a man's head. He had once in frustration nipped at her nipple; she had socked his head with both fists. Levin had never imagined such as she his, her insufficiencies, discontents. Consider too the burden of her ambient: prior claimant, husband-in-law; the paraphernalia of her married life—love her, love her past. With her possibly take kids and their toys. Not for me, he told himself. He wanted no tying down with ropes, long or short, seen or invisible—had to have room to move so he could fruitfully use freedom. If, ecstasied out of his senses he let down his guard—was leapt on by fate—Lord help Levin!

But if he loved her why loved he her? You are comely, my love. Your self is loveliness. You make me rich in feeling. You have grace, character. I trust you. He loved because she had one unforgettable day given herself to a city boy in a forest. And for the continuance of her generosity in bed (was he less generous?) abating desire as she made it grow, taking serious chances (did he not chance as much?). Or was he moved to love because her eyes mirrored Levin when he looked? Or, to drag truth closer, because he was compelled by his being to be in love with her open, honest, intelligent, clearly not very happy self? (Why do I feel I have chosen her because I am her choice?) The catechism made little difference, for he knew fait accompli when accomplished. Who was he kidding, or what pretending to delay or dress in camouflage? "The truth is I love Pauline Gilley." His confession deeply moved him. What an extraordinary only human thing to be in love. What human-woven mystery. As Levin walked the streets under a pale moon he felt he had recovered everything he had ever lost. If life is not so, at least he feels it is. The world changed as he looked. He thought of his unhappy years as though they had endured only minutes, black birds long ago dissolved in night. Gone for all time. He had made too much of past experience, not enough of possibility's new forms forever. In heaven's eye he beheld a seeing rose.

. . . But Levin had long ago warned himself when he arrived at this intensity of feeling—better stop, whoa. Beware the forms of fantasy. He had been, as a youth, a luftmensch, sop of feeling, too easy to hurt because after treading on air he hit the pavement head first. Afterwards, pain-blinded, he groped for pieces of reality. "I've got to keep control of myself. I must always know where I am." He had times without number warned himself, to harden, toughen, put on armor against love.

It snowed heavily.

The snow fell in buffeted veils. It bent shrubs and small evergreens and broke branches everywhere. There hadn't been such a snowfall in years, Mrs. Beaty said. Gilley's Marathon night passed and Pauline did not visit Levin. He accused himself, then blamed the snow, until after three warm days it vanished and she still had not appeared. Had his antics, while avoiding the bed, scared her away? He hungered to call her or write, but she had once asked him not to. Another Marathon night went by and Levin's desperation grew. He felt he had lost her.

When Pauline appeared in his room ten days after he had discovered he loved her, Levin was moved by the glow of her, the lovely form she achieved in being. How love perfects each imperfect thing. What she was was beauty. With breasts she couldn't possibly be the one he loved. I mustn't forget this, he thought, it's worth remembering.

Yet as she entered the room he knew at once—it smote him—that her detachment, almost unconcern—was something more than of the moment; and if desire, no more than that, the little she wanted from him, for which he castigated himself. She scanned his face and finding him fit plucked off her earrings. Hearing no objections to the contrary, she undressed for bed. When he embraced her she stiffened momentarily in his arms. When he spoke of love she whispered she had only an hour. Levin was thinking of forever. He felt he had loved her from the time he had laid eyes on her at the railroad station last summer—years ago. They had looked guardedly at one another. Had she guessed he would love her and turned away as though the thought was burdensome? Could she ever know that before meeting her he had loved the idea of Pauline Gilley? Didn't that make him worthy of her love?

But what had tilted Levin into love had not tipped her. In bed she dispatched the act with an easy cry. He loved her, wanting as he loved. She fell asleep as he lay awake thinking of the unyielding irony of his life.

Afterward she said, "You've been so strange."

He apologized. "I had some trouble but it's gone now."

"Is that the truth?"

"Pauline, the truth is I love you."

She said after silence, "How like a woman to want to love the one you sleep with."

"I do."

She held her hands to her ears.

He shut his mouth, eyes, his life. She dressed and quickly left. He wasn't looking.

Each day passed excruciatingly, he tried not to count. He fought thinking of her, a mockery—she was in every thought. He beat his brains to destroy her place in his mind without maiming himself. How to be, please God, not Levin? How to live loveless or not live? Once more he paid for who he was, a dirty deal.

Late one night she tapped on his window and nervously entered. Levin, putting down a book he couldn't read, faced her with what dignity he could muster, concealing love in his own defense, and the pain her presence invoked.

"I saw your light," she said.

He answered nothing.

"I tried not to come," Pauline said. "It isn't fair to you."

Fair or foul, he would settle for sex.

"Considering what I know about your life—what you've been through—I have no right to love you or expect your love, my poor darling."

He rose with an aching heart.

"I love you," she was saying, "although I try not to. I tried to be fair to you, to Gerald, and my children."

They embraced. She dug her nails into his back. He beat her with his heart.

"I love you, Lev. That's my name for you. Sy is too much like sigh, Lev is closer to love. I love you, I'm sorry, you deserve better."

"I deserve you."

"I should never have let you that day in the woods. But I love the kind of man you are, the kind I have to love."

"I love you willingly, with all my heart."

"Oh, my darling, we must do something with our lives."

My God, thought Levin, "What hath God wrought?"

IT WAS easy to duck Gilley whether on campus or some downtown street. From afar his red head flared; Levin spun around and walked another way. In Humanities Hall he cut out tea to stay out of the coffee room. He could not avoid him at department meetings but didn't go near his office—hadn't since Albert Birdless. If it were possible to escape the sight of him, Levin escaped. Yet when they met at somebody's house, since Pauline was there he felt less self-conscious with Gerald than he thought he would be, guilt diminished because divided. (She glanced at him; he looked at her; she looked away.) Gilley and he sometimes talked shop, or the sportsman described how to wallop a little white ball across the grass or pull a half-dead fish out of water. He teaches me, thought Levin, and felt, in spite of all, a mild affection for the man, a sort of third cousin by marriage. But when he was alone, Levin worried. He feared the HUSBAND of the wife, ashamed of eating his apple, spitting on his manhood, betraying him in a way the betrayer would have died to be betrayed.

Levin had only casually tied morality to sex, the act, that is. Sex was where it grew, where with luck he found it, manna when least expected. What was for free was for free so long as nobody got hurt. If the lady was willing nature approved. But the matter became moral when, in getting at sex, a man interfered with another's "rights." Though he loved Pauline he had no right to her at present. Gilley had staked his claim and she had agreed, the marriage contract. Destroy the value of that and every personal right lost value. And pretense to Gerald, at the moment he was sleeping with his wife, that their relationship—such as it was—continued to be what it had been, ladled hypocrisy on deceit. He was also ashamed of old-fashioned disloyalty to someone who had favored him with a job that pointed to a future. For which Levin (bearded witch riding Gilley's corpse) repaid him with kicks where it hurt most, once, God forbid, he knew he had been kicked.

Yet he tried to convince himself not to let his conscience weigh too heavily. Gilley was, after all, not guiltless; he erred too. Indifferent to his wife in vital ways, did he deserve her fidelity? His "rights" were formal, less than right because he hadn't used them very well, at the very least to keep her from sexual hunger; and rely on more than two adopted kids to hold the marriage together. He had flubbed his best chances. As to what Levin could do for her, what his chance amounted to (beyond love itself) he did not know for sure. Since she was not free it was a matter for the future; they would have to wait for the right time. Pauline, after confessing her love, had thus far said nothing that reached past present, suggested no startling changes in their lives. He would have worried if she had, was still bound by the plans he had come with. If they were to live together some day, it would have to be arranged with the greatest care; neither of them could afford to make the wrong compromises. He thought good must eventually come from their love, willy nilly Gilley; and when it came, would the ex-husband profit less from more in the world? Although such reflections induced no great peace, at least Levin knew where he stood, and wasn't knowledge a blessing, even when it weighed on the head like lead? So he continued to avoid Gilley wherever possible, a bit of a feat because they used the same classroom three mornings a week at contiguous hours. When the bell rang the instructor bolted but had twice managed to run into arms that had held Pauline.

One day, shortly after lunch, Gilley knocked on Levin's office door, the instructor fabricating a cracked smile as the condemned man entered. Levin felt an odd abashed gratitude to him for coming in, as though he were a dear friend (apart from the fact they shared a wife) who by his appearance in his office guaranteed his once and future innocence. By definition: a friend was not an enemy. Or as though the husband, present without a club to bash his brains in, was proof of innocence or, at the very least, of gentle pardon. The instructor, flipping open a folded handkerchief, hastily blew his nose, for he felt a tense discomfort until Gilley, visibly on edge, on noticing Levin's collection of sample textbooks in the bookcase, suggested it might be a good idea to call a meeting of the textbook committee sometime soon. Levin then felt a little relieved.

"We'll still be using *The Elements* in comp next fall," Gerald said with that innocence that made him seem so simple in a complex world, "but you could be thinking ahead about a new freshman reader since we do change that every few years or so."

Levin agreed to call the meeting, still concerned about what might have upset Gerald. An uneasy conscience plastered peril everywhere.

Gerald, red behind both ears and back of his neck, lingered a minute over the view through the cracked window before turning again to Levin, who could not help sighing.

"Haven't seen much of you lately, Sy. Don't you drink tea any more?"

"Once in a while," said Levin.

"You aren't sore about anything in particular?"

"Not me."

"About the Birdless boy?"

"Not any more."

"Good. I didn't think you'd carry a grudge."

"Can't stand them."

"I'll try to remember to get that window fixed," Gilley said absently.

"No hurry."

"But that's not what I came to say."

Levin, as though in a sudden blizzard, feared the worst until Gerald explained he had been upset by something that had happened in Professor Fairchild's office that morning.

"I started out to tell George about it, but he's gone so I thought I'd tell you."

Sunshine devoured blizzard; Levin cautiously relaxed.

"It was embarrassing, Sy, though I came in at the tail end, after Orville, who had borne the brunt of it, sent Milly to get me. What happened was this. The father of one of Dr. Kuck's girl students—he's a millhand in town—was waiting in Orville's office when he returned from his cup of coffee. The man was about fit to be tied. He shouted he wouldn't have his daughter reading dirty stuff even if this is a college. He was objecting to a Hemingway short story Leopold had assigned in his survey of literature class. Orville tried to talk sensibly to the man but didn't get very far. He pounded with his fist on Orville's desk and broke the plate glass cover. He also brought on one of Orville's high blood pressure headaches. Finally Orville promised to look into the anthology we've been using in that course. He asked me to do it and report to him. Then he left for home, looking like something the cat had mauled."

"What story was he objecting to?" Levin said, fiddling with his whiskers.

"'Ten Indians.' Do you know it?"

"I don't remember anything wrong with it."

"They object—the girl and her father—to the sex parts."

Levin rubbed his nose. "I don't remember anything—er—particularly outstanding."

"It has a raw touch of subject matter. The boy in the story has been having intercourse with this Indian girl. The girl's father—the one in Leopold's class—her father—said his daughter came to him so embarrassed she couldn't look him in the eye when she asked his opinion of the story. After reading it he forbade her to open the book again. He told Orville if he didn't get rid of that book he'd go to President Labhart, and if *he* didn't give him any satisfaction he'd take it up with the governor, and I believe he would. That was when Orville called me in and it was all I could do to calm the man down. I read the story at lunch time and, frankly, I think we ought to drop the anthology."

Levin, suppressing excitement, hesitantly rose.

"You can't do that. Didn't you tell the man what literature is, why we study it?"

"There was no telling him a thing. He was absolutely enraged. I thought he was going to sock Orville, he was that sore."

"Maybe you should have asked him to leave?"

Gilley made a face. "The townspeople are just as good as we are, Sy."

"I wouldn't doubt it," said Levin, "but are ideas equal?"

"My policy with complaints is to hear them out, not antagonize anybody further."

"Fine—but—er—censorship is dangerous business."

"I'm not sure I'd call it censorship." Gerald had to clear a rough spot in his voice.

"Whatever you call it, that's what it is."

"I'd like to ask you what kind of budget you think this college would rate if this man's complaint reached the legislature? It's more than likely they'd see it pretty much as he does. We have to watch our step nowadays, or the next thing you know they'd be accusing us of something a lot worse than teaching sexy stories."

"A college is no place to show contempt for art or intellect. If you drop the book, you'll be making cowards of us all."

Gilley frowned. "Aren't those pretty strong words, Sy?"

Conscious of nervous knees, Levin sat down.

Gerald spoke mildly. "You sound as though I were out to hurt the institution, although what I was thinking of first and foremost was our welfare. Let me tell you what happened in one of our colleges of education last year. This art instructor they hired from some California college got a nude model to pose in his painting class, which nobody knew anything of till he exhibited the pictures they had painted of her. Well, the exhibition lasted about an hour, but that was long enough to raise a fuss and smell that the newspapers carried all over the state. The next thing everybody knew, it was reported in *Time*. Only last month one of my former students, who is now in oil in Venezuela, sent me a clipping of it in Spanish. But the worst of it was this. Although the art instructor was canned, in traveling around the state I still hear occasional smutty talk about what the students are learning in the Northern Cascadia College of Education. It wouldn't at all surprise me if their graduates are having trouble finding teaching jobs in the state, and maybe out. Now we can't afford to have that sort of thing happening here. The reputation of an institution of higher learning is sacred. That's why I did everything I could to pacify the man instead of antagonizing him, as you suggested. Besides, the girl was just nineteen, and you know how sensitive they are at that age."

"Maybe she doesn't belong in college," Levin said.

"Any Cascadia high school graduate is by law eligible to enter Cascadia College."

"If the course is too much for her she ought to drop it."

"That's not the point. All she does is object to a story I can't legitimately defend."

"If you'll pardon my saying so, I think you're wrong."

"Have you read it recently?"

"No, but I've never heard any criticism of it as an improper story."

"Leopold had gone through the anthology before he recommended it to Orville, who at that time was too busy to read it, but he admits he might have slipped up on that particular story. For one thing, the boy's father seems to have approved the son's illicit relationship with the Indian girl, even though he had told him—his son—that he—the father—had witnessed the girl having intercourse with somebody else in the woods. Now would you defend that as a story for classroom discussion?"

Though Levin felt hot under his beard and was contemplating a sarcastic remark, he had quick second thoughts. *In the woods?* For a wild minute he was convinced Gilley had followed Pauline into the forest that day and was leading up to a devastating accusation. The instructor felt tense and sweaty, but as he guardedly studied Gerald's face he knew his annoyance was for something less than a mortal wound. Again he felt secret relief.

"What would you have done if you were in my shoes?" Gilley asked.

Levin, limp, said he wasn't sure.

"I'll bet you'd have done pretty much what I had to. I've read *Areopagitica*, too, Sy, but we have to be practical as well as idealistic. Suppose we kept on teaching the story and one of our Indian students, or somebody with Indian blood in him, objected to it as degrading the American Indians? They're pictured as drunks, even if there was a Fourth of July celebration in the story. It wouldn't be long, I bet, before we'd have the Un-American Committee here investigating us and making all sorts of nasty charges. Then where would we be?"

Staring out of the window, Levin noticed that the cracked glass resembled forked lightning. He drew a wavering breath but said nothing.

"It's a question," Gilley was saying, "of our bread and butter."

"Not of our immortal souls?" Levin laughed unwillingly.

Responsive to smiles and laughter, Gilley beamed. "I knew you'd see it my way. We may disagree here and there, Sy, but I think we value the same things."

In shame, Levin looked away.

After rereading Hemingway's innocent little story he felt

faint, disgusted with himself for the ineffectuality of his protest.

Standing at the lone urinal in the second floor lavatory he tried to think what he could possibly do to save the anthology. The voice of Dr. CD Fabrikant penetrated the thin wall from his classroom, and Levin, as though staring the man in his hypnotic big eye, listened. He had on this spot previously heard portions of lectures on "The Noble Savage in James Fenimore Cooper," "Nightmare in Edgar Allan Poe," "Huck Finn's River Journey," "The American Past," and parts of other discourses. One heard in Fabrikant's dehydrated rumble a breath of excitement in the expression of ideas, perhaps his only emotion after too many dry years; still, he was able to communicate that ideas can excite, and Levin considered him a good teacher. He was at the moment lecturing on Emerson, and the instructor after a while listened with half an ear, still thinking of his upsetting talk with Gerald.

Particularly since the Birdless hassle, Levin had thought he would like to suggest an improvement or two in department principles and methodology, subtly or otherwise, if not to Gilley perhaps to Fairchild through some of the men on good terms with both. Since overcoming his drunkenness, perhaps as interest received on what he had accomplished, or what learned from what he had been through, he had from time to time felt the return of the courage of his convictions. As of old, Levin felt the human lot could be infinitely improved, but what was he doing about it? The true liberal, in his moral fervor, kept alive the visionary ideal, in the long run perhaps the decisive thing, and fought at every opportunity to translate it into a better life for people; but not Levin. The ideal got no farther than the inside of his head. Although thoughts of "making things better" continued to arrive by inspiration, at Cascadia College he restrained them. He did nothing to resist the status quo. He was, after all, a newcomer here; of the same race as the Cascadians, true, but a distant relative. And if not abysmally timid, not terribly courageous. Too often, in the midst of discussions with those who found his liberalism distasteful, Levin—as though his nervous system voted conservative—broke into hot sweat and his knees softened; lockjaw set in.

He blamed this unwilled reaction partly on his personal history, partly it was the effect of the times. He had dragged through the past a weight of shame and sense of exclusion from normal life, engineered by his father, Harry the goniff, misfit turned thief—he stole from everyone and his own left hand—whose fantastic thieving was the talk of every neighborhood they had to move out of. Levin had his whole life felt imperiled. In recent years he had come to pity his father but was still influenced by his distortions. Add to a backlog of personal insecurity his portion of the fear that presently overwhelmed America. The country was frightened silly of Alger Hiss and Whittaker Chambers, Communist spies and Congressional committees, flying saucers and fellow travelers, their friends and associates, and those who asked them for a match or the time of day. Intellectuals, scientists, teachers were investigated by numerous committees and if found to be good Americans were asked to sign loyalty oaths. Democracy was defended by cripples who crippled it. At Cascadia College the American fear manifested itself, paradoxically, in what was missing: ideas, serious criticism, a liberal position. Levin remarked this only to Bucket, who nodded once. No one, for instance, disagreed with Professor Fairchild's daily dispraise of "Roosevelt socialism"; if one did, disagreement was silent. Levin's protective coloration was to pretend he thought like everyone else. The specter of Duffy haunted his head, beware his *fate*. You have only one life to live, the instructor counseled himself, why lose it here, cut down in your prime at a cow college in a backwoods town for bucking the petrified order? For who, after all, was Levin but a poor man trying to make an honest living, a tough-enough proposition for him in the best of times. Therefore be smart, mind your business, don't make trouble.

Yet because others were more timid than he (who was striving, as Chekhov said, to squeeze the slave out of himself) perhaps Levin, mixing feelings of weakness with intimations of strength, was brave by default; for even as he whispered warnings to himself the word within sometimes was, "Speak up, do what you must to uphold the common good"—emphasis on the issues, Levin, conservative radical, loyal opposition, master of the gentle tactic, patient persuader, calm reasoner. He must *on principle* not be afraid. "The little you do may encourage the next man to do more. It doesn't take a violent revolution to change a policy or an institution. All it takes is a good idea and a man with guts. Someone who knows that America's historically successful ideas have been liberal and radical, continuing revolt in the cause of freedom. 'Disaster occurs if a country finally abandons its radical creative past'—R. Chase. Don't be afraid of the mean-spirited. Remember that a man who scorns an idealist scorns the secret image of himself." (Levin's notebook: "Insights.") Don't be afraid of names. Your purpose as self-improved man is to help the human lot, notwithstanding universal peril, anxiety, continued betrayal of freedom and oppression of man. He would, as a teacher, do everything he could to help bring forth those gifted few who would do more than their teachers had taught, in the name of democracy and humanity. (Whistles, cheers, prolonged applause.) The instructor took a bow at the urinal.

Such being his mood these days he felt the need to make an issue of the book censorship business, all but convinced that Fairchild and Gilley would retreat if they ran into unexpected opposition. But Levin though feeling free and energetic, remembered he was in love with Pauline Gilley and stood speechless.

If not I, who shall lead? he eventually asked. Listening to Fabrikant's voice, the instructor wondered if he ought to ally himself with the scholar, and if Fabrikant managed to come into power, become useful through him? There seemed no doubt that an election was on its way, though no one could say just when. Fabrikant, according to Bucket, was still eager to become the next head of department, and Levin thought he would offer his support, at least a vote added to Joe's and a few others' who seemed to take the scholar's candidacy seriously. Levin had considered this course of action before but hadn't made up his mind because he was still not entirely sold on Fabrikant. CD wasn't exactly the open type; he offered little of self. Sought out, he could be hospitable, laugh you his short laugh, even invite you to come again, but if you didn't he wouldn't miss you. He was not warm even to warmth. Scowers called him "soured—he has lost too many battles." Leopold Kuck had remarked that privacy represented more than a privilege to him. "He enjoys it as an exclusion of those he thinks don't appreciate him." Levin knew what they meant but tended to explain certain of Fabrikant's limitations as brought on or intensified by his hard life during the Depression, and, for that matter, his kind of luck. He was a man who had never run ahead of the life he lived. Maybe so, Levin thought, and he wears white socks, and his shoes squeak but what matters are his principles and record.

He knew George Bullock didn't think much of either. George had once said that CD had never fought a major battle. "Okay, he's got good marks for plugging for salary increases, more promotions, freer sabbatical rules, and a better retirement system than we now have on the books. He's also for academic freedom, but who isn't outside of Congress? I hear tell he did used to go see Marion Labhart every now and then and urge him to support this or that item, but once when he took a dim view of a policy of required attendance at department meetings, Marion blasted him out of his office, and, as I understand it, CD has never gone back in. If you want to know what's mostly on his mind, read some of the letters he's written in the past few years to the local rag and the college daily. On campus he's against reports in triplicate, fraternities, and student apathy in college elections. His letters to the *Commercial Budget* protest the inefficiency of county government. He's against indiscriminate garbage dumping and dogs that run loose and murder his chickens. He's also got no use for chlorine and fluorides in the drinking water. 'What this country needs is a pure glass of water.' If he's written one letter on that subject, I swear I've read five. Do you call that a record?"

On the other hand, Gilley, so far as Levin could learn, had fought not even for a pure glass of water. Beyond his good nature and lovely wife, he had little to recommend him. At the very least Fabrikant stood on principle. Gilley, totally congenial, was blown by every wind, in particular Fairchild's. Fabrikant, though maybe a little eccentric—give him credit—showed in his independence a strength of sorts. Gilley's strength was to persist in his weaknesses. Fabrikant might grow as an administrator as he loosened to life, once it had at last rewarded him; Gilley would remain as he was, gregarious, generous, ungrown. Of these two most possible choices it seemed to Levin the better was Fabrikant.

Through the wall came his dry voice reading Emerson: "'Whoever would be a man must be a non-conformist. He who would gather immortal palms must not be hindered by the name of goodness . . .' That is to say," said Fabrikant, "not 'goodness' but 'the name of goodness.' 'Nothing at last is sacred but the integrity of your mind.'"

"Amen," sighed Levin.

The bell in the hall rang. He checked his fly and turned to the sink. Standing there was Professor Fairchild, watching him with interest.

"All yours," Levin stammered.

On his way out of the building that afternoon he visited Fabrikant in his office and in a low voice told him the story of the censored anthology. The scholar, his thick brows pressed together, listened gloomily.

"It's been that way as long as I can remember."

"Couldn't you talk to Fairchild?"

"It wouldn't do any good. Once his mind's made up he's stubborn as a goat."

"Even if you talked to him?"

"Even if Teddy Roosevelt did."

"Shouldn't we at least try?"

"It wouldn't come to anything. I'd advise you not to worry about that book. One battle isn't the war."

"Unless it is," said Levin.

"It isn't. This isn't the time to fight each petty tyranny or idiocy that comes along but to wait and overthrow the tyrant."

"You think it's possible?"

"A lot depends on popular support."

Levin said quietly, "I would like to offer my—assistance in your campaign, in some way."

"Fine, but you must understand I can't show my hand just yet, though I will soon. I have one or two other irons in the fire. Fairchild has promised my long overdue promotion and I want to be sure that's gone through before I antagonize him again. I should know in a month."

"Don't wait too long," Levin advised. "Anyway," he said,

"I'm your man. I meant to tell you before this." He felt not quite at ease saying it but said it.

"Call me CD." Fabrikant cordially offered a cigar.

Levin refused a light but to be sociable sat with the cigar in his mouth. Feeling foolish, he thrust it into his breast pocket. "I'd better be getting home. I have a load of papers to go through tonight."

"Feel free to come in."

The instructor thanked him. He almost walked into Gilley in the corridor. Levin tried to hide the cigar but failed though he crushed it into his pocket. Gilley nodded coolly, his expression suggesting suspicion. Levin, wondering which perfidy he knew, absently lifted his hat.

If Gilley were alive to political affront, he showed not the slightest sign he was aware of a situation that insulted his manhood; and Levin's passion for his wife grew, fed by the secrecy it lived in. His heart was a taut string played hard by love, one further note of longing and it would snap in its face. Secrecy was an intensifying component, another that he saw her rarely now, and lived much in images of desire. At the time of his deepest need (one way of tormenting himself was to imagine spending twenty-four normal hours in her company) Gilley's winter extension course ended and he did not reschedule it for spring. The trout season wouldn't open till April, and freshman recruitment was temporarily over until a last intensive week in May. Gerald was therefore either home with Pauline or out with her. She saw Levin for occasional short visits, but was now hesitant to give as her excuse for going out, nonexistent civic meetings. A Mrs. Bowie, whose house she was supposed to be at, had called one night, and Gilley was mystified until Pauline (fresh from love with Levin) said she had remembered the meeting had been postponed and so had dropped in at Jeannette's. She had become again "deathly afraid." It's the town, Levin thought; too tight to maneuver in. Too much is visible to the naked eye. When they met it still took her a while to stop being afraid. She looked sometimes as though it were all too much for her. Levin said that one night but she denied it. "It's just that I sometimes worry what would happen to the children." He had not much thought of them, but now he thought, though not much. She made him promise faithfully never to mention her name to anyone.

Though the Gilleys entertained more frequently now, Pauline thought it best not to invite Levin. "It's hard to pretend no-love when I feel so much for you." Therefore though they made plans to be together more often, they saw each other less. As always he "had" again as have-not; hadn't bargained for this much longing, this much not having what was his to have. Missing her became work. He reveried a warm floral time when they'd be inseparably together, in various stages of dress or undress, bed or board. My God, if I could only walk in the street with her. He dreamed of her as his wife, but on her belly was tattooed "Mrs. Gilley." She wrote him suddenly, a spate of letters in official-looking brown envelopes, which he was not permitted to answer because Gilley made a point of going to the box after the mail delivery during the lunch hour; and Levin, after carrying it in his inside pocket, reading and rereading it, burned each letter in the fireplace because she had asked him to. The letters he couldn't write her were a further loss. He was in his heart a poet these days; each thought of her was crammed with beauty. It's what you don't say that counts. But she let him telephone if he made sure Gerald was either at his desk or in class. Levin went into a phone booth in the Student Union to make his call, his heart thumping like a hand on a bull fiddle. They exchanged endearment and hung up. On Saturday mornings she called from downtown, if she could. If Mrs. Beaty, deaf or not, was too close by, she could tell from his voice and said goodbye. If not, each praised the other and both praised love. Afterwards Levin walked unknown distances.

They had met rarely by chance before they became lovers, but in March, as though for compensation, he began to see her almost every time he left the house, and he left the house to see her. Walking downtown he would spot her driving the family Buick, tall in the seat, her straight hair touching her shoulders, nose pointing direction—where Levin must go. They met by accident in the post office, library, market. She greeted him vaguely and hurried the kids on. He would pass her on the street and tip his hat. Last fall, when they had met, she had stopped to exchange a word; he was the one in a hurry. Now her greetings were hesitant, formal. She hid love, a concealment painful to him. But there were times when for the slightest second her eyes were in love with him. Sometimes he saw her alone across the street; he liked her brisk high-heeled walk. Each noticeable new thing about her was an event: what she wore: a split skirt showing a bit of white slip against her leg. Long dark blue socks awoke forest memories. He knew when she had washed her hair. Once in a food market, Gilley and both kids waiting outside in the car, when Levin approached Pauline dropped a can of tuna fish she had just taken off the shelf. It rolled along the floor. He bent for it, remembering the casserole she had ladled into his lap the night they had met. As he gave her the can their fingers touched and his heart grew flowers. Leaving the store, she glanced back at him. He lived on that for a week.

One Saturday morning when she had not telephoned, Levin hurried downtown hoping for a glimpse of her. Wherever he went, she wasn't. At noon he was returning in disappointment to his car when he passed a photographer's shop displaying some enlarged shots of the Cascadia basketball team in its window. An intuition stopped Levin and he went to the window. Almost at once he discovered Pauline in a picture ("Profs and Wives Cheer Team"), nothing less than revelation. While the photographer was posing a bridal party in the studio at the rear of the store, Levin entered, plucked the picture out of the window, folded it once, and slipped it into his pocket. He drove home in a hurry and in his room cut out her intense, open, lovely face. Levin then tore up Gilley, the Bullocks, and the rest of the crowd he had extracted her from. He kept this little picture of her hidden among the best thoughts in his notebook and would often gaze at it.

Now and then he saw her at people's houses, a star, a flower amid the full-breasted faculty wives. What they lacked she had. What she hadn't nobody needed. It was high adventure for him when she walked in, even with Gilley, even if she hardly seemed to recognize her lover. Better that than not appear; that broke the night. At these social gatherings talk was small and wit rare, but hospitality and warmth were undeniable; Levin eagerly laid hold of any invitation that might produce her. He was surprisingly often invited where she was, almost as though people sensed romance and fostered it, though he hoped not. Whenever they met the action was as before: although they had talked together casually in the past, now, as on the street, she gave him little more than hello, how are you? She was no actress. He loved, therefore, behind the eyes; always conscious of what she was doing, when alone, talking to Jeannette, Alma or another woman, or to men and which men, when in the kitchen, on the sofa, or momentarily gone to the bathroom. He must know where she was. From where Levin observed, standing among others apart from her, sitting near her at a dinner table, trying not to stare, or watching from the next room, her face was gentle and luminous, sometimes a little sad; he created her quality as love created him; her loveliness enriching her clothes, the air around her. Once she drew back a lock of hair to adjust a barrette and revealed an ear pinned like a jewel to her head. Another time she was wearing her hair in a bun and he whispered, "Your neck is stupendous." Pauline, in spite of herself, laughed. Lord, thought Levin, how beautiful women are, and how hungry my heart is. But how short life, how soon gone. Where will I find the patience to go on hungering? Love entitled him to create her beauty but never to embrace it when he most desired.

They sat in circles and talked; or, depending on the specialty of the house, watched slides, listened to records, or acted charades. He was pleased when his play acting amused her. There was no mood to a party but Levin's own. Once after dancing with her at Bullocks, he followed her into a bedroom. Pauline returned his kiss then drew back. "Please don't when Gerald's around." She walked out as he wiped his lips clean. He felt there was no future in their love, until a few minutes later, when as they met in a momentarily empty hall, she took his hand and pressed it to her cheek.

Although during the evening he could blot Gilley out of his mind, what most tormented him was their leaving together, Levin locked out, a dirty trick on a lover. At midnight one of the women mentioned her baby sitter, her husband automatically stood up, and the whole company rose in a body. That ended the party, a blow to a bachelor who slept with his beard. Gilley gave his wife the eye and she went for her coat. They left for what lands, what voyages Levin couldn't make. He sometimes walked downtown and ordered a meal, to eat up his hunger.

One night at Bullocks she stayed as far from him as she could. She clung to Gilley, on her fourth drink without George's assistance. He recalled the time she had said she hoped for a revival of Gerald's love. He doesn't deserve it, Levin thought; but he felt she loved short of his love for her—his usual fate. Pauline saw him watching her and went into another room. She stayed apart from him all night. He was embittered, desolate. At midnight when the Bullocks served their elaborate buffet—coffee and cake was the customary nightcap elsewhere—Pauline filled up a plate and brought it to Gilley. He took it with a grin, placing a public arm around her. Levin, jealous of the years and substance of her Gerald had had, put down his glass and went out into the garden. It had begun to drizzle. As he was thinking he would leave from the garden and come around tomorrow for his coat, he heard footsteps on the patio. She was in his arms before he could turn.

"Forgive me, darling, Gerald's been awfully sweet, and I've felt very guilty. At times I hate myself."

"Don't feel bound to me."

"The truth is I do."

"Then don't feel guilty."

"If it were only that easy."

"Is that why you're drinking?"

"To forget you a little."

They kissed. "I'd better go," she said.

He took her hand. "You're so lovely."

"I feel lovely with you."

"My heart aches for you."

"I for you."

"When can you come?"

"I'll try tonight."

"Don't if you feel bad."

Pauline said she would try.

It was past two when she tapped on the glass. She had slept in Erik's room after Gilley had fallen asleep. When Erik called for his water she gave it to him, then changed the baby in her sleep and left. "I can only stay a few minutes."

"Did you take the car?"

"I was afraid of the noise it would make."

"I'll drive you back."

"Not all the way."

But she had not touched her earrings.

"Aren't you going to undress?"

She looked at him then looked away. "I can't tonight. Gerald wanted to and I couldn't say no."

He was struck by a grave sadness.

A few nights later she came in at nine. "I'm supposed to be at a late movie he doesn't want to see, and I've got to be home just after it lets out."

It was a time of fulfillment. Afterwards Levin said, "I hate to see you so scared. We've got to think of something we can do."

"What, for instance?"

"Whatever you say."

"What about your plans?"

"Sometime we'll have to tell him the truth."

"Not yet," she said. Then she said, "Let's wait till summer, then we'll talk about it."

"Why till summer?"

"To see how things go."

"Don't you think we have a future together?"

"Sometimes I do and sometimes not."

"When do you think so?"

"When it suddenly looks possible. I feel calm and see it that way."

"When doesn't it?"

"When I feel you ought to have someone with fewer problems to bring you."

"Forget that. How does it look now?"

"Possible."

"That creates the future," Levin said.

Before she left he asked, "Are you sure you love me?"

"So much it takes me time to think how much. Why do you ask so often?"

"All my life I've been engaged in wanting."

"Love makes a long journey in you."

"Your love inspires me. It always will."

"Don't make me cry, darling," Pauline said.

*

She left at midnight, it was raining. She had stayed longer than she had intended; but she had taken the precaution of dropping in at the Scowers' before, to say she had been there too if Gerald asked anything.

"The lies shame me most," she said.

He lit her way down the stairs with a flashlight and watched her leave the yard, regretting her going. Tonight the room was empty after she had gone. Levin switched off the light and tried to fall quickly asleep. He was beginning to doze when he heard a knock on his door and roused himself.

The landlady, her gray hair in braids, held her battery box in her hand. She was upset.

"I'm sorry, Mr. Levin, but I have my self-respect to think of. I asked Mrs. Gilley not to come here again. I'm sorry for her and I'm sorry for you, but it's not right, and I have the reputation of my house to think of."

He listened with battered heart and stone ear.

"A few nights ago when I awoke to get my medicine I thought I saw her coming out of the alley with you. Since then I waited up every night, and tonight I missed her going in but I heard her high heels come down your stairs. At first I was going to talk to you, but then I decided to talk to her. She isn't the right person for you, Mr. Levin, and you'll get into real trouble at the college if you go on with her. Whether you do or you don't, I don't want her coming here any more."

"It would have been merciful if you had spoken to me."

"I'm not sure that a married woman carrying on deserves much mercy. I feel sorry for Mr. Gilley."

"What did she say when you spoke to her?"

"All she did was run away."

Levin groaned.

After the old woman went downstairs he felt a furious desperation. What had happened now seemed inevitable. He dressed and left the house. Levin walked in the rain to Pauline's. Her house was dark except for the white tree on the front lawn. He stood across the street, wanting her through walls. Half the night he wandered in the rain.

In the morning he was impatient to call her but Gilley wasn't at his desk during his office hours and Levin did not want to risk it. Later he found a letter in his office mailbox, a blue envelope addressed in block letters. She had never written him here before.

"Just a word, dearest. I suppose you know?—I'm awfully sorry. I was afraid of something like this. I can't tell you how bad I feel, God knows how I'll get through the night. I'm writing this in Erik's room. Call me Thurs. between 9 & 10, no later. I just had to get in touch. I love you. I miss you so. Destroy this. Pauline."

He kissed the letter.

Thursday at nine he called. Hearing her voice made him feel as though they had been separated for years.

"When can I see you?" he asked.

"Lev, I'm frightened to death. Let's be careful. Not for a while is best."

"I could look for another room or maybe a small apartment with a private entrance?"

"If you move now she may tell people. If she lets you stay I doubt she'd talk. Has she said anything to you?"

"Just only what happened. She hasn't asked me to move but we ought to have plans."

"You have plans, Lev."

"I mean in case something happens."

"I don't want anything else to happen, nothing, nothing."

"Don't be scared."

"I was brought up to be."

"If I could just see you."

"Not for a while, please. Just call me Tuesdays and Thursdays, about this time. I may write but please don't you. I'm terribly sorry—I shouldn't have come so often. She wasn't nasty but I felt awful. I'm sorry I'm not somebody else, I mean someone not married. You don't deserve this."

"I deserve you."

"I'd better hang up. I don't want to cry on the phone."

Though he telephoned twice a week for a brief word of love, he saw her only in passing, in motion away from him. He thought of her with such intensity it was like waking when he stopped thinking. So Levin lived, famished, except for the sound of her voice on the phone and an occasional letter to the office, which he dutifully tore up. Beyond the word he lived on memory: her heart-easing presence in his arms. Levin inspired, by her embrace, breath, beauty, the smell and feel of her, their consummation, and aftermath, when because of love's possibilities the previous minute's love was deepened. Otherwise hunger.

"I never see you," he said on the phone. "Where are you besides in my heart?"

"Here," she said, "at this end."

"We've got to meet."

"Where would we go?"

"I'll find some place," he said.

"A beautiful place, a forest."

At night Levin haunted her street. After a walk to the river, or the hills, he came to her house when it was late and unlikely Gilley would step out with milk bottles or the cat. Levin stood across the street near the flowering plum tree thick with deep-hued pink blossoms. He watched for a touch of Pauline, a glimpse of her dress as she passed the half-shaded window, or whatever morsel luck would let fall into his empty hands.

In his thoughts he crossed the street and entered his house. She was waiting for him. They ate together, then when the kids were in bed, talked, read, listened to music. They went to bed and made love without ache or fear—was there ever such a life? Anyway, it was love and he had it, until he was standing alone across the street as she lay in bed with a stranger . . .

Levin was startled by a touch on the arm. A cop, staring at his beard, said a taxpayer had called and complained of a peeping Tom.

"Not me," said Levin.

"Could I see some I.D.?"

Levin produced his automobile license.

The cop looked at it and returned the card.

"Could you tell me why you're standing here?"

"Resting after a walk. Such a beautiful night."

"Right in the middle of the sidewalk?"

"I love this tree."

"The lady that phoned said you had been here more than an hour. She thought you might be casing one of the houses across the street."

"That long?" said Levin. He left, heavy-hearted.

One early spring night when a brimming moon in the white sky gilded houses, trees, and spring flowers, a moon-drenched Levin wandered along Pauline's street and paused at the flowering plum. He crossed the street and stood, hat in hand, a few feet from her partly-open, dark bedroom window. Come to the window for a minute, my dearest, and I'll be content for a month. But no one appeared, though he thought of it often. In the stillness he heard the rhythmic creaking of a bed, and then on the night—a bird, catch it, hold it—the soft cry of a woman at the height of her pleasure.

Gilley had, in an inspired moment, satisfied her for him.

They made plans to be together but for one reason or another abandoned them. She was afraid they might be seen wherever they met. "It would be absolutely cruel if Gerald found out through gossip." "Am I never to be with you?" "Be patient, Lev." He cursed the day Mrs. Beaty had seen her in the alley. One morning when he was famished for a look at her, she let him watch from down the block as she entered the food market. When she came out, she looked in his direction for several seconds, then walked to her car. This can't go on, he thought.

Learning on Thursday morning that she was going with Gilley to a post-season basketball game on Saturday night, Levin hurried to the Basketball Palace and with luck got a reserved seat in the balcony, facing the faculty section. On Saturday night he was there early, amid an enormous crowd of students and townspeople. Levin spent most of his time scanning faces with his birdwatching binoculars. Once the glasses met a pair directed at him, a hard eye for an eye. A chill ran through him as he recognized the flushed half-bald dome and expressionless features of Dr. Marion Labhart. Levin had sulfurous visions of himself as Arthur Dimmesdale Levin, locked in stocks on a platform in the town square, a red A stapled on his chest, as President Labhart stood over him, preaching a hellfire sermon denouncing communist adulterers, the climax of which was the public firing of Levin out of the college. Next to the president sat Dean Lawrence Seagram of the Liberal Arts Service Division. When Levin first saw him in September the dean was a clean-shaven youngish type; now he was middle-aged and wore a grizzled Van Dyke but at least looked human.

Seeking Pauline, Levin located Gilley with an empty seat at his side, a gap for Levin. Above in the next row were both Bullocks. Levin, focusing on the empty seat, wondered what had happened to Pauline; he waited impatiently for the two-hour sight of her. From a man at his side he learned that Cascadia was playing Los Angeles for the Western Conference Championship. The floor of the court blazed with reflected light, practice went on, and two bands blared. Among the rally girls on the Cascadia side Levin recognized Nadalee Hammerstad. She shook red pompoms, danced and twirled, revealing her slim thighs and frisky black-tighted behind. She performed directly below Pauline's empty seat, and Levin was uneasy at how life related events and people.

When the game started, Pauline had still not come. He considered running downstairs to telephone to make sure she was all right but he was caught in the prevailing excitement and stayed. The L.A. band had antagonized him. Costumed in hard straw hats, red bow ties, shorts and hairy legs, it created a jazz uproar, drowning out the pep songs of the white-shirted Cascadians. If the strategy was to keep their own players hopped up, they did the same for all present, setting Levin's teeth on edge, and arousing in him a strong antagonism to the State of California. From the whistle Los Angeles broke into the lead, and Levin, realizing the home town was the underdog, found himself cheering it. For a minute he studied himself with a sour eye yet went on as before.

Though he had not since college watched basketball, he was gripped by the game. More than once he jumped out of his seat to cheer a good play or boo a bad call. What a bad call was he left to the crowd. He shouted encouragement to the players, in particular Whitey Barker, a skinny, long-chested type, a solid C minus student in Levin's last term's class, but on the court, canny, alert, graceful, wise. He defended like a matador enclosing the bull, and on offense hit baskets with every kind of shot. His rebounding was outstanding. The instructor waving his hat, cheered himself hoarse for his former student—although he suspected the boy had complained to Bullock about the grade he had got, because George had been cold to Levin for a while at the end of the winter term. Peering with his binoculars at the faculty section to study George's face, he discovered Pauline sitting next to Gerald.

A little ashamed of having forgotten her, he focused his glasses and was moved by her drawn face. She had lost weight. He could hear the game going on, ten men thundering back and forth, pitching a ball at two hoops, but now he kept his glasses tightly on her, taking his excitement from her presence. Pauline seemed, after a while, to be squirming this way and that; he realized she had become aware of him and was trying either to shrink or hide from his magnified eyes. Levin lowered his glasses and absent-mindedly watched the last few minutes of play. At the end he did not know who had won.

As he was leaving the Palace he thought he had at least shared the town's big emotion. He would not, if he could, deny them basketball if once in a while the big emotion came from a good book.

Going down the stairs, he overheard one beanied freshman he knew talking to another.

"Did you see that cat with the black whiskers who had those binocks in front of us? That's my comp prof."

"So what?"

"He's supposed to be nuts about some dame. Maybe he could see her naked in those glasses."

When Levin arrived home, he snipped off his beard with scissors and shaved the rest.

When they met, on a street at the southern edge of town, Pauline looked at him in disbelief then wept, though Levin said it wasn't too bad. He had searched long in the mirror, felt ill but lived. Too much face, the eyes still sad candles, blunt bent nose, lips without speech telling all, but the jaw looked stronger, possibly illusion.

"Why did you do it?" she asked. "It had gotten to look so rich and silky. I hope it isn't bad luck."

He waited until she stopped talking about it.

They tried to think where to go to be alone. He suggested the woods or the riverbank but it rained every day and they had to settle for motels near outlying towns. This was during a time Gilley was beginning to go fishing again. Levin registered and she stayed in the car, her face averted. Alone, they kissed, he tasting on her tongue the Scotch she had had to relax her. She was still mistress of the quick lay, and once it was over he dozed by her side, dreaming of her. Longing was long, the consummation brief. Satisfaction bred quick hunger. It saddened him he couldn't be contented for more than minutes. Levin held her in his arms, longing for Pauline. The thought of all the time that would go by before he saw her again oppressed him.

She wanted, of course, not to be nervous but usually was. "I hate motels. Your room was so nice. I felt at home in it." He offered to move to Marathon, where nobody knew them. "That's not good either," she said. "You'd be miles away and I'd have less time to be with you. And after a while, no matter where you lived, somebody would find out I was coming to see you and this would start again."

One night when there was not much time and they had worked themselves into desire in Levin's car, parked by the riverbank, she joked about the back seat, then grew depressed. The result was nothing achieved, his loss, for she seemed soon to feel better, as though she had exchanged nothing for something. He had lost more than a lay. But loss enlarged love, or so they said. And part of the experience of paradise was when it was no longer paradise. This thought had come to him in a former time when he was struggling to accept fate without making less of experience.

She said, as he was driving her to the street where she usually got out and walked home, "I've been thinking if only something very good happened to Gerald it would be easier to think of leaving him. Please don't oppose him for the headship. I'm sure he'll be good at it."

"There are better men around," Levin said.

"Last night I dreamed he found us in bed and took the children away from me."

"That won't happen."

"I always knew I would fall in love again but I wasn't prepared to feel ravaged so soon."

"Love is life."

"I wish you hadn't cut your beard."

"What can I do to make things easier for you?" Levin asked her. "I could stay away for a month, even till summer if you'd feel any better. Then in the summer we could come to a decision."

"Could you stay away that long?"

"I could for you."

"I don't think I could stand it, I'd worry about you."

"What worry?"

"About how you were and if you still loved me."

"You know I would."

"No, I don't want that kind of worry. I'd rather have this."

Afterwards he wanted to send her something—flowers—but what would she say if Gilley asked her where they had come from? So he settled for a pair of gold hoop earrings which he bought for more than he could afford. But when could she wear them except with him, and where would she hide them later? He kept them for her in his notebook drawer.

The next time they talked on the phone she said, "Don't think of me as poor Pauline, think of me as rich. I may have fears but I have you. I have lovely thoughts of you. I want to give you what you haven't had. I want to make up for all you've been through in the past. I want to make you happy with me."

He said he was happy.

In bed, the next time, she failed to achieve satisfaction. Since this was twice in a row Levin was disappointed.

"Don't make anything out of it," she said, "I've been sleeping badly and I'm usually tired. The kids tire me, and it's not easy to live with one man and be always thinking of another. I worry he senses something is wrong. And I worry about the strain on you."

"Don't worry about me."

"Now you have her, now you don't is no life for a man. And I worry about a definite break with Gerald. I guess I was not passionately attached to him but I've never been able to unlove anyone I ever loved."

"We'll settle it in the summer."

"I already have settled it but my nervous system hasn't. That's what flopped just now—not me. But I'll be myself next time."

Next time was in a little hotel about thirty miles out of Easchester—she was insisting they not go back to the motels they had been to. After a while, Pauline, her brow wet, said, "Don't wait for me, I don't think I can."

"Are you sure?"

"Come without me."

Finally he did.

"I'm really beat," she said.

"Is that it?"

She said, "Gerald is ardent again. I think he senses something. I told you he might. Sometimes I get so tired of sex."

Now we have truly come to adultery, Levin thought.

"I would have skipped it if you had asked me," he said.

She caressed his beardless face. Her eyes were tired, her nose thin. "Please don't worry. I go through these periods. I was in a bad period with Gerald just before the first time with you. But he's used to me and doesn't seem to mind."

"I mind."

"Don't idealize sex, Lev."

"Not sex, you."

After the fourth fruitless, songless time, one end-of-April night, Levin lay awake while she slept, grinding her teeth. She had looked imperiled. He felt he had to do something to help her or this might get beyond her. Since it was almost certainly too late to start writing around for a new job, if he could get an assistantship somewhere, and Pauline a part-time job, things might work out. But making new plans worried Levin; it was as if those he had come West with had been wrong to begin with. If that was the case would he ever in his life make the right plans? Yet he felt for her a deep tenderness and dreamed of a decent life for them. When he awoke it was almost six-thirty and Pauline was frantic.

They were racing through a thick fir forest. Levin had said he would take her to the Easchester bus station where she could get a cab, and she had in silence agreed, her face calmly locked in fright.

"What will you do if he's awake?" Levin asked.

"I'll lie."

"Could I go in with you?"

"No."

Above the trees the light brightened, yellow, then foggy gold. "'Tis the rising, not the setting sun,'" he said.

"Who said so?"

"B. Franklin."

"He was wrong."

The fake forest, Levin thought.

As he was speeding out of it, a siren sounded behind them. A state trooper in an unmarked car waved the Hudson to the side.

Levin cursed. Pauline shut her eyes. Any minute he expected to see gray in her hair.

The trooper talked for ten minutes before handing Levin the ticket. Pauline stared ahead, her stomach rumbling. She bent to hide it but couldn't.

Finally they were off again at fifty.

"I'd better go in with you."

"No, please no."

They parted at the Easchester bus station. She hurried into a cab, forgetting goodbye, Until We Meet Again, or even to wave. He watched the taxi turn the corner on a dull gray morning.

Afterwards Levin sweated it out in his room. He had visions of disaster for all, particularly himself. Yes, she loved him, but she also loved Gilley and she loved the kids. If she had loved Levin as he loved her, she would already have made up her mind to leave Gilley. To go on as they had been, would prolong the torture and destroy what was left of the joy of love. He stayed in the house Saturday and Sunday, waiting for a word from her but none came. Only Pauline lived in his thoughts. He thought of her as she had been when they were first in love and how worn out and unhappy she had looked lately. Levin struck himself for the harm he had done her. He promised that if, by some stroke of luck she had got in without Gilley knowing it, he would not see her till summer. The rest would do her good.

When he went to work on Monday morning, after his first desperate glance at Gerald, Levin knew Pauline had got in safely. Out of love he gave her up.

MAY SUNBURSTS flooded the windows, making the mourner invisible; he sat, when he came in, unable to move, even a breath unsettling pain. He secretly waited for a word, a sign she loved him, would never let him give her up. She had once seized his flesh: "I'll never let you go." He waited for her to redeem the pledge. Through long days he waited, loving her, giving her up, trying to forget the last hours with her, memory repeating memory. But when she appeared—through Mrs. Beaty on guard, thick walls, a ring of flame, the salt sea—he sneaked her home past her husband at indecent hours; then in his mind (to save her from this) parted from her forever, the worst place to part from anyone. The landlady left a plate of oatmeal cookies at his door.

He secretly waited. She did not write or phone; nor appeared in the universe. After relief at her escape he ate himself slowly; his heart like a vessel of pain against bare bones; the mourner attended his perpetual funeral. He had expected in the ruined aftermath a diminished misery, reason the shield, since he had himself brought the affair to its broken end; but a surgeon operating on himself does not excise the pain, and now he knew the majesty of his. Having betrayed his nature, his deepest need, he had surrendered something of life to death. In pain he mortified what he was attempting to kill, his short-lived love, self-created freedom. Ah, the soaring anticipation of Pauline Gilley; possessing her in feeling's fullness; dreaming of what he had had. Dreams dead by suicide.

Silence burdened ache. Why had she not told him she had got in safely, knowing how intensely worried he would be? He could only explain it that she had given him up at the same moment he had abandoned her, breaking off before impossible got worse, ultimately relieved to be done with an unhappy affair. It tormented him that he had left her, in the end, unsatisfied. Why does the last event condition the quality of the past? In his most desperate moments he felt a hatred of her that relieved the fundamental pain, but with such frightening other effects he preferred the pain. In the midst of which, in some shaded place within, dwelt Levin's Pauline, tender, lovely girl of the graceful shoulders and shapely can, their own fine art; the woman he had least expected to be in love with, source of his discoveries of her beauty (as when her hand or the wind touched her hair). Thoughts such as these made his loss unbearable.

After he had endured all he thought he could, there was more; he had in a former existence lowered the threshold of heartbreak. Ah, sweet mastery of life—if only Levin could. The more he suffered, no matter how frequent or pure his resolutions to change himself, the more he suffered. For whatever unknown or unpredictable cause. He did not kid himself, he was his own bad cause, causing what caused him pain ("Which way I flie is Hell; myself am Hell."); somewhere along the line he had erred, his life gone wrong, wronger. And when Levin erred the result was serious, no matter how often he promised to take life more lightly, less frantic seeking of a hold to throw it with. He laughed seriously and suffered merrily, miserere.

The sorrows of Levin: his mouth thickened with thirst. He hid a brown bottle under the bed, then slept with it. Ache turned at teasing times to prurience (original original sin) within which he imaged a bearded billy goat chewing Someone's pubic hair, the lady responding to the tickle and other jests in 167 satisfying ways. He plowed through the black pants she wore. Pricked with pins her bubless nipples. Clobbered her with sex, though she sobbed no, then begged for more, satisfaction levitating her a foot in the air. Amid such pleasures Mrs. Beaty's white cat fell in love with him, laying a broken-feathered bird at his door, fat headless robin. He asked the landlady to keep the cat out of the house but pussy in love was faithful, finding more ways in than he could block off, depositing another bloody-breasted bird. "Eat my heart," he cried and kicked the beast down the stairs. Ascending on three legs she delivered a mangled rat, then went into heat, her raucous cries sounding throughout the house. He considered taking off with packed bags, but to return where he had failed was failure. Depression dug a fast hole and in it he sat drowning. Alas, Levin, ever-drowning sailor. What had he done to his poor self? . . .

But time, though he hid from it, rained him in the face and change changed against the will. He rose once more to the surface, not the same man but who was? Apathy followed, worse yet. "A grief without a pang, void, dark, and drear,/ A stifled, drowsy, unimpassioned grief,/ Which finds no natural outlet, no relief,/ In word, or sigh, or tear." This went on too long, till he was ready to secede from the world; until a fissure appeared in the windowless wall and he wriggled through. No-feeling, purged, left mildewed melancholy. Each day introduced its own variation and quantity of ache. He felt sadness for every living thing. Even a tree, when Levin looked, looked sad. He was his own pathetic fallacy.

The bright flags of loneliness unfurled and flapped in the breeze. He knew it in every size and shape, hard, soft, black, blue, concrete city-type recalled; and woodsy-leafy country-kind. He had lived in dark small rooms in anonymous tenements on gray streets amid stone buildings crowding the sky; loneliness tracked him in the guise of strangers. In the country it dwelt in the near distance under vast umbrella skies. In the city, compressed; spacious in the country. Space plus whatever you feel equals more whatever you feel, marvelous for happiness, God save you otherwise. God save Levin. He longed for her to share the burden of his incompletion, the cheat of being human; longed for a past that was now memory pickled in regret. The unhappy clever purpose of the disease was to compel him to expel it. It would never succeed. Despite all his exertions to forget her, Levin remembered and desired; the town was small and she lived nearby. He had one day seen Erik scraping the sidewalk in her long shoes.

To get away from what he could not escape he drove his car on dusty country roads leading nowhere. Sometimes he stopped and shouted in the stillness. Lonely crows flew up from the fields. White farmhouses and rain-stained barns were lonely, cows and horses, every living thing. Trees were lonely, fences, so was the horizon. That somehow was the worst. The dust blew up behind him as he sped home. He knew that the only way to fight his sadness of spirit was to be among people but he did nothing to be. Throughout these weeks he managed to teach students, then escaped his office. Though an occasional invitation to someone's house came his way he did not accept, not to see her. He was certain she didn't want to see him; this made him deathly lonely. He often doubted she had truly loved him. He was at times desperately moved to write her but wrote nothing. If she wanted it ended, he would keep it ended. He would help her resist him if she were resisting.

Levin resisted with the same arguments: She was, for the thousandth time, a married woman with a family. She had caused herself to love out of discontent, although her discontents were tolerable. Gilley was good to her; she had a better than average home, kids she loved. Maybe she was bored but she wasn't desperate; she probably could go on living with him forever. If diversion was what she had wanted, a little love on the side, she wasn't made for it, the pleasure butchered by anxiety and shame. She wasn't the type who could give "all" for love. And he doubted he could inspire such love, the limits of her passion conditioned by the man he was. He might awaken love but not madness, although maybe it was mad to chance what she had chanced; maybe she understood he too was unwilling to give "all." He had lived through too much, become wary to the frazzled ends of his nerves of too many "lessons." He was, in love, not Seymour Gordon Lord Byron, but a modest man and would not complain if all he got was no more than he gave. He left to Casanova or Clark Gable the gourmandise, the blasts and quakes of passion. He wanted love like a fountain in the wind. He wanted in a woman loveliness and feeling, of course, but character, constancy. He wanted someone free to love so he could freely love.

Whenever Levin saw Gilley he thought of his treachery to him; it was wrong to have continued to see his wife under the circumstances. Sneaking love in his room, in motels; the hiding and guilt had hurt them both. He would have done better to have kept his door shut against her; only if she were willing to give up Gilley was the way. If she were, there might have been no problem. If she were that willing he might have run from her, over the hills and far away; at least tipped his hat and backed off. In the street they would nod to each other, a lanky lady and a bearded gent, and hurry by. He would not then have been incapacitated before her husband when there was an issue to fight for, a principle to defend. Somebody should have fought for the retention of the short story anthology; he was the coward in that affair. Now, if he expected to be of any help to Fabrikant he had to quit wanting to duck whenever he saw a red head in Humanities Hall. That was no career for a man with a future, future as man.

Morality—awareness of it—perhaps in his reaction to his father's life, or in sympathy with his mother's, or in another way, had lit an early candle in Levin's. He saw in good beauty. Good was as if man's spirit had produced art in life. Levin felt that the main source of conscious morality was love of life, anybody's life. Morality was a way of giving value to other lives through assuring human rights. As you valued men's lives yours received value. You earned what you sold, got what you gave. That, if not entirely true, ought to be. Our days are short, thought Levin, our bodies frail. The universe is unknown, remorseless. We have no certain understanding of Nature's intentions, nor God's if he intends. We know the meagerness, ignorance, cruelty of too many men and too many societies. We must protect the human, the good, the innocent. Those who had discovered their own moral courage, or created it, must join others who are moral; these must lead, without fanaticism. Any act of good is a diminution of evil in the world. To make himself effectual Levin must give up Pauline, or what was principle for? The strongest morality resists temptation; since he had not resisted he must renounce the continuance of the immoral. Renunciation was what he was now engaged in; it was a beginning that created a beginning. What an extraordinary thing, he thought: you could be not moral, then you could be. To be good, then evil, then good was no moral way of life, but to be good after being evil was a possibility of life. You stopped doing what was wrong and you did right. It was not easy but it was a free choice you might make, and the beauty of it was in the making, in the rightness of it. You knew it was right from the form it gave your life, the moving esthetic the act created in you.

I must give her up, he thought, if I haven't.

He had for half his life in wintertime yearned for spring. In the East, as early as February he woke sniffing the breeze for the first vernal fragrance still locked in a future month. Yet when spring burst into life he continued to hunger for it as though it weren't there, secretly knowing that what he desired did not grow on trees. In the Northwest this year spring had leapfrogged over winter's back before habit could rouse the spirit's hunger. And when he became aware of spring he was already involved with Pauline and spring made little difference. But now the green and floral season overwhelmed him, for with all its beauty it could not return to him an iota of the happiness he had lost. Sitting in his room on the very day they had parted (an act in aftermath) he watched the cherry tree blossom outside his window. In the morning sunlight a single moldy branch broke into flower and by evening the whole tree wore white. Up the block the hawthornes surprised: a flood of rose-hued blossoms capped the tiny dark-green leaves. And the chestnuts raised their white flambeaux. Everything was in flower around the corpse; and the corpse flowered in desire. Unable to resist the beauty of this spring night, love still tormenting despite all his exertions, he left his dreary room and walked in the direction of Pauline's house.

He had seen her downtown that day, a slim, pale woman with a distracted lovely face. Torn by the sight of her he had turned away, dizzied, drunk from seeing, desiring her from every pore. He ached beyond belief, famished, struggling to steel himself before he was overwhelmed. Levin cursed his particular body, inept apparatus; nothing brought relief. He prayed the night would, but it appeared in profuse beauty, a perfume of new flowers stirring pain. As he walked, a tree came alive with chirping birds. Bullfrogs were noisy in the distance; beyond that, the lowing of a cow. Realizing how close he had come to where he wasn't going, Levin halted. Was a man no more than a pawn to the season's mood? Why had he suffered if not to be his own master?

A woman in a light dress was coming toward him in the dark. Good God, it's Pauline. What will I do?

He waited for her to approach, or on recognition run the other way, but it wasn't Pauline. . . . It was Avis Fliss, her baggy chest stiff in a pink cotton dress stained by sweat around the armpits. She looked as lonely as he felt. Have I invented her? Levin thought.

"Why, good evening, Seymour. I almost didn't recognize you without your beard. Congratulations, if I may. If you hadn't been staring at me I would have walked right past you. Isn't tonight out of this world?"

They had returned to first names after being thrown together at people's houses during the winter, the old maid and lonely bachelor. She had lately shown signs she had forgotten her irritation with him.

"Are you enjoying an evening stroll?" Avis asked.

He nodded, watching her like a hawk, suspecting she was waiting to see which way he would go. He had noticed, when she was present at parties, Avis' livening of attention when he had stood near Pauline or their hands had brushed in passing.

"Were you by any chance going to the Gilleys'?"

He said nothing.

"I wasn't meaning to pry," she said. "I thought I might save you a trip if you were, because I'm just coming from there and they're about to go out. I walked this way after supper to give Gerald a little thing I had just finished writing on teaching remedial grammar. I have copies if you'd care to read it. Gerald was delighted to have it. He offered to drive me home but I preferred to walk. When I was a little girl in Louisville, on nights like this everybody walked. Daddy often used to take me and sister Cora out and I can recall many young couples courting, holding hands in Charity Park. I realize the automobile is necessary to our economy, Seymour, but don't you think it has caused something gracious to leave our lives?"

He grunted. Avis' eyelids fluttered. "Are you bound somewhere in particular?"

He had no particular place in mind.

"Would you care to continue your walk with me? I—I've wanted to say something to you, Seymour."

Levin walked with her. They went toward the campus. It seemed to him that all he could smell of the night now was her overpowering orange blossom. He would walk another block or two, then ditch her and go back.

They passed Humanities Hall, all dark for once. Under the maple tree Avis turned to him breathlessly. "Mr. Levin—I mean Seymour—I shan't allude to this again, but I do want you to know I am most sincerely grateful to you for—for your self-control that time. It isn't often a gentleman will assist a lady to preserve her virtue."

Levin laughed badly.

She said quickly, "But that isn't what I meant to say. I've

wanted to discuss with you a matter that concerns the welfare of our department, something I'm sure you'll be discreet about for obvious reasons. Let's just walk out of the campus, shall we? Voices carry here."

He went with her across the quadrangle and lower campus in the direction of the river. They came to a wooded area by the water, to a stone bench dimly lit. Two students who had been necking got up and walked off. She had brought him to Lovers' Lane.

Lighting a cigarette, Avis crossed her legs. She puffed without inhaling, Levin motionless. She glanced at him nervously, then said in a low voice, "Just how much have you been told of the past?"

"Whose?" he asked drearily.

Her eyelids were in action. "Specifically, Leo Duffy's and, frankly, Pauline Gilley's."

"Specifically," he said slowly, "I know she liked and sympathized with him."

"Yes, that's true, but did you know?"—her strained breathiness broke—"that they were lovers"—she wet her lips—"actually?" Avis stared in another direction.

Levin sat there with a splitting headache. Though his impulse was to choke Avis he lived through torment to a clear understanding of Pauline's anxiety and fear: she had been through it before. Amid the rocks in his heart he silently groaned. What hurt most was the realization there had been in his relationship with her more than he knew, something that explained the end it had come to. What he had assumed to be the unique truth of their love was less than that. That she had had a lover before him he might forgive, but to keep from him that he had followed, under Gilley's nose, smack in another man's footsteps was deceit. He felt a rage of helplessness, again the victim of a lying life.

It changes nothing, he desperately thought. At the same time he knew it changed everything, even the past.

Avis, squirming on the bench, apologized for her news. "Please understand I tell you this only because it has some reference, more than indirect, to the future of our department." She spoke with eyes shut.

It took Levin a minute to speak through his misery, a

complex self-renewing institution. But he hid what he felt so that he could learn what was left to know, afraid to be ignorant of anything that concerned him.

"Gerald knew?"

"Yes." She stepped on her cigarette and sat very still. "It all came out when he—when he developed the picture."

"What picture?"

She was restless again. The sweat marks around her armpits spread.

"Hadn't—hadn't you heard of it? I was sure Dr. Fabrikant had told you."

"No."

She hesitated, then quickly said, "Gerald took a photograph of them on the beach one day at the coast. They were both naked. I assumed you knew, or I—I wouldn't—"

He lived through a nauseating sense of having been here before.

"He—he had followed them. It was when Pauline and he were seriously considering divorce and he was collecting evidence—as he had every right to do. He took it with a certain kind of lens, from a distance. They had been in the water and as they were coming out, Gerald snapped."

"Was there a mess?"

"Not quite. Although he had consulted an attorney, Gerald did not file for the divorce. And once Leo was discharged from his position by President Labhart, that's what people talked about. Apparently they hadn't been seen together. Shortly after Leo had left, Gerald and Pauline dropped their plans for divorce, mainly because their adoption of Erik had come through. I assume Pauline had discovered that her heart was in domestic life after all, and that helped bring them together."

"Was the picture the only proof they were lovers?"

"I believe," Avis answered, "that Pauline had admitted that fact to Gerald."

"He told you that?"

"I'm not really at liberty to say."

"Did you see the picture?"

"It was described to me. You ought to know that Pauline has not seen it. She doesn't know of its existence, Seymour. Gerald was going to show it to her but when she confessed she loved Leo, he did not have to. It would only hurt her to know about it—that's why it's so important to be discreet."

"Who knows about it?"

"Not many. Counting—ah—you, about a dozen people. The wonderful thing was that everyone closed ranks behind Gerald to protect him and Pauline from further embarrassment, although perhaps that was more than she deserved."

Levin asked her if Bucket knew.

"He may possibly have heard from Dr. Fabrikant."

"Who told him?"

"Gerald, I believe."

He now understood.

"We've all been careful not to talk much about it," Avis said uneasily. "But I was certain you had heard, or I would never to my dying day, I assure you, have told you. I felt you ought to know the truth, since there are one or two people who have criticized Gerald for having taken the picture. I give you my word of honor that was my one and only reason for revealing this to you, Seymour, otherwise I would not have under any circumstances. I was told that Dr. Fabrikant—to be perfectly honest he told me himself—he said that he considered you to be one of those supporting his candidacy for department head, and I assumed, though perhaps I should not have, that he had won your confidence by telling you about the picture without describing the extenuating circumstances." She was unable to sit comfortably on the bench.

"I honestly did not wish to impugn Pauline's reputation," Avis went on. "I was thinking of no more than the welfare of our department, as I've said. If you knew Dr. Fabrikant as well as some of us, you'd understand he is not the most suitable person for head of department. He may indeed be a scholar, and I personally have nothing against him, but he's barely civil to other people. I'm not asking you to support Gerald—I wouldn't presume to—however, I thought it wasn't fair for you to go around with a wrong impression."

After a long, hopeless silence, Levin got up. Spring was gone, an interior army had murdered it with hammers.

"If I had to know," he muttered, "I had to know. I don't hold it against you."

"Against me?" she said hotly.

He wandered off.

"Mr. Levin—" she called after him.

He went without hearing, without judgment of her, or memory. He had saved her virtue and she had preserved him as a moral man.

When he attempted, after a period of renewed misery, to grow a beard, the stubble, to his horror, was sprinkled with gray, so he abandoned it.

Q. "What have I done to deserve my fate?"

A. "I am worthy of no other."

He saw in the strewn garbage of his life, errors, mishaps, ignorance, experience from which he had learned nothing.

He was as a man inadequate, in the sense of being powerless to achieve the most meager happiness. He had been left far behind by Purpose—those chances for self-fulfillment that spring up around the man who is not fortune's fool.

Whatever strayed into Levin's orbit wrecked it. He could not make happen to him what happened to all but the poor bastards of the world, a use of the better choices of life; with, sooner or later, some sense of accomplishment—however slow if visible.

And love, for Jesus' sake, so that he have not lived in vain.

He was not ambitious for power, wanted no extraordinary rewards; he wanted most to break through the hardened cement of self-frustration, to live in the world and enjoy it.

He felt, as always, the need of change—in and of himself, but no longer knew where to begin. His life was a sad hash of beginnings.

He could not understand why he chose so badly, why he invariably wound up with just that woman who was most clearly wrong for him, verboten, bound to bring him to broken bloody knees.

But as the days passed, there were whole hours in which he no longer thought of her, and though she still appeared, deviously, trickily in the mind, her image was thin, abstract. Yet it wearied Levin that he should be aware of her so continuously: open an eye in sleep and she was pallidly present. Close it and she trailed across a dream. He had locked himself behind a double-barred door—her rejection of him and the revelation of her true tie to Duffy, consequently, of his own; namely that he was a dead fish to begin with. Her easy way out: she had loved him to repeat Duffy, or possibly forget him, both reasons amounting to the same thing. She appeared and disappeared, hiding behind her transparent skirts Gilley parboiled before the second cuckoldry. God knows what else.

If in his thoughts she failed him, in fairness, in the same country he failed her. Levin, pipsqueak coward, who had not loved no matter what. "Love alters not with his brief hours and weeks,/ But bears it out even to the edge of doom." He could say, as he often did, I quit to help her, for her, not me; but Duffy, exposed by Avis, made fast the trembling quittance. He had therefore left her for what she had withheld, the Irishman and his aftermath in her life. Aftermaths breed aftermaths. "Strangers are welcome," the magicians of love who pass in the night. Bearded and beardless whoremasters. He felt for a time a corrosive self-soiling jealousy of a ghost; Levin, contaminated substance of Duffy's shade. He endured to be unhaunted, the last of love in its rotting coffin.

After an oppressive time, the hours few but endless, his "spirit" a foggy mishap, as if he were in perpetual sleepwalk, Levin found himself looking for something to do in his "spare time." "But tasks in hours of insights will'd,/Can be through hours of gloom fulfill'd." Not that he could will or fulfill anything, but he hoped to transform the mind from the vinegar-soaked sponge it had become, or broken bottle full of broken glass, once more into a functioning instrument. He secretly meant to prove there was reason to be alive although he scarcely believed it. In working, one at least worked to an end. With luck some small purpose might come to something larger, possibly a purpose to live for. At this he snickered for he was repeating himself. Still, one sought a task to escape the impoverishing richness of time. Every minute made Levin poorer. If I were a poet, he thought, my miseries would have value; but what does a teacher teach if he can't teach what he is? He considered a philosophy project, to work towards a unity of Plato and Aristotle? Or maybe learn Russian and read Pushkin in the original? Or take up the guitar or recorder, Bach on both? Maybe paint weekends, not that he could weekdays. He had no heart for any of these things, then wondered if he could begin to collect material for a critical study of Melville's whale: "White Whale as

Burden of Dark World." "Moby-Dick as Closet Drama." He liked the idea of an intellectual task, the whale on his head, relief through balancing the weight on the heart, a disguise and punishment in perpetuity, a means of keeping his poor ego from shattering into bits. Under a burden some found freedom. It had happened to slaves.

Levin began to read and make notes but gave up the whale when he discovered it in too many critical hats. He wrote down possible other titles for a short critical essay: "The Forest as Battleground of the Spirit in Some American Novels." "The Stranger as Fallen Angel in Western Fiction." "The American Ideal as Self-created Tradition." Levin wrote, "The idea of America will always create freedom"; but it was impossible to prove faith. After considering "The Guilt-ridden Revolutionary of the Visionary American Ideal," he settled on "American Self-criticism in Several Novels." Limiting himself, to start, to six books Levin read and reread them, making profuse notes. Almost with the first words he wrote, he was disappointed in how ill-prepared he was to evaluate ideas and express them. But he forced himself to keep on—if nothing else this might lead to a subject for a future dissertation. He wrote for a week, into the early morning hours, pushing himself, exasperated, suffering for having heaped punishment on punishment, yet ultimately producing a ten-page paper which Milly typed for him. After he had proofread it, the essay looked useless. He reread it with growing hatred, wanting to burn it, but decided to let someone else read it first. He thought of Dr. Fabrikant, thought no, then yes, and finally delivered it to the scholar, apologizing for taking his time. An hour or so later he found the paper in his mailbox with attached note: "I find this an illuminating insight and will be happy to advise where it might be sent. Am glad you have decided to publish. We sorely need that kind of thing in this institution. In the future I would hope to encourage it. CD." Levin thought of sending the paper out at once, but doubt lingered so he decided to try one more opinion. He considered Bullock but abandoned the thought and left the little essay on Bucket's desk. "Would appreciate any comment. No hurry. S.L."

After several days no word from Bucket, not even an acknowledgment he had got, or was reading, the paper; but Levin waited patiently. Two more days made him restless. He had come up with a new idea but did not want to work on it until he knew how good the first paper was. If Bucket agreed with CD he could see the article already in print. S. Levin, essayist and critic, the start of a new career. Patience, he counseled, knowing how busy poor Bucket was. His dissertation had been newly rejected and he had begun a "final" revision: Uncle Toby once more at his sorry fortifications. In a rare free moment he was still hammering boards on the addition to his still uncompleted house. Algene was pregnant. The little Buckets, Levin knew, had been trading illnesses since November. Joe himself had come down with chicken pox, "an humiliating experience." To pay doctors, medicine, and other bills he had added to his odd-job schedule several hours in a gas station where he had worked as a boy. (He had once lubed Levin's car.) And he still had themes, preparations, quizzes to take care of. Levin was now sorry he hadn't thought twice before wishing the article on him, even if only ten pages.

He considered asking him to return it, but then worried he might be offended—Bucket could be touchy—if Levin got in the way of his making up his mind what he wanted to do, or seemed to be pressing. The instructor had learned in the West that his Eastern timing was often on the tightly wound side for many of the people he dealt with. He was concerned with time even when he had on hand more than he knew what to do with; you couldn't knit with it or purl. None of his colleagues seemed to grow jittery about where time went. Perhaps it was the climate, no clearly marked seasons to make a man conscious of, and impatient with, passing time: Time's winged chariot walked. Such being so, best wait, Levin advised himself, till the assistant professor either returned the paper unread or indicated he had read it and was willing to express an opinion.

Although Levin saw him at least once daily, Bucket never alluded to the essay. By now the instructor felt he must do something about it, or he might not see it for years. There were that type; you didn't know who until you dealt with them. Since he had made the mistake of leaving Bucket the original copy, and not wanting to pay Milly for another from the carbon if it wasn't worth doing, Levin reluctantly decided to drop him a note. He would say he needed the original to send out but would gladly leave the carbon if Bucket had time to read it; if he hadn't Levin understood. But when he entered his office after his last morning class, the manuscript, somewhat worn—the first page looked as though it had kissed a lollipop—lay on his desk. He thumbed through hastily for comments and found none. Levin searched the floor, under the desk, even the wastebasket, for a note that might have fallen off but there was no such thing.

Seeing Bucket in the hall later he thought he would speak to him, but then it seemed to Levin that the assistant professor was pretending not to see him; Levin said nothing. He returned to his office, his heartbeat in his ears, but blaming his sensitivity lately, heightened by every sort of dissatisfaction. Have I done something to him that I shouldn't have? he wondered. Had he perhaps heard about Levin and Pauline and thus shown his disapproval? Ironic if so at this stage, yet not likely. If he knew something he minded his business, his virtue his fault. He wasn't a puritan, nor addicted to gossip. It must be something else—but what? He recalled a pleasant cup of coffee with Bucket in the Student Union the day after he had left the paper, neither mentioning it; still it was pleasant. Was he, despite that, secretly annoyed that his customary good nature had earned him an unwanted task when he had so much to do? If so, why not say it instead of putting on the mask of Fu-Manchu? Whatever the answer, from the look of the ms., he was certain Bucket had read it; yet he seemed not to have the slightest intention of saying what he thought of it. Levin, now greatly irritated, didn't know what to do next.

Maybe there had been a misunderstanding? No, his request for the man's opinion was clear; the least he could do was acknowledge he had read it. Or maybe Bucket was worried about something—he had his worries, all right. Could he, for instance, be ill? A secret cancer? Levin saw him later, in the hall, looking healthy as an ox. I don't understand, he thought. He's a nice guy, affable, honest; but isn't it just good manners to say something: "Sorry, I couldn't get to it," or "Sorry I did." Was he too timid to say the paper was bad, in fact, stank? If Bucket had a weakness it was his small-town timidity—the departmental disease, or how could they have lived so long with *The Elements* and the damned d.o., to say nothing of how Fairchild and Gilley, seemingly equalitarian, autocratically ran things? Climate or moral climate? "We all have our weaknesses," Levin sighed. But Bucket had never before held back criticism of his ideas, so why begin now? Could he have gone through some private crisis while reading the paper? Jealous because the instructor wrote not badly whereas he (evidence: the oft-returned dissertation) wrote like a clod? Professional jealousy?

He considered every possibility but none satisfied him. He often peeked into Bucket's office to see if he had a minute to talk, but his day was always booked solid with students. Standing unseen near his door, Levin had once heard him go on—he estimated twenty minutes—to a not fully awake freshman, concerning the uses of the semi-colon. For semi-colons he had all day, for a colleague's paper not a minute. Infuriating. Levin considered waiting downstairs on the porch until Bucket left for home, and walking with him a bit to sneak in a question or two. But pretense of this sort bothered him (his little moralities). So time went by without satisfaction. One day Levin had to speak to Bucket about a book committee meeting and the assistant professor seemed his cordial self, tempting the instructor to pop a question then and there. But before it popped, out of pride he swallowed, then chewed his bitter cud all day. From Bucket's behavior who would think he had ever seen the manuscript? Or had he in a former existence? or was he mesmerized when reading, or had been hit on the head by a brick and no longer remembered he had seen the paper? How else explain the mystery? Apparently what was important to Levin did not exist for Joe B. How far apart men are, strangers to each other's needs. In anger he thought, Be damned to the bastard, I swear I'll never say a word to him about that cursed article. Either he brings it up or he can go to hell. What could he have expected from a man who had not once in all these months invited him to his house for a little talk and hospitality? He had made not the slightest effort to be more than an acquaintance despite Levin's desire to have him as friend; the instructor had clearly shown this by his good will for Bucket that still—mind you—lived in his breast. He doesn't need me, so his theory is I don't need him. Knock on his door and you knock on wood, nobody answers. I hate his small guts. Levin worked himself into fits of rage. Whatever he looked at looked black. Once he had to run home and take a cold shower to calm down.

When they passed each other in the hall he wouldn't look at the man, his skinny frame, oversize goggles, meaty ears. He envisioned punishment fallen on him, some sad misfortune: One day J.B. collapsed at his desk and died at home. Levin came uninvited to the wake. The former assistant professor was laid out in the still unfinished parlor, in wool sweater and brown socks, shoeless. He lay on a soft fir slab he had cut himself, his trusty crosscut saw at his side. During the services, Levin, assisting wherever possible, held a dripping candle over his waxen face. As the five little Buckets prayed for their father's return he prayed with them, but Bucket had entered his last long silence.

The next morning Levin awoke with wet cheeks. He woke inspired: what a unique man Joe Bucket was! This was *he*, his personal quality, the only one in the world who could be Joseph P. Bucket. He had acted on his rights as a free man, the right not to say, for whatever reason, under no matter what provocation, what he didn't feel like saying. He did not care to say anything about Levin's paper, probably to save someone pain—himself, both, either. He wasn't talking, his natural and constitutional right. And it was his free choice as a man *not* to choose Levin, not to have him in, not to make a bosom buddy of him, not to utter a single syllable in his presence if he so pleased. And he pleased. Marvelous! "Man, the wonder of the world!" The instructor threw aside his covers and hopped out of bed. He found his article in a drawer, and gritting his teeth, read through it. He was slowly nauseated. He fought contempt for Fabrikant, but after tearing up and burning both copies of the paper, did not blame CD. Probably he was, in his way, trying to be kind. The article was trivial, not an original thought in ten typewritten pages. He had inflicted gratuitous punishment on a friend by asking him to read it, then worsened the situation because the poor guy wouldn't confess the agony he had undergone. The unpardonable affront was Levin's. He hated his sick pride.

I must be humble, he told himself. Humility is its own virtue, sweet, if true. I must be generous, kind, good. He wanted to embrace Bucket and ask his forgiveness. He vowed he would forever be his friend, no matter whose friend *he* was. This was Levin's own choice. He drove to town to buy Bucket a present. Sweet are the uses of humility. He left a potted white carnation on his desk. Without a word, nameless, for the wrong he had done him.

Levin was moved to discover he cherished what he had best cherished. For the first time since he had parted from Pauline the world seemed home, welcome. He had, as men must, given birth to it; he was himself reborn. Proof: leafy trees stippling green of earth on sky. Flowers casting bright color everywhere. Vast fires in cosmic space—all nature flowing in Levin's veins. He felt tender to the grass. "God's handkerchief," Whitman called it. He watched with pleasure a flat-footed bluejay hopping up and down branches in the blooming cherry tree. He was amiable even to Mrs. Beaty's cat, licking herself on the lawn at night, her whiteness, light. And Levin wanted, still, to be closer to men than he had been. The good you did for one you did for all; it wasn't a bad way to love.

He had visions of service to others, the truest form of freedom, a secret he had unlocked. It stared him in the face like a crown of violets, diamonds, plums and wild pink roses. When he wore it on his head he created invisible miracles. He had become an extraordinary physician, S. Levin, M.D., F.A.C.S., an experienced man with a bony bald head, craggy face, kind eyes, sparse gray beard, and thin-fingered confident hands. He healed the sick, crippled, blind, especially children. When not practicing medicine he wrote, played the harpsichord, or spun his spinning wheel. In his tiny room only a cot, table, chair, and shelf of books. He lived on dried dates and goats' milk. He often fasted for days. Levin read and reflected to know for tomorrow. He lived everywhere. Every country he came to was his own, a matter of understanding history. In Africa he grafted hands on the handless and gave bread and knowledge to the poor. In India he touched the untouchables. In America he opened the granaries and freed the slaves.

Alas, the picture blew up in his face. What dreadful egoism, willed humility, inverse, ass-scratching pride. Saintliness was for his betters. Levin was a small man, constantly in error, and had to live practically.

He changed to his students. He had allowed his disappointment in their mediocre work, their sameness as people, to sour him against them, though this bothered him in afterthought. Levin's freshmen, when he met them, were eighteen and warm. Many were fine people, earnest, ambitious in uncomplicated ways, some obviously bright, but very few he knew were committed to ideas or respected intellectualism. They showed almost no interest in the humanities and arts ("electives"). They overvalued "useful" knowledge and confused vocational training with humanistic education. They consistently applied standards of technical efficiency to the values and purposes of life; so did too many of their professors. Even their fears were unimaginative: not that civilization was imperiled and might be destroyed, but that if their grades were not high enough they would miss out on the "good jobs" and have to settle for a "lower standard of living." They were badly informed about themselves and the world. Their intelligence, their lives, were absorbed in triviality. They had lost much without knowing it. They had not earned their innocence. This wasn't, of course, true for all, but it was true for too many.

Still they were human and possible. Although they were responsible for tomorrow, they had not invented the world or the values they had found in it. He could not blame them for being uneducated to begin with; he blamed them for their resistance to ideas they had not inherited. For their unexamined lives. Still, a teacher's job was patiently to teach them. It was the nature of the profession: respect those who seek learning and help them learn what they must know. So Levin, although now spending solid hours trying to catch up with papers he had neglected during the time he had felt so bad, opened his office to them. There he sat in full view of the multitudes in the corridor, WELCOME tacked on the wall above his head. Though he hadn't Bucket's forbearance in explaining punctuation rules, he had his students read them again and answered questions. Although their personal lives were none of his business he asked them who they were and what they were living for. He said the wealth of life lay within, keeping his fingers crossed because he hadn't learned all the lessons he taught. He advised the students he had not already frightened away, to study more of the liberal arts before they became technicians, even if it meant transferring to Gettysburg. He quoted Mill: "Men are men before they are lawyers or physicians or manufacturers . . ." He loaned out his best books and asked those who read them to come back for more. Once he caught a glimpse of George Bullock easing an ear close to his door. Levin suspected there had been complaints—that he was a communist propagandist, homosexual, corrupter of youth. But he continued to say: The liberal arts, you can't get enough. They teach what's for sale in a commercial society, and what had better not be. That democracy is a moral philosophy and can't be defended by lopping off its head. A man can find an ideal worth living for in the liberal arts. It might inspire him to work for a better society. It takes only one good man to make the world a little better.

Holy smoke, Levin thought, suppose *I* were head of the department?

One morning shortly after his avowal of service, humility, good will to men, after the wars in the soul had more or less subsided, Levin ran into his old self across the hall in George Bullock's office. Having knocked and got no answer, he had unlocked the door, to leave on George's desk a reader he had asked Levin's committee to consider for fall-term use. As he put the book down near the phone—Gilley's gift to Bullock—the instructor's eyes momentarily lighting on a picture of Jeannette in a bathing suit, fell on a typewritten list of names, among which, without trying, a second after sensing he would, he found his own. Stapled to the list was a note from George addressed to Lon Lewis, the head football coach: "For your personal information. These are lukewarm if not downright unsympathetic to athletes. I frankly can't advise your key men to take their classes. In fact I'd say lay off unless emergency threatens, and then not to unless they've talked to me first. Best ever, George."

After reading this twice and finding himself in a state of high excitement, Levin shut the door and studied the names on the paper, at the same time trying to think what he would say if Bullock walked in. With Levin on the list were Bucket, Fabrikant, O. E. Jones, Haddock, Scowers, Merdith Schultz, Sprinkle, and surprise—Farper. To rate inclusion, Levin figured, you had to be considered prejudiced to athletes, a tough marker, or an irritable pest like Farper. Conversely, those not listed, though not necessarily scoundrels, might be expected to give the boys an easier time and possibly a "break" if needed. What angered Levin was Bullock's gratuitous defamation of his colleagues, the harm a list of this kind could do—probably had done, no doubt there had been others. Since shopping for grades was endemic at Cascadia College, there was already a good amount of prejudging professors and courses in terms of grades given, on other students' say so; but George's document worsened the disease as it destroyed reputations. Levin now understood why, this term, he hadn't had one of the usual letters from the coaches asking how their boys were doing; simply, the athletes had avoided his classes. Alternating between flush and tremble, he felt feverishly eager to confront Bullock with his list. Levin began to copy down the names but had to stop. He tore up what he had written, picked up the book he had come to return and was about to leave when the postscript of a letter on George's paper-cluttered desk caught his eye. This, after a swift unsuccessful pushing match with his conscience, turned out to be a financial report from George's father: "Your personal worth as of today's date is $104,337.31." The telephone rang and Levin left.

Staring through his cracked window (Was Duffy cracked? flitted through his mind) he was unable to stop thinking of Bullock's dirty list, going to the P.E. department, surreptitiously to most of the football players—only a few were good students—then no doubt to their girls, *their* sorority sisters, and where not—everybody knowing who had been proscribed but the professors themselves. Something ought to be done and Levin tried to think what. He could of course speak to Bullock, but that had its disadvantages; Levin would be on the defensive simply in knowing about the list; and if Bullock said, "So what?" Levin was powerless to stop him. Somebody had strongly to tell him where he got off. Who? The instructor felt helplessly without a source of appeal. Gilley? He would find some way to defend Bullock. Fairchild? He would deny the list existed, then gently lecture Levin for having read George's correspondence. The list seemed to imply more than an individual act of Bullock's; it hinted at a way of life. Levin wasn't sure, if he made a public issue of it, that he wouldn't be jumped on by somebody in the administration "for impugning the integrity of the institution." Then he'd be the traitor and Bullock would assist at the funeral—Levin's. So he did nothing, unwilling to jeopardize his job—he shuddered at the chances he had taken with Pauline—a job that was more precious to him with every jeopardy. Here he had begun his career as college professor, sweet dream of his life; here, as a result of some miraculous batting of both eyes by fate he had gone almost a year without being kicked out. One more and he would have enough respectable experience to make a change to a better place. Therefore be prudent, the more the better. Easy does it, Levin thought, you've got to live with all kinds in this world.

But the decision to do nothing was like a bird imprisoned in his chest. A worrisome hour later he was in Fabrikant's office, relating in confidence what he had discovered, and urging the associate professor to give George some fatherly advice; if possible, get him to destroy his list before it went out.

CD, not the least surprised to learn of the existence of the paper, after several minutes of reflection, urged caution.

"As I said before on a similar occasion, the way to fight this is not piecemeal but by getting at the source of a rotten situation. In the meantime let's not tip our hand but keep our powder dry." He winked his big eye.

"But why hide where we stand?" Levin asked. "Everybody knows there's a contest between you and Gerald. Time's fantastically short if it's going to be held this term."

"I'm not so sure that it is," CD said gloomily. "So far as I am concerned it's still no more than a rumor."

"Gilley's positive it's coming off soon, so is Bullock."

"I've already indicated to you why I must proceed carefully."

"The promotion?"

Fabrikant nodded.

"Hasn't that gone through yet?"

"I understand it's in the president's office now."

"Avis told me you said I was supporting you. Surely you know she's for Gilley and anything you tell her will get back to him?"

"I may have been indiscreet," CD admitted. "I hope I didn't cause you embarrassment by speaking of you as a possible ally?"

"No," Levin said impatiently. "It would have to come out sooner or later. I hear there are others with us. Can I ask who?"

"Bucket, you, and I, as of now, but there are several who will join us when the time is ripe, Merdith Schultz and Jones, I have reason to believe, and others. As for tactics at present, we can keep a record of grievances, including this incident and the censorship of the textbook." He laughed dryly. "I can supply a lot more of a similar nature going all the way back to 1932. Once the dean announces the election, whether my promotion has come through or not, we can begin to discuss these matters privately with various members of the department. Then if word of what we're saying gets back to the higher-ups, as I don't doubt it will, no one can accuse us of muckraking, or fuss for the sake of fuss. We'll be engaged in the legitimate American activity of practical politics."

"I see the point," Levin said.

But the point—he didn't see it steadily or whole—gave way to an inspiration that made Levin nervous. After leaving CD he spent an hour trying to get rid of it, but inspiration prevailed. Late that afternoon, after Marv Beal had swept up and left, and even Avis had gone home, Levin sneaked across the hall. The letter and list, though he wished them annihilated, still lay on Bullock's desk. Not allowing himself to think, the instructor slipped them into a folder and hurried to the library. There he had the papers photostated, then returned them to a memorized spot on the desk. "Practical politics," he told himself. He had, however, a brutal headache, and went early to bed.

The next morning he found in his mailbox a letter from Dean Seagram and a folded note "from the desk of Gerald Gilley." The dean's mimeographed letter officially announced an election for a new head of the English department. It was co-signed, as a matter of form, by Professor Fairchild, who had more than once stated in the coffee room that it was foolish to make a simple thing complicated—seniority was the most sensible means of promotion. "If a man's good enough to hold down a job for twenty years, he is good enough to advance to a position of responsibility. And if he's already done that, he should have first choice at something higher." The details of the election were at least simple. It was scheduled for the day after Commencement, in the office of the dean, by secret ballot. Nominations were open and would be received at once. If in the voting no candidate won a two-thirds majority (14 votes) after three ballots, a temporary chairman would be appointed by the dean and a new election held on the fifth of next January.

Gilley's handwritten note asked Levin to drop in to see him at his convenience. Levin, knowing the two communications were related, shuddered. The election, for so long no more than a possibility, was about to become an event. He had looked forward to it—always enjoyed a contest—but now felt no pleasure in the announcement, although the thought of Bullock's list still irritated him and any even remote comeuppance for him, for instance through Fabrikant's election, was something to look forward to. Although he would gladly have skipped seeing Gilley—forever, without missing him—Levin ran into him in the hall. The director of composition was his tall, loose-figured self, and although a bit reserved, still friendly in speech. He said at once, "Why don't we just go into my office for a minute, Sy? What I have to say won't take so long." The instructor dumbly followed him down the hall.

Gilley looked uncertainly at Levin across his half acre of desk, covered with the apparatus of his picture history of American literature. On the desk lay a portrait of Henry Ward Beecher leering up at Levin. He shut his eyes. When he opened them, Gilley seemed tired to him and older by more than just the number of months that had gone by since they had met at the railroad station last summer. His face was motionless yet unsettled, the eyes mirroring Levin's own unease. Whether he knew it or not, he had lived through much since January. He showed, however, not the slightest sign of suspicion, or knowledge of betrayal, and Levin doubted he could have hidden his wound once he knew he had it. It was as if gossip, if any, had stopped dead at his ear—so much for her anxious fears of exposure. A curious thing about a small town: if it didn't destroy you, it protected you. He was of course glad she hadn't been found out. Her luck was still running strong. But had or hadn't, he felt shame before the man; yet when he thought of the picture he had taken of his naked wife, a betrayal perhaps worse than hers of him, Levin was conscious of renewed disgust, although who was he to measure sin? His own moral calipers were badly bent. In the end he boiled up a scum of sympathy for Gilley as victim—Levin's (his favorite sport since Albert Birdless); he felt almost affection for the vulnerable hackee, cheated by his wife and a man he had surely hired to vote for him in the election, a fellow victim, taken over the rocks by the same woman and somebody named Duffy; one's fate is long on the loom before he knows what has happened to him. I owe him something, Levin thought, for the harm I've done him.

Gilley, running his hand through his hair, spoke huskily,

although pretending voice normal, relations unchanged, business as usual.

"Sy," he said, evoking cheeriness, "though we've had our small differences they're nothing I myself take too seriously, and I know that holds for you. You don't seem to me to be the type that goes around holding grudges against people for not agreeing with him. Not only that, but as time goes by I am sure we'll understand each other better and our occasional hassles will give way altogether."

He beamed tentatively as Levin, about to stroke his beard, found it missing, and smiled vaguely.

"Anyway," Gilley said, after a pause, "I thought I'd better ask you where you stand in the election we seem to be having in June. I suppose you've seen the dean's notice?" Having stated the question, he pulled his handkerchief out of his back pocket and blew his nose.

Levin admitted he had seen the notice.

Gilley brushed his nostrils both ways, carefully tucked away the handkerchief and buttoned his pocket.

"Have you made up your mind who you're going to support?"

Though the question basically insulted, Levin found it hard to look the man in the eye, although he attempted a decent approximation of the act after fighting down a suspicion that Gerald, probably through Avis, knew where he stood and was leading up to something else.

What shall I tell him? he thought. That I can't vote for him because he's a mediocre leader, no matter how many years he has coveted the job or been Fairchild's Friday to get it? Or that I can't trust him for the pictures he takes (my God, who can trust me?)? Or shall I say I can't vote for him because I've betrayed him with his wife?

"First let me ask you something," he said hesitantly. "Suppose you—er—had found out that somebody in this department had typed up a list of his colleagues he recommended for athletes to take; or possibly the names of ten people whose courses he told the boys to stay away from. And that he had sent these names to the P.E. department, specifically to one of the coaches, for distribution among the players. Could I ask you what you would do about that?"

"Is there," Gilley asked, his eyes narrowing, "that kind of list?"

"Suppose there was?"

"I wouldn't believe everything I heard around here. I don't listen to most of it myself."

"Suppose I saw it?"

Gerald leaned back in his chair. "I'm not for any such kind of list."

"Could I ask what you would do about it? Would you, for instance, talk to the one who had compiled it, tell him he had made a serious mistake and the best thing he could do would be to withdraw and destroy it? And would you firmly say he must cut out that kind of thing in the future?"

"I might," said Gerald, reaching for a ruler on the desk and absently measuring his hand. Glancing up, he said, "I may not be for that kind of list, Sy, but I'll tell you this. I frankly don't see anything wrong with anybody wanting to look out for the boys on our teams. They have their place in college as well as anybody else. You know what the Greeks said about physical fitness and the well-rounded man. Athletes set certain standards of perfection which is part of your liberal education. Sports mold character. Besides that, practically speaking these boys bring us a lot of exciting games and keep the town interested and grateful to the college. It builds good will all over the state and even intersectionally in some of the bigger games. You could say they're really playing for America. People appreciate that and are solidly behind our sports programs, even in the public schools. Just between us, one of the Easchester school board members personally told me that if it came to a choice between funds for a further developed high school athletics program, or none for kindergartens, he'd vote to abolish the kindergartens. I say this not because I necessarily agree with him—Erik will be ready for kindergarten in '53—but you ought to know what people think. A lot of them in Cascadia give very loyal support to the state colleges because of our teams, and that's mighty important when it comes to funds for new buildings and raises for us all. Don't kid yourself that spectator interest in athletics doesn't influence legislators. The fact of it is that our athletes do a lot for all of us and we ought to admit it and be thankful. I know George tries to assist those who need some help here and there, but in case you don't know it he has more than once been personally thanked by President Labhart. And I suppose you know how fond of him Orville is?"

Levin slowly fanned his face with his hand.

"Let's face the facts," Gilley said. "People *should* be doing things for these boys who break their backs for Cascadia. Sure, most of them have their athletic scholarships for which they have to put in seventy hours a month in the off seasons, but just how far do you think eighty bucks a month goes in these times? And keep this in mind, Sy. The boys on the football squad are out on the field sometimes while you and I are snug in bed, practicing in every kind of dirty weather. They get hit hard, often landing in the mud under a ton of beef. And if they break an arm or leg, or something a lot worse, you never hear them complaining. Spring practice is already on. And when the boys get back in the fall, a whole month before everybody else, they'll be at it day after day until the season ends. By nightfall they barely have the strength to get their clothes off and hit the sack, yet there are plenty of them who keep up good grades. We need people to help them pick courses and advise them generally. Please note no one is asking you to do it."

"I'm not belittling what they do," Levin said, "only that we think they have to do it." He brought up the list again. "Wouldn't you say it was an unethical business?"

"Whose list is it?"

"Well," said Levin, "I'll tell you off the record, although we both know whose it is."

"Then what's the sense of talking about it? Unofficially I can't do anything."

"Not even talk to him?"

"I might do that."

"Tell him to cut it out," said Levin.

Gilley laid down his ruler. "Which brings me back to the original question I asked you before." He did not repeat it.

"I'm thinking of supporting CD," Levin said.

Gilley's expression was momentarily blank; he then shot Levin a look of genuine hatred. The instructor's scalp crawled yet by an act of will he kept himself seated. Gerald hadn't known he was supporting Fabrikant. Avis had probably kept her mouth shut, possibly fearing that if he confronted Levin with previous knowledge of his vote the instructor might say who had told him about the picture; but now Gerald knew and apparently couldn't believe that somebody he thought was in the bag, wasn't.

It then occurred to Levin he had done a foolish thing in saying who he was voting for. He ought to have answered, "Yes, I've made up my mind," and then mum, or just the simple statement that he would not reveal his vote. Gilley would have said no more than he hoped Levin would support him. That would have kept peace between them until the school year ended. Next year was next year.

I told him because of all I haven't told him, Levin thought.

Gilley said bitterly, "I assume that's in the nature of thanks for all I've done for you."

Levin, shoulders hunched, waited for a thunderous revelation of Gilley's service, gift, sacrifice—a statement that would unstitch his skull and destroy him.

"I got you this job—I gave you your office and other privileges—"

"You did more than that—" Levin's voice cracked. He bit his compulsive tongue.

Gerald stirred. "Fabrikant," he muttered. "What makes you think he's such a hot bargain? He doesn't know beans about administering any department, and he can't meet people. A fine mess of public relations he'd make. In no time he'd have us in a snafu so thick it'd take an act of Congress to unravel it."

"He wouldn't have sacrificed the anthology."

"God damn it," Gilley said, "I had Orville on my back on that. If I had been my own boss I'd've had a committee consider it."

"Committees can be cowards—"

"Who are you calling coward?" Gerald glowered.

"Excuse me," Levin said. "All I meant is that one determined man could have saved that book."

"You know," said Gilley, "I'm beginning to think you consider yourself some sort of fount of wisdom put on earth to tell us how to run our affairs. The next thing, you'll be advising the prexy to step aside so you can take over and run the college."

"Oh no," said Levin, perspiring under his clothes. "And don't think I don't appreciate your good qualities, Gerald—I do. But these are dangerous times, and since education is so important this college has to be more effective—"

"Who says we're not effective?"

"*More* effective."

"In the first place, this isn't Harvard, you know. There are thousands of places just like us. In the second, I already told you I expected to make changes in the department once I was in a position to."

"We'd need more than those changes," Levin said.

Gilley glared at him for a tense minute, and Levin looked around to see where the door was, but the director of composition sat back, shaking his head.

"You have a rare nerve to criticize, with no experience to speak of to back it up. You haven't even taught a full year in a college. How knowledgeable do you think you are, for instance? How much have you studied our practical problems—the budget, our mode of operation, the philosophy of the land grant colleges, et cetera? Until you do, what's your big hurry to give out advice about changes *you* think we ought to make? Those of us with experience, who have faced problems of administration, know what we have to do and how much we can sensibly accomplish in any given time. I've told you more than once Cascadia is a conservative state. One thing you so-called liberals can't get into your heads is we *want* it that way. Also remember taxes are way too high. Rural people tend to be frugal and the state legislature is a rural power. We can do what they want us to do. If you don't start with that premise you are off-balance to begin with."

"New ideas cost nothing," said Levin. "Some things are easy to change. And sometimes the college has to lead the community."

"What do you think is so wrong with English?"

"With reference to composition, if you'll pardon my saying so, the course is half dead. We have to get rid of *The Elements* and those damn workbooks. We have to abolish the d.o. because everyone's teaching for it and not beyond it. And we ought to introduce some literature into the course so the students know that good writing means something more than good report writing."

"We have all the lit courses we need. Composition is writing, not studying the forms of literature."

"Just enough lit for inspiration, to liven it up, to ease the heart."

"We're not teaching comp for the sake of the instructor, I'll tell you that."

"Nor for the students, if you ask me. If we were we'd be giving a full liberal arts and science program along with the other stuff."

"If you know anything about educational trends you'd know that pure liberal arts programs are dying out all over the country."

"In that case we may die with them."

"What do you expect me to do?" Gilley then asked. "You know darn well I can't arrange the kind of program you want, all by myself. What about Dr. Labhart? I have heard him say that Plato, Shelley, and Emerson have done more harm than good to society."

"God save us all!"

"Don't underrate him. This place has just about doubled in size and scope during his tenure. He's a first-rate organizer. As a student he paid his way through graduate school by founding and running a successful used-car business that his brother still carries on in Boise."

Levin sighed.

"You know," Gilley said with renewed anger, "one thing I have never liked about you is the way you look around with an eye that says 'I've seen better.' If you took the trouble to check into figures you'd find that our kids on the average get more education per person than yours in the East. And we send a larger percentage to college than you do. Our literacy rate is one of the highest of all the states. I didn't expect you to know that because you have the New Yorker's usual cockeyed view of the rest of the country. You are still an outsider looking in."

"I don't feel like an outsider."

"That has nothing to do with it. It's how you act here that counts."

Pushing back his chair, Gerald strode over to his long closet and pulled out a fishing rod, assembled and ready to strike. "This is a spinning rod," he said. "Do you know it from a fly fishing rod or an African spear? This is the reel, the line—monofilament, eight pound test which I use for steelhead—dropline, lure. I bet you thought we use worms."

Levin admitted it.

"You've been here for almost a year and have never once, so far as I know, gone fishing. If you did that now and then and a few other things I might mention you wouldn't be so dissatisfied. I'll bet you'd be less impatient with your students and colleagues. I personally don't think you enjoy your life, or you wouldn't have that pain-in-the-gut look you have gone around with in the past weeks. If you don't watch out you'll wind up with high blood pressure and will someday keel over while tying your shoelaces. You ought to get out into the open and tone up your muscles. We have some of the best fishing streams in the world in Cascadia. Ernest Hemingway has fished here. How will you ever teach Thoreau, once you have your Ph.D., without ever in your life having been to a wild place?—"

"I've been to Walden Pond—" Levin said.

"God knows I'm not against books," Gilley said, "but I'm against only books."

"I too," said Levin.

Gerald raised his rod and flipped it as if casting. "I don't think you can imagine what it means to wade into a swift icy mountain stream—"

"I can imagine—"

Gilley moved into the cold, fast flowing stream.

"The fisherman estimates the pull of the current from the froth on the water so he knows how deep he can go in without being knocked over and carried away. One wrong step could mean his life. He's got to be mighty careful with his footing when he jumps from one slippery scum-covered rock to another."

He raised his foot, jumped, and made it.

Bravo, thought Levin.

"Now he's in the water up to his chest," Gerald said, extending the rod over the desk, "his arms moving rhythmically as he searches the stream for a fish, pitting his sportsman's knowledge against the instinctive wisdom of the species. This is contentment, this is the good life."

Levin pictured himself in cold water up to his heart (ah the balm of it) enjoying the good life.

"Half the fun is knowing what to do," Gerald went on, "when to fish upstream, when down. He knows just where to drop the lure—or dry fly if he's a real aficionado—a steelhead coming up to a floating fly is a thrill he never forgets. He knows how far to wade in after a struck fish before he's close enough to land it. And when he does that's perfection. And even if you don't catch a single one, you are a better man for the day's work."

"All my life I've wanted to fish—"

"You have seen almost nothing of this country. In the winter and spring vacations you stayed home. What the hell did you buy a car for?"

"I drive into the country," Levin said. "This spring I saw Scotch brume for the first time in my life, pure gold in the fields—marvelous. In the sky the drama of the clouds never ends—"

"I'm not talking about what you can see in the city parks," Gerald said. "I'm talking about *nature*. I mean *live* in it. Camp *alone* in it. I mean *climb* a real mountain. Then you'd know what this country means. And the same holds true for Cascadia College. After you've been here five years you can think about reforming us."

Levin got up. "I wish you luck in the election, Gerald."

Gilley rose, still flushed. "I suppose I got what I deserve for hiring you, also overlooking the harm you've done here, including advising your students to transfer to Gettysburg."

"Did Bullock tell you that?"

"Never mind who told me. It's an act of disloyalty to the institution that pays you your salary. If the University gets ahead of us student-wise, they'll collect most of the budget and we'll get beans. You'd better cut it out."

Levin swallowed. "I'll do what I have to."

"Then you'd better keep this in mind. If I win the election, and I have a darn good chance to, let me tell you there won't be much of a future for you here. And when you leave, don't bother to ask me for a reference. I have nothing good to say about you." Picking up his shears he snipped a picture out of a magazine. "No more New Yorkers, goddammit."

Levin returned to his office. His knees were trembly as he stood at the window, watching his career fly off to a faraway world. Yet the day was serene, the sky blue to the mountains. Not a cloud anywhere but in his head.

A knock on the door. He expected Bucket but Gilley appeared. He had calmed down, though his eyes were still moody.

"Maybe I let myself get a little out of hand," he said, "though I still honestly think I will do a better job than CD once I am on my own here. Anyway, what I wanted to say is this. I just happened to come across a quotation in *Time*, that gives me a better understanding of the type you are." He read from a tiny clipping. "It's by George Santayana and says, 'Americans are eminently prophets; they apply morals to public affairs; they are impatient and enthusiastic.'"

Levin said, "He also said if you don't remember the past you were condemned to relive it." He laughed his broken laugh, and Gilley, once more in a benign ambient, smiled.

"What I thought I would suggest is this," he said. "Of course I'd still like to have your support—" he was gazing out of the window "—but if you can't honestly give it to me, at least don't vote against me."

But Levin said he couldn't do that.

Fourteen votes for Fabrikant were no small picnic to arrange, but since four or five were presumably on hand, nine or ten more, according to Bucket, "seemed not impossible." Levin for some time had had certain hesitations about Fabrikant, including one that really troubled him, but CD was the only candidate other than Gilley who evoked some expression of respect, and since Gerald was almost certainly (inevitably) his enemy now, Levin's situation in the department, so long as it lasted, and future, insofar as it depended on recommendations, would do better under someone else as head, if that could be arranged. He urged CD, now that the dean's notice was out, to carry on a vigorous campaign in the few weeks that remained before Commencement. There had been as yet little serious talk on anyone's behalf, for although Gerald had begun to sound like a candidate as far back as last September, nobody had felt the matter was especially pressing. CD told Levin that he would do what he could short of aping Gilley buttonholing people in the hall and asking for their votes. For that Levin couldn't blame him, but he asked for permission to speak to some of their colleagues in CD's behalf, Bucket to try others. Fabrikant consented. Since Joe felt he would be more comfortable on the second floor, Levin went upstairs among the young instructors, those whom Fabrikant called "the unknown quantities." He called on them with reluctance because a month of salesmanship had once harrowed him to the core. However he was received with the usual amicability, and was courteously listened to, except by Ferris Farper, who glowered as Levin nervously talked, then said he would never vote for anyone a buttinsky supported. But most of the other men seemed no more than mildly interested in what was going on. Either they hid their interest for reasons of their own, or it was a case of "whoever wins is good enough for me," equalitarianism at its most desperate. For good or ill no one expressed any fervid loyalty to Gilley; some lowered their voices or sneaked a glance at the door when speaking his name. Levin sensed more dissatisfaction with the director of composition than he had anticipated, although he was aware that any administrator was bound to annoy some people just in existing. Still it was good there was no strong feeling Gerald was a sure thing.

Levin suggested the department was in the doldrums and needed a shove by someone with a few ideas; it astonished him that several of the men wanted to know what was wrong with the way the department was being run. They weren't kidding. The instructor was at first irritated; they deserved Gilley. Then, annoyed with his annoyance, he patiently explained what ought to be improved and they nodded and said nothing. He expected hot commitment but would have to get used to commitment withheld. He felt heavy-handed and big-booted among them, shaken by their blandness and reticence. Yet gently pinned down, they agreed the better the leader, the better the department. CD, they admitted, had merit as a candidate. He had in the past, they had heard, pushed faculty benefits. No doubt he would do things Gilley mightn't care to try. It was rumored CD would give each instructor a lit class to teach and would insist that everyone in the professorial ranks take a comp class. Levin realized he had started the rumor by talking of it as a "possibility." He hastily denied it was a plank in Fabrikant's platform. But almost everyone complained

Fabrikant was not very sociable. He never went to anyone's house and invited no one to his; he never appeared in the coffee room; he practically lived in his office. "How the hell am I supposed to vote for him," Scowers said, "if I'm not even sure what he looks like?" Fitznogle remarked, "I have a hunch he might be stubborn in close quarters with anybody who didn't agree with him. I'd be afraid of that." And Purtzer said, "Wouldn't it be better to ask the dean to drop the election and bring a new man in from the outside? I've seen these elections before. They leave a lot of bad feeling and are more trouble than they're worth."

Levin went again to Fabrikant. "CD, I think it might pay you to talk to some of the men upstairs. I think they'd like to make your acquaintance and hear your ideas about what ought to be changed around here."

But Fabrikant was not so sure he wanted to visit the third floor. "Let them come down here," he suggested.

"I suppose you know Gerald's been up there twice this week?"

"That's his privilege. I don't think it's dignified to knock on doors and ask the instructors to vote for me. Furthermore, I don't like the antagonisms this competition arouses."

"A campaign is a campaign," Levin said.

"That may be," CD said uneasily, "but if Gilley wins the election I'll still have to live with him."

"Granted, as he will have to with you, if you win."

"He has his full professorship; I haven't. He doesn't need my assistance but I may need his cooperation in the future if the president turns down my promotion. It's been on his desk long past the usual time," he said glumly.

"Why would he turn it down?"

"I don't know but I don't want to encourage it. Gilley is one of his white-haired boys. They play golf and pinochle together. Things I can't and won't do." He looked unhappy.

Levin nodded.

"However, I'll see anybody who wants to see me."

"Fine, I'll tell them."

"One by one, please. I hate crowds."

Levin left him, troubled.

He still vaguely held it against CD that he had not told him his article was half baked. And what's he hiding from in his office—still the Depression? sex? the frustrations of life? Is he the best possible man around or can we do better? But what most troubled Levin was the old question why CD had dropped the defense of Leo Duffy.

He telephoned Bucket at supper time. "Joe, maybe this is the wrong question right now, but do you have any serious reservations about Fabrikant?"

Bucket laughed self-consciously. "I have reservations about everyone, not excepting myself."

"Do you think he'd make a better head than Gilley?"

"I would say so."

"Does he stand a chance to be elected?"

"It seems to me he does."

"Joe, why don't you run?" Levin asked. "I bet people would support you."

The phone was silent for a minute, then Bucket said, "That's very kind but I don't care for administrative responsibility."

Levin said it was just a thought. He had been about to ask if Fabrikant had told him about the picture of Pauline and Duffy, but if Bucket knew, the instructor wanted him to mention it first.

The next morning he found a sealed note in his mailbox, his first written communiqué from Bucket: "Although I genuinely admire CD in several ways and will unquestionably vote for him, I'd be less than honest not to admit one reservation—his withdrawal of assistance to Leo in the Academic Freedom subcommittee of our AAP. Having said that, I hope you will excuse me from further comment."

Levin hunted him up after the end of the hour.

"Excuse me, Joe—I hate to ask, but could you give me a little more information?"

Bucket refused. "All I will add is that secrecy in this matter is not merely willful on my part."

He knows, thought Levin.

"Thanks," he said. "I think I'll talk to CD again."

He had come to a reluctant decision and all day postponed doing something about it although he felt he must. In the late afternoon he knocked on Fabrikant's office door but he wasn't in. That evening, as the sun was setting, Levin drove to his farm and came upon the candidate on his horse in the meadow. The brown horse was a big-bodied animal on short legs, and Fabrikant resembled Napoleon with a cigar. Was he planning a new melon patch or a pitched battle? Austerlitz or Waterloo? Defense in front or rear?

Levin waded out to him through the knee-deep grass. The scholar, in a mellow mood, removed his cigar. "Nice of you to come by." He gestured at the twilit sky.

"So peaceful," Levin said, and paused, hat in hand.

Fabrikant waited, alert. The horse stirred in the grass.

"You recall," Levin began, "I once asked you about Mr. Duffy, why you gave up defending him?"

Fabrikant, chewing his cigar, remarked, "I recall."

Levin cleared his throat. "If you'll pardon me, CD, why did you?"

"That's a private matter."

"Wasn't it also a public one?"

After a silent minute the instructor said, "I'm not referring to the picture."

Fabrikant frowned. "What picture do you have in mind?"

"The one Gerald took of his wife."

The horse moved forward. Fabrikant checked her.

"Did he tell you about that?"

"No. Someone else did—not Bucket."

The scholar grunted. The horse whinnied. "Whoa, Isobel."

"Specifically," Levin said, "what I'd like to know is, was it just the picture that made you change your mind about helping Duffy, or was it something else—or both?"

Fabrikant let out a puff of smoke. A statement followed: "When the photograph was called to my attention I realized there was more to the mess than I had guessed. An ethical problem presented itself which, until then, I had no knowledge of."

"Did you tell the AAP committee about the picture?"

"I told them I no longer intended to defend Mr. Duffy."

"That killed the entire defense?"

"More or less."

"Wasn't that too an ethical matter? That his rights had been violated and no one did anything about it?"

"It was my opinion that the introduction of that photograph cast a different light on his previous trouble."

"All the picture showed—didn't it?—was that they were naked coming out of the water?"

"I wouldn't care to discuss that."

"I'm trying to understand what—er—actually happened."

"It was an indecent business."

"The picture, or the sex angle?"

"Call it what you will."

"Er—Did Duffy ever say anything—in explanation?"

"I don't know. You can ask Gilley."

"Did you tell Bucket?"

Fabrikant coughed. "He had sympathized with Duffy and asked me to explain my action. I afterwards promised myself I wouldn't discuss it with anyone again, nor have I until this evening."

"Excuse me for pursuing this," Levin said nervously, "but it's very important. Did Gilley say, when he showed you the picture, that his wife and Duffy were lovers?—that she had conf—admitted that to him?"

"He didn't say anything. He stopped in my office and handed me the photograph. I took one look and handed it back. There was no further communication on the subject, except his remark later that his wife didn't know about the picture and he would rather she didn't."

Fabrikant turned his horse and Levin had to step back. "I find this discussion unpleasant, Seymour."

"Excuse me for asking," Levin said, "but surely you must have assumed they had—they had been intimate, because there's no moral issue in going for a swim naked."

"What I assumed is my own business."

"I'm on my way," Levin said, "but I want to be clear about one thing. Before you saw the picture—correct me if I'm wrong—you were willing to stand up for Duffy, but then you changed your mind. The main issue, the one that influenced you to offer your help was that he had been fired publicly for being a troublemaker. He had not been given notice, which I understand is contrary to universally approved policy. There was no bill of particulars, or a hearing by any organization on campus, so far as I know. Anyway, what I'm specifically asking is whether the issue on which you decided the matter in your own mind—the reason you wouldn't go on defending him—whether it was based on the merits of the case or just on your seeing the picture?"

"I don't see how you can separate one thing from the other. The evidence was clear."

"Evidence of what?"

"Of his character, of their relationship—do I have to be franker?"

"But did you ask for—er—any other proof? I mean, could I ask whether you gave Duffy the benefit of a reasonable doubt—for instance that he might just have happened to go swimming in the nude with a woman—let's say on impulse—hers—and otherwise the relationship might have been perfectly innocent? It's possible." Levin ended with his voice off pitch.

Fabrikant testily answered, "I decided he was a pestiferous nuisance, not worth the fuss he had kicked up, and washed my hands of the whole annoying business."

"Ah," said Levin. He put on his hat.

Night had fallen. The fragrant warmth of late spring rose from the fields. A crescent moon and single green star glowed overhead as a garden of blue stars evolved in the sky.

Levin sighed. "I'm sorry, CD, but after thinking it over I'm not sure I can support your candidacy any more. I want you to know I like you personally but it's the principle involved."

Fabrikant's big-pupiled eye, reflecting a star, throbbed and sparkled. His horse moved restlessly as he tried to steady her.

"Mr. Levin," he said, cold, aloof, "as you grow older, and I hope wiser, you'll learn there's more to mature behavior than snap absolute judgments. Are you being principled in supporting Gilley?"

"Not him," said Levin.

"Then who?"

His dry lips parted. "Myself."

"That smacks of sickening pride." Fabrikant rose in his stirrups and flung his cigar away. He galloped thunderously across the dark field.

Why should an unlocked door make Levin itchy in his pants, prurient? To say nothing of how the heart throbbed in anticipation. He knew why but pretended not to, to stay put in his office. Coming in just before eleven, after hours of walking after he had visited Fabrikant, on going down the hall to the water cooler he had noticed Gerald's door ajar, his office dark; this rarely happened. Back at his desk, temptation tempted Levin. Gilley's lock did not respond to the common key so it was now or never. He knew that inside Gerald's office was a filing cabinet with a drawer marked "composition personnel." In it was Duffy's folder, probably his history and imperfections described, possibly with pictorial illustrations. This thought roused Levin's prurience. He decided to go home and be done with temptation, but once in the hall he walked the wrong way. For safety's sake he knocked first, softly, and listened to utter silence throughout the building. Levin's legs were so wobbly he had to trek back to his office. He rested his head on his arms on the desk. Go home, he warned himself. In the distance a church bell thinly tolled midnight. What's the sin, he asked, in knowing the truth? Is it ever wrong to know? He rose from his seat at the thought and hastened down the hall, non-stop into Gilley's office, leaving the door partly open in case he had to make a quick exit. I'm always breaking into something of his, he thought, someday he will justifiably shoot me. In the dark he tugged at the top drawer of the filing case. Locked. Good. Levin go home! But he stayed, ensnared in flouting verboten. A door, for some unknown reason, had been left open. You walked in if you were the type. A drawer was closed, you hunted the key. If he found it, what Pandora's horrors would he fall into? A boxful of doors, Levin. The nature of evil: one wrong door opened untold others.

He was feeling for the key in Gilley's drawer when steps going down the stairs froze him. He went quickly to the door and listened as someone walked slowly down from the third to the first floor. Then the footsteps moved in his direction. Yet they were going down the stairs to leave the building. He realized there were two sets of footsteps. Too late to escape, Levin ducked behind the desk. If Gilley came in, what in God's name could he say he was doing there in the pitch dark? He pictured himself caught. Total disgrace as a thief, his father's fate, not unexpected. The steps stopped, the door slowly creaked open. A light played on the wall, filing case, desk. Someone waited, breathing heavily. Levin, cowering on the floor, pictured a cop. That was it, the campus police! He had forgotten their midnight inspection of buildings, putting off lights, shutting doors. He held his breath to the point of madness. When the door shut, for a desperate moment he thought the cop had closed it to prevent his escape; but as the lock snapped he felt he had exploded into freedom. Ten minutes later he dragged his mangled self to his office.

At one A.M., Levin opened Gilley's door, cunningly left ajar; he drew the blinds, put on the light, and located the key to the filing cabinet. In the file in his own folder was his letter of application and signed loyalty oath. Duffy's folder was empty.

PROFESSOR O. FAIRCHILD, on his way home, bent to pick a daisy at the edge of someone's lawn. Levin, dawdling half a block behind, saw him stoop for the flower in a wavering way. Slowly rising, the professor tottered as though the daisy were too much for him. He paused to draw its stem through his buttonhole, smoothing the white petals; always meticulous, everything where it should be. Then he strolled on as though concentrating on a line drawn to infinity. Possibly the sidewalk boxes made the long line difficult to follow. When he walked off it, trying to get back, he put his foot in the wrong place. He stepped on the grass. This happened twice. The professor looked at the sky, loosened his collar, then neatly drew his tie tight. A passing car honked. His arm half rose in greeting; he almost turned to watch it go by. With his neatly folded silk handkerchief he patted his forehead. For half a minute he studied his watch and then walked on slowly. Could he be drunk? Levin wondered. Does he secretly tipple from an office bottle, his father's fate long since caught up with him? The instructor shivered. He had left the office late, and seeing the old grammarian walking on ahead, had not wanted to catch up.

A few days before, Levin had been summoned into the professor's office (Strangers are still welcome . . .) via a short typed note in a sealed envelope, sure trouble. He had knocked nervously, not because he had much of a career to lose (although he had foolishly been wondering would the old gent, in a burst of pre-retirement good will, write him at least a mild recommendation "to whom it may concern"?), but because he felt he had earned his displeasure. Professor Fairchild sat at his desk scanning galleys, the sun flaring his white hair; he looked as though he hadn't budged since the time Levin had visited him in this many-windowed room last August. He had the impression he had seen him then for all time. Since summer he doubted they had exchanged a hundred words. The old man, bags heavy under his eyes, laid down a galley page and focused on Levin a watery blue frown.

Maybe I should have worked up a little hatred of him, the

instructor thought. If he had been strong we would all be stronger. He created the wrong past:

Here Lies Orville Fairchild, Lost Leader
He Ran the Cheapest English Department on the West Coast
Requiescat and Please Omit Flowers

Now the head of department was supporting Gerald Gilley for his place, as Gilley was grooming George Bullock, his man Saturday, for his. (Levin's Law I: Weak leaders favor weak leaders, the mirror principle in politics.) He saw himself sternly accusing the old man of a lack of concern for those who came after him, the professor cowering as S. (for Savonarola) Levin lectured him.

Instead Levin stared at his shoes. The professor, after inviting the instructor to sit, said in his vibrant voice, not unkindly, "Mr. Levin, I have asked you into this office not to protest your enmity to my grammar text—which in its twenty-eighth year, thirteenth edition, and twelve hundred and sixth adoption, needs no defense; nor your disrespect for Dr. Gilley, your immediate superior, and the person most responsible, may I say, for putting you on here; nor because of your presumption in other matters which do not concern you; but to insist you show a decent respect for the opinions of mankind."

If he forgives me, I'll forgive him.

"And I advise you," the professor said sternly, "not to have anything more to do with the wives of your colleagues. They're married women."

All is lost, I lost it.

"Yes, sir."

"My wife tells me there's talk you've been seen with several faculty wives. Is that true?"

"Several, sir?"

"That's right."

"No, sir. I did—ah—see one but that's all past tense."

"Well, keep it so. I warned you very strongly against that sort of thing and I renew my warning. I am being tolerant only out of charity, to keep you from destroying your career at its inception. To subdue your passion to interfere with others as well as criticize everything in sight, you might profitably begin with some much-needed reforms of yourself."

"How true, sir."

"Remember the sad fate of Leo Duffy."

"I do."

"I speak to you as a father to a son."

Levin, choked up, had to blow his nose. "Thank you, sir."

"Be humble. We must all be, especially those who teach others."

Levin nodded.

"Be good—"

He promised faithfully . . .

The old professor, lifting his coattails, had without a backward glance, sat down on the grass. He sat in the shade of a leafy linden tree on a small round grassy island amid three intersecting streets deserted at the supper hour. A little girl in a red dress, on one skate, was watching him as Levin came by. The professor had lain back, his eyes watery, lips blue, nose shrinking.

"Oh God," cried Levin.

On his knees he loosened the old man's collar, his chest heaving as he gasped for breath. Levin ran across the street, frantically pushed a door bell and asked the woman to call an ambulance. He returned to tell her to call Mrs. Fairchild, then raced back to the island. The little girl had skated away.

Although he seemed not to know where he was, the old man appeared to recognize Levin. He hoarsely whispered something and Levin bent low to hear.

"'—Shot—an arrow—into the—air, it fell—'"

"Don't say a word," Levin begged. "I've called an ambulance. You'll surely get better."

He's dying, he thought. Where's everybody?

"'All are—archi-tects—of—fate—'"

The old man smiled with wet eyes. His face was smaller now. His lips twitched as he tried to speak. Levin leaned very close.

"Try to rest."

"The mys—mystery—of the in-fin—in-fin—in-fin—"

"Infinite."

"In-fin-i-tive. Have—you con-sidered—its possi-bil-i-ties? To be—"

He paused, gazed intently at Levin, and muttered, "Poor Papa." His mouth shut sternly. He died.

Gerald made all the funeral arrangements. Pauline, at the church and graveside on a coldish day clung to her husband's arm, a thin-faced mourner unable to look at an open grave. The department was present en masse, including all the young instructors and their wives who looked like girls. President Labhart, pink-skulled and grim-visaged, Dean Seagram, ex-Dean Feeney, small and unpressed after retirement, were present with their modest wives. Fabrikant and his sister came in white faces and dark clothes. Probably the saddest man present was Joe Bucket, who had lost an old friend and benefactor. Gilley bore up. Bullock's face was serious but inexpressive. Pauline looked lost in the crowd, in black dress, small veilless hat, nose aimless, her hair dark gold in the afternoon sun. Levin gazing across the coffin met her sad eyes. He felt regret, a sense of loss beyond all loss, like death in childhood, that somehow passed. She looked away. His heart remained heavy. The professor was buried at the foot of two gnarled fir trees in a new section of the cemetery, not too far from the graves of pioneers with their weather-beaten wood, and eroded stone, markers.

Afterwards rumors flew that Gerald, Fabrikant, Leopold Kuck, George, and even Bucket were being considered for acting head; and Levin hoped for Joe or anyone who wasn't Gilley or Bullock; even CD. It turned out, according to Avis, who had got it from a reliable source, that although the dean was considering everyone, President Labhart, after reading a sealed letter left by Professor Fairchild, "in the event of my death before retirement," proposed Gerald because he knew the department from A to Z, where everything was and went. Gilley was duly appointed, Levin's hopes for a change for the better suffering a not unexpected blow. Almost at once Gerald moved across the hall. People going into Milly's office for a stencil or to get their mail could see him through a connecting door, closed during Fairchild's tenure but now always open, sitting at his predecessor's desk. He had got a haircut and new brown suit and was no longer visible in shirt sleeves. It seemed strange to see him where the old professor had been but Levin soon got used to it. Gerald's first official communication was a dittoed sheet in praise of the late head, followed by an announcement that department policy for the few weeks he was acting head would remain unchanged. He expected everyone would, of course, pitch in to keep things moving as usual. In a subsequent notice he announced that the departmental elections, contrary to false rumors, would take place as scheduled. In the meantime he was at your service. "Feel free to come in."

Although department policy remained ostensibly as usual, Gilley himself showed an alteration or two, nothing serious. Though he looked smaller in a large room, he seemed to have gained weight in a matter of days, noticeable around the middle and jowls; wore bright bow ties and button-down collars, and looked surer of himself, less preoccupied than in the recent past. He was healthy, happy, flourishing. His color had picked up, brilliant in the light that swirled around his red head. He still impressed Levin as everybody's boy, but modified, as if events had proved his mettle, fait accompli, no hands on his part; for hadn't the mantle of office fallen smack on his shoulders? He strove less yet managed to campaign without seeming to do so, whereas Fabrikant, according to Bucket, hardly talked of his aspirations. Wasn't it politicking when Gerald sent out, more often than necessary, notices signed "Gerald Gilley, Acting Head"? He functioned with assurance, to be expected considering his long apprenticeship for the role. What he was doing he had done for years—perhaps a few more decisions to make, and his signed notices more prominently displayed on the bulletin board; otherwise his activities were as before, emphasis on freshman comp. He looked as if he were ready to stay forever where he was unless someone did something about it.

Things were the same only more so. A few days after Gerald had entered the new office, he had his own large desk moved in and continued to clip pictures for his book. He put in the usual time in the coffee room, alone meditating on the twists and turns of fortune; joking with instructors; or discussing the college baseball picture with Marv Beal and Doug Womack, Milly's husband, in cowboy hat and black windbreaker, who waited hours to transport her in his one-ton truck, wherever she had to go. Gerald was friendly as ever to anyone who approached him, the same congenial democratic soul, five-eighths affection for people, Levin guessed, three-eighths fear, as though his well-being depended on *everybody's* good will. Besides clipping and pasting, he read *Field and Stream*, liked to enter in his class record book the objective test scores of his students, which he also graphed; and sometimes read popular fiction to light music on the radio. On days it wasn't seriously raining he golfed during the lunch hour, napped after eating, and returned to the office raring to go. Whenever Cascadia College scheduled a home baseball game he was there as official scorer, reward for years of perfect attendance.

The acting head made no attempt to hide his dislike of Levin. Apparently he told Avis, who told someone who slipped it to the instructor, that he was annoyed with him for "campaigning for Fabrikant behind my back." As a result of Levin's underhandedness, Gilley seemed to have grown doubts of his honesty. The doubts were valid if grown in truth; he was admittedly dishonest but not in the small, ratty ways Gilley seemed to think. For instance, when in Milly's absence Levin extracted a three-cent stamp from the cigar box in her drawer, a customary procedure when she was not at her desk, Gerald watched him hawk-eyed through the open door to see that he paid three pennies. When the instructor came in for paper, pencils, chalk, the acting head, peeking out, noted on a pad what supplies Milly gave him. And Gerald once sent her to ask Levin if "he had happened to see" two missing rolls of scotch tape. Levin was often reminded he was a chip off his father's block.

Gilley's suspicions of the instructor were perhaps evidence of an increased sensitivity to him as implied "chief critic of everything," particularly when the acting head was diddling at something that wasn't work. At times Gerald seemed nervous in Levin's even momentary presence. He became conscious of his cup of coffee if the instructor happened to be passing while he was imbibing. Once at Levin's approach to the water cooler Gerald, standing in the hall, quickly thrust into his pockets some film negatives (Pauline in the bathroom?) he was showing Leopold Kuck. Even Kuck seemed embarrassed. The next day Gerald hurriedly removed his feet from his desk when the instructor walked into Milly's office to inspect his generally useless mail. In a further complication of cause and effect Levin had a sudden desperate feeling he was Gilley's unwilling nemesis. (Levin's Law II: One becomes his victim's victim. III. Stand for something and somebody around will feel persecuted.)

The cold war between Gerald and himself, plus the hot

between his conscience and natural timidity, was exhausting Levin. One morning he went very reluctantly into the acting head's office to report the selections of the textbook committee at their final meeting. Gilley slipped a magazine into his top drawer, locked it with a key, and glumly faced Levin.

"I just came to tell you," Levin said, aware of the thick beat in his breast, "that our committee has voted to recommend the use of *The Elements* in the 'Grammar for Teachers' course. In the comp classes we'd like to substitute Smith and McGinnis' *Composition and Handbook of Grammar*. We also suggest a better—more suitable reader, Guffey's *Experience in Fact and Fiction*."

"Where do you think that'll get you?" Gilley asked sarcastically. Without waiting for an answer he said, "You might at least have waited until Professor Fairchild's corpse was cold in his grave."

"I'm reporting the committee's decision."

"I'll bet you led them by the nose."

"Our decision was unanimous. You can poll Bucket, Jones, Scowers and Carson Fitch if you don't believe me."

"We'll see about that."

He had flushed darkly and Levin felt his stomach flip. "Gerald," he said, trying to keep his voice steady, "if you countermand these recommendations I'll have to go to everybody and tell them about Bullock's shit-list that you did nothing about."

"Don't you use that kind of language in this office." Gerald looked indignantly to see if Milly had heard but she was in the lavatory.

"I will also tell them, if they don't already know, that Bullock invites the outstanding athletes into his own classes so he can look after them personally, and no one has done a thing to discourage that either. On top of that he tutors those who are too stupid to get a C, and gets paid for it by the P.E. department. That's twice for the same student. How do you think the Cascadia taxpayers would feel about that?"

Gerald got up and shut both doors.

"Are you trying to blackmail me?"

Levin denied it.

"Nothing is being done that the president doesn't know about. It's all on the up and up, so don't try to make it sound like some kind of secret conspiracy," Gerald said, his fury subdued but showing. "George had the initiative to start this tutoring program on his own. The P.E. department insisted on paying him for his time, he didn't ask for it, he doesn't need the money. I personally mentioned it to the president and he didn't think it important enough to comment on."

"Have you told him about the list?"

"Nobody has any proof of that."

"Why don't you ask George if it exists? If he admits it you can then tell him to cut it out. You could also ask him to stop tutoring those he teaches."

"I don't see what difference it makes who tutors them," Gerald said, "so long as he's qualified to do it, and I'd like to point out to you that George, who is three years younger than you, has had his Ph.D. for the last two years, the youngest man in this department with the degree. He is eminently well qualified to teach or tutor anybody. Now I want to tell you that you're not fooling me with your complaints. I know darn well that you and Fabrikant, and Joe Bucket, are playing these things up because you want to discredit me and win the election for CD. But I'll tell you this: it won't work because everybody in the department knows that things aren't as bad as you try to make them out to be."

"They're a lot worse."

Gilley sat down looking miserable. "Sometimes I curse the day I brought you here. You're not fit to be a college instructor."

"Why did you?"

"I was a damn fool."

"To get my vote for giving me a job?"

"If I did I don't want it any more. Listen, Levin, why don't you go back where you came from—to the stinking goddamn New York subways?"

"I'm here to stay." Levin barely believed it.

"That's what somebody else thought who is no longer with us. We'll get rid of you just as we did him."

Though the instructor had borne up fairly well till then, Gilley's threat made him wilt. He might have discovered his ass on the floor, had he not then heard the acting head's desperate voice asking him to be reasonable. Afterwards he felt a dark sense of isolation. He was meant for a peaceful life.

He tried again to persuade Bucket to run, but the assistant professor said he had already committed himself as far as he could.

"If Gilley wins," Levin said, "I'll be kicked out for sure."

"Not without good cause."

"I've given good cause."

"And I've given five hostages to fortune," Bucket said, "not counting a presently pregnant wife, a not unsizeable company to consider."

"I am my only hostage," Levin sighed.

Home, he lay on his bed for hours, staring at the wall.

That night, while picking up a box of crackers in the neighborhood grocery, Levin spied Dean Seagram hefting grapefruit at the fruit counter, and his heart skipped a beat. With his Van Dyke and pinched nose he looked slightly aristocratic but Levin suspected he was approachable. Though the dean had brought nothing particularly new to the Liberal Arts Service Division, he had at least upset the English department with his plans for an election. Levin had more than once seen him in this store; usually they nodded and each went his way, but tonight the instructor felt a desire to talk to the dean. Lately he had been thinking of discussing with him Bullock's concern with athletes but it was too much like snitching. Tonight something else was on his mind.

He waited outside the store and when the dean appeared carrying a huge paper sack loaded with grapefruit, Levin lifted his hat.

"Good evening, I'm in the English department, S. Levin." This took an effort but less than he had imagined.

"I recognized you," the dean said. "You've cut your beard—a pity."

"Oh that." Levin laughed in embarrassment. He fell in step with the dean; they crossed the street at the corner and walked on.

"Do you live this way, Mr. Levin?"

"No, sir, the other. I—ah—thought I'd like to speak to you about an idea I have."

He laid his hand on his chest to calm the galloping organ. It had occurred to him that the dean might have had a bad report of him from Gerald and he now regretted having approached him. Still, here he was, so he spoke.

"I've been wondering if this mightn't seem like a possible good idea to you: to introduce a Great Books program here, something we might carry on at night in the college library? I would be willing to do whatever running around is necessary, et cetera, to get it started."

"I don't understand," said the dean. "Do you mean a Great Books course for our students?"

"No sir. They could come if they want to—everybody welcome including townspeople—but I had the faculty in mind mostly. That is if you think the idea is practicable. What I've been hoping is to get a mixed group together—liberal arts people, scientists, technologists, and business school people—so we can explain these books to each other. Most of them are classics of literature and the rest are from science and the social sciences. What I've been thinking is this: After we've talked about some of the books maybe the others would understand us a little better, at least what the humanities are and why they're necessary to our existence. I realize," he went on quickly, "understanding is a two-way street—some of us know dismally little about science, but in Cascadia College it's obvious who the second-class citizens are, as Dr. Fabrikant calls them. The technologists barely know we're alive and hardly seem to care. Our people have almost no status and accept their fate; some, as I understand it, don't even defend the importance of the subjects they teach. How can they when we're so service-oriented, if I—er—may ask? One can guess the effect of this on their students—"

The dean nodded.

He was about to remark something but Levin hastened on. "I figure if we could keep the program going for a while it might eventually create a climate of opinion in favor of the return of the liberal arts to this college. And maybe this group could become a sort of nucleus of a faculty forum? That is—er—if nobody objects."

Shifting his grapefruit bag, the dean looked intently at Levin.

God damn me for a miserable fool, thought the instructor, why do I never learn?

"Now there's an interesting suggestion."

"You think so?" Levin drew a jagged breath in relief.

"No doubt about it, if we could get the right sort of group. Maybe the approach should be to ask the Council of Deans informally to sponsor the project so that it doesn't look like a propaganda job of the Liberal Arts Service Division? I'll tell you what, Mr. Levin, why don't you drop up to my office some time shortly after Commencement and let's talk about it? We might make a stab at getting such a thing started next fall. I have my doubts as to what the response will be but it's worth trying. Even if we can't get any technologists to join, it'd do some of our people no harm to become re-acquainted with the Great Books—or should I say acquainted?" He laughed hesitantly. "If we could get half a dozen participants from all the other schools, we'd be doing unusually well. It's a unique idea. I congratulate you."

They walked on, Levin with light step. One more idea like that, he thought, and he'd give me a bang up reference.

"Ah—there's something else I wanted to mention," he said after another block. "This election we're having soon—can anybody run?—I mean an instructor?" He was beginning to laugh hollowly and choked it off. "It may sound silly but all sorts of people run in elections. What would happen if—ah—an instructor won?"

The dean shifted the grapefruit bag to his other arm. "I haven't given a thought to that possibility. Generally the men at the upper ranks are the likely candidates; still if an instructor managed to win fourteen votes I imagine we'd commission him on the battlefield. I'd suggest he be immediately promoted to assistant professor, with all the privileges and emolument thereof—not much of either, I'm afraid. But there might be something additional for administering the department, though not so much as a man of higher rank would get. However, in the unlikely event an instructor won, just to be cautious I think I'd urge that the chairmanship be made rotating—say a new man every two years, at least for a while."

"Fair enough," Levin said.

"Are you interested in running?"

"I'm not sure." He aborted a mad snicker. "Is it—it isn't too late for further nominations?"

"Yes, it is. I sent out a poop sheet to you people this afternoon, with the names of the nominees. However you were nominated, along with Drs. Gilley, Fabrikant and Bullock. The latter called me at home this evening and asked to have his name withdrawn."

"Me?" said Levin in joyful surprise. Bucket did it, he thought. Or Jones, or maybe Scowers. He wondered if the dean thought he had nominated himself, since names had been entered on unsigned sheets. He laughed nervously.

Dean Seagram laughed too. An oncoming car separated them in the street, Levin waiting as the dean ran ahead.

"Look out," he yelled.

The dean, glancing back to see what had become of the instructor, was heading into a phone pole. He stopped short of it but not before his grapefruit bag had hit the pole and split apart.

The grapefruit went rolling into the street. Levin, clucking, rescued an armful. At the dean's insistence he piled a few on those he had in his arms but what he couldn't carry Levin did.

In fine fettle for being so helpful, almost without thinking he asked the dean how much notice anyone who was not going to be re-hired usually got.

"Well, sir," said the dean, hugging his fruit, "the Administrative Regulations require us, after the first year, to give twelve months' notice to faculty members without tenure. But if you're referring to someone serving his probationary year, he's got to have notice in writing by the latest at the beginning of the spring term that we won't be renewing his contract for the fall."

I've had nothing in writing, Levin thought with elation. Though he realized he had asked a foolish question he could not help thinking that a man had no true idea of his possibilities until he had investigated them. Even with Gilley as head of department, in another year, given a break or two, he might recoup his fortune at Cascadia College if he played it right. Therefore, no further questions.

"But dismissal is summary," the dean went on cheerily, "on any sort of morals charge. I understand that that, ultimately, was the justification for getting rid of Mr. Duffy."

In a minute they were scrambling after grapefruit after Levin had walked into a tree.

Am I worthy? he asked himself. Me, jailbird's son, ex-drunk, unfrocked idealist, sinner re-sinned, mistake-maker-of-every-kind? How can a man who has so often failed in obedience think of himself as a possible leader? Do I dare, with my nature, weaknesses, history of failures, seek any task other than that which fosters humility, cleans conscience, and/or balances the mistakes of the past? Levin had never before even remotely considered running for office, had never been a candidate for anything but punch-ball captain at twelve, and later for a couple of college degrees. A worthy leader means man of virtue and wisdom, virtue embodying courage; he had not much of either, mostly he had good intentions. Still a good-intentioned administrator who was not afraid to try a worthwhile idea once in a while might do all right. Of course it was a hell of a nerve for an instructor with so little experience in a college, an Easterner not long in the West, until recently a stranger to most of his colleagues, to ask them to elect *him* head of department. Yet maybe that sort of shock was what they needed here. If that happened, anything might.

He reveried accomplishment, Levin the leader; foresaw an effective if necessarily short career. What mightn't he achieve at Cascadia if he devoted himself to the task: a hundred needed reforms—raising the department from mediocrity to excellence. And while at that, who knows if, working every which way, he mightn't succeed in starting a campaign to bring back to Cascadia a liberal arts majors program? Easchester would flower. One good thing led to another once somebody dared. Good institutions proliferate good deeds. They might, in town, build a concert hall and public forum, start an art gallery, theatre group, show foreign films, even open a bookstore that sold books. An enlightened public opinion! Easchester, Athens of the Northwest! And when Levin left to take up a new career (Why leave if he had created the conditions of his survival? A woman one was bound to meet sooner or later.), the good people of the town, inspired to communal gratitude would parade him up and down Main Street amid Lions, Elk, Women of the Moose, Odd Fellows, the Easchester Taxpayers

Association, cheers, tears and a brassband. Levin, benefactor, Culture Hero, Seymour J. P. Bunyanseed, Fautor et Cultor Bonorum, American Patriot! He had to slap himself to leave off.

Though he detested asking people for their votes, to raise himself above them, hated the indignity of campaigning, it was what he had to do. He counted, three, maybe four, votes in hand, but there was a way of inducing a half dozen others, even more if he could do the dirty thing he contemplated doing. If he did, it was doubtful he could make fourteen votes, but possible. If not, the trick was to prevent Gilley's election in the hope that somebody neutral would be appointed acting head, though the instructor had doubts of that too, since Gerald was already serving. Still, Levin's plan was to keep him from certain power until he had landed a job in another college. What happened after he left was their business; if they voted Gilley in, they deserved to have him. Gerald was sure he had the inside track but Levin, upstart shmo, had a photostat of Bullock's shit-list; and since there was little time, began—an uneasy Machiavelli—(I'm telling them for their own good; ignorance is not bliss) to show it cautiously around. He had cut off from the letter Bullock's signature. When people guessed who had compiled the names, he neither affirmed nor denied it, saying only that he had called the paper to Gerald's attention but he had refused to take action against the perpetrator of the list, the original copy of which now reposed amid the football coach's papers, a filed defilement. No one particularly hit the ceiling in surprise or indignation but several people were disturbed, Bucket and O. E. Jones to the point of quiet misery. One or two were frightened to see their names on the list. "How can I get off?" they asked Levin.

As if to compensate for the first document, he produced another, mimeographed in secret late at night: "S. Levin, PLATFORM: To maintain our self-respect, OUT with *The Elements* (as recommended by the composition textbook committee), ALSO the d.o., ditto the policy of unwilled favoritism to athletes; and censorship of responsibly selected texts; fear of the public and distrust of staff; the composition room and assorted gadgets. IN, a writing-centered comp course; one literature class to each man insofar as possible; the ideal of the humanities—foundation of democracy." He went on, in talk, almost without meaning to: held these truths to be self-evident: there is more to democracy, even in the American West, than equalitarianism. Equality means equal justice under law, equal suffrage, equal opportunity through free education; it doesn't mean every man is as good as the next—that there is no such thing as aristocracy of mind, spirit, attainment. Jefferson (his italics) to Adams; to Levin: "There is a natural aristocracy among men, the grounds for this are *virtue and talents.* The natural aristocracy I consider to be the most precious gift of nature, *for the instruction, the trusts and the government of society.*" Equality is not achievement of the identical average. Nor are "ideas" equal in value because they were thought up by friendly people. A man seeks excellence through education and accomplishment. When its leaders are great, democracy is. Levin, his armpits sizzling, was at this point usually stammering, on the verge of disconnected sentences, the felt disjunction of his worth with what he must say. When he was asked why he no longer supported Fabrikant he said he thought the department needed a stronger man, and when his auditor inspected him with a critical eye, in a canny moment the instructor offered to quit his candidacy if the dean would appoint as head a capable man from the outside. O. E. Jones said he and Ed Purtzer would at once suggest that to Dean Seagram.

Levin stirred up, during the last days of the term, a terrible discord. He was, and knew it, the subject of much talk and rancor. He lived on the edge of things, on edge, his nerves ragged, yet forcing himself to push his campaign to get himself elected. Those who agreed with his criticisms and suggestions for improvement of the department, seemed to be as much annoyed with him as those who disagreed, who thought *The Elements* was fine, Gilley's policies fine, the way things went, fine. He was accused of starting trouble and disturbing people's peace. He was accused of exaggerating, lying. He was called to his face by Leopold Kuck, usually a mild sort, "the main victim of your own presumptuous desire for power." He quoted Lord Acton and informed Levin he had never trusted him. "You don't understand us," he all but yelled in his office. "You have no idea of decorum. You're as bad as Leo Duffy, without his virtues. You oughtn't to be teaching in a college." Ferris

Farper—Levin had been expecting this—called him a "lousy goddamn un-American radical." I'm a poor substitute for one, Levin thought, but here a little goes a long way. He felt like a viper. His heart palpitated when he was doing nothing. He feared the name-callers, satisfied with what they had, wanted more of the same, three cars in every garage. Anyone who suggested that to be too contented with one's life or society was a subtle form of death, was clearly off his rocker, alien, without doubt a Red.

A few days before year-end exams began, George Bullock, his sharp face florid, encountering Levin in the hall, threatened to knock his block off. "Where the hell do you get your fat nerve copying my private correspondence and showing it around?"

"I cut your name out of the letter," said Levin. "I didn't mention whose list it was."

"You mentioned it to Gerald."

"The list, not your name. He guessed whose it was."

"You can't make a crime where none was intended," Bullock said angrily. "The athletes are the only ones around who achieve anything worth talking about. I have every right to protect them from the likes of you. Jesus, what a sucker I was to invite you to my home. You betrayed my hospitality."

"I'm sorry—I was grateful for it."

"Like hell you were. You and that foul beard, the minute I laid eyes on it I knew I couldn't trust you."

"Don't blame my beard—"

"You won't get a single goddamn vote more than your own."

Gilley, listening down the hall, smiled grimly; Fabrikant, on his way to the men's room, glowered.

Levin's isolation deepened. He was weary of making enemies, sick to death of fighting alone, living alone, of his lonely mind. The battle had become more than he could stand; he wanted desperately to quit.

But that same day Bucket came to him and said he had, after much contemplation, decided to support his candidacy.

"Ah," sighed the instructor, "only don't do anything you'll be sorry for."

"'The more my uncle Toby pored over his map, the more

he took a liking to it.'" Bucket cackled a bit. "I'll do what little I can to help."

As Levin, moved to celebrate the acquisition of an ally, was sitting in the men's room later, a voice from the next stall asked, "Mr. Levin?"

"Speaking."

"I thought that was you talking to yourself. This is Merdith Schultz." Levin had seen him, other than at department meetings, maybe twice during the year although their offices were next to each other.

"I've been following your career with great interest," said Merdith Schultz. "You have more friends than you know."

Levin went home in an improved frame of mind.

During final-exam week some of the animosity seemed to evaporate from the air. Now and then people passing Levin in the hall, smiled. He had the feeling he might make it; it was "not impossible."

On the Saturday night before finals Levin went to his office to average grades and after a few minutes became restlessly conscious of a scent he recognized. He put his head out of the window and breathed the cold air, then sniffed inside and was convinced the warm odor was orange blossom. His scalp prickled; he had lately got the feeling he was being watched—ridiculous. He had blamed it on his nerves—now he suspected Avis had been in his office. He quickly went through a mess of papers in his top drawer and was moved and frightened to find among them a letter of Pauline's he was positive he had destroyed, the one she had written after running into Mrs. Beaty. The paper seemed alive in his hand and he sensed Avis had read it. Levin tore it up and burned it in the wastebasket. Then he opened a book and waited.

In about an hour he heard Avis shut her door and walk up the hall. She hastened past his office. He listened to her crooked heels clacking down the stairs, gave himself seven minutes, then let himself into her office. Her desk drawer was locked but he pried it open with a screw driver he had got in Marv Beal's closet. In her perfumed, neat, old-maid's drawer, he found several notebooks labeled "Lesson Plans." Flipping through them one by one, Levin discovered that a portion of the most recent book had been converted into a rough diary of his "movements." Avis had for the last month been listing his comings and goings. She had recorded the number of girl students who had entered his office, and whenever possible, the length of time each had stayed. She had also listed the names of colleagues who had been in to see him, Bucket's name most often but at one time or another everyone on Bullock's list. The last entry, dated tonight, was Pauline's letter copied in Avis' girlish hand.

"Just a word, dearest. I suppose you know?—I'm awfully sorry. I was afraid of something like this. I can't tell you how bad I feel, God knows how I'll get through the night. I'm writing this in Erik's room. Call me Thurs. between 9 & 10, no later. I just had to get in touch. I love you. I miss you so. Destroy this. Pauline."

His impulse was to rip up the notebook, but he rolled it up and slipped it into his pocket. Pulling the drawer out as far as it would go, he discovered several packs of letters bound by rubber bands, arranged chronologically within the pack, going back to Avis' first year in Cascadia. Levin sat down and looked through them. They were for the most part from her family and Louisville friends, reporting local chitchat. But among the letters he found an unstamped yellow envelope addressed "Avis" in strong, thick-stroked writing. Inside were two thin sheets of papers, short handwritten notes. The first, dated 18 October, 1948, read: "Dear Avis—I am most grateful for last night. Yours, Leo." The second, 3 April, 1949, said: "Dear Miss Fliss: I'll thank you to keep your nose out of my business. Leo Duffy."

Levin returned both notes into the envelope and pocketed it. From Milly's office he dialed Avis, saying he wanted to see her. She answered, after a short pause, that she had already hung up her dress but would be pleased to see him in the morning.

"Put something on," said Levin. "I'm coming over."

"Have you been drinking?"

"Not yet."

She hesitated. "All right, you may come."

She was waiting for him on the porch in her pink—he thought at first, nightgown—but it was a summer dress though the night was cold. She gave forth orange scent and her bosom was quietly agitated.

"Avis," said Levin, "I would appreciate the truth. Have you already told Gerald about the letter you copied into your notebook tonight?"

She stamped her foot. "Oh, you are vile." Her hand went to her chest and her knees buckled but as he reached out to help her she grabbed the porch rail. Her eyelashes fluttered endlessly. At last she moaned and lowered herself into a chair. When she spoke her body was rigid, voice expressionless.

"No, I haven't—"

"Good," said Levin.

"I won't promise not to. You both betrayed Gerald. I suspected it. I felt you were hiding something and when you began to take George's letter around I thought you deserved a similar treatment. Not only do you want Gerald's job, you want his wife. Your inhumanity knows no bounds—"

"The notebook," said Levin, "also contains the names of some of our colleagues who have nothing to do with Pauline or me, and who might seriously object to being spied on. I also have two notes from Leo Duffy to you."

Tears filled her eyes. "You contemptible, perfectly awful person, don't you dare show them to anyone or I'll have you arrested."

"I have no intention to, but I ask the same consideration from you. The lady and I no longer see each other. She's reconciled with her husband. It would help nobody if you told him about her letter."

She sat motionless.

He said gently, "You were in love with Duffy?"

She seemed to come to after a while. "For a short time," she said. "However I retained my virtue though he tried endlessly to persuade me to bow to his will."

"Later he became interested in Pauline?"

"She threw herself at him," Avis said bitterly. "She enticed and seduced him."

He hadn't the courage to deny it.

HE BEHELD her through the musty curtains of the front door, his hand resting on the knob. How can it be? he thought; that's in the past. It was a cold early morning; he had been getting up at five to work on a paper about a white whale. It was an awesome burden and woke him in the dark every morning. At a quarter of eight he had drunk his coffee and was about to leave the house to give his first exam when he saw her through the curtain, standing across the street. The day was overcast, intensifying color. Behind her were purple irises and a flaming azalea bush. She stood at the curb under a tree and he thought at first she was waiting for someone to give her a lift, though why at this hour, or why here, or where she might be going, he didn't know. He was, however, moved to see her and memorized this picture of her standing across the street alone.

May, in its middle, had turned disappointingly cold. June came in as bad. Heavy vaporous clouds, on the move from the Pacific, hid the sun except for unexpected minutes of light. It rained on and off. In the late afternoon the sun bloomed gold but give it a welcoming cheer and it sank in a red sea. Mrs. Beaty recalled many a wet cold summer. She wore long underwear, thick around the ankles under heavy stockings, and often drank hot tea. They decided to continue the furnace full time, for a while had been using no more than a half hopperful of sawdust each morning to flush the chill. The chill was there especially because it wasn't supposed to be, less than three weeks to summer.

He watched her from deep within, his hand still on the knob, nothing new about her that he could see. She wore her raincoat and black headscarf. Though she was a plain woman he could still see wherein she was lovely. It was this thought that had momentarily moved him. Also a sense of the waste of life. Of experience lived to what purpose? He knew she was waiting for him.

Levin went up the stairs and out by the back way. He climbed the fence, crossed a muddy yard, then over another wet fence to come out on a side street. He hurried to Humanities Hall by a roundabout route. All morning he wondered how long she had waited. He stayed in his office, grading papers. When he got back to the house, toward six, there was a note on the hall table, that Mrs. Gilley had called. He was both surprised that she would and that Mrs. Beaty would tell him so casually. Upstairs on his bureau lay a blue envelope addressed in Pauline's writing; it had been mailed yesterday. He put it into a drawer. Later that night, after returning from a walk he hadn't particularly wanted to take, Levin got out the letter and tore it open. He read it with spy glass from a distant planet. Then, by an effort of the will, he read it in his room. "I must see you—*please*. Can you call me? Pauline." An overwhelming sadness settled in him. If suffering was for something what had he suffered for? Levin burned her letter.

What renunciation was supposed to do he assumed it had done. Occasionally there were still unexpected moments of warm recall—his first sight of her in the forest, their falling in love, the bed at its best; but remembrance of the bed invariably led to thoughts of their last failures, nature uncooperative, hers. What he felt now—felt?—was abstraction, no more than the memory of memory. She stayed in the mind in the act of dropping into his unwilling lap the hot contents of a tuna fish casserole, mopping same with baby's diaper; he thought of her as the small town lady who talked of a new life but had been consistently afraid of it, never daring beyond the frontier of sex. He was at times harsh in judging her, Avis Fliss once removed. Wasn't that renunciation?

At his worst he blamed her for Duffy. Not that she had invented him; the man had an existence in history that Levin, almost from the moment of hearing his name, had in self-love been drawn to. But he blamed her for having used the Irishman against him, as it were, in a sense negating Levin's value as Levin. What she had probably wanted was someone like Duffy at a Duffyless time, so she settled for him come disguised with a beard. He held against her her never revealing the repetition she had fabricated, never told him whose carbon copy he was. She had not once whispered of her wild Irish lover, who, although he hadn't created it, had most recently lived the myth Levin fell into, or was dragged into assways. She had caused him to believe he was her first true love, Gilley not qualifying beyond somebody who had married her in a desperate moment (hers), although Levin had seen in her picture album also a Guggenheim scholar she had girlishly given her heart to, who had given it back. Before that, innocence; after, Duffy. Once he had heard about Leo from Avis, during the bad time he was having Levin thought he had lost the will to be Levin; that he was, so to say, the extension of Duffy's ghost. This sort of thing could become dangerous if it went too far. What most enraged him was clear evidence of the continued weakness of his old self.

He was thus affected until, as events developed, he had reason to distrust Avis as informant and began to wonder at some of his recent judgments of Pauline. From nothing to speak of he had more than once in his life erected fantastic structures, complicated Babels on stilts, overwrought constructions that collapsed under a single cold fact, or in whiff of sober sense. In talking with Fabrikant that night in his melon patch, Levin had realized doubts of his own suspicions that Pauline and Leo Duffy had been lovers. He knew only circumstantial details of an affair between them; her rumored confession to Gilley, authored, however, by Avis, author of the spying notebooks and the story of a picture she hadn't seen but could describe. If the photo existed, and Levin assumed it did, all it proved was that Pauline and Duffy had once gone swimming bareass together. End of evidence. What it proved about Gilley was a jackass of another color. From the supposition of the existence of the picture it was of course no trick to infer an affair between two discontented adults; yet a man of more than ordinary imagination, with good reason might infer nothing of the sort. Two and two was sometimes not two and two. If they had been lovers it would somehow have come out. She spoke openly of her life even when trying not to.

Having arrived here, Levin, explorer, ventured farther. Suppose there had been something between them—love, affair, love affair, what did that subtract from *him*, appearing on the scene two years later, Duffy, if not forgotten, long since gone? Nothing, if the mind stopped overreaching itself in creating analogies. As for telling or not telling him, so she hadn't—out of modesty, shame, pain—who knows how many motives lead to a single omission. Had he, for instance, told her about

Nadalee Hammerstad, for all her knowledgeability in bed not much more than a kid? Must Pauline confess who first had slipped his subtle fingers under her skirt; or he go back to age five, when he had packed earth in a little girl's backside through failure to think boldly? All this plus and minus in a long long world was nobody's business if privacy had any meaning. What Levin dwelt on was this: Was her love for him when it was love, less true because she had once loved Duffy, if she had loved Duffy? Why the obsessive linking of himself with the fabricated protoytpe, no more than just another guy trying to run into the meaning of his life, raising a little Cain in the process, and, in the nature of things, disappearing for good in all but name. There was enough in life to sneeze at without sniffing in dusty time. Let's admit—wherever Levin had been, someone had been before (no Chingachgook he, even in the primeval forest, even forest of the night). Two men with similar temperaments, possibly backgrounds and ideas, showing up after a short interval at the same all-but-unchanged locale, would see the same birds and flowers, walk the same streets, create similar adventures, and, not impossibly, love the same woman. What was wrong with my head? he asked himself. He blamed his overworked emotions and resolved to forget the long-departed Duffy.

Where did all this involved thinking leave him? It left him, a week before the election, electioneering. It left him much where one is left, he thought, who had suffered and renounced. Wherever he was he was left; if Levin, still in doubt. Recalling how deeply, tenderly, fervently—to the twisted core of his being—he had loved her, he could not understand how he had brought himself to give her up. Was it cowardice calling itself reason, or a true, even talented, reading of the hopelessness of the situation? It was hopeless; he had fled love to dispel her anxiety and misery. He had suffered to free her from suffering. He felt he had done the right thing; he sensed she had willed their break; he had carried it out for her.

Therefore, when he saw her through the front door he left by the back.

She was there, the image in the curtain, the next morning. Watching, he tried to feel something for her but felt nothing. I get this way, he thought. Levin escaped the back way, tearing his pants leg on a nail as he climbed the fence. A man in the neighboring house shook his fist at him. In the office a blue letter—guess who?—lay on his desk. He tore it up. Simply hopeless. Then he regretted what he had done, then tried not to.

Mrs. Beaty that afternoon nervously reported two phone calls. "She asked me if you knew she had been trying to get in touch with you and I said I thought you did. She said nothing after that, just hung up the phone."

"Thanks," he said. The old woman waited for more but got nothing.

Another call came while he was lying in bed, watching the rain. He had told her if it was Pauline to say he had gone out.

She walked slowly up the stairs and said through the door, though he pretended to be sleeping, "I told her what you told me to say, Mr. Levin, but please, you'll have to tell her yourself if she calls again."

He asked, after minutes, if she was lowering the drawbridge; she wanted to know what he meant.

"Aren't we still protecting the honor of your house?"

"Please don't be sarcastic with me, I'm an old woman. I'm sorry for her and I'm sorry for you."

"I'm in an election. I have my future to think of."

"Tell her yourself."

He tried to think what he could tell her but told her nothing. He reveried his life as a drunkard. He had suffocating dreams of walking miles for a bottle but when he got to the store he had no money. When he had got the money the store was closed. When the store opened he dropped the bottle on the sidewalk. Then he lay in a dank cellar watching his shoes burning. He woke apprehensive.

Looking out early on Wednesday he spied her coming up the back stairs. Like old times. Levin slipped out the front way as she was knocking upstairs. He called himself nasty names but saw no profit in the chase. The time to have come was a month ago.

Glancing out of his office window later he saw her, with Erik and Mary, in front of the Student Union. She waved, he retreated. She's surely mad. He stayed out of sight till she had left. Home, he tacked a sheet of heavy wrapping paper over the back door window, long overdue. Levin ate on the run and ran to a movie. He had considered leaving a note: "What can I give you? For Christ's sake, let's keep it quits." He lived in fear she would pop in at night, he would wake to find her in bed pumping his organ. But she did not appear; maybe Gilley kept a wide-open eye on her now.

Though he hungered to stay in bed the next morning, because he had slept badly and had no exam, he was dressed early to be out of the house before she appeared. He figured another day or two and the chase would end. He had waked heavy-hearted, a weight of sadness in every movement. He had felt this way, on and off, since the day she had reappeared. For three days he had tried to beat the mood but couldn't; he was uneasy that it persisted. Lifting the wrapping paper he looked cautiously out at one corner. Nothing but the wet world. He detested having to climb wet fences. At half-past seven Levin went downstairs and looked through the front door. She was standing in the rain under the dripping sycamore, with both kids. His teeth were on edge.

He went up to his room. It's useless, he thought. I can't outrun her.

Mrs. Beaty labored up the creaking stairs. "It's raining hard. The children are getting wet."

"Have you talked to her?"

"Just for a minute."

"What does she want?"

"She'll have to tell you herself."

For five minutes he listened to her breathing at his door.

"Ask her to come in," said Levin.

He heard her go down and open the front door. Then he heard her speaking and Pauline saying something to her, and they all came in.

Levin looked at himself in the mirror and looked away. He went to the window and gazed at the back fences but returned to the mirror. He did not remember going to the stairs, only going down them.

Pauline, holding Mary on her arm, ground her teeth. The little girl began to cry.

Mrs. Beaty took her. "We'll make coffee." She took Erik's hand and they went into the kitchen.

When they were alone Pauline said, "I'm sorry, I wanted to leave them but I couldn't get anyone to sit at this hour."

She looked weary, harried, lonely. Her face was taut, small, her dark eyes, restless. "Why did you run from me?" she said bitterly. "Why didn't you call when I asked you to?"

"Does Gerald know you came here?"

"No. He's always at the office early during exam week."

"Come inside."

They entered the small parlor off the hall. She sat in one stiff-backed chair at the wet window, he in the other at the wall opposite. The clock ticked above his head. She had removed her wet raincoat and scarf; her hair hung in dark rattails. Turning her head away from him she wiped her eyes with her fingers. Outside it was raining steadily. He listened to the sound of the rain.

"Not much of a spring, I guess." She had slipped off her shoes, twisting one long foot behind the other. "I hope you don't mind, my shoes are damp."

The depression Levin felt, hung in him like a dead animal. Where's my love gone? He wanted to warn her something was wrong; instead he hid it.

She asked, then, why he had stopped seeing her.

Levin, after long silence, spoke. "At first to help you. After a while I felt you no longer wanted to see me. I got used to it."

"It's true," she said. "I didn't."

"I figured that, I tried to help you."

"If you had written once at least."

"I hoped you would, it had to be by your choice. What could I do under the circumstances? You didn't let me know how you had got into the house—or if you had got in though you knew I'd be sweating it out. Not hearing from you I felt you wanted to call it quits."

"I didn't call purposely. I did it for *you*, not to involve you further in my confusions. I ate myself about you but I was terribly unhappy about Gerald and the children. I had got into the house without the least trouble. He wasn't there, he had left at four to go fishing with George. He thought I had come in and gone to sleep in Erik's room, and didn't want to wake me—I'd been sleeping so badly. The kids were alone in the house from four till almost eight. There were signs Mary had waked and cried herself back to sleep. Erik had gone looking for me and then began to play with his toys. When I got back, he cried as though he had found out for all time what a bitch I was. That I wasn't his mother and never would be. What if there had been a fire? I would have killed myself. That was my state of mind for most of a week and I decided I must give you up—my love for you. I imagined you would know, when you saw Gerald, that I had got in safely."

He said he had known.

"I swore to myself I'd be a better mother, and wife. I did everything I could to suit myself to him, to be less critical, to enjoy life with him. I did everything, short of cutting my throat, to forget you."

"Ah—" said Levin.

"The more I tried—I hope you don't mind hearing this—the less I could. There were days when I almost didn't think of you, when I felt I had killed you in me, but the very thought renewed my feeling of loss so profoundly that sometimes I felt I had left drops of blood where I was standing when I had thought of you last. But I kept trying to end you in me, and I was, bit by bit, until I saw you at Orville's funeral. When I saw you then, your face so lonely without the beard you had cut off to protect me, what was left of my heart beat itself silly trying to get to you. I realized then how much beyond recall I was in love with you. If you had come over to me and said I was to go with you, I would have gone. Afterwards I fought against myself for your sake—to save your plans—until I no longer could. Then I thought, I must go to him, and that's what I did."

Levin sat like a broken statue. The destruction of love she could not commit he had accomplished.

The landlady brought in two cups of coffee on a silver tray.

Pauline had her handkerchief to her eyes.

"I'm sorry for your trouble," Mrs. Beaty said.

"And I to trouble you."

"There's none at all. The children are playing with my pots and pans."

"We'll be leaving soon—"

The landlady set the coffee cups on the small tables near each chair and returned to the kitchen.

Pauline held her cup in her palms.

Levin did not touch his. He grew desperate to leave.

"When we got home from the funeral," she was saying, looking at the cup in her hands, "I went upstairs and tried to sleep. But I thought about Gerald, about all the kind things he had done for me. I found myself thinking that my character had deteriorated with his. I overlook too much in both of us that I oughtn't to. I try to be honest and I'm not when I want most to be. He knows I no longer love him but he can stand it so long as I keep my mouth shut and we go on living together. He gives me little, I give him less. I try but fail with him, we fail together. I don't want to any more. I want a better life. I want it with you."

He listened in petrification.

"Lev, I love you. Be my love again."

He muttered what of her husband.

"I've made up my mind to ask for a divorce. I feel I'm entitled to my love for you. I've worn out the obligation—if it is that—of living half a life. I want to be your wife."

He rose hastily, upsetting the cup on the table. Levin watched the stain spreading on the rug. He ran to the kitchen for something to mop it with.

Why don't I keep on running?

But he returned with a cloth and dabbed at the rug. She wanted to do it but he wouldn't let her.

When he came back from the kitchen again she was standing barefoot at the window, watching the rain. She turned to him with eyes like sad flowers.

I've got to be honest with her, Levin thought. That may be all I have left to give.

"Pauline," he said heavily, "I'm sorry for the way I am now—"

"Don't you feel well?"

"I'm not myself—"

"Have I upset you?"

"To tell the truth, I wasn't expecting this—"

"That I would come back?"

"Yes—" She went to him, put her arms around him. "Hold me, please hold me."

He held her.

"Hold me tightly."

Levin tightened his arms. She gazed at him as though he had just returned from a long voyage and she was trying to remember what he was like in a former time.

"Don't you love me any more?"

"Love—" he said with a heavy heart. "Who knows what I've mangled—"

She seemed to shrink, then held him harder. "I love you, say you love me. Say it the way you used to."

Holding her, he strove to say it, groping from one obscure thought to another for an explanation, the secret of what afflicted him, anything that might free him to love her. At last Levin said, "Why didn't you tell me you and Leo Duffy were lovers?"

She pushed him away. "Oh God, is that what's bothering you?"

"I don't know—"

"I thought you knew, that Avis or someone had told you but you never mentioned it to be kind to me. If I loved him what difference would it make?"

"I want to know the truth—"

"The truth is we were lovers, sexually, once. I slept with him the day he was publicly fired. If you want to know where, it was in his car that night. I've had that experience too—"

"Did you love him?"

"Not then, but I fell in love with him after he had gone. Now you know what I'm like—"

"Are you sure you still don't love him?"

She smiled sadly. "Leo's dead."

Levin shuddered. "Dead?"

"He died last year. His mother wrote in the spring that he had killed himself in January. I don't know the circumstances and couldn't bring myself to ask—"

"I'm sorry—"

"He left a note: 'The time is out of joint. I'm leaving the joint.'"

Levin sprang to her and they desperately embraced.

He packed both bags and drove off along a lonely road lined with black cypresses, past a railroad crossing, full granary, and deserted farmhouse. He was making good time when the car gave out with a clunk. Abandoning suitcase and valise, he took off on foot, the dust of the road settling on him. He had run through the day and was on night's tail when an obscure figure appeared on the road, coming at him from a mirror, the opposing self or its spitting image.

QUO VADIS, LEVIN?

Towards freedom.

Loud laughter in the wings.

He awoke clammy, and spent half the night wandering amid the crosses row by row in a graveyard of mangled hopes, purposes, schemes. Hadn't he planned—it said in his notebook—to be a college professor? To Straighten Out His Life? Come To Something? He hadn't planned to be entangled with a married woman. To be anyone's second husband before he was somebody's first. To be this unsettled, confused, tormented, at this time of his life. He suffered from Unfinished Business. He wanted to win the election. Now that classes were over, he was moved by an oppressive desire to rush to Humanities Hall and teach all who would listen, the mysteries of the infinitive.

Flight flew in him. He wasn't fleeing yet fled, unable to determine whom he was running from, himself or her. He blamed the flight, paradoxically a pursuit of feeling, on the fact that too much had happened in too short a time. He couldn't cram it all in, experience leaked out, confusing subjectivity. He had, since their separation, harbored a secret belief that they had through love marked each other for future use; he hadn't expected the future to explode in his face, shattering all he had to think, decide, do. The responsibility was terrifying—taking away another man's wife, the miserable mess of divorce, having to fit himself to her, all her habituations and impedimenta, to suit to her clutter his quiet bachelor's life, needs, aspirations, plans, which though more than once destroyed and replaced, remained essentially what they had been, except that their fulfillment was farther in front of the nose with every step he took. He was distended by the fast thrust of events, of too many revived possibilities—where would he put them all? He feared his destiny had been decided apart from him, by chance, her, not him. She called the signals and he awoke running in the play. He had grave doubts, if he took her on again, that he could be master of his fate to any significant degree; he had already lost—the terrible thing—his freedom to feel free.

Levin beat himself into a concrete frenzy to resuscitate his love for her, but try breathing green, purple, rose. He tried every way he could, by every use of the imagination, to recapture love as it had been in fullest flower, as though the mind could recreate what it apparently rejected. Memory was a dark door leading through dark doors floating in space to Orpheus always descending. Levin a whirlwind of enraged impotence at what had become of him. In love he had unwillingly pulled the stopper, ug glug, no further feeling. This though he told himself he *must* still love her. Love for her was in him as experience, as valued idea, pleasure received, which he wanted to repeat. Except it wasn't where it had been, or should be. He had had and hadn't it. What in Christ's name had he done with the love he had only a month ago felt for her? Had he butchered it in the vise of will, sublimated it beyond repair, or recall, like a magician prestidigitating a girl into a tree, then forgetting the hocus pocus so that when he wanted a woman he embraced wood? Was such a thing even remotely possible? These thoughts drew others equally unhappy into their orbit. Was it love murdered or love imperfect, less than love to begin with? Had he loved her for the lay and not much else, giving it a tainted reciprocity of feeling? Was it a guilty response to experience he should have accepted as one accepts sunlight? Why must he forever insist on paying for being alive?

And with the lay as good as gone—he had believed—had he then, after a show of self-castigation to make himself look decent in the mirror, stopped loving the little he had loved? Or would this, in time, have happened anyway, out of boredom, without the necessity of a sudden decisive surrender of her? Or was his interest in Pauline basically that she belonged to someone else—life's initial tease—and once he had her as far as she went, when her thing broke down in various motels, best send her back to daddy, the lover's gut glutted? Who knows the answer? Not Levin. But why scratch sores to see what lies under them? "Thought is a disease of the flesh." T. Hardy said it, not the diseased Levin. Levin couldn't stop scratching: if it was none of these things then wasn't it really as in the past—the thought returned—the suffocating quasi-deadness (alas poor Duffy) of going through more than he could stand, nervously frazzled to the point of immobility? Can I give out with only three pints of feeling before the well runs dry? Is it nerves, glands, the broken machine itself? What's to blame: the poor quality of his love, how beat to death, or the imperfections of an imperfect man? Or, please God, that he had simply gone through her, she no longer interested him as a person—perfectly normal and he was making a sickness out of it? Conscience the rotting onion in the mind's stomach. Whatever the answer or answers, the doubt most in his mind was What to Do: Was it best to stall for time—wait it out and hope to approach her again with a full heart, to which she was entitled; or must he commit himself now, no matter how bad he felt, or couldn't feel? In her mind she had parted from Gilley and was alone in his house, possibly frightened at all that lay ahead to be done. He felt for her a blunted compassion, not enough to give relief but at least a response.

Everdrowning Levin saw the thirsty world from under the sea. It wasn't the world, it was more of the sea. He was a lone fish poking its snoot into bursting bubbles. On the bank sat Gilley with hook, line, sinker. The poor fish fled. Levin in watery flight followed confused currents. Every way out was his way in. He fantasied self-destruction, fish hooking self, funny for a fish. (Duffy, proud bird, had blown his coop.) . . . He woke in terrible thirst and frantically searched for a bottle in the bottom drawer until remembering he had long ago dumped it into the garbage can. He tried drowning thirst in water, drinking glass after glassful until his stomach bloated. He bathed in Mrs. Beaty's tub, thirstily soaping himself six times over but still was thirsty, thick as toothache, fire in the mouth, boiling lead dripping down his salted gullet. Levin dressed in the dry middle of the night and walked in rain till the rain stopped. He stood on the riverbank watching the thirsty-fingered dawn on the surface of the hidden water. For hours he wandered in downtown streets, his eyes glazed as he gazed through glass, thirsting to dive into a whiskey bottle. What sweet relief to feel the searing stuff go through his tortured throat. To feel the sodden spirit soar. To be in peace not Levin. To lie pickled thirstless, satisfied. Wandering, he cast love-sick glances at both brown-bottled tavern windows, drunk with emptiness, wrenching himself along in rectangular circles, until broken by weariness he pushed through a door and stood solemnly at a bar.

"What'll it be?" said the hairy bartender.

"Love," Levin said, and as the man looked for the bottle, fled.

Hiding under the rattling boards of the old river bridge as the sun set, dust sifting into his hair whenever a car rumbled overhead, Levin, the machinery of his existence creaking, in a private place in the mind put things together thus: that he, S. Levin, the self again betrayed by the senses (if not vice-versa), did not presently desire her, in no way diminished her as one worthy of love (his), and what is worth loving is worth love, or the other way around. What I had from forest to last frustration was worth having—I respect what it was. If I could have it again, I would. I have no cause now not to love her, granted I loved; I grant. I loved her; we loved. She loves me still, I have never been so loved. That was the premise, and the premise you chose was the one you must live with; if you chose the wrong one you were done to begin with, your whole life in jail. You cheated yourself of the short freedom you had in the world, the little of life to be alive in. He craftily told himself time alters everything, premises wear out, change produces incompatibles. He sniffed out reasons to escape, go where he pleased, unbound, unburdened, where fancy fancied and the feet followed. . . . Then by devious ways he returned to the premise: She was his love, changed by it only as he by hers. What had changed beyond that was badly willed, now unwilled. A man sentenced to death may regain freedom; so may love. It was possible, it surely had happened. No matter what he had suffered or renounced, to what degree misused or failed feeling, if Pauline loving him loves; Levin with no known cause not to will love her. He would without or despite feeling. He would hold on when he wanted terribly to let go. Love had led him, he would now lead love. Having reasoned thus he cursed reason.

They talked that night in his car, parked on a country road, black fields on both sides. He had for an hour felt relief at a decision made, had begun, he had thought, to anticipate seeing her. But after picking her up on a street not far from her house, he knew it still wasn't right. The feeling he had tried to feel, had in her presence disappeared like a flight of birds sucked into an underworld; or maybe blown the other way, scattered and lost in the sky. He once more hid imprisonment.

It was a cold spring night. Fog drifted in patches across the road. Gray clouds hung low; the quarter moon when it momentarily slipped through, looked lusterless, odd. Levin was his stiff, numb, shattered self. Pauline rubbed her cold nose against his rigid jaw. She teased him to kiss her. More than once he told himself he was no longer in love with her. The reason didn't matter, the condition did. Having thought it he denied it, weary of denial.

She was bright with plans for them. He had his own: delay, let her say nothing to Gilley, forestall any final commitment. He must see the election through. Win or lose, he wanted another year at the college. He hoped for the dean's recommendation. Next year would be soon enough to talk of marriage.

But when he suggested that, she asked whether he expected her to go on living with Gerald.

I'm sure you understand I can't. And when I move out of his house what sort of recommendation do you think you'll get once he lets it be known why we have separated?

She urged him to let her tell Gerald tonight—she could no longer stand keeping it from him. They would settle things, and when Levin had his grades in, would leave. She spoke of a Nevada divorce so they would not have to wait a year to get married. She had a little money that her father had left her, and the divorce could be got comparatively cheaply if she stayed with a college friend in Carson City, the girl she had told him about, with the mismatched breasts. He could live, meanwhile, in San Francisco, more beautiful, less overpowering than New York City. After she got back from the divorce, if he had decided to return to graduate school in the fall they could get married and go. They would somehow get along. The references he needed he could get from the professors he worked under. If he would rather give up teaching, her uncle in San Francisco would help him find a job.

She's got it all planned. He wrestled a rage against her, answered nothing.

Then shall I tell him? she asked. He senses something's wrong but doesn't know what. He tends to wait for a situation to disappear and this one won't. I feel sorry for him. I think we ought to tell him.

The moon had gone again, the fog risen. He felt spasms of irritation and self-disgust.

What's the matter, darling? You're so quiet. Aren't you well?

He denied it.

Don't keep anything from me, like that time you had the pain I didn't know about.

Though Levin craftily warned himself to keep his yap shut to protect his undiminished pride, to keep whole her image of him as a man, he at last confessed how tormented he still was.

I feel as though I no longer can love, as though all feeling were buried in me under a rock. I'm in that again. I told you about it that time in the woods. It's a hellish thing.

In the dark she turned pale, embraced him tightly, blamed herself for his trouble, for not knowing her own mind.

I should long ago have agreed to leave Gerald. Her eyes glistened. Don't you feel anything for me?

I'm worn out. It's a terrible emptiness.

Suppose the truth is you just don't love me any more?

He said, after long hesitation, he had no reason not to.

Then maybe you ought to see a doctor?

No, said Levin, I've been through it before. I know what it is.

What will you do?

Wait it out.

How long did it last the last time?

Months. Maybe a year. I'm not sure.

It needn't again.

No?

You're not alone any more.

He had forgotten.

Are you afraid? Pauline asked.

More of the world than anything else.

My darling, she said. They held each other.

Levin recalled their fruitless nights in motels. Should we go somewhere? he said.

Go where?

To my room, or maybe in the field now. We both have our coats.

But she said no. I've thought of that but decided not to. If we get married—if we ever do—I'd rather not till then. I want to come to you with a little innocence saved up.

Abstaining makes you a virgin?

I'm withholding it from myself. Help me to a little virtue, Lev.

Virtue lies between the legs?

It's a way of being despite what you've been.

Then she kissed him with cold lips. I'll sleep with you if you have to prove something to yourself.

No.

Please love me, she said. Don't not love me. Please protect me. I'm afraid to be alone. She began to cry.

Don't cry, Levin said. I love you.

I'm crying for the way things are.

He let her cry.

She wiped her eyes with a handkerchief. If we broke up you couldn't be sure, could you, that it would be what you really wanted?

No.

I believe in you, do you in me?

He said he did.

Then hadn't I better tell Gerald?

He said the hard thing was to make decisions without confidence in his feelings. Couldn't we wait till the end of summer? I might have it licked by then.

It will take till then till I get my divorce. I think we ought to do what I suggested before. I'll leave Gerald and we'll go to San Francisco. After that if things turn out well, they turn out well. If they don't, we won't get married.

Her eyes misted again.

Secretly relieved, he sat in silence.

Only I don't believe in that kind of end for us, do you? she asked.

He said no.

Then shall I tell Gerald?

He said yes.

*

He woke in the dark, both arms flailing. A light blinded him. Papers fluttered in the room as a cold wind blew in through the open door. I got to lock it, Levin thought, struggling to sleep.

A figure emerged at the foot of the bed.

Levin sat upright. "Don't shoot."

Gilley stood there in shirt sleeves, his face agitated, eyes lit in hatred of the one in bed.

"You goddamn two-faced, two-assed, tin-saint hypocrite, preaching reform all the while you were committing adultery with my wife!"

Levin lay back, groaning.

"Don't deny it, you slimy do-gooder, false pretender to virtue. You ought to be strung up—"

"I confess I loved—do love—her—"

"Preach one thing, practice the opposite, a dirty thief throwing up a filthy smoke screen while stealing a man's wife from him."

"We were in love—"

"You're two of a kind—"

Levin slowly sat up. "Are you so innocent?"

"What do you mean?" Gilley thundered.

"You drove her to it, a man not above taking a picture of his naked wife and showing it to a dozen people."

Gilley's jaw sagged. He raised his arm as if to defend himself and couldn't. Looking wearily around he located a chair but didn't get to it. His eyes had turned glassy, his mask of misery fitted his face.

"CD told you?" he sighed.

"Your pal Avis—"

"She shouldn't have. She gave— You haven't told Pauline, have you? She doesn't know about it."

"I'd be ashamed to."

"I was desperate."

"I'll bet you look at it every day."

Gilley shook his head miserably. "It's been destroyed. Not by me, I'll admit, though I would have by now if he hadn't. Duffy did it. I hid the one print I had developed, and the negative, in his folder in my files. One night he sneaked into my office—I'll never know how unless he picked my lock—I wouldn't put that past him—and he stole everything in the folder, all his incriminating records, and the picture of them, and burned it in my wastebasket. I found the ashes the next morning."

"Bravo!"

"She drove me to it," Gerald said heavily. "First she took up for him, then with him. I suspected something was fishy and watched her, as I ought to have done with you around if I hadn't been so stupid in underestimating what you were capable of. One day I got wind they were going to the coast and I followed them. My Leica was in the glove compartment of the car. I always keep it loaded—"

"It was loaded so you snapped."

"Spare me, for Pete's sake. Both of my ears hurt. You're in no position to be preaching to me."

"My error," muttered Levin.

"I admit that taking that picture was a mistake, although I thought I might need it for a divorce, but that certainly doesn't excuse you for all the harm you've done here. I want to warn you about one thing, don't bet on her love for you, if that's what it is. All she sees in you is a certain resemblance to somebody else."

"Explain that one."

"I will," said Gilley. "A few months after she found out Leo Duffy had bumped himself off, or however he did it, she picked your application out of a pile I happened to be studying. I had my strong doubts about that but in a minute of foolishness let her. She was still in a funk about him and blaming herself for his suicide. I felt bad myself, though I honestly had no reason to, so I let her."

"Let her what?"

"Pick your application as the one we would take. I had brought home a pile half a foot high from people looking for jobs. We had had a man renege out of his appointment because he had got a better offer, and I had to replace him on very short notice. I had previously put you in the discards as unsuitable, but Pauline was reading the newspaper at the dining table where I was working and her eye just happened to light on your picture among the discarded applications. She picked up yours and read through it. The next thing I knew she was advising me to hire you, a thing she usually keeps out of. I was suspicious right off but wanted to show I was sympathetic to how she was feeling, so I said I would. What a cockeyed mistake that was."

"Why did she pick me?"

"She said she thought your experience was good and liked the letter you had written about your ideas of teaching composition, which I thought was pretentious when I read it. I guess it also appealed to her that you were from New York. Duffy was from the East."

"Chicago?"

"That's East out here. There were other resemblances between you both."

"Why did you let her if you didn't trust her choice?"

"Frankly, I didn't think she could be interested in you after seeing your picture. Yet I admit I did feel that if I took her suggestion I'd live to regret it."

"Was Duffy a handsome man?"

"In his way. But that was a good trick of yours coming with a beard."

"Trick?"

"Pauline has always had odd tastes."

"I tricked her and she tricked you?"

"She'll do the same to you. She's a discontented woman and I could tell you more. If you were to marry her you'd find that out soon enough, and I'd pity you when you did."

"If that's the case why do you want to keep her?"

"I love her," he said miserably.

Levin socked himself hard on the chest.

Gilley then came up with a proposition: "We've both made mistakes, though I wouldn't have done to you half of what you did to me. What I have to say is that I'm willing to forgive and forget if you will resign and leave. I promise you good references."

But Levin sadly shook his head.

"She's all I've got," Gerald said brokenly.

The instructor lay back with both eyes shut.

On Monday the acting head let it be known through Avis Fliss and George Bullock that he and his wife were separating, with an assist by Mr. S. Levin. The halls were thick with talk as department members came in to hand in their grades and get on their gowns for the Commencement ceremony. People avoided Levin and he avoided them. The next day the election was held in Dean Seagram's office. Levin did not attend. Neither did Bucket. The first and final vote for head of department was Gilley 17, Fabrikant 2, Levin 0. Though he had expected nothing less, Levin, poor man's Parnell, somewhere in his buried self felt shame and loss. He might have led.

In his mailbox was a note from Gilley. "I am willing to let you stay on for one last year, provided you promise not to see my wife again, or otherwise interfere in our lives. G. Gilley, Head of Dept. P.S. In thinking it over we will use the books your committee recommended. G.G."

Levin did not reply. Later in the day he received by messenger an official communication from President Marion Labhart, terminating his services "as of today, in the public interest, for good and sufficient cause of a moral nature." He referred to the ex-instructor, among other things, as a "frustrated Union Square radical."

Levin put his fist through Duffy's bloody window.

HE AWOKE with Pauline in his arms. She had kissed him awake. "Mrs. Beaty let me come up when I told her I was upset and had to see you."

Levin, realizing it was no dream, sat up slowly. She moved back on the bed, looking worn, tired, lonely. She was hastily dressed and in doubt.

"How's your hand?"

"Better."

He lit a cigarette with his bandaged hand.

"I never saw you smoke before."

"I go back to it sometimes."

"What else do you go back to?"

"What do you have in mind?"

"Nothing really. I'm sorry I'm nervous." She asked, "How do you feel?"

"I slept badly, thinking of the job."

"But you knew you would lose it. Even if you had won the election you would have lost your job once people knew why I was leaving Gerald."

"For a short time in my life I felt I was able to say what would happen to me next."

"There are other jobs," Pauline said. "But if you think you're sacrificing the right thing for the wrong woman, you can call it off. Don't be too proud to admit defeat."

He said he wasn't.

Pauline said, "Gerald left last night and went to the hotel until I leave the house. We had a nasty argument about the children. He said he'd contest my divorce and not let me have them. He accused me of deserting them in spirit long ago. I said the truth was I had long ago deserted him but hadn't the courage to say so. Our marriage was in shreds after Leo left, but the children kept it together until I fell in love with you."

She got her handkerchief out of her bag. "I've never seen him so hurt and unyielding. He asked me not to leave him, and when I said it was for the good of us all he got very bitter and said if it was a question of whose good it was, he would keep Erik and Mary."

She blew her nose. "I'm blowing my nose," she said. "He has been an affectionate father but I've always thought of them as more mine than his. I was the one who really wanted them. He made me wait almost six years before we put in adoption papers. After he left I kept waking up every hour and wanting to look at the kids. I went upstairs several times. I've been so positive he would let me have them and I almost died when he said no. Please help me get them, Lev."

He had always known she would want them. I'm in so far already, he thought.

He said he would help her.

"I hate to burden you further," she said. "But you really don't have to marry me."

"We've gone through all that," he said.

"Why are you then?"

"I've told you."

"Tell me again."

"I love you."

"Without feeling?"

"As I am."

"You love me on principle?"

"Yes."

"Is that all?"

"No."

"How else?"

He was silent.

"I get afraid," Pauline said. "It's so easy to make a serious mistake." She said, after a minute, "Will you talk to him? He wouldn't listen to me."

"Would it be so bad to leave them with him?"

"What would he do with them? Either he'd have to bring someone in to take care of them or send them to his parents. I don't want strangers bringing up my children."

"Couldn't he take one and we'd have the other?"

"I couldn't do that, they both need me. They're still babies."

"Suppose I said I didn't want them?"

"I don't think you would."

Levin asked, "What do you want me to do?"

"Talk to Gerald and persuade him to let us keep them."

"What makes him think he could take them from you?"

"He said he would tell the court I wasn't a fit mother."

"Don't cry."

"I wouldn't if you put your arms around me."

He did that, thinking he hadn't planned to see Gilley again, either.

Pauline waited downstairs while he shaved and dressed. It took him longer than usual, partly because of his bandaged hand. When Levin came down, they were all in the kitchen, the kids playing with Mrs. Beaty's pots. Pauline was having a cup of coffee with the landlady.

"Good wishes if I may, Mr. Levin," Mrs. Beaty said.

"Lev want to marry Mama," said Erik.

"Would you like a cup of coffee?" Pauline asked, reddening. "Mrs. Beaty very kindly made a fresh potful."

"I'll eat later."

"You can now, there's no rush."

"I'd rather go now."

Levin called the office but Milly said Dr. Gilley was staying at the Covered Wagon Hotel. They drove downtown in Levin's car. Summer had come, the day was warm. They said little.

In the hotel lobby Levin asked, "Are we all going up?"

Pauline, tense, shook her head. "I'd rather not. I will though if you want me to."

"Wait here," said Levin.

"Tell him I want Erik and Mary and mean to have them. If he wants to go to court that's all right with me."

Then she said, "Maybe you'd better not say it that way. Speak to him nicely. Maybe he'll relent. Do you think he will?"

"I don't know."

"Try not to make him angry—any more than he is."

He said he would try.

She pressed his hand.

In the elevator he thought: I've slept with his wife and here I come asking for his kids. He felt he wanted to give Gilley back everything he had taken from him and more.

Levin stood in front of the door five minutes before he knocked.

Gerald, in a seersucker robe, unshaven, dark half-moons under his eyes, opened the door.

"Oh, it's you."

"Sorry to bother you again," Levin said, "but there's one last thing I have to see you about." He was ready to step back if Gilley slammed the door in his face.

"Come in," Gerald said. The magazines and newspapers he had been reading were strewn around the armchair and base of the lit pink lamp in the darkish hotel room.

He looks like a misplaced bachelor, Levin thought, and I feel long since married.

"Pardon the small room," Gilley said. He sat in the armchair, crossing his long red-haired legs. "I was hoping you'd show up."

Levin sat on the edge of a hard chair. "I'm sorry I've been such a thorn in your side, Gerald."

"More a pain in the ass," Gilley said. "And if you're so goddamn sorry, why don't you close up shop and go haunt some other neighborhood? Why did you have to pick on me? I've worked doggone hard in my life and don't know why I shouldn't be allowed to live in peace with my wife and kids and enjoy the fruits of my labor."

"The reason I've come," Levin said, "is to ask for the children. They'll miss their mother. She says they'd only be in your way."

"If their mother wants them so much why didn't she act like one? Why didn't she consider their welfare before breaking up their home?"

He was haughty, embittered, so unhappy Levin found it hard to look at him.

Neither of them spoke until Gerald, uncrossing his legs, said, "I thought you'd be more than glad for me to take them off your hands, but if you're asking to have them for her, that shows you don't really have any true idea what you're in for. Up to now you've had a free ride on my back, although I can't blame you entirely, I suppose. I know darn well it wasn't all your fault, and that's why I opened the door to you just now instead of punching your eye. But the way you're acting convinces me, if I haven't already been convinced along other lines of the same thing, that you are a very inexperienced person. I mean with women as they really are and not as they pretend to be, or as they are when it's a question of going to bed with them. I don't doubt you're in love with my wife. Duffy was too, but that's not the whole of it. A lot you don't know will pop up the minute you begin to live as man and wife under the same roof. Up to then the picture might as well be something you think you're seeing whereas the real thing is something else again after it's been developed. That's why I thought I ought to talk to you before you go on with this."

"I appreciate it," Levin said, "but I know what you mean."

"You can't," said Gilley, "unless you've been married to her for years. First off, she has some qualities that would drive even the most patient man, and I am one of them—crazy. If you want to know why I want her back if that's the case, and after she has twice deceived and humiliated me, the reason is understandable. I'm used to her and know what to expect. She can't surprise me any more, good or bad, though this would be her last chance with the bad. I've had it. Yet I'd be a liar not to admit there are some wonderful things about Pauline or why am I bothering to talk to you now? But as somebody thinking of marrying a woman who has been married a dozen years, the best and freshest of her youth, you are due for some unpleasant surprises, and I wouldn't be surprised myself in the least to hear that you and she break up within six months if you are so foolish as to marry her. In order to save you unforeseen trouble I'll give you some idea what she's like."

"I know what she's like—"

"You think you do. I've already told you she is never contented, but I don't think you understand what that means. She was born dissatisfied, as some people are—Fabrikant comes to mind, and I could mention others—or maybe she was brought up that way. Whatever it is, even when as a student she turned in some very good term papers to me, which I gave high A's to, she never was satisfied. She always said she felt she should have done better. Not that she *could*, mind you, but that she *should* have, as though all you have to do to execute a better performance is to wish for it. I blame her old man for this, to some extent. I understand he was a fine physician and a nice thoughtful person—I've suffered myself from his virtues—but it's plain to me that he gave her a blown-up idea of herself. She was an only child, too, be that as it may. If you make the mistake of tying yourself to her, more than once—I guarantee—you'll wake up at six A.M. to hear her already going on about her life and how it didn't pan out as she wanted it to. When you ask her what she had expected, all she can tell you is that she wanted to be a better person than she is. And this, as is obvious, from a woman who admits to two extra-marital lovers in the last three years. Then you will hear in long detail everything she thinks she has done wrong, or those things she tried to do and had to give up, or everything she now does and does badly. She will never once tell you what she does well, which can get pretty monotonous. After that she'll blame you for as much as she blames herself, because you married her—in my case when she was twenty—and didn't do what she calls 'bring me out,' meaning make out of her something she couldn't make out of herself though you may have broken your back trying to think up new ways to do it. I've suggested courses, taken her on trips, kept her on a decent budget even when I couldn't so well afford it, given her a position in the community, a car, fine home, children just as real and lovable as anyone else's, although adopted, and in general tried everything I know to make her happy. And when she's through with that complaint she will have worked herself up into a nervous jag, so that unless you get out of the house early you'll be having an argument with her that may run through the day and into the night, just to the time, let's say, when you might be thinking of a little natural satisfaction. The next day it'll take her half the morning to wake up because she hasn't slept well, which happens more often than you would think. I'm not saying I hold these things against her, and I'm willing to bet that if you asked her right now she'll admit I've always been considerate. Maybe it's just the way her nervous system is built. It might be what used to be called 'delicate.' Almost anything can throw off her balance and start you both being miserable."

Levin shifted in his chair.

Gilley went on: "If you happen to want someone who is a good housekeeper and will keep the house as neat and orderly as I've seen your office—I'm not talking about those fireballs who do canning, baking, gardening, civic activities, refinishing furniture, bean picking in summer, and play tennis besides keeping up the usual household chores—I am talking about a reduced scale of domestic efficiency—well, you'd better forget it. She has her periods of efficiency, I admit, usually in the spring and early fall, but there are times when for one reason or another she can't get organized enough to clean the toilet and I have to do it after a full day's work, especially on a day she has spent most of the time with a pile of cookbooks around her, cooking a dinner that should take two hours to prepare instead of seven, and is not anything super-special anyway. That's why we don't entertain as much as I would like. She doesn't care for housework—it bores her, and even on days she is concentrating on getting it done, her resistance to it cuts down on her accomplishment. That's why I frankly thought we were better off not adopting for a while because I knew she'd be more swamped than ever. As soon as I could afford a cleaning woman for her twice a week I agreed to having the kids. I know how finicky you are to order and punctuality, but if you marry her you can bury your clock for all the good it will do you. Not only does she resist time, she makes it her enemy."

"I'm not such good friends with it either," Levin sighed.

"What I mean is that for years—this started in her twenties—she has been keeping track of her wrinkles and lamenting the passing of her youth, which, I take it, was from eighteen to twenty-five, and I can't convince her otherwise. With me around she has the advantage of my forty-five years as a comparison to her thirty-two, but with you and your thirty or thirty-one, you can imagine what that might do to her morale. She'll be older with you than she is with me, older at every age and, believe me, you won't find any advantage to it. Living with Pauline though it can be pleasant is generally no bed of roses."

"I have never slept on flowers."

"And then there are her health problems."

"I'd rather not hear—"

"It won't take a minute. I won't call her health bad but she has her problems that you'd better know about. After thirty a woman doesn't get any younger. She sometimes has constipation, which I won't go into, but the real nuisance is her female troubles on and off. When you least expect it, she goes into her nine-day-or-so period that is caused by what they call anovulatory cycle or some such name. The doctor says that with her it's more a nuisance than anything serious and could clear up on its own, which it sometimes does, but the result is that you never know where you stand when your instincts are up. No doubt she saved her best times for you but you'll be making a mistake if you take her for a sexy babe. Once you're married to her you can bet your boots that many times when you are looking forward to your satisfaction there is nothing doing that night. You might just as well beat your brains out then as argue with her to go to see a doctor. She's afraid of them and resists till she gets so wound up from worry that when she finally does go, your bill is twice as high as it should have been. Think of that on your salary."

"Excuse me," Levin said. "What I came about is the children—"

"I was getting to that," said Gilley. "They also have their troubles, as all kids do. Little Mary is generally healthy but has eczema all summer, and the pediatrician has warned Pauline she could go into asthma overnight—it's some kind of strong allergic condition. She gets shots that are costing me over a hundred dollars a year. And Erik never stops having colds he can't shake off, that either go into bronchitis or ear infections. One month this past winter his antibiotics bill alone came to sixty dollars. He's also had strep throat three times and the pediatrician is always testing for a possible low-grade rheumatic fever as a result of the streptococcus. He doesn't think Erik is such a sick kid but Pauline has yet to stop worrying about him, and when she worries, brother, you worry."

Levin, fanning himself with his good hand, continued to listen.

"I said before there are some wonderful things about Pauline—I wouldn't in the least call her a flop. Though you mightn't guess it she plays a good game of golf. She also began to learn how to ski a few years back, but I can't, so we don't go often. She's also good around the garden. She reads a lot, listens to music—I built her a hi-fi—and she has knitted me some nice sweaters and socks. She has wanted to go to work but I'd rather have her at home because that's what needs the most attention. It all boils down to what I said before, that she is dislocated by nature, and in the end there is a better than even chance she will tell you what she has told me, that maybe the cause of it is she didn't really love me when she married me. I'll tell you this," Gerald said with bitterness, "I know love in a woman when I see it, and believe me, I saw it in her. I have her letters to prove it. Once she begins to question herself, nothing is sacred any more. And to top it all, at times she'll get so low and unhappy that more than one night I've had to comfort her, as for instance after she had deceived me with Duffy. You may be doing the same with her some day over some other third party. Don't think your situation will be much better than mine."

"It's the chance you take—"

"The odds are not in your favor."

Levin again mentioned the children. "She'd be miserable without them. We could work out some sort of arrangement so that you could have them part of the year—maybe the summer."

Gilley stared at him. "You expect to go on with this after what I've told you?"

Levin laughed badly.

Gilley snapped off the lamplight and rose. "In that case she can't have them. When she deserts me, she deserts them."

Levin sat humidly on the hard chair. "How can you hurt her if you say you love her?"

"The same way she hurts me. The way you do. The way I want to hurt you."

His eyes were dark with distaste and anger. "If you want so much to have the kids, there's only one way—"

Levin, in pain of anticipation, leaned forward.

"Are you willing to give me your promise you will give up college teaching?" Gerald said.

Levin jumped up in rage. "Are you crazy? That's a fantastic blackmail."

"Take it or leave it."

"It's unconstitutional," Levin shouted. "Inhuman, barbaric, immoral."

"And what is it when you steal a man's wife and children from him?" Gilley thundered. "Is that so g.d. moral, since you use the word so much?"

"Pauline is a free agent."

"Can you say the kids are, or that she deserves to have them, a woman who had two lovers?"

"Will you use them any better than you used her?"

"She used me. She played me for a sucker."

"How am I supposed to support them if I can't teach?"

"I didn't say you couldn't teach. I said not in any college. You can go back to a high school. They generally pay better anyway."

"What's the difference whether I teach in a high school or college?"

"You'd do less harm in high school. You're not fit to teach at the college level."

"What a low form of revenge."

"It's your own fault. I want to get at least something out of this mess."

"I won't agree to it. We'll fight for the kids in court."

"You won't get anything in court when I testify she engaged in adultery with Duffy, then with you, during which—as she has admitted to me—she sometimes left the kids unattended. She isn't a fit mother."

"You're not in your right mind if you say that."

"I'll argue about it when the time comes."

"You'll have no evidence. She won't testify against herself."

"I have all the evidence I need—on tape."

Levin groaned from his shoes up. "You mean you took a tape of her talking, without her knowledge?"

Gilley blanched. "So would you."

"These goddamn gadgets will destroy you. I'll testify as to the kind of pictures you took of her."

"Picture, damn it, and *she* was naked in it with a man, not I. I wish now I had had the sense to print more than one copy. As for whatever evidence you have to give, I'd advise you not to or the judge might be interested in hearing a lot more about you. I don't want to bring this up just yet because I haven't finished investigating it, but one of the boys at the Alpha Zeta fraternity, which I am the faculty adviser to, recently became engaged to a girl who told him one night in his car that she had had intimate relations with one of her English profs, who she didn't name. Out of curiosity I looked up her record and found that three people in the department had taught her, Avis this spring, Leopold Kuck last winter, and you back in the fall. Both of them gave her C's. You gave her a C first, then petitioned to change it to a B. I remember that business very well and was suspicious when you wanted to raise her grade. Her name's Nadalee Hammerstad."

Levin felt as though Gilley had broken a lead pipe on his head; but the bleeding was internal.

"The grade she got was the grade she earned," he muttered.

"You are now shown up for the first-class scum you are."

What else could I expect, Levin thought, given who I am?

"Well, take it or leave it," Gilley said.

"I'll speak to Pauline."

"Tell her how goddamn moral you are."

He descended three flights of stairs in a stupefying daze. Pauline was sitting on the lobby couch, Mary on her lap, Erik by her side, turning the pages of a picture book.

She looked at Levin in fright. "What happened?"

He told her Gilley's terms and she was furious. "Oh, that's awful. We'll see my lawyer. I'll sue for the children."

"You may not get them," Levin said. "Why did you tell him you had left them alone while you were with me?"

"It slipped out as we were arguing. I was afraid to tell you I had told him."

"Suppose his lawyer asks on the stand if you had slept with Duffy. What would you say?"

"Please lower your voice," she said, lowering hers.

"Would you deny it?"

"No."

"And with me?"

"I lie so badly."

"You'd never get the kids."

She hugged the baby.

"Under the circumstances are you willing to give them up?"

"No."

Erik, still looking at the pictures, began to cry.

"Don't cry, Erik," Pauline said. "Lev wants me to have you and Mary."

"Suppose the court doesn't?"

"I'd die."

Erik continued to cry and the baby began.

"Then we have no choice," Levin said.

"I can't ask you to give up your career for us. The whole

thing's mad. It's Gerald's revenge against me. Isn't there some other way?"

"Not that he offers."

"What will this get him? When he's himself again I don't believe he'll hold you to it."

"When he's himself will he let you have the kids?"

"I'm afraid to take the chance. But I don't want you to hate me all my life for bringing this on you."

"I brought it on myself."

She opened her purse.

"Don't cry."

"I have to."

Levin climbed up the stairs to Gilley's room.

"I agree to your terms."

"You're batty," said Gilley. "You're cutting your throat."

"You're cutting it. Do you want me to sign anything?"

"I'll take your word, you're a fanatical type."

"Isn't there some better way?"

"Yes, go away and leave my wife and family alone."

Levin opened the door.

"Goodbye to your sweet dreams," Gilley called after him.

"I hope yours are sweet."

"An older woman than yourself and not dependable, plus two adopted kids, no choice of yours, no job or promise of one, and other assorted headaches. Why take that load on yourself?"

"Because I can, you son of a bitch."

They drove to the house. Levin went unwillingly in, the signs of the husband still around. Pauline fed the kids, then put them down for naps. She made sandwiches and they sat in the kitchen. Levin ate, looking at the stump of the leaning birch tree in the back yard; Pauline said Gerald had chopped it down in the spring.

After coffee she said, "He gets the house and car and I get a cash settlement. All I'll take are my clothes and the children's things. I'll send the crib and Erik's bed, my two trunks, some books and records, to my uncle's, and we'll have three bags for the trip, plus yours."

"How long will it take to get there?"

"Two days without rushing. Three if we want to look at things along the way. Don't worry about the driving. I'll spell you."

"Let's make it two days. I want to get there and look around."

"You'll have weeks while I'm in Nevada."

"I want to get started."

"How do you feel now?"

"The same."

"Please take my hand. My feeling for you is an ache."

He took her cold hand across the table.

"It makes me sad that you're still this way," she said, "but now that you're with me I feel you'll want me again. Maybe not so intensely but so long as it's love I'll have no kick."

He said nothing.

"My maiden name was Josephson," Pauline said. "Think of me as Pauline Josephson. Joseph was my father's name and he wanted a son but I was his best-beloved daughter."

She was looking out of the window. "Imagine, we've never been for a walk together."

Afterwards Levin asked her why she had picked his application out of the pile Gilley had discarded.

"You had attached a photograph," Pauline said, "although you weren't asked to."

"It was an old picture. I wanted them to know what I looked like."

"You looked as though you needed a friend."

"Was that the reason?"

"I needed one. Your picture reminded me of a Jewish boy I knew in college who was very kind to me during a trying time in my life."

"So I was chosen," Levin said.

That night, after packing his few possessions, he caught sight of his doubtful face in the mirror. Am I in my right mind? He sat in a chair, head in his hands. His doubts were the bricks of a windowless prison he was in, where Gilley's voice endlessly droned the reasons he ought to quit. Every reason was part of the structure. The prison was really himself, flawed edifice of failures, each locking up tight the one before. He had failed at his best plans, who could say he wouldn't with her? Possibly he already had and would one day take off in the dark as she lay in bed. Unless the true prison was to stick it out chained to her ribs. He would look like a free man but whoever peered into his eyes would see the lines of a brick wall.

He left the house and walked to the river. What if he beat it now, sneaked back, and when the old lady was snoring away with her ears turned off he would lug his suitcase and valise down to the car and drive away? He could head north to Canada, and then east. No one would know where he was or was going. He would leave a note, "Sorry, I don't think it will work. Too much has happened. I do this for you as well as myself. Sincerely, and with regret, S. Levin." He would slip that under her door and fade away. All she had to do when she found it was unpack and call Gilley at the hotel. She would cry a little but could say, "He wasn't worth your little finger. I made a dreadful mistake. The children miss you—please take us back." And Gilley, the forgiver, would hotfoot it home, holding flowers. They'd go on as before.

Or if she were really sick of him, she could take the train to SF and stay with her uncle. She would feel bad for a while but sooner or later some middle-aged gent would show up who would want to marry her; she was that type. Let somebody else marry her, Levin thought. He had from the first resisted becoming her savior, or victim. She had in a moment of unhappiness after the death of a former flame picked him by chance from a pile of discards. She had marked him x in a distant port and summoned him across the continent. Did this casual selection make him responsible for her for life? Was he forever bound to the choice she had made? That was stretching kismet too far. Who was a man if he surrendered freedom in a prior time?

The town was quiet as he walked, all but deserted since the college students had gone, the houses dark, silent. He met no one. At the river, after watching the moving water, he turned back, avoiding downtown and his reflection in store windows, still roaming, after so many years, the stone streets of the past. The city haunted him tonight. While others were sleeping Levin, in stinking clothes, had sneaked out of the bug-infested room he hid in during the day and wandered along long dark streets, peering into the houses of strangers for drops of light. Many a night he had walked in anguished desire of a decent future; failing that, another bottle. He drove the seasons away after hounding them to appear: winter, sniffing the icy wind for the scent, the breath, of spring; yet a time of flowers drove him wild; amid summer foliage, in ascetic heat, he obsessively hunted dead leaves and found them under every bush; autumn inspired his own long death. This went on for too many years to remember.

He came by a roundabout way to her house and stood under the ornamental plum tree across the street. The house looked already empty, except the lit living room where, through a half-open window, he could see her packing. She wore a shapeless shirt and her toreador pants, and with a cigarette in her mouth, was putting kids' things into a suitcase. Who is she? Levin thought. What do I really know about her? He thought if after she got back from Nevada he was still not sure how it would work out, he would call it quits. That would finish the promise to Gilley and he would, after a year in graduate school, try again to get into a small liberal arts college and teach there. With luck he might make it.

Pauline was holding a yellow dress against herself to see how it looked. She put it down and with a cloth, rubbed something on the table. When she picked it up and placed it under her chin it was a violin. She tried the bow, then played. Levin listened till he recognized the music.

Overslept, he awoke with a bang and was splashing cold water on his face when the landlady knocked. "Mrs. Gilley called and said to come right over, it's very important."

This could go too far. He hurriedly dressed, shaved, and left the house, leaving behind both his bags for protection.

When he drove up, Pauline, watching at the window, opened the door for him.

"What's wrong?"

She seemed not to want, or be able, to look at him. A massive excitement seized Levin.

Meeting his eyes at last, she murmured, "I'm about two months' pregnant."

He remembered then to remove his hat. The blood in his brain gave his head the weight of a rock.

"Mine?" he asked.

She smiled wanly. "Not Leo's."

"I mean Gerald—no, I guess I don't."

"I suspected something last month," Pauline said, "but thought no because I had a slight flow at the more-or-less usual time."

"I didn't think of the possibility of conception those last times."

"You want the right feeling for every event?"

"Don't you?"

"Yes," she said. "I called you as soon as I knew for sure. I happened to think last night that my period was late. Then I checked the calendar and it was very late. I called the doctor and was examined this morning. There isn't any doubt I'm pregnant. I didn't want you to think I had come back to you because of that. I thought I'd tell you before we left in case you want to call it off."

"What would you do if I did?"

"I frankly don't know. I could try to abort."

"No."

"Are you saying that with your steely will or pity for the human race?"

"I want the child."

Pauline said, "I'm so relieved. I wasn't sure how you'd take it." Then she said, "Touch my breasts, they're beginning to grow."

Levin touched them.

"They'll shrink after the baby is weaned but at least you'll know how I look with little ones."

He returned for his bags, passed up eating from the cherry tree and said goodbye to Mrs. Beaty. On the way back he saw Bullock in a new red station wagon. George had expected to be director of comp but Gerald, Pauline had said, was combining that job with his own.

Pauline was ready with both kids but instead of three bags she had four, a duffel bag, and a violin case. Levin, in a sweat, was thinking of a luggage rack for the roof of the car, but then the Buckets came along, Algene heavy-bellied in her ninth month; Joe helped Levin get five bags in the trunk, and two, with the violin case and his umbrella, they put in the back of the car.

"No rack needed yet," Bucket said. "'A penny saved is a penny earned.'"

"It's the earned penny that worries me," said Levin.

"'God tempers the wind to a shorn lamb.'"

"Lev's no lamb," said Pauline.

"I speak for myself," Bucket said.

Levin lifted Erik into the back seat. "I'm your father now."

"I want my real daddy."

When they were in, five counting Pauline's baby, Levin started the Hudson and the Buckets waved them off. What if I had bought a seven-passenger car? Levin thought.

Mary sat in the baby seat, in front, the sores on her arms covered with ointment. Pauline's hair, brushed bright, was drawn into a bun. He thought she would be wearing the yellow dress he saw last night but she wore the sleeveless white linen he had first seen her in. When they drove off she gazed back at the house, then turned away.

Levin drove to the edge of town for a last look at the view to the mountains. The clouds were a clash of horses and volcanoes.

"Beautiful country."

"If beauty isn't all that happens."

They drove through the campus, the trees in full leaf, arched above the narrow streets, shading the green lawns.

"I failed this place," Levin said.

"You got *The Elements* kicked out after thirty years."

"A hell of a revolution."

"Gerald is also thinking of offering some of the instructors doing graduate work a literature class."

"I still want to teach," he said.

"Don't undersell yourself."

"It's what I do best."

"What else have you tried?"

"Too much."

They saw Fabrikant, a stogie in his mouth, hurrying to the office.

"He's growing reddish whiskers," said Pauline.

"I hear the dean asked him to handle the Great Books program."

"That was your idea," Pauline said. She said, "Gerald wouldn't keep that promise if he had made it to you."

"That's the point," Levin said.

She rested her head on his shoulder. "Trust me, darling. I'll make you a good wife."

Her body smelled like fresh-baked bread, the bread of flowers.

"Wear these." He gave her the gold hoop earrings he had kept for her.

She fastened them on her ears. "God bless you, Lev."

"Sam, they used to call me home."

"God bless you, Sam."

Two tin-hatted workmen with chain saws were in the maple tree in front of Humanities Hall, cutting it down limb by leafy limb, to make room for a heat tunnel. On the Student Union side of the street, Gilley was aiming a camera at the operation. When he saw Levin's Hudson approach he swung the camera around and snapped. As they drove by he tore a rectangle of paper from the back of the camera and waved it aloft.

"Got your picture!"

THE FIXER

For Paul

"Irrational streams of blood are staining earth . . ."

YEATS

"O yonge Hugh of Lyncoln—slayn also
With cursed Jewes, as it is notable,
For it is but a litel while ago—
Preye eek for us, we synful folk unstable,
. . ."

CHAUCER

I

FROM THE small crossed window of his room above the stable in the brickyard, Yakov Bok saw people in their long overcoats running somewhere early that morning, everybody in the same direction. Vey iz mir, he thought uneasily, something bad has happened. The Russians, coming from streets around the cemetery, were hurrying, singly or in groups, in the spring snow in the direction of the caves in the ravine, some running in the middle of the slushy cobblestone streets. Yakov hastily hid the small tin can in which he saved silver rubles, then rushed down to the yard to find out what the excitement was about. He asked Proshko, the foreman, loitering near the smoky brickkilns, but Proshko spat and said nothing. Outside the yard a black-shawled, bony-faced peasant woman, thickly dressed, told him the dead body of a child had been found nearby. "Where?" Yakov asked. "How old a child?" but she said she didn't know and hurried away. The next day the *Kievlyanin* reported that in a damp cave in a ravine not more than a verst and a half from the brickworks, the body of a murdered Russian boy, Zhenia Golov, twelve years old, had been found by two older boys, both fifteen, Kazimir Selivanov and Ivan Shestinsky. Zhenia, dead more than a week, was covered with stab wounds, his body bled white. After the funeral in the cemetery close by the brick factory, Richter, one of the drivers, brought in a handful of leaflets accusing the Jews of the murder. They had been printed, Yakov saw when he examined one, by the Black Hundreds organizations. Their emblem, the Imperial double-headed eagle, was imprinted on the cover, and under it: SAVE RUSSIA FROM THE JEWS. In his room that night, Yakov, in fascination, read that the boy had been bled to death for religious purposes so that the Jews could collect his blood and deliver it to the synagogue for the making of Passover matzos. Though this was ridiculous he was frightened. He got up, sat down, and got up again. He went to the window, then returned hastily and continued to read the newspaper. He was worried because the brick factory where he worked was in the Lukianovsky District, one in which Jews were forbidden to live. He had been living there for months under an assumed name and without a residence certificate. And he was frightened of the pogrom threatened in the newspaper. His own father had been killed in an incident not more than a year after Yakov's birth—something less than a pogrom, and less than useless: two drunken soldiers shot the first three Jews in their path, his father had been the second. But the son had lived through a pogrom when he was a schoolboy, a three-day Cossack raid. On the third morning when the houses were still smoldering and he was led, with a half dozen other children, out of a cellar where they had been hiding he saw a black-bearded Jew with a white sausage stuffed into his mouth, lying in the road on a pile of bloody feathers, a peasant's pig devouring his arm.

2

Five months ago, on a mild Friday in early November, before the first snow had snowed on the shtetl, Yakov's father-in-law, a skinny worried man in clothes about to fall apart, who looked as though he had been assembled out of sticks and whipped air, drove up with his skeletal horse and rickety wagon. They sat in the thin cold house—gone to seed two months after Raisl, the faithless wife, had fled—and drank a last glass of tea together. Shmuel, long since sixty, with tousled gray beard, rheumy eyes, and deeply creased forehead—dug into his caftan pocket for half a yellow sugar lump and offered it to Yakov who shook his head. The peddler—he was his daughter's dowry, had had nothing to give so he gave favors, service if possible—sucked tea through sugar but his son-in-law drank his unsweetened. It tasted bitter and he blamed existence. The old man from time to time commented on life without accusing anyone, or asked harmless questions, but Yakov was silent or short with answers.

After he had sipped through half his glass of tea, Shmuel, sighing, said, "Nobody has to be a Prophet to know you're blaming me for my daughter Raisl." He spoke in sadness, wearing a hard hat he had found in a barrel in a neighboring town. When he sweated it stuck to his head, but being a religious man he didn't mind. Otherwise he had on a patched and padded caftan from which his skinny hands hung out. And very roomy shoes, not boots, which he ran in, and around in.

"Who said anything? You're blaming yourself for having brought up a whore."

Shmuel, without a word, pulled out a soiled blue handkerchief and wept.

"So why, if you'll excuse me, did you stop sleeping with her for months? Is that a way to treat a wife?"

"It was more like weeks but how long can a man sleep with a barren woman? I got tired of trying."

"Why didn't you go to the rabbi when I begged you?"

"Let him stay out of my business and I'll stay out of his. All in all he's an ignorant man."

"Charity you were always short of," the peddler said.

Yakov rose, enraged. "Don't talk to me about charity. What have I had all my life? What have I got to give away? I was practically born an orphan—my mother dead ten minutes later, and you know what happened to my poor father. If somebody said Kaddish for them it wasn't me till years later. If they were waiting outside the gates of heaven it was a long cold wait, if they're not still waiting. Throughout my miserable childhood I lived in a stinking orphans' home, barely existing. In my dreams I ate and I ate my dreams. Torah I had little of and Talmud less, though I learned Hebrew because I've got an ear for language. Anyway, I knew the Psalms. They taught me a trade and apprenticed me five minutes after age ten—not that I regret it. So I work—let's call it work—with my hands, and some call me 'common' but the truth of it is few people know who is really common. As for those that look like they got class, take another look. Viskover, the Nogid, is in my eyes a common man. All he's got is rubles and when he opens his mouth you can hear them clink. On my own I studied different subjects, and even before I was taken into the army I taught myself a decent Russian, much better than we pick up from the peasants. What little I know I learned on my own—some history and geography, a little science, arithmetic, and a book or two of Spinoza's. Not much but better than nothing."

"Though most is treyf I give you credit—" said Shmuel.

"Let me finish. I've had to dig with my fingernails for a living. What can anybody do without capital? What they can do I can do but it's not much. I fix what's broken—except in the heart. In this shtetl everything is falling apart—who bothers with leaks in his roof if he's peeking through the cracks to spy on God? And who can pay to have it fixed let's say he wants it, which he doesn't. If he does, half the time I work for nothing. If I'm lucky, a dish of noodles. Opportunity here is born dead. I'm frankly in a foul mood."

"Opportunity you don't have to tell me about—"

"They conscripted me for the Russo-Japanese War but it was over before I got in. Thank God. When I got sick they booted me out. An asthmatic Jew wasn't worth the trouble. Thank God. When I got back I scraped again with my broken nails. After a long runaround which started when I met her, I married your daughter, who couldn't get pregnant in five and a half years. She bore me no children so who could I look in the eye? And now she runs off with some stranger she met at the inn—a goy I'm positive. So that's enough—who needs more? I don't want people pitying me or wondering what I did to be so cursed. I did nothing. It was a gift. I'm innocent. I've been an orphan too long. All I have to my name after thirty years in this graveyard is sixteen rubles that I got from selling everything I own. So please don't mention charity because I have no charity to give."

"Charity you can give even when you haven't got. I don't mean money. I meant for my daughter."

"Your daughter deserves nothing."

"She ran from one rabbi to another in every town I took her, but nobody could promise her a child. She ran to the doctors too when she had a ruble, but they told her the same thing. It was cheaper with the rabbis. So she ran away—may God protect her. Even a sinner belongs to Him. She sinned but she was desperate."

"May she run forever."

"She was a true wife to you for years. She shared your every misfortune."

"What she caused she shared. She was a true wife to the last minute, or the last month, or the month before that, and that makes her untrue, a black cholera on her!"

"God forbid," cried Shmuel, rising. "On you!"

Eyes agitated, he thickly cursed the fixer and fled from the house.

Yakov had sold everything but the clothes on his back, which he wore as peasants do—embroidered shirt belted outside his trousers, whose legs were stuffed into wrinkled high boots. And a peasant's worn and patched, brown sheepskin coat, which could, on occasion, smell of sheep. He had kept his tools and a few books: Smirnovsky's *Russian Grammar*, an elementary biology book, *Selections from Spinoza*, and a battered atlas at least twenty-five years old. He had made a small bundle of the books with a piece of knotted twine. The tools were in a flour sack tied at the neck, the crosscut blade protruding. There was also some food in a cone of newspaper. He was leaving behind his few ruined sticks of furniture—a junkman had wanted to be paid to take them—and two sets of cracked dishes, also unsaleable, that Shmuel could do with whatever he wanted—use, ax, or fire—they were worth nothing. Raisl had had two sets for her father's sake, for herself it made not much difference. But in exchange for the horse and wagon the peddler would get a fairly good cow. He could take over his daughter's little dairy business. It could hardly pay less than peddling. He was the only person Yakov knew who peddled nothing and sold it, in bits and slices, for real kopeks. Sometimes he traded nothing for pig bristles, wool, grain, sugar beets, and then sold the peasants dried fish, soap, kerchiefs, candy, in minute quantities. That was his talent and on it he miraculously lived. "He who gave us teeth will give us bread." Yet his breath smelled of nothing—not bread, not anything.

Yakov, in loose clothes and peaked cap, was an elongated nervous man with large ears, stained hard hands, a broad back and tormented face, lightened a bit by gray eyes and brownish hair. His nose was sometimes Jewish, sometimes not. He had to no one's surprise—after Raisl ran away—shaved off his short beard of reddish cast. "Cut off your beard and you no longer resemble your creator," Shmuel had warned. Since then he had been admonished by more than one Jew that he looked like a goy but it had caused him neither to mourn nor rejoice. He looked young but felt old and for that he blamed nobody, not even his wife; he blamed fate and spared himself. His nervousness showed in his movements. Generally he moved faster than he had to, considering how little there was to do, but he was always doing something. After all, he was a fixer and had to keep his hands busy.

Dumping his things into the open wagon, a rusty water bucket hanging under it between the back wheels, he was displeased with the appearance of the nag, a naked-looking animal with spindly legs, a brown bony body and large stupid eyes, who got along very well with Shmuel. They asked little from each other and lived in peace. The horse did mostly as he pleased and Shmuel indulged him. After all, what difference did a short delay make in a mad world? Tomorrow he would be no richer. The fixer was irritated with himself for acquiring this decrepit beast, but had thought better a lopsided exchange with Shmuel than getting nothing for the cow from a peasant who coveted her. A father-in-law's blood was thicker than water. Although there was no railroad station anywhere around, and the coachman came for travelers only every second week, Yakov could have got to Kiev without taking over the horse and wagon. Shmuel had offered to drive him the thirty or so versts but the fixer preferred to be rid of him and travel alone. He figured that once he got into the city he could sell the beast and apology-for-dray, if not to a butcher, then at least to a junk dealer for a few rubles.

Dvoira, the dark-uddered cow, was out in the field behind the hut, browsing under a leafless poplar tree, and Yakov went out to her. The white cow raised her head and watched him approach. The fixer patted her lean flank. "Goodbye, Dvoira," he said, "and lots of luck. Give what you got left to Shmuel, also a poor man." He wanted to say more but couldn't. Tearing up some limp yellowing grass, he fed it to the cow, then returned to the horse and wagon. Shmuel had reappeared.

Why does he act as though he were the one who had deserted me?

"I didn't come back to fight with anybody," Shmuel said. "What she did I won't defend—she hurt me as much as she did you. Even more, though when the rabbi says she's now dead my voice agrees but not my heart. First of all she's my only child, and since when do we need more dead? I've cursed her more than once but I ask God not to listen."

"Well, I'm leaving," Yakov said, "take care of the cow."

"Don't leave yet," Shmuel said, his eyes miserable. "If you stay Raisl might come back."

"If she does who's interested?"

"If you had been more patient she wouldn't have left you."

"Five years going on six is enough of patience. I've had enough. I might have waited the legal ten, but she danced off with some dirty stranger, so I've had my fill, thanks."

"Who can blame you?" Shmuel sighed sadly. He asked after a while, "Have you got tobacco for a little cigarette, Yakov?"

"My bag is empty."

The peddler briskly rubbed his dry palms.

"So you haven't, you haven't, but what I don't understand is why you want to bother with Kiev. It's a dangerous city full of churches and anti-Semites."

"I've been cheated from the start," Yakov said bitterly. "What I've been through personally you know already, not to mention living here all my life except for a few months in the army. The shtetl is a prison, no change from the days of Khmelnitsky. It moulders and the Jews moulder in it. Here we're all prisoners, I don't have to tell you, so it's time to try elsewhere I've finally decided. I want to make a living, I want to get acquainted with a bit of the world. I've read a few books in recent years and it's surprising what goes on that none of us knows about. I'm not asking for Tibet but what I saw in St. Petersburg interested me. Whoever thought of white nights before, but it's a scientific fact; they have them there. When I left the army I thought I would get out of here as soon as possible, but things caught up with me, including your daughter."

"My daughter wanted to run away from here the minute you got married but you wouldn't go."

"It's true," said Yakov, "it was my fault. I thought it couldn't get worse so it must get better. I was wrong both ways so now enough is enough. I'm on my way at last."

"Outside the Pale only wealthy Jews and the professional

classes can get residence certificates. The Tsar doesn't want poor Jews all over his land, and Stolypin, may his lungs collapse, urges him on. Ptu!" Shmuel spat through two fingers.

"Since I can't be a professional on account of lack of education I wouldn't mind being wealthy. As the saying goes, I'd sell my last shirt to be a millionaire. Maybe, by luck, I'll make my fortune in the outside world."

"What's in the world," Shmuel said, "is in the shtetl—people, their trials, worries, circumstances. But here at least God is with us."

"He's with us till the Cossacks come galloping, then he's elsewhere. He's in the outhouse, that's where he is."

The peddler grimaced but let the remark pass. "Almost fifty thousand Jews live in Kiev," he said, "restricted to a few districts, and all in the way of the first blow that falls if a new pogrom should come. And it will fall faster in the larger places than it falls here. When we hear their cries we will rush into the woods. Why should you walk straight into the hands of the Black Hundreds, may they hang by their tongues?"

"The truth of it is I'm a man full of wants I'll never satisfy, at least not here. It's time to get out and take a chance. Change your place change your luck, people say."

"Since the last year or so, Yakov, you're a different man. What wants are so important?"

"Those that can't sleep and keep me awake for company. I've told you what wants: a full stomach now and then. A job that pays rubles, not noodles. Even some education if I can get it, and I don't mean workmen studying Torah after hours. I've had my share of that. What I want to know is what's going on in the world."

"That's all in the Torah, there's no end to it. Stay away from the wrong books, Yakov, the impure."

"There are no wrong books. What's wrong is the fear of them."

Shmuel unstuck his hat and wiped his brow with his handkerchief.

"Yakov, if you want to go to foreign parts, Turks or no Turks, why not to Palestine where a Jew can see Jewish trees and mountains, and breathe the Jewish air? If I had half a chance there's where I'd go."

"All I've had in this miserable town is a beggarly existence. Now I'll try Kiev. If I can live there decently that's what I'll do. If not, I'll make sacrifices, save up, and head for Amsterdam for a boat to America. To sum it up, I have little but I have plans."

"Plans or none you're looking for trouble."

"I've never had to look," said the fixer. "Well, Shmuel, good luck to you. The morning's gone so I'd better go."

He climbed up onto the wagon and reached for the reins.

"I'll ride with you as far as the windmills." Shmuel got up on the seat on the other side.

Yakov touched the nag with a birch switch the old man kept in the holder, a hole bored into the edge of the seat, but the horse, after an initial startled gallop, stopped short and stood motionless in the road.

"Personally I never use it," the peddler remarked. "It's there as a warning. If he dawdles I remind him it's there. He seems to like to hear me talk about it."

"If that's the case I'm better off walking."

"Patience." Shmuel smacked his lips. "Gidap, beauty—he's very vain. Whenever you can afford it, Yakov, feed him oats. Too much grass and he's prone to gas."

"If he's prone to gas let him fart." He flicked the reins.

Yakov didn't look back. The nag moved along a crooked road between black plowed fields with dark round haystacks piled up here and there, the peasant's church visible on the left in the distance; then slowly up the narrow stony cemetery road, a few thin yellow willows amidst the graves, and around a low tombstone-covered hill where Yakov's parents, a man and woman in their early twenties, lay buried. He had considered a visit to their weed-strewn graves but hadn't the heart at the last minute. The past was a wound in the head. He thought of Raisl and felt depressed.

The fixer snapped the rod against the nag's ribs but got no increase of motion.

"I'll get to Kiev by Hanukkah."

"If you don't get there it's because God wills it. You won't miss a thing."

A shnorrer in rags called to the fixer from beside a tilted tombstone. "Hey, there, Yakov, it's Friday. How about a two-kopek piece for a Sabbath blessing? Charity saves from death."

"Death is the last of my worries."

"Lend me a kopek or two, Yakov," said Shmuel.

"A kopek I haven't earned today."

The shnorrer, a man with ugly feet, called him goy, his mouth twisted, eyes lit in anger.

Yakov spat in the road.

Shmuel said a prayer to ward off evil.

The nag began to trot, drawing the rickety wagon with its swinging bucket banging the axle past the cemetery hill, down the winding road. They drove by the poorhouse, a shabby structure with an addition for orphans, which Yakov averted his eyes from, then clop-clopped across a wooden bridge into the populous section of the town. They passed Shmuel's hut, neither of them looking. A blackened bathhouse with boarded windows stood near a narrow stream and the fixer felt suddenly itchy for a bath, thinking of himself in the thick steam, slapping his soapened sides with a twig brush as the attendant poured water on his head. God bless soap and water, Raisl used to say. In a few hours the bathhouse, steaming from its cracks, would be bulging with Jews washing up for Friday night.

They rattled along a rutted dusty street with thatched cottages on one side, open weedy fields on the other. A big-wigged Jewess, sitting on her doorstep, plucked a bloody-necked hen between her knees, as she cursed out a peasant's sow rooting in the remnants of her potato garden. A pool of blood in the ditch marked the passage of the ritual slaughterer. Farther on, a bearded black goat with a twisted horn, tethered to a post, baaed at the horse and charged, but the rope around his neck held and though the post toppled, the goat was thrown on its back. The doors of some of the cottages hung loose, and where there were steps they sagged. Fences buckled and were about to collapse without apparent notice or response, irritating the fixer, who liked things in place and functioning.

Tonight the white candles would gleam from the lit windows. For everybody else.

The horse zigzagged towards the marketplace, and now the quality of the houses improved, some large and attractive, with gardens full of flowers in the summertime.

"Leave it to the lousy rich," the fixer muttered.

Shmuel had nothing to say. His mind, he had often said, had exhausted the subject. He did not envy the rich, all he wanted was to share a little of their wealth—enough to live on while he was working hard to earn a living.

The market, a large open square with wooden houses on two sides, some containing first-floor shops, was crowded with peasant carts laden with grains, vegetables, wood, hides and whatnot. Around the stalls and bins mostly women clustered, shopping for the Sabbath. Though the market was his usual hangout, the fixer waved to no one and no one waved to him.

I leave with no regret, he thought. I should have gone years ago.

"Who have you told?" Shmuel asked.

"Who's there to tell? Practically nobody. It's none of their business anyway. Frankly, my heart is heavy—I'll tell the truth—but I'm sick of this place."

He had said goodbye to his two cronies, Leibish Polikov and Haskel Dembo. The first had shrugged, the other wordlessly embraced him, and that was that. A butcher holding up by its thick yellow feet a squawking hen beating its wings saw the wagon go by and said something witty to his customers. One of these, a young woman who turned to look, called to Yakov, but by then the wagon was out of the marketplace, scattering some chickens nesting in the ruts of the road and a flock of jabbering ducks, as it clattered on.

They approached the domed synagogue with its iron weathercock, a pock-marked yellow-walled building with an oak door, for the time being resting in peace. It had been sacked more than once. The courtyard was empty except for a black-hatted Jew sitting on a bench reading a folded newspaper in the sunlight. Yakov had rarely been inside the synagogue in recent years yet he easily remembered the long high-ceilinged room with its brass chandeliers, oval stained windows, and the prayer stands with stools and wooden candleholders, where he had spent, for the most part wasted, so many hours.

"Gidap," he said.

At the other side of the town—a shtetl was an island surrounded by Russia—as they came abreast a windmill, its patched fans turning in slow massive motion, the fixer jerked on the reins and the horse clopped to a stop.

"Here's where we part," he said to the peddler.

Shmuel drew out of his pocket an embroidered cloth bag.

"Don't forget these," he said embarrassed. "I found them in your drawer before we left."

In the bag was another containing phylacteries. There was also a prayer shawl and a prayer book. Raisl, before they were married, had made the bag out of a piece of her dress and embroidered it with the tablets of the Ten Commandments.

"Thanks." Yakov tossed the bag among his other things in the wagon.

"Yakov," said Shmuel passionately, "don't forget your God!"

"Who forgets who?" the fixer said angrily. "What do I get from him but a bang on the head and a stream of piss in my face. So what's there to be worshipful about?"

"Don't talk like a meshummed. Stay a Jew, Yakov, don't give up our God."

"A meshummed gives up one God for another. I don't want either. We live in a world where the clock ticks fast while he's on his timeless mountain staring in space. He doesn't see us and he doesn't care. Today I want my piece of bread, not in Paradise."

"Listen to me, Yakov, take my advice. I've lived longer than you. There's a shul in the Podol in Kiev. Go on Shabbos, you'll feel better. 'Blessed are they who put their trust in God.'"

"Where I ought to go is to the Socialist Bund meetings, that's where I should go, not in shul. But the truth of it is I dislike politics, though don't ask me why. What good is it if you're not an activist? I guess it's my nature. I incline toward the philosophical although I don't know much about anything."

"Be careful," Shmuel said, agitated, "we live in the middle of our enemies. The best way to take care is to stay under God's protection. Remember, if He's not perfect, neither are we."

They embraced quickly and Shmuel got down from the wagon.

"Goodbye, sweetheart," he called to the horse. "Goodbye, Yakov, I'll think of you when I say the Eighteen Blessings. If you ever see Raisl, tell her her father is waiting."

Shmuel trudged back towards the synagogue. When he was

quite far away Yakov felt a pang for having forgotten to slip him a ruble or two.

"Get on now." The nag flicked an ear, roused itself for a short trot, then slowed to a tired walk.

"It'll be some trip," the fixer thought.

The horse stopped abruptly as a field mouse skittered across the road.

"Gidap, goddamit"—but the nag wouldn't move.

A peasant passed by with a long-horned bullock, prodding the animal with a stick.

"A horse understands a whip," he said across the road in Russian.

Yakov belabored the beast with the birch rod until he drew blood. The nag whinnied but remained tightly immobile on the road. The peasant, after watching a while, moved on.

"You son-of-a-bitch," said the fixer to the horse, "we'll never get to Kiev."

He was at the point of despair when a brown dog rustling through a blanket of dead leaves under some trees came onto the road, yelping at the horse. The nag hurried forward, Yakov barely grabbing the reins. The dog chased them, barking sharply at the horse's hooves, then at a turn in the road, disappeared. But the wagon rolled on, bucket rattling, its wheels wobbling, the nag trotting as fast as it could.

It clip-clopped along the hard dirt road, on one side of which flowed a mild stream below a sloping embankment; and on the other were the scattered log huts of a peasant village, their roofs covered with rotting straw. Despite poverty and the antics of too many pigs the huts looked better than the shtetl cottages. A bearded peasant chopped wood, a woman pumped water from the village well. They both stopped to stare at him. A verst from his town and he was a stranger in the world.

The horse trotted on, Yakov gazing at the fields, some plowed under, where oats, hay, sugar beets had grown, the haystacks standing dark against the woods. A crow flew slowly over the stubble of a wheatfield. The fixer found himself counting sheep and goats grazing in the communal meadows under lazy thick clouds. It had been a dank and dreary autumn, the dead leaves still hanging on half the trees in the woods around the fields. Last year at this time it had already snowed.

Though as a rule he enjoyed the landscape, Yakov felt a weight on him. The buzz and sparkle of summer were gone. In the violet distance the steppe seemed melancholy, endless.

The cut on the horse's flank, though encrusted, still oozed red droplets and drew fleas he switched away without touching the animal. He thought his spirits would rise once he was out of the shtetl but felt no relief. The fixer was troubled by discontent, a deeper sense that he had had no choice about going than he wanted to admit. His few friends were left behind. His habits, his best memories such as they were, were there. But so was his shame. He was leaving because he had earned a worse living—although he hadn't become a gravedigger—than many he knew with fewer brains and less skill. He was leaving because he was childless husband—"alive but dead" the Talmud described such a man—as well as embittered, deserted one. Yet if she had been faithful he would have stayed. Then better she hadn't been. He should be grateful to be escaping from a fruitless life. Still, he was apprehensive of going to a city of strangers—Jews as well as gentiles, strangers were strangers—in a sense a forbidden place. Holy Kiev, mother of Russian cities! He knew the towns for a dozen versts around but had only once, for a week in summer, been in Kiev. He felt the discontent of strangeness, of not knowing what was where, unable to predict or clearly visualize. All he could think of were the rows of shabby crowded tenements in the Podol. Would he go on in the same useless poverty and drab experience amid masses of Jews as poor as he, or somehow come to a better way of life? How at his age?—already thirty. Jobs for him were always scarce. With just the few rubles in his pocket how long would he last before starving? Why should tomorrow be better than today? Had he earned the privilege?

He had many fears, and since he rarely traveled long distances, had fears of traveling. The soles of his feet itched, which meant, the old wives said: "You will journey to a far-off place." So, good, but would he ever get there? The horse had slowed down again, a black year on its stupid head. Suppose those clouds, grown dark and heavy, cracked open on their undersides and poured snow upon the world. Would the horse make it? He pictured the snow falling thickly, in a few minutes turning the road and fields white so you couldn't see where one ended and the other began, the wagon filling up with snow. The nag would stop. Yakov might switch him till his bones gleamed through the blood but the animal was the type that would quietly lie down in the snow to spite him. "Brother, I'm tired. If you want to go on in this storm, go in good health. But not me. I'll take sleep and if it's sleep forever, so much the better. At least the snow is warm." The fixer saw himself wandering in drifts until he perished.

But the horse said nothing, and it didn't look like snow—or rain either. It was a brisk day beginning to be windy—it raised the nag's mane—and though the horse moved leisurely it moved steadily. Yet as they went through a grove of black-branched trees, the leafless twigs darkly intertwined high above Yakov's head, the small wood grew gloomy, and the fixer still searching for a change in the weather became actively nervous again. Shading his eyes in the queer light, he peered ahead—a winding road, absolutely snowless. Enough of this, he thought, I'd better eat. As though it had read his mind the nag came to a stop before he pulled the reins. Yakov got down off the seat, and taking hold of the bridle, drew the horse to the side of the road. The horse spread its hind legs and spattered a yellow stream on the road. Yakov urinated on some brown ferns. Feeling better, he tore up several handfuls of dry tussocky grass, and since he could locate no feedbag in the wagon, fed it in fistfuls to the nag. The horse, its sides heaving, chewed with its eroded yellow teeth until the grass foamed. The fixer's stomach rumbled. He sat under a sunlit tree, raised his sheepskin collar, and opened the food parcel. He ate part of a cold boiled potato, chewing slowly, then half a cucumber sprinkled with coarse salt, with a piece of sour black bread. Ah, for some tea, he thought, or if not that, some sweetened hot water. Yakov fell asleep with his back to the tree, awoke in a hurry, and climbed up on the wagon.

"It's late, goddamit, come on, move."

The nag wouldn't budge. The fixer reached for the switch. On second thought he climbed down, unhitched the rusty bucket and went looking for water. When he found a little stream the pail leaked, but he offered it, half full, to the horse, who wouldn't drink.

"Games I don't play." Yakov poured out the water, hitched

the bucket on the hook under the wagon, and stepped up to the seat. He waved the switch till it whistled. The nag, lowering his ears, moved forward, if one could call it movement. At least it wasn't where it had been before. The fixer again whistled the air with the switch, and the horse, after an indecisive minute, began to trot. The wagon rattled on.

They had gone on a while when the wagon caught up with an old woman, a pilgrim walking slowly in the road, leaning on her long staff, a heavy peasant in black, wearing men's shoes and carrying a knapsack, a thick shawl wrapped around her head.

He drew over to the side to pass her but as he did Yakov called out, "A ride, granny?"

"May Jesus bless you." She had three gray teeth.

Jesus he didn't need. Bad luck, he thought. Yakov helped pull her up to the wagon seat and touched the nag with the birch whip. To his surprise the horse took up his trot. Then as the road turned, the right wheel struck a rock and broke with a crunch. The wagon teetered and sagged at the rear, the left wheel tilted inward.

The old woman crossed herself, slowly climbed down to the road, and walked on with her heavy stick. She did not look back.

Yakov cursed Shmuel for wishing the wagon on him. Jumping to the ground he examined the broken wheel. Its worn metal ring had come off. The wooden rim had caved in, splintering two spokes. The split hub leaked axle grease. He groaned.

After five minutes of stunned emptiness he got his tool sack out of the wagon, untied it and spread out the tools on the road. But with hatchet, saw, plane, tinsmith's shears, tri-square, putty, wire, pointed knife and two awls, the fixer couldn't fix what was broken. Under the best conditions it would take him a day to repair the wheel. He thought of buying one from a peasant if he could get one that fitted, or nearly fitted, but if so where was the peasant? When you didn't need them they were in your beard. Yakov tossed the pieces of broken wheel into the wagon. He tied up his tools and drearily waited for someone to come. Nobody came. He considered returning to the shtetl but remembered he had had enough. The wind was colder, sharper, got under his coat and between the shoulder blades. The sun was setting, the sky turning dark.

If I go slow maybe I can make it on three wheels to the next village.

He tried it, sitting lightly as far to the left on the seat as he could, and begged the nag to take it easy. To his relief they went forward, the back wheel squeaking, for half a verst. He had caught up with the pilgrim and was about to say she couldn't ride when the other rear wheel, grinding thickly against the axle, collapsed, the back of the wagon hitting the road with a crashing thud, the bucket crushed. The horse lurched forward, snorted and reared. The fixer, his body tipped at a perilous angle, was paralyzed.

Eventually he got down off the seat. "Who invented my life?" Behind him was the empty treeless steppe, ahead the old woman. She had stopped before a huge wooden crucifix at the side of the road, crossed herself, and then slowly sinking to her knees, began to hit her head against the hard ground. She banged it until Yakov had a headache. The darkening steppe was here uninhabited. He feared fog and a raging wind. Unhitching the horse and drawing him out from under the wooden yoke, Yakov gathered together the reins. He backed the nag to the wagon seat, and climbing up on it, mounted the animal. No sooner up than down. The fixer placed his tool bag, book bundle, and parcels on the tilted seat, wound the reins around him, and remounted the horse. He slung the tools over his shoulder, and with his left hand held the other things as they rested on the horse's back, his right hand grasping the reins. The horse galloped forward. To Yakov's surprise he did not fall off.

They skirted the old woman, prostrate at the cross. He felt foolish and uncertain on the horse but hung on. The nag had slowed to a trot, then to a dejected walk. It stood stock still. Yakov cursed it into eternity and eventually it came to life, once more inching forward. When they were on the move, the fixer, who had never sat on a horse before—he couldn't think why except that he had never had a horse—dreamed of good fortune, accomplishment, affluence. He had a comfortable home, good business—maybe a small factory of some kind—a faithful wife, dark-haired, pretty, and three healthy children,

God bless them. But when he was becalmed on the nag he thought blackly of his father-in-law, beat the beast with his fist, and foresaw for himself a useless future. Yakov pleaded with the animal to make haste—it was dark and the steppe wind cut keenly, but freed of the wagon the horse examined the world. He also stopped to crop grass, tearing it audibly with his eroded teeth, and wandering from one side of the road to the other. Once in a while he turned and trotted back a few steps. Yakov, frantic, threatened the switch, but they both knew he had none. In desperation he kicked the beast with his heels. The nag bucked and for a perilous few minutes it was like being in a rowboat on a stormy sea. Having barely survived, Yakov stopped kicking. He considered ditching his goods, hoping the lightened load might speed things up, but didn't dare.

"I'm a bitter man, you bastard horse. Come to your senses or you'll suffer."

It availed him nothing.

By then it was pitch dark. The wind boomed. The steppe was a black sea full of strange voices. Here nobody spoke Yiddish, and the nag, maybe feeling the strangeness of it, began to trot and soon came close to flight. Though the fixer was not a superstitious man he had been a superstitious boy, and he recalled Lilith, Queen of Evil Spirits, and the Fish-witch who tickled travelers to death or otherwise made herself helpful. Ghosts rose like smoke in the Ukraine. From time to time he felt a presence at his back but would not turn. Then a yellow moon rose like a flower growing and lit the empty steppe deep into the shadowy distance. The distance glowed. It'll be a long night, the fixer thought. They galloped through a peasant village, its long-steepled church yellow in moonlight, the squat thatched huts dark, no lights anywhere. Though he smelled woodsmoke he saw none. Yakov considered dismounting, knocking on a strange door and begging for a night's lodging. But he felt that if he got off the horse he would never get back on. He was afraid he might be robbed of his few rubles, so he stayed put and made uncertain progress. The sky was thick with stars, the wind blowing cold in his face. Once he slept momentarily and woke in shivering sweat from a nightmare. He thought he was irretrievably lost, but to his amazement, before him in the distance rose a vast height glowing in dim moonlight and sprinkled sparsely with lights, at the foot of which ran a broad dark river reflecting the half-hidden moon. The nag stopped jogging and it took them an almost endless hour to make the last half verst to the water.

3

It was freezing cold but the wind was down on the Dnieper. There was no ferry, the boatman said. "Closed down. Closed. Shut." He waved his arms as though talking to a foreigner although Yakov had spoken to him in Russian. That the ferry had stopped running sharpened the fixer's desire to get across the river. He hoped to rent a bed at an inn and wake early to look for work.

"I'll row you across for a ruble," the boatman said.

"Too much," Yakov answered, though deadly tired. "Which way to the bridge?"

"Six or eight versts. A long way for the same thing."

"A ruble," the fixer groaned. "Who's got that much money?"

"You can take it or leave it. It's no easy thing rowing across a dangerous river on a pitch-black night. We might both drown."

"What would I do with my horse?" The fixer spoke more to himself.

"That's none of my business." The boatman, his shoulders like a tree trunk, and wearing a shaggy grizzled beard, blew out one full nostril on a rock, then the other. The white of his right eye was streaked with blood.

"Look, mate, why do you make more trouble than it's worth? Even if I could haul it across, which I can't, the beast will die on you. It doesn't take a long look to see he's on his last legs. Look at him trembling. Listen to him breathing like a gored bull."

"I was hoping to sell him in Kiev."

"What fool would buy a bag of old bones?"

"I thought maybe a horse butcher or someone—at least the skin."

"I say the horse is dead," said the boatman, "but you can save a ruble if you're smart. I'll take him for the cost of the trip. It's a bother to me and I'll be lucky to get fifty kopeks for the carcass, but I'll do you the favor, seeing you're a stranger."

He's only given me trouble, the fixer thought.

He stepped into the rowboat with his bag of tools, books, and other parcels. The boatman untied the boat, dipped both oars into the water and they were off.

The nag, tethered to a paling, watched from the moonlit shore.

Like an old Jew he looks, thought the fixer.

The horse whinnied, and when that proved useless, farted loudly.

"I don't recognize the accent you speak," said the boatman, pulling the oars. "It's Russian but from what province?"

"I've lived in Latvia as well as other places," the fixer muttered.

"At first I thought you were a goddam Pole. Pan whosis, Pani whatsis." The boatman laughed, then snickered. "Or maybe a motherfucking Jew. But though you're dressed like a Russian you look more like a German, may the devil destroy them all, excepting yourself and yours of course."

"Latvian," said Yakov.

"Anyway, God save us all from the bloody Jews," the boatman said as he rowed, "those long-nosed, pock-marked, cheating, bloodsucking parasites. They'd rob us of daylight if they could. They foul up earth and air with their body stink and garlic breaths, and Russia will be done to death by the diseases they spread unless we make an end to it. A Jew's a devil—it's a known fact—and if you ever watch one peel off his stinking boot you'll see a split hoof, it's true. I know, for as the Lord is my witness, I saw one with my own eyes. He thought nobody was looking, but I saw his hoof as plain as day."

He stared at Yakov with the bloody eye. The fixer's foot itched but he didn't touch it.

Let him talk, he thought, yet he shivered.

"Day after day they crap up the Motherland," the boatman went on monotonously, "and the only way to save ourselves is to wipe them out. I don't mean kill a Zhid now and then with a blow of the fist or kick in the head, but wipe them all out, which we've sometimes tried but never done as it should be done. I say we ought to call our menfolk together, armed with guns, knives, pitchforks, clubs—anything that will kill a Jew—and when the church bells begin to ring we move on the Zhidy quarter, which you can tell by the stink, routing them out of wherever they're hiding—in attics, cellars, or ratholes—bashing in their brains, stabbing their herring-filled guts, shooting off their snotty noses, no exception made for young or old, because if you spare any they breed like rats and then the job's to do all over again.

"And then when we've slaughtered the whole cursed tribe of them—and the same is done in every province throughout Russia, wherever we can smoke them out—though we've got most of them nice and bunched up in the Pale—we'll pile up the corpses and soak them with benzine and light fires that people will enjoy all over the world. Then when that's done we hose the stinking ashes away and divide the rubles and jewels and silver and furs and all the other loot they stole, or give it back to the poor who it rightfully belongs to anyway. You can take my word—the time's not far off when everything I say, we will do, because our Lord, who they crucified, wants his rightful revenge."

He dropped an oar and crossed himself.

Yakov fought an impulse to do the same. His bag of prayer things fell with a plop into the Dnieper and sank like lead.

II

WHERE DO you go if you had been nowhere? He hid at first in the Jewish quarter, emerging stealthily from time to time to see what there was to see in the world, exploring, trying the firmness of the earth. Kiev, "the Jerusalem of Russia," still awed and disquieted him. He had been there for a few hot summer days after being conscripted into the army, and now, again, he saw it with half the self—the other half worried about his worries. Still, as he wandered from street to street, the colors were light and pretty. A golden haze hung in the air in the late afternoons. The busy avenues were full of people, among them Ukrainian peasants in their native dress, gypsies, soldiers, priests. At night the white gas globes glowed in the streets and there were thick mists on the river. Kiev stood on three hills, and he remembered his first trembling sight of the city from the Nicholas Bridge—dotted with white houses with green roofs, churches and monasteries, their gold and silver domes floating above the green foliage. He wasn't without an eye for a pretty scene, though that added nothing to his living. Still, a man was more than a workhorse, or so they said.

The other way, across the glassy brown river—the way he had come on a dying horse—the steppe stretched out into the vast green distance. Only thirty versts and the shtetl was invisible, gone—poof!—lost, maybe expired. Though he felt homesick he knew he would never return, yet what would it come to? More than once Raisl had accused him of being afraid to leave and maybe it was true but at last it wasn't. So I left, he thought, what good will it do me? Was she back? he wondered. He cursed her when he thought of her.

He went where he had not been before, speaking in Russian to anyone who spoke to him—testing himself, he explained it to himself. Why should a man be afraid of the world? Because he was, if for no other reason. Numb with fear that he would be recognized as a Jew and ordered out, he stealthily watched from the gallery of a church as the peasants, some with knapsacks on their backs, knelt and prayed at the altar before a tall gold crucifix and a jeweled ikon of the Madonna, as the priest, a huge man in rich thick vestments, chanted the Orthodox service. The fixer had the shivers as he looked, and the strange odor of incense increased his nervousness. He almost rose out of his boots as he was touched on the arm and saw at his side a black-bearded hunchback who pointed to the peasants below smacking their heads against the flagstone floor and kissing it passionately. "Go thou and do likewise! Eat salted bread and listen to the truth!" The fixer quickly left.

Stupefied that he dared the adventure, he afterwards descended to the Lavra catacombs—under the old monastery on the Pechersky hill overlooking the Dnieper—amid a group of frightened, pasty-faced peasants holding lit candles. They moved in a loose line along low, damp-smelling passages, where through barred windows he caught glimpses of the saints of the Orthodox Church lying in open coffins, covered with shabby cloths of red and gold. Small red lamps glowed in the walls under their ikons. In a candle-lit cell, as the line moved on, a monk with rattail hair to his shoulders held out a relic of "the hand of St. Andrew" for the faithful to kiss, and each knelt to touch the parchmented hand to his lips. But though Yakov had considered a quick kiss of the bony fingers, when his time came to kneel, he blew out his candle and groped his way on in the dark.

Outside there was a crowd of beggars, some of them armless and legless cripples from the late war. Three were blind. One rolled his eyes inward. One bulged his so that they looked like fish eyes. And one read sonorously "by divine inspiration" from a book of gospels which he held in his hands. He stared at Yakov and Yakov stared at him.

2

He lived in the heart of the Jewish quarter in the Podol District in a teeming tenement hung with mattresses airing and rags of clothing drying, above a courtyard crowded with wooden workshops where everyone was busy but no one earned much of anything. They stayed alive. The fixer wanted better, at least better than he had had, too much of nothing. For a while, during the cold rains of late autumn, he confined himself to the Jewish section, but after the first snowfall in the city—about a month after he had arrived—he began to edge out again, looking for work. With his tool sack slung over his shoulder he trudged from street to street through the Podol and Plossky, the flat commercial districts reaching to the river, and went up the hills into neighborhoods forbidden to Jews to work in. He sought, he continued to say to himself, opportunities, though in seeking them he sometimes felt like a spy behind enemy lines. The Jewish quarter, unchanged in ages, swarmed and smelled. Its worldly goods were spiritual goods; all that was lacking was prosperity. The fixer, having left the shtetl, resented the lack. He had tried working for a brushmaker, a man with a foaming beard who had promised to teach him the business. The wages were soup. So he had gone back to being a fixer and it came also to nothing, sometimes soup. If a window was broken they stuffed it with rags and said a blessing. He offered to replace it for a pittance, and when he had done the work they gave him thanks, blessings, a plate of noodle soup. He lived frugally in a low-ceilinged cubicle, in a printer's assistant's flat—Aaron Latke's, sleeping on a bench covered with a burlap sack; the flat was crowded with children and smelly feather beds, and the fixer, as he parted with kopeks and earned none, grew increasingly anxious. He must go where he could make a living or change his craft, maybe both. Among the goyim his luck might be better, it couldn't be worse. Besides, what choice has a man who doesn't know what his choices are? He meant in the world. So he walked out of the ghetto when no one was looking. In the snow he felt anonymous, in a sense unseen in his Russian cap and coat—any unemployed worker. Russians passed him without looking at him and he passed them. Having been told he did not look Jewish he now believed it. Yakov trudged in the snow up the hill to the Kreshchatik, the broad main street, trying kiosks, shops, public buildings, but finding little to do, a few odd jobs, payment in greenish coppers. At night in his cubicle, a glass of hot tea cupped in his reddened hands, when he thought of returning to the shtetl he thought of death.

Latke, when the fixer said this aloud, looked at him in popeyed horror. He was a man with arthritic hands and eight half-starving children. The pain hindered his work but not his labor.

"For God's sake, patience," he said. "You're not without brains and that's the beginning of luck. Afterwards, as they say, your ox will calve."

"To have luck you need it. I've had little luck."

"You've just come green from the country, so at least be patient till you know where you are."

So the fixer went looking for luck.

One desperate evening, the gas lamps casting a greenish glow on the snow, Yakov, trudging at twilight in the Plossky District, came upon a man lying with his face in the trodden snow. He hesitated a minute before turning him over, afraid to be involved in trouble. The man was a fattish, bald-headed Russian of about sixty-five, his fur cap in the snow, his heavy face splotched a whitish red and blue, snow on his mustache. He was breathing and reeked of drink. The fixer at once noticed the black and white button pinned to his coat, the two-headed eagle of the Black Hundreds. Let him shift for himself, he thought. Frightened, he ran to the corner, then ran back. Grabbing the anti-Semite under the arms he began to drag him to the doorway of the house in front of which he had fallen, when he heard a cry down the street. A girl wearing a green shawl over a green dress was running crookedly towards them. At first he thought she was a crippled child but then saw she was a young woman with a crippled leg.

She knelt, brushed the snow from the fat man's face, shook him and said breathlessly, "Papa, get up! Papa, this can't go on."

"I ought to have gone for him," she said to Yakov, cracking her knuckles against her breast. "This is the second time this month he's fallen in the street. When he drinks in the tavern it becomes an impossible situation. Kindly help me get him home, sir. We live only a few doors from here."

"Take his legs," said Yakov.

With the girl's help he half carried, half dragged the fat Russian up the street to the three-story yellow brick house with a wrought-iron awning above the door. The girl called the porter, and he and the fixer, she hobbling up after them, carried her father up the stairs into a large-roomed, well-furnished flat on the first floor. They laid him on a leather couch near the tile stove in the bedroom. A Pekinese began to yelp, then growled at the fixer. The girl picked the dog up, deposited it in another room, and at once returned. The dog barked shrilly through the door.

As the porter removed the man's wet shoes he stirred and groaned.

"With God's help," he muttered.

"Papa," said his daughter, "we owe thanks to this good man for assisting you after your accident. He found you face down in the snow. If not for him you would have smothered."

Her father opened his humid eyes. "Glory be to God." He crossed himself and began quietly to cry. She crossed herself and dabbed at her eyes with a handkerchief.

As she was unbuttoning her father's overcoat, Yakov, after staying for a last deep breath of the warmth, left the flat and went down the stairs, relieved to be out.

The girl called to him in a tight high voice from the top of the stairs and quickly hobbled down after him, holding to the banister. Her face was sharp, her green eyes searching, hungry. She seemed about twenty-five, slightly built, her torso long, with thick honey-colored hair that she wore loose around the shoulders. She wasn't pretty but she wasn't plain, and although he was sorry for her crippled leg he felt for her a strange momentary revulsion.

She asked him who he was, not quite looking at him, her eyes lowered, then shifting to a direct glance. She stared at the sack of tools on his shoulder.

He told her little: he was a stranger, recently from the provinces. It occurred to him then to remove his cap.

"Please come back tomorrow," she said. "Papa says he would like to thank you when he is in a better frame of mind, but I will tell you frankly you may expect something more than mere thanks. My father is Nikolai Maximovitch Lebedev—semiretired—he was already retired but had to take over his brother's business affairs at his death—and I am Zinaida Nikolaevna. Please call on us in the morning when Papa is himself. He's usually at his best then, though never at his very best since my poor mother's death."

Yakov, without giving his name, said he would return in the morning and left.

Back in his cubicle in Aaron Latke's flat, he wondered what was "more than mere thanks." Obviously the girl meant some sort of reward, possibly a ruble or two, and with luck, five. But he had doubts whether to go back there. Should he take a reward from a self-advertised Jew hater? He hadn't for a minute been comfortable in his presence, or the girl's. Then either better not go, or tell the old man who he was indebted to and leave. But that wasn't what he wanted to do. Yakov sweated in his thoughts, the drunkard's two-headed eagle staring him in both eyes. He slept badly and woke with a new thought. Why not a ruble or two if it kept a Jew alive? What better service from an anti-Semite? He recalled a Russian saying: "A fearful wolf should stay out of the forest," but decided to go anyway, take a chance, or how would he know what went on in the world?

So he returned to the house in the Plossky without his bag of tools, though he could not dress up, nor did he want to. Zinaida Nikolaevna, wearing an embroidered peasant blouse and skirt, with two green ribbons plaited into her hair and some strings of yellow glass beads at her throat, led him to her father's bedroom. Nikolai Maximovitch, in a loose wadded robe with a fur collar, sat at a table by a curtained window, a huge book open before him. On the wall behind hung a large chart in the form of a tree showing by way of white printed slots on its thickest black branches the descent of Nicholas II from Adam. A framed portrait of the Tsar sitting with the pale-faced Tsarevitch hung above that. The house was overheated. The little dog snarled at the fixer and had to be carried out of the room by the cook.

Nikolai Maximovitch rose slowly, an old man with wrinkled, red-rimmed, wet melancholy eyes, and welcomed Yakov without embarrassment. The fixer, thinking of his Black Hundreds button felt for him contempt, and a portion of the same for himself. His throat tightened. Though he wasn't trembling he felt he might be.

"Nikolai Maximovitch Lebedev," the fat Russian said, offering his soft pudgy hand. A thick gold watch-chain hung on his paunch, and his vest was dusty with snuff grains.

Yakov, after a slight hesitation, shook hands, answering as he had planned, "Yakov Ivanovitch Dologushev." To have given his name might have finished off the reward. Yet he felt ashamed and sweaty.

Zinaida Nikolaevna busied herself with the samovar.

Her father indicated a chair for the fixer.

"I have a good deal to thank you for, Yakov Ivanovitch," he said, resuming his seat. "I lost my footing in the snow, no doubt there was ice under it. You were very kind to assist me—not everyone would have. Once, under quite different circumstances—I began to drink only after the death of my beloved wife, a woman of exceptional qualities—Zina will affirm the truth of what I am saying—I fainted from illness on Fundukleyevsky Street, in front of a coffee shop, and lay on the pavement with a gash in my head for an unconscionable time before anyone—in this case a woman who had lost a son at Port Arthur—bothered to come to my assistance. Nowadays people are far less concerned about their fellow humans than in times past. Religious feeling has shrunk in the world and kindness is rare. Very rare indeed."

Yakov, waiting for him to come to the reward, sat tightly in the chair.

Nikolai Maximovitch regarded the fixer's worn sheepskin coat. He took out his snuffbox, inserted a pinch in both nostrils, blew his nose vigorously in a large white handkerchief, sneezed twice, then after a few futile attempts, succeeded in thrusting the box back into his robe pocket.

"My daughter informs me you were carrying a bag of tools yesterday. What is your trade, if I may ask?"

"Repairs, et cetera, of all kinds," Yakov answered. "I do carpentering, also painting, and roofing."

"Is that so? Are you presently employed?"

The fixer, without thought, said he wasn't.

"Where are you from if you don't mind saying?" said Nikolai Maximovitch. "I ask because I have a curious nature."

"From the provinces," Yakov answered, after a moment's hesitation.

"Ach—really?—a country boy?—and a good thing, may I say. The country virtues are not to be denied. I'm from the region of Kursk myself. I've pitched hay in my time. Do you come to Kiev as a pilgrim?"

"No, I came for work." He paused. "Also, if possible, for a little education."

"Excellent. You speak well although with a provincial accent. But grammatically. Have you had some schooling?"

Blast his questions, the fixer thought.

"I've read a little on my own."

The girl was watching him through lowered eyelids.

"Do you also read in the Holy Scriptures?" asked Nikolai Maximovitch. "I presume you do?"

"I know the Psalms."

"Wonderful. Did you hear, Zina?—the Psalms, wonderful. The Old Testament is admirable, the true prophecy of Christ's coming and his redemption of us through death. However, it is in no way equal to the preachings and parables of Our Lord, in the New Testament. I have just been rereading this." Nikolai Maximovitch glanced down at the open book and read aloud: "'Blessed are the poor in spirit; for theirs is the kingdom of heaven.'"

Yakov, grown pale, nodded.

Nikolai Maximovitch's eyes were humid. He had again to blow his nose.

"He always cries when he reads the Sermon on the Mount," said Zinaida Nikolaevna.

"I always cry." Clearing his throat, Nikolai Maximovitch read on: "'Blessed are the merciful; for they shall obtain mercy.'"

Mercy, the fixer thought, it makes him cry.

"'Blessed are they which are persecuted for righteousness' sake; for theirs is the kingdom of heaven.'"

Come already to the reward, thought Yakov.

"Ah, this is most moving," Nikolai Maximovitch said, having to wipe his eyes again. "You know, Yakov Ivanovitch, I am in some ways a miserable man, melancholic, a heavy drinker, yet something more than that although I recently set my clothes on fire while smoking a cigarette when a piece of hot ash fell on my trousers, and if Zina had not alertly poured a pitcher of water over me, I would now be a burnt corpse. I drink because I happen to be more sensitive than most—I feel much too keenly the sorrows of life. My daughter will attest to that."

"It's true," she said. "He is a man of more than ordinary feeling. When our former little dog Pasha died of a distemper, Papa couldn't eat for weeks."

"When Zina was a child, after her severe illness I wept every night over her poor crippled leg."

"It's true," she said, her eyes moist.

"I tell you this so that you may know the kind of person I am," Nikolai Maximovitch said to Yakov. "Zina, please serve the tea."

She brought the tea to the marble-top table on a thick silver tray, with two clay pots of whole-fruit jam, raspberry and peach; and Viennese rolls, and butter.

It's mad, I know, Yakov thought. Tea with rich goyim. Yet he ate hungrily.

Nikolai Maximovitch poured a little milk into his tea and ate a buttered roll. He ate with gulping noises, as though drinking what he ate. Then he sipped again from the hot glass and set it down, patting his snuff-swollen lips with a linen napkin.

"I would like to offer you a modest reward for your timely assistance."

Yakov hastily put down his glass and rose.

"I ask for nothing. Thanks for the tea and I'd better be off."

"Spoken like a Christian, but please sit down and listen to what I have to say. Zina, fill Yakov Ivanovitch's glass and put plenty of butter and conserves on his roll. Yakov Ivanovitch, what I have to say is this. I have an empty flat on the next story, recently vacated—the tenants proved entirely unsuitable—four fine rooms that need painting and repapering. If you care to undertake the task I offer forty rubles, which is more than I would ordinarily pay, considering the fact that I furnish the paint and other materials; but the circumstances in this case are different. It is, of course, a matter of gratitude, but wouldn't you rather work than peremptorily receive from me some silver coins? Is money ever valuable if it is come by without labor? An offer of work is an appreciation of merit. Notwithstanding you did me the greatest of favors—I might have suffocated in the snow, as Zina points out—isn't my offer of work a more estimable reward than a mere payment of money?" He looked eagerly at Yakov. "Therefore will you accept?"

"In the way you put it, yes," said Yakov. He got up quickly, said he had to be going, and after stumbling into a closet on his way out, hurriedly left the apartment.

Though he worried what he was getting into and changed his mind every half hour as he lay restlessly on his bed-bench that night, the next morning he went back. He returned for the same reason he had gone the first time—to collect his reward. What he earned for his work in this case was the reward. Who could afford to say no to forty rubles—a tremendous sum? Therefore why worry about returning? Go, do the job quickly, collect the money, and when you have it in your pocket, leave the place once and for all and forget it. After all it's only a job, I'm not selling my soul. When I'm finished I'll wash up and go. They're not bad people. The girl's direct and honest in her way, though she makes me uneasy, and as for the old man, maybe I misjudged him. How many goyim have I known in my life? Maybe someone stuck that Black Hundreds pin on his coat when he was drunk in the tavern. Still, if it's really his own I'd like to ask him straight out, "Nikolai Maximovitch, will you please explain how you can cry for a dead dog yet belong to a society of fanatics that urges death on human beings who happen to be Jews? Explain to me the logic of it." Then let him answer that.

What also troubled the fixer was that once he went to work, even though the "reward" made it different from work though not less than work, he might be asked to produce his passport, a document stamped "Religious Denomination: Judaic," which would at once tell Nikolai Maximovitch what he was hiding from him. He chewed his lips over that but decided that if the passport was asked for he would say the police in the Podol had it; and if Nikolai Maximovitch insisted he must produce it, that was the time to quit or there would be serious trouble. It was therefore a gamble, but if you were against gambling, stop playing cards. He guessed the Russian was probably too muddled to ask for the passport although he was required to by law. Still, after all, it was a reward, maybe he wouldn't. Yakov was now somewhat sorry he hadn't at once identified himself as a Jew by birth. If that had killed off the reward, at least there would be no self-contempt. The more one hides the more he has to.

He did an expert job on the flat—scraped the walls clean of paper, and the ceilings of flakes and loose patches. He plastered where he had to, then thickly calcimined the ceilings—nothing but the best for Nikolai Maximovitch. And he pasted the wallpaper neatly though his experience with papering was limited—in the shtetl only Viskover, the Nogid, was that fancy. Yakov worked all day and into the night by yellow gaslight to get the job done, collect his rubles, and disappear. The landlord, stopping now and then to catch his breath, labored up the stairs each morning to see how the work was progressing, and expressed himself as most pleased. In the afternoon he got out his vodka bottle, into which he had cut strips of orange peel, and by sunset was drunk. Zina, unseen during the day, sent up the cook, Lidya, with a snack at lunchtime—a fish pie, bowl of borscht, or some meat dumplings so delicious it seemed to the fixer he would have done the job for the food alone.

One night Zina limped up the stairs, expressing surprise he was working so late. She asked Yakov if he had eaten since lunch, and when he said he was not hungry she suggested, nervously laughing, that he eat supper with her, Papa having already retired and she liking company. The fixer, greatly surprised by the invitation, begged off. He had, he explained, too much to do, and apologized for his clothes. Zina said not to mind that. "Clothes can be shed in a minute, Yakov Ivanovitch, but whether they are or not cannot change a man's nature. He's either kind or he isn't, with or without clothes. Besides I don't care for excessive formality." He thanked her but said he couldn't take the time off from work. There were two more rooms to do. The next evening she came up again and somewhat agitatedly confessed she was lonely; so they ate together in the kitchen downstairs. She had dismissed Lidya and throughout the meal talked constantly, mostly of her childhood, the young ladies' school she had attended, and the pleasures of Kiev in the summertime.

"Days are long and hot, but nights are languorous and starlit. People refresh themselves in their flower gardens and some walk in the parks, drink kvass and lemonade, and listen to the symphonies. Have you ever heard *Pagliacci*, Yakov Ivanovitch? I think you would love Marinsky Park."

He said he did not mind parks.

"The Contract Fair opens in the spring, it's most entertaining. Or if you like there's a cinematograph to go to on the Kreshchatik."

Her eyes darted glances as she spoke and when he looked at her she glanced away. Afterwards the fixer, made nervous by her chatter, excused himself to go back to work, but Zina followed him up the stairs to watch him paste on the wallpaper she had selected, bunches of blue roses. She sat on a kitchen chair with her legs crossed, the good one over the crippled, and cracked and ate dried sunflower seeds, rhythmically swinging her leg as she watched him work.

Then she lit and awkwardly smoked a cigarette.

"You know, Yakov Ivanovitch, I couldn't possibly treat you as an ordinary common laborer for the simple reason that you aren't one. Certainly not in my eyes. Really you are a guest who happens to be working here because of Papa's idiosyncratic ways. I hope you realize that?"

"If you don't work you don't eat."

"Quite true, but you are more intelligent and even genteel—at any rate, sensitive—please don't shake your head over that—than the average Russian laborer. I can't tell you how exasperating they can be, particularly Ukrainians, and really we dread having repairs or improvements made. No, please don't deny it, anyone can sense you are different. And you told Papa you believe in the necessity of an education and would like to further your own. I heard you say that and approve very much. I too love to read, and not only romances. I'm sure you'll find excellent opportunities for yourself in the future, and if you are alert may some day be as comfortably off as Papa."

Yakov went on papering.

"Poor Papa suffers dreadfully from melancholia. He gets quite drunk by nightfall and has no appetite, to speak of, for supper. He usually falls asleep in his chair, Lidya removes his shoes, and with Alexei's help we get him to bed. At night he awakes and says his prayers. Sometimes he undresses himself, and it's almost impossible to find his clothes in the morning.

Once he put his socks under the rug, and I found his drawers, all wet, in the water closet. Usually he isn't awake till mid-morning. It's hard on me, of course, but I can't complain because Papa's had a difficult life. And there's no one to keep me company in the evening but Lidya and at times Alexei when he happens to be fixing something, but quite frankly, Yakov Ivanovitch, neither of them has an idea in his head. Alexei sleeps in the basement, and Lidya's small room is at the back of the flat off the terrace beyond Papa's bedroom; and since I would rather read at night than listen to her go on and on, I dismiss her early. Sometimes it gives me pleasure to be the only one up in the house at night. It's very cozy. I light the samovar, read, write letters to old friends and crochet. Papa says I make the most remarkable lace doilies. He marvels at the intricacy of the patterns. But most of the time," she sighed, "to tell the truth, it can be dreadfully lonely."

She chewed a sunflower seed disconsolately, then remarked that although she had been crippled through illness as a child, she had always been considered attractive by the opposite sex and had had more than one admirer.

"I don't say this to flaunt myself or be brazen but because I don't want you to think of me as being at a disadvantage with regard to the normal experiences of life. I am nothing of the sort. I have a quite attractive figure and many men notice me, especially when I'm dressed up. Once in a restaurant a man ogled me so insistently Papa went over to him and demanded an explanation. The man humbly apologized and do you know, Yakov Ivanovitch, when I got back home I broke into sobs."

Gentlemen called on her of course, Zina went on, but unfortunately not always the most sensitive or worthy, a situation more than one of her friends had to put up with. Sensitive, dependable men were rare, although such persons could be found in all classes, not necessarily gentry.

He listened with one ear, aware that her glance traced his every move. Why does she bother? he asked himself. What can she see in a man like me whose advantages are all disadvantages if I have it right? I have little wit in Russian, it's a heavy language for me. And if I said "Jew" aloud she'd run in six directions. Yet she often entered his thoughts. He had been a long time without a woman and wondered what it would be like to be in bed with her. He had never had a Russian woman, though Haskel Dembo had slept with a peasant girl and said it was the same as with any Jewess. The crippled leg, Yakov thought, would not bother him.

He finished papering the fourth room that night and except for the woodwork the job was done. Two days later when it was all but finished, Nikolai Maximovitch unsteadily ascended the stairs to inspect the flat. He went from room to room, running his fingers over the wallpaper, looking up at the ceilings.

"Outstanding," he said. "Quite outstanding. An honest and attractive piece of work, Yakov Ivanovitch. I congratulate you."

Later he said as though in afterthought, "You must excuse me for asking, but what are your political predilections? Surely you're not a Socialist? I ask in the strictest confidence without attempting to pry, and not in the least accusatorily. I ask, in a word, because I am interested in your future."

"I am not a political person," Yakov answered. "The world's full of it but it's not for me. Politics is not in my nature."

"Very good, indeed. Neither am I, and much better off in the bargain if anyone should ask. Yakov Ivanovitch, don't think I will soon forget the quality of your craftsmanship. If you should care to go on working for me, though in another, and may I say, advanced capacity, I would be more than happy to employ you. The truth of the matter is that I am the owner of a small brickworks nearby, although in a contiguous district. I inherited it from my elder brother, a lifelong bachelor who went to his final reward half a year ago after suffering from an incurable disease. I tried to sell the factory but the offers were so disgraceful that, although I have little heart or, at this time of my life, head for business, I have kept it going, although, I confess, barely profitably. My foreman Proshko is in charge, an excellent technical person who is otherwise an ignorant man, and confidentially, the drivers who work under him have not been accounting for every brick that leaves the yard. I would like you to go in as a sort of overseer to handle accounts and, on the whole, look after my interests. My brother was involved in every phase of the operations, but I have little patience with bricks."

Yakov, though he had listened with excitement to the proposition, confessed he was without experience in business. "I know nothing about bookkeeping."

"Common sense is what's needed in business once honesty is assured," said Nikolai Maximovitch. "What there is to learn you will learn as you go along. I usually visit for an hour one or two mornings a week, and what you don't know I'll try to help you with, though I frankly confess my knowledge is limited. There's no need to protest, Yakov Ivanovitch. My daughter, whose judgment in these matters I respect, has the highest opinion of your merit, and you may believe me, I thoroughly share it. She considers you a man of sobriety and sound sense, and I am confident that after you have mastered the fundamentals you will do a responsible and effective job. During the period of your—ah—apprenticeship I will pay you forty-five rubles monthly. I hope that's satisfactory. But there is another advantage for you that I should mention, frankly one that will work to our mutual benefit. My brother converted part of a loft over the brickyard stable into a warm and comfortable room, and you may live there without payment of rent if you accept my offer."

The forty-five rubles astounded and tempted the fixer.

"What is it an overseer does? Excuse the question, but I'm not a man of the world."

"Worldliness is vanity, it doesn't appeal to me. The overseer manages the business end of the enterprise. We manufacture about two thousand bricks daily—many fewer than we used to—a thousand or so more during the building season, not quite so many this time of the year; and it has been fewer lately although we have a contract with the Kiev Municipal Council for several thousands of bricks. The Tsar himself has given orders for civic improvements to be made before the Romanov Jubilee, and the Municipality is tearing up wooden walks and laying down entire streets of brick sidewalk, though this is done of course when the weather permits, not in the winter snow. And we also hold a small contract for bricks for the restoration of certain fortifications above the Dnieper. Yes, I would expect you to keep track of orders received and, to be sure, of the exact number of bricks manufactured as well as those carted out. These figures you will get from Proshko, but there are ways of checking. You will also send out statements requesting payment and enter payments received in the ledger. Once or twice weekly you will turn over bank drafts and other monies to me, and in the meantime keep them safe in the strongbox. Proshko will of course retain the responsibilities of the technical foreman, and I will tell him I expect him to place all orders for supplies through you. You will also make out the wages inventory and pay the workers at the end of the month."

Though beset by self-doubt and every kind of fear, Yakov was thinking this might be his important chance. A few months' experience at this kind of work and other opportunities might open up for him. "I'll think it over carefully," he said, but before Nikolai Maximovitch had descended the stairs, he had accepted.

The landlord returned with a vodka bottle to wet the bargain. Yakov had two drinks and his uneasiness wore off. He was preparing himself for a better future, he told himself. He slept for a while on the floor and later finished the last of the woodwork, once more uneasy.

It was nightfall. After he had swept and cleaned up, soaked the paintbrushes in turpentine, and washed, he heard Zina limping up the stairs. She was wearing a dress of blue silk, her hair up and encircled with a white ribbon, her cheeks and lips delicately rouged. She invited Yakov to eat with her again. "In celebration of the completion of your fine work, and most of all, to your future relationship with Papa, though he has already retired and we shall be alone."

He had the old excuses, was even a little irritated by the invitation and wanted to escape, but she would not hear of it. "Come, Yakov Ivanovitch, there's more to life than work."

It was news to him. Still, he thought, the job's done here and this is the last I'll see of her. So what's wrong with farewell?

On the kitchen table Zina had laid out a feast, even some food he had never seen before. There were stuffed cucumbers, raw Danube herring, fat sausages, pickled sturgeon with mushrooms, assorted meats, wine, cakes and cherry brandy. The fixer, overwhelmed by the spread, felt at first self-conscious. If you've had nothing you're afraid of too much. But he swept that aside and ate hungrily those things he had eaten before. He sucked the red wine through delicious chunks of white bread.

Zina, open and happy, and looking more attractive than he had ever seen, picked here and there at sweet and spicy things and filled her wineglass often. Her sharp face was flushed, she talked about herself and laughed at nothing at all. Although he tried to think of her as possibly a friend she remained strange to him. He was strange to himself. Once, staring at the white tablecloth, he thought of Raisl but put her out of his mind. He finished the meal—he had never in his life eaten so much—with two glasses of brandy, and only then began to enjoy the "party."

When she cleared the table Zina's breath was heavy. She brought out a guitar, plucked it, and in a high thin voice sang, "Ech, my pack is heavy." It was a sad song and filled him with mild melancholy. He had thought of getting up to leave, but the kitchen was warm and it was pleasant to sit there listening to the guitar. Then she sang, "Come on, come on, my darling angel, come and dance with me." When she put down her guitar, Zina looked at him in a way she never had before. Yakov understood at once where they were. Excitement and foreboding flowed into one feeling. No, he thought, it's a Russian woman. If she slept with me and found out who I was she'd cut her throat. Then he thought, it's not always so, there are some who wouldn't mind. For himself he was willing to experience what there was to experience. But let her lead.

"Yakov Ivanovitch," Zina said, pouring herself another glassful of wine which she at once drank down, "do you believe in romantic love? I ask because I think you guard yourself against it."

"Whether I do or don't it doesn't come easily to me."

"I heartily agree that it oughtn't to come too easily," Zina said, "but it seems to me that those who are serious about life—perhaps too serious—are slow to respond to certain changes in the climate of feeling. What I mean to say, Yakov Ivanovitch, is that it's possible to let love fly by like a cloud in a windy sky if one is too timid, or perhaps unable to believe he is entitled to good fortune."

"It's possible," he said.

"Do you love me—just a little, Yakov Ivanovitch?" she asked quickly. "I've sometimes noticed you looking at me as though you might. For instance, you smiled at me quite delightfully a few minutes ago, and it warmed my heart. I dare ask because you yourself are very modest and tend to be conscious—overconscious, I would say—that we are from different classes, though I believe much alike as people."

"No," he said. "I can't say I love you."

Zina flushed. Her eyelids fluttered. After a long minute she sighed and said in a smaller voice, "Very well, then, do you like me at all?"

"Yes, you have been kind to me."

"And I like you too, indeed I do. I think you are serious and a well-informed person."

"No, I am half an ignoramus."

She poured herself some cherry brandy, sipped from the glass and put it down.

"Oh, Yakov Ivanovitch, please for a moment let up on your seriousness and kiss me. I dare you to kiss me."

They got up and kissed. She groped for him, her body clinging tightly to his. He felt for an instant an anguished pity for her.

"Shall we stay here longer?" she whispered, breathing heavily, "or would you care to visit my room? You've seen Papa's but not mine."

She looked him full in the face, her green eyes lit dark, her body hot, still clinging. She seemed to him an older woman, possibly twenty-eight or -nine, someone used to looking out for herself.

"Whatever you say."

"What do *you* say, Yakov Ivanovitch?"

"Zinaida Nikolaevna," he said, "excuse me for asking you this question but I don't want to make a serious mistake. I've made my share of them—every kind you can think of—but there are some I don't want to make again. If you are innocent," he said awkwardly, "it would be better not to go any further. I say this out of respect for you."

Zina reddened, then shrugged and said frankly, "I'm as innocent as most, no more nor less. There's nothing to worry about in that regard." Then she laughed self-consciously and said, "I see you're an old-fashioned person and I like that, although your question to me was hardly discreet."

"If one why not another? What about your father? What I

mean to ask is, is it likely he might find out if we go to your room?"

"He never has," she said. He was momentarily surprised at her answer and then accepted it without another question. Why wrestle with a fact?

They went silently along the corridor, Zina hobbling, Yakov tiptoeing behind her, to her perfumed bedroom. The Pekinese, lying on the bed, looked at the fixer and yawned. Zina picked it up and went again down the hall to lock it in the kitchen.

Her room was full of knickknacks on numerous small tables, and pictures of kerchiefed girls on the wall. Peacock feathers stuck out from behind the frame of a mirror. In the corner of the room hung an ikon of the Holy Mother with a small red oil lamp lighted before it.

Should I stay or should I go? Yakov thought. On the one hand it's been a long season without rain. A man is not a man for nothing. What do the Hasidim say? "Hide not from thine own flesh." On the other hand what does this mean to me? At my age it's nothing new. It means nothing.

When she returned he was sitting on the bed. He had taken off his shirt and undershirt.

Yakov watched uneasily as Zina, after removing her shoes, knelt at the ikon, crossed herself, and for a moment prayed.

"Are you a believer?" she asked.

"No."

"I wish you were, Yakov Ivanovitch," she sighed.

Then she rose and asked him to undress in the lavatory while she got ready in the bedroom.

It's her leg, he thought. She'll be under covers when I come in. Better that way.

He removed his clothes in the lavatory. His hands still stank of paint and turpentine, and he soaped them twice with her pink bar of perfumed soap. He smelled them again but now they stank of the perfume. If there's a mistake to make I'll make it, he thought.

Seeing himself naked in the mirror he was at first uneasy, then sickened by what he was about to do.

Things are bad enough, so why make them worse? This isn't for me, I'm not the type, and the sooner I tell her the better. He went into the bedroom, carrying his clothes.

Zina had braided her hair. She stood naked, her bosom full, sponging herself from a white bowl, in the gaslight. He saw a dribble of bright blood run down her crippled leg and said, stupefied, "But you are unclean!"

"Yakov!—You startled me." She covered herself with the wet cloth. "I thought you would wait till I called you."

"I didn't know your condition. Excuse me, I had no idea. You didn't mention it, though I realize it's personal."

"But surely you know this is the safest time?" Zina said. "And there's no inconvenience to speak of, the flow stops the minute we begin."

"Excuse me, some can but I can't."

He was thinking of his wife's modesty during her period and until she had been to the baths, but could not say that to Zina.

"Excuse me, I'd better be going."

"I'm a lonely woman, Yakov Ivanovitch," she cried, "have mercy a little!" but he was already dressing and soon left.

3

One night in the dead of winter, in the cold thick dark at 4 A.M., after the drivers Serdiuk and Richter had come for two teams of horses—leaving six horses in the stalls—and he had heard them clomp out of the stable and clack dully across the snow-covered cobblestones, Yakov, who had been two days in the brickyard, got quickly out of bed, lit a short candle and hurriedly dressed. He sneaked down the outer stairs from his room above the stable and went along the fence of palings, past the squat brickkilns to the cooling shed. Motionless in the wet cold, he watched the drivers and their helpers, in steaming sheepskins, the horses' flanks steaming, loading the straw-covered long wagon-trucks with large heavy yellow bricks. The work progressed slowly, helper tossing a brick to helper, who tossed it to the driver on the wagon, who laid it in place. After what seemed to him an endless time standing in the dark, blowing on his hands and trying soundlessly to stamp the cold out of his boots, Yakov had counted three hundred and forty bricks loaded into one wagon, and four hundred and three into another. Three other wagons at the shed went unused. But in the morning when Proshko, the foreman, presented him with the voucher in the stuffy low-ceilinged shack where Yakov sat at a table stacked with ledgers and bundles of useless papers from the past, the badly written numbers scrawled on a torn piece of wrapping paper came to a total of six hundred ten bricks, instead of seven hundred forty-three, and the fixer ground his teeth in anger at the cold-blooded nerve of the thievery.

Though Yakov was desperately eager for work, he had reluctantly accepted Nikolai Maximovitch's offer, at the last minute almost in panic trying to back out when he learned that the Lukianovsky, where the brickyard was located—near a cemetery, with a few houses and trees scattered around and beyond it, more heavily on the far-off side about half a tombstoned verst away—and where he was expected to live, was a district forbidden to Jews to reside in. He had then told the owner of the brickworks that he would not take the job because he had many doubts he could do the work as it should be done. But Nikolai Maximovitch, advising him not to be hasty, had pooh-poohed his doubts.

"Nonsense, you will do better than you suppose. You must learn to have confidence in your natural abilities, Yakov Ivanovitch. Just follow my late brother's method with the ledger—old-fashioned but accurate—and you will master the system as you go along." Yet puzzled somewhat, he raised his offer by three rubles a month, and Yakov trying every way to convince himself to take the job, then suggested it would be more convenient for him if he could go on living in the Podol—he never said where in the district—and come to work very early each morning. It wasn't too far a walk from where he lived. The electric trolley, which stopped close by the brickyard, did not run after dark.

"Unfortunately you won't be of much use to me living in the Podol," said Nikolai Maximovitch. They were talking in the brickyard on a cloudy end-of-January day—a pall of black smoke hung over the kilns—and Nikolai Maximovitch still wore his Black Hundreds button on his coat, which Yakov, when speaking to him—he saw himself unable to detach his eye if once he stared at it—had to ignore or look around, for the button loomed large and unsettling.

"It is not what goes on here during the workday that

worries me so much," the anti-Semite said, "although I assure you that worries me too; but I am deeply concerned with what happens in the early morning hours when the wagons are being loaded for the first deliveries. Daylight is too strong for a thief. It's in the dark when the ghosts are flying and good people are lying abed that he does his dirty work. My late-lamented brother, who had little respect for sleep—one must respect it or it will not respect him—was here at 3 A.M. in every weather to oversee each and every wagonload. I am not asking you to do the same, Yakov Ivanovitch. That sort of dedication to a business enterprise is fanatic and in his case led, I am convinced, to my brother's early death." Nikolai Maximovitch crossed himself with eyes shut. "But if you were to look in on them in the early morning hours, and also unexpectedly during other loadings, counting off aloud a close estimate of the number of bricks in the trucks, it might tempt them not to overdo it. I expect some thievery—humans are humans—but of necessity there has to be a limit. It would be impossible for me to get a reasonably just price for this factory if it should go bankrupt."

"How do they steal?" the fixer had asked.

"I suspect the drivers under Proshko's supervision or connivance. They take out more than they account for."

"Then why don't you give him the boot?"

"More easily said than done, my dear boy. If I did I would have to shut down the plant. He is an excellent technical man—one of the best, my brother used to say. I confess it is not my purpose to catch him thieving. As a religious person I want to keep him from it. And wouldn't you say it was the more sensible as well as charitable thing? No, let's arrange it as I say. Take the room above the stable, Yakov Ivanovitch. It's yours without a single kopek of rent."

Since he had not mentioned the fixer's papers—neither the passport necessary for new employment, nor the residence certificate he would need, Yakov uneasily took the chance and accepted the job. He had for a fleeting minute again considered saying he was a Jew—just quietly informing Nikolai Maximovitch: "Well, you ought to know what the situation is. You say you like me; you know I'm an honest worker and don't waste the boss's time, then maybe it won't surprise you to hear

I was born Jewish and for that reason can't live in this district." But that was of course impossible. Even supposing—a fantastic suppose—that Nikolai Maximovitch, two-headed eagle button and all, overlooked the confession in his own interests, still the Lukianovsky was not for Jews, with certain unusual exceptions, and if a poor fixer were exposed as one living there he would be in serious trouble. It was all too complicated. For the first week Yakov was daily on the verge of leaving, escaping from the place, but he stayed on because he had heard from Aaron Latke that counterfeit papers of various kinds were available to prospective buyers at a certain printing establishment in the Podol, for not too large a sum, and though the thought of acquiring such papers gave him severe sweats, he decided he ought to keep it in mind.

When Proshko brought in the voucher the morning after Yakov had spied on the drivers loading the wagons, though the fixer's heart beat loudly when he saw the false figure on the paper, he informed the foreman that Nikolai Maximovitch had told him to be present at night when the wagons were loaded, and since it was his responsibility, he would be there from now on. Proshko, a burly, thick-eared man with a rough beard, who wore high rubber boots muddy with yellow clay and a long dirty leather apron, gazed at the fixer with intense small eyes.

"What do you think goes on in the wagons at night? Are the drivers on their knees fucking their mothers?"

"What goes on goes on," said Yakov nervously, "but the number of bricks that you loaded last night and this figure on your paper don't agree, if you'll excuse me for saying so."

He then wished he had said it differently, though how was it possible to say it differently to a thief?

"How would you know how many bricks were loaded?"

"I stood near the shed last night, counting them, according to Nikolai Maximovitch's direction. In other words, I did as he told me." His voice was thick with emotion, as though the bricks belonged to him, although the strange thing was they belonged to an anti-Semitic Russian.

"Then you counted wrong," Proshko said, "this is the number we loaded." He tapped a thick finger on the paper on the table. "Listen, my friend, when a dog puts his nose into shit, he gets it dirty. You have a long nose, Dologushev. If you don't believe me look in a mirror. A man with a nose like that ought to be careful where he puts it."

He left the shack but returned in the afternoon. "What about your papers," he said, "have you registered them yet? If not, hand them over here and I'll have them stamped by the District Police."

"I'm obliged to you," Yakov said, "but that's already been seen to and done. Nikolai Maximovitch took care of it. You don't have to trouble yourself."

"Tell me, Dologushev," said Proshko, "why is it you talk Russian like a Turk?"

"And what if I am a Turk?" The fixer smiled crookedly.

"He who runs too fast raises the wind against him." Lifting his leg Proshko farted.

Afterwards Yakov felt too uneasy to eat supper. I'm the wrong man to be a policeman, he thought. It's a job for a goy.

Yet he did what he was asked to. He appeared in the shed every morning in the 4 A.M. cold and counted the bricks in the wagons. And when he looked out the shack window and saw them loading up during the daylight hours, he went outside to watch. He did it openly, preventing the thieves from their thievery. When Yakov appeared at the shed, no one spoke but the drivers sometimes stopped their work to stare at him.

Proshko no longer turned in vouchers each morning, so Yakov wrote his own. The bookkeeping was not so difficult as he had thought—he had caught on to the system, and besides there wasn't that much business. Once a week Nikolai Maximovitch, more drearily melancholic, arrived by sledge for receipts to be deposited in his bank, and after a month Yakov received a long congratulatory letter from him. "Your work is diligent and effective, as I foresaw, and I shall continue to vest in you my utmost confidence. Zinaida Nikolaevna sends her regards. She too applauds your efforts." But no one else did. Neither the drivers nor their helpers paid any attention to him, even when he tried to make conversation. Richter, the heavy-faced German, spat in the snow at his approach, and Serdiuk, a tall Ukrainian who smelled of horse sweat and hay, watched him, breathing heavily. Proshko, passing the fixer in the yard, muttered, "Bastard stool pigeon!" Yakov pretended not to hear. If he heard "Jew" he would dive into the sky.

Except for these he was on more or less decent terms with the other workers in the yard—he paid them on time, about fifty left from almost two hundred employed when the yard had turned out six or seven thousand bricks a day—and this was so despite the fact that Proshko was spreading nasty stories about him; one that Skobeliev, the yardkeeper, had told him was that the fixer had once done time as a convicted thief. But no one sought him out as friend or kept him company when the brickyard was closed, so he was mostly alone. After work Yakov stayed in his room. He read by lamplight—though Nikolai Maximovitch had promised to install an electric bulb—for hours each night. His reading in the past was what he had accidentally come across; he now read what he wanted to know. He continued to study Russian, wrote out long grammatical exercises and read them aloud. And he devoured two newspapers every day, though they often gave him the shivers, both things reported as fact, and things hinted at; for instance, Rasputin and the Empress, new plots of terrorists, threats of pogroms, and the possibility of a Balkan war. So much was new to him, how is one to know all he ought to know? He began then to haunt the bookshops in the Podol in his free time, searching for inexpensive books. He bought a *Life of Spinoza* to read during the lonely nights in his stable room. Was it possible to learn from another's life? And Russian history fascinated him. He went through stacks of pamphlets on the shelves in the rear of the shops. He read some on serfdom, the Siberian penal system—a terrifying account he had found in a bushel the bookseller had winked at. He read about the revolt and destruction of the Decembrists, and a fascinating account of the Narodniki, idealists of the 1870's who had devoted themselves to the peasants in an impulsive attempt to stir them to social revolution, were rebuffed by them, and turned from peasant-mysticism to terrorism. Yakov also read a short biography of Peter the Great, and after that a horrifying account of the bloody destruction of Novgorod by Ivan the Terrible. It had entered the madman's head that the city intended treason to him, so he had ordered a wooden wall built around it to prevent escape. Then he marched in with his army, and after putting his subjects through the cruelest tortures, daily slaughtered thousands of them. This went on in increasing savagery, the sound of horror rising to the sky as the wailing mothers watched their children being roasted alive and thrown to wild dogs. At the end of five weeks, sixty thousand people, maimed, torn, broken apart, lay dead in the foul-smelling streets as disease spread. Yakov was sickened. Like a pogrom—the very worst. The Russians make pogroms against the Russians—it went on throughout their history. What a sad country, he thought, amazed by what he had read, every possible combination of experiences, where black was white and black was black; and if the Russians, too, were massacred by their own rulers and died like flies, who were then the Chosen People? Fatigued by history, he went back to Spinoza, rereading chapters on biblical criticism, superstition, and miracles which he knew almost by heart. If there was a God, after reading Spinoza he had closed up his shop and become an idea.

When he wasn't reading, Yakov was composing little essays on a variety of subjects—"I am in history," he wrote, "yet not in it. In a way of speaking I'm far out, it passes me by. Is this good, or is something lacking in my character? What a question! Of course lacking but what can I do about it? And besides is this really such a great worry? Best to stay where one is, unless he has something to give to history, like for instance Spinoza, as I read in his life. He understood history, and also because he had ideas to give it. Nobody can burn an idea even if they burn the man. On the other hand there was the activist Jan De Witt, Spinoza's friend and benefactor, a good and great man who was torn to pieces by a Dutch mob when they got suspicious of him although he was innocent. Who needs such a fate?" Some of the little essays were criticisms of "Certain Conditions" as he had read about them in the newspapers. He read these over and burned them in the stove. He also burned the pamphlets he could not resell.

Something that unexpectedly bothered him was that he was no longer using his tools. He had built himself a bed, table, and chair, also some shelves on the wall, but this was done in the first few days after he had come to the brickyard. He was afraid that if he didn't go on carpentering he might forget how and thought he had better not. Then he got another letter, this from Zina, her handwriting full of surprising thick black strokes, inviting him—with her father's permission—to call on her. "You are a sensitive person, Yakov Ivanovitch," she wrote, "and I respect your ideals and mode of behavior; however, please don't worry about your clothes, although I am sure you can purchase new ones with the improved salary you are earning." He had sat down to reply but couldn't think what to say to her, so he didn't answer the letter.

In February he went through a period of severe nervousness. He blamed it on his worries. He had visited the place where he could get counterfeit papers, had found they were not impossibly expensive although they were not inexpensive, and he was thinking of having a passport and residence certificate made out under his assumed name. When he awoke, hours before he had to, to check the number of bricks in the trucks his muscles were tight, his chest constricted, breathing sometimes painful, and he was uneasy when he dealt with Proshko. Even to ask him the most routine questions troubled the fixer. He was irritable all day and cursed himself for trifling mistakes in his accounts, a matter of a kopek or two. Once, at nightfall, he drove two boys out of the brickyard. He knew them as troublemakers, one a pale-faced pimply boy of about twelve, the other like a peasant with a head of hair like hay, about the same age. They came into the yard after school, in the late afternoon, and pitched balls of clay at each other, broke good bricks, and hooted at the horses in the stable. Yakov had warned them to stay out of the yard. This time he caught sight of them through the shack window. They had sneaked into the yard with their book satchels and threw rocks at the smoke curling up from the kilns. Then they hit the chimneys with pieces of brick. Yakov had rushed out of the shack, warning them to leave, but they wouldn't move. He ran towards them to scare them. Seeing him coming, the boys hooted, touched their genitals, and clutching their satchels, sped past the supply sheds and scrambled up a pile of broken bricks at the fence. They tossed their book satchels over the fence and hopped over it.

"Little bastards!" Yakov shouted, shaking his fist.

Returning to the shack, he noticed Skobeliev watching him slyly. Then the yardkeeper hurried with his stick to light the gas lamps. After a while they glowed in the dusk like green candles.

Proshko, standing at the door of the cooling shed, had also been looking on. "You run like a ruptured pig, Dologushev."

The next morning a police inspector visited the fixer to ask if anyone in the brick factory was suspected of political unreliability. The fixer said no one was. The official asked him a few more questions and left. Yakov was not able to concentrate on his reading that night.

Since he was sleeping badly he tried going to bed just after he had eaten. He fell asleep quickly enough but awoke before midnight, totally alert, with a sense of being imperiled. In the dark he feared calamities he only occasionally thought of during the day—the stable in flames, burning down with him in it, bound hand and foot unable to move; and the maddened horses destroying themselves. Or dying of consumption, or syphilis, coughing up or pissing blood. And he dreaded what worried him most—to be unmasked as a hidden Jew. "Gevalt!" he shouted, then listened in fright for sounds in the stable to tell him whether the drivers were there and had heard him cry out. Once he dreamed that Richter, carrying a huge black bag on his back, was following him down the road by the graveyard. When the fixer turned to confront the German and asked him what he was carrying in the bag, the driver winked and said, "You." So Yakov ordered and paid for the counterfeit papers, though weeks went by and he did not claim them. Then for no reason he could think of he began to feel better.

He went through a more confident period, when for the first time in his life he spent money as though it was nothing more than money. He bought more books, paper to write on, tobacco, a pair of shoes to relieve him from boots, a luxurious jar of strawberry jam, and a kilo of flour to bake bread with. The bread did not rise but he baked it and ate it as biscuit. He also bought a pair of socks, a set of drawers and undershirt, and an inexpensive blouse, only what was necessary. One night, feeling an overwhelming hunger for sweets, he entered a candy store to sip cocoa and eat cakes. And he bought himself a thick bar of chocolate. When he counted his rubles later, he had spent more than he had bargained for and it worried him. So he returned to frugality. He lived on black bread, sour cream and boiled potatoes, an occasional egg, and when he was tempted, a small piece of halvah. He repaired his socks and patched his old shirts until there was nowhere he hadn't made a stitch. He saved every kopek. "Let the groats accumulate," he muttered. He had serious plans.

One night in April when the thick ice of the Dnieper was cracking, and Yakov—after selling the books he had recently bought and afterwards wandering in the Plossky District—was returning late to the brickyard, it began to snow unexpectedly. Coming up the hill approaching the cemetery, he saw some boys attacking an old man and scattered them with a shout. They ran like frightened rabbits through the graveyard. The old man was a Jew, a Hasid wearing a caftan to his ankles, a round rabbinic hat with a fur brim, and long white stockings. He slowly bent and retrieved from the snow a small black satchel tied with brown twine. He had been hurt on the temple and the blood dripped down his hairy cheek into his tousled two-forked gray beard. His eyes were dazed. "What happened to you, grandfather?" the fixer said in Russian. The Hasid, frightened, backed off, but Yakov waited and the old man replied in halting Russian that he had come from Minsk to see a sick brother in the Jewish quarter and had got lost. Then some boys had attacked him with snowballs embedded with sharp stones.

The streetcars were no longer running, and the snow was falling in thick wet flakes. Yakov was uneasily worried but thought he could take the old man into the brickyard, let him rest while he applied some cold water to his wound, then get him out before the drivers and their helpers came in.

"Come with me, grandfather."

"Where are you taking me?" said the Hasid.

"We'll wipe the blood off you, and when the snow stops I'll show you which way to the Jewish quarter in the Podol."

He led the Hasid into the brickyard and up the stairs to his room above the stable. After lighting the lamp, Yakov tore up his most tattered shirt, wet it, and wiped the blood off the old man's beard. The wound was still bleeding but it didn't bother the Hasid. He sat in Yakov's chair with his eyes shut, breathing as though he were whispering. Yakov offered him bread and a glass of sweetened tea but the Hasid would not accept food. He was a dignified man with long earlocks and asked the fixer for some water. Pouring a little over his fingers over a bowl, he then withdrew a small packet from his caftan pocket, some matzo pieces wrapped in a handkerchief. He said the blessing for matzos, and sighing, munched a piece. It came as a surprise to the fixer that it was Passover. He was moved by a strong emotion and had to turn away till it had gone.

When he looked out the window the snow was still falling but there were signs of a moon, a circle of dim light within the falling snow. It'll soon stop, he thought, but it didn't. The glow disappeared and once more it was dark and snowy. Yakov thought he would wait till the drivers arrived, quickly count the bricks, and when the snow stopped, sneak the old man out after the wagons had left and before Proshko came. If the snow didn't stop, the old man would have to leave anyway.

The Hasid slept in the chair, woke, stared at the lamp, then at the window and slept again. When the drivers opened the stable door he awoke and looked at Yakov, but the fixer made a sign for silence and left to go down to the shed. He had offered the Hasid his bed but when he returned the old man was sitting up awake. The drivers had loaded the wagons and were waiting in the shed for daylight. They had wrapped chains around the horses' hooves but Serdiuk had said if the snow got deeper they would not leave the yard. Now Yakov was worried.

In his room, huddled in his sheepskin coat, he stood watching the snow, then rolled and smoked a cigarette and made himself a glass of tepid tea. He drank a little, fell asleep on his bed, and dreamed he had encountered the Hasid in the graveyard. The Hasid had asked, "Why are you hiding here?" and the fixer had struck him a blow on the head with a hammer. It was a terrible dream and gave him a headache.

He awoke to find the old man staring at him, and his nervousness returned.

"What's wrong?" he asked.

"What's wrong is wrong," said the old man. "But now the snow has stopped."

"Did I say anything in my sleep?"

"I wasn't listening."

The sky had lightened and it was time to go, but the Hasid dipped the tips of his fingers into water, then unknotted the twine around his satchel, opened it, and removed a large striped prayer shawl. From the pocket of his caftan he took out a phylactery bag.

"Where is the east?" asked the old man.

Yakov impatiently indicated the wall with the window. Saying the blessing for phylacteries, the Hasid slowly wound one around his left arm, the other on his brow, binding the strap gently over the crusting wound.

He covered his head with the capacious prayer shawl, blessing it, then prayed at the wall, rocking back and forth. The fixer waited with his eyes shut. When the old man had said his morning prayers, he removed the shawl, folded it carefully and put it away. He unbound the phylacteries, kissed them, and packed them away.

"May God reward you," he said to Yakov.

"I'm much obliged but let's move on." The fixer was sweating in his cold clothes.

Asking the old man to wait a minute, he went down the snow-laden stairs and walked around the stable. The yard was white and still, the roofs of the kilns covered with snow. But the wagons, though loaded with bricks, had not yet left and the drivers were still in the shed. Yakov hurried up the stairs and got the Hasid and his satchel. They hastened through the spring snow to the gate. He led the old Hasid down the hill to the streetcar stop, but while they were waiting a sledge with tinkling bells drove by. Yakov hailed it and the sleepy driver promised he would take the Jew to his street in the Podol. When Yakov got back to the brickyard he felt he had been through a long night. He felt out of sorts and unreasonably depressed. On the way to the stable he met Proshko in high spirits.

When he entered his room Yakov had the sudden feeling that someone had been in it while he was out with the Hasid. He had the impression things had been moved, then set back not exactly in place. He suspected the foreman. The smell of horse manure and rotting hay seeped up from the stable. He hastily searched among his few possessions but could find nothing missing, neither household articles, his few books, nor rubles in the tin can. He was glad he had sold some of the books and burned the pamphlets; they were about history but some history was dangerous. The next day he heard that a body had been found in a cave nearby, then he read with fascinated horror a newspaper account of the terrible murder of a twelve-year-old boy who had lived in one of the wooden houses near the cemetery. The body was found in a sitting position, the boy's hands tied behind his back. He was clad in his underwear, without shoes, one black stocking hanging on his left foot; scattered nearby were a bloodstained blouse, a schoolboy's cap, a belt, and several pencil-smeared copy books. Both the *Kievlyanin* and *Kievskaya Mysl* carried a picture of him, Zhenia Golov, and Yakov recognized the pimply-faced boy he had chased out of the yard with his friend. One newspaper said the boy had been dead for a week, the other said two. When the Police Inspector had examined his swollen face and shrunken mutilated body, he had counted thirty-seven wounds made by a thin pointed instrument. The boy, according to Professor Y. A. Cherpunov of the Kiev Anatomical Institute, had been stabbed to death and bled white, "possibly for religious purposes." Marfa Vladimirovna Golov, the bereaved mother, a widow, had claimed the body of her son. There was a picture of her in both newspapers, pressing the boy's poor head to her grief-stricken bosom, crying desolately, "Tell me, Zheniushka, who did this to my baby?"

That night the river overflowed its banks, flooding the lower reaches of the city. Two days later the boy was buried in the cemetery, a few short steps from his home. Yakov could see from the window of his stable the trees still powdered with April snow, and wandering amid them and the thin tombstones, the black crowd, among them some pilgrims with staves. When the coffin was lowered into the grave, hundreds of leaflets exploded into the air: WE ACCUSE THE JEWS. A week later the Kiev Union of Russian People, together with members of the Society of the Double-headed Eagle, placed a huge wooden cross on the grave of the boy—Yakov watching from afar—at the same time calling on all good Christians, according to the newspapers that night, to preach a new crusade against the Israelitic enemies. "They want nothing less than our lives and country! People of Russia! Have pity on your children! Avenge the unfortunate martyrs!" This is terrible, Yakov thought, they want to start a pogrom. In the brickyard Proshko sported a Black Hundreds button on his leather apron. Very early the next morning the fixer hurried to the printer's for his counterfeit papers but when he arrived he found the place had burned down. He ran back to the stable and hastily counted his rubles to see if he had enough to get to Amsterdam and possibly New York. Wrapping up his few things, and slinging his bag of tools onto his shoulder, he was on his way down the stairs when a man who identified himself as Colonel I. P. Bodyansky, the red-mustached head of the Secret Police in Kiev, with several other officials, fifteen gendarmes wearing white looped cords across the breasts of their uniforms, a detachment of police, several plainclothes detectives, and two representatives of the Office of the Chief Prosecuting Attorney of the District Superior Court, about thirty in all, rushed up the stairs with drawn pistols and swords, confronting the fleeing Yakov.

"In the name of His Majesty Nicholas the Second," said the red-headed colonel, "I arrest you. Resist and you are dead."

The fixer readily confessed he was a Jew. Otherwise he was innocent.

III

IN A long, high-ceilinged cell under the District Courthouse, a dismal faded stucco structure in the commercial section of the Plossky a few versts from the brickyard in the Lukianovsky, Yakov, in a state of unrelieved distress, could not blot out the sight of himself marching manacled between two tall columns of gendarmes on horses, their sabers drawn and spurs clinking as they hurried him along snowy streets tracked slushy by sledge runners.

He had begged the colonel to let him walk on the sidewalk to lessen his embarrassment, but was forced into the wet center of the street, and people on their way to work had stopped to watch. They gazed at first quietly, then in deep silence, broken by whispers, muttering and a few jeers. Most seemed to wonder what the parade was about, but then a uniformed schoolboy in a blue cap and silver-buttoned coat, poking his fingers up like horns over his head, danced in the snow behind the prisoner, chanting, "Zhid, Zhid," and that awoke murmurs, hoots, mockery. A small crowd, including some women, began to follow them, jeering at the fixer, calling him dirty names, "murdering Jew." He wanted to break and run but didn't dare. Someone flung a block of wood at him but it struck a horse that broke into a wild gallop, kicking up snow and running two squares before it was controlled. Then the colonel, a huge man in a fur cap, raised his saber and the crowd scattered.

He delivered the prisoner first to Secret Police Headquarters, a one-story brown building in a side street; then after a long annoyed telephone conversation, fragments of which the frightened prisoner sitting on a bench in an anteroom surrounded by gendarmes, overheard, the colonel escorted Yakov directly to an underground cell in the District Courthouse, leaving behind two gendarmes who patrolled the corridor with naked sabers. Yakov, alone in the cell, wringing his hands, cried out, "My God, what have I done to myself? I'm in the hands of enemies!" He hit his chest with his fist, bewailed his fate, envisioned terrible things happening to him, ending by being torn apart by a mob. Yet there were also moments of sudden hope when he felt that if he only *explained* why he had done what he had done, he would be at once released. He had stupidly pretended to be somebody he wasn't, hoping it would create "opportunities," had learned otherwise—the wrong opportunities—and was paying for learning. If they let him go now he had suffered enough. He blamed also egotism and foolish ambition, considering who he was, and promised himself it would be different in the future. He had learned his lesson—again. Then he jumped up and cried aloud, "What future?" but nobody answered. When an orderly brought in tea and black bread, he could not eat though he had eaten nothing that day. As the day wore on he groaned often, tore his hair with both fists, and knocked his head repeatedly against the wall. A gendarme saw him and strictly forbade it.

Towards evening, the prisoner, sitting immobile on a thin mattress on the floor, heard footsteps in the corridor other than the measured tread of the armed guard who had replaced the two gendarmes. Yakov scrambled to his feet. A man of medium height carrying a black hat and fur coat hurried along the dimly lit corridor to the dark cell. He ordered the guard to open the cell door, lock him in with the prisoner, and leave. The guard hesitated. The man waited patiently.

"I was ordered not to leave, if it's all the same to your honor," said the guard. "The Prosecuting Attorney said not to let the Jew out of my sight because it's a most important case. That's what I was told by his assistant."

"I am here on official business and will call you when I need you. Wait outside the corridor door."

The guard reluctantly opened the cell, locked the man in with Yakov and left. The man watched till the guard had gone, then took a candle stub out of his coat pocket, lit it and set it in some drops of wet wax in a saucer. He held the saucer in his hand, studying Yakov for a long moment, then put it down on the table in the cell. Seeing his cold breath in the light he drew on his fur coat. "I am subject to lingering colds." He wore a darkish beard, pince-nez, and a thick scarf wrapped around his neck. Facing the fixer, who was standing stiffly at attention, inwardly trembling, he introduced himself in a quiet resonant voice.

"I am B. A. Bibikov, Investigating Magistrate for Cases of Extraordinary Importance. Please kindly identify yourself."

"Yakov Shepsovitch Bok, your honor, though there's nothing extraordinary about my foolish mistakes."

"You are not Yakov Ivanovitch Dologushev?"

"That was a stupid deception. I admit it at once."

Bibikov adjusted his glasses and looked at him in silence. He lifted the candle to light a cigarette, then changed his mind, set it down, and thrust the cigarette into his pocket.

"Tell me truly," said the Investigating Magistrate in a severe voice, "did you murder that unfortunate child?"

A fog of blackness rose before Yakov's eyes.

"Never! Never!" he cried hoarsely. "Why would I kill an innocent child? How could I have done it? For years I wanted a child but my luck was bad and my wife couldn't have one. If in no other way at least in my heart I'm a father. And if that's so how could I kill an innocent child? I couldn't think of such a thing, I'd rather be dead."

"How long have you been married?"

"Five years going on six, though I'm not really married now because my wife left me."

"Is that so? Why did she leave you?"

"To make it short and simple she was unfaithful. She ran off with an unknown party and that's why I'm in jail now. If she hadn't done that I would have stayed where I belonged, which means where I was born. This very minute I'd be sitting down to supper, such as it was, but it could have been worse. When the sun went down, whether I had earned a kopek or not, I headed straight for my hut. It wasn't such a bad place to be, now that I think of it."

"You're not from Kiev?"

"Not the city, the province. I left my village a few months after my wife left me and I've been here since November. I was ashamed to stay on there with things as they were. There were other reasons but that was what bothered me most."

"What other reasons?"

"I was fed up with my work—no work at all. And I hoped, with a bit of luck, to get myself a little education. They say in America there are schools where a grown man can study at night."

"You were thinking of emigrating to America?"

"It was one of my thoughts, your honor, though I've had many such and they've all come to nothing. Still in all, I'm a loyal subject of the Tsar."

The Investigating Magistrate found the cigarette in his pocket and lit it. He smoked silently, standing on the other side of the table, still studying Yakov's tormented face in the candlelight.

"I saw among your possessions when you were arrested a few books, among others a volume of selected chapters from the work of the philosopher Spinoza."

"That's right, your honor. Could I get them back? I'm also worried about my tools."

"In due course, if you are not indicted. Are you familiar with his writings?"

"Only in a way of speaking," said the fixer, worried by the question. "Although I've read the book I don't understand it all."

"What is its appeal to you? First let me ask you what brought you to Spinoza? Is it that he was a Jew?"

"No, your honor. I didn't know who or what he was when I first came across the book—they don't exactly love him in the synagogue, if you've read the story of his life. I found it in a junkyard in a nearby town, paid a kopek and left cursing myself for wasting money hard to come by. Later I read through a few pages and kept on going as though there were a whirlwind at my back. As I say, I didn't understand every word but when you're dealing with such ideas you feel as though you were taking a witch's ride. After that I wasn't the same man. That's in a manner of speaking of course, because I've changed little since my youth."

Though he had answered freely, talking about a book with a Russian official frightened the fixer. He's testing me, he thought. Still when all's said and done, better questions about a book than a murdered child. I'll tell the truth but speak slowly.

"Would you mind explaining what you think Spinoza's work means? In other words if it's a philosophy what does it state?"

"That's not so easy to say," Yakov answered apologetically. "The truth is I'm a half-ignorant man. The other half is half-educated. There's a lot I miss even when I pay the strictest attention."

"I will tell you why I ask. I ask because Spinoza is among my favorite philosophers and I am interested in his effect on others."

"In that case," said the fixer, partly relieved, "I'll tell you that the book means different things according to the subject of the chapters, though it's all united underneath. But what I think it means is that he was out to make a free man out of himself—as much as one can according to his philosophy, if you understand my meaning—by thinking things through and connecting everything up, if you'll go along with that, your honor."

"That isn't a bad approach," said Bibikov, "through the man rather than the work. But you ought to explain the philosophy a little."

"Who knows if I can," the fixer said. "Maybe it's that God and Nature are one and the same, and so is man, or some such thing, whether he's poor or rich. If you understand that a man's mind is part of God, then you understand it as well as I. In that way you're free, if you're in the mind of God. If you're there you know it. At the same time the trouble is that you are bound down by Nature, though that's not true for God who is Nature anyway. There's also something called Necessity, which is always there though nobody wants it, that one has to push against. In the shtetl God goes running around with the Law in both hands, but this other God, though he fills up more space, has less to do altogether. Whoever you end up believing in, nothing has changed much in the world if you're without work. So much for Necessity. I also figure it means that life is life and there's no sense kicking it into the grave. Either that or I don't understand it as well as it's said."

"If a man is bound to Necessity where does freedom come from?"

"That's in your thought, your honor, if your thought is in God. That's if you believe in this kind of God; that's if you reason it out. It's as though a man flies over his own head on the wings of reason, or some such thing. You join the universe and forget your worries."

"Do you believe that one can be free that way?"

"Up to a point," Yakov sighed. "It sounds fine but my experience is limited. I haven't lived much outside the small towns."

The magistrate smiled.

Yakov snickered but caught himself and stopped.

"Is such a thing as you describe it, true freedom, would you say, or cannot one be free without being politically free?"

Here's where I'd better watch my step, the fixer thought. Politics is politics. No use fanning up hot coals when you have to walk across them.

"I wouldn't know for sure, your honor. It's partly one and partly the other."

"True enough. One might say there is more than one conception of freedom in Spinoza's mind—in Necessity, philosophically speaking; and practically, in the state, that is to say within the realm of politics and political action. Spinoza conceded a certain freedom of political choice, similar to the freedom of electing to think, if it were possible to make these choices. At least it is possible to think them. He perhaps felt that the purpose of the state—the government—was the security and comparative freedom of rational man. This was to permit man to think as best he could. He also thought man was freer when he participated in the life of society than when he lived in solitude as he himself did. He thought that a free man in society had a positive interest in promoting the happiness and intellectual emancipation of his neighbors."

"I guess that's true, your honor, if you say so," said Yakov, "but as far as I myself am concerned what you said is something to think about, though if you're poor your time is taken up with other things that I don't have to mention. You let those who can, worry about the ins and outs of politics."

"Ah," Bibikov sighed. He puffed on his cigarette without speaking. For a moment there was no sound in the cell.

Did I say something wrong? Yakov thought wildly. There are times it doesn't pay to open your mouth.

When the magistrate spoke again he sounded once more like an investigating official, his tone dry, objective.

"Have you ever heard the expression 'historical necessity'?"

"Not that I remember. I don't think so though maybe I could guess what it means."

"Are you sure? You've not read Hegel?"

"I don't know his name."

"Or Karl Marx? He too was a Jew, though not exactly happy to be one."

"Not him either."

"Would you say you have a 'philosophy' of your own? If so what is it?"

"If I have it's all skin and bones. I've only just come to a little reading, your honor," he apologized. "If I have any philosophy, if you don't mind me saying so, it's that life could be better than it is."

"Yet how can it be made better if not in politics or through it?"

That's a sure trap, Yakov thought. "Maybe by more jobs and work," he faltered. "Not to forget good will among men. We all have to be reasonable or what's bad gets worse."

"Well, that's at least a beginning," the magistrate said quietly. "You must read and reflect further."

"I will just as soon as I get out of here."

Bibikov seemed embarrassed. The fixer felt as though he had disappointed him, although he was not sure why. Probably too much inexact talk. It's hard to make sense when you're in trouble, considering also your other natural disadvantages.

The magistrate after a while absently asked, "How did you bruise your head?"

"In the dark, in desperation."

Bibikov reached into his pocket and offered the fixer his cigarette box. "Have one, they're Turkish."

Yakov smoked in order not to affront the man, though he could not taste the cigarette.

Taking a folded paper and pencil stub out of his suit coat pocket the magistrate placed them on the table, saying, "I leave this questionnaire with you. We will have to know more biographical details since you have no police record. When you have answered each question and signed your name, call the guard and give him the paper. Be accurate in everything you say. I'll leave the candle with you."

Yakov stared at the paper.

"I have to hurry now. My boy has a fever. My wife gets frantic." The Investigating Magistrate buttoned his fur coat and put on a wide-brimmed black fedora that looked large for his head.

Nodding to the prisoner, he said quietly, "Whatever happens you must have fortitude."

"My God, what can happen? I'm an innocent man."

Bibikov shrugged. "It's a touchy thing."

"Have mercy, your honor; I've had little in my life."

"Mercy is for God, I depend on the law. The law will protect you."

He called the guard and left the cell. As the door was being locked he hurried away in the dimly lit corridor.

The fixer felt at once a sense of intense loss.

"When will you come back?" he shouted after him.

"Tomorrow." A distant door shut. The footsteps were gone.

"It's a long tomorrow," said the guard.

2

The next morning a new guard unlocked the cell, searched Yakov thoroughly for the third time since he had awakened, manacled him tightly with heavy handcuffs attached by a short thick chain, and in the presence of two other armed guards, one of whom cursed the prisoner and prodded him with his pistol, escorted Yakov, about as dead as he was alive, up two flights of narrow booming wooden stairs into the Investigating Magistrate's office. In the large anteroom some clerks in uniform sat at long tables scratching on paper with wet pens. They gazed at him with intense interest, then looked at each other. Yakov was led into a brown-walled smaller office. Bibikov was standing at an open window, waving his hand back and forth to thin out the cigarette smoke. As Yakov entered he quickly shut the window and seated himself in a chair at the head of a long table. The room contained a bulky desk, several shelves of thick books, two large green shaded lamps, and a small ikon in the corner; on the wall hung a large sepia portrait of Tsar Nicholas II, bemedaled and immaculately barbered, staring critically at the fixer. The picture added to his discomfort.

The only other person in the room was Bibikov's assistant, a pimply-faced man in his thirties, with a thin beard through which his small chin was visible. He was sitting next to the magistrate at the short end of the table, and Yakov was told to take his seat at the other end. The three escorting guards at the magistrate's request waited in the antechamber. He, after barely glancing at the prisoner—almost distastefully the fixer thought—fished among some official documents in a pile before him and drew forth a thick one whose pages he thumbed through. He whispered something to the assistant, who filled a heavy fountain pen from a large bottle of black ink, wiped the nib with an ink-stained rag, and began to write quickly in a notebook.

Bibikov, looking ill-at-ease and tired, seemed changed from last night, and for a moment Yakov nervously wondered if it was the same man. His head was large, with a broad forehead and a pelt of dark graying hair. As he read he nibbled on his thin underlip; then he put down the paper, blew at his pince-nez, adjusted them with care and sipped from a glass of water. He spoke in a voice without warmth, addressing the fixer across the table: "I will now read you a portion of the deposition of Nikolai Maximovitch Lebedev, factory owner of the Lukianovsky District; that is, his factory is in the Lukianovsky—" Then his official voice changed and he said quietly, "Yakov Shepsovitch Bok, you are in a difficult situation and we must straighten things out. Listen first to a statement of the witness Lebedev. He says it was your intent from the outset to deceive him."

"It isn't true, your honor!"

"Just one minute. Please contain yourself."

Bibikov took up the document, turned to an inside page and read aloud:

"'N. Lebedev: He whom I knew as Yakov Ivanovitch Dologushev, although he did me, by chance, a personal favor of some magnitude, for which I generously rewarded him, and my daughter treated him most considerately, was a less than honest man—more accurately, a deceitful one. He concealed from me, for reasons that are obvious—and well he might for I would never have employed him had I known what I do now—that he was in truth, although he attempted to hide it, a member of the Jewish Nation. I confess I felt a tremor of suspicion when I observed his discomfiture at a query I addressed him concerning the Holy Scriptures. In response to my question whether he had made it a habit to read the Holy Bible, he replied he was familiar only with the Old Testament, and blanched greatly when I proceeded to read him some telling verses from the New Testament, in particular from the Sermon on the Mount.'

"'Investigating Magistrate: Anything else?'

"'N. Lebedev: I also noticed an odd hesitancy, a sort of bumbling when he spoke his name for the first time, that is to say the assumed name, which he was as yet unfamiliar with. It did not, need I say, your honor, fit his Jewish tongue. Furthermore, for an ostensibly poor man he showed extreme reluctance—perhaps this is to his credit—to accept my generous offer of a position in my brickworks, and my suspicions were further aroused because he seemed uneasy when I had broached the matter of his living in the room above the stable on the factory grounds. He wanted to work for me and yet he was afraid to, naturally enough. He was troubled and nervous, constantly wetting his lips and averting his eyes. Since I am somewhat incapacitated in health—my liver gives me trouble and I suffer a marked shortness of breath—I had need of an overseer who would live on the premises and see that my affairs were kept in order. However, since the Jew had helped me when I became suddenly ill and collapsed in the snow, my suspicions were not long lasting, and I offered him the position. I believe he knew full well, when he accepted my unwitting offer, that the Lukianovsky District is sacred territory and forbidden to Jews for residence, except, as I understand it, for exceptional services to the Crown; and I take that to be the reason he made no attempt to turn over to me his papers so that I might deliver them to the District Police.'

"'Investigating Magistrate: Did you ask for them?'

"'N. Lebedev: Not directly. Yes, perhaps I did once and he made me some sort of fishy Jewish excuse or other, and then as I was having trouble with my health I neglected to remind him again. Had I done that and he refused my request, I would at once have ordered him off my property. I am a generous and lenient man, your honor, but I would never have tolerated a Jew in my employ. Please note, if you will, the sigillum on my coat lapel. I consider it a mark of this man's insolence that he was not quailed by it in my presence. For your information I am a former recording secretary of the Society of the Double-headed Eagle.'"

The magistrate laid down the paper, removed his glasses and rubbed his eyes.

"You have heard the deposition," he said to Yakov. "I have also read your questionnaire and am familiar with the responses, but I must now ask you to comment on the remarks of the witness Lebedev. Is the substance of them correct? Be careful in your reply. This, though not a trial, is a police investigation to see if an Act of Indictment is warranted."

Yakov rose in excitement. "Please, your honor, I don't know much about the law, and it isn't always simple to say yes and no in the right place. Would you let me speak to a lawyer for advice? I might even have a few rubles to pay if the police will return my money to me."

"Yes and no take care of themselves if a man tells the truth. As for consulting a lawyer, that is not possible at this stage. In our legal system the indictment comes first. After the preliminary examination the Investigating Magistrate and Prosecuting Attorney consult, and if both believe the suspect to be guilty, an Act of Indictment is drawn up and sent to the District Court, where it is either confirmed or disapproved by the judges. The defense may begin after the accused is informed that the indictment has been voted, and he is then given a copy of it. Within a week or so, possibly a bit more, the accused may select his counsel and inform the court."

"Your honor," Yakov said in alarm, "suppose a man is innocent of what they say he did? What's it all about is a confusion in my mind. One minute I think it's as clear as daylight and the crime we're talking about is a small one, no more than a mistake you might say, and the next minute you say things that make me shiver. For my little sin why should anybody accuse me of a big one? If I gave a false name to someone does that mean there's bound to be an indictment?"

"We will know in due course what is bound to be."

The fixer, sighing heavily, sat down, his manacled hands twitching in his lap.

"I have asked you to comment on the witness Lebedev's remarks," Bibikov said.

"Your honor, I give you my word I meant no harm. What I did wrong—even Nikolai Maximovitch admits it—I did with reluctance, against my will. The truth is I found him drunk in the snow. As a reward he offered me a job I didn't ask for. I could've refused it and I did once or twice, but my money was going fast, I had rent to pay and et cetera. I was getting desperate for work—my hands complain when they have nothing to do—so I finally took what he offered me. He was satisfied with the paint and papering job I first did, and he also told me I was a good overseer in the brickworks. I used to get up half past three every night to inspect the loading of the wagons. If he said it once he said it more than once. Ask him yourself, your honor."

"True, but didn't you give him a false name as your own? In effect, a gentile name? That was no accident I take it? That was your intent, wasn't it?"

The magistrate had forcefully thrust his face forward. Was this the man who said he admired Spinoza?

"It's my mistake, I admit it," said Yakov. "I gave him the first name that popped into my head. I wasn't thinking, your honor, and that's how a man comes to grief. When you're faced with a worrisome situation it's not so easy to keep your mind on what comes next. Dologushev is a one-eyed peasant near my village who slaughters pigs. But the truth of it is I really didn't want to live on the factory grounds. It got so I couldn't sleep from worrying so much. Nikolai Maximovitch mentions that I was afraid to take his offer to live in the stable. He says so himself in this paper you just read to me. I asked him if I could live in the Podol instead and walk to the job, but he said no, I had to live there. In other words it wasn't my idea in the first place. And he's mistaken if he thinks he asked for my passport. Maybe he thought he did but he didn't. He's a melancholy man and sometimes vague in his thoughts. I swear he never asked me. If he had, that would have ended it then and there. I would have thought the jig's up and gone home. It would have saved me a lot of misery."

"Still, you did live in the Lukianovsky, though fully aware it was illegal for you to do so?"

"That's as you say, your honor, but I didn't want to lose the job. I was hoping for a better life than I had." His voice had begun to plead, but noticing the magistrate's compressed lips and stern gaze, Yakov stopped speaking and inspected his hands.

"In the questionnaire," said Bibikov, snapping on his glasses and consulting another paper, "you state you are a Jew 'by birth and nationality.' Do I sense a reservation, and if so what is it?"

The fixer sat silent a minute, then looked up uncomfortably. "What I meant by that is I'm not a religious man. I was when I was young but lost my belief. I thought I mentioned that when we talked last night, but maybe I didn't. That's all I meant by that."

"How did it happen? I refer to your loss of religion."

"I guess there's more than one reason even though I don't recall them all. In my life, the way that it's turned out, I've had a lot to think about. One thought breeds another. Give me an idea and in two minutes there's a second pushing out the first. Also I've been reading a little here and there, as I mentioned to you, your honor, and have picked up a few things I never knew before. It all adds up."

The magistrate leaned back in his chair. "You haven't by some chance been baptized along the way? It might be convenient if you had."

"Oh, no, your honor, nothing at all like that. What I mean to say is I'm a freethinker."

"I understand that, though to be a freethinker assumes one would know how to think."

"I try my best," said Yakov.

"What do you think freethinker means?"

"A man who decides for himself if he wants to believe in religion. Maybe an agnostic also. Some do and some don't."

"Do you think it adds to your stature to be irreligious?"

My God, what have I said? the fixer thought. I'd better keep this simple and small or I'll dig my grave and they'll lay me in it.

He said hastily, "It's as you say, your honor, yes and no fall into place if you tell the truth. I'm telling the truth."

"Let's not complicate matters unnecessarily." Bibikov sipped from his water glass. "Legally you are a Jew. The Imperial Government considers you one even though you twist and squirm. You are so recorded on your passport. Our laws concerning Jews apply to you. However, if you are ashamed of your people, why don't you leave the faith officially?"

"I'm not ashamed, your honor. Maybe I don't always like what I see—there are Jews of all sorts, as the saying goes, but if I'm going to be ashamed of anyone, it might as well be myself." As he said this his color heightened.

Bibikov listened with interest. He glanced down at his notes, then looked up with eyes narrowed. Ivan Semyonovitch, the assistant, who reacted quickly to his remarks, often taking on the same facial expression as the magistrate, glancing at the notes from where he sat, leaned forward intently.

"The absolute truth, please," said the Investigating Magistrate sternly. "—Are you a revolutionary, either as a theorist or activist?"

Yakov felt the force of his pounding heart.

"Does it say that anywhere in your papers, your honor?"

"Please answer my question."

"No, I'm not. God forbid. That's beyond me, if you know what I mean. It's not my nature. If I'm anything I'm a peaceful man. 'Yakov,' I used to say to myself, 'there's too much violence in the world and if you're smart you'll stay out of it.' It isn't for me, your honor."

"A Socialist or member of any Socialist parties?"

The fixer hesitated. "No."

"Are you certain?"

"I give you my earnest word."

"Are you a Zionist?"

"No."

"Do you belong to any political party whatsoever? That would include Jewish parties."

"To none at all, your honor."

"Very well. Have you noted the responses, Ivan Semyonovitch?"

"Every word, sir. I have it all," said the pimply assistant.

"Good," said Bibikov, absently scratching his beard. "Now there is another matter I wish to question you about. Wait till I find the paper."

"Excuse me, I don't mean to interrupt," Yakov said, "but I would like you to know that my passport was stamped 'Permission Granted' when I left my village. And when I got to Kiev, the very next day after my arrival which happened late at night—the next day I brought it to the passport section of the Police Station of the Podol District. It was also stamped there, your honor."

"That is already noted. I've examined the passport and your remarks are substantially correct. However, that isn't the matter I was about to bring up."

"It was only in the Lukianovsky, if you'll excuse me, your honor, that I didn't register. That was where I made a mistake."

"That is also noted."

"If you don't mind, I'd like to mention that I served for a short time in the Russian Army."

"Noted. A very short time, less than a year. You were discharged for illness, were you not?"

"Also because the war was over. There was no use for any more soldiers at that time."

"What was the illness?"

"Attacks of asthma, on and off. I would never know when they would hit me next."

"Are you still troubled with this ailment?" the magistrate said conversationally. "I ask because my son has asthma."

"Mostly it's cleared up though sometimes on a windy day I find it hard to draw a breath."

"I'm glad it's cleared up. Now permit me to go on to the next item. I will read from the deposition of Zinaida Nikolaevna Lebedev, spinster, age thirty."

This is terrible, the fixer thought, squeezing his hands. Where will it all end?

The door opened. The magistrate and his assistant looked up as two officials strode into the room. One, in a red and blue uniform with gold epaulets, was the officer who had arrested Yakov, Colonel Bodyansky, a heavy man with a cropped red mustache. The other was the Prosecuting Attorney Grubeshov, Procurator of the Kiev Superior Court. He had that morning gone down to stare at the fixer in his cell without addressing a word to him. Yakov had stood frozen against the wall. Five minutes later the prosecutor had walked away, leaving him in a sweaty state of unrest.

Grubeshov placed on the table a worn portfolio with straps. He was a stoutish man with a fleshy face, sidewhiskers, thick eyebrows and hawklike eyes. A roll of flesh on the neck hung over his stiff collar, the tabs of which were bent over a black bow tie. He wore a dark suit with a soiled yellow vest and seemed to be repressing excitement. Yakov was again apprehensive.

Bibikov's assistant had at once arisen and bowed. At a warning glance from the magistrate, the fixer hastily got up and remained standing.

"Good morning, Vladislav Grigorievitch," said Bibikov, a little flustered. "Good morning, Colonel Bodyansky, I am examining the suspect. Kindly be seated. Ivan Semyonovitch, please shut the door."

The colonel brushed his fingers over his mustache, and the Prosecuting Attorney, smiling slightly at nothing in particular, nodded. Yakov, at the magistrate's signal, shakily resumed his seat. Both officials studied him, the Prosecuting Attorney, once more intently, almost as though appraising the fixer's health, weight, stamina, sending chills down his back; or as though he were a new animal in the zoo. But the colonel looked through him as though he did not exist.

He wearily wished he didn't.

Bibikov read part way down the typewritten first page of the paper in his hand, then flipped through several more pages before he glanced up.

"Ah, I have it here," he said, clearing his throat. "This is the key statement: 'Z. N. Lebedev: I felt from the first he was different or odd in some way but could not guess how basically so, or I would never have had anything to do with him, you may believe me. He seemed to me somewhat foreign, but I explained to myself that he was from the provinces and obviously lacking in education and cultivation. I can only say I was on the whole uncomfortable in his presence, although of course truly grateful that he had assisted Papa that time he slipped in the snow. Afterwards I detested him because he tried to assault me. I told him firmly I never wished to see him again—'"

"It's not true, I didn't assault her," Yakov said, half rising. "It's not true at all."

"Please," said Bibikov, staring at him in astonishment.

"Silence," said Colonel Bodyansky, pounding his fist on the table. "Sit down at once!"

Grubeshov drummed with his fingertips.

Yakov quickly sat down. Bibikov glanced at the colonel in embarrassment. To the fixer he said firmly, "You will please control yourself, this is a legal investigation. I shall continue to read: 'Investigating Magistrate: Are you charging sexual assault?'

"'Z. N. Lebedev: I'm sure he intended to assault me. By this time I had begun to suspect he might be a Jew but when I saw for certain I screamed loudly.'

"'Investigating Magistrate: Explain what you mean that you saw "for certain."'

"'Z. N. Lebedev: He—I saw he was cut in the manner of Jewish males. I could not help seeing.'

"'Investigating Magistrate: Go on, Zinaida Nikolaevna, after you have calmed yourself. You may be embarrassed but it is best to speak the truth.'

"'Z. N. Lebedev: He realized I would not tolerate his advances and left the room. That was the last I saw of him, and I thank God.'

"'Investigating Magistrate: Then there was no assault in the true sense of the word, if you will pardon me? He did not touch you or attempt to?'

"'Z. N. Lebedev: You may say that but the fact remains he undressed himself and his intentions were to have relations with a Russian woman. That's what he hoped for, or he wouldn't have undressed and appeared naked. I'm sure you wouldn't approve of that, your honor.'

"'Investigating Magistrate: There is no approval expressed or implied either of his conduct or yours, Zinaida Nikolaevna. Did you afterwards inform your father, Nikolai Maximovitch, of this incident?'

"'Z. N. Lebedev: My father is not well and hasn't been in good health or spirits since the death of my poor mother. And his only brother died a year ago of a lingering illness, so I didn't wish to upset him further. He would have wanted to horsewhip the Jew.'"

"It is noted that at this point the witness wept copiously."

Bibikov laid down the paper.

"Will you say now," he asked Yakov, "whether you attempted to force yourself upon Zinaida Nikolaevna?"

Ivan Semyonovitch filled the magistrate's water glass from a porcelain pitcher on the table.

"Absolutely not, your honor," Yakov said hastily. "We ate together twice on her invitation while I was working in the upstairs flat, and the last night—the night I finished painting—she afterwards invited me to her bedroom. Maybe I shouldn't have gone—that's obvious now—but it's not such a hard thing to do when you consider a man's nature. Anyway, I had doubts and the minute I saw she was unclean, if you'll excuse me for saying so, your honor, I left. That's the honest truth and I could try from now to the Day of Judgment and not make it truer."

"What do you mean 'unclean'?"

The fixer was distraught. "I'm sorry to mention such things but if a man is in trouble he has to explain himself. The truth of it is she was having her monthlies."

He lifted his manacled hands to wipe his face.

"Any Jew who approaches a Russian woman ought to be strung up," said Colonel Bodyansky.

"Did she state such was her condition?" Grubeshov spoke with a slight thickness of speech.

"I saw the blood, your honor, if you'll excuse me, while she was washing herself with a cloth."

"You saw the blood?" the Prosecuting Attorney said sarcastically. "Did that have some religious meaning to you as a Jew? Do you know that in the Middle Ages Jewish men were said to menstruate?"

Yakov looked at him in surprise and fright.

"I don't know anything about that, your honor, although I don't see how it could be. But getting back to Zinaida Nikolaevna Lebedev, what her condition meant to me was that it wouldn't do either of us any good, and I was a fool to agree to go to her room in the first place. I should have gone home the minute I finished my work and not be tempted by a table full of all kinds of food."

"Relate what happened in the bedroom," Bibikov said. "And please confine yourself to the question at hand."

"Nothing happened, your honor, I swear it with my whole heart. It's as I said before—and also the young lady in the paper you just read—I got dressed as quickly as I could and left. I assure you of that, and it was the last I saw of her. Believe me, I'm sorry it happened."

"I do believe you," said Bibikov.

Grubeshov, sharply startled, stared at the Investigating Magistrate. Colonel Bodyansky shifted uncomfortably in his chair.

Bibikov, as though justifying himself, said, "We found two letters, both identified by the witnesses as written in their hand. One was from Nikolai Maximovitch addressed to Yakov Ivanovitch Dologushev, praising his diligence as an overseer of the Lebedev Brickworks, and the other was from the daughter, Zinaida Nikolaevna, on a sheet of perfumed blue letter paper, inviting the suspect to call on her at her home and expressly stating in the letter that she was writing it with the permission of her father. I have both letters in my files. They were turned over to me by Captain Korimzin of the Kiev City Police, who found them in the office of the brickworks."

The colonel and Prosecuting Attorney sat like statues.

Again addressing Yakov, the magistrate said, "I gather from the date that the letter from the young lady was written after the incident already described?"

"That's right, your honor. I was working in the brickworks then."

"You did not write her as she requested?"

"I didn't answer the letter. I figured I was born with a lot more trouble than I needed and there was no sense searching for more. If you're afraid of a flood stay away from the water."

"Her later remarks to me though of informal nature," the magistrate said, "affirm your statement. Therefore, considering the circumstances—this does not mean that I admire your behavior, Yakov Bok—I will recommend to the Prosecuting Attorney that you not be charged with attempted sexual assault."

He turned to his assistant, who, nodding, wrote hastily.

The Prosecuting Attorney, flushing through his sidewhiskers, picked up his portfolio, pushed back his chair and got up noisily. Colonel Bodyansky also arose. Bibikov reaching for the water glass, knocked it over. Jumping up, he dabbed at the spilled water on the table with his handkerchief, assisted by Ivan Semyonovitch, who in dismay quickly gathered up the papers and began to dry those that had got wet.

Grubeshov and Colonel Bodyansky, neither speaking a word, strode sullenly out of the room.

When he had blotted up the water, the Investigating Magistrate sat down, waited till Ivan Semyonovitch had dried and sorted the papers, and though embarrassed at the incident, picked up his notes, and clearing his throat, once more addressed the fixer in his resonant voice.

"We have laws, Yakov Bok," he said grimly, "directed against any member of your faith, orthodox or heretic, who assumes or counterfeits a name other than that entered in his official birth records, which is to say for the purpose of one sort of deception or another; but since there are no forged or counterfeited documents involved in this case, and since there is at present no record of similar previous offenses by you, I shall be lenient this time and not press this charge, although I personally feel, as I have already informed you, that your deception was repugnant and it is only by the greatest good fortune that it did not become an even more reprehensible situation—"

"I thank you kindly, your honor—" The fixer wiped his eyes with his fingers.

The magistrate went on. "I shall, however, ask the court to charge you for taking up residence in a district forbidden to Jews, except under certain circumstances which do not in any way appertain in your case. In this regard you have disobeyed the law. It is not a capital crime but you will be charged and sentenced for a misdemeanor."

"Will I be sent to jail, your honor?"

"I am afraid so."

"Ach. But how long in jail?"

"Not very long—a month at least, possibly less, depending on the magistrate who sentences you. It will teach you a lesson you are apparently in need of."

"Will I have to wear prison clothes?"

"You will be treated the same as other prisoners."

There was a knock on the door and a uniformed messenger

entered. He handed an envelope to Ivan Semyonovitch, who quickly passed it to Bibikov.

The Investigating Magistrate, his hand trembling a little, tore it open, read the handwritten note, slowly cleaned his glasses, and hastened out of the room.

Though he knew he could expect trouble—although he had half hoped he would be let off with a warning or even a severe dressing down and sent running back to the Jewish quarter—oh, with what pleasure he would run!—Yakov, after his first disappointment, felt relief that things weren't a lot worse. A month in jail is not a year, and three weeks are less; besides, if you wanted to look at it that way, rent was free. After his manacled march through the snowy streets, the mutterings of the crowd, and the terrible question the Investigating Magistrate had put to him last night in his cell, he had expected a calamity if not worse. Now things had calmed down. Practically, there was only this minor charge, and perhaps a lawyer could get the sentence reduced to maybe a week or nothing at all? It meant, of course, goodbye to some rubles from his savings—surely the police would return them to him—but a ruble he could earn, if not in a day, then in a week or month. Better a month spent grubbing for one than a month in prison. It didn't pay to worry over rubles. The main thing was to be free, and once they freed him, Yakov Bok would be less foolish in his dealings with the law.

The magistrate's assistant had hesitantly reached over to read the note that Bibikov had crumpled up and left on the table. After glancing at it he smiled vaguely; but when the fixer attempted a smile in return, the assistant vigorously blew his nose.

Then the Investigating Magistrate returned, breathing through his mouth, his face drawn and grim, followed into the room by Grubeshov and Colonel Bodyansky. Once more they seated themselves at the table, the Prosecuting Attorney again unstrapping his portfolio. Ivan Semyonovitch gazed at them with concern, but neither of the officials spoke. The assistant tested his pen, and held it ready to write. Grubeshov's smile was gone, his lips set. The colonel's expression was deadly serious. One look at them and a vast fear again surged through

Yakov. Cold sweat prickled his back. Once more he expected the worst. At least almost the worst.

"The Prosecuting Attorney will now ask you a few questions," Bibikov said quietly though hoarsely. He sat back and fiddled with his pince-nez string.

"If you please, first my question," said the colonel, nodding to Grubeshov, who was peering into the compartments of his portfolio. The Prosecuting Attorney, looking up, assented.

"Will the prisoner state," Colonel Bodyansky's voice boomed out in the room, "whether he is a member of certain political organizations I shall now name: Social Democrats, Socialist-Revolutionists, or any other groups including the Jewish Bund, Zionists of whatever ilk or stripe, Seymists, or Volkspartei?"

"I've already gone into that," Bibikov said with a touch of impatience.

The colonel turned on him. "Mr. Investigating Magistrate, the task of protecting the Crown from its enemies is under the jurisdiction of the Secret Political Police. Already there has been too much interference in our affairs."

"Not at all, colonel, we are investigating a civil offense—"

"Even a civil offense may be lèse majesté. I ask you not to intrude on my questions and I won't interfere with yours. Tell me," he said, turning to Yakov, "are you a member of any of those so-called political parties I have just named, or of any secret terroristic or nihilistic organizations? Answer truthfully or I will send you to the Petropavlovsky Fortress."

"No, sir, none, not one," Yakov replied hastily. "I've never belonged to a political party or any secret organizations such as you just mentioned. To tell the truth I don't know one from the other. If I were a better educated man I might, but as it is now whatever you ask me about them I can tell you very little."

"You will be severely punished if you are lying."

"Who's lying, your honor? As a former soldier, I swear I am not lying."

"Save your breath," said the colonel in disgust, "I've never met a Jew I could call a soldier."

Yakov's face turned a fiery red.

The colonel wrote furiously on a slip of paper, thrust it into his tunic pocket and nodded to the Prosecuting Attorney.

Grubeshov had drawn a black oilskin-covered notebook out

of his portfolio and was, with arched brows, studying one of its closely handwritten pages. Then he put the notebook down, and though he stared at the fixer, seemed to be in a pleasant state of mind as he remarked in a dry but slightly thick voice, "Well, we have been amusing ourselves, Mr. Yakov Shepsovitch Bok, alias Dologushev, alias I know not what else, but I now have some serious questions to put to you and I request that you give them your most serious attention. By your own admission you are guilty of certain flagrant violations of Russian law. You have confessed to certain crimes and there is good reason—excellent reason—to suspect others, one of so serious a nature that I shall not name it until we have further sifted the evidence, which I propose to continue to do now, with the permission of my colleagues."

He bowed to Bibikov, who, smoking, gravely nodded in return.

"Oh, my God," groaned Yakov, "I swear to you I am innocent of any serious crime. No, sir, the worst I am guilty of is stupidity—of living in the Lukianovsky without permission, that the Investigating Magistrate says I can get a month in prison for—but certainly not of any serious crimes."

God forgive me, he thought in terror. I'm in a bad spot now, worse than quicksand. That's what one gets for not knowing which way he's running, to begin with.

"Answer this question precisely," said Grubeshov, referring to his notebook. "Are you a 'Hasid' or 'Misnogid'? Please take down his answers with extreme accuracy, Ivan Semyonovitch."

"Neither. I'm neither one nor the other," said Yakov. "As I told his other honor—if I'm anything at all it's a freethinker. I say this to let you know I'm not a religious man."

"That won't do you any good," said the prosecutor, suddenly irritable. "I was expecting just such a response, and of course it's nothing more than an attempt to divert the questioning. Now answer me directly, you are a circumcised Jew, aren't you?"

"I'm a Jew, your honor, I'll admit to that and the rest is personal."

"I've already gone through all this, Vladislav Grigorievitch," said Bibikov. "It's all in the notes of the testimony. Read it to him, Ivan Semyonovitch, it will save time."

"I must ask the Investigating Magistrate not to interrupt,"

Grubeshov said testily. "I have no interest in saving time. Time is immaterial to me. Please let me go on without useless interruption."

Bibikov lifted the pitcher to pour himself a glass of water but it was empty.

"Shall I refill it, your honor?" whispered Ivan Semyonovitch.

"No," said Bibikov, "I'm not thirsty."

"What's this freethinker business about?" said the colonel.

"Not now, Colonel Bodyansky, I beg you," said Grubeshov. "It is not a political party."

Colonel Bodyansky lit a cigarette.

Grubeshov addressed Yakov, reading aloud certain words from his notebook and pronouncing them slowly.

"There are those among you—are there not?—Jews who are called 'tzadikim'? When a Jew wishes to harm a Christian, or as you call him, 'goyim,' he goes to the 'tzadik' and gives him a 'pidion,' which is a fee of some sort, and the 'tzadik' uses the power of the word, in magical incantations, to bring misfortune on the Christian. Isn't that a true fact? Answer me."

"Please," said Yakov, "I don't understand what you want of me. What have I to do with such things?"

"You'll find out, if you don't already know, only too soon," said Grubeshov, flushing. "In the meantime answer me truthfully and directly without vomiting a mouthful of irrelevant questions in return. Tell me now, what do you Jews mean by 'afikomen'? I want the truth without varnish."

"But what has this got to do with me?" Yakov said. "What do I know about these things you're asking me? If they're strange to you they're strange to me."

"Once more I will direct you to limit yourself to my questions. I will tell you patiently for the last time that I am not interested in your personal comments. Keep in mind that you are already in very serious trouble and curb your tongue."

"I am not positive," said the fixer, disheartened, "but it's a matzo of some kind that's used in the Passover ceremony for protection against evil spirits and evil men."

"Write that all down, Ivan Semyonovitch. Is it magic?"

"To my way of thinking it's superstition, your honor."

"But you say it's the same as matzos?"

"Practically the same, I think. I'm not an expert in these things. If you want to know the truth I haven't much use for such matters. I have nothing against those who want to follow the customary ways, but for myself I'm interested in what's new in the world."

He glanced at the Investigating Magistrate, but Bibikov was looking out the window.

Grubeshov slid his fingers into the portfolio and withdrew something covered with a handkerchief. He slowly peeled the four corners of the handkerchief and triumphantly held up a triangle of broken matzo.

"This was found in your habitat in the stable at the brick factory. What have you to say now?"

"What can I say, your honor? Nothing. It's matzo. It's not mine."

"Is it 'matzo shmuro'?"

"I wouldn't know if it was or wasn't."

"I understand that 'matzo shmuro' is eaten by very religious Jews."

"I think so."

"How does it differ from ordinary matzo?"

"Don't ask me, your honor. I don't really know."

"I'll ask what I please. I'll ask until your eyes pop out. Do you understand that?"

"Yes, sir."

"Did you bake this matzo?"

"No."

"Then how did it get into your habitat? That's where the police found it."

"It was brought in by an old man, a stranger to me. I give you my earnest word. He was lost one night near the cemetery and I took him in till it stopped snowing. Some boys had hit him with rocks. He was frightened."

"Near the cemetery in the Lukianovsky this occurred?"

"Where the brickworks is."

"Was he a 'tzadik'?"

"Even suppose he was, what has that got to do with me?"

"Answer with respect!" The Prosecuting Attorney struck the table with his palm. The piece of matzo fell to the floor. Ivan Semyonovitch hastily retrieved it. He held it up for all to see, it had not broken. Bibikov wet his dry lips. "Answer courteously," he said.

Yakov, in a dull state, nodded.

Grubeshov again bowed to the magistrate. "My deepest thanks." He paused as though to say more, then changed his mind. "Did your friend the 'tzadik' come often to the stable?" he asked Yakov.

"He came that once. He was a stranger to me. I never saw him again."

"That was because you were arrested not long after his departure."

Yakov could not argue the point.

"Is it true that you hid other Jews in the stable and trafficked with them in stolen goods?"

"No."

"Did you steal systematically from your employer, Nikolai Maximovitch Lebedev?"

"As God is my judge, never a single kopek."

"Are you certain you did not yourself bake this matzo? A half bag of flour was found in your habitat."

"With respect, your honor, it's the wrong flour. Also I'm not a baker. I once tried to bake bread to save a kopek or two but it didn't rise and came out like a rock. The flour was wasted. Baking isn't one of my skills. I work as carpenter or painter most of the time—I hope nothing has happened to my tools, they're all I've got in the world—but generally I'm a fixer, never a matzo baker. What there is to fix I fix though it pays little and generally my luck in jobs has been bad. But I'm not a criminal, your honor."

Grubeshov listened impatiently. "Answer strictly to the point. Did the 'tzadik' bake the matzos?"

"If so not in my house. Who knows if elsewhere, he didn't tell me but I don't think so."

"Then some other Jew did?"

"It's probably true."

"It's more than probable," said the Prosecuting Attorney, glaring at him. "It's the truth of God."

When Yakov saw him peering again into his evil portfolio, he wrung his manacled hands under the table.

Grubeshov now slowly drew forth a long, stained rag.

"Have you seen this before?" He danced the stained rag over the table with his fingers.

Bibikov watched the dancing rag, absently polishing his glasses; Ivan Semyonovitch stared at it in fascination.

"I will describe it to you," said the Prosecuting Attorney. "It is part of a peasant's blouse similar to the one you are presently affecting. Was this rag, by some chance, formerly a possession of yours?"

"I don't know," said Yakov wearily.

"I advise you to think more carefully, Yakov Bok. If you've eaten no garlic your breath won't stink."

"Yes, your honor," Yakov said desperately, "it's mine more or less, although that's nothing to worry about. The old man I mentioned to you was hit on the head by a rock, and I used part of an old shirt I was no longer wearing—it fell apart on my back—to wipe the blood away. That's God's own truth and all there is to it, I swear."

"So you admit it's bloodstained," shouted the Prosecuting Attorney.

Yakov felt his tongue turn to dust.

"Did you ever chase any children in the brickworks yard in the vicinity of the kilns, in particular a twelve-year lad by the name of Zhenia Golov?"

The fixer was unable to reply.

Grubeshov, after glancing at Bibikov, smiled broadly as he mincingly asked the fixer, "Tell me Yankel Jew, why are you trembling?"

3

Why does a man tremble?

When he was locked in the cell again there were three filthy straw pallets on the floor. One was his—what a misery that he could think of it as his; and two new prisoners were lying on the others. One was a hairy man in rags, the other a living skeleton. Both stank across the room, of dirt and poverty. Though neither paid any attention to him, the ragged one blinking at the wall, the other snoring, the fixer kept to the far corner of the cell. He felt abandoned, lost to the world.

"What will happen to me now?" he asked himself. And if it

happens bad who will ever know? I might as well be dead. Recalling his father-in-law and wife, he could conjure neither of them close. Especially the wife. He thought of his father and mother, young people in their weedy graves, and their fate gave him no comfort. His frustrated innocence outraged him. He was unjustly accused, helpless, unable to offer proof or be believed. What horror would they accuse him of next? "If they knew me could they say such things?" He tried to comprehend what was happening and explain it to himself. After all, he was a rational being, and a man must try to reason. Yet the more he reasoned the less he understood. The familiar had become evil. What happened next was weighted with peril. That he was a Jew, willing or unwilling, was not enough to explain his fate. Remembering his life filled him with hatred for the way things went and were going. I'm a fixer but all my life I've broken more than I fix. What would they accuse him of next? How could a man defend himself against such terrible hints, insinuations, *accusations*, if no one was willing to believe him? Panic gnawed him. He was full of desperate thoughts of what to do next—somehow to sneak out of the cell and seek in the ghetto for the old man to tell the Russians that he had been hit on the head by a rock and Yakov had wiped away the blood?

The fixer goes from house to house, knocking on each thin door and asking for the tzadik but nobody knows him; then in the last house they know him, a saintly man, but he had long ago gone away. The fixer hurriedly travels on the train to Minsk and after months of desperate searching meets the old man, the moon on his rabbinic hat, coming home one evening from the synagogue.

"Please, you must go back to Kiev with me and prove my innocence. Tell the officials I didn't do what they say I did."

But the old tzadik does not recognize the fixer. He looks at him long but shakes his head. The wound on his temple has healed and he cannot now recall the night Yakov says he had spent with him in the room above the stable.

When the fixer remembered where he was he tore at his hands with his nails, and he tore at his face.

The snorer awoke with a gasp. "Akimytch," he cried out. "Formerly a tailor. I am innocent," he whimpered. "Don't beat me."

The other one snickered.

"Have you got a cigarette, Potseikin?" the former tailor asked the one on the other mattress. "A piece of butt?"

"Fuck yourself," said the blinker, a man with bloodshot eyes.

"Have you got a cigarette?" Akimytch asked Yakov.

"My bag is empty," said the fixer. He held it up.

"I'll bet you don't know why I'm here," Akimytch said.

"No."

"Neither do I. It's mistaken identity with me. I never did what they say I did, may they choke to death on their mothers' milk. They mistook me for an anarchist."

He began to weep.

"I'm here because of a pack of pamphlets or whatever you call 'em," Potseikin said. "Some poor bastard, a man with wild eyes and a thick greatcoat says to me on Institutsky Street, 'Brother,' he says, 'I have to piss, so hold my bundle a minute, and when I come back here I'll slip you a five-kopek piece, on my honor.' What can you say to a man who has to piss? Could I say no to that? Then he might piss on me. So I held onto his bundle and in two minutes a pig-eyed detective comes running across the street and jabs a gun in my gut so hard it almost busts, and then he marches me off to the Secret Police without listening to a word I say. When we get there three big ones give me a going over with fat sticks till all my bones are cracked, and they show me where the pamphlets say to overthrow the Tsar. Who wants to overthrow the Tsar? Personally, I have only the highest regard for Nicholas the Second and the royal family, especially the young princesses and the poor sick boy, who I love as my own. But nobody believed me and that's why I'm here. It's all the fault of those bastard pamphlets."

"It's mistaken identity with me," said Akimytch. "What's it with you, pal?"

"The same," said Yakov.

"What did they say you did?"

He thought he oughtn't to tell them, but it came out quickly, in accusation of the accusers.

"They say I killed a boy—it's a dirty lie."

There was a deep silence in the cell. Now I've blundered, Yakov thought. He looked for the guard but he had gone for the soup pail.

The two on the straw pallets, their heads together, whispered in each other's ears, first Akimytch whispering, then Potseikin.

"Did you?" Akimytch asked Yakov.

"No, of course not. Why would I kill an innocent child?"

They whispered once more and Potseikin said in a thick voice, "Tell us the truth, are you a Jew?"

"What difference would it make?" Yakov said, but when they were whispering again he was afraid.

"Don't try anything or I'll call the guard."

The one in rags got up and approached the fixer, sneering. "So you're the bastard Jew who killed the Christian boy and sucked the blood out of his bones? I saw it in the papers."

"Leave me in peace," Yakov said. "I've done nothing like that to anybody, not to speak of a twelve-year-old child. It's not in my nature."

"You're a stinking Jew liar."

"Think as you like but let me alone."

"Who else would do anything like that but a motherfucking Zhid?"

Potseikin pounced on the fixer and with his rotten teeth tried to bite his neck. Yakov shoved him off but Akimytch, foul-breathed, was on his back beating the fixer's head and face with his clammy bony hands.

"Christkiller!"

"Gevalt!" cried Yakov, flailing his arms. Though he whirled, ducked, and struck out with his fists, Potseikin hit him with a knee in the back as Akimytch struck him on the neck with both fists. The fixer went down, his mind darkened in pain. He lay motionless as they kicked him savagely, and felt as he passed out, a terrible rage.

Afterwards he woke on his mattress, and when he heard their snoring, retched. A rat scuttled across his genitals and he bolted up in horror. But there was a bit of horned moon at the small high barred window and he watched for a while in peace.

IV

THE STABLE had burned to the ground in a matter of minutes, Proshko said, spitting at the fixer's feet, and it wouldn't surprise him if it were done with Jewish magic. He pointed to the blackened remains of the stalls where four maddened, rearing, trumpeting horses had died, and a crisscross pile of burnt and broken planks and timbers had fallen from the roof.

The mustached and bearded officials in the brickyard, some uniformed and booted, a few carrying umbrellas although it was no longer raining, and the Secret Police gendarmes, plainclothes detectives, and Kiev City Police—among them also an Imperial Army general with two rows of gold buttons and one of medals across his chest—looked on in silence as the foreman spoke. Grubeshov, in English bowler, mud-spattered gaiters, and rain cape, flushed at Proshko's testimony, whispered in Colonel Bodyansky's lowered ear, clutching his hand tightly, and the colonel earnestly whispered something in return as Yakov licked his dry lips. Bibikov, with small, yellow-muddy, ankle-length shoes, his winter scarf and large hat, standing behind two tight-faced Black Hundreds representatives wearing their accusatory buttons, chain-smoked cigarettes from a box he amiably offered around. Nearby, the pimply Ivan Semyonovitch accompanied an oldish priest of the Orthodox Church, Father Anastasy, a "specialist," Yakov had heard it whispered, "of the Jewish religion"; he was a round-shouldered man with a streaked beard, thin hands, and restless dark eyes, dressed in flowing vestments and round pot-hat which he pressed down with his palm when the wind blew. What he was expected to add to the miserable state of Yakov's affairs the fixer didn't know and was afraid to guess. Manacled, his legs chained, nervously exhausted, his body in flight though he tried with ten fingers to hold onto his mind, he stood with five armed guards at his back, apart from the rest. Though almost a month had gone by since his arrest he could still only half believe this had happened to him, someone who did not recognize himself in the dream he was dreaming; and listened stunned to Proshko, as though the accusation of the monstrous crime were both true and an irrelevancy, as though it had happened to someone he didn't know very well, in truth a stranger, although he clearly remembered fearing that something like this might happen to him.

Otherwise the brickyard was deserted on a gray and green overcast Sunday afternoon in what had been a cold May. None of the workers was around except for the drivers Richter and Serdiuk, who listened without speaking and occasionally spat, the Ukrainian holding his cap in his large red hand, ill at ease, the German staring darkly at the former overseer. Nikolai Maximovitch had been expected but Yakov knew it was too late in the day for him to leave the house sober. After a morning fog had thinned and lifted, it began to rain heavily; and it poured again in the afternoon. The horses drawing the half dozen carriages that had left at intervals from the District Courthouse in the Plossky, and met first in the brickyard, had splashed through puddles, and the motorcar carrying Yakov, Colonel Bodyansky and the gendarmes, had got stuck in the mud on a road in the Lukianovsky, drawing several people, and irritating the Prosecuting Attorney, who made it known to the chauffeur that he didn't want "the matter getting out." Not very much about the fixer had appeared in the newspapers. All they seemed to know was that a Jew from the Podol had been arrested "as a suspicious person," but not who or why. Grubeshov had promised more information at a later date in order not, presently, to impede the investigation. Bibikov, before they left the courthouse, had managed to convey this to Yakov, but not much else.

"Start from the beginning," Grubeshov said to Proshko, dressed in his Sunday thick-trousered suit with short jacket. "—I want to hear your earliest suspicions."

The Prosecuting Attorney had planned this re-enactment, he had told the accused, "to let you know the inescapable logic of our case against you so that you may act accordingly and for your own benefit."

"But how for my benefit?"

"It will become clear to you."

The foreman blew his nose, wiped it in two strokes and thrust the handkerchief into his pants pocket.

"On one look I knew he was a Jew, even though he was faking that he was a Russian. It's easy enough to tell an onion from a radish if you're not color blind." Proshko laughed a little from the chest. "Yakov Ivanovitch Dologushev, he called himself, but I knew from the sound of it on his tongue that the name didn't fit him. A name belongs to you as your birthright, but it hung on him like a suit of stolen clothes. I felt in my blood he was a Jew the same way as you feel in the dark the presence of a ghost. Wait up, little brother, I thought to myself, something smells fishy here. Maybe it's his natural smell, or the way he talks Russian, or maybe it's the flatfooted way he runs when he chases young boys, but when I looked with both of my eyes open I saw what I already knew—he was a Zhid and no two ways about it. You can't make a gentleman out of a toad, as the saying goes, and a born Jew can't hide the Zhid in his face. This is a foxy bastard, I thought to myself, and he thinks he's got it hidden because he wears a belted sheepskin coat and has shaved off his Jewish whiskers and curls, and maybe it'll be a little slow smoking him out of his hole now that he's fooled Nikolai Maximovitch, but smoke him out I will, and with God's help it's what I did."

"Tell the details," said Grubeshov.

"It wasn't more than fifteen minutes after I first saw him that I went back to the office shack and asked him for his papers so as to hand them over to the District Police, and right off he showed me who he was. He lied that he had given them to the boss and he had registered them with the police. If a man talks crooked, I thought to myself, he's crooked elsewhere, and I'll watch out to see where else. I didn't have long to wait. Once when he was nosing around the kilns for purposes of his own, I sneaked into the shack and checked up on his figures in the books. He was crooked in his accounts and every day entered smaller amounts than he should so he could keep some rubles for himself—not so many, a Jew is cunning—maybe three or four or five a day that Nikolai Maximovitch had no suspicions of, and he saved himself a nice little pile in a tin can in his room."

"You're a liar," Yakov said, trembling, "you're the thief and you're putting it on me. You and your drivers stole thousands of bricks from Nikolai Maximovitch, and you hated me for watching you so you couldn't steal more."

Nobody was listening.

"What did he do with the rubles you say he stole?" Bibikov asked the foreman. "There were about ninety in the tin can, if I remember correctly. If he was stealing four rubles a day, let us say, he should have had many more."

"Who knows what a Jew does with money. I've heard it said they take it to bed with them and give it a fuck once in a while. I bet he gave most of it to the Zhidy synagogue in the Podol. They have plenty of uses for a Russian ruble."

"The Secret Police confiscated altogether one hundred and five rubles," Grubeshov announced after conferring with Colonel Bodyansky. "Keep your mouth shut," he said to Yakov. "Answer when you're spoken to."

"What's more," Proshko went on, "he sneaked other Jews into the brickyard, and one was one of those Hasids with a round hat, or whatever you call them, who prayed up there in the stable with this one here. The other one came when they thought nobody was around to watch them. They both tied horns on their heads and prayed to the Jewish God. I watched them through the window and saw them praying and eating matzos. I figured they baked some in the stove up there and I was right, there was half a sack of flour hidden under the bed that the police got. I kept track of them because I had my own suspicions, like I told you. I saw this one here sneaking around like a ghost at night, his face white and eyes strange, looking for something, and I also saw him chasing the boys that I told you about. I was worried he would do them some kind of harm, little knowing how right I was. One day two or three school kids came in the yard with their book satchels. I saw him chase them but they got away over the fence. Once I asked him, 'Yakov Ivanovitch, why did you chase those young school kids, they are good boys and all they want to do is to see how we make brick,' but he answered me, 'If they are so innocent Jesus Christ will protect them.' He thought Proshko wouldn't know what he meant by that but I did."

Yakov groaned.

"That's why I kept my eye on him and when I couldn't I told the drivers to watch him."

"That's so." Serdiuk, still smelling of horse, nodded, and Richter said yes.

"I saw them praying with their little black hats on, and I spied on them when they were baking those matzos. Then when the boy was murdered and they found him in the cave with all those wounds the morning it was snowing—when the snow came again in April—I saw this one take the other Jew with the round hat down the stairs and they left the brickyard in a hurry. I went up there, walking right in their footsteps in the snow so he wouldn't see I had been there, and that was the day I found pieces of matzos they had baked, half a bag of flour under the bed, his sack of tools, and that bloody rag I told you about. The devil scatters his dung wherever he goes.

"After that he wanted to set the stable on fire to burn the evidence but he saw I had my eye on him. When I met him in the brickyard the blood ran out of his face and he couldn't raise his eyes at me. That was after they had killed the kid. After the funeral I went to the police, and in a week they came and arrested him. They took the matzos away and the other things that I told you about, but I went up there with Serdiuk and Richter here, to tear up the floorboards—some had certain dark stains on them that we wanted to show the police. Just then we see an old graybeard Jew run out of the stable, and the next thing the place was up in roaring flames, and the whole stable burned down in less than five minutes, so it was just by luck we saved any of the horses. We saved six and lost four. If the fire had been an ordinary kind we would've saved the whole ten, but being as it was, there was something that made it burn as if the wind was caught in it, and it cried out like people were dying and ghosts were going to meet them. They had said some magic words from a Zhidy book, I'll swear to God, and upstairs where this one here had lived before they arrested him, the flames turned an oily green such as I never saw before, and then yellow, and then almost black, and they burned twice as fast as the fire in the stalls even though the loft was full of hay. In the stalls the fire burned orange and red, and it was slower, more like an ordinary fire, so we got six horses out of the burning stalls and lost the other four."

Richter swore every word was true and Serdiuk crossed himself twice.

2

Father Anastasy stiffly embraced Marfa Golov, the haggard mother of the martyred boy, a tallish, scrawny-necked woman with red-rimmed, wet, flecked gray eyes, and dark skin drawn tautly over her face, who tried to curtsy and collapsed in the priest's arms.

"Forgive us our transgressions, Father," she wept.

"You must forgive us, my child," said the priest, in a nasal voice. "The world has sinned against you. In particular, those who sin against our Lord."

He crossed himself, his hand like a bird, and so did some of the officials.

Marfa Golov, when Yakov first saw her waiting for the officials to arrive, was standing, with a thick-shawled neighbor who quickly ran off when the carriages appeared, on the sagging steps of a two-story wooden house with a peaked corrugated tin roof. The house overlooked a low-walled cemetery, and in the distance the brickyard, which Bibikov stopped to stare at, its chimneys smokeless on Sunday. It was a boxlike house that had once been painted white but was now weathered gray and peeling. The grassless front yard, muddy from the rain, was surrounded by a high unpainted fence, held together horizontally on the street side by long uneven darkly weathered boards. The road in front of the house where the carriages and motorcar waited was pitted and muddy, and the carriages looked like those of a funeral party except that there was no visible hearse. Marfa, thirty-nine, the newspaper had said, and vaguely pretty, with a tense distracted manner, eyes glancing in every direction, a drawn unhappy mouth and slight chin, wore for the occasion a dark-flowered blouse, long green skirt, and pointed two-tone button shoes. She had pinned a discolored cameo at her worn throat and thrown a light scarf over her shoulders. And she had on a new white hat topped with a bunch of bright cherries that caused some interested glances. When the fixer was led through the gate into the yard, Marfa burst into sobs. One of the officials in the Prosecuting

Attorney's office and a gendarme nearby cursed the prisoner under their breaths yet loud enough for him to hear.

"It's surely the one," Marfa gasped.

"Which one is that?" Bibikov asked, snapping on his silver-rimmed pince-nez and staring at her.

"The Jew Zhenia told me about, who had chased him with a long knife."

"Note the identification," said Grubeshov to Ivan Semyonovitch. The assistant hadn't his notebook with him, but he mentioned it to one of the policemen, who wrote it down.

There was a green mildewed stone well in the yard and Bibikov peered down it but could see nothing.

He dropped a small stone down the well and after a while there was a splash. The officials looked at one another but the Investigating Magistrate walked away.

"The room's upstairs, your honor," Marfa said to the Prosecuting Attorney. "It's small as you'll see, but Zhenia was small himself for a lad his age. That's not from me, you'll notice, because I don't lack size, but from his cowardly father who deserted us." She smiled nervously.

Marfa led them in and hurried upstairs to show the officials where the poor child had slept. They wiped their feet on a muddy rag at the door and went up in small hushed groups to stare into the dark tiny cubicle between a large untidy bedroom with a two-pillowed brass bed, and a room with a locked door Marfa said was a storeroom.

"What can a widow do with so many bedrooms? Generally I store things. When my aunt died she left me her furniture although I have enough of my own."

Yakov was ordered to go up after the others had seen the boy's room. He wanted not to go but knew that if he said so they would drag him up. He went slowly up the stairs in his clanking leg chains that rubbed his ankles sore, followed by three booted gendarmes who waited for him on the landing with drawn pistols. Marfa, Father Anastasy, Grubeshov, Ivan Semyonovitch and Colonel Bodyansky were in the corridor as the Jew glanced furtively into the boy's room. They watched him intently, Grubeshov's lips pursed. The fixer had wanted to look calmly and with dignity but had been unable to. It was as though he expected a wild animal in the room to spring out at him. He glanced fearfully into the tiny cubicle with torn wallpaper and unmade cot, the crumpled bedsheet gray, soiled, the faded blanket torn. Though the room and cot were strange to him, Yakov had a momentary hallucinatory thought he had seen them before. He then recalled his cubicle in the printer's flat in the Podol. This was what he remembered but he worried they thought he was thinking of something that would surely convict him were it known what.

"My darling Zhenechka hoped to be a priest," Marfa whispered loudly to Father Anastasy, dabbing at her reddened eyes with a scented handkerchief. "He was a religious child and worshipped God."

"It was reported to me that he was being prepared for the seminary," said the priest. "One of the monks told me he was a dear boy, in some respects a saintly boy. I understand he had already had a mystical experience. I was also told he loved our priestly vestments and hoped some day to wear them. His death is God's loss."

Marfa wept miserably. Ivan Semyonovitch's eyes clouded and he turned away and wiped them on his coat sleeve. Yakov felt like crying but couldn't.

Then Father Anastasy came down and Bibikov went up the stairs, squeezing past the gendarmes. He glanced casually into Zhenia's small room, looked around absently, then got down on his knees, and lifting the bedsheet, peeked under the bed. He touched the floor and examined his soiled fingertips.

"The floor may be dusty," Marfa said quickly, "but I always empty the chamber pot."

"Never mind that," said Grubeshov distastefully. "Well, what have you discovered?" he asked Bibikov.

"Nothing."

The Investigating Magistrate glanced quickly into Marfa's bedroom and stopped at the locked door of the other room as if he were listening, but did not try the knob. He then wandered downstairs. Marfa hurriedly attempted to make the boy's bed up but Grubeshov ordered her to leave it alone.

"It will take me only a minute."

"Leave it as it is. The police prefer it that way."

They went downstairs. Although it was drizzling outside, some of the officials were gathered in the yard. The others, including the prisoner and gendarmes who guarded him, met in Marfa's dusty disordered parlor that smelled of tobacco smoke, stale sweet beer, and cabbage. At Grubeshov's request, she pulled open the window vent, and with a dirty rag hastily wiped the seats of a half dozen chairs nobody sat down in. The prisoner was afraid to sit. Marfa tried to do something to the floor with a broom but the Prosecuting Attorney took it from her.

"This can wait, Marfa Vladimirovna. Please give us your fullest attention."

"I just thought I'd clean up a bit," she hurriedly explained. "To tell the truth, I wasn't expecting so many high officials. I thought the prisoner was coming to see what he had done and why should I clean up for a dirty Jew?"

"That'll do," Grubeshov said. "We're not interested in your household affairs. Go now into the story of what happened to your son."

"Ever since he was little he wanted to be a priest," Marfa wept, "but now he's a dead corpse in his grave."

"Yes, we all know that and it's a tragic story, but perhaps you ought to limit yourself to what you know about the details leading up to the crime."

"First shouldn't I serve tea, do you think, your honor?" she asked, distracted. "The samovar's boiling."

"No," he said. "We are very busy and have much to do before we can return to our homes. Please tell the story—specifically of Zhenia's disappearance and death—how, for instance, you learned of it."

"You," he said to Yakov, who was gazing out the window at the rain in the chestnut trees, "you know well this concerns you so pay attention." In the time the fixer had been in prison the city had turned green and there were sweet smelling lilacs everywhere but who could enjoy them? Through the open window he could smell the wet grass and new leaves, and where the cemetery ended there were birches with silver trunks. Somewhere nearby an organ grinder was playing a waltz that Zinaida Nikolaevna had played for him once on her guitar, "Summer Is Gone Forever."

"Go on, please," Grubeshov said to Marfa.

She lifted both hands to straighten her hat, then caught his eye and dropped them.

"He was an earnest boy," Marfa quickly began, "and never gave me much trouble as boys do. As for myself I'm a widow of stainless character, pure and simple. My husband, who was a telegrapher, deserted me, as I mentioned before, your honor, and a couple of years later died of galloping consumption, which served him right for the way he mistreated us. I support myself by hard work and that's why my house that you're in isn't the neatest, but my child has always had a roof over his head, and my life has been one of irreproachable toil. If you work like a horse you can't live like the gentry, if you'll pardon my frankness. We got along without the deserter. This house doesn't belong to me, I rent it and sometimes let out a room or two, though one has to be careful of riffraff, especially those not given to paying what they owe to others. I didn't want my child associating with such, so I rarely took boarders in—even though I had to work that much harder—and then only if they were genteel people. But even if he didn't have all the advantages, Zhenia had what he needed and wasn't above showing his appreciation by giving me help—not like some boys I could name you, for instance Vasya Shiskovsky in the next house from here. My own was an obedient lad, an angel. He once asked me if he should leave the ecclesiastical school and become a butcher's apprentice but I advised him, 'Zhenia, my good darling, it's best to go on with your lessons. Get an education and when you're rich some day, you can support your poor mother in her old age.' 'Mamenka,' he answered me, 'I will always take care of you even when you are old and sick.' He was a saintly child, and it didn't in the least surprise me when he came back from his Bible lesson one day and said he wanted to be a priest. My eyes were full of tears that day."

She glanced nervously at Grubeshov, who nodded slightly.

"Go on, Marfa Vladimirovna, tell now what happened towards the end of March, a few short weeks before the Jewish Passover this year. And speak more slowly so that we can comprehend everything you say. Don't slur your words."

"Are you paying attention?" he asked Yakov.

"The closest, your honor, though I honestly don't understand what this has to do with me. It's all so strange."

"Only be patient," Grubeshov said. "It will be as familiar and close as the nose on your face."

Several of the officials, including the army general, laughed.

"On the morning in the week you mention," said Marfa, darting a glance at the Jew, "it was a Tuesday I'll never forget in my life, Zhenia woke up and got dressed in his black stockings that I had bought him for his name day and left for school as usual at six in the morning. I had to work until long after dark that day, then attend to the marketing so I naturally didn't get home until late. Zhenia wasn't in the house and after I had rested a while—I've had painful varicose veins since giving birth to my child—I went to Sofya Shiskovsky, my neighbor in the next house down a ways, whose Vasya was in Zhenia's form in school, and asked him where my boy was. Vasya said he didn't know because though he had seen Zhenia after school, Zhenia hadn't come home with him as was usual. 'Where did he go?' I said. 'I don't know,' he answered. Ach, I thought, he is at his grandmother's, I won't worry. But on the same night I caught the flu. I had the shakes and shivers for three days and stayed in bed in a weak condition for three more, only getting up, if you'll excuse me, to go to the toilet, or boil up a little rice and water to stop diarrhea. Zhenia was missing for about a week—six or seven days to be exact, and when I made up my mind to get dressed and report it to the police he was found dead in a cave with forty-seven stabs on his body. The neighbors came into my house with slow steps and sad faces—they looked like dead folk and frightened me before they spoke—then when they told me what horror had happened to me, I cried out, 'My life is over because I've lost my reason to live!'"

Marfa put her hand to her eyes and tottered. Two of the officials stepped towards her but she held onto a chair and remained upright. The men withdrew.

"Excuse me," Bibikov said gently, "but how is it you waited six or seven whole days before thinking to report that your son was missing? If it were my son I would have reported it at once—at the very latest on the night he had not yet appeared in the house. It's true that you were sick but even sick people have been known to pull themselves out of bed and act in emergencies."

"It all depends on how sick they are, if you please, your honor. Whether it's your son or mine, when you're running a high fever and are nauseous besides, your thoughts aren't always at their best. I worried about Zhenia and had terrible nightmares besides. I was afraid he was in some kind of horrible trouble, but I thought I dreamed that because I was feverish. And while I was so sick with the flu, so was my neighbor Sofya, and also Vasya. No one came to knock on my door, as usually happens two or three times during the day. And Yuri Shiskovsky, Sofya's husband, is as likely to knock on a person's door when you need him as Father Christmas. We don't get along at all but that's a story for a winter night. Anyway, if someone had come into my house during those five or six days I would have split both his ears crying out my fears for my poor child, but nobody ever did."

"Let her go on with the story," Grubeshov said to Bibikov. "If necessary you can ask questions later."

The Investigating Magistrate nodded to his colleague. "I assure you it's necessary enough, Vladislav Grigorievitch, but as you please, I'll ask later. As for what else may be necessary, or even not so necessary, for instance this entire procedure during a time of investigation, I think we ought to discuss that too, at least in principle if for no other reason."

"Tomorrow," said Grubeshov. "We'll talk over everything tomorrow."

"Come now to the point of the matter, Marfa Vladimirovna," he said. "Tell us what Zhenia and Vasya Shiskovsky told you about the Jew before the fatal incident."

Marfa had listened intently to the exchange between the men, alternating uneasiness with apparent boredom. When Bibikov was speaking she cast nervous glances around her but lowered her eyes if anyone looked at her.

"Vasya also told me what I heard Zhenia say more than once—that they were afraid of the Jew in the brickyard."

"Go on, we're listening."

"Zhenia told me that one day when he and Vasya were playing in the factory yard they saw two Jews—it was toward nightfall—sneak through the gate and go up the stairs where this one lived."

She glanced at the fixer, then averted her eyes. He was standing with his head bowed.

"Excuse me for interrupting," Bibikov said to the Prosecuting Attorney, "but I would like to understand how the boys identified the two men as Jews?"

Colonel Bodyansky guffawed and Grubeshov smiled.

"Easily, your honor," Marfa said in excitement, "they were wearing Jewish clothes and had long rough beards, not nicely trimmed ones like some of the gentlemen here. Also the boys used to peek in the window and saw them praying. They wore black hats and robes. The boys were frightened and ran home here. I asked Vasya to stay for a cup of cocoa and slice of white bread with Zhenia, but he was scared sick and said he wanted to go home to his own house."

Grubeshov listened, standing with his thumbs locked behind him. "Please go on."

"I heard from the boys that this one here brought other Jews up in his stable. One was an old man with a black satchel that the Lord knows what they did with. Zhenia once told this one to his face that he would tell the foreman if he chased him again. 'And if you do that I'll kill you once and for all,' said the Jew. One day Zhenia saw him running after another boy in the brickyard, a lad not eight years old from the neighborhood around here, Andriushka Khototov, whose father is a street sweeper. The boy luckily got out through the open gate, thank the Lord. Then the Jew saw my Zhenia and chased him, but my Zhenia climbed the fence and escaped that time, though he told me his heart hurt because he did not think he would get over the fence before the Jew grabbed him. One day, hiding by the kiln, Zhenia saw two of the Jews try to catch a Russian child and drag him into the stable. But the boy was a smart one and bit, clawed, and screamed so loud they got frightened and let him go. I warned Zhenia more than once not to go back there or he might get kidnapped and killed, and he promised me he wouldn't. I think he didn't for a time, then one night he came home frightened and feverish, and when I cried out, 'Zhenia, what ails you, tell me quickly what happened?' he said that the Jew had chased him with a long knife in the dark among the gravestones in the cemetery. I got down on my knees to him. 'Zhenia Golov, in the name of the Holy Mother, promise me not to go near that evil Jew again. Don't go in that brickyard.' 'Yes, dear Mamenka,' he said, 'I will promise.' That's what he said, but he went back in there again, anyway. Boys are boys, your honor, as you already know. God knows what draws them to danger, but if I had kept him under lock and key in this house as I sometimes did when he was a little boy he'd be alive today and not a corpse in his coffin."

She fervently crossed herself.

"Marfa Vladimirovna, please tell us what else you were told by the two boys," Grubeshov said to her.

"I was told they had seen a bottle of blood on the Jew's table."

The army general gasped and the officials looked at each other in horror. Yakov stared whitely at Marfa, his lips working in agitation. "There was no bottle of blood on my table," he cried out. "If there was anything it was a jar of strawberry jam. Jam is not blood. Blood is not jam."

"Be quiet!" Grubeshov ordered. "We will inform you when it is your time to speak."

One of the gendarmes pointed his revolver at Yakov.

"Put that foolish gun away," Bibikov said. "The man is chained and manacled."

"Did you personally see 'the bottle of blood'?" he asked Marfa.

"No, but both of the boys did, and they told me about it. They could hardly talk. Their faces were green."

"Then why didn't you report that to the police? It was your duty to, as well as the other incidents you just enumerated, as for instance the suspect chasing your son with a knife. That is a criminal act. This is a civilized society. Such things must be reported to the police."

She answered at once: "Because I've had my fill of the police, if you won't mind me saying so, your honor, and with apologies to those of them present that never bothered me. I once complained to them that Yuri Shiskovsky, for reasons that will be kept to myself, struck me on the head with a block of wood, and all morning they kept me in the police station answering personal questions while they filled out long forms, as if I myself were the criminal and not that madman who they let go, although I had a bloody gash in my scalp, and even an idiot would know who had hit who. I can't afford to lose my time like that. I have to earn a living and that's why I didn't report what the boys told me."

"Which is understandable enough," said Grubeshov—turning to the general, who nodded—"although I agree with the Investigating Magistrate that such things should be reported at once. Now finish your story, Marfa Vladimirovna."

"I have finished, there's no more to tell."

"In that case," said the Prosecuting Attorney, addressing the officials, "it's best to move on."

He pulled a thin gold watch from his yellow waistcoat pocket and consulted it closely.

"Vladislav Grigorievitch," Bibikov said, "I must insist on my prerogative to question the witness."

Marfa's intent gaze at him changed from fear to anger.

"What have I done to you?" she cried out.

"Neither of us has done anything to the other, that's not the point. Marfa Golov, I would like to ask you a question or two. Please, Vladislav Grigorievitch, I insist. Unfortunately, I can't go into certain things just now, but one or two questions I insist on asking and I would like them answered honestly and directly. Is it true, for instance, Marfa Golov, that you receive stolen goods from a gang of thieves, one of whom is or was your lover who often visits this house?"

"You needn't bother to answer that," Grubeshov said, flushing. "It's irrelevant to the matter at issue."

"I insist it is not so irrelevant, Vladislav Grigorievitch."

"No, I don't receive such goods," said Marfa, white-lipped, her eyes darkening. "That's a filthy rumor spread by my enemies."

"Is that your response?"

"Of course it is."

"Very well, then. Is it true that a year ago last January you threw the contents of a phial of carbolic acid into the eyes of your lover and blinded him for life, a man whom you have since become reconciled with?"

"Is he the one who reported me?" she asked, enraged.

"Reported you?"

"Told you these filthy lies?"

"Boris Alexandrovitch, as your superior in rank, I forbid these questions," Grubeshov said, irritated. "If you have anything of that nature to ask, please do so in my office tomorrow morning, though I personally don't see how such irrelevancies can matter. They do not change the weight of the significant evidence. We must absolutely get on now. It's Sunday and we all have obligations to our families."

"What is the 'significant evidence' you refer to?"

"The evidence we have been engaged in collecting, including the evidence of history."

"History is not law."

"We will see about that."

"I must insist on a reply from Marfa Golov."

"I have no more to say than I've already said," Marfa answered haughtily. "He used to beat me up and I defended myself. My legs and back were black and blue for months where he beat me, and once he smashed me in the eye so hard it ran pus for three weeks."

"Is it true that he also beat your son, once so severely that the boy lost consciousness?"

"I forbid you to answer," Grubeshov shouted.

"Don't be a fool," Colonel Bodyansky said to Bibikov.

"The Jew killed my child," Marfa cried out. "Somebody ought to scratch his eyes." She ran to the window and called out of the open vent to the gravestones in the cemetery, "Zhenia, my baby, come home! Come home to your mother!"

She wept heartbrokenly.

She's insane, thought Yakov. So is her hat with the cherries.

"See how he glares at me like a starving wolf from the forest," Marfa, turning to the fixer, shouted. "Make him stop!"

There was a stir among the officials. Two of the gendarmes pinned the prisoner by his arms.

Marfa, glaring at him, attempted then to remove her hat. Her eyelids fluttered, and moaning she sank to the floor. The hat rolled off her head, but before fainting she gazed loosely around to see where it was. Father Anastasy and Colonel Bodyansky bent to assist her.

When Marfa recovered only the police and gendarmes were in the room with her and the prisoner. Bibikov, to Yakov's misery, had left first, and he saw him, through the window, walk down the muddy road and get into a carriage alone. The dead boy's mother asked for her hat, blew on it, and put it carefully away in a sideboard drawer.

She covered her head with a coarse black shawl.

3

Grubeshov, in his bowler and wet rain cape, hovered over Father Anastasy with a large black umbrella as the wet-lipped priest, standing on a low flat rock, his voice rising and falling sometimes out of context with what he was saying, nasally recited the blood guilt of the Jewish Nation.

The group of officials and police had abandoned the carriages and motorcar at the bottom of an inclined street paved with rocks, lined on one side by a row of blackened shanties from which people stared at them out of windows and doorways, but no one came out to watch. A flock of pigeons rose in the street and two small white dogs, barking shrilly, darted into the houses as the crowd of officials approached. On foot they climbed first up the steps of a terraced hill from which the winding Dnieper was visible in the distance, then descended into a muddy ravine, and along it to the bottom of an almost perpendicular rocky hill with some caves in its face, in one of which the body of Zhenia Golov had been found. This cave, minutely described in the newspapers Yakov had read on the day of the discovery of the boy's body, one of those cut into the hill by religious hermits centuries ago, was about fifteen feet up its face. To get up into it one climbed the rough steps that had been hewn into the rocky hill. On top of it was a sparse birchwood grove with thin-trunked white trees full of chirping swallows, and beyond that lay a flat section of the outskirts of the city consisting of scattered houses and empty lots, about two versts from Nikolai Maximovitch's brick factory.

"There is from here an almost straight road from the brick factory where Zhenia was presumed to be killed," Grubeshov said.

"But, permit me, Vladislav Grigorievitch, to draw your attention to the fact that the road from Marfa Golov's house is just as straight and a little shorter," said Bibikov.

"In any case," the Prosecuting Attorney answered, "the most important evidence will be the testimony of the experts."

The priest, a long-haired, large-nosed man whose breath smelled of garlic, was standing under Grubeshov's umbrella before a loose semicircle of listeners but the Prosecuting Attorney had Yakov brought up close, the officials giving way as he was pushed forward, his chains rattling, by his guards. Bibikov, standing in the rear, looked on, impassively smoking. It was still drizzling and the fixer had lost his cap, unsettling him further, more than he thought possible in his present condition. It's only a cap, not my life; but the thought was a terrible one, because it was the first time he had admitted to himself he was afraid for his life. Fearing he was about to hear some secret fact that would absolutely condemn him once it was known, he stood inch-deep in the mud, breathing thickly, listening transfixed.

"My dear children," said the priest to the Russians, wringing his dry hands, "if the bowels of the earth were to open to reveal the population of human dead since the beginning of the world, you would be astonished to see how many innocent Christian children among them have been tortured to death by Christ-hating Jews. Throughout the ages, as described in their holy books and various commentaries, the voice of Semitic blood directs them to desecrations, unspeakable horrors—for example, the Talmud, which likens blood to water and milk, and preaches hatred of gentiles, who are characterized as being not human, no more than animals. 'Thou shalt not kill' does not apply to us, for do not they also write in their books: 'Murder the good among gentiles'? This perfidy, too, is prescribed in their Kabbala, the book of Jewish magic and alchemy, wherein the name of Satan is invoked; hence there have been multitudes of slaughtered innocent children whose tears have not moved their murderers to mercy."

His eyes darted over the faces of the officials but no one moved.

"The ritual murder is meant to re-enact the crucifixion of our dear Lord. The murder of Christian children and the distribution of their blood among Jews are a token of their eternal enmity against Christendom, for in murdering the innocent Christian child, they repeat the martyrdom of Christ. Zhenia Golov, in the loss of his own warm blood, symbolizes to us our Lord's loss of his precious lifeblood, drop by cruel drop, as he hung in pain on the wooden cross to which the anti-Christ had nailed him. It is said that the murder of the gentile—any gentile—hastens the coming of their long-awaited Messiah, Elijah, for whom they eternally leave the door open but who has never, during all the ages since his first coming, bothered to accept the invitation to enter and sit in the empty chair. Since the destruction of their Temple in Jerusalem by the Legions of Titus there has been no sacrificial altar for animals in their synagogues, and it has come about, therefore, that the killing of gentiles, in particular innocent children, is accepted as a fitting substitute. Even their philosopher Maimonides, whose writings were suppressed in our country in 1844, orders Jews to murder Christian children. Did I not tell you they think of us as animals?

"In the recorded past," said Father Anastasy in his nasally musical voice, "the Jew has had many uses for Christian blood. He has used it for purposes of sorcery and witches' rituals, and for love potions and well poisoning, fabricating a deadly venom that spread the plague from one country to another, a mixture of Christian blood from a murdered victim, their own Jewish urine, the heads of poisonous snakes, and even the stolen mutilated host—the bleeding body of Christ himself. It is written that all Jews require some Christian blood for the prolongation of their lives else they die young. And in those days they considered our blood to be—this too is recorded—the most effective therapeutic for the cure of their diseases. They used it, according to their old medical books, to heal their women in childbirth, stop hemorrhages, cure the blindness of infants, and to alleviate the wounds of circumcision."

One of the Kiev police officials, Captain Korimzin, a man in a damp coat and muddy boots, secretly made the sign of the cross. Yakov felt faint. The priest, staring at him intently for a minute, went on, and although he spoke calmly his gestures were agitated. The Russians continued to listen with grave interest.

"There are those among us, my children, who will argue that these are superstitious tales of a past age, yet the truth of much I have revealed to you—I do not say it is all true—must be inferred from the very frequency of the accusations against the Jews. None can forever conceal the truth. If the bellman is dead the wind will toll the bell. Perhaps in this age of science we can no longer accept every statement of accusation made against this unfortunate people; however we must ask ourselves how much truth remains despite our reluctance to believe. I do not say that all Jews are guilty of these crimes and that pogroms should therefore be instituted against them, but that there are certain sects among them, in particular the Hasidim and their leaders, the tzadikim, who commit in secret crimes such as I have described to you, which the gentile world, despite its frequent experience with them, seems to forget until, lo! another poor child disappears and is found dead in this fashion: his hands tied behind his back, and his body punctured by a sharp weapon in several places, the number of wounds according to magic numbers: 3, 7, 9, 13, in the manner of such crimes of former times. We know that their Passover, though they ascribe to it other uses, is also a celebration of the crucifixion. We know that is the time they kidnap gentiles for their religious ceremonials. Here in our Holy City, during the Polovostian raids in the year 1100, the monk Eustratios was abducted from the Pechera Monastery and sold to the Jews of Kherson, who crucified him during Passover. Since they no longer dare such open crimes they celebrate the occasion by eating matzos and unleavened cakes at the Seder service. But even this act conceals a crime because the matzos and cakes contain the blood of our martyrs, though of course the tzadikim deny this. Thus through our blood in their Passover food they again consume the agonized body of the living Christ. I give you my word, my dear children, that this is the reason why Zhenia Golov, this innocent child who wished to enter the priesthood, was destroyed!"

The priest wiped one eye, then the other, with a white handkerchief. Two of the guards standing nearest the fixer edged away from him.

But then Yakov cried out, "It's all a fairy tale, every bit of it. Who could ever believe such a thing? Not me!" His voice quavered and his face was bloodless.

"Those who can understand will believe," said the priest.

"Be respectful if you know what's good for you," Grubeshov said heatedly in an undertone. "Listen and learn!"

"How can it be so if the opposite is true," the fixer shouted, his throat thick. "It's all right to theorize with a fact or two but I don't recognize the truth in what's been said. If you please, your reverence, everybody knows the Bible forbids us to eat blood. That's all over the book, in the laws and everything. I've forgotten most of what I knew about the sacred books, but I've lived among the people and know their customs. Many an egg my own wife would throw out to the goat if it had the smallest spot of blood on the yolk. 'Raisl,' I said, 'take it easy. We can't afford to live like kings,' but there was no getting the egg back on the table, either by hook or by crook, once she took it off, even admitting anyone wanted to, which I never did—you get used to the customs. What she did was final, your reverence. I never said, 'Bring back the bloody egg,' and she would have thrown it at me if I had. She also soaked for hours the little meat or chicken we ate, to wash out every fleck of blood, and then sprinkled it with salt so as to be sure she had drained out every last drop. The rinsings with water were endless. That's the truth of it, I swear. I swear I'm innocent of this crime you say I did, not you personally, your reverence, but some of the officials here. I'm not a Hasid and I'm not a tzadik. I'm a fixer by trade, it's a poorer trade than most, and formerly for a short time I was a soldier in the Imperial Army. In fact, to tell the whole truth, I'm not a religious man, I'm a freethinker. At first my wife and I quarreled about this but I said a man's religion is his own business, and that's all there is to it, if you'll pardon me for saying so, your reverence. Anyway, I never touched that boy or any boy in my life. I was a boy myself once and it's a time I find hard to forget. I'm affectionate to children and I would have been a happy man if my wife had given birth to a child. It's not in my nature to do anything such as has been described, and if anyone thinks so it's mistaken identity for sure."

He had turned to the officials. They had listened courteously, even the two Black Hundreds representatives, though the shorter of them could not hide the distaste he felt for the fixer. The other now walked away. One man in a round cloth cap smiled sweetly at Yakov, then gazed impassively into the far distance where the golden cupolas of a cathedral rose above the trees.

"You'd be better off confessing," Grubeshov said, "instead of raising this useless stink." He asked the priest's pardon for his language.

"Confessing what, your honor, if as I told you I didn't do it? I can confess to you some things but I can't confess this crime. You'll have to excuse me there—I didn't do it. Why would I do such a thing anyway? You're mistaken, your honor. Somebody has made a serious mistake."

But no one would admit it and a heavy sadness settled on him.

"Confessing how it was done," Grubeshov replied. "How you enticed the boy into the stable with sweets, and then two or three of you pounced on him, gagged his mouth, tied him hand and foot, and dragged him up the stairs to your habitat. There you prayed over him with those black hats and robes on, undressed the frightened child, and began to stab him in certain places, twelve stabs first, then another making thirteen wounds—thirteen each in the region of the heart, on the neck, from which most of the blood is drawn, and on the face —according to your cabalistic books. You tormented and terrified him, enjoying the full shuddering terror of the child victim and his piteous pleas for mercy, in the meanwhile collecting his dripping lifeblood into bottles until you had bled him white. The five or six litres of warm blood you put into a black satchel, and this, if I understand the custom, was delivered by a hunchback Jew to the synagogue in time for making the matzos and afikomen. And when poor Zhenia Golov's heart was drained of blood and he lay on the floor lifeless, you and the tzadik Jew with the white stockings picked him up and carried him here in the dead of night and left his corpse in the cave. Then you both ate bread and salt so that his ghost would not haunt you and hurried away before the sun rose. Fearing the discovery of the bloodstains on your floor, you later sent one of your Jews to burn down Nikolai Maximovitch's stable. That is what you ought to confess."

The fixer, moaning, wrung his hands and beat them against his chest. He looked for Bibikov but the Investigating Magistrate and his assistant had disappeared.

"Take him up to the cave," Grubeshov ordered the guards.

Shutting his umbrella, he quickly preceded them, scampering up the steps, and entered the cave.

The leg chains were too short for Yakov to climb the steep steps, so he was seized under the arms by two of the gendarmes and dragged and pushed up, the other guards following directly behind. Then one guard went into the cave and the others shoved the fixer in through the narrow stone opening.

Inside the dank cave, smelling of death, in the dim light of a semicircle of dripping candles fastened on the wall, Grubeshov produced Yakov's tool sack.

"Aren't these your tools, Yakov Bok? They were found in your habitat in the stable by the driver Richter."

Yakov identified them in the candlelight.

"Yes, your honor, I've had them for years."

"Look at this rusty knife and these awls cleansed of blood with this rag, and now deny these instruments were used by you and your gang of Jews to perforate and bleed the body of a sweet and innocent Christian child!"

The fixer forced himself to look. He gazed at the gleaming point of the awl, and beyond it, into the depths of the cave which he now saw clearly, everyone present, among them Marfa Golov, her head wrapped in a black shawl, her wet eyes reflecting the candle lights, wailing on her knees at the bier of her Zhenia, disinterred from his grave for the occasion, lying naked in death, the wounds of his gray shrunken pitiful body visible in the light of two long thickly dripping white candles burning at his large head and small feet.

Yakov hastily counted the wounds on the child's bloated face, and cried out, "Fourteen!"

But the Prosecuting Attorney replied these were two magic groups of seven, and Father Anastasy, the stink of garlic rising from his head, fell on his knees and with a quiet moan began to pray.

V

THE DAYS were passing and the Russian officials were waiting impatiently for his menstrual period to begin. Grubeshov and the army general often consulted the calendar. If it didn't start soon they threatened to pump blood out of his penis with a machine they had for that purpose. The machine was a pump made of iron with a red indicator to show how much blood was being drained out. The danger of it was that it didn't always work right and sometimes sucked every drop of blood out of the body. It was used exclusively on Jews; only their penises fitted it.

In the morning the guards came into the cell and awakened him roughly. He was searched carefully and ordered to dress. Yakov was manacled and chained, then marched up two flights of stairs—he had hoped to Bibikov's office but it was to the Prosecuting Attorney's across the hall. In the anteroom, on a bench against the wall in the rear two men in threadbare suits looked up furtively at the prisoner, then lowered their eyes. They are spies, he thought. Grubeshov's office was a large high-ceilinged room with a long ikon of a crucified blue-haloed Christ on the wall behind the prosecutor's desk, where he sat reading legal documents and referring to open law books. The fixer was ordered to sit in a chair facing Grubeshov, and the guards lined up behind him.

The day was uncomfortably warm, the windows shut against the heat. The prosecutor wore a light greenish suit with the same soiled yellow vest and black bow tie. His sidewhiskers were brushed, and he mopped his moist face and palms and wiped the back of his heavy neck with a large handkerchief. Yakov, disturbed by his bad dream of that morning, and almost unable to look at the Prosecuting Attorney since his performance at the cave, felt he was suffocating.

"I have decided to send you to the preliminary confinement cell in the Kiev Prison to await your trial," Grubeshov said, blowing his nose and cleaning it slowly. "It is, of course, not easy to predict when it will begin, so I thought I would inquire whether you had become more cooperative? Since you have had time to reflect on your situation, perhaps you are now willing to tell the truth. What do you say? Further resistance will gain you only headaches. Cooperation will perhaps ease your situation."

"What else is there to say, your honor?" the fixer sighed sadly. "I've looked in my small bag of words and I have nothing more to say except that I'm innocent. There's no evidence against me, because I didn't do what you say I did."

"That's too bad. Your role in this murder was known to us before you were arrested. You were the only Jew living in the district, with the exceptions of Mandelbaum and Litvinov, Merchants of the First Guild, who weren't in Russia during the time of the commission of the crime, perhaps on purpose. We suspected a Jew at once because a Russian couldn't possibly commit that kind of crime. He might cut a man's throat in a fight, or suddenly kill a person with two or three heavy blows, but no Russian would maliciously torture an innocent child by inflicting forty-seven deadly wounds on his body."

"Neither would I," said the fixer. "It's not in my nature, whatever else is."

"The weight of the evidence is against you."

"Then maybe the evidence is wrong, your honor?"

"Evidence is evidence, it can't be wrong."

Grubeshov's voice became persuasive. "Tell me the honest truth, Yakov Bok, didn't the Jewish Nation put you up to this crime? You seem like a serious person—perhaps you were unwilling to do it but they urged it on you, made threats or promises of certain sorts, and you reluctantly carried out the murder for them? To put it in other words, wasn't it their idea rather than yours? If you'll admit that, I'll tell you frankly—I'll put it this way—your life would be easier. We will not prosecute to the full extent of our powers. Perhaps after a short while you will be paroled and your sentence suspended. In other words, there are 'possibilities.' All we ask is your signature—that's not so much."

Grubeshov's face glistened, as though he were making a greater effort than was apparent.

"How could I do such a thing, your honor? I couldn't do such a thing. Why should I blame it on innocent people?"

"History has proved they are not so innocent. Besides I don't understand your false scruples. After all, you're an admitted freethinker, this admission occurred in my presence. The Jews mean very little to you. I size you up as a man who is out for himself, though I can't blame you. Come, here is an opportunity to free yourself from the confines of the net you have fallen into."

"If the Jews don't mean anything to me, then why am I here?"

"You are foolish to lend yourself to their evil aims. What have they done for you?"

"At the very least, your honor, they've let me alone. No, I couldn't sign such a thing."

"Then keep in mind that the consequences for you can be very grave. The sentence of the court will be the least of your worries."

"Please," said the fixer, breathing heavily, "do you really believe those stories about magicians stealing the blood out of a murdered Christian child to mix in with matzos? You are an educated man and would surely not believe such superstitions."

Grubeshov sat back, smiling slightly. "I believe you killed the boy Zhenia Golov for ritual purposes. When they know the true facts, all Russia will believe it. Do you believe it?" he asked the guards.

The guards swore they did.

"Of course we believe it," Grubeshov said. "A Jew is a Jew, and that's all there is to it. Their history and character are unchangeable. Their nature is constant. This has been proved in scientific studies by Gobineau, Chamberlain and others. We here in Russia are presently preparing one on Jewish facial characteristics. Our peasants have a saying that a man who steals wears a hat that burns. With a Jew it is the nose that burns and reveals the criminal he is."

He flipped open a notebook to a page of pen-and-ink sketches, turning the book so that Yakov could read the printing at the top of the page: "Jewish noses."

"Here, for instance, is yours." Grubeshov pointed to a thin high-bridged nose with slender nostrils.

"And this is yours," Yakov said hoarsely, pointing to a short, fleshy, broad-winged nose.

The Prosecuting Attorney, though his color had deepened, laughed thinly. "You are a witty man," he said, "but it won't do you any good. Your fate is foreseen. Ours is a humane society but there are ways of punishing hardened criminals. Perhaps I ought to remind you—to show you how well off you are—how your fellow Jews were executed in the not too distant past. They were hanged wearing caps full of hot pitch and with a dog hanging beside them to show the world how despised they were."

"A dog hangs a dog, your honor."

"If you can't bite don't show your teeth." Grubeshov, his neck inflamed, slashed the fixer across the jaw with a ruler. Yakov cried out as the wood snapped, one piece hitting the wall. The guards began to beat his head with their fists but the Prosecuting Attorney waved them away.

"You can cry to Bibikov from now to doomsday," he shouted at the fixer, "but I'll keep you in prison till the flesh rots off your bones piece by piece. You will beg me to let you confess who compelled you to murder that innocent boy!"

2

He feared the prison would go badly for him and it went badly at once. It's my luck, he thought bitterly. What do they say?—"If I dealt in candles the sun wouldn't set." Instead, I'm Yakov Fixer and it sets each hour on the stroke. I'm the kind of man who finds it perilous to be alive. One thing I must learn is to say less—much less, or I'll ruin myself. As it is I'm already ruined.

The Kiev Prison, also in the Lukianovsky, was a high-walled old gray fortress-like building with a large interior muddy yard, strewn on the iron gate side with junk piles—a broken wagon, rotting mattresses, blackened boards, barrels of rubbish, rock and sandpiles where prisoners sometimes worked with cement. A clear area between the administrative offices on the west and the main cell block was the promenade grounds. Yakov and his guards had got to the prison on a trolley, a ride of several versts from the District Courthouse where he had been in jail until then. At the prison the fixer was greeted by the cross-eyed warden, "Hello, blood-drinker, welcome to the Promised Land." The Deputy Warden, a lean, narrow-faced man with depthless eyes and a four-fingered right hand, said, "Here we'll feed you flour and blood till you shit matzos." The sub-officials and clerks rushed out of their offices to see the Jew, but Warden Grizitskoy, a man of sixty-five, with a limp yellowish gray beard, a khaki uniform with gold epaulets, and a visored cap, shoved open a door and led the fixer into an inner office, where he sat down at his desk.

"I don't want your kind here," he said, "but I have no choice in the matter. I'm the Tsar's servant and follow his orders faithfully. You are the lowest of Jewish scum—I've read of your deeds—but nevertheless a charge of his Imperial Majesty Nicholas the Second. So here you'll stay till they tell me otherwise. You'd better behave yourself. Follow the rules and regulations and do as you're told. Quickly does it. Under no circumstances are you to attempt to communicate with any person outside this prison unless I authorize it. If you make trouble you will be shot in your tracks. Understood?"

"How long must I stay here?" Yakov managed to ask. "I mean considering I haven't yet been tried."

"As long as the proper authorities deem necessary. Now keep your questions to yourself and go along with the sergeant. He will tell you what to do."

The sergeant, a man with drooping mustaches, led the fixer down the corridor past some dingy offices from whose doorways the clerks were staring out, to a long room with a counter and several benches where he was ordered to undress. Yakov changed into a sack-like white jacket, smelling of human sweat, and a pair of shapeless linen trousers. He was handed a shirt without buttons and a worn greatcoat that had once been brown and was now gray, to sleep in or under at night. As he was pulling off his boots to change into a pair of stiff prison shoes, a wave of oppressive darkness swept over him. Though he felt like fainting he wouldn't give them the satisfaction.

"Sit down in that chair for your haircut," the sergeant ordered.

Yakov sat down in a straightback chair, but as the prison barber was about to crop his hair with a pair of large clippers, the sergeant, checking his official paper, stopped him.

"Never mind that. The orders say let him keep his head of hair."

"It's always like that," said the barber, incensed. "These pricks are born with privileges."

"Cut it off!" shouted Yakov, "cut off my hair!"

"Silence!" ordered the sergeant. "Learn to follow orders! Move on!"

He unlocked a metal door with a large key and followed the fixer down a dimly lit dank corridor to a large crowded cell with a barred grating on one side, and a wall on the other containing two high small dirty windows through which little light penetrated. A smelly urinal, no more than an open drain, ran along the rear wall of the cell.

"It's the thirty-day cell," said the sergeant. "You stay here for a month and either you go on trial or they transfer you elsewhere."

"Where elsewhere?"

"You'll find out."

Wherever it is what difference does it make? the fixer thought blackly.

The noise in the cell quieted as the door clanked open, and the silence deepened as though a quilt had been thrown over the prisoners as they watched Yakov enter. After the door shut behind him they began talking and moving again. There were about twenty-five men in the room, their searing stench in the almost airless cell nauseating. Some sat on the floor playing cards, two men danced closely together, a few wrestled or sparred, fell over each other, got kicked and cursed at. An old fanatic jumped repeatedly from the seat of a broken stool. A man with a sick sunken face hammered his shoe with the heel of another. There were a few benches and tables in the cells but no cots or mattresses. The prisoners slept on a low wooden platform along the outer wall, raised a centimeter from the damp filthy floor. Yakov sat alone in the farthest corner, reflecting on his wretched fate. He would have torn out fistfuls of his hair but was afraid to be noticed.

3

A guard with a gun outside the grating shouted "Supper!" and two other guards opened the cell door and delivered three steaming wooden pails of soup. The prisoners ran with a roar to the pails, crowding around each. Yakov, who had eaten nothing that day, got up slowly. A guard handed out a wooden spoon to one prisoner in each group around the three pails. Sitting on the floor before his pail, the prisoner was allowed to eat ten spoonfuls of the watery cabbage soup, thickened with a bit of barley, then had to pass the spoon to the next one in line. Those who tried to take extra spoonfuls were beaten by the others. After each prisoner had had his quota, the first began again.

Yakov edged close to the nearest pail but the one eating the soup, a clubfoot with a scarred head, stopped spooning, reached into the pail, and with a shout of triumph plucked out half a dead mouse, its entrails hanging. The prisoner held the mouse by the tail, hastily spooning down the soup with his other hand. Two of the prisoners violently twisted the spoon out of his hand and shoved him away from the pail. The clubfoot limped over to the men at the next pail and dangled the mouse in front of their faces, but though they cursed him into the ground no one left the pail. So he clumsily danced around with his dead mouse. Yakov glanced into the second pail, already empty except for a few dead cockroaches floating at the bottom. He did not look into the third pail. Nor did he care for the colorless tea that was served in tin mugs without sugar. He had hoped for a bit of bread but was given none because his name had not been entered on the bread list by the sergeant. That night when the other prisoners were snoring side by side on the platform, the fixer, wrapped in his greatcoat, though it was not a cold night, walked back and forth the length of the cell in the thick dark until the nails in his shoes bit into his feet. When he lay down exhausted, covering his face with half a sheet of newspaper he had found in the cell, to keep off the flies, he was at once awakened by the clanging bell.

At breakfast he gulped down the weak tea that smelled like wood rotting but could not touch the watery gray gruel in the pails. He had heard the wooden pails were in use in the bathhouse when they were not filled with soup or gruel. He asked for bread but the guard said he was still not on the list.

"When will I be?"

"Fuck you," said the guard. "Don't make trouble."

The fixer noticed that the mood of the prisoners to him, neutral to begin with, had altered. The men were quieter, subdued. During the morning they congregated in groups close to the urinal, whispering, casting glances at Yakov. The clubfoot from time to time appraised him with shrewd and cunning eyes.

Yakov felt icicles sprout in his blood. Something has happened, he thought. Maybe somebody told them who I am. If they think I killed a Christian boy they might want to kill me.

In that case should he cry out to the guard and ask to be transferred to another cell before they murdered him in this? And if he did would he live long enough to get there? Suppose the prisoners rushed him and the guards made no move to defend him?

During the morning "promenade," the ten-minute exercise break when the men marched in double lines of twelve around the yard, ten paces between each group, as armed guards, some with coiled bullwhips, stood at the foot of the high thick walls, the clubfoot, who had slipped into line next to Yakov, said in a whisper, "Why isn't your head shaved like the rest of us?"

"I don't know," Yakov whispered. "I told the barber to go ahead and do it."

"Are you a stool pigeon or squealer? The men are suspicious of you."

"No, no, tell them I'm not."

"Then why do you sit apart from us? Who the hell do you think you are?"

"To tell the truth my feet hurt in these shoes. Also it's my first time in prison. I'm trying to get used to it but it's not so easy."

"Are you expecting any food packages?" asked the clubfoot.

"Who would send me packages? I have nobody to send me a package. My wife left me. Everyone I know is poor."

"Well, if you get one, share and share alike is my motto. That's the rule here."

"Yes, yes."

The clubfoot limped along in silence.

They don't know who I am, Yakov thought. From now on I'd better be sociable. Once they find out it will be blows, not questions.

But when the prisoners had marched back into the cell there were whispered arguments among them, and Yakov, remembering how he had been beaten in the District Courthouse cell, felt himself sweating hotly.

Afterwards, another prisoner, a tall man with humid eyes, detached himself from a group of others and approached Yakov. He was heavily built, with a pale hard intense face, an almost black neck, and thin bent legs. He walked forward slowly, oddly, as though afraid something might fall out of his clothes. The fixer, sitting on the floor with his back to the wall, scrambled up quickly.

"Listen, little brother," the other prisoner began, "I am Fetyukov. The prisoners have sent me to talk to you."

"If you're worried that I'm a stool pigeon," Yakov said hastily, "you've got the wrong worry. I'm here like everybody else, waiting for my trial. I haven't asked for any privileges, not that they would give me any. I'm not even getting a bread ration. As for my hair, I told the barber to go ahead and cut it off but the sergeant said not to, though don't ask me why."

"What are you accused of?"

The fixer touched his lips with a dry tongue. "Whatever they've accused me of I didn't do. I give you my word. It's too complicated to go into without turning it into a wearying tale, something I don't understand myself."

"I'm a murderer," said Fetyukov. "I stabbed a stranger at the inn in my village. He provoked me so I stabbed him twice, once in the chest, and when he was falling, once in the back. That was the end of him. I had had more than a drop or two, but when they told me what I had done I was greatly surprised. I'm a peaceful man, I never make trouble if you don't provoke me. Who would've thought I could murder anybody? If you had told me any such thing I would have laughed at you to your face."

The fixer, staring at the murderer, edged sideways along the wall. At the same time he saw two other prisoners sneaking up on him, one from either side. As he cried out, Fetyukov reached behind him whipping a short heavy stick out of his trousers. He struck Yakov a hard blow on the head. The fixer went down on one knee, holding both hands over his pain-wracked, bloody head, then fell over.

He awoke, lying on the clammy wooden platform. His head ached sickeningly and a searing pain throbbed on the left side of his skull. His fingers sought out the wet swollen cut on his scalp. Blood dripped from it. He was anguished. Would he be beaten every time he was moved to another cell and met other prisoners? The fixer dizzily sat up, blood trickling down his face.

"Wipe it off," advised an old man with cracked eyeglasses, peering down at him. It was the slop-pail man who took care of the excrement buckets, brought in drinking water, and occasionally swept the wet floor. "Use the water bucket by the door."

"Why do you hit a man who has done nothing to you? What have I done to you?"

"Listen, matey," the old man whispered, "wash the blood off before the guard comes or the men will kill you."

"Let them kill me," he shouted.

"I told you he's a shitnose squealer," the clubfoot said from the other side of the cell. "Finish him off, Fetyukov."

A nervous murmur rose among the prisoners.

Two guards came running in the corridor, one carrying a shotgun. They peered through the grating.

"What's going on here? Cut out the noise, you pigs, or you'll live on half rations for a week."

The other guard stared through the barred grating into the gloomy cell.

"Where's the Jew?" he called.

There was dead silence. The prisoners looked among themselves; some glanced furtively at Yakov.

After a while Yakov said he was there. A low murmur came from the prisoners. The guard pointed a shotgun at them and the murmur ceased.

"Where?" said the guard. "I can't see you."

"Here," said Yakov. "There's nothing to see."

"The sergeant wrote your name on the bread list. You'll get your six ounces tonight."

"In the meantime you can dream of matzos," said the guard

with the gun. "Also the blood of Christian martyrs, if you know what I mean."

When the guards left the prisoners talked excitedly among themselves. Yakov felt renewed fright.

Fetyukov, the murderer, approached again. The fixer rose tensely, his hand clawing the wall.

"Are you the Jew they say has murdered a Russian lad?"

"They lie," Yakov said hoarsely, "I'm innocent."

The mutterings of the prisoners filled the cell. One of them shouted, "Jew bastard!"

"That's not why I hit you," said Fetyukov. "Your head wasn't shaved and we thought you were a spy. We did it to see if you would report us to the guard. If you had done that it would have finished you off. The clubfoot would have knifed you. We are going on trial and don't want anybody testifying what he has heard in this cell. I didn't know you were a Jew. But if I had I wouldn't have hit you. When I was a boy I was apprenticed to a Jew blacksmith. He wouldn't have done what they say you did. If he drank blood he would have vomited it up. And he wouldn't have harmed a Christian child. I'm sorry I hit you, it was a mistake."

"It was a mistake," said the clubfoot.

Yakov went unsteadily to the water bucket. The bucket stank but he sank to his knees and poured some water over his head.

After that the prisoners lost interest in him and turned to other things. Some of them went to sleep on the platform and some played cards.

That night Fetyukov woke the fixer and gave him a piece of sausage he had saved from a package his sister had sent him. Yakov gobbled it up. The murderer also handed him a wet rag to press down the swollen cut on his head.

"Tell the truth," he whispered, "did you kill that lad? Maybe you did it for a different reason? You might have been drunk."

"For no other reason," Yakov said. "And I wasn't drunk. It never happened, I'm innocent."

"I wish I were innocent," sighed Fetyukov. "It was a terrible thing I did. The man was a stranger to me. One must protect strangers, it says so in the Book. I had had a drop, you understand, and the next thing I knew I grabbed up a knife and he was dead at my feet. God, who gives us life, lets it hang by a thread. One blow and it's torn away. Don't ask me why unless the devil is the stronger. If I could give that man his life again I would. I would say take your life and don't come near me again. I don't know why I did it but I don't want to be a murderer. Things are bad enough as they are, who needs worse? Now they'll pack me off to a prison camp in Siberia and if I live out my term I'll have to stay there the rest of my days.

"Little brother," he said to Yakov, making the sign of the cross over him, "don't lose hope. The stones of the bridge may crumble but the truth will come out."

"And till then," sighed the fixer, "what of my wasted youth?"

4

His youth dribbled away.

He had been imprisoned almost three months, three times longer than Bibikov had predicted and God only knew when it would end. Yakov nearly went mad trying to figure out what was happening to him. What was a poor harmless fixer doing in prison? What had he done to deserve this terrible incarceration, no end in sight? Hadn't he had more than his share of misery in a less than just world? He tried desperately to put together a comprehensible sequence of events that had led inevitably from his departure from the shtetl to a prison cell in Kiev; but to think of all these strange and unexpected experiences as meaningfully caused by related events confused him. True, the world was the kind of world it was. The rain put out fires and created floods. Yet too much had happened that didn't make sense. He had committed a few errors and paid for them in more than kind. One dark night a thick black web had fallen on him because he was standing under it, and though he ran in every direction he could not extricate himself from its sticky coils. Who was the spider if it remained invisible? He sometimes thought God was punishing him for his unbelief. He was, after all, the jealous God. "Thou shalt worship no other Gods before me," not even no Gods. He also blamed the goyim for their eternal hatred of Jews. Things go badly at a historical moment and go that way, God or no God, forever. Did it *have* to be so? And he continued to curse himself. It could have happened to a more dedicated Jew, but it had happened instead to a recent freethinker because he was Yakov Bok. He blamed his usual mistakes—he could not always tell those of the far-off past from those that had led directly to his arrest in the brickyard. Yet he knew there was something from the outside, a quality of fate that had stalked him all his life and threatened, if he wasn't careful, his early extinction.

He hungered to explain who he was, Yakov the fixer from a small town in the Pale, an orphan boy who had married Raisl Shmuel and had been deserted by her, a curse on her soul; who had been poor all his life, had grubbed for a living, and was poor in other ways too—if he was that one what was he doing in prison? Who were they punishing if his life was punishment? Why put a harmless man into a prison with thick stone walls? He thought of begging them to let him go simply because he was not a criminal—it was a known fact—they could ask in the shtetl. If any of the officials—Grubeshov, Bodyansky, the warden—had known him before, they would never have believed he could commit such a monstrous crime. Not such as he. If only his innocence were written on a sheet of paper, he could pull it out and say, "Read, it's all here," but since it was hidden in himself they would know it only if they sought it, and they were not seeking. How could anyone look twice at Marfa Golov, note her suspicious ways and those crazy cherries on her hat, and not suspect she knew more about the murder than she was willing to admit? And what had happened to the Investigating Magistrate whom he hadn't seen now in more than a month? Was he still loyal to the law, or had he joined with the others in their vicious hunt for a guilty Jew? Or had he merely forgotten an expendable man?

During Yakov's first days in the courthouse jail the accusation had seemed to him almost an irrelevancy, nothing much to do with his life or deeds. But after the visit to the cave he had stopped thinking of relevancy, truth, or even proof. There was no "reason," there was only their plot against a Jew, any Jew; he was the accidental choice for the sacrifice. He would be tried because the accusation had been made, there didn't have to be another reason. Being born a Jew meant being vulnerable to history, including its worst errors. Accident and history had involved Yakov Bok as he had never dreamed he could be involved. The involvement was, in a way of speaking, impersonal, but the effect, his misery and suffering, were not. The suffering was personal, painful, and possibly endless.

He felt entrapped, abandoned, helpless. He had disappeared from the world and nobody he could call friend knew it. Nobody. The fixer berated himself for not having listened to Shmuel's advice and staying where he belonged. He had got himself in a terrible mess, for what? Opportunity? An opportunity to destroy himself. He had fished for a herring and had been snatched by a shark. It wasn't hard to guess which of them would eat meat. And though he had now, at last, a little understanding of what was going on, or thought he had, he could of course still not resign himself to what had happened. In a philosophical moment he cursed history, anti-Semitism, fate, and even, occasionally, the Jews. "Who will help me?" he cried out in his sleep, but the other prisoners had their own anguish, their own bad dreams.

One night a new guest was let into the cell, a fattish heavy-faced young man with a blondish beard and small hands and feet, who wore his own clothes. At first his manner was morose and he returned furtive glances to anyone who looked in his direction. Yakov observed him from the distance. The young man was the only fat one in a cellful of skinny prisoners. He had money, bribed the guards for favors, lived well on packages from the outside—two large ones in a week—and wasn't stingy with food or cigarettes. "Here, boys, eat hearty," and he would hand out whatever there was to spare, yet keep himself well supplied. He even passed around green bottles of mineral water. He seemed to know how to get along, and some of the prisoners played cards with him. The clubfoot offered to be his personal servant but he waved him away. At the same time he was a worried man, muttered to himself, shook his head in disagreement, and sometimes tore at his round wrists with dirty fingernails. One by one he pulled off the buttons of his shirt. Yakov, though wanting to talk to the man, skirted him in the beginning, possibly because he didn't know what to say to people with money, partly because the man obviously didn't want to be bothered, and partly for reasons he could not explain to himself. The new prisoner dispensed his favors with pretended cordiality, his eyes unable to conceal the fact that he was not a cordial man, and then withdrew. He sat alone often, muttering. Yakov sensed this one was aware of him. They both minded their business and looked each other over. One morning, after the promenade in the prison yard, they began to talk in a corner of the cell.

"You're a Jew?" said the fat young man, in Yiddish.

Yakov admitted it.

"I, too."

"I thought so," said the fixer.

"If you thought so why didn't you come over?"

"I thought I'd wait a little."

"What's your name?"

"Yakov Bok the fixer."

"Gronfein, Gregor. Shalom. What are you in here for?"

"They say I killed a Christian child." He still couldn't say it keeping his voice steady.

Gronfein looked at him in astonishment.

"So you're the one? My God, why didn't you tell me right away? I'm happy to be in the same cell with you."

"Why should you be happy?"

"I heard they had accused somebody of killing the Russian boy they found in the cave. Of course the whole thing is a manufactured fake, but there's a rumor running around in the Podol that a Jew was arrested, though nobody has seen you or knows who. Whoever he is he's a martyr for us all. Is it really you?"

"It's me, I wish it wasn't."

"I had my doubts that such a person exists."

"Only that and no more," the fixer sighed. "My worst enemies should exist like this."

"Don't grieve," said Gronfein. "God will help."

"He will or he won't as it suits him, but if he doesn't I hope somebody else will soon, or they might as well put me in the ground and cover me up with earth and grass."

"Patience," Gronfein said absently. "Patience. If there's not one way, there's another."

"Another what?"

"As long as a man stays alive he can't tell what chances will pop up next. But a dead man signs no checks."

He began to talk about himself. "Of course I'm better off than some I can think of," Gronfein said, looking at Yakov to see if he agreed. "I have a first-class lawyer already working for me in what you could call unofficial ways, and I'm not afraid to part with a few hundred rubles if I have to, because there's more where they come from. What I do is I'm a counterfeiter. It's not honest but pays well, and so what if it takes away from Tsar Nicholas—he's got plenty he takes from the Jews. Still, if a bribe doesn't work this time I don't know what will. I've got a wife and five children and I'm getting a little worried. This is the longest I've spent in a cell. How long have you been here yourself?"

"Here about a month. Altogether three months since I was arrested."

"Whew." The counterfeiter gave Yakov two cigarettes and a piece of apple strudel from his last package, and the fixer ate and smoked gratefully.

Next time they talked, Gronfein asked Yakov questions about his parents, family, and village. He wanted to know what he had been doing in Kiev. Yakov told him this and that but not too much. He did, however, mention Raisl, and Gronfein squirmed.

"Not so much of a Jewish daughter I'd say. My wife couldn't have such thoughts, not with a goy anyway, let alone do such a thing."

The fixer shrugged. "Some do, some don't. And some who do are Jewish."

Gronfein started to ask something, looked around cautiously, then whispered he would be interested in knowing what exactly had happened to the boy. "How did he die?"

"How did who die?" the fixer said, astonished.

"That Russian boy who was murdered."

"How would I know?" He drew away from the man. "What they say I did I didn't do. If I weren't a Jew there'd be no crime."

"Are you sure? Why don't you confide in me? We're both in the same pot."

"I have nothing to confide," said Yakov coldly. "If there was no fowl there are no feathers."

"It's tough luck," said the counterfeiter amiably, "but I'll do what I can to help you. Once they let me out of here I'll speak to my lawyer."

"For that I'll thank you."

But Gronfein had grown depressed, his eyes clouding, and said no more.

The next day he sidled up to Yakov and whispered, worried, "They say on the outside that if the government brings you up on trial they might start a pogrom at the same time. The Black Hundreds are making terrible threats. Hundreds of Jews are leaving the city as if fleeing the plague. My father-in-law is talking of selling his business and running to Warsaw."

The fixer listened in silence.

"Nobody's blaming you, you understand," Gronfein said.

"If your father-in-law wants to run away at least he can run away."

As they talked, the counterfeiter, from time to time, nervously glanced in the direction of the cell door, as if he were watching for the guard.

"Are you expecting a package?" Yakov asked.

"No no. But if they don't let me out of here I'll soon go mad. It's a stinking place and I'm worried about my family."

He drifted away, but was back in twenty minutes with the remnants of a package.

"Guard what's left here," he said to Yakov, "maybe I'm getting some action after all."

A guard opened the door and Gronfein disappeared from the cell for half an hour. When he returned he told the fixer they were letting him out that evening. He seemed satisfied but his ears were flaming, and afterwards he muttered much to himself for more than an hour. Later he was calmer.

That's how it goes with money, Yakov thought. If you've got it you've got wings.

"Something I can do for you before I go?" Gronfein whispered, slipping the fixer a ten-ruble note. "Don't worry, it's guaranteed good."

"Thanks. With this I can get myself a few things. They won't give me my own money. Maybe I can buy a better pair of shoes from one of the prisoners. These hurt my feet. Also if your lawyer can help me I'll be much obliged."

"I was thinking maybe you want to leave me a letter to send to somebody?" said Gronfein. "Just write it out with this pencil and I'll mail it along. I have paper and an envelope or two in my pack. Stamps I'll paste on on the outside."

"With the greatest of thanks," Yakov said, "but who have I got to write to?"

"If you have nobody to write to," said Gronfein, "I can't manufacture you a correspondent, but what about your father-in-law that you told me about?"

"He's a poor man all his life. What can he do for me?"

"He's got a mouth, hasn't he? Let him start yelling."

"A mouth and a stomach but nothing goes in."

"They say when a Jewish rooster crows in Pinsk they hear him in Palestine."

"Maybe I'll write," said Yakov.

The more he thought about it, the more he wanted to write. He had a desperate desire to make known his fate. On the outside, as Gronfein had said, they knew somebody was in prison but not who. He wanted everyone to know it was Yakov Bok. He wanted them to know his innocence. Somebody had to know or he would never get out. Maybe a committee of some sort could be formed to help him? Maybe, if you knew the law, it was possible for a lawyer to see him before the indictment; if not that, he could at least urge them to produce the document so they could begin his defense. In another week it would be thirty days in this smelly detention cell and he had heard from no one. He considered writing to the Investigating Magistrate but didn't dare. If he should turn over the letter to the Prosecuting Attorney things might go worse. Or if he didn't maybe his assistant, Ivan Semyonovitch, might. In any case, it was too great a chance to take.

The fixer then slowly wrote two letters, one to Shmuel, and another to Aaron Latke, the printer who had rented him a room in his flat.

"Dear Shmuel," wrote Yakov. "As you predicted I got myself into serious trouble and am now in the Kiev Prison near Dorogozhitsky Street. I know it's impossible but try to help me as soon as you can. Who else can I appeal to? Your son-in-law, Yakov Bok. P.S. If she's back I'd rather not know."

To Aaron Latke he wrote, "Dear friend Aaron, your recent boarder Yakov Bok is now in the Kiev Prison, in the thirty-day cell. After thirty days God knows what will happen to me. What's happened already is bad enough. I am accused of killing a Russian child by the name of Zhenia Golov, who I swear I didn't touch. Do me a favor and take this letter to some Jewish journalist or maybe to a sincere philanthropist, if you happen to know of one. Tell them if they can get me out of here I'll work hard my whole life to pay them back. Only hurry because it's a desperate situation and getting worse. Yakov Bok."

"Good," said Gronfein, accepting the sealed letters, "that should do it. Well, the best of luck to you, and don't worry about the ten rubles. You can pay me when you get out. Where there's that there's more."

The guard opened the cell door and the counterfeiter hurriedly disappeared down the corridor, the prison guard trotting after him.

Fifteen minutes later Yakov was called to the warden's office. He handed the remnant of Gronfein's package to Fetyukov to watch, promising to divide it with him.

Yakov hurried through the hall with the guard's gun at his back. Maybe it's the indictment, he thought in excitement.

Warden Grizitskoy was in his office with the Deputy Warden and a stern-faced inspector in a uniform like a general's. In the corner sat Gronfein, his hat on and eyes shut.

The warden waved the two letters, out of their envelopes, that the fixer had just written.

"Are these yours? Answer truthfully, you son-of-a-bitch."

The fixer froze, his heart sinking. "Yes, your honor."

The warden pointed to the Yiddish script. "Translate these bird droppings," he said to Gronfein.

The counterfeiter opened his eyes long enough to read the letters aloud in Russian, in a quick monotone.

"You Zhid bloodsucker," said the warden, "how dare you break prison regulations? I personally warned you not to try to get in touch with anybody on the outside without my express permission."

Yakov said nothing, staring, sickened to the pit of his stomach, at Gronfein.

"He turned them over to us," the Deputy Warden said to the fixer. "A law-abiding citizen."

"Don't expect a moral man," Gronfein said to nobody in particular, his eyes still clamped shut. "I'm only a counterfeiter."

"You bastard stool pigeon," Yakov shouted at him, "why did you trick an innocent man?"

"Watch your language, you," warned the warden. "A foul heart, a foul tongue."

"It's every man for himself," Gronfein muttered. "I have five small children and a nervous wife."

"What's more," said the Deputy Warden, "we have it in writing that you also tried to bribe him to poison the yardkeeper who saw you attempting to kidnap the boy in the brickyard, and also to pay Marfa Golov not to testify against you. Isn't that the truth?" he asked Gronfein.

The counterfeiter, sweat trickling from under his hat down his dark lids, nodded once.

"Where would I get the money to pay for those bribes?" Yakov asked.

"The Jewish Nation would supply it," answered the inspector.

"Get him out of here," said the old warden. "The Prosecuting Attorney will call you when he needs you," he said to Gronfein.

"Stool pigeon!" Yakov shouted, "bastard traitor—it's a filthy lie!"

Gronfein, as though blind, was led out of the room by the Deputy Warden.

"This is the sort of assistance you can expect from your compatriots," the inspector said to Yakov. "It would be best for you to confess."

"We won't have our rules flouted by such as you," the warden said. "To strict confinement you go, and if you have any more letters to write you'll write them in your own blood."

5

He was being boiled alive in the smothering heat of the small solitary cell they had thrust him into, the sweat drenching his back and flowing from his armpits; but on the third night the bolt was shot back, a key grated in the lock, and the door opened.

A guard ordered him downstairs to the warden's office. "Get a move on, you fuck, you're more trouble than you're worth."

The Investigating Magistrate was there, sitting in a chair, fanning himself with a wilted yellow straw hat. He wore a crumpled linen suit and a white silk tie, his pallid face contrasting with his dark short beard as he talked earnestly with the Deputy Warden, an uneasy-eyed man with smelly polished boots, flushed, and self-consciously irritated when Yakov entered. When the prisoner, ghastly gray and close to shock, limped into the room, the two officials momentarily stopped talking. The Deputy Warden, gnawing his lip, remarked, "It's an irregular procedure if you ask my opinion"; but Bibikov patiently differed. "I'm here in the pursuit of my official duties as Investigating Magistrate, Mr. Deputy Warden, so there is nothing to fear."

"So you say, but why close to midnight when the warden's away on vacation and the other officials are sleeping? It's a strange time to come here on business, if you ask me."

"It's a dreadful night after a dreadfully hot day," the magistrate said huskily, coughing into his fist, "but much cooler at this hour. In fact there's a veritable breeze off the Dnieper once you are in the street. To be frank, I was already in bed, but the heat in the house was unbearable and the bedsheets perspired more than I did. I tossed and turned, then I thought, it's useless, I'll get up. Once I had dressed it occurred to me it would be helpful if I got on with official matters rather than lay around drinking cold drinks that give me gas, and curse the heat. Fortunately, my wife and children are at our dacha on the Black Sea, where I will go to join them in August. Do you know the heat rose to 40.5 in the shade this afternoon, and must now be hovering around 33.8? I assure you it was all but impossible to work in my office today. My assistant complained of nausea and had to be sent home."

"Go on, then, if you want to," said the Deputy Warden, "but I have to insist that I stay here as a witness to your questions. The prisoner's under our jurisdiction, that's clear enough."

"May I remind you that your function is custodial and mine investigatory? The suspect has not yet been tried or sentenced. In fact there is no indictment up to now. Nor has he officially been remanded to prison by administrative decree. He is simply here as a material witness. If you will allow me, I am within my rights to question him alone. The time may be inconvenient, but it is so in a formal sense only; therefore I beg you to absent yourself for a brief period, say not more than a half hour."

"At least I ought to know what you're going to ask him about in case the warden wants to know when he gets back. If it's about his treatment in this prison, I warn you flatly the warden will be annoyed if you ask about that. The Jew hasn't been made any exception of. If he follows the rules and regulations he gets the same treatment as everybody else. If he doesn't he's in for trouble."

"My questions will not refer to his prison treatment, although I hope it is always humane. You may tell Warden Grizitskoy that I was checking some testimony of the accused made before me at a previous date. If he would like more precise information, let him telephone me."

The Deputy Warden withdrew, casting a sullen glance at the prisoner.

Bibikov, after sitting a minute with two fingers pressed to his lips, moved quickly to the door, listened intently, then carried his chair and one for Yakov to the windowless far corner of the office, and motioned him to sit down.

"My friend," he said hurriedly in a low voice, "I can see from your appearance what you have been through, and I beg you not to think me remiss or without feeling if I do not comment on it. I have promised the Deputy Warden to confine myself to other matters, and besides our time is short and I have much to say."

"That's fine with me, your honor," muttered Yakov, struggling with his emotions, "but I would like to know if you could get me a different pair of shoes. The nails in these hurt my feet though nobody believes me. Either let them give me a different pair or lend me a hammer and pliers so I can fix them myself."

He sucked in his breath and wiped an eye with his sleeve. "Excuse me for being out of order, your honor."

"I see we're wearing similar linen garments," Bibikov joked, fanning himself slowly with his limp hat. He remarked in an undertone, "Tell me your size and I'll send you a pair of shoes."

"Maybe it's better not to," Yakov whispered, "or the Deputy Warden would know I complained to you."

"You understand it wasn't I but the Prosecuting Attorney who ordered your imprisonment?"

The fixer nodded.

"Would you care for a cigarette? You know my Turkish beauties?"

He lit one for him but after a few puffs Yakov had to put it out. "Excuse me for wasting it," he coughed, "but it's hard to breathe in this heat."

The magistrate put away his cigarette box. He reached into his breast pocket for his pince-nez, blew on them, and settled the glasses on his perspiring nose. "I would like you to know, Yakov Shepsovitch—if I may—that your case holds an extraordinary interest for me, and only last week I returned in a beastly stuffy, crowded train from St. Petersburg, where I had consulted the Minister of Justice, Count Odoevsky."

He leaned forward and said quietly, "I went there to submit the evidence I had already gathered, and to request that the charge against you be limited, as I had already suggested to the Prosecuting Attorney, strictly to the matter of your residing illegally in the Lukianovsky District, or perhaps even dropped altogether if you left Kiev and returned to your native village. Instead I was expressly directed to continue my investigation beyond the slightest shadow of a doubt. I will tell you in the strictest confidence what most troubled me is that although the Minister of Justice listened courteously and with obvious interest, I left with the unmistakable impression that he expects the evidence to confirm your guilt."

"Vey iz mir."

"This was not stated so specifically, you must understand—it was an impression and I may possibly be misinterpreting, although I don't think so. Frankly, the matter seemed to revolve around an imprecise use of language, further confused by hints, hesitations, odd questions I did not fully understand, shadowy remarks, and so forth. Nothing—even now—is said absolutely directly, yet I am under pressure, as it were, to uncover evidence close to the prevailing belief. The Minister of

Interior also has been telephoning me regularly. I will admit these pressures have made me nervous. My wife tells me I am more difficult than usual to live with, and there are signs of gastric disturbances. In her letter today she urged me to see a doctor. And tonight," he went on, lowering his voice to the dimmest whisper, "I had the impression on my way here that my carriage was being followed by another, though no doubt I am suggestible in my present state of nerves."

He thrust his pallid face close to Yakov's, continuing to whisper: "But that's neither here nor there. To return then to the facts: Count Odoevsky at one point offered to relieve me of the 'burden' of this case if I felt 'pressed or unwell,' or the work had become 'distasteful' or seemed to go against what he referred to as 'your creed.' And I believe I caught a clear hint that the purposes of justice might better be served by an indictment of murder for ritual reasons, an accusation which is of course poppycock."

"As for the murder," said Yakov, "if I had a hand in it let me live forever a cripple in hell."

The Investigating Magistrate fanned himself slowly with his hat. After again glancing at the door he said, "When I told the Minister of Justice—quite directly told him, nothing minced or hedged, shadowy remarks do not explicate or uphold the law—that my evidence pointed in the opposite direction, towards acquittal of the major charge, he shrugged his shoulders—the count is an imposing man, handsome, well-spoken, discreetly perfumed—as though perhaps to indicate I had not yet achieved true wisdom. And that's apparently where we left it, with a shrug that may mean much or little, but in any case a doubt. I can say in his favor that he is a gentleman. But I will tell you frankly that with the Prosecuting Attorney, my colleague Grubeshov, there are not even the slightest doubts. He has, I would say, convinced himself, perhaps almost before the fact. I say this after careful consideration. Grubeshov has more than once emphatically requested from me—in fact he has insisted on it—a severe indictment of you, mincing no words—for Zhenia Golov's murder, and I have categorically refused. Of course that adds to my nervousness. Yet for all practical purposes you should know this matter can't go on in such a way much longer. If I don't draw up the indictment someone else will. They will get rid of me, if they possibly can, and then I'll be of no use to you whatever. Therefore I will pretend to cooperate with them while I continue my investigation, until I have a foolproof case. I will then once more submit the evidence to the Ministry of Justice, and if they insist on a prosecution, I may reveal my findings to the press, which could conceivably cause a scandal. I would hope so. In fact I am already planning anonymously to give out selected information to one or two highly placed journalists as to the true state of affairs regarding the nature of the evidence against you, which up to now consists in nothing more than anonymous accusations and provocative articles published by the reactionary press. I decided this as I lay awake tonight. My visit to you, which I decided on impulsively, is to inform you of my plans so that you will not think you are without a friend in the world. I know you are falsely accused. I am determined to continue this investigation to the best of my ability and powers in order to discover, and if necessary, publish the whole truth. I am doing this for Russia as well as for your sake and mine. I therefore request, Yakov Shepsovitch, though I understand how difficult your trials are, your confidence and patience."

"Thanks, your honor," said Yakov with a tremor in his voice. "If you're used to stepping out of the hut once in a while to take a breath of fresh air in your lungs while you look at the sky to see if it's going to rain tomorrow—not that it makes any difference—it's hard to go on living in a small dark solitary cell; still now I know there's somebody who knows what I did and what I didn't do, and who I trust, though I would like to hear what you mean about 'the true state of affairs' that you mentioned before when you were talking about the journalists."

Bibikov went again to the door, opened it softly, peered out, closed it carefully and returned to his chair, once more bringing his face close to Yakov's.

"My theory is that the murder was committed by Marfa Golov's gang of criminals and housebreakers, in particular her blinded lover, one Stepan Bulkin, who, thus, perhaps, revenged himself on her for the loss of his eyesight. The boy was grossly neglected by his mother. She is a wicked woman, stupid yet cunning, with the morals of a hardened prostitute. Zhenia had apparently threatened, possibly more than once, to expose their criminal activities to the District Police, and it is possible that the lover convinced her the child had to be done away with. Perhaps the incident occurred during a time of general drunkenness. The boy was killed, I am all but certain, in his mother's house, Bulkin taking the leading role in the beastly sacrifice. They obviously tortured the poor child, inflicting a large number of wounds on his body and soaking up the blood as it spurted forth, in order not to leave any telltale stains on the floor—I would imagine they burned the bloody rags—and finally plunging the knife deep into the child's heart. I have not been able to determine whether Marfa witnessed his death or had passed out drunk."

The fixer shuddered. "How did you find out about that, your honor?"

"I can't tell you except to say generally that thieves quarrel, and as I said before, Marfa is stupid, canny as she is. The true story will come out in time if we work patiently. We have reason to believe she kept her son's body in the bathtub for a week before it was removed to the cave. We are searching for one of the neighbors who is believed to have seen it there and soon thereafter moved out of the vicinity, frightened out of her wits I would guess, by Marfa's threats. To save their own necks, naturally the thieves are going along with the blood ritual accusation against you. How that originated we are not exactly sure. We suspect Marfa herself wrote an anonymous letter suggesting that Jews did the evil work. The original letter to the police was signed 'A Christian.' I know that, though I have not been able to put my hands on the document yet. At any rate the thieves will do whatever they can to uphold the charge, even if it means testifying against you as eyewitnesses to your 'crime.' They are frightened and dangerous men. And my assistant, Ivan Semyonovitch, has ascertained that Proshko and Richter burned down Nikolai Maximovitch's stable, though without the help of any Jewish demons."

"So that's how it is," sighed Yakov. "Behind the world lies another world. Excuse me, but does the Prosecuting Attorney also know what you just told me?"

Bibikov fanned himself leisurely with his hat.

"To be absolutely truthful I don't know what he knows or doesn't. I am not one of his confidants—but I suspect he knows more than he admits. I also know he is an ambitious and opportunistic man, a restless careerist. In his youthful days he was a strong Ukrainophil, but since attaining public office he has become more Russian than the Tsar. Someday, if God's mercy does not intervene, he will be a justice of our Supreme Court—it is without a doubt what he wants most. If that should happen there will be 'justice' without justice." The magistrate caught himself and paused. "I will be grateful to you if you do not repeat this, Yakov Shepsovitch, or my other remarks to you, to anyone. Like most Russians I talk too much; however I wanted in particular to ease your mind a bit. I ask this for our mutual protection."

"Who would I repeat it to even if there was somebody here who wasn't my enemy? But what I want to ask is, does the Prosecuting Attorney truly think I killed the boy, and does he really believe those things the priest said at the cave?"

"As to his true beliefs I must again confess my ignorance although I see him often in the course of official business. He tends to believe, in my opinion, what those around him believe. I don't pretend to know how much claptrap and superstition there is in his soul or what purpose it serves. But he is not a fool, I assure you. He knows our history and is quite familiar with the law though not greatly responsive to its spirit. He surely knows that Alexander I, in 1817, and Nicholas I, in 1835, by official ukase prohibited blood libels against Jews living on Russian soil, although it is quite true that these libels have been revived within the last generation to provoke pogroms for political purposes. I do not have to tell you there has been a disappointing retreat of progress in recent times, whatever it is we call progress, especially disappointing because of the little we have had since the Emancipation. There's something cursed, it seems to me, about a country where men have owned men as property. The stink of that corruption never escapes the soul, and it is the stink of future evil. Still, the original decrees have not been withdrawn and are therefore the law. If Grubeshov has at all looked into this subject, as I have recently, he will also know, for instance, that certain Roman Catholic Popes, including an Innocent, a Paul, a Gregory, and a Clement, whose numerical designations I have forgotten, issued certain interdictions against this accusation. I believe one of them called it 'a baseless and wicked invention.' Interestingly, I learned that this very same blood accusation made against the Jews was used by pagans of the first century to justify the oppression and slaughter of the early Christians. They too were called 'blood drinkers,' for reasons you would understand if you knew the Catholic mass. The blood mystique arose in a belief of primitive people that there is a miraculous power in blood. It is, of course, a most dramatic substance in color and composition."

"So if the Pope said no, why does the priest say yes?"

"Father Anastasy is a charlatan. He has written a stupid anti-Semitic brochure in Latin which brought him to the attention of the United Nobility, who have urged him to testify against you. Around him much of the pogrom agitation is centered. It is interesting to me that quite shortly after the appearance of his brochure, Zhenia Golov was murdered. He is a defrocked Catholic priest, for some disgraceful act, we think an embezzlement of church funds, who only latterly came from Poland and joined the Orthodox Church, whose Synod, incidentally, does not support the accusation against you, although it does not deny it. The Metropolitan of Kiev has informed me he will not issue a statement."

"That won't keep the water from boiling," the fixer muttered.

"I'm afraid not. Do you know any French, Yakov Shepsovitch?" Bibikov asked.

"Not that I can think of, your honor."

"The French have a saying, 'The more it changes, the more it remains the same.' You must admit there may be a certain truth to that, especially with reference to what we call 'society.' In effect it has not changed in its essentials from what it was in the dim past, even though we tend loosely to think of civilization as progress. I frankly no longer believe in that concept. I respect man for what he has to go through in life, and sometimes for how he does it, but he has changed little since he began to pretend he was civilized, and the same thing may be said about our society. That is how I feel, but having made that confession let me say, as you may have guessed, that I am somewhat of a meliorist. That is to say, I act as an optimist because I find I cannot act at all, as a pessimist. One often feels helpless in the face of the confusion of these times, such a mass of apparently uncontrollable events and experiences to live through, attempt to understand, and if at all possible, give order to; but one must not withdraw from the task if he has some small thing to offer—he does so at the risk of diminishing his humanity.

"Be that as it may," he went on, "if the Prosecuting Attorney had indulged in a bit of Old Testament research he would, I am sure, be familiar with the prohibitions in Leviticus that Jews may not eat any manner of blood. I can't quote it exactly—my notes are on my desk at home—but the Lord warned that whoever ate blood, Israelite or stranger, He would cut him off from his people. Nor would He afterwards allow King David to raise a temple to Him, because he had fought in many wars and spilled much blood. He is a consistent God, if not gentle. I have also learned from certain Russian authorities of the Old Testament and other Jewish sacred texts that there does not exist in those writings a record of any law or custom which permits a Jew to use blood, or specifically Christian blood, for religious purposes. According to those I have consulted—secretly, you understand—the prohibition against using any blood whatsoever for whatever purpose was never retracted or altered in later Jewish writings of law, literature, or medicine. There is not, for instance, any record of a prescription of blood for use in medicine, internal or external. Et cetera, et cetera. There are many such facts that Grubeshov ought to have familiarized himself with—and I assure you I am strongly contemplating submitting him a summary of my researches for his reflection. Frankly, Yakov Shepsovitch, I am embarrassed to belittle a colleague to you in this manner but I have come to the unhappy conclusion that whatever he knows, or may know through my intervention, that might be helpful to you in establishing your innocence is, if not actually useless, then at least antithetical to his aims and purposes. He also would like to have you convicted."

Yakov wrung his hands. "If so what am I to do, your honor? Will I be abandoned to die in this prison?"

"Who has abandoned you?" the Investigating Magistrate asked, looking at him gently.

"Not you, of course, and I thank what little luck I have for that. But if Mr. Grubeshov has no use for your evidence I might rot here for years. After all, how long are our lives? Couldn't you put out an indictment of some small sort against me so that I could at least see a lawyer?"

"No, that wouldn't work at all. Murder is what I would be compelled to charge you with. I'm afraid to start off that way. Your lawyer will appear in due course. But at present no lawyer can do as much for you as I, Yakov Shepsovitch. And when the time comes that he can, I'll see to it that you have a good one. I already have in mind someone who is a vigorous and courageous man of the most excellent reputation. I will sound him out in the near future, and I am sure he will agree to represent you."

The fixer thanked him.

Bibikov, after looking at his watch, suddenly rose. "Yakov Shepsovitch, what more can I tell you? Take heart in the truth and endure your trials. Sustain yourself in your innocence."

"It's not so easy, your honor. I'm not suited for this kind of life. I find it hard to imitate a dog. That's not exactly what I mean but turned around a bit it is. What I mean is that I'm sick of prison, also I'm not a brave man. To tell the truth I have terrible fears that never leave me, day or night."

"No one says it's easy. Still, you are not alone."

"In my cell I'm alone. In my thoughts I'm alone. I don't want to sound bitter to you because I'm thankful for your help—"

"My dear friend," said Bibikov gravely, "your bitterness doesn't offend me. My worry is not to fail you."

"Why should you fail me?" the fixer said, anxiously rising.

"Who can say?" Bibikov put on his limp hat. "Partly it is our situation in this unfortunate country that causes me doubt. Russia is such a complex, long-suffering, ignorant, torn and helpless nation. In one sense we are all prisoners here." He paused, combed his beard with his fingers, then said, "There is so much to be done that demands the full capacities of our hearts and souls, but, truly, where shall we begin? Perhaps I will begin with you? Keep in mind, Yakov Shepsovitch, that if your life is without value, so is mine. If the law does not protect you, it will not, in the end, protect me. Therefore I dare not fail you, and that is what causes me anxiety—that I must not fail you. Now permit me to say good night. Let us both somehow try to sleep and perhaps tomorrow will be better. Thank God for tomorrow."

Yakov seized his hand to press to his lips but Bibikov had gone.

6

A prisoner, an anguished and desperate man, was locked in the next cell. The minute in, he began to pound with his shoe, or both shoes, against the wall. The noise came through distantly and Yakov pounded back with his shoe. But when the man shouted he could somehow be heard, though not his words. They shouted to each other at various times of the day and night as loudly as they could—it sounded to the fixer as though someone was trying to tell him a heartbreaking tale, and he wanted with all his heart to hear and then tell his own; but the man's shouts, cries, questions, were muffled, indistinguishable. So were his, the fixer knew.

The isolation cells were rectangular cubicles, the walls of brick and cement, the outer wall containing a single three-barred window a half meter above the prisoner's head. The door was made of solid iron with a peephole at eye level, through which the guard, when he was there, peered; and though Yakov could understand what was yelled at him from the corridor, when either prisoner shouted at the other through the spy hole, neither could understand. The openings were small, and reverberations in the corridor muffled the words and turned them into noise.

Once a guard with a dark face and stupid eyes, appearing in the cell block, heard them shouting to each other and cursed them both. He ordered the other prisoner to shut up or he would beat his head to a pulp, and to Yakov he said, "No more noise out of you or I'll shoot your Jew cock off." When he was gone both men resumed beating on the wall. The guard came once a day with a bowl of watery, insect-ridden soup, and a slice of stale black bread; he also checked the cells at unpredictable intervals. Yakov would be sleeping on the floor, or pacing back and forth the meager distance of the cell; or sitting with his back to the wall, his knees drawn up, lost in despondent thought, when he became aware of a malevolent eye staring at him, which was at once withdrawn. From the number of doors opening in the morning when the guard and his assistant delivered the food, the fixer knew there were only two prisoners in that wing of cells. The other prisoner was on his left, and on the right the guards retreated fifty steps to another door which they opened with a key, then shut with a terrible thump and locked from the other side. Sometimes in the early morning hours, when the huge prison was steeped in darkness and silence although hundreds of men, more likely thousands, dreamed, moaned, snored and farted in their sleep, the prisoner in the next cell woke and began beating on the wall between them. He did this in quick bursts of sound, then slowly, as though he were trying to teach the fixer a code, and though Yakov counted the beats and tried to translate them into letters of the Russian alphabet, the words he put together made no sense and he cursed himself for his stupidity. He banged but what did it mean? Sometimes they uselessly banged on the wall at the same time.

To be imprisoned alone was the greatest desperation the fixer had known. He hadn't the wit, he told himself, to be this much alone. When the guards came with his bread and soup on his twelfth morning of solitary confinement, Yakov begged for relief. He had learned his lesson and would uphold every regulation if they kindly returned him to the common cell, where there were, at least, other faces and some human activity. "If you will tell this to the warden I'll thank you with my whole heart. It's hard to live without a little conversation once in a while." But neither of the guards answered a word. It wouldn't have cost them a kopek to give his message to the warden, but they never did. Yakov sank into silence, sometimes imagining himself in the Podol, talking casually to someone. He would stand under a tree in the tenement courtyard with Aaron Latke and say how badly things were going. (How bad was bad if you were free?) Just a homey few words, better in Yiddish, but good enough in Russian. Or since freedom, at the moment, was out of the question, if he had his tools he could, after a morning's work, break a small hole through the wall and talk with the other prisoner, maybe even see his face if he stepped back a little. They could tell each other the story of their lives and stretch it out for months, then start over again if necessary. But the other prisoner, either because he was disheartened or sick, had stopped beating on the wall, and neither of them shouted to the other.

If he had forgotten the man he suddenly remembered him. One night a distant moaning broke into his sleep. He awoke and heard nothing. The fixer beat on the wall with his heavy shoe but there was no response. He dreamed he heard footsteps in the corridor, then a smothered cry awakened him again, terrified. Something's wrong, he thought, I must hide. A cell door clanged and there were steps of more than one man in the corridor. Yakov waited tensely in the pitch gloom, about to cry out if his door moved, but the steps went past his cell. The heavy door at the end of the corridor thumped shut, a key turned in the lock, and that was the end of the noise. In the terrible silence that followed, he could not get back to sleep. He beat on the wall with both broken shoes, shouting until he was hoarse, but could rouse no response. The next morning he was not brought food. They are leaving me to die, he thought. But at noon, a drunken guard came in with his soup and bread, muttering to himself. He spilled half the soup over Yakov before the prisoner could grab the bowl.

"Here he kills a Russian child and lords it over us," the guard muttered, his breath thick with alcohol.

When he had gone it came to the fixer, as he was very slowly chewing his black bread, that the guard had not locked and bolted the door. The hair on the back of his neck prickled. He got up in excitement, thrust two fingers through the peephole and almost fainted as the door slowly opened inward.

Yakov was overwhelmed in confusion and fright. If I step out they'll kill me for sure. Someone must be waiting on the outside. He peered through the hole but could see no one. Then he shut the door softly and waited.

An hour, if not longer, went by. Again he opened the creaking door and this time quickly looked into the hall. To the right, at the end of the cell block the concrete door stood ajar. Had the drunken guard forgotten to lock that too? Yakov slunk along the corridor, stopped a few feet from the door and at once hurried back. Yet he did not go into his cell. Once more he approached the heavy door and was about to pull it open when it came to him thunderously that he was acting faster than he could think. So he ran back to his cell, entered, and slammed the door shut. There he waited, his flesh freezing, his heart a growing pain. No one came. But the fixer had thought it out and was certain the guard had left the door open on purpose. If he went through it and sneaked down the stairs, at the bottom another guard would confront him, the one with the stupid eyes. He would look at Yakov and slowly raise his pistol. In the prison log the warden would write: "The prisoner Yakov Bok shot in the stomach while attempting to escape."

But he slid out into the corridor again, his thoughts flooded with freedom, this time going the other way, astonished he hadn't thought of that before. He looked cautiously to the left and right, then peered through the peephole into the other prisoner's cell. A bearded man, swinging gently, hung from a leather belt tied to the middle bar of the open window, a fallen stool nearby. He was staring down where his pince-nez lay smashed on the floor under his small dangling feet.

It took the fixer an age to admit it was Bibikov.

VI

IN THE luminous dark the ghost of Bibikov appeared wearing a large white hat. He had no glasses pinched to his nose, they were gone, and he rubbed the bridge in embarrassment.

"A terrible thing has happened, Yakov Shepsovitch. These men are without morality. I fear they will kill you, too."

"No, no," cried Yakov. "I don't believe in superstition."

The Investigating Magistrate lit a rose-papered cigarette and sat silent; then tried to say something and began to fade. He slowly disappeared in the dark, his white self dimming, as though evening had come and then night; and the soft glow of the cigarette diminished until it was out. All that remained was the dark memory of him hanging from the window, his bulbous eyes staring at his smashed glasses on the floor.

All night the fixer sat huddled in the corner of the cell, filled with the dread of dying. If he slept a minute his sleep was steeped in the taste, smell, horror of dying. He lay motionless in a graveyard, rigid, terrified. In the black sky were black stars. If he stirred he would topple into an open grave, amid the rotting dead, their dead flesh and putrefying bones. But more than death he feared torture. He feared being torn and broken before he died. He saw them dragging into the cell terrible instruments, monstrous wooden machines that racked and crushed the body; they hung his remains from a window bar. At dawn, when the dirty eye staring through the hole in the door touched him, he woke from shadowy sleep begging for his life. As the door creaked open he cried out; but the guards did not strangle him. One of them, with his foot, shoved in a bowl of gruel without a cockroach in it.

All day the fixer walked in his cell, sometimes he ran, five steps, three, five, three, breaking the circuit to hurl himself against the wall, or smash his fists against the metal door with prolonged cries of grief. He mourned Bibikov with great sorrow, great bitterness. For weeks he had lived with this potential savior in his thoughts, this just and gentle man; depended on him somehow to free him from prison, the trap laid for him, from the crime itself, the horrifying accusation. His only peace had come from these thoughts, that a good man was assisting him, and because of him, when the trial came, he would be judged not guilty. He had pictured himself freed, hurrying back to the shtetl, or running off to America if he could raise the funds. But now these hopes and expectations, these reveries on which he had lived, were gone, snatched from him without warning. Who would help him now, what could he hope for? Where Bibikov had lived in his mind was a hopeless hole. Who would now expose the murderess, Marfa Golov, and her accomplices, and proclaim his innocence to the newspapers? Suppose she left Kiev, fled to another city—or country—would they ever lay eyes on her again? How would the world ever learn about the injustice that had been committed against an innocent man? Who could help him if no one but his jailers knew where he was? For aught he meant to anyone, Yakov Bok did not exist. If they had no plans to kill him outright, then they would kill him slowly by burying him alive in prison forever.

"Mama—Papa," he cried out, "save me! Shmuel, Raisl—anybody—save me! Somebody save me!" He walked in circles, forgetting he was walking, inventing fantastic plans to escape, each making his heart ache because each was impossible. He walked all day and into the night, until his shoes fell apart, and then walked in his bare feet on the lacerating floor. He walked in almost liquid heat with nowhere to go but his circular entrapment, striking himself on his journey—his chest, face, head, tearing his flesh, lamenting his life.

His crooked feet hurt unbearably. Yakov lay down in exhaustion on the floor. Torture by his own instrument—pain of body on deep depression. His pulpy feet, the soles covered with live scabs and red pussing sores, were like bags blown up about to burst. Then the ankles disappeared as the swelling moved up his legs. The fixer lay on his back, breathing badly, noisily. At least if it were cooler. How long can I stand this? His feet felt as though they were bound in chains and laid on fire. Both legs bulged to the knees. He lay on his back wishing for death. A cold eye stared at him. Ultimately he placed it at the peephole, an eye gazing at his suppurating feet, but the one who looked had nothing to say; and said nothing. "Help my poor feet," Yakov cried out, "it's a terrible pain." Whoever he was, if he heard, said nothing. Then the eye in the hole was gone. The fixer, feverishly shivering, his clothes wet, moaned through another night of pain. In the morning a key turned in the door and Warden Grizitskoy entered. Thinking of Bibikov, Yakov shrank from him. But the cross-eyed warden looked real and even human, and what he had seen in the next cell, dream-like, unreal; he was at times not sure he had seen it. He didn't dare ask about the Investigating Magistrate. If they knew he knew they might kill him at once.

"What tricks are you up to now?" the warden demanded.

"Please," Yakov said, "my feet are infected from the nails in my shoes. I need a doctor."

"There are no doctors for the likes of you."

The fixer wearily shut his eyes.

The warden left. In the afternoon he returned with an aid from the prison infirmary.

"He's poisoned his feet," said the aid.

"Is it serious?" said the warden, "or will it go away by itself?"

"Both feet are full of pus. It might become gangrene."

"It would serve the bastard right," said the warden.

"All right," he said to Yakov, "go down to the infirmary. I'd let you rot here but I don't want the cell to stink any more than it does, or it will get infected from your germs. Move quickly now."

"How can I walk?" said Yakov. "Could Fetyukov or somebody help me?"

"Perfect company for a fellow murderer," said the warden. "Fetyukov is no longer present. He was shot for disobeying orders and resisting a guard."

"Shot?" said the stunned fixer.

"For insubordination. He insulted a guard. Let that be a lesson to you. Now move along quickly."

"I can't walk. How can I go if I can't walk?"

"If you can't walk, crawl. The devil take you."

Like a dog, thought Yakov. On his hands and knees he moved out into the corridor, then painfully toward the door leading to the stairs. Though he crawled slowly the pressure hurt his knees and he could not keep his battered feet from scraping the floor. But he forced himself not to cry out. The warden and infirmary aid had left, and a guard with a shotgun followed the fixer as he moved toward the concrete door. Going down the steep wooden steps, he had the weight of his body on his trembling arms, his feet bumping each step, and he more than once almost fell headlong down the stairs. When he paused, the guard prodded him with the butt of his gun. By the time Yakov reached the bottom of the stairs both his hands were scraped raw, and both knees bled. His back was black with sweat and the veins bulged on his neck as he crawled forward along the corridor and out the prison door into the yard.

The infirmary was in the administration section, on the other side of the quadrangle from the prison cells. It was the time of the ten-minute afternoon promenade, and the prisoners opened their double files for the fixer as they watched him haltingly crawling across the dirt yard.

"Five kopeks on the Zhid mule," shouted the clubfoot. A prisoner in a torn greatcoat turned and struck him across the mouth. A guard beat the prisoner.

If I live will I make it? Yakov, nauseated, was close to fainting. Halfway across the yard his trembling arms gave out and he collapsed. Several prisoners broke from their lines, but the guard with the whip shouted it was forbidden. The sentries patrolling the yard pointed their rifles at the prisoners and they returned to the lines, but not the slop-pail man, the one with the cracked eyeglasses. He fished some burlap rags from a garbage pile in the corner of the yard and ran towards Yakov. Hurriedly he wound the rags around the fixer's hands and knees. The guard cursed but looked on. When the rags were tied he prodded Yakov with his foot.

The fixer got up on his raw hands and bleeding knees and went on, blindly crawling across the yard. He climbed up the stone steps into the infirmary.

The surgeon, a bald-headed man in a soiled white linen coat that smelled of carbolic acid and tobacco, inspected Yakov's feet, smeared them with a thick yellow acrid salve out of a can, and after bandaging both feet with dirty bandages and swabbing his hands and knees with alcohol, ordered the fixer into bed. This was the first bed he had been in since his arrest. He slept for a day and a half. When he awoke, the surgeon, smoking a cigar, unwound the bandages and operated on his feet. He cut into the pussing sores with a scalpel, without anesthetic. The prisoner, biting his lips to be silent, cried out at each cut.

"This is good for you, Bok," said the surgeon. "Now you know how poor Zhenia felt when you were stabbing him and draining his blood, all for the sake of your Jewish religion."

That night as he lay in bed in the infirmary Yakov had trouble breathing. Though he took in great gulping hot breaths through his mouth, the air seemed thin and insufficient. He did not at first fear asthma because he had often had trouble breathing under stress yet had not been seriously sick for years. But then the air turned heavy and stale. It was like trying to breathe metal. His chest heaved. His lungs weighed like rock, his breathing turned heavily raspy and he felt sick. The fixer clawed the mattress. "Please, who needs more? I have enough." He sat up, gasping for help but none came. Yakov got out of bed, his bandaged feet oozing blood, and tottered to the barred window. He lay under it, wheezing as he fought to draw into his lungs a few drops of air. In the midst of his exertions he fell into an exhausted and perilous half-sleep, dreaming he was expiring in a windowless cell, seeing in his drowning dreams the miserable orphans' home, a crumbling tilted shack he had spent his childhood in; Raisl running from him in terror as though he had threatened her with a meat cleaver; and his imprisonment for a lifetime in Siberia for the murder of a boy whose suffering dead face haunted him still. He dreamed he had come upon him in the woods, a child carrying his schoolbooks, and had grabbed and choked him unconscious on impulse; then with Proshko's help, as the boy lay on the ground still twitching, he stabbed him thirteen times in the chest and drained five litres of his bright blood, a magnificent liquid. All night Grubeshov, standing with both yellow gaitered feet on Yakov's chest, harangued the victim in a thick-voiced tirade, and though the fixer frantically implored Bibikov's help, the Investigating Magistrate, at his desk in another room, would or could not be disturbed.

2

The warden assigned him to a new cell, a large dampish one on the ground floor of the solitary block of the south building of the prison, to the right of the administrative section and infirmary.

"It's just to keep you closer to my eye," he said. "There's talk you might try to escape with the assistance of your Jewish cohorts, which I strongly warn you against, because if you attempt it you're sure to get shot."

He pointed to the notice on the wall:

Obey all rules and regulations without question. If the prisoner is insubordinate or insulting to a guard or prison official, or he attempts in any way to breach the security of this prison, he will be executed on the spot.

"Furthermore," said the old warden, "the guard receives a monetary commendation for defending the regulations, so watch yourself. A smart dog recognizes the whip and avoids the lash."

He helped himself to a pinch of snuff and sneezed twice.

Yakov asked if he could have another prisoner, some decent person, for company. "It's hard to live without another soul to talk to, your honor. How is one to ease his heart a little?"

"That's the least of my worries," said the warden.

"Then could I have some kind of an animal to keep, either a cat or maybe a bird?"

"A cat out of your rations?—you'd both starve. Either he'd eat you or you'd eat him. Anyway, this is a prison for criminals, and not a tea parlor or clubhouse. You're not here for comforts or coddling but for strict punishment for the mean murder you committed against a harmless child. Only you Jew prisoners have the nerve to make such requests. I've had enough of it."

In the fall the weather was bad, rainy and cold, and Yakov could see his breath in the cell. The asthma was not bothersome until he caught a cold, then it came on again, usually badly. Some mornings the outer wall of the cell, fronting the prison yard, was covered with lacy areas of frost. The inside walls, a foot thick, of brick, broken stone and cement, were scabby and cracked. After a heavy rain the greater part of the stone-paved floor was moist with seepage from the earth. Part of the ceiling above the window dripped. On fair days the small barred window, about a meter above the fixer's head, though dirty, let in light. The light was dim and on rainy days disappeared in the dark. After supper Yakov was given a small smelly kerosene lamp without its glass chimney, that burned until morning and was then removed. But one night the lamp was not given to him because, the Deputy Warden said, kerosene cost money. The fixer asked for a candle instead, and the Deputy Warden said he would see about that, but the fixer never got the candle. The cell was pitch black all night. I'll get the candle when I get the indictment, Yakov thought.

When the wind was strong on the outside, cold air floated through the cracked window into the cell. Yakov offered to fix it if they would let him have a little putty and a ladder, but no one was interested. The cell was cold but at least he had a mattress, a thin lumpy straw pallet whose last occupant—Zhitnyak, the small-eyed, black-fingered day guard, told him—had died of jail fever. The fixer kept the mattress on the dry part of the floor. There were bedbugs in it but he managed to beat out and kill some. His back ached after he had slept on it, and the straw in the sacking stank of mold, but it was better than sleeping on the stone floor. In November they gave him a ragged blanket. He also had a three-legged stool in the cell and a greasy small wooden table, one leg shorter than the other three. He had a jug of water in one corner of the cell; and in the opposite corner he kept the smelly can he urinated and defecated in, when there was something to defecate. Once a day he was allowed to empty the slop can into one of the barrels that were trundled past the cells by another prisoner, who wasn't allowed to speak to the fixer and whom Yakov was forbidden to address. He could tell from where the trundle stopped in the corridor that the cells on both sides of him were empty. It was a solitary solitary.

The bolted cell door was made of three sheets of iron, once painted black but now largely rusted; it had a peephole at eye level covered by a metal disk that the guard slipped aside to look in. Once every hour or so during the day a single eye roamed the cell. Zhitnyak was usually there in the daytime and Kogin at night; some days their times overlapped, and occasionally they exchanged shifts. When Yakov secretly pushed aside the disk and looked through the peephole, he could see Zhitnyak sitting in a large chair against the wall, hacking with his pocket knife at a stick, looking at pictures in a magazine, or dozing. He was a heavy-shouldered man with hairy nostrils and blackened stubby fingers, as though he had once worked with grease or lampblack that he had never got off. When he stepped into the cell he smelled of sweat and cabbage. Zhitnyak had a pock-marked face and an impatient manner. He was surly and unpredictable and sometimes struck the fixer.

Kogin, the night guard, was a tall man with a gaunt face and watery eyes, worn with worry. He spoke in a deep voice that seemed to rise from the ground. Even his whisper was low and heavy. Often he paced the corridor as if he were the prisoner; Yakov could hear his boots going back and forth on the concrete floor. At night Kogin opened the spy hole and listened to the fixer's asthmatic breathing and when he talked or shouted in his sleep. Yakov knew he was there, because when his nightmares or sleep-shouting woke him, he saw the dim light from the hall through the hole, and he saw the disk slowly moved back into place. Sometimes he woke up as Kogin was shining a torch through the peephole. Sometimes he could hear the guard's heavy breathing at the cell door.

Zhitnyak was the more talkative of the two, though he said little enough. Kogin at first did not speak to the fixer, but once after he had been drinking he complained that his son had come to nothing. "He does no steady work," the guard said in his deep voice. "When will he get himself a job? I've waited thirty years for him to become a man and I'm still waiting. 'Wait,' I tell myself, 'he will change. He will become a man,' but he never does. He even steals from me and I am his father. My wife says it's my fault for not hitting him when he was a child and up to bad tricks, but that's not my nature. I had enough of that from my own father, may he rot in his grave. What's more, the daughter doesn't behave well either, but I won't go into that. The son will one day end up in prison the same as you, and it will serve him right. That's all that comes from a father's love."

In October Yakov had begged the guards to light the brick stove in the cell, but the Deputy Warden at first refused to spare the wood. Then one day in November Zhitnyak opened the door and two close-cropped prisoners, who sneaked looks at Yakov, brought the fixer a small load of wood tied in bundles. He had had a cold and asthma, and maybe one of the guards had reported it to the warden, who perhaps felt he had to keep the prisoner alive. The warden, as Yakov saw him, was not a vicious man. He was at best a disciplinarian, at worst, stupid. The Deputy Warden was something else. The fixer shuddered at the man's depthless eyes, narrow face, and four-fingered hand. Whatever he looked at he seemed to gnaw a little. His small mouth was crafty and hiddenly hungry. His boots stank of dog turd or whatever he used to polish them with. The guards wore guns in their holsters, but the Deputy Warden had a large gun on each hip. He had taken his time giving his permission for Yakov to have wood. The fixer disliked and feared him more than anyone in the prison.

The tall upright yellow brick stove leaked smoke at the top through a cracked brick, but Yakov preferred the smoke to the cold. He asked for the stove to be lit in the early morning, to get the frost off the wall although a small puddle formed on the floor when the cell warmed up; and he asked for a lit stove before supper so that he could eat in comfort. If the cell was too cold he could not taste the few bits of cabbage in his soup. If the cell was warm he tasted each morsel. To save wood he let the stove go out in the late morning. Afterwards, with his fingers he scraped the cold ashes out of the pit under the grate, put in a little kindling and some pieces of wood, then before supper, Zhitnyak came in to relight it. He did not seem to mind doing that, though he would sometimes curse as he was doing it. Yakov's hair was still not cropped but once was clipped a little by the prison barber; he was not permitted to shave, and his beard was growing long.

"That's to keep you looking more like a Jew," Zhitnyak said through the peephole. "They say the warden is going to make you wear a Zhid caftan and a rabbi's round hat, and they're going to twist earlocks out of your hair over your ears so you'll look kosher. That's what the Deputy Warden said they'll do."

The prisoners in the other solitary cells down the hall were served their meager food by other prisoners who were not allowed to serve the Jew. In Yakov's case they had to give the food to Zhitnyak, or Kogin, and he handed it to the fixer. This annoyed Zhitnyak, and sometimes when he brought Yakov's gruel or cabbage soup and bread, he said, "Here's your bowl of Christ's blood, drink hearty, mate." To enter the cell, the guard on duty, sometimes backed up by another guard in the hall holding a shotgun, more often alone, unlocked the six three-ringed bolts that had been attached on the door the day Yakov had been put into this cell. Hearing the six bolts being snapped back one by one, four or five times a day, put the fixer on edge.

During the late autumn Yakov did not see the warden, then one day he appeared in the cell "for purposes of official business."

"They've found a fingerprint on Zheniushka's belt buckle so we'd better take yours."

A detective appeared with an ink pad and paper and took Yakov's fingerprints.

A week later the warden entered the cell with a large pair of scissors.

"They've found some hairs on the boy's body, and we want to compare them with yours."

Yakov uneasily gave him permission to cut his hair.

"You cut it," said Warden Grizitskoy. "Cut off six or eight hairs and put them in this envelope." He handed Yakov the scissors and envelope.

The fixer snipped off several of his hairs. "How do I know you won't take these hairs and put them on the boy's corpse and then say you found them there in the first place?"

"You are a suspicious type," said the warden. "That's true of all your race."

"Excuse me, but why should the warden of a prison look for evidence of a crime? Is he a policeman?"

"That's none of your damn business," said the warden. "If you're so innocent let's have the proof of it."

A louse fell into the envelope with the hairs but Yakov let it stay.

One morning the warden entered the cell with a pen, bottle of black ink, and several sheets of foolscap paper for some samples of Yakov's handwriting. He ordered him to write in Russian, "My name is Yakov Shepsovitch Bok. It is true that I am a Jew."

Later the warden returned and asked the fixer to write the

same words, lying on the floor. Then he had Zhitnyak hold the prisoner's legs as he stood on his head while writing his name.

"What's this for?" asked Yakov.

"To see if the change in position changes your writing any. We want all possible samples."

And twice a day since he had been in this cell there were inspections of the fixer's body; "searches" they were called. The bolts of the door were shot back, and Zhitnyak and the Deputy Warden, with his smelly boots, came into the cell and ordered the fixer to undress. Yakov had to remove his clothes—the greatcoat, prison jacket, buttonless shirt, which were never washed though he had asked that he be allowed to wash them; and then he dropped his trousers and long drawers. He was allowed to keep on his threadbare undershirt, possibly so he wouldn't freeze to death. They also made him remove the torn socks and wooden clogs he had worn since the time the surgeon had lanced the sores on his feet, and to spread his toes apart so that Zhitnyak could inspect between them.

"Why do you do this?" Yakov had asked at the time of the first search.

"Shut your trap," said Zhitnyak.

"It's to see you haven't hidden any kind of weapon up your ass or in your clothes," said the Deputy Warden. "We have to protect you."

"What weapons could I hide? Everything was taken from me."

"You're a foxy sort but we've dealt with your kind before. You could be hiding small files, nails, pins, matches or such; or maybe even poison pills the Jews gave you to commit suicide with."

"I have none of those things."

"Spread your ass," said the Deputy Warden.

Yakov had first to raise his arms and spread his legs. The Deputy Warden probed with his four fingers in Yakov's armpits and around his testicles. The fixer then had to open his mouth and raise his tongue; he stretched both cheeks with his fingers as Zhitnyak peered into his mouth. At the end he had to bend over and pull apart his buttocks.

"Use more newspaper on your ass," said Zhitnyak.

"To use you have to have."

After his clothes were searched he was permitted to dress. It was the worst thing that happened to him and it happened twice a day.

3

He sank into deep gloom. I'll be here forever. The indictment will never come. I can beg on both broken knees but they won't give it to me. They will never bring me to trial.

In December, frost appeared on the four walls in the morning. Once he awoke with his hand stuck to the wall. The air was dead icy air. The fixer walked all day to keep from freezing. His asthma was worse. At night he lay on the straw mattress in his greatcoat, covered with the blanket, gasping, snoring thickly, wheezing as he desperately fought to breathe. The one listening at the peephole shut it and moved away. One morning Zhitnyak helped Yakov pile up a new load of bundles of wood almost chest high against the outer wall. And in the evening there were pieces of meat floating in the cabbage soup, and some round flecks of fat.

"What's happened?" the fixer asked.

The guard shrugged. "The higher-ups don't want you dying on them. You can't try a corpse in court, as the saying goes." He winked and laughed a little.

Maybe this means the indictment is coming, Yakov thought in excitement. They don't want me looking like a skeleton in the court.

Not only was the food better, there was more of it. In the morning there were two extra ounces of bread and the gruel was thicker, barley with watery hot milk. And there was a half lump of sugar for the tea, which diluted the rotten taste a little. The fixer chewed slowly, savoring what he was eating. A cockroach in the bowl no longer bothered him. He plucked it out and ate, afterwards licking the bowl with his tongue. Zhitnyak brought the food into the cell and left at once. But he sometimes watched Yakov eat, through the spy hole, although the prisoner as he ate usually sat on the stool with his back to the iron door.

"How's the soup?" Zhitnyak asked through the hole.

"Fine."

"Eat hearty." When Yakov had finished the guard was gone.

Though there was more to eat, the fixer hungered for more. The minute after he had eaten he was hungry. He had visions of Zhitnyak appearing one day with a huge plate of well-seasoned chicken soup, thick with broad yellow noodles, a platter of meat kreplach, and half a hallah loaf from which he would tear hunks of sweet foamy bread that melted on the tongue. He dreamed of rice and noodle pudding with raisins and cinnamon, as Raisl had deliciously baked it; and of anything that went with sour cream—blintzes, cheese kreplach, boiled potatoes, radishes, scallions, sliced crisp cucumbers. Also of juicy tomatoes of tremendous size that he had seen in Viscover's kitchen. He sucked a ripe tomato till it dribbled from his mouth, then, to get to sleep, finally had to finish it off, thickly salted, with a piece of white bread. After such fantasies he could hardly wait for the guard to come with his breakfast; yet when it came at last he restrained himself, eating very slowly. First he chewed the bread until its hard texture and grain flavor were gone, then bit by bit swallowed it down. Usually he saved part of his ration for nighttime, in bed, when he got ravenously hungry thinking of food. After the bread he ate the gruel, sucking each barley grain as it melted in his mouth. At night he worked every spoonful of soup over his tongue, each pulpy cabbage bit and thread of meat, taking it in very small sips and swallows, at the end scraping the bowl with his blackened spoon. He was grateful for the somewhat more satisfying portions he was getting, and although he was never not hungry, after this somewhat better, more plentiful food, he was a little less hungry than he had been.

But in a week his hunger was gone. He awoke nauseated one morning and waited a long day for it to go away but only felt worse. He felt sick in his mouth, eyes, and in the pit of his bowel. It's not asthma, he thought, then if so what's wrong with me? His armpits and crotch itched, he was cold inside himself and his feet were ice. He also had diarrhea.

"What's going on here?" said Zhitnyak when he entered the cell in the morning. "You didn't eat your last night's soup."

"I'm sick," said the fixer, lying in his greatcoat on the straw mattress.

"Well," said the guard as he scrutinized the prisoner's face, "maybe you might have jail fever."

"Couldn't I go to the infirmary?"

"No, you had your turn already but maybe I'll tell the warden if I see him. In the meantime you better eat this barley gruel. It's got hot milk in with the barley, and that's good for sickness."

"Couldn't I get out in the yard for a breath of air? The cell stinks and I've had no exercise for a long time. Maybe I would feel better outside."

"The cell stinks because you do. You can't go out in the yard because that's against the regulations when you're in strict confinement."

"How long will I be kept that way?"

"You'd better shut up your questions. That's for the higher-ups to say."

Yakov ate the gruel and threw it up. He sweated violently, the mattress soaked. In the evening a doctor came into the cell, a young man with a sparse beard and brown fedora. He took the prisoner's temperature, examined his body, and felt his pulse.

"There is no fever," he said. "It's some kind of harmless stomach complaint. You also have a rash. Drink your tea and never mind the solid food for a day or two, then you can go back on regular fare."

He left quickly.

After fasting two days the fixer felt better and went back to gruel and cabbage soup, though not to black bread. He hadn't the energy to chew it. When he touched his head hairs came off on his fingers. He felt listless, despondent. Zhitnyak watched him through the hole, peeking in from the side. The diarrhea occurred more frequently, and after it Yakov lay, enervated and panting, on the mattress. Though he was very weak he kept up the fire in the stove all day and Zhitnyak did not say no. The fixer still felt cold and nothing seemed to warm him. The one good thing was that there were now no searches.

He asked again to be sent to the infirmary but when the Deputy Warden came into the cell, he said, "Eat your food and cut out malingering. Starving is what makes you sick."

Yakov forced himself to eat and after a few spoonfuls it was not too bad. Later he vomited. He vomited repeatedly although there was nothing left in his stomach. And at night he had terrible dreams, visions of mass slaughter that left him sleepless, moaning. When he dozed again people were being cut down by Cossacks with sabers. Yakov was shot running into the woods. Yakov, hiding under a table in his hut, was dragged forth and beheaded. Yakov, fleeing along a rutted road, had lost an arm, an eye, his bloody balls; Raisl, lying on the sanded floor, had been raped beyond caring, her fruitless guts were eviscerated. Shmuel's split and broken body hung from a window. The fixer awoke in nausea, afraid to sleep although when he was awake the thick foul-smelling sickness was worse to bear than his nightmares. He often wished for death.

One night he dreamed of Bibikov hanging over his head and awoke with a heavy taste in his mouth, as if his tongue had turned to brass.

He sat up in fright. "Poison! My God, they're poisoning me!"

He wept for a while.

In the morning he would not touch the food Zhitnyak had brought in, nor drink the tea.

"Eat," ordered the guard, "or you'll stay sick."

"Why don't you shoot me?" the fixer said bitterly. "It would be easier for both of us than this bastard poison."

Zhitnyak turned pale and hurriedly left the cell.

He returned with the Deputy Warden.

"Why do I have to spend so much time on one goddamned Jew?" said the Deputy Warden.

"You're poisoning me," Yakov said hoarsely. "You have no true evidence against me so you're poisoning my food to kill me off."

"It's a lie," said the Deputy Warden, "you're out of your head."

"I won't eat what you give me," Yakov cried. "I'll fast."

"Fast your ass off, it'll kill you just the same."

"Then it's your murder."

"Look who's accusing other people of murder," said the Deputy Warden, "the blood killer of a twelve-year-old Christian lad."

"You shithead," he said to Zhitnyak as they left the cell.

The warden soon hastily came in. "What are you complaining about now, Bok? It's against the prison regulations to refuse food. I warn you that any more unorthodox behavior will be severely punished."

"You're poisoning me here," Yakov shouted.

"I know of no poison," the warden said sternly. "You're inventing this tale to make us look ridiculous. The doctor reported you had a stomach cold."

"It's poison. I can feel it in me. My body is sick and shrunken and my hair is falling out. You're trying to kill me."

"To hell with you," said the cross-eyed warden as he left the cell.

In a half hour he was back. "It's not my doing," he said. "I never gave such orders. If there's any poisoning done it's on the part of your fellow Jews who are the most notorious well-poisoners of all time. And don't think I've forgotten your attempt, in this prison, to bribe Gronfein to poison or kill Marfa Golov so that she couldn't testify against you in court. Now your Jewish compatriots are trying to poison you out of fear you will confess your true guilt and implicate the whole nation. We just found out that one of the cook's assistants was a disguised Jew and packed him off to the police. He's the one who was poisoning your food."

"I don't believe it," said Yakov.

"Why would we want you to die? We want you sentenced to a severe life imprisonment as a lesson for all to see of Jewish perfidy."

"I won't eat what you give me. You can shoot me but I won't eat."

"If you expect to eat, eat what you get. If not you'll starve."

For the next five days Yakov starved. He exchanged the sickness of poisoning for the sickness of starving. He lay on the mattress, sleeping fitfully. Zhitnyak threatened him with a whipping but nothing came of it. On the sixth day the warden returned to the cell, his cross-eye watering and face flushed. "I command you to eat."

"Only out of the common pot," Yakov said weakly. "What the other prisoners eat I will eat. Let me go to the kitchen and take my gruel and soup out of the common pot."

"It cannot be allowed," said the warden. "You mustn't leave your cell. You are under strict confinement. Other prisoners are not allowed to look at you. It's all in the regulations."

"They can turn their heads while I draw my rations."

"No," said the warden. But after Yakov had fasted another day he consented. Twice a day the fixer, accompanied by Zhitnyak holding his drawn pistol, went to the prison kitchen in the west wing. Yakov drew his bread rations in the morning and filled his bowl from the common pot as the prisoners working in the kitchen momentarily faced the wall. He did not fill the bowl too full because if he did Zhitnyak poured some of it back.

He returned to half starvation.

4

He begged for something to do. His hands ached of emptiness, but he got nothing. The fixer offered to repair furniture, build tables, chairs, other pieces they might need—all he asked for was a few boards and his sack of tools. He missed his crosscut saw with the taped handle, his small German plane, the hammer and tri-square. He could still feel each tool with his fingers and remembered how each worked. The sharp saw could rip through a six-inch board in ten seconds. He liked the touch and smell of wood shavings. There were times he heard in his thoughts the two-toned buzz of the crosscut and the responsible knock of the hammer. He remembered things he had built with his tools, and sometimes in his thoughts he built them again. If he had the tools—if not his own, any tools—and some pieces of wood, he might earn himself a few kopeks to buy underdrawers, a wool vest, a warm pair of socks—other things he needed. If he earned a little money he secretly hoped he might pay someone to smuggle out a letter; or if not a letter then a message to Aaron Latke. But the tools and wood were refused him, and he cracked his knuckles constantly to do something with his hands.

He asked for a newspaper, a book of some sort, anything he could read to forget the tedium. Zhitnyak said the Deputy Warden had told him reading matter was forbidden to prisoners who had violated the regulations. So were paper and pencil.

"If you hadn't written those sneaky letters you wrote, you wouldn't be in strict confinement now." "Where would I be then?" Yakov asked. "Better off. You might still be in the common cell." "Do you know when my indictment is supposed to come?" "No, and neither does anybody else, so don't ask me." Once Yakov said, "Why did you try to poison me, Zhitnyak, what did I do to you?" "Nobody said there was poison in that food," the guard said uneasily. "All they told me was to give it to you." Later he said, "It wasn't my fault. Nobody wanted to hurt you. The Deputy Warden thought you might confess faster if you got sick. The warden gave him a tongue lashing." The next morning Zhitnyak brought the prisoner a birch twig broom. "If you want to have it here, then keep your mouth shut from now on. The Deputy Warden says he's fed up of you talking to me. I'm not supposed to listen any more."

The broom was a stick with a bunch of thin birch twigs tied to it with cord. Yakov used it to sweep the cell every morning, working not too hard at first because he still felt weak from his sickness; yet he needed exercise to keep his strength up. He had again asked to be let out in the yard once in a while but, as he expected, the request was denied. Every day he thoroughly swept the stone floor, the wet parts and the dry. He swept in the corners of the cell, lifted his mattress and swept under that. He swept in the crevices between stones and once uncovered a centipede. He saw it escape under the door and the thought of that gave him a headache. He also used the broom handle to beat the mattress, its covering threadbare and split on both sides, the discolored straw visible so that he stopped beating it lest it fall apart. And when he beat it the mattress gave off a stench. Yakov patted it with his hands each morning as though to freshen it.

As much as he could he tried to arrange things so as to break the monotony of long stretches of time. When the bell rang in the corridor at 5 A.M. he arose in the cold dark, quickly cleaned the ashes out of the stove with his hand, raising dust he could smell, sweeping the small pile of ashes into a box they had given him for the purpose. Then he filled the stove with kindling, dry twigs, and some larger pieces of wood and waited for Zhitnyak, sometimes Kogin, to come in and light it. Formerly, the guard lit the stove when he brought in the prisoner's breakfast, and now that Yakov went to the kitchen for it, he lit the fire after the fixer returned with his food. Twice a day Yakov was permitted to go to the kitchen, not willing, when the warden suggested it, to give up the privilege of leaving the cell for a few minutes, although the warden gave his personal assurance that the food would be "perfectly healthful" if it were once again brought from the kitchen by the prisoners who delivered it to the guards.

"You have nothing to fear from us, Bok," he said. "I can assure you that the Prosecuting Attorney is most eager, as are all the other officials, to bring you to trial. No one would want to kill you off. We have other plans."

"When will my trial be?"

"I can't say," said Warden Grizitskoy. "They're still collecting evidence. It takes time."

"Then if you don't mind I'd rather keep on going to the kitchen."

As long as I can, he thought. I've paid for the privilege. He thought they were letting him continue to go only because they knew he knew they had tried to poison him.

After that the number of searches of Yakov's person was increased to three a day. His heart raced after these experiences, hatred thickened in it, and it took him a while to calm down. Sometimes after a search, to get the vile taste of it out of him, he swept the cell a second and third time. Or he collected the ashes out of the pit and had the wood ready for lighting long before Zhitnyak came in to take him to the kitchen to draw his supper rations. Though the stove was smoky the fixer ate near it, and after he had drunk the last of his tea, he threw in another stick or two of wood and lay down on the mattress with a sigh, hoping he could fall asleep before the stove went out and the cell became freezing. Sometimes the drinking water was ice in the morning and he had to melt it.

Passing water was another way to pass time. He urinated often, listening to the noise as the water rose in the tin can. Sometimes he held his water until it came forth with such heat and force his teeth hurt. When the can was collected was another momentary diversion. And every second day one of the guards filled the jug of water from which he drank and washed. There were no towels and he dried his hands on his ragged coat, or at the stove, rubbing them till they were dry. Fetyukov had given him a broken comb with which the fixer combed his hair and beard. Twice, thus far, he had been allowed into the bathhouse in the presence of a guard, when none of the other prisoners was there, and was permitted to wash his naked body with tepid water from a wooden bucket. He was worried to see how thin he had become. They would not touch his hair but once when his head was very lousy, the prison barber doused it with kerosene and let him comb the dead lice out with a fine comb. His beard went uncut though nobody objected that he kept it combed. Occasionally when Yakov complained that his nails were too long, Zhitnyak cut them for him. He would not allow the fixer to hold the scissors. Afterwards the guard collected the nail parings and put them into an oilskin pouch.

"What's that for?" asked Yakov.

"For an analysis they want to make," said the guard.

One morning something new appeared in Yakov's cell. An old prayer shawl and a pair of phylacteries had been left there after he had gone to the kitchen for his food. He examined the phylacteries, then put them aside, but he wore the prayer shawl under his greatcoat to help keep him warm. He was wearing a heavier prison suit than the one he had first got, though much used by other prisoners in the past and already falling apart. He also had a small cap with ear flaps that did not fit him, which he wore with the flaps down. The seams of his greatcoat had split in places. Zhitnyak loaned him a darning needle and some thread to sew them with; and Yakov received a blow in the face from the guard when he told him, afterwards, that he had lost the needle. He really hadn't; he had hidden it inside the stove. But the coat seams opened again and there was no thread. His wooden clogs had been taken from him and he now wore bast shoes without laces; he was not allowed to have a belt. When Yakov put the prayer shawl on, Zhitnyak watched through the spy hole, often looking in unexpectedly as though hoping to catch the fixer at prayer. He never did.

Yakov spent hours pacing in the cell. He walked to Siberia and back. Six or eight times a day he read the prison regulations. Sometimes he sat at the shaky table. He could eat at the table but there was nothing else to do at it that he could think of. If he only had some paper and pencil he might write something down. With a knife he could whittle a piece of firewood, but who would give him a knife? He blew on his hands constantly. He feared he might go crazy doing nothing. If only there were a book to read. He remembered how he had studied and written in his stable room in the brickyard, at the table he had built himself with his tools. Once, just after Zhitnyak had peeked in, the fixer quickly piled up the loose wood at the wall and climbed up on top of the pile to see if he could look out the window into the prison yard. He thought the prisoners might be there on their promenade. He wondered whether any of those he knew were still in prison, or had they got out. But he could not reach the window bars with his hands and all he saw out of it was a piece of leaden sky.

5

The newspaper strips he was given to clean himself with Zhitnyak forbade him to read though Yakov managed to read some of them anyway.

"It's because you're an enemy of the state," the guard said through the peephole. "They're not allowed to read anything."

During the endless empty days, to forget his misery a little, the fixer tried to remember things he had read. He remembered incidents from Spinoza's life: how the Jews had cursed him in the synagogue; how an assassin had tried to kill him in the street, for his ideas; how he lived and died in his tiny room, studying, writing, grinding lenses for a living until his lungs had turned to glass. He had died young, poor and persecuted, yet one of the freest of men. He was free in his thoughts, his understanding of Necessity, and in the construction of his philosophy. The fixer's thoughts added nothing to his freedom; it was nil. He was imprisoned in a cell, and even in memory because so much that had happened to him during a life that had perhaps, at times, seemed free, now seemed designed to lead to this imprisonment. Necessity freed Spinoza and imprisoned Yakov. Spinoza thought himself into the universe but Yakov's poor thoughts were inclosed in a cell.

Who am I to compare myself?

He tried to recall the biology he had studied, and reflected on as much of history as he could bring to mind. They say

God appeared in history and used it for his purposes, but if that was so he had no pity for men. God cried mercy and smote his chest, but there was no mercy because there was no pity. Pity in lightning? You could not pity anything if you weren't a man; pity was a surprise to God. It was not his invention. And Yakov also recalled tales by Peretz, and some pieces he had read in the papers by Sholem Aleichem, and a few little stories he had read in Russian by Chekhov. He recalled things from the Scriptures, in particular, fragments of psalms he had read in Hebrew on old parchment. He could, in a sense, smell the Psalms as well as hear them. They were sung weekly in the synagogue to glorify God and protect the shtetl from harm, which they never did. Yakov had chanted them, or heard them chanted, many times, and now in a period of remembrance he uttered verses, stanzas that he did not think he knew. He could not recall a whole psalm, but from fragments he put together one that he recited aloud in the cell in order not to forget it, so that he could have it to say. In the morning he said it in Hebrew, and in the dark as he lay on his mattress, he tried to translate the verses into Russian. He knew Kogin listened when he said them aloud at night.

"Behold, he travaileth with iniquity;
Yea, he conceiveth mischief, and bringeth forth
falsehood.
He hath digged a pit, and hollowed it,
And is fallen into the ditch which he made."

"I am weary with my groaning;
Every night make I my bed to swim;
I melt away my couch with my tears."

"For my days are consumed like smoke,
And my bones are burned as a hearth.
My heart is smitten like grass, and withered;
For I forget to eat my bread."

"Unrighteous witnesses rise up;
They ask me things that I know not."

"For I have heard the whispering of many,
Terror on every side;

While they took counsel together against me,
They devised to take away my life."

"Arise, O Lord; O God, lift up Thy hand;
Forget not the humble."

"Break Thou the arm of the wicked."

"Thou shalt make them as a fiery furnace
in the time of Thine anger."

"He bowed the heavens also, and came down;
And thick darkness was under His feet."

"And He sent out His arrows, and scattered them;
And He shot forth lightnings, and discomfited them."

"I have pursued my enemies, and overtaken them;
Neither did I turn back till they were consumed."

He thought of himself pursuing his enemies with God at his side, but when he looked at God all he saw or heard was a loud Ha Ha. It was his own imprisoned laughter.

6

I scratch at memory. I think of Raisl. I'm in prison so what difference does it make? The first time I saw her she was riding in her father's rickety wagon, drawn by the bony nag of late memory. She sat with the sick mother amid their few shreds of household goods. Shmuel was on the seat talking to himself, or the horse's tail, or God; he went where the nag pulled, but wherever he went he was going backward. They were coming from some place, where I don't know. Where can you come from in the Pale that's so different from where you're going? Everywhere he tried to make a better living, and everywhere he couldn't so he tried some place else. He came to our town, and the mother, fed up with adventure, died on the spot. After that her grave kept him in one place. Also from such a hard-luck father what kind of daughter could you expect, so I stayed away from her. Naturally I stayed away for the months I was in the army, but I also stayed away from her when I got back, though not for long. (She would have done me a favor to have got married while I was gone.) Anyway, she was a pretty girl, intelligent and dissatisfied, with even then a sad face. At least the right eye was sad; the left was neutral, it reflected me. I saw her many times in the market before I got up the nerve to talk to her. She scared me, I wasn't sure I had what she wanted. I was afraid she would rub my nose in my future. Anyway I saw the other young men looking at her and I looked too. She was a thin lanky girl with small breasts. I remember her dark hair in braids, deep eyes, and a long neck. She wore in the morning what she had washed out at night; sometimes the clothes were damp. The father wanted her to work as a servant girl but she wouldn't. She bought a few eggs from a peasant woman and set up a little stall in the market. Whenever I could I bought an egg from her. She lived with Shmuel in a hut off the road near the bathhouse stream. When I came for a visit they seemed glad to see me, especially the father. He was looking for a husband for her and a dowry didn't exist. If it existed it was a cherry pit. But he knew my type, that I wouldn't ask questions and he wouldn't mention it.

We walked together in the woods by the water, she and I. I showed her my tools and once cut down a small tree with my saw. I fixed up their hut a little, made a bench, a cupboard, and a few shelves out of some boards I was saving. If there was a little chicken to eat I came also on Friday nights. Raisl blessed the candles and served the food, it was very nice. We liked each other but both had doubts. I think she thought, He won't move, he isn't ambitious, he'll stay here forever. What kind of future is that? I thought to myself, She's a complicated girl and won't be easy to satisfy. What she wants she'll drive me wild to get. Still, I liked to be with her. One day in the woods we became man and wife. She said no but took a chance. Later it bothered her. She was afraid for her child once she had one, that it would be born crippled or with seven fingers. "Don't be superstitious," I said. "If you want to be free, first be free in your mind." Instead she began to cry. After a while I said, "All right, you've cried enough, so before it happens again let's get married. I need a wife and you need a husband." At this her eyes got big and once again were full of tears. She didn't answer me. "Why don't you talk?" I said. "Say yes or no." "Why don't you say love?" she said. "Who talks about love in the shtetl?" I asked her. "What are we, millionaires?" I didn't say so but it's a word that makes me nervous. What does a man like me know about love? "If you don't love me I can't marry you," she answered me. But by then the father had his nose in my ear. "She's a doll, a marvelous girl, you can't go wrong. She'll work hard and both together you'll make a living." So I said love and she said yes. Maybe my poor future looked better than her own.

After we were married, all she talked about was we must get out of Russia, including the father, because things were getting worse, not better. Worse for us and worse for the Russians. "Let's sell everything and leave while we can." I answered her, "Even if we sell everything we'll have nothing. Believe me, there's no shortage of places to go to in this wide world, but first I'll work hard and we'll save a few rubles, and in that case who knows where we'll get to. Maybe it'll take a year or two and then we'll leave." She looked at me with a tight face. "After another year you'll never go; you're afraid to leave." Maybe she was right but I said, "Your father changed places every time he breathed and all he's collected is air. I'll stay in one place and build up a little capital, and then I'll think of leaving." That wasn't strictly the truth. I was in no hurry to run to another country. Some men are by nature explorers; my nature is to stay under the same moon and stars, and if the weather is wet, under the same roof. It's a strange world, why make it stranger? When I was in the Tsar's army I was less afraid of the world but once I got home again enough was enough. In other words, in those days to make me move, somebody had to push. So she pushed. But we didn't get along so badly until another year or two went by and we still had no capital, and we had no children. Raisl was depressed and either said nothing, or wept, and never left off complaining. Our hut was divided into two small rooms. At night she stayed in bed while I sat in the kitchen. It was at this time that I began to read more. I picked up books here and there, a few I stole, and read by the lamp. Many times after I read I slept on the kitchen bench. When I was reading Spinoza I stayed up night after night. I was by now excited by ideas and I tried to collect a few of my own. It was the beginning of a different Yakov. I thought of things I had never thought of before, and then when I began to read a little history and also a pamphlet about Nicholas I, the Tsar's father, I said to myself, "She's right, we ought to get out of here and the sooner the better."

But without a living where can you go? We went nowhere. By now it was coming to six years that we were married and still had no children. I said nothing but I was, in my heart, a disappointed man. Who could I look in the face? In her heart Raisl was frantic. She blamed it on her sins. Maybe on my sins. She was running again, in her big wig, to the rabbis, who had never helped her, if not in our town, then in the others. She tried magic and she tried spells. She recited verses from the Scriptures and drank potions squeezed out of parts of fish and hares. I don't believe in this kind of business. Anyway, as one might expect, nothing happened. "Why has God cursed me?" she cried. "What God?" I said. She was a desperate woman. "Will I be just like my father, will I always have *nothing*? Will I have less than my father?" By this time I was worn out living in a storm. She ran this way and that, she wept, she cursed her life. I said less and read more though the books didn't bring me a kopek unless I sold them. I thought I would take her to a big doctor in Kiev, but who would pay for it? So nothing happened. She stayed barren and I stayed poor. Every day she begged me to leave so our luck would change. "Leave," I said, "on whose wings?" Then I said, "Like your father's luck changed." So she looked at me with hatred. I began to stay away from the house. When I came in at night I slept in the kitchen. The next thing I knew they were talking about her in the taverns. Then one day she was gone. I opened the door and the house was empty. At first I cursed her like somebody in the Bible curses his whorish wife. "May she keep her miscarrying womb and dry breasts." But now I look at it like this: She had tied herself to the wrong future.

7

You wait. You wait in minutes of hope and days of hopelessness. Sometimes you just wait, there's no greater insult. You sink into your thoughts and try to blot out the prison cell. If you're lucky it dissolves and you spend a half hour out in the open, beyond the doors and walls and the hatred of yourself. If you're not lucky your thoughts can poison you. If you're lucky and get out to the shtetl you might call on a friend, or if he's out, sit alone on a bench in front of his hut. You can smell the grass and the flowers and look at the girls, if one or two happen to be passing by along the road. You can also do a day's work if there's work to do. Today there's a little carpentering job. You work up a sweat sawing wood apart and hammering it together. When it's time to eat you open your food parcel—not bad. The thing about food is to have a little when you want it. A hard-boiled egg with a pinch of salt is delicious. Also some sour cream with a cut-up potato. If you dip bread into fresh milk and suck before swallowing, it tastes like a feast. And hot tea with lemon and a lump of sugar. In the evening you go across the wet grass to the edge of the wood. You stare at the moon in the milky sky. You breathe in the fresh air. An ambition teases you, there's still the future. After all, you're alive and free. Even if you're not so free, you think you are. The worst thing about such thoughts is when they leave you and you're back in the cell. The cell is your woods and sky.

Yakov counted. He counted time though he tried not to. Counting presupposed an end to counting, at least for a man who used only small numbers. How many times had he counted up to a hundred in his life? Who could count forever?—it piled time on. The fixer had torn some splinters off sticks of firewood. The long splinters were months, the short, days. A day was a bad enough burden of time but within the day even minutes could do damage as they piled up. When one had nothing to do the worst thing to have was an endless supply of minutes. It was like pouring nothing into a million little bottles.

At five in the morning the day began and never ended. In the early evening dark he was already lying on his mattress trying to sleep. Sometimes he tried all night. During the day there were the regular checks through the spy hole, and three depressing searches of his body. There was cleaning out ashes, and making and lighting the stove. There was the sweeping of the cell to do, urinating in the can, walking back and forth until one began to count; or sitting at the table with nothing to do. There was the going for, and eating of, his meager meals. There was trying to remember and trying to forget. There was the counting of each day; there was reciting the psalm he had put together. He also watched the light and dark change. The morning dark was different from the night dark. The morning dark had a little freshness, a little anticipation in it, though what he anticipated he could not say. The night dark was heavy with thickened and compounded shadows. In the morning the shadows unfurled until only one was left, that which lingered in the cell all day. It was gone for a minute near eleven he guessed, when a beam of sunlight, on days the sun appeared, touched the corroded inner wall a foot above his mattress, a beam of golden light gone in a few minutes. Once he kissed it on the wall. Once he licked it with his tongue. After the sun had gone, light from the window descended more darkly. When he stole a newspaper strip to read, the darkness was on the paper. It was night at half past three in the afternoon in December. Yakov put wood in the stove and Zhitnyak, after they had gone for the night rations, lit it. He ate in the dark or by the light through the stove door left ajar. There was still no lamp, no candle. The fixer set a small splinter aside to mark the lost day and crawled onto his mattress.

The long splinters were months. He figured it was January. Zhitnyak wouldn't tell him, nor would Kogin. They said they were forbidden to answer such questions. He had been arrested in the brickyard in mid-April and had served in the District Courthouse jail for two months. He figured he had been in this prison another seven months, a total of nine, if not more. It would soon—soon?—be a full year of prison. He did not, could not, think past a year. He could not foresee any future in the future. When he thought about the future all he thought about was the indictment. He imagined the warden snapping back the six bolts and bringing in the indictment in a thick brown envelope. But in this thought, after the warden had left, the indictment had still not come and he was still counting time. How long would he wait? He waited with months, days, minutes on his heavy head, and with the repetitive cycles of light and dark piled on top of the long and short pieces of time. He waited with boredom sticking its fingers down his throat. He waited for an unknown time, a time different from all the time on his head. It was unending waiting for something that might never happen. In the winter, time fell like hissing snow through the crack in the barred window, and never stopped snowing. He stood in it as it piled up around him and there was no end to drowning.

One wintry day, sickened of time, he tore off his clothes. The rags fell apart in his hands.

"Bastards!" he shouted through the peephole at the guards, prison officials, Grubeshov, and the Black Hundreds. "Anti-Semites! Murderers!"

They let him stay naked. Zhitnyak would not light the stove. The fixer's body turned blue as he walked frantically in the freezing cell. He shivered on the mattress, shook, with the prayer shawl and ragged blanket wrapped around him.

"By morning," the Deputy Warden said when he came in with the guard for the last search of the day, "you won't need clothes. You'll be frozen stiff. Spread your filthy ass."

But the warden entered before nightfall and said it was indecent to have a naked Jew parading around in the cell. "You could have been shot for less than this."

He flung at Yakov another threadbare suit of prison clothes, and another ragged greatcoat. Zhitnyak then lit the stove, but it took the fixer a week to get the ice out of his spine, and the cold hurt worse than before.

Then he began to wait again.

He waits.

8

The warden, in full uniform, delivered a message from Prosecuting Attorney Grubeshov to Yakov in his solitary cell.

"You're to get dressed in your street clothes and go to the Plossky Courthouse. Your indictment is ready."

The fixer, stunned, shut his eyes. When he opened them the warden was still there.

"How shall I go, your honor?" His voice broke.

"A detective will accompany you. Since it's a short distance you can go by streetcar. You will be allowed out for no more than an hour and a half. That is the time the Prosecuting Attorney requisitioned you for."

"Must my legs be chained again?"

The warden scratched in his beard. "No, but you'll be handcuffed and there'll be strict orders to shoot you dead if you try anything in the least irregular. Furthermore, two Secret Police officers will be following you and the detective in case any of your cohorts attempt to communicate with you."

In half an hour Yakov was outside the prison, waiting with the detective for a trolley. Though the day was dreary and cold, the streets white in every direction, the leafless trees black against the frozen sky, everywhere he looked brought tears to the fixer's eyes. It seemed to him he was seeing for the first time how the world was knit together.

On the trolley he watched the shops and passers-by in the street as though he were in a foreign country. How moving it was that a peasant entered a store. The detective sat next to him, one hand in his overcoat pocket. He was a heavy-bellied man with eyeglasses and a gray fur cap, who sat silent. All the way to the courthouse the fixer worried what the indictment would say. Would it accuse him simply of murder, or of murder "for ritual purposes"? The evidence was non-existent, "circumstantial" at best, but he feared their ingenuity. When the purpose was frame-up, the evidence could be arranged. Yet whatever the indictment said, the important thing to him now was getting it so that he could talk to a lawyer. Once he had done that maybe they would not keep him in solitary confinement. Even if they put him in with a murderer it would be better than being so desperately alone. The lawyer would tell everyone who he was. He would say, "This is a decent man, he could never have killed a child." The fixer worried about getting the proper lawyer, wondering who Bibikov had had in mind, "a vigorous and courageous man of excellent reputation." Would Ivan Semyonovitch know, if he were permitted to ask him? Was the lawyer a Russian or a Jew? Which was best? And how would he pay him? Could a lawyer advise him if he had no money to give him? And even if he had a good lawyer, would he be able to defend him if Bibikov's files had fallen into the hands of the Black Hundreds?

Despite these worries, and though he was tightly handcuffed, a prisoner out of jail for a few minutes, Yakov enjoyed the trolley ride. The people around him and the movement of the car created an illusion of freedom.

At the next stop two men boarded the streetcar, and passing the fixer, saw his manacled hands. They whispered to each other, and when they sat down, whispered to others. Some of the passengers turned their heads to stare at him. Noticing this he shut his eyes.

"It's that bastard killer of a Christian child," a man in a knitted wool hat said. "I saw him once in a motorcar in front of Marfa Golov's house after they arrested him."

Some of the men in the car began to mutter among themselves.

Then the detective spoke calmly. "Everything is in good order, my friends. Don't excite yourselves for nothing. I am accompanying the prisoner to the courthouse, where he will be indicted for his crime."

Two bearded Jews wearing large hats hastily got off the trolley at the next stop. A third tried to speak to the prisoner but the detective waved him away.

"If they convict you," the Jew shouted at Yakov, "cry, 'Sh'ma, Yisroël, the Lord our God, the Lord is one!'" He jumped off the moving trolley, and the two secret police, who had risen, sat down.

A woman in a hat with velvet flowers, when she went by, spat at the fixer. Her spittle dribbled from his beard. Soon the detective nudged him and they left the trolley at the next stop. They were trudging along on the snowy sidewalk when the detective stopped to buy an apple from a street vendor. He handed it to the fixer, who gobbled it down in three bites.

In the courthouse building Grubeshov had moved into a larger office with six desks in the anteroom. Yakov waited with the detective, nervously impatient to see the indictment. It's strange, he thought, that an indictment of murder should be so precious, yet without it he could not make the first move to defend himself.

He was summoned into the inner office. The detective, hat in his hand, followed him in and stationed himself at attention behind the prisoner but Grubeshov dismissed him with a nod. The Prosecuting Attorney sat stolidly at a new desk regarding the prisoner with squinting eyes. Little had changed but his appearance. He looked older and if that was so, how much older did Yakov look? He saw himself as bushy-haired, bearded, swimming in his clothes, and frightened to death.

Grubeshov coughed seriously and glanced away. Yakov saw

no papers on his desk. Though he had made up his mind to be controlled before this archanti-Semite, he could not help himself and began to shiver. He had been trembling within and had suppressed it, but when he thought of what had happened to Bibikov, and how he himself had been treated and what he had endured because of Grubeshov, a bone of hatred thickened in his throat and his body shook. It trembled violently as though it were trying to expel a poisonous substance. And though he was ashamed to be shivering as though feverish or freezing in front of this man, he could not stop it.

The Prosecuting Attorney looked on in puzzlement for a minute. "Are you suffering a chill, Bok?" The slightly thick voice attempted sympathy.

The fixer, still uncontrollably shaking, said he was.

"Have you been ill?"

Yakov nodded, trying to mask his contempt for the man.

"A pity," said the prosecutor. "Well, sit down and try to control yourself. Let's get on with other matters."

Unlocking his desk drawer, he took out a pack of closely typewritten long sheets of blue paper. There were about twenty pages.

My God, so many? Yakov thought. His trembling subsided and he sat forward anxiously.

"So," said Grubeshov, smiling as though he understood the matter for the first time, "you have come for the indictment?" He fingered the papers.

The fixer, staring at them, wet his lips.

"I suppose you find incarceration a not very pleasant experience?"

Though moved to shriek, Yakov nodded.

"Has it altered your thinking, yet?"

"Not of my innocence."

Grubeshov laughed a little, pushing his chair away from the desk. "A stubborn man walks with both feet tied. I am surprised at you, Bok. I wouldn't exactly have called you stupid. I think you know your future is nil if you continue to be stubborn."

"Please, when can I see a lawyer?"

"A lawyer won't do you the least good. You may take my word for it."

The fixer sat tensely, silent but wary.

Grubeshov began to walk on his oriental rug. "Even with six or seven lawyers you will be convicted and sentenced to total solitary confinement for the rest of your life. Do you think a jury of patriotic Russians will believe what some shyster concocts for you to say?"

"I will tell them the truth."

"If the 'truth' is what you have told us, no sane Russian will believe you."

"I thought you might, your honor, since you know the evidence."

Grubeshov paused in his pacing to clear his throat. "I least of all, though I have given thought to the possibility that you were once a virtuous man who became the expiatory victim of his co-religionists. Would it interest you to know that the Tsar himself is convinced you committed the crime?"

"The Tsar?" said Yakov in astonishment. "Does he know about me? How could he think such a thing?" His heart sank heavily.

"His Majesty has taken an active interest in this case since he read of Zhenia's murder in the newspapers. He at once sat down at his desk and wrote me in his own hand the following: 'I hope you will spare no pains to unearth and bring to justice the despicable Jewish murderer of that lad.' I quote from memory. His Majesty is a most sensitive person and some of his intuitions are extraordinary. Since then I've kept him informed of the progress of the investigation. It is conducted with his full knowledge and approval."

Ah, it's bad luck, the fixer thought. After a while he said, "But why should the Tsar believe what isn't true?"

Grubeshov quickly returned to his desk and sat down. "He is convinced, as we all are, by the accumulative evidence conveyed in the testimony of the witnesses."

"What witnesses?"

"You know very well which witnesses," Grubeshov said impatiently. "By Nikolai Maximovitch Lebedev, for instance, and his daughter, refined and genteel people. By Marfa Golov, the long-suffering mother of an unfortunate son, a tragic but pure woman. By the foreman Proshko and the two drivers. By the janitor Skobeliev, who saw you offering sweets to Zhenia, and will testify in court that you chased the boy several times in the brickyard. It was through your intervention, Nikolai Maximovitch tells us, that the man was discharged from his job."

"I never knew he was discharged."

"There's a lot you don't know that you will find out."

Grubeshov went on naming witnesses. "I shall also cite testimony by your Jewish cellmate, Gronfein, whom you urged, as a favor to the Jewish community, to bribe Marfa Vladimirovna so she wouldn't testify against you. By a beggar woman who once asked you for alms, which you refused her, and who saw you enter a shop where knives are sharpened. By the proprietor of that establishment and his assistant, who will say two of your knives were sharpened to the highest pitch and then returned to you. By certain religious figures, scientists of Jewish history and theology, and alienists who are authorities on the Jewish mind. We have already gathered more than thirty reliable witnesses. His Majesty has read all the relevant testimony. When he last visited Kiev shortly after your arrest, I had the honor to inform him, 'Sire, I am happy to report that the guilty culprit in Zhenia Golov's murder has been apprehended and is now in prison. He is Yakov Bok, a member of one of the Jewish fanatic groups, the Hasidim.' I assure you His Majesty bared his head in the rain and made the sign of the cross to express his thanks to the Lord for your apprehension."

The fixer could see the Tsar crossing himself, bare-headed in the rain. For the first time he wondered if it were a matter of mistaken identity. Could they have confused him with someone else?

The prosecutor opened a side drawer of his desk and took out a folder of newspaper clippings. He read from one: "'His Majesty expressed himself as justified in his belief that the crime was the dastardly work of a Jewish criminal who must be properly punished for his barbaric deed. "We shall do whatever is necessary to protect our innocent Russian children and their anxious mothers. When I think of my own wife and children I think of them."' If the ruler of the Russian State and its people is wholeheartedly convinced of your guilt, what chance do you think you will have for a verdict of not guilty? None, I assure you. No Russian jury will free you."

"Still," said the fixer, sighing brokenly, "the question is of the worth of the evidence."

"I have no doubts of its worth. Do you have any better evidence?"

"What if certain anti-Semitic groups committed the murder to cast suspicion on the Jews?"

Grubeshov banged his fist on the desk. "What a monstrous canard! It takes a Jew to shift the blame of his crime onto his accusers. You are apparently unaware of your own admissions, yes, confessions of guilt." He had begun to sweat and his breath whistled in his nose.

"Mine?" said Yakov, on the verge of panic. "What admissions? I have made none."

"You may think not but there is already a record of more than one confession you have made in your sleep. The guard Kogin has compiled it in his notebooks, and the Deputy Warden also heard you when he listened at the cell door at night. It's obvious that your conscience is heavily burdened, Yakov Bok, and for good and sufficient reason. There is much crying out against the abhorrent nature of your crime, sighs, ejaculations, grunts, even sobs of remorse. It is because you obviously feel some sorrow for what you have done that I am willing to talk to you in this kindly way."

Yakov's eyes again crept to the papers on the desk.

"Could I see the indictment, your honor?"

"My advice to you," Grubeshov said, wiping his neck with a handkerchief, "is to sign a confession saying you committed the murder unwillingly, under the influence of your religious cohorts. Once that's done, as I informed you the last time I talked to you, something to your advantage may be arranged."

"I have nothing to confess. What can I confess to you? I can only confess my miseries. I can't confess the murder of Zhenia Golov."

"Listen, Bok, I speak to you for your own good. Your position otherwise is hopeless. A confession by you will have more than one beneficial effect. For your fellow Jews it may prevent reprisals. Do you know that at the time of your arrest Kiev was on the verge of a massive pogrom? It was only the fortuitous appearance of the Tsar to dedicate a statue to one of his ancestors that prevented it. That won't happen a second time, I assure you. Think it over, there are strong advantages for you. I am willing to see to it that you are secreted out of prison and taken to Podvolochisk on the Austrian border. You will have a Russian passport in your pocket and the means of transportation to some country outside of Europe. This includes Palestine, America, or even Australia, if you choose to go there. I advise you to consider this most carefully. The alternative is to spend your lifetime in prison under circumstances much less favorable than those you are presently enjoying."

"Excuse me, but how will you then explain to the Tsar that you let a confessed murderer of a Christian child go?"

"That part doesn't concern you," said Grubeshov.

The fixer didn't believe him. A confession, he knew, would doom him forever. He was already doomed.

"The warden said you would give me the indictment."

Grubeshov uneasily studied the top sheet of the paper, then put it down. "The indictment requires the signature of the Investigating Magistrate. He is away on official business and has not yet returned to his office. In the meantime I want to know what your response is to my more than reasonable proposal?"

"I have enough to confess but not that crime."

"Ach, you are a stupid Jew."

Yakov readily agreed.

"If you have hopes of the sympathy and perhaps assistance of Magistrate Bibikov, you had better give them up. He has been replaced by another."

The fixer clamped his teeth tight to keep from going into shudders again.

"Where is Mr. Bibikov?"

Grubeshov spoke restlessly. "He was arrested for peculating from official funds. While awaiting trial, overwhelmed by his disgrace, he committed suicide."

The fixer shut his eyes.

When he opened them he said, "Could I speak to his assistant, Mr. Ivan Semyonovitch?"

"Ivan Semyonovitch Kuzminsky," said the Prosecuting

Attorney coldly, "was taken into custody at the Agricultural Fair last September. He did not remove his hat when the band played 'God Save the Tsar.' If my memory is correct he was sentenced to a year in the Petropavlovsky Fortress."

The fixer gasped silently.

"Do you get the point?" Grubeshov's face was taut, sweaty.

"I am innocent," the fixer shouted hoarsely.

"No Jew is innocent, least of all a ritual assassin. Furthermore, it is known you are an agent of the Jewish Kahal, the secret Jewish international government which is engaged in a subterranean conspiracy with the World Zionist Organization, the Alliance of Herzl, and the Russian Freemasons. We also have reason to believe that your masters are dickering with the British to help you overthrow the legitimate Russian government and make yourselves rulers of our land and people. We are not exactly naïve. We know your purposes. We have read the 'Protocols of the Elders of Zion,' and the 'Communist Manifesto,' and fully understand your revolutionary intentions!"

"I am not a revolutionist. I am an inexperienced man. Who knows about such things? I am a fixer."

"You can deny it all you want, we know the truth," Grubeshov shouted. "The Jews dominate the world and we feel ourselves under their yoke. I personally consider myself under the power of the Jews; under the power of Jewish thought, under the power of the Jewish press. To speak against the crimes of the Jews means to evoke the charge that one is either a Black Hundred, an obscurantist, or a reactionary. I am none of these things. I am a Russian patriot! I love the Russian Tsar!"

Yakov stared miserably at the indictment papers.

Grubeshov grabbed them and locked them in the drawer.

"If you come to your senses, let me know through the warden. Until then you will continue to give off your stink in prison."

Before Yakov was permitted to leave the office, the Prosecuting Attorney, his face darkened by blood, reading from his notebook, asked the prisoner if he was related to Baal Shem Tov or Rabbi Zalman Schneur of Ladi, and whether there had ever been a shochet in his family. To each question Yakov, shivering uncontrollably, replied no, and Grubeshov painstakingly recorded his answers.

9

He sat in his prison clothes in the dark cell, his beard tormented, eyes red, head burning, the acid cold cracking his bones. The snow hissed on the window. The wind seeping through the split glass sank on him like an evil bird, gnawing his head and hands. He ran in the cell, his breath visible, beating his chest, waving his arms, slapping blue hands together, crying anguish. He sighed, he wailed, called to the sky for help, until Zhitnyak, one nervous eye at the spy hole, ordered him to shut up. When the guard lit the evening fire the fixer sat at the smoky stove with its door open, the collar of his greatcoat raised above his ears, the light of the flames heatless on his face. Except for the glowing, crackling, moaning fire the cell was black, dank, heavy with wet stink. He could smell the rotten odor of himself in the enduring stench of all the prisoners who had lived and died in this miserable cell.

The fixer shivered for hours, plunged in the deepest gloom. Who would believe it? The Tsar himself knew of him. The Tsar was convinced of his guilt. The Tsar wanted him convicted and punished. Yakov saw himself locked in combat with the Russian Emperor. They wrestled, beard to beard, in the dark until Nicholas proclaimed himself an angel of God and ascended into the sky.

"It's all a fantasy," the fixer muttered. "He doesn't need me and I don't need him. Why don't they let me alone? What have I truly done to them?"

His fate nauseated him. Escaping from the Pale he had at once been entrapped in prison. From birth a black horse had followed him, a Jewish nightmare. What was being a Jew but an everlasting curse? He was sick of their history, destiny, blood guilt.

VII

HE WAITS.

The snow turned to rain.

Nothing happened.

Nothing but the long winter; not the indictment.

He felt the change of weather in his head. Spring came but stayed outside the bars. Through the window he heard the shrilling of swallows.

The seasons came faster than the indictment. The indictment was very slow. The thought that it might sometime come made it so slow.

In the spring it rained heavily. He listened to the sound of the rain and liked the thought of the outside wet, but he didn't like the inside wet. Water seeped through the wall on the prison yard side. Lines of wet formed on the cement between the exposed bricks. From an eroded part of the ceiling above the window, water dripped after the rain had stopped. After the rain there was always a puddle on the floor. Sometimes the dripping went on for days. He awakened at night listening to it. Sometimes it stopped for a few minutes and he slept. When the dripping began again he awoke.

I used to sleep through thunder.

He was so nervous, irritable, so oppressed by imprisonment he feared for his sanity. What will I confess to them if I go mad? Each day's oppressive boredom terrified him. The boredom and the nervousness made him think he might go insane.

One day, out of hunger for something to do, for a word to read, he cracked open one of the phylacteries that had been left in the cell. Holding it by the thongs he hit the box against the wall till it burst with a puff of dust. The inside of the phylactery box smelled of old parchment and leather, yet there was a curious human odor to it. It smelled a little like the sweat of the body. The fixer held the broken phylactery to his nose and greedily sucked in the smell. The small black box was divided into four compartments, each containing a tightly rolled little scroll, two with verses from Exodus and two from Deuteronomy. Yakov puzzled out the script, remembering the words faster than he could read. The bondage in Egypt was over, and in one scroll Moses proclaimed the celebration of Passover. Another scroll was the Sh'ma Yisroël. Another enumerated the rewards for loving and serving God and the punishment for not: the loss of heaven, rain, and the fruit of that rain; even life. In each of the four scrolls the people were commanded to obey God and teach his words. "Therefore you shall lay up these my words in your heart and in your soul, and bind them for a sign upon your hand, that they may be frontlets between your eyes." The sign was the phylactery and it was the phylactery that Yakov had broken. He read the scrolls with excitement and sadness and hid them deep in the mattress straw. But one day Zhitnyak, his eye roving at the peephole, caught the fixer absorbed in reading them. He entered the cell and forced him to give them up. The appearance of the four scrolls puzzled the guard, although Yakov showed him the broken phylactery; and Zhitnyak turned them over to the Deputy Warden, who was greatly excited to have this "new evidence."

A few weeks later, Zhitnyak, while in the cell, sneaked the fixer a small green paper-covered New Testament in Russian. The pages were worn and soiled with use. "It's from my old woman," Zhitnyak whispered. "She said to give it to you so you could repent for the wrong you did. Besides, you're always complaining you have nothing to read. Take it but don't tell anyone who gave it to you or I will break your ass. If they ask you say that one of the prisoners in the kitchen slipped it in your pocket without you knowing it, or maybe one of those who empty the shit cans."

"But why the New Testament, why not the Old?" Yakov said.

"The Old won't do you any good at all," Zhitnyak said. "It's long been used out and full of old graybeard Jews crawling around from one mess to the other. Also there's a lot of fucking in the Old Testament, so how is that religious? If you want to read the true word of God, read the gospels. My old woman told me to tell you that."

Yakov would at first not open the book, having from childhood feared Jesus Christ, as stranger, apostate, mysterious enemy of the Jews. But with the book there his boredom grew deeper and his curiosity stronger. At last he opened it and began to read. He sat at the table reading through the darkness on the page, though not for long periods because he found it hard to concentrate. Yet the story of Jesus fascinated him and he read it in the four gospels. He was a strange Jew, humorless and fanatic, but the fixer liked the teachings and read with pleasure of the healing of the lame, blind, and of the epileptics who fell into fire and water. He enjoyed the loaves and fishes and the raising of the dead. In the end he was deeply moved when he read how they spat on him and beat him with sticks; and how he hung on the cross at night. Jesus cried out help to God but God gave no help. There was a man crying out in anguish in the dark, but God was on the other side of his mountain. He heard but he had heard everything. What was there to hear that he hadn't heard before? Christ died and they took him down. The fixer wiped his eyes. Afterwards he thought if that's how it happened and it's part of the Christian religion, and they believe it, how can they keep me in prison, knowing I am innocent? Why don't they have pity and let me go?

Though his memory gave him trouble he tried to learn by heart some of the verses he liked in the gospels. It was a way to keep his mind occupied and his memory alert. Then he would recite to himself what he had learned. One day he began to say verses aloud through the peephole. Zhitnyak, sitting in his chair in the corridor, hacking at a stick with his knife, heard the fixer recite the Beatitudes, listened to the end, then told him to shut his mouth. When Yakov could not sleep at night; or when he had slept a little and was waked by some dream or noise, he passed part of his waking time reciting in the cell, and Kogin as usual kept his ear to the spy hole, breathing audibly. One night, the guard, lately morose with worry, remarked through the door in his deep voice, "How is it that a Jew who killed a Christian child goes around reciting the words of Christ?"

"I never even touched that boy," said the fixer.

"Everybody says you did. They say you had a secret dispensation from a rabbi to go ahead and do it and your conscience wouldn't hurt you. I've heard it said you were a hardworking man, Yakov Bok, but you still could have committed the crime because in your thinking it was no crime to murder a Christian. All that blood and matzo business is an old part of your religion. I've heard about it ever since I was a small boy."

"In the Old Testament we're not allowed to eat blood. It's forbidden," said Yakov. "But what about these words: 'Truly, truly, I say to you, unless you eat the flesh of the Son of man and drink His blood, you have no life in you; he who eats My flesh and drinks My blood has eternal life, and I will raise him up on the last day. For My flesh is food indeed, and My blood is drink indeed. He who eats My flesh and drinks My blood, abides in Me, and I in him.'"

"Ah, that's a different load of fish altogether," said Kogin. "It means the bread and wine and not the real flesh and blood. Besides, how do you know those words that you just said? When the Devil teaches scripture to a Jew they both get it wrong."

"Blood is blood. I said it the way it was written."

"How do you know it?"

"I read it in the Gospel of John."

"What's a Jew doing reading the gospels?"

"I read them to find out what a Christian is."

"A Christian is a man who loves Christ."

"How can anyone love Christ and keep an innocent man suffering in prison?"

"There is no innocent Christ-killer," Kogin said, shutting the disk over the spy hole.

But the next night as the rain droned steadily in the prison yard and drops of water dripped from the ceiling, the guard came to hear what else Yakov had memorized.

"I haven't been in a church in years," Kogin said. "I'm not much of a body for incense and priests but I like to hear the words of Christ."

"'Which of you convicts me of sin?'" said Yakov. "'If I tell the truth, why do you not believe me?'"

"Did he say that?"

"Yes."

"Go on to another one."

"'But it is easier for heaven and earth to pass away, than for one dot of the law to become void.'"

"When you say the words they sound different than I remember them."

"They're the same words."

"Go on to another one."

"'Judge not, that you be not judged. For with the judgment you pronounce you will be judged and the measure you give will be the measure you get.'"

"That's enough," said Kogin. "I've had enough."

But the next night he brought a candle stub and match.

"Look, Yakov Bok, I know you're hiding a book of the gospels in your cell. How did you get it?"

Yakov said someone had slipped it into his pocket when he went to get his rations in the kitchen.

"Well, maybe, and maybe not," said Kogin, "but since you have the book in there you might as well read me something. I'm bored to my ass out here all alone night after night. What I really am is a family man."

Yakov lit the candle and read to Kogin through the hole in the door. He read him of the trial and suffering of Christ, as the yellow candle flame dipped and sputtered in the damp cell. When he came to where the soldiers pressed a crown of thorns on Jesus' head, the guard sighed.

Then the fixer spoke in an anxious whisper. "Listen, Kogin, could I ask you for a small favor? It isn't much of one. I would like a piece of paper and a pencil stub to write a few words to an acquaintance of mine. Could you lend them to me?"

"You better go fuck yourself, Bok," said Kogin. "I'm onto your Jew tricks."

He took the candle, blew it out, and did not again come to hear the verses of the gospels.

2

Sometimes he caught the scent of spring through the broken window when a breeze that had passed through the flowering bushes and trees left him with a remembrance of green things growing on earth, and his heart ached beyond belief.

One late afternoon in May, or possibly June, after the fixer had been imprisoned more than a year, a priest in gray vestments and a black hat appeared in the dark cell, a pale-faced young man with stringy hair, wet lips, and haunted, dark eyes.

Yakov, thinking himself hallucinated, retreated to the wall.

"Who are you? Where do you come from?"

"Your guard opened the door for me," said the priest, nodding, blinking. He coughed, a complex fit it took him a while to get through. "I've been ill," he said, "and once as I lay in bed in a fever I had an extraordinary vision of a man suffering in this prison. Who can it be? I thought, and at once it came to me, it must be the Jew who was arrested for killing the Christian child. I was covered with perspiration and cried out, 'Heavenly Father, I thank you for this sign, for I understand you wish me to be of service to the imprisoned Jew.' When I had recovered from my illness, I wrote at once to your warden asking him to permit me to see you. At first it seemed impossible, but after I had prayed and fasted, it was finally arranged with the Metropolitan's assistance."

Seeing the ragged, bearded fixer in the gloom, standing with his back to the sweating wall, the priest fell to his knees.

"Dear Lord," he prayed, "forgive this poor Hebrew for his sins, and let him forgive us for sinning against him. 'For if you forgive men their trespasses, your heavenly father also will forgive you; but if you do not forgive men their trespasses, neither will your father forgive your trespasses.'"

"I forgive no one."

Approaching the prisoner on his knees, the priest tried to kiss his hand but the fixer snatched it away and retreated into the shadows of the cell.

Groaning, the priest rose, breathing heavily.

"I beg you to listen to me, Yakov Shepsovitch Bok," he wheezed. "I am told by the guard Zhitnyak that you religiously read the gospels. And the guard Kogin says that you have memorized many passages of the words of the true Christ. This is an excellent sign, for if you embrace Christ, you will have truly repented. He will save you from damnation. And if you are converted to the Orthodox faith, your captors will be compelled to reconsider their accusations and ultimately to release you as one of our brothers. Believe me, there is none so dear in the eyes of God as a Jew who admits he is in error and comes willingly to the true faith. If you agree I will begin to instruct you in the Orthodox dogma. The warden has given his permission. He is a broad-minded man."

The fixer stood mute.

"Are you there?" said the priest, peering into the shadows. "Where are you?" he called, blinking uneasily. He coughed with a heavy rasp.

Yakov stood in the dim light, motionless at the table, the prayer shawl covering his head, the phylactery for the arm bound to his brow.

The priest, coughing thickly, his handkerchief held to his mouth, retreated to the metal door and banged on it with his fist. It was quickly opened and he hurried out.

"You'll get yours," said Zhitnyak to the fixer, from the hall.

Afterwards a lamp was brought into the cell and Yakov was stripped of his clothes and searched for the fourth time that day. The Deputy Warden, in a foul mood, kicked at the mattress and found the New Testament in the straw.

"Where the hell did you get this?"

"Somebody must've slipped it to him in the kitchen," said Zhitnyak.

The Deputy Warden floored the fixer with a blow.

He confiscated the phylacteries and Zhitnyak's New Testament but returned in the morning and flung at Yakov a handful of pages that flew all over the cell. They were pages from the Old Testament in Hebrew, and Yakov collected them and patiently put them together. Half the book was missing and some of the pages were covered with muddy brown stains that looked like dry blood.

3

The birch twig broom came apart. He had used it for months and the twigs had worn out on the stone floor. Some had snapped off in the sweeping and he was given nothing to replace them with. Then the frayed cord that bound the twigs wore away and that was the end of the broom. Zhitnyak would not supply twigs or a new cord. Yakov had asked for them, but he took the broomstick away instead.

"That's so you won't hurt yourself, Bok, or try any more of your dirty tricks on anybody else. Some say you clubbed the poor boy unconscious before you stuck him with your knife."

The fixer talked less with the guards, it was less wearying; they said little to him, once in a while a gruff command, or a curse if he was slow. Without the broom his thin routine began to collapse. He tried to hang on to it but now there was no stove to make or tend, or wait to be lit, and he was no longer permitted to go to the kitchen to get his rations. The food was brought to him in the cell, as it had been before. They said he had stolen things from the kitchen. The New Testament Bible, for instance. And a knife had been "found" during an inspection of his cell. That ended the excursions he had looked forward to, sometimes with excited eagerness, twice a day. "It's only right," said the warden. "We can't have a Jew going around flouting the rules. There have been mutterings among some of the other prisoners." What was left of the routine was to be waked by the prison bell in the morning, to eat meagerly not once but twice a day, and three times each day to be searched to desperation.

He had stopped keeping track of time with the long and short splinters. Beyond a year he couldn't go. Time was summer now, when the hot cell stank heavily and the walls sweated. There were mosquitoes, and bugs hitting the walls. Yet, better summer; he feared another winter. And if there was a spring after the winter it would mean two years in prison. And after that? Time blew like a steppe wind into an empty future. There was no end, no event, indictment, trial. The waiting withered him. He was worn thin by the struggle to wait, by the knowledge of his innocence against the fact of his imprisonment; that nothing had been done in a whole year to free him. He was stricken to be so absolutely alone. Oppressed by the heat, eaten by damp cold, eroded by the expectation of an indictment that never came, were his gray bones visible through his skin? His nerves were threads stretched to the instant before snapping. He cried out of the deepest part of him, a narrow pit, but no one appeared or answered, or looked at him or spoke to him, neither friend nor stranger. Nothing changed but his age. If he were tried, convicted, and sentenced to

Siberia, that at least would be something to do. He combed his hair and beard until the teeth of the comb fell out. No one would give him another although he begged, wheedled; so he combed with his fingers. He picked his nose obsessively. His flesh, containing girls who had never become women, tempted him, but that upset his stomach. He tried unsuccessfully to keep himself clean.

Yakov read the Old Testament through the stained and muddied pages, chapter by fragmentary chapter. He read each squat letter with care, although often the words were incomprehensible to him. He had forgotten many he once knew, but in the reading and rereading some came back; some were lost forever. The passages he could not understand and the missing pages of the book did not bother him; he knew the sense of the story. What wasn't there he guessed at, or afterwards recalled. At first he read only for a few minutes at a time. The light was bad. His eyes watered and head swam. Then he read longer and faster, gripped by the narrative of the joyous and frenzied Hebrews, doing business, fighting wars, sinning and worshipping—whatever they were doing always engaged in talk with the huffing-puffing God who tried to sound, maybe out of envy, like a human being.

God talks. He has chosen, he says, the Hebrews to preserve him. He covenants, therefore he is. He offers and Israel accepts, or when will history begin? Abraham, Moses, Noah, Jeremiah, Hosea, Ezra, even Job, make their personal covenant with the talking God. But Israel accepts the covenant in order to break it. That's the mysterious purpose: they need the experience. So they worship false Gods; and this brings Yahweh up out of his golden throne with a flaming sword in both hands. When he talks loud history boils. Assyria, Babylonia, Greece, Rome, become the rod of his anger, the rod that breaks the heads of the Chosen People. Having betrayed the covenant with God they have to pay: war, destruction, death, exile—and they take what goes with it. Suffering, they say, awakens repentance, at least in those who can repent. Thus the people of the covenant wear out their sins against the Lord. He then forgives them and offers a new covenant. Why not? This is his nature, everything must begin again, don't ask him why. Israel, changed yet unchanged, accepts the new covenant in order to break it by worshipping false gods so that they will ultimately suffer and repent, which they do endlessly. The purpose of the covenant, Yakov thinks, is to create human experience, although human experience baffles God. God is after all God; what he is is what he is: God. What does he know about such things? Has he ever worshipped God? Has he ever suffered? How much, after all, has he experienced? God envies the Jews: it's a rich life. Maybe he would like to be human, it's possible, nobody knows. That's this God, Yahweh, the one who appears out of clouds, cyclones, burning bushes; talking. With Spinoza's God it's different. He is the eternal infinite idea of God as discovered in all of Nature. This one says nothing; either he can't talk or has no need to. If you're an idea what can you say? One has to find him in the machinations of his own mind. Spinoza had reasoned him out but Yakov Bok can't. He is, after all, no philosopher. So he suffers without either the intellectual idea of God, or the God of the covenant; he had broken the phylactery. Nobody suffers for him and he suffers for no one except himself. The rod of God's anger against the fixer is Nicholas II, the Russian Tsar. He punishes the suffering servant for being godless.

It's a hard life.

Zhitnyak watched him as he read. "Rock back and forth like they do in the synagogue," he said through the spy hole. The fixer rocked back and forth. The Deputy Warden was called to see. "What else would you expect?" he said as he spat.

Sometimes Yakov lost sight of the words. They were black birds with white wings, white birds with black wings. He was falling in thoughtless thought, a stupefying whiteness. The fixer lost track of where he was, a forgetting so profound he ached on coming out of it. This occurred often now and went on for hours. Once he fell into this state in the morning, sitting at the table reading the Old Testament, and came back to the present in the late afternoon, standing naked in the cell, being searched by the Deputy Warden and Zhitnyak. And he sometimes walked across Russia without knowing it. It was hard on the feet and had to be controlled because he wore out the soles of his bast shoes and nobody wanted to give him another pair. He walked in his bare feet over a long rocky road and afterwards found both feet battered and blistered. He awoke to find himself walking and it frightened him when he recalled the pain of the surgeon's scalpel. He willed himself to attention when he began to walk. He took a step or two on the long road and awoke in fright.

Yakov reveried the past; the shtetl, the mistakes and failures of his life. One white-mooned night, after a bitter quarrel about something he couldn't remember now, Raisl had left the hut and run in the dark to her father. The fixer, sitting alone, thinking over his bitterness and the falseness of his accusations, had thought of going after her but had gone to sleep instead. After all, he was dead tired doing nothing. The next year the accusation against her had come true, although it wasn't true then. Who had made it come true? If he had run after her then, would he be sitting here now?

He turned often to pages of Hosea and read with fascination the story of this man God had commanded to marry a harlot. The harlot, he had heard it said, was Israel, but the jealousy and anguish Hosea felt was that of a man whose wife had left his bed and board and gone whoring after strangers.

> "And let her put away her harlotries from her face,
>   and her adulteries from between her breasts;
> Lest I strip her naked,
> And set her as in the day that she was born,
> And make her as the wilderness,
> And set her like dry land,
> And slay her with thirst.
> And I will not have compassion on her children;
> For they are the children of harlotry.
> For their mother hath played the harlot,
> She that conceived them hath done shamefully;
> For she said: 'I will go after my lovers,
> That give me bread and my water.
> My wool and my flax, mine oil and my drink!'
> Therefore, behold, I will hedge up thy way with
>   thorns,
> And I will make a wall against her,
> That she will not find her paths.
> And she shall run after her lovers,
>   but she shall not overtake them,

And she shall seek them, but shall not find them;
Then shall she say: 'I will go and return to my first
husband:
For then was it better with me than now.'"

4

One morning Zhitnyak brought the prisoner a thick letter in a soiled white envelope with a long row of red stamps. The stamps were portraits of the Tsar in military tunic, wearing a medallion of the royal coat of arms, the double-headed eagle. The letter had been opened by the censor and resealed with a strip of gummed paper. It was addressed to "The Murderer of Zhenia Golov" and sent in care of the Prosecuting Attorney of the Superior Court, Plossky District, Kiev.

Yakov's heart palpitated when he took the letter. "Who is it from?"

"The Queen of Sheba," said the guard. "Open and see."

The fixer waited until the guard had gone. He put the letter down on the table to get it out of his hand. He stared at it for five minutes. Could it be the indictment? Would they address it like that? Yakov clumsily ripped open the envelope, tearing it across, and found in it a sixteen-page letter written in Russian in a woman's spidery handwriting. There were blots of ink on every page, many words misspelled, and some heavily crossed out and rewritten.

"Sir," it began, "I am the bereaved and unfortunate mother of the martyred Zhenia Golov, and I take my pen in my hand to beg you to do the right and decent thing. In God's name give an ear to a mother's pleas. I am worn out by the wicked insults and insinuations that have been wrongfully cast on myself by certain worthless people—including certain neighbors I have now cut myself off from, without any proof whatsoever. *On the contrary* with all the proof directed against you, and I beg you to clear the air up by a complete and candid confession. Although I admit your face, when I saw it in my household, didn't look too Jewish, and maybe you really wouldn't commit such a dreadful crime murdering a child and taking out his precious lifeblood if you hadn't been egged on to do it by fanatical Jews—you know the kind I mean. Still you probably did it because they threatened you with death, although maybe you didn't want to, I don't know. But now I know for a certainty that it was these old Jews with long black coats and nasty beards that warned you you had to make the kill and they would hide my child's corpse in the cave when you did. Just the same night before Zheniushka disappeared I dreamed of one of them carrying a satchel, with wild glaring eyes and bright red spots in his beard, and my former neighbor Sofya Shiskovsky told me she had dreamed the same dream that I had on the same night.

"I am asking you to own up because the evidence is all against you. One thing you might not know is that after Zheniushka confided to me you had chased him with a knife in the cemetery, I had you followed by a gentleman friend of mine to find out what other criminal activities you were engaged in. It is a known fact that you were involved in certain illegal acts in secretly dealing with other Jews in the brickyard who pretended they were not Jews, and also in the cellar of the synagogue, where you all met in the Podol District. You smuggled, robbed, and traded in goods that didn't belong to you. Zheniushka found out all about this and other of your illegalities, and that's another reason why you bore him such a violent hatred, and why you had him in your mind as the victim as soon as you were chosen to find one and drain his blood for the Jewish Easter. You also acted as a fence for this gang of Jews who broke into the homes of the Gentry as well as in certain commercial stores, and houses in the Lipki District, where the aristocratic houses are, and took out all sorts of loot in money, furs and jewels, not to mention other precious objects of different kinds. Also you paid your gang only a part of the real price the goods were worth because as the saying is, each Jew cheats the other. Which is nothing new to anybody because the whole world knows they are born criminals. A Jew wanted to lend a friend of mine money to build a house, but she went to the priest for advice and he began to tremble and advised her to take nothing from a cursed Jew, in Christ's name, because they will defraud and cheat you because it is their nature and they can't do otherwise. This priest said their Jewish blood itches when they aren't engaged in evil. If it weren't for that maybe you would have resisted the murder of a saintly boy when they egged you to do it. And I suppose you know there have been attempts to bribe me not to testify against you when your trial comes. One fat Jew in silk clothes offered me the sum of 40,000 rubles to leave Russia and he would pay me the sum of another 10,000 rubles, on arriving in Austria, but even if he and your fellow Jews had offered me 400,000 rubles, I would still spit in their faces and say *absolutely no* because I prefer the honor of my good name to 400,000 rubles of Jewish blood money.

"My gentleman friend also saw you spit on the ground one day when you walked around on the outside of St. Sophia's Cathedral after spying out the school in the courtyard where Zhenia went. He saw you turn your head as though you might go blind if you didn't, when you looked up on the golden crosses on top of the green domes, and you spat fast so no one should see you, but my friend saw you. I was also told you practice black magic religious ceremonies and certain cabalistic superstitions.

"Also, don't think I don't know the sordid part of the story. Zhenia told me about the times you enticed him to come to your room in the stable and there with the promise of bonbons and sweets you got him to open the buttons of his pants and with your hand caused him intense excitement. There were other lewd things you performed which I can't even write because I get very faint. He told me that after you did those awful things you were afraid he would tell me and I would denounce you to the police, so you used to give him ten kopeks not to say anything to anybody. He never did at the time this all happened, although once he told me about what went on up there, because he was worried and frightened, but I haven't breathed a word of it to anyone, not even to my closest neighbors because I was ashamed to say anything, and also because your crime of murder is enough to answer for, and you will probably suffer the tortures of the cursed for that alone. Yet I will honestly and frankly tell you that if people go on making suspicious and vile remarks about me behind my back, I will tell all the facts of the case whether I blush or not to the Prosecuting Attorney who is first of all a gentleman. I will also tell everybody the sordid things you did to my child.

"I will petition the Tsar to defend my good name. Besides

losing my child I have led an irreproachable life of toil. I have been an honest person and a pure woman. I have been the best of mothers even though I was a working woman with no time to herself and two people to support. Those who say I didn't weep for my poor boy at his funeral are saying a filthy lie and I will some day sue someone for libel and character assassination. I looked after my Zhenia as though he were a prince. I attended to his clothes and all of his other needs. I cooked special dishes that he liked most of all, all sorts of pastries and expensive treats. I was a mother and also a father to him since his own weakling of a father deserted me. I helped him with his lessons where I could and encouraged him and said yes when he wanted to be a priest. He was already in a preparatory church school to prepare for the priesthood when he was murdered. He felt to me the way I felt to him—he loved me passionately. Rest assured of that. Mamashka, he said, I only love you. Please, Zheniushka, I begged him, stay away from those evil Jews. To my sorrow he did not follow his mother's advice. You are my son's murderer. I urge you as the martyred mother of a martyred child to confess *the whole truth* at once and clear the evil out of the air so that we can breathe again. If you do, at least you won't have to suffer so much in the afterworld.

"Marfa Vladimirovna Golov"

The excitement of receiving the letter had increased in the reading and Yakov's head throbbed at the questions that ran through his mind. Was the trial she had mentioned already on its way or only assumed to be by her? Probably assumed, yet how could he be sure? Anyway the indictment would still have to come, and where was the indictment? What had caused her to write the letter? What were the "wicked insults and insinuations," and the "suspicious and vile remarks" she referred to? And who was making them? Could it be she was being investigated, yet by whom if not Bibikov? Certainly not Grubeshov, yet why had he let the letter, mad as it was, go through to him? Had she written it with his help? Was it to demonstrate the quality of the witness, to show Yakov what he was up against and thus again to warn or threaten him? To say we assure you she will say these things and more you can never guess, and she will convince a jury of people like her, so why not confess now?

They were multiplying the accusations and disgusting motives, and would not rest until they had trapped him like a fly in a gluepot; therefore he had better confess before other means of escape were impossible.

Whatever her reason for sending it the letter seemed close to a confession by her, maybe a sign something else was going on. Would he ever know what? The fixer felt his heartbeat in his ears. He looked around for a place to hide the letter, hoping to pass it on to the lawyer, if he ever had one. But the next morning after he had finished eating, the letter was missing from his coat pocket and he suspected he had been doped, or they had got it some other way, possibly while he was being searched. Anyway the letter was gone.

"Can't I send her an answer?" he asked the Deputy Warden before the next search, and the Deputy Warden said he could if he was willing to admit the wrongs he had done.

That night the fixer saw Marfa, a tallish, scrawny-necked woman with a figure something like Raisl's, enter the cell and without so much as a word begin to undress—the white hat with cherries, the red rose scarf, green skirt, flowery blouse, cotton petticoat, pointed button shoes, red garters, black stockings and soiled frilly drawers. Lying naked on the fixer's mattress, her legs spread apart, she promised many goyish delights if he would confess to the priest at the peephole.

5

One night he awoke hearing someone singing in the cell and when he listened with his whole being the song was in a boy's high sweet voice. Yakov got up to see where the singing was coming from. The child's pale, shrunken, bony face, corroded copper and black, shone from a pit in the corner of the cell. He was dead yet sang how he had been murdered by a black-bearded Jew. He had gone on an errand for his mother and was on his way home through the Jewish section when this hairy, bent-back rabbi caught up with him and offered him a lozenge. The instant the boy put the candy into his mouth he fell to the ground. The Jew lifted him onto his shoulder and hurried to the brickworks. There the boy was laid on the stable floor, tied up, and stabbed until the blood spouted from the orifices of his body. Yakov listened to the end of the song and cried, "Again! Sing it again!" Again he heard the same sweet song the dead child was singing in his grave.

Afterwards the boy, appearing to him naked, his stigmata brightly bleeding, begged, "Please give me back my clothes."

They're trying to unhinge me, the fixer thought, and then they'll say I went mad because I committed the crime. He feared what he might confess if he went crazy; his suffering to defend his innocence would come to nothing as he babbled his guilt and the blood guilt of those who had put him up to it. He strove with himself, struggled, shouted at him to hold tight to sanity, to keep in the dark unsettled center of the mind a candle burning.

A bloody horse with frantic eyes appeared: Shmuel's nag.

"Murderer!" the horse neighed. "Horsekiller! Child-killer! You deserve what you get!"

He beat the nag's head with a log.

Yakov slept often during the day but badly. Sleep left him limp, depressed. He was being watched by many eyes through the spy hole for the minute he went mad. The air throbbed with voices from afar. There was a plot afoot to save him. He had visions of being rescued by the International Jewish Army. They were laying siege to the outer walls. Among the familiar faces he recognized Berele Margolis, Leib Rosenbach, Dudye Bont, Itzik Shulman, Kalman Kohler, Shloime Pincus, Yose-Moishe Magadov, Pinye Apfelbaum, and Benya Merpetz, all from the orphans' home, although it seemed to him they were long since gone, some dead, some fled—he should have gone with them.

"Wait," he shouted. "Wait."

Then the streets around the prison were noisy, the crowds roaring, chanting, wailing; animals mooing, clucking, grunting. Everyone ran in several directions, feathers floating in the air, *gevalt* they were killing the Jews! A horde of thick-booted, baggy-trousered, sword-swinging Cossacks were galloping in on small ferocious ponies. In the yard the double-eagle banners were unfurled and fluttered in the wind. Nicholas the Second drove in in a coach drawn by six white horses, saluting from both sides the hundreds of Black Hundreds aching to get at the prisoner and hammer nails into his head. Yakov hid in his cell with chest pains and heartburn. The guards were planning to murder him with rat poison. He planned to murder them first. A Zhid shits on Zhitnyak. Kog on Kogin. He barricaded the door with the table and stool, then smashed them against the wall. While they were battering the door down to get at him he sat cross-legged on the floor, mixing blood with unleavened flour. He kicked savagely as the guards lugged him through the corridor, raining blows on his head.

The fixer crouched in a dark place trying to hold his mind together with a piece of string so he wouldn't confess. But it exploded into a fountain of rotting fruit, one-eyed herrings, birds of Paradise. It exploded into a million stinking words but when he confessed he confessed in Yiddish so the goyim couldn't understand. In Hebrew he recited the Psalms. In Russian he was silent. He slept in fear and waked in fright. In dreams he heard the voices of screaming children. Dressed in a long caftan and round fur hat he hid behind trees, and when a Christian child approached, compulsively chased him. One small-faced boy, a consumptive type, ran from him frantically, his eyes rolling in fright.

"Stop, I love you," the fixer called to him, but the child never looked back.

"Once is enough, Yakov Bok."

Nicholas II appeared, in the white uniform of an admiral of the Russian Navy.

"Little Father," said the fixer on both knees, "you'll never meet a more patriotic Jew. Tears fill my eyes when I see the flag. Also I'm not interested in politics, I want to make a living. Those accusations are all wrong or you've got the wrong man. Live and let live, if you don't mind me saying so. It's a short life when you think of it."

"My dear fellow," said the blue-eyed, pale-faced Tsar in a gentle voice, "don't envy me my throne. Uneasy lies the et cetera. The Zhidy would do well to understand and stop complaining in a whining tongue. The simple fact is there are too many Jews—my how you procreate! Why should Russia be burdened with teeming millions of you? You yourselves are to blame for your troubles, and the pogroms of 1905–6 *outside* the Pale of Settlement, mind you, were proof positive, if proof is needed, that you aren't staying where you were put. The ingestion of this tribe has poisoned Russia. Who ever wanted it? Our revered ancestor Peter the Great, when asked to admit them into Russia, said, 'They are rogues and cheats. I am trying to eradicate evil, not increase it.' Our revered ancestor, the Tsarina Elizabeth Petrovna, said, 'From the enemies of Christ I wish neither gain nor profit.' Hordes of Jews were expelled from one or another part of the Motherland in 1727, 1739, 1742, but still they crawled back and we have been unable to delouse ourselves of them. The worst of it happened, our greatest error, when Catherine the Great took over half of Poland and inherited the whole filthy lot, a million poisoners of wells, spies against us all, cowardly traitors. I always said it was the Poles' plot to ruin Russia."

"Have mercy on me, your Majesty. So far as I'm concerned, I am an innocent man. What have I seen of the world? Please have mercy."

"The Tsar's heart is in God's hands." He stepped into his white sailboat and sailed away on the Black Sea.

Nikolai Maximovitch had lost weight, the girl limped badly and would not look at the fixer. Proshko, Serdiuk and Richter came in on three skittish horses whose droppings were full of oats he longed to get at. Father Anastasy sought to convert him to Roman Catholicism. Marfa Golov, wept dry-eyed and haggard, offered him a bribe to testify against himself; and the Deputy Warden, in the uniform of a naval officer, for personal reasons insisted on continuing the searches. The guards promised the fixer anything if he would open up and name names, and Yakov said he might for a heated cell in wintertime, a daily bowl of noodles and cheese, and a firm clean hair mattress.

Shots were fired.

He passed through time he had no memory of and one day awoke to find himself in the same cell, not a new one with six doors and windows he had dreamed of. It was still hot but he couldn't be sure it was the same summer. The cell seemed the same, possibly a bit smaller, with the same scabby sweating walls. The same wet stone floor. The same stinking straw mattress; its smell had never killed the bugs. The table and three-legged stool were gone. Scattered over the wet floor were pages of the Old Testament, stained and muddied. He could not find the phylacteries but still wore the ragged prayer shawl.

And the last of the firewood had been removed and the cell hosed down as though to make it fit for him to stay forever.

"How long was I gone?" he asked Zhitnyak.

"You weren't gone. Who says you were gone?"

"Was I sick then?"

"They say you ran a fever."

"What did I say when I ranted and raved?" he asked uneasily.

"Who the hell knows," said the guard impatiently. "I have my own troubles. Try and live on the lousy wages they pay you here. The Deputy Warden listened to you twice a day but couldn't make out heads or tails. He says you have a filthy mind but nobody expected otherwise."

"Am I better now?"

"That's up to you, but if you break another piece of furniture, we'll smash your head."

Though his legs trembled, he stood at the peephole, looking out. Moving the disk aside with his finger, he stared out into the corridor. A yellow bulb lit the windowless wall. The cells on both sides of him, he remembered, were empty. He had more than once hit a log against the walls but there was never any response. Once an official passing by in the corridor saw his eye staring out and ordered him to shut the hole and move away from the door. After the man had gone Yakov looked out again. All he could see on the left was the chair the guards sat on, Zhitnyak whittling a stick, Kogin sighing, worrying. The other way a dusty bulb lit up a broken barrel against the wall. The fixer stood for hours staring into the corridor. When Zhitnyak came over to look in, he saw the fixer's eye staring out.

6

One midsummer night, long past midnight, Yakov, too long imprisoned to sleep, was staring out the peephole when his eye throbbed as if it had been touched, and slowly filled with the pained sight of Shmuel.

The fixer cursed himself, withdrew his eye, and tried the other. Whether vision or visitor it looked like Shmuel, though older, shrunken, grayer, a scarecrow with a frightened beard.

The prisoner, in disbelief, heard a whisper. "Yakov, it's you? Here is Shmuel, your father-in-law."

First the Tsar and now Shmuel. Either I'm still crazy or it's another mad dream. Next comes the Prophet Elijah or Jesus Christ.

But the figure of the fragile old man in shirt-sleeves and a hard hat, standing in the yellow light, his fringed garment hanging out under his shirt, persisted.

"Shmuel, don't lie, is it really you?"

"Who else?" said the peddler hoarsely.

"God forbid you're not a prisoner, are you?" the fixer asked in anguish.

"God forbid. I came to see you though I almost didn't. It's erev shabbos but God will forgive me."

Yakov wiped his eyes. "I've dreamed of everybody so why not you? But how did you get in? How did you come here?"

The old man shrugged his thin shoulders.

"We came in circles. I did what they told me. Yakov, for more than a year I tried to find you but nobody knew where. I thought to myself he's gone for good, I'll never see him again. Then one day I bought for a few kopeks a hill of rotting sugar beets from a sick Russian. Don't ask me why but for the first time in my life what I bought for rotten was not all rotten. More than half the beets turned out good, God's gift to a poor man. The sugar company sent some wagons and took them away. Anyway, I sold the beets for forty rubles, my biggest profit since I'm in business. Also I met Fyodor Zhitnyak, the brother of the one here—he peddles in the Kiev market. We got to talking and he knew your name. He told me that for forty rubles he could arrange it so I could speak to you. He spoke to the brother and the brother said yes if I came late at night and wasn't too ambitious. Who's ambitious, so here I am. For forty rubles they will let me stand here just ten minutes, so we must talk fast. Time I've had like dirt my whole life but now it's worth money. Zhitnyak, the brother who's the guard here, changed shifts with another one who took the night off because his son got arrested. That's how it goes, I wish him luck. Anyway, Zhitnyak will wait for ten minutes down the hall by the outside door but he warned me if somebody comes he might have to shoot. He might as well, if they see me I'm lost."

"Shmuel, before I faint from excitement, how did you know I was in prison?"

Shmuel moved his feet restlessly. It wasn't a dance though it looked like one.

"How I know, he asks. I knew because I knew. I know. When it came out in the Yiddish papers last year that a Jew was arrested in Kiev for murdering a Christian child, I thought to myself who can this poor Jew be, it must be my son-in-law Yakov. Then after a year I saw your name in the newspaper. A counterfeiter by the name of Gronfein got sick from his nerves and went around saying that Yakov Bok was in the Kiev prison for killing a Russian child. He saw him there. I tried to find this man but he disappeared and those who are hopeful hope he's alive. Maybe he went to America, that's what they hope. Yakov, maybe you don't know, it's a terrible tumult now all over Russia, and to tell you the truth, the Jews are frightened to death. Only a few know who you are, and some say it's a fake, there's nobody by that name, the goyim made it up to cast suspicion on the Jews. In the shtetl those who never liked you say it serves you right. Some have pity and would like to help you but we can't do a thing till they give you an indictment. When I saw your name in the Jewish paper I wrote you right away a letter and they sent it back—'No such prisoner.' I also sent you a little package, not much in it, just a few little things, but did you ever get it?"

"Poison I got but no package."

"I tried to get in here to see you and nobody would let me till I made my profit on the sugar beets and I met the brother Zhitnyak."

"Shmuel, I'm sorry for your forty rubles. It's a lot of money and what are you getting for it?"

"Money is nothing. I came to see you, but if it paves my way a foot into Paradise it's a fine investment."

"Run, Shmuel," the fixer said, agitated, "get out while you can or they'll shoot you in cold blood and call it a Jewish conspiracy. If that happens I'm doomed forever."

"I'm running," said Shmuel, cracking his knuckles against

his bony chest, "but tell me first why they blame you for this terrible crime?"

"Why they blame me? Because I was a stupid ass. I worked for a Russian factory owner in a forbidden district. Also I lived there without telling him my papers were Jewish."

"You see, Yakov, what happens when you shave your beard and forget your God?"

"Don't talk to me about God," Yakov said bitterly. "I want no part of God. When you need him most he's farthest away. Enough is enough. My past I don't have to tell you, but if you knew what I've lived through since I saw you last." He began to say but his voice cracked.

"Yakov," said Shmuel, clasping and unclasping his excitable hands, "we're not Jews for nothing. Without God we can't live. Without the covenant we would have disappeared out of history. Let that be a lesson to you. He's all we have but who wants more?"

"Me. I'll take misery but not forever."

"For misery don't blame God. He gives the food but we cook it."

"I blame him for not existing. Or if he does it's on the moon or stars but not here. The thing is not to believe or the waiting becomes unbearable. I can't hear his voice and never have. I don't need him unless he appears."

"Who are you, Yakov, Moses himself? If you don't hear His voice so let Him hear yours. 'When prayers go up blessings descend.'"

"Scorpions descend, hail, fire, sharp rocks, excrement. For that I don't need God's help, the Russians are enough. All right, once I used to talk to him and answer myself, but what good does it do if I know so little in the first place? I used to mention once in a while the conditions of my life, my struggles, misfortunes, mistakes. On rare occasions I gave him a little good news, but whatever I said he never answered me. Silence I now give back."

"A proud man is deaf and blind. How can he hear God? How can he see Him?"

"Who's proud if I ever was? What have I got to be proud of? That I was born without parents? I never made a decent living? My barren wife ran off with a goy? When a boy was murdered in

Kiev, out of three million Jews in Russia they arrested me? So I'm not proud. If God exists I'll gladly listen to him. If he doesn't feel like talking let him open the door so I can walk out. I have nothing. From nothing you get nothing. If he wants from me he has to give first. If not a favor at least a sign."

"Don't ask for signs, ask for mercy."

"I've asked for everything and got nothing." The fixer, after a sigh, spoke close to the peephole. "'In the beginning was the word,' but it wasn't his. That's the way I look at it now. Nature invented itself and also man. Whatever was there was there to begin with. Spinoza said so. It sounds fantastic but it must be true. When it comes down to basic facts, either God is our invention and can't do anything about it, or he's a force in Nature but not in history. A force is not a father. He's a cold wind and try and keep warm. To tell the truth, I've written him off as a dead loss."

"Yakov," said Shmuel, squeezing both hands, "don't talk so fast. Don't look for God in the wrong place, look in the Torah, the law. That's where to look, not in bad books that poison your thoughts."

"As for the law it was invented by man, is far from perfect, and what good is it to me if the Tsar has no use for it? If God can't give me simple respect I'll settle for justice. Uphold the Law! Destroy the Tsar with a thunderbolt! Free me from prison!"

"God's justice is for the end of time."

"I'm not so young any more, I can't wait that long. Neither can the Jews running from pogroms. We're dealing nowadays with the slaughter of large numbers and it's getting worse. God counts in astronomy but where men are concerned all I know is one plus one. Shmuel, let's drop this useless subject. What's the sense of arguing through a little hole where you can barely see part of my face in the dark? Besides, it's a short visit and we're eating up time."

"Yakov," said Shmuel, "He invented light. He created the world. He made us both. The true miracle is belief. I believe in Him. Job said, 'Though He slay me, yet will I trust in Him.' He said more but that's enough."

"To win a lousy bet with the devil he killed off all the servants and innocent children of Job. For that alone I hate him, not to mention ten thousand pogroms. Ach, why do you make me talk fairy tales? Job is an invention and so is God. Let's let it go at that." He stared at the peddler with one eye. "I'm sorry I'm making you feel bad on your expensive time, Shmuel, but take my word for it, it's not easy to be a freethinker in this terrible cell. I say this without pride or joy. Still, whatever reason a man has, he's got to depend on."

"Yakov," said Shmuel, mopping his face with his blue handkerchief, "do me a favor, don't close your heart. Nobody is lost to God if his heart is open."

"What's left of my heart is pure rock."

"Also don't forget repentance," said Shmuel. "This comes first."

Zhitnyak appeared in a great hurry. "That's enough now, it's time to go. Ten minutes is up but you talked longer."

"It felt like two," Shmuel said. "I was just about to say what's on my heart."

"Run, Shmuel," Yakov urged, his mouth pressed to the peephole. "Do whatever you can to help me. Run to the newspapers and tell them the police have imprisoned an innocent man. Run to the rich Jews, to Rothschild if necessary. Ask for help, money, mercy, a good lawyer to defend me. Get me out of here before they lay me in my grave."

Shmuel pulled a cucumber out of his pants pocket. "Here's a little pickle I brought you." He attempted to thrust it through the spy hole but Zhitnyak grabbed it.

"None of that," the guard loudly whispered. "Don't try any Jew tricks on me. Also you shut up," he said to Yakov. "You've had your say and that's enough now."

He grabbed Shmuel by the arm. "Hurry up, it's getting towards morning."

"Goodbye, Yakov, remember what I told you."

"Raisl," Yakov called after him. "I forgot to ask. Whatever happened to her?"

"I'm running," said Shmuel, holding on to his hat.

VIII

SHMUEL'S VISIT left the fixer with a heavy burden of excitement. Something must happen now, he thought. He will run to people on my behalf. He will say this is my son-in-law Yakov and look what happened to him. He will tell them I'm in prison in Kiev and what for. He will cry out my innocence and beg for help. Maybe a lawyer will then go to Grubeshov and ask for the indictment. He will say, "You must give it to us before this man dies in his cell." Maybe he will even petition the Minister of Justice. If he's a good lawyer he will think of other things to do. He won't neglect me here.

Instead the warden appeared in the cell, tense and agitated. His good eye gleamed. His mouth was loose with anger. "We'll give you escape, you bastard. We'll give you conspiracy."

A prisoner in strict confinement nearby had heard voices that night and had informed on Zhitnyak. The guard was arrested and after a while confessed that he had let an old Jew in to talk to the murderer.

"This time you overreached yourself, Bok. You'll wish you had never laid eyes on this other conspirator. We'll show you what good outside agitation will do. You'll wish you had never been born."

He demanded to know who the conspirator was, and the fixer excitedly answered, "Nobody. He was a stranger to me. He didn't tell me his name. A poor man. He met Zhitnyak by accident."

"What did he say to you? Come out with it."

"He asked me if I was hungry."

"What did you answer?"

"I said yes."

"We'll give you hunger," shouted the warden.

Early the next day two workmen entered the cell with boxes of tools, and after laboring all morning with steel hammers and long metal spikes, drilled four deep holes in the inner wall, in which they cemented heavy bolts with attached rings. The workmen also constructed a bed-size platform with four short wooden legs. The foot of the "bed" was a stock for enclosing the prisoner's legs, that would be padlocked at night. The window bars were strengthened and two more were added, reducing the meager light in the cell. But the cracked window was left cracked, and six additional bolts were fastened to the outside of the iron door, making twelve altogether, plus the lock that had to be opened by key. There was a rumor, the Deputy Warden said, that the Jews were planning a ruse to free him. He warned the fixer a lookout tower was being constructed on the high wall directly opposite his cell, and the number of guards patrolling the yard had been increased.

"If you try to escape out of this prison we'll slaughter the whole goddamn gang of you. We'll get every last one."

In Zhitnyak's place a new guard was stationed at the cell door during the day, Berezhinsky, an ex-soldier, a dark-faced man with pouched, expressionless eyes, swollen knuckles and a broken nose. There were patches of hair on his cheekbones and neck even after he had shaved. At times, out of boredom, he thrust a rifle barrel through the spy hole and sighted along it at the prisoner's heart.

"Bang!"

The fixer was chained to the wall all day, and at night he lay on the bedplank, his legs locked in the stocks. The leg holes were tight and chafed his flesh if he tried to turn a little. The straw mattress had been removed from the cell. At least that smell was gone, and the bedbugs, though some still inhabited his clothes. Since the fixer slept on his side when he slept, it took a while before he could begin to fall asleep on his back. He lay awake until he could no longer stand it, then seemed to faint into sleep. He slept heavily for an hour or two and woke. If he slept again the slightest movement of his body awakened him.

Now in chains, he thought the searches of his body might end, but they were increased to six a day, three in the morning and three in the afternoon. If the Deputy Warden went off duty early, the six searches were carried out in the morning. Berezhinsky went in with him in place of Zhitnyak. Six times a day his key grated in the lock, and one by one the twelve bolts were snapped back, each with a noise like a pistol shot. Yakov put his hands to his head, obsessed by the thought that someone was hitting him repeatedly. When the searchers appeared he was unchained and ordered to strip quickly. Though he tried to hurry, his fingers were like lead; he could not open his few buttons, and the guard booted him for not moving fast enough. He begged them to examine half his body at a time, with his jacket and shirt on and pants off; then with his pants on and the other clothes off, but they wouldn't. All he was allowed to keep on was his undershirt. It was as though, if that were not removed, the search could not be such a bad thing whatever else they did to him. During the search Berezhinsky grabbed the fixer's beard in his fist and tugged. When Yakov complained, he yanked his penis.

"Ding-dong, giddyap. A Jew's cock's in the devil's hock."

The Deputy Warden's color heightened. He laughed with a gasp and during the search his mouth wore a smile.

After each search, Yakov, exhausted, bleak, fell into depression. At first he had waited with hope that *anyway* something might come of Shmuel's visit. Then he began to fear that the peddler had been arrested. At times he wondered whether Shmuel had really come to see him, and if he had, he now wished he hadn't. If he had not come, there would now be no chains. For the chains he cursed him.

The second winter in prison was worse than the first. The outside weather was worse, less snow and sleet but more clear freezing days, especially cold when a wind was blowing. The wind bayed at the window like starving wolves. And the inside weather was worse. The cold glowed in the cell. It sometimes struck him with pain, pressing his chest so hard it hurt to breathe. He wore his cap with earflaps, the ragged prayer shawl looped around it, twice around the head, and knotted on top. He wore it until it fell apart and then kept a piece of it for a handkerchief. He tried to get his coat sleeves under the manacles but couldn't. The icy shackles encircled his bare legs. They threw him a horse blanket which he wore over his head and shoulders in the worst of winter, for though there were now a few bundles of wood in the cell, Berezhinsky was never in a hurry to light the stove, and most of the day the fixer's bones were like ice-covered branches of a tree in the winter woods. The searches in the freezing cold were terrible; the cold plunged knives into his chest, armpits, anus. His body shriveled and teeth chattered. But when Kogin came in, in the late afternoon, he built a fire. Sometimes he lit one late at night. Since the arrest of his son, the guard's eyes were almost glazed. He usually said nothing, puffed on a dead butt. After Yakov had cleaned out his supper bowl and lain down, Kogin locked his feet in the bed stocks and left.

During the day the fixer sat in chains on a low stool they had given him. The Old Testament pages had been taken from the cell the day he was chained to the wall, and the Deputy Warden said they had been burned. "They went up like a fart in the breeze." Yakov had nothing to do but sit and not think. To keep his blood from freezing he would often get up, move one step to the right, then two to the left; or one to the left and two to the right. He could also move a step back to the frozen wall, then one step forward. This was as far as he could go, and whichever way he moved he dragged the clanking chains with him. He did this for hours during the day. Sometimes he sobbed as he strained to pull the chains out of their sockets.

He was allowed to do nothing for himself. To urinate he had to call the guard and ask for the can. If Berezhinsky was not at the door, or was too lazy to hear, or Yakov could not stand the sound of the bolts hitting his head, he held his water till it cut like a knife. When he could no longer hold it he pissed on the floor. Once he held it so long the stream burst forth, wetting his pants and shoes. When Berezhinsky came in and saw what had happened he slapped the fixer's face with one hand, then with the other until the day blotted out.

"You cocksucker Zhid, I ought to make you lick it up off the floor."

When Berezhinsky delivered the gruel, Yakov often begged him to remove the manacles for a few minutes while he ate, but the guard refused. Once after eating, while the guard was gone, Yakov turned sideways, used the spoon handle to dig a little at the cement around one of the bolts. But the guard saw this through the spy hole, entered the cell, and bloodied the prisoner's mouth. After that Berezhinsky had the cell searched by a detail of five guards. Nothing was turned up at first, but they came again later in the week and found the blackened needle Yakov had long ago borrowed from Zhitnyak and carefully hidden in a crevice in the stove. To punish the fixer, his stool was removed for a week. He stood in chains all day and at night slept the sleep of the dead.

Thus the days went by. Each day went by alone. It crawled along like a dying thing. Sometimes, if he thought about it, three days went by, but the third was the same as the first. It was the first day because he could not say that three single days, counted, came to something they did not come to if they were not counted. One day crawled by. Then one day. Then one day. Never three. Nor five or seven. There was no such thing as a week if there was no end to his time in prison. If he were in Siberia serving twenty years at hard labor, a week might mean something. It would be twenty years less a week. But for a man who might be in prison for countless days, there were only first days following one another. The third was the first, the fourth was the first, the seventy-first was the first. The first day was the three thousandth.

Yakov thought how it used to be before he was chained to the wall. He remembered sweeping the floor with the birch broom. He remembered reading Zhitnyak's gospels, and the Old Testament pages. He had saved and counted the wood splinters and kept track of the days and months when it seemed a sort of reward to add up time. He thought of the minutes of light on the scabby wall. He thought of the table he had once had to sit at reading before he smashed it in a fit of madness. He thought of being free to walk back and forth in the cell, or in circles, until he was too tired to think. He thought of being able to urinate without having to call the guard; and of only two searches a day instead of a terrifying six. He thought of lying down on the straw mattress any time he wanted to; but now he could not even lie down on the wooden bed except when they released him to. And he also thought of the time he was allowed to go to the kitchen to fill his bowl; and also of tending the stove in winter, and Zhitnyak, who was not too bad, coming in twice a day to light it. The guard had permitted him a good fire. He allowed Yakov to put in plenty of wood; then before leaving the cell he lit it with a match and watched until it really blazed. Yakov thought he would be glad if things went back to how they had once been. He wished he had enjoyed the bit of comfort, in a way of freedom, he had had then. In chains all that was left of freedom was life, just existence; but to exist without choice was the same as death.

He had secret, almost pleasurable thoughts of death, had had from the time he had stolen Zhitnyak's needle. He had thought, if I want to die sometime I can use the needle to cut my veins. He could do it after Kogin left, and bleed all night. In the morning they would find a corpse. He had these thoughts more intensely now. After a while all he thought of was death. He was terribly weary, hungry to rid himself of the hard chains and the devilishly freezing cell. He hoped to die quickly, to end his suffering for once and all, to get rid of all he was and had been. His death would mean there was one last choice, there always is, and he had taken it. He had taken his fate in his hands. How will I do it? He thought of a hunger strike but that would take too long, slowly starving. He had no belt but could tear up his clothes and the blanket, braid the strips together, and if he did not first freeze to death, hang himself from the window bars. But he couldn't reach the window bars, and even if he found some way to get the rope behind them and down to him, hanging himself was not what he wanted. It would leave them out of it. He wanted them involved. He thought of Fetyukov shot by the guard. That's how I have to do it. They want me to die but not directly by their hand. They'll keep me in chains, making searches until my heart gives out. Then they can say I died of natural causes "while awaiting trial." I'll make it unnatural causes. I'll make it by their hand. I'll provoke them to kill me. He had made up his mind. He planned to do it during the sixth search of the next day, when they were at their most irritable, so they would react without thought, mechanically, instantly. He would refuse to undress, and when they ordered him to, he would spit into the Deputy Warden's eye. If he were not at once shot he would try to wrestle a gun out of one of his holsters. By then Berezhinsky would have shot him through the head. It would be over in minutes, and the guard would later receive five or ten rubles for meritorious service. The Tsar would read about it in the St. Petersburg newspapers and at once sit down at his desk to write out a telegram to Grubeshov. "I heartily congratulate you for paying back in his own coin the Jewish murderer of

Zhenia Golov. You will hear from me soon regarding advancement. Nicholas." But then the officials would have to explain his death, and whatever they said, they could never say they had proved his guilt. Who would believe them? It might even create a tumult on the outside.

Let the Tsar jig on his polished floor. I shit my death on him.

2

It is late afternoon. The sun is sinking behind the cold treetops. A black carriage appears in the distance (coming from what city?) drawn by four black horses. He loses it amid traffic on the Kreshchatik, among other carriages, droshkies, trolleys, wagon-trucks, a few motorcars. The trees are now black. It is night again. Kogin is restlessly pacing back and forth in the corridor. He has often stood by Yakov's cell door, the spy hole open, listening to his noisy wheezing, the guard's breathing audible as he wets his pencil and writes in the notebook what Yakov cries out in his sleep. But tonight, a blizzarding night, the snow swirling thickly around the prison, after hours of walking back and forth past Yakov's cell door, knowing the prisoner is awake, the guard stops and sighs through the spy hole, "Ah, Yakov Bok, don't think you're the only one with troubles. They're piled on my head like snows on a mountain top."

He walks away and then returns to say that his son Trofim has murdered an old man while robbing a house in the Podol. "That's what it comes to, you see."

After a long silence he says, "I had trouble enough with my daughter, who got herself pregnant by a man of my age, a goddamn drunk, but no sooner do I get her married off to someone," Kogin says through the spy hole, "than the boy takes to robbing a house, a thing that never entered his mind before. He stole from me but never from anybody else until this night he went into a house by the Dnieper, and while he was in there, killed the old man who lived in it. He was a harmless old man, and anyone in his right mind could see from the outside of the house that there wasn't likely to be anything of any value in it, not a thing. He knew it, but in that case why did he do it, Yakov Bok? Was there anything on his mind but to pay me back with worries for the years of love I gave him? When the old man caught him in his house he grabbed Trofim's coat and hung onto it, and he, in fright, he says, beat the old man on the head with his fists until he let go, but by that time it was too late—the old man had had some kind of stroke and died. That was the end of him. Trofim came in, as you might say, to partake of his hospitality, and he stayed on there to light the funeral candles and maybe say a prayer over the remains. He returned to the house that morning as I was taking my boots off after a night's work and told me what he had done. So I put my boots on again, and we went together to the District Police and there inscribed him for murder. A few months ago he was tried in court and sentenced to the highest penalty, twenty years at forced labor in Siberia. He's on his way there now. They started out across the Nicholas Bridge on a freezing day in December, and God only knows where they are now in all this snow and wind. Just imagine, twenty years—it's a lifetime."

"It's only twenty years," says Yakov.

"I won't see him, if we both live that long, till he's fifty-two, which is the age I am now."

The guard's low voice rumbles in the cell so he goes on in a thick whisper.

"I asked him why he had done that thing, and he said he had no particular reason. Can you imagine a more ridiculous statement, Bok? He came to the end I had predicted for him, all of a father's love gone for nothing. That's how it goes. You plan one thing and get another. Life plays no favorites and what's the use of hoping for it? The children were ruined by their mother, a woman of unsettled character and lax ways. My son was always hard to control because of her ways with him, and I thought for a time he would murder one of us in spite of all the love I had for him, but it turned out that he murdered somebody else."

Kogin sighs, pauses a minute, and asks Yakov if he wants a cigarette.

Yakov says no. He breathes deeply so the guard can hear the whine in his chest. A cigarette would make him sick.

"But if you open the stocks for a minute," he says, "it would ease my stiff legs."

Kogin says he can't do that. He stands silently at the spy hole for a few minutes, then whispers heavily, "Don't think I am not aware of your misfortunes, Bok, because I am. It's a terrible thing to see a man in chains, whoever he is, and have to lock his feet in stocks every night, but to be frank with you I don't allow myself to dwell on it much. I try not to think of you there in chains all day long. The nerves can take just so much, and I already have all the worry I can stand. I think you know what I mean by that."

Yakov says he does.

"You're sure about a cigarette? It's a small infraction of the rules. Some of the guards sell them to prisoners here, and if you ask me the warden knows it. But if I opened your stocks I could get myself shot."

After a while Yakov thinks the guard has gone away but he hasn't.

"Do you still have the gospels in there?" Kogin asks.

"No, they're gone."

"What about the sayings you used to say by memory? Why don't you say any of them any more?"

"I've forgotten them."

"This is one I remember," says the guard. "'But he who endures to the end will be saved.' It's either from Matthew or Luke, one or the other."

Yakov is moved so deeply he laughs.

The guard walks away. Tonight he is restless and in a half hour returns to the cell door, holding a lamp to the hole, peering above it to see what he can see. The light falls on the fixer's imprisoned feet, waking him again. Kogin is about to say something but doesn't. The light goes out. Yakov moves restlessly, lying awake listening to the guard walking back and forth in the corridor as though he were walking to Siberia along with his son. The prisoner listens until exhaustion overtakes him, then goes on with the dream he was having.

He locates the black carriage once again, only it is a rickety wagon coming from the provinces, carrying a coffin made of weatherbeaten pine boards. For me or who else? he thinks. Afraid to name names he struggles to wake up and instead finds himself in an empty room standing by a small black coffin, like a trunk locked with chains.

It's Zhenia's coffin, he thinks. Marfa Golov has sent it to me as a present. But when he unlocks the rusty chains and raises the coffin lid, there lies Shmuel, his father-in-law, with a prayer shawl covering his head, a purple hole in his forehead and one eye still wet with blood.

"Shmuel, are you dead?" the fixer cries, and the old man, if not in peace, at least in repose, for once has nothing to say.

The fixer awakens, grieving, his beard damp with salt tears.

"Live, Shmuel," he sighs, "live. Let me die for you."

Then he thinks in the dark, how can I die for him if I take my life? If I die I die to fuck them and end my suffering. As for Shmuel, he's already out in the cold. He may even die for my death if they work up a pogrom in celebration of it. If so what do I get by dying, outside of release from pain? What have I earned if a single Jew dies because I did? Suffering I can gladly live without, I hate the taste of it, but if I must suffer let it be for something. Let it be for Shmuel.

The next day he is searched six times in the bitterly cold cell, standing barefoot on the floor, each stone like a block of ice, as they poke their filthy fingers into his private parts. The sixth search, when he has planned to die, is the most dreadful of all. He struggles with himself to keep from leaping on the Deputy Warden, to murder him a little with his bare hands before he is shot to death.

He tells himself he mustn't die. Why should I take from myself what they are destroying me to take? Why should I help them kill me?

Who, for instance, would know if he dies now? They'll sweep his remains off the bloody floor and throw them into a wet hole. A year or two later they'd say he died attempting to escape. Who would question it after a year or two? It was a natural thing for prisoners to die in prison. They died like flies all over Russia. It was a vast country and there were many prisons. There were more prisoners than there were Jews. And what difference if the Jews said they didn't believe he had died naturally? They would have other headaches then.

Not that he is afraid to die because he is afraid of suicide, but because there is no way of keeping the consequences of his death to himself. To the goyim what one Jew is is what they all are. If the fixer stands accused of murdering one of their children, so does the rest of the tribe. Since the crucifixion the crime of the Christ-killer is the crime of all Jews. "His blood be on us and our children."

He pities their fate in history. After a short time of sunlight you awake in a black and bloody world. Overnight a madman is born who thinks Jewish blood is water. Overnight life becomes worthless. The innocent are born without innocence. The human body is worth less than its substance. A person is shit. Those Jews who escape with their lives live in memory's eternal pain. So what can Yakov Bok do about it? All he can do is not make things worse. He's half a Jew himself, yet enough of one to protect them. After all, he knows the people; and he believes in their right to be Jews and live in the world like men. He is against those who are against them. He will protect them to the extent that he can. This is his covenant with himself. If God's not a man he has to be. Therefore he must endure to the trial and let them confirm his innocence by their lies. He has no future but to hold on, wait it out.

He is enraged by what has happened—is happening to him—a whole society has set itself against Yakov Bok, a poor man with a few grains of education, but in any case innocent of the crime they accuse him of. What a strange and extraordinary thing for someone like himself, a fixer by trade, who had never in his life done a thing to them but live for a few months in a forbidden district, to have as his sworn and bitter enemies the Russian State, through its officials and Tsar, for no better reason than that he was born a Jew, therefore their appointed enemy, though the truth of it is he is in his heart no one's enemy but his own.

Where's reason? Where's justice? What does Spinoza say—that it's the purpose of the state to preserve a man's peace and security so he can do his day's work. To help him live out his few poor years, against circumstance, sickness, the frights of the universe. So at least don't make it any worse than it is. But the Russian State denies Yakov Bok the most elemental justice, and to show its fear and contempt of humankind, has chained him to the wall like an animal.

"Dogs," he cries out.

He beats his chains against the wall, his neck cords thick. He is in a rage to be free, has at times glimmerings of hope, as though imagining creates it, thinks of it as close by, about to happen if he breathes right, or thinks the one right thought. Maybe a wall will collapse, or sunrise burn through it and make an opening as large as a man's body. Or he will remember where he has hidden a book that will tell him how to walk with ease through a locked-and-twelve-times-bolted door.

"I'll live," he shouts in his cell, "I'll wait, I'll come to my trial."

Berezhinsky opens the spy hole, inserts his rifle, and sights along the barrel at the fixer's genitals.

Yakov sits in the pit. An angelic voice, or so he thinks, calls his name, but he isn't sure he has heard right; his hearing is dulled in the right ear since Berezhinsky hit him there. The sky rains and snows on him. Or it may be bits of wood or frozen time. He doesn't reply. His hair is matted and long. His nails grow until they break. He has dysentery, dirties himself, stinks.

Berezhinsky douses him with a bucket of cold water. "It's no secret why Jews won't eat pig. You're blood brothers and both live on shit."

He sits on the grass under a leafy tree. The fields are full of flowers. He talks to himself not to forget. Some things he remembers astonish him. Are they memories or thoughts of things he had hoped to do? He is shrouded in thick clouds of yellow fog. Sometimes in painful stretches of light. Memories thin out and fall away. Events of the past he has difficulty recalling. He remembers having gone mad once. Where do you look if you lose your mind? That's the end of it. He would, in his mind, be forever locked in prison, no longer knowing why or what he is locked in. Locked in his final fate, the last unknowing.

"Die," says Berezhinsky. "For Christ's sake, die."

He dies. He dies.

Kogin says he has received a letter that his son is dead. He has drowned himself in a river in Irkutsk on the way to Novorosiisk.

3

"Remove your cap," said the warden, standing in his cell.

He removed his cap, and the warden handed him a sheaf of papers.

"It's your indictment, Bok, but that doesn't mean your trial is necessarily on its way."

Afterwards, crouched on his stool in chains, Yakov very slowly read the papers. His heart raced as he read but the mind ran ahead of the heart; this Jew they were talking about had committed a terrible crime and then stepped into a trap, and at once the prisoner saw him dead and buried in a thin grave. Sometimes the words on the paper grew blurred and disappeared under water. When they rose to the surface he read them one by one, saying each aloud. After reading three pages he hadn't the strength to concentrate longer. The papers weighed like oakwood and he had to put them down. Soon, though the barred window was still lit, it was too dark to read. At night he awoke famished to devour the words. He thought of begging Kogin for a candle but had visions of the paper catching fire and burning. So he waited for morning, once dreaming he was trying to read the indictment but the language was Turkish. Then he awoke and frantically felt for the papers. They were in his greatcoat pocket. He waited impatiently for daylight. In the morning, when there was enough light the fixer avidly read through the whole document. It seemed to him that the story had changed from how he read it yesterday, but then he realized it had changed from how he knew it as he had pieced it together from the questions he had been asked, and the accusations that had been made. The crime was the same but there were details that he had not heard before, some fantastic ones; and some of the old ones had been altered and a new mystery created. Yakov read, straining to find a combination of facts that would make them, by virtue of this arrangement, truer than they were when he first heard them; or as though, if he comprehended them in some way others did not, he would at once establish his innocence. And once he established it they would have to release him from his chains and open the prison doors.

This "Court Indictment," typed on long sheets of blue paper, retold the murder of Zhenia Golov, much as Yakov knew it, but now the number of wounds was unaccountably forty-five, "3 groups of 13, plus 2 additional groups of 3." There were wounds, the paper said, on the boy's chest, throat, face, and skull—"around the ears"; and the autopsy performed by

Professor M. Zagreb of the Medical Faculty of Kiev University, indicated that all the wounds had been inflicted on the body when the boy's heart was still strong. "But those in the principal veins of the neck had been inflicted when the heart was weakening."

On the day the boy was found murdered in the cave, his mother, when she heard the news, fainted. This had been noted on the police record of the case. Then came some details Yakov read quickly but had to go back and read slowly. The collapse of Marfa Golov, the indictment said, "was noted here with particular interest" because it was later observed that she was composed at the funeral and did not weep at her son's burial, although others, "mere strangers," had wept without restraint. Some "well-meaning spectators" and others "perhaps not so well-meaning," were disturbed by this, and "foolish rumors" began at once to circulate "concerning the possible involvement of this good woman, through a former and seriously incapacitated friend, in the murder of her own child." Because of this baseless rumor, but in the interests of arriving at the truth, she was arrested and thoroughly investigated by the police. They searched her house more than once and found "nothing in the least incriminating." Thus, after days of painstaking investigation she was released with the apologies of the police and other officials. The Chief of Police concluded that the rumors previously referred to were false and unfounded, "probably the invention of the enemies of Marfa Golov, or possibly of certain sinister forces," for Marfa Golov was a devoted mother, "blameless of any crime against her child." Such suspicion was contemptible. Her composed behavior at her son's funeral was the "behavior of a dignified person in control of her sentiments although involved in a profound personal loss." For "not all who are sad, weep" and "guilt is not a matter of facial expression but of evidence." "How much this unfortunate woman had mourned and endured *prior* to the child's funeral no one had inquired." However, witnesses had testified that Marfa Golov had been a more than ordinarily conscientious mother, and a "hardworking virtuous woman of unstained character, who without any assistance to speak of, had provided for her child since the desertion and death of the irresponsible father." It was therefore concluded that the attempts to destroy her reputation were "the work of unknown subversive alien groups" for the purpose of "concealing the guilt of one of its members, the true murderer of Zhenia Golov, the jack-of-all-trades, Yakov Bok."

"Vey is mir," said Yakov.

The fixer had been suspected from the beginning. Even before the funeral, rumors had begun to fly through the city that "the real culprit responsible for the murder of the boy was a member of the Hebrew faith." Then came a summary of reasons why Bok had come to the attention of the police "as a suspicious person": First, because it had come out he was a Hebrew using a false name and living in the Lukianovsky District, a district forbidden by special law to all members of his faith except Merchants of the First Guild and some professionals. Second, while representing himself as a Russian, one Yakov Ivanovitch Dologushev, this same Yakov Bok had made improper advances, and even attempted physical assault of Zinaida Nikolaevna, the daughter of Bok's employer, Nikolai Maximovitch Lebedev. "By good fortune she thwarted his nefarious purposes." Third, Yakov Bok was suspected by certain of his fellow employees at the brickworks, in particular "the observant foreman Proshko," of systematically peculating from funds belonging to the business enterprise of Nikolai Maximovitch Lebedev. Fourth, he was seen on certain occasions by the yardkeeper Skobeliev, the foreman Proshko, and "other witnesses," chasing boys in the brickyard, near the kilns. These were Vasya Shiskovsky, Andrei Khototov, the deceased Zhenia Golov, and other even younger children, all of them boys. And fifth, Zhenia Golov had one night been pursued among the tombstones in the cemetery close to the brickyard by the same Yakov Bok "clasping in his hand a long thin carpenter's knife." The frightened boy had related this to his mother. In Bok's living quarters in the stable the police had unearthed his bag of tools, which included "certain bloodstained awls and knives." Some bloody rags also were recovered in this room.

The fixer sighed and went on reading.

"In addition to the above-listed evidence, Marfa Golov has testified that Zhenia complained Yakov Bok had interfered with him sexually and had feared the boy would expose him to the authorities." "Zhenia, a bright and perceptive lad," had "on certain occasions" followed Bok and discovered that he sometimes met "with a group of other Hebrews, suspected smugglers, housebreakers, and other criminal elements, in the cellar of the synagogue." Her son, according to the mother, threatened to report these illegal activities to the police. Furthermore, Vasya Shiskovsky and Zhenia Golov had once or twice "in the manner of boys," angered Bok by flinging rocks at him and taunting him about his race, and he was determined to take revenge on them. "Zhenia Golov, to his great misfortune, was the one who had fallen into Bok's evil hands, but by great good luck Vasya Shiskovsky had escaped his poor friend's fate."

He read quickly through the section where he had killed the boy. ("Skobeliev testified that he had seen Bok carrying something heavy in his arms, a large squirming package of some sort that resembled a human body, up the stairs to his quarters. There, the evidence is clear, the boy was tortured and then murdered by Yakov Bok, probably with the assistance of one or two of his co-religionists.") "While in prison," the indictment went on, "the said Yakov Bok had attempted to influence the counterfeiter Gronfein, a friend and fellow religionist, to bribe Marfa Golov not to testify against him. The sum of money for that purpose was to be raised by subscription in the Hebrew communities of the Jewish Pale of Settlement. Another bribe was offered to Marfa Golov herself at a later date, the large sum of 40,000 rubles if she would flee across the Austrian border, but she indignantly refused."

The last paragraph read: "It is therefore the fully considered opinion of the Investigating Magistrate, the Prosecuting Attorney, and the President of the Superior Court of the Kiev Province, where the Court Indictment is this day filed, that Yakov Bok, an admitted Hebrew, had with premeditation, and for purposes of torture and murder, stabbed to death Yevgeny Golov, age 12, the beloved son of Marfa Vladimirovna Golov, for the reasons stated above; in sum, an overweening and abnormal desire for revenge against an innocent child who had discovered his participation in criminal activities. However, the crime was so wicked and debased that an additional element may be said to have been present. Only a criminal of the worst sadistic instincts could have engaged in such an unnatural act of unprovoked hostility and degraded bestiality."

The indictment was signed by Yefim Balik, Investigating Magistrate; V. G. Grubeshov, Prosecuting Attorney; and P. F. Furmanov, President of the Superior Court.

Yakov squeezed his throbbing head after reading the papers. Though his eyes ached—he felt as though he had read the words through sand and glue—he at once reread them, and again, in increasing astonishment and disbelief. What had happened to the charge of ritual murder? Holding each sheet up for better light he searched it in vain. There was no such charge. Every reference to a religious crime, though hinted at, led up to, had in the end been omitted. The Jews had become Hebrews. Why? The only reason he could think of was that they could not prove a charge of ritual murder. And if they couldn't prove that, what could they prove? Not these stupid lies, vile, ridiculous, some snipped directly out of Marfa's insane letter. They can't prove a thing, he thought, that's why they've kept me in solitary imprisonment for almost two years. They know the mother and her lover murdered the boy. He fought a deepening depression. With this "evidence" they'll never bring me to trial. The weakness of the indictment showed they had no intention to.

Still it was an indictment and he was wondering if they would now let him see a lawyer, when the warden appeared again in the cell and ordered him to hand over the papers.

"You may not believe this, Bok, but they were issued through an administrative error. I was supposed to look them over but not give them to you."

They're afraid of the trial, the fixer thought bitterly, after the warden had left. Maybe people are asking when it will begin. Maybe this has them worried. If I live, sooner or later they'll have to bring me to trial. If not Nicholas the Second, then Nicholas the Third will.

4

When his chains were unlocked and he was permitted to lie on his bed-bench as long as he liked with his legs free, or to walk around, he could not comprehend what had happened and for a while suffered from excitement. Yakov limped around the cell but mostly lay, breathing through his mouth, on the wooden bed. "Is it another indictment, or maybe is the trial coming?" he asked Berezhinsky, but the guard wouldn't say. One day the fixer's hair was trimmed a bit and the beard combed. The barber, glancing stealthily at a yellowed photograph in his tunic pocket, combed out curls over his ears. He was then given another suit of prison clothes, permitted to wash his hands and face with soap, and called to the warden's office.

Berezhinsky pushed him out into the hall and commanded him to move along, but the prisoner limped slowly, stopping often to recover his breath. The guard prodded him with his rifle butt, then the fixer ran a step and limped two. He worried how he would make it back to the cell.

"Your wife is here," said Warden Grizitskoy, in his office. "You can see her in the visitors' room. There'll be a guard present, so don't presume any privileges."

He felt, in towering astonishment, this could not be true, they were deceiving him to extend the torture. And when, as he watched the warden and guard, he believed it, the fixer gasped as though fire had scorched his lungs. When he could breathe he was frightened.

"My wife?"

"Raisl Bok?"

"It's true."

"You'll be allowed to speak to her for several minutes in the visitors' room, but watch your step."

"Please, not now," said Yakov wearily. "Some other time."

"That'll do," said the warden.

The fixer, shaken, upset, his thoughts in turmoil, was led in a limping trot by Berezhinsky through a series of narrow corridors to the prisoners' pen in the visitors' room. At the door Yakov tried to straighten himself, entered, and was locked in. It's a trick, he thought, it's not her, it's a spy. I must be careful.

She sat on a bench, separated from him by a heavy wire grating. On the far side of the bare-walled boxlike room, a uniformed guard stood behind her, his rifle resting against the wall, slowly rolling a cigarette.

Yakov sat stiffly opposite her, hunched cold, his throat aching, palms clammy. He felt a dread of cracking up, going mad in front of her—of will failing him once they talked and how would he go on after that?

"Get along with your business," said the guard in Russian.

Though the visitors' room was dimly lit it was brighter than his cell, and the light hurt his eyes before he could get used to it. The woman sat motionless, her coat threadbare, a wool shawl covering her head, her fingers clasped like spikes in her lap. She was watching him mutely, eyes stricken. He had expected a hag, but though she was worn, tensely embarrassed, and had abandoned the wig she had never liked to wear, she looked otherwise the same, surprising how young though he knew she was thirty, and not bad as a woman. It's at my expense, he thought bitterly.

"Yakov?"

"Raisl?"

"Yes."

As she unwound her shawl—her own dark hair cut short, the hairline damp—and he looked fully into her face, at the long exposed neck, both eyes sad, she was staring at him with fright and feeling. He tried twice to speak and could not. His face ached and mouth trembled.

"I know, Yakov," Raisl said. "What more can I say? I know."

Emotion blinded him.

My God, what have I forgotten? I've forgotten nothing. He experienced a depth of loss and shame, overwhelming—that the feelings of the past could still be alive after so long and terrible an imprisonment. The deepest wounds never die.

"Yakov, is it really you?"

He shook away the beginning of tears and turned his good ear to her.

"It's me. Who else could it be?"

"How strange you look in earlocks and long beard."

"That's their evidence against me."

"How thin you are, how withered."

"I'm thin," he said, "I'm withered. What do you want from me?"

"They forbade me to ask you any questions about your conditions in this prison," Raisl said in Yiddish, "and I promised not to but who has to ask? I have eyes and can see. I wish I couldn't. Oh, Yakov, what have they done to you? What did you do to yourself? How did such a terrible thing happen?"

"You stinking whore, what did *you* do to me? It wasn't enough we were poor as dirt and childless. On top of that you had to be a whore."

She said tonelessly, "It's not what I alone did, it's what we did to each other. Did you love me? Did I love you? I say yes and I say no. As for being a whore, if I was I'm not. I've had my ups and downs, the same as you, Yakov, but if you're going to judge me you'll have to judge me as I am."

"What are you?"

"Whatever I am I'm not what I was."

"Why did you marry me for I'd like to know? 'Love,' she says. If you didn't love me why didn't you leave me alone?"

"You can believe me I was afraid to marry you, but you were affectionate then, and when a person is lonely it's easy to lean toward a tender word. Also I thought you loved me although you found it hard to say so."

"What can a man say if he's afraid of a trap? I was afraid of you. I never met anybody so dissatisfied. I am a limited man. What could I promise you? Besides that, your father was behind me, pushing with both hands: If I married you the world would change, every day a rainbow. Then you got me in the woods that day."

"We were to the woods more than once. You wanted what I wanted. It takes two to lie down, one on top of the other."

"So we got married," he said bitterly. "Still, we had a chance. Once we were married you should have been faithful. A contract is a contract. A wife is a wife. Married is married."

"Were you such a fine husband?" Raisl said. "Yes, you always tried to make a living, I won't say no, though you never did. And if you wanted to stay up all night reading Spinoza I had nothing against that either, though it wasn't Torah, except when it was at my expense, and you know what I mean. What bothered me most were the curses and dirty names. Because I slept with you before we were married you were convinced I was sleeping with the world. I slept with no one but you until you stopped sleeping with me. At twenty-eight I was too young for the grave. So, as you advised, I stopped being superstitious and at last took a chance. Otherwise I would soon have been dead. I was barren. I ran in every direction. I flung myself against trees. I tore at my dry breasts and cursed my empty womb. Whether I stayed or left I was useless to you, so I decided to leave. You wouldn't so I had to. I left in desperation to change my life. I got out the only way I could. It was either that or death, one sin or worse. I chose the lesser sin. If you want to know the truth, Yakov, one reason I left was to make you move. Whoever thought it would come to this?"

She cracked her white knuckles against her chest. "Yakov, I didn't come here to fight about the past. Forgive me, forgive the past."

"Why did you come?"

"Papa said he saw you in prison, it's all he talks about. I went back to the shtetl last November. I was first in Kharkov, then in Moscow, but couldn't get along any more, so I had to go back. When I found out you were in Kiev Prison I came to see you but they wouldn't let me in. Then I went to the Prosecuting Attorney and showed him the papers that I was your wife. He said I couldn't see you except under the most extraordinary circumstances, and I said the circumstances were extraordinary enough when an innocent man is kept in prison. I went to see him at least five times and finally he said he would let me in if I brought you a paper to sign. He told me to urge you to sign it."

"A black year on his papers to sign. A black year on you for bringing it."

"Yakov, if you sign you can go free tomorrow. It's at least something to think about."

"I've thought," he shouted. "It's nothing to think about. I'm innocent."

Raisl stared at him mutely.

The guard came over with his rifle. "Nobody's supposed to be talking Yiddish here," he said. "You're supposed to be talking Russian. This prison is a Russian institution."

"It takes longer in Russian," she said. "I speak very slowly in Russian."

"Hurry up with the paper you're supposed to give him."

"The paper has to be explained. There are advantages but there are also disadvantages. I have to tell him what the Prosecuting Attorney said."

"Then tell him, for Christ's sake, and be done with it."

Taking a small key out of his pants pocket, he unlocked a small wire door in the grating.

"Don't try to pass anything but the paper he has to sign or it'll go hard on you both. I've got my eyes wide open."

Raisl unclasped a grayed cloth handbag and took out a folded envelope.

"This is the paper I promised I would give you," she said in Russian to Yakov. "The Prosecuting Attorney says it's your last chance."

"So that's why you came," he said in vehement Yiddish, "to get me to confess lies I've resisted for two years. To betray me again."

"It was the only way I could get in," Raisl said. "But it's not why I came, I came to cry." She gasped a little. Her mouth fell open, the lips contorted; she wept. Tears flowed through her fingers as she pressed them to her eyes. Her shoulders shook.

He felt, as he watched her, the weight of the blood in his heart.

The guard rolled another cigarette, lit it, and smoked slowly.

This is where we left off, thought Yakov. The last time I saw her she was crying like this, and here she is still crying. In the meantime I've been two years in prison without cause, in solitary confinement, and chains. I've suffered freezing cold, filth, lice, the degradation of those searches, and she's still crying.

"What are you crying for?" he asked.

"For you, for me, for the world."

She was as she wept, a frail woman, lanky, small-breasted, worn and sad. Who would have thought so frail? As she wept she moved him. He had learned about tears.

"What's there to do here but think, so I've thought," Yakov said after a while. "I've thought about our life from beginning to end and I can't blame you for more than I blame myself. If you give little you get less, though of some things I got more than I deserved. Also, it takes me a long time to learn. Some people have to make the same mistake seven times before they know they've made it. That's my type and I'm sorry. I'm also sorry I stopped sleeping with you. I was out to stab myself, so I stabbed you. Who else was so close to me? Still I've suffered in this prison and I'm not the same man I once was. What more can I say, Raisl? If I had my life to live over, you'd have less to cry about, so stop crying."

"Yakov," she said, when she had wiped her eyes with her fingers, "I brought this confession paper here so they would let me talk to you, not because I want you to sign it. I don't. Still, if you wanted to what could I say? Should I say stay in prison? What I also came to tell you is maybe not such good news. I came to say I've given birth to a child. After I ran away I found out I was pregnant. I was ashamed and frightened, but at the same time I was happy I was no longer barren and could have a baby."

There's no bottom to my bitterness, he thought.

He flailed at the wooden walls of the pen with both fists. The guard sternly ordered him to stop, so he beat himself instead, his face and head. She looked on with shut eyes.

Afterwards, when it was over, except what was left of his anguish, he said, "So if you weren't barren, what was the matter?"

She looked away, then at him. "Who knows? Some women conceive late. With conception you need luck."

Luck I was short of, he thought, so I blamed her.

"Boy or girl?" Yakov asked.

She smiled at her hands. "A boy, Chaiml, after my grandfather."

"How old now?"

"Almost a year and a half."

"It couldn't be mine?"

"How could it be?"

"Too bad," he sighed. "Where is he now?"

"With Papa. That's why I went back, I couldn't take care of him alone any more. Ah, Yakov, it's not all raisins and almonds. I've gone back to the shtetl but they blame me for your fate. I tried to take up my little dairy business but I might just as well be selling pork. The rabbi calls me to my face, pariah. The child will think his name is bastard."

"So what do you want from me?"

"Yakov," she said, "I'm sorry for what you're suffering. When I heard it was you I tore my hair; but I figured you'd also be sorry for me. Please, it might make things easier if you wouldn't mind saying you are my son's father. Still, if you can't you can't. I don't want to add to your burdens."

"Who's the father, some goy I'll bet."

"If it makes you feel better he was a Jew, a musician. He came, he went, I forgot him. He fathered the child but he's not his father. Whoever acts the father is the father. My father's the father but he's only two steps from death's door. One knock and I'm twice widowed."

"What's the matter with him?"

"Diabetes, though he drags himself around. He worries about you, he worries about me and the child. He wakes up cursing himself for not having been born rich. He prays every time he thinks of it. I take care of him the best I can. He sleeps on a bag of rags pushed to the wall. He needs food, rest, medicine. The little we get comes from charity. One or two of the rich send their servants over with this or that, but when they see me they hold their noses."

"Has he talked to anybody about me?"

"To everybody. He runs everywhere, sick as he is."

"What do they say?"

"They tear their hair. They beat their chests. They thank God it wasn't them. Some collect money. Some say they will make protests. Some are afraid to do anything because it may annoy the Christians and make things worse. Some are pessimistic but a few have hope. Still, there's more going on than I know."

"If it doesn't go faster I won't be here to find out what."

"Don't say that, Yakov. I went myself to see some lawyers in Kiev. Two of them swear they will help you but nobody can move without an indictment."

"So I'll wait," said Yakov. Before her eyes he shrank in size.

"I've brought you some hallah and cheese and an apple in a little pack," Raisl said, "but they made me leave it at the warden's office. Don't forget to ask for it. It's goat's cheese but I don't think you'll notice."

"Thanks," said Yakov wearily. He said, after a sigh, "Listen, Raisl, I'll write you a paper that the child's mine."

Her eyes glistened. "God will bless you."

"Never mind God. Have you got a piece of paper, I'll write something down. Show it to the rabbi's father, the old melamed. He knows my handwriting and he's a kinder man than his son."

"I have paper and pencil," she whispered nervously, "but I'm afraid to give them to you with this guard in the room. They warned me not to hand you anything but the confession and to take nothing but that from you or they would arrest me for attempting to help you escape."

The guard was restless and again came forward. "There's nothing more to talk about. Either sign the paper or go back to your cell."

"Have you got a pencil?" the fixer asked.

The guard took a fat fountain pen from his tunic pocket, and gave it to him through the opening in the grating.

He stayed to watch but Yakov waited until he had withdrawn.

"Give me the confession," he said to Raisl in Russian.

Raisl handed him the envelope. Yakov removed the paper, unfolded it, and read: "I, Yakov Bok, confess that I witnessed the murder of Zhenia Golov, the son of Marfa Golov, by my Jewish compatriots. They killed him on the night of March 20, 1911, upstairs in the stable in the brickyard belonging to Nikolai Maximovitch Lebedev, merchant of the Lukianovsky District."

Under that a heavy line was drawn on which to sign his name.

Yakov placed the paper on the shelf before him and wrote in Russian on the line for his name: "Every word is a lie."

On the envelope, pausing between words to remember the letters for the next, he wrote in Yiddish, "I declare myself to be the father of Chaim, the infant son of my wife, Raisl Bok. He was conceived before she left me. Please help the mother and child, and for this, amid all my troubles, I'll be grateful. Yakov Bok."

She told him the date and he wrote it down, "February 27, 1913." Yakov passed it to her through the opening in the grating.

Raisl slipped the envelope into her coat sleeve and handed the guard the confession paper. He folded it at once, and thrust it into his tunic pocket. After examining the contents of Raisl's handbag and tapping her coat pockets he told her to go.

"Yakov," she wept, "come home."

IX

He was chained to the wall again. Things went badly. Better not have been unchained, the getting back was so bad. He beat the clanking chains against the wall until it was scarred white where he stood. They let him beat the wall. Otherwise he slept. But for the searches he would have slept through the day. He slept the sleep of the dead with his feet in stocks. He slept through the end of winter and into spring. Kogin said it was April. Two years. The searches went on except when he was sick with dysentery. The Deputy Warden did not come near him then, though Berezhinsky sometimes searched him alone. Once after the fixer was sick the cell was hosed down and a fire started in the stove. An old pink-faced man came into the cell dressed in winter clothes. He wore a black cape and black gaiters and grasped a gnarled cane. Berezhinsky followed him in, carrying a slender chair with a delicate back, and the old man sat in it erectly, several feet from the fixer, holding the cane with gray-mittened hands. His watery eyes wandered. He told Yakov he was a former jurist of high repute, and that he came with good news. An excitement so thick it felt like sickness surged through the fixer. He asked what good news. The former jurist said this was the year of the three-hundredth anniversary of the rule of the House of Romanov and that the Tsar, in celebration, would issue a ukase amnestying certain classes of criminals. Yakov's name would be listed among them. He was to be pardoned and permitted to return to his village. The old man's face flushed with pleasure. The prisoner clung to the wall, too burdened to speak. Then he asked, Pardoned as a criminal or pardoned as innocent? The former jurist testily said what difference did it make so long as he was let out of prison. It was impossible to erase the sins of the past, but it was not impossible for a humane ruler, a Christian gentleman, to forgive an evil act. The old man sneezed without snuff and peered at his silver watch. Yakov said he wanted a fair trial, not a pardon. If they ordered him to leave the prison without a trial they would have to shoot him first. Don't be foolish, said the former jurist, how can you go on suffering like this, caked in filth? The fixer moved his chains restlessly. I have no choice, he said. I have just offered you one. That's not choice, said Yakov. The former jurist tried to convince the prisoner, then gave up in irritation. It's easier to reason with a peasant. He rose and shook his cane at the fixer. How can we help you, he shouted, if you are so pigheaded? Berezhinsky, who had been listening at the spy hole, opened the door and the old man left the cell. The guard came in for the chair but before taking it, he let Yakov urinate in the can, then dumped the contents on his head. The fixer was left in chains that night. He thought that whenever he had been through the worst, there was always worse.

One day, during Yakov's third summer in prison, his manacles and shackles were unlocked. Immediately his heart beat heavily and when he touched it with his hand the hand beat like his heart. In an hour the warden, who had aged since the fixer had last seen him and walked with shorter steps, brought in a new indictment in a brown envelope, a sheaf of papers twice thicker than the last. The fixer took the papers and read them slowly and frantically, fearing he would never get to the end of them; but he had discovered at once what he had expected: that the blood murder charge had been violently revived. Now they are serious again, he thought. The reference to sexual experiences with the boy, and to activities with a gang of Jewish housebreakers and smugglers operating out of the cellar of the Kiev synagogue—all the insane lies from Marfa Golov's letter—were omitted. Once again Yakov Bok was accused of murdering the innocent boy in order to drain his body of blood necessary for the baking of Passover matzos and cakes.

This was affirmed by Professor Manilius Zagreb, who with his distinguished colleague, the surgeon Dr. Sergei Bul, had twice performed the autopsy of Zhenia's remains. Both categorically stated that the vicious wounds had been inflicted in prearranged clusters with a time interval between each cluster in order to prolong the torture and facilitate the bleeding. It was estimated that one litre of blood was collected from each set of wounds, and that a total of five litres of blood was collected in bottles. Such was also the conclusion of Father Anastasy, the well-known specialist in Jewish affairs, who had made a close study of the Talmud, his reasons given in minute detail for eight single-spaced pages. And it was also the conclusion of Yefim Balik, the Investigating Magistrate. He had carefully reviewed the entire evidence and agreed with its "direction and findings."

How the bloodthirsty crime was committed was described in this indictment much as it had been by Grubeshov at the cave, more than two years ago, "with careful note taken of the fanatic Hasidic tzadik, seen in the brickyard by the foreman Proshko; who had no doubt helped the accused drain the necessary blood from the boy's still living body, and also assisted him in transporting the corpse to the cave where two horrified boys had found it." And related evidence omitted from the previous indictment was included in this. It was stated that half a bag of matzo flour was "hidden away" in Yakov Bok's stable room, together with certain hard pieces of already baked matzo no doubt containing the innocent blood, which both the Jews "in all probability" had eaten. And the usual bloodstained rag, "admitted by the accused to be a piece of his shirt," had been uncovered in the same room. According to the testimony of Vasya Shiskovsky, a bottle of bright-red blood was seen by him and Zhenia on a table in Bok's stable room, but it had disappeared when the police searched for it. And a sack of carpenter's tools containing bloodstained awls and knives had been found in the same room after the fixer's arrest, "despite a plot later carried out by Jewish co-conspirators to destroy this and other significant evidence by burning down the brickyard stable, a plot which they ultimately achieved."

Towards the end of this wearying, terrifying document a new subject was introduced, "the matter of Yakov Bok's self-proclaimed atheism." It was noted that although the accused, when first examined by the authorities, had confessed he was a Jew "by birth and nationality," he had however claimed for himself "an atheistic status; to wit, that he was a freethinker and not a religious Jew." Why he should make "such an odious self-description" was understandable to anyone who reflected for a moment on the matter. It was done to create "extenuating circumstances" and "obfuscating details" in order "to deflect the legal investigation by hiding the motive for this dastardly crime." However this assertion of atheism could not be defended, for it was observed by reliable witnesses, including prison guards and officials, that Yakov Bok, while incarcerated and awaiting trial, "though persisting in his false claim of irreligion, had in his cell secretly prayed daily in the manner of Orthodox Jews, wrapped in a prayer shawl, with black phylacteries entwined around his brow and left arm." He was also seen piously reading an Old Testament Bible, "which, like the previously mentioned Orthodox religious instruments, had been smuggled into his cell by fellow Jews of the synagogue." It was clear to all who observed him that he was engaged in the performance of a devout religious rite. He had continued to use the prayer shawl until he had worn it out, and "even now he kept a remnant of this sacred garment in his coat pocket."

It was the opinion of investigators and other officials that this self-incriminating atheism "was a fabrication of Yakov Bok's, in order to hide from the legal authorities that he had committed a vile religious murder of a child for the sole and evil purpose of providing his Hasidic compatriots with the uncorrupted human blood needed to bake the Passover matzos and unleavened cakes."

After he had finished reading the document the fixer, in exhaustion, thought, There's no getting rid of the blood any more. It's stained every word of the indictment and can't be washed out. When they try me it will be for the crucifixion.

The fixer grew more intensely worried. Now that he had this paper would they withdraw it and later issue another? Was this the newest torture? Would they hand him indictments, time after time, for the next twenty years? He would read them till he died of frustration or his dry brain exploded? Or would they, after this indictment, or the third, seventh, or thirteenth *at last* bring him to trial? Could they make a strong enough circumstantial case against him? He hoped they could. Anyway, just barely. If not, would they keep him in chains forever? Or were they planning a worse fate? One day as he was about to clean himself with a scrap of newspaper he read on it, "THE

JEW IS DOOMED." Yakov frantically read on to find out why, but that part was torn off.

2

He had been told a lawyer was on his way to the prison, but when the cell door was opened on a hot July night, it was not the lawyer, it was Grubeshov, in evening dress. The fixer awoke when Kogin, holding a dripping candle, unlocked his feet. "Wake up," said the guard, shaking him, "his honor is here." Yakov awoke as though coming up out of deep dirty water. He beheld Grubeshov's moist fleshy face, his sidewhiskers limp, his redshot eyes, lit, restless. The public prosecutor's chest rose and fell. He began pacing in the cell, unsteadily, then sat down on the stool, one hand on the table, an enormous shadow on the wall behind him. He stared for a moment at the lamp, blinked at it, and gazed at Yakov. When he talked, the stink of rich food and alcohol on his breath drifted across to the fixer, nauseating him.

"I am on my way home from a civic banquet in honor of the Tsar," Grubeshov, breathing with a whistle, said to the prisoner. "Since my motorcar happened to be in this district, I ordered the driver to go on to the prison. I thought I would speak to you. You are a stubborn man, Bok, but perhaps not yet beyond reason. I thought I would talk to you one last time. Please stand up while I am speaking."

Yakov, sitting on the wooden bed with his bony bare feet on the clammy floor, slowly got up. Grubeshov, gazing at his face, shuddered. The fixer felt a violent hatred of him.

"First of all," said Grubeshov, patting the back of his flushed neck with a large humid handkerchief, "you oughtn't to let your expectations rise too high, Yakov Bok. You will be disappointed if they do. Don't think just because an indictment has been issued that your worries are over. On the contrary—now begin your worst troubles. I warn you, you will be publicly unmasked and seen for what you are."

"What do you want from me here, Mr. Grubeshov? It's late at night. I need my little rest for the chains in the morning."

"As for the chains, that's your fault; learn to follow orders. It's none of my affair, I came on other business. Marfa Golov, the victim's mother, visited me in my office today. She knelt before me with holy tears streaming from her eyes, and swore before God that she had told the absolute truth regarding Zhenia and his experiences with you that led to the murder. She is a totally sincere woman and I was deeply affected by her. I am more than ever convinced that a jury will believe what she says, and so much the worse for you. Her testimony and the sincerity of her appearance will demolish whatever case you think you can make."

"Then let her give her testimony," Yakov said. "Why don't you begin the trial?"

Grubeshov, who squirmed on the stool as though it were the top of a hot stove, answered, "I have no intention of engaging in an argument with a criminal. I came to tell you that if you and your fellow Jews continue to press me to bring you to trial before I have gathered every last grain of evidence, or investigated all courses of action, then you ought to know what dangers you are creating for yourself. There can be too much of a good thing, Bok, if you understand my meaning. The kettle may steam but don't be surprised if the water is boiled off."

"Mr. Grubeshov," said Yakov, "I can't stand up any more. I'm tired and must sit down. If you want to shoot me call the guard, he has a gun."

Yakov sat down on the bedplank.

"You're a cheeky one," Grubeshov said, his voice emotional. "The Russian people are sick to their souls of your Jewish tricks and deceptions. That holds also for your investigators, your complaints, your libels from all over. What is happening, Bok, obviously reveals the underground involvement of the Jewish conspiracy in Russian affairs, and I warn you to take rational notice that there is bound to be a tumultuous reprisal against the enemies of the state. Even if by some trickery you were to succeed in swaying a jury to render a judgment against the weight of the true evidence, then you can believe me that the Russian people in justifiable wrath will avenge this poor Zhenia for the pain and torture that you inflicted on him. You may wish for the trial now, but remember this: even the judgment that you are guilty will set off a bloodbath in this city that will outdo the ferocity of the so-called Kishinev massacres.

A trial will not save you nor your fellow Jews. You would be better off confessing, and after a period of time when the public has settled down, we could announce your death in prison, or something of the sort, and spirit you out of Russia. If you insist on the trial, then don't be surprised if bearded heads roll in the street. Feathers fly. Cossack steel invades the tender flesh of young Jewesses."

Grubeshov had risen from the hot stool and was pacing again, his shadow going one way on the wall as he went the other.

"A government has to protect itself from subversion, by force if it can't persuade."

Yakov stared at his white crooked feet.

The public prosecutor, in the grip of his excitement, went on: "My father once described to me an incident involving a synagogue cellar full of Jews, men and women, who attempted to hide from the Cossacks during a raid on their village. The sergeant ordered them to come up one by one and at first none of them stirred, but then a few came up the steps holding their arms over their heads. This did do them not the least good as they were clubbed to death with rifle butts. The rest of them, though they were like herrings stuck together in a stinking barrel, would not move although they had been warned it would go worse with them. And so it did. The impatient Cossacks rushed into the cellar, bayoneting and shooting every last Jew. Those who were dragged out still alive were later thrown from speeding trains. A few, beginning with their benzine-soaked beards, were burned alive, and some of the women were dropped in their underclothes into wells to drown. You can take my word for it that in less than a week after your trial, there will be a quarter-million fewer Zhidy in the Pale."

He paused to breathe, then went on thickly. "Don't think we don't know that you wish to provoke just such a pogrom. We know from Secret Police reports that you are plotting to bring down on yourselves a violent reaction for revolutionary purposes—to stimulate active subversion among Socialist revolutionaries. The Tsar is informed of this, you can be sure, and is prepared to give you increased doses of the medicine I have described if you persist in trying to destroy his authority. I warn you, there is already a detachment of Ural Cossacks quartered in Kiev."

Yakov spat on the floor.

Either Grubeshov did not see or pretended he hadn't. Now, as though he had spent his anger, his voice became calm. "I am here to tell you this for your own good, Yakov Bok, and for the ultimate good of your fellow Jews. It's all I will say now, absolutely all. I leave the rest to your contemplation and judgment. Have you any suggestions on how to forestall such an appalling, catastrophic—and I say frankly—useless tragedy? I appeal to your humanitarian impulses. One can imagine all sorts of compromises a person in your situation might be willing to make to tip the balance against disaster. I'm very serious. Have you something to say? If so, speak up."

"Mr. Grubeshov, bring me to trial. I will wait for the trial, even to my death."

"And death is what you will get. It's on your head, Bok."

"On yours," said Yakov. "And for what you did to Bibikov."

Grubeshov stared at the fixer with white eyes. The shadow of a huge bird flew off the wall. The lamps went out and the cell door clanged.

Kogin, in a foul mood, slammed the stocks on the fixer's feet.

3

The lawyer had come and gone, Julius Ostrovsky.

He had appeared one day a few weeks after the Prosecuting Attorney's visit, whispered with the prisoner an hour, filling his ear with what was going on, some that the fixer already had guessed, much that astonished him. He was astonished that strangers knew more than he of the public cause of his suffering and that the complications were so fantastic and endless.

"Tell me the worst," Yakov had begged, "do you think I will ever get out of here?"

"The worst is that we don't know the worst," Ostrovsky had answered. "We know you didn't do it, the worst is they know it too but say you did. This is the worst."

"Do you know when my trial is coming—if ever?"

"What can I answer you? They won't tell us what's happening today, so what can we expect to find out about tomorrow? Tomorrow they also hide from us. They hide even the most basic facts. They're afraid that anything we might know is a Jewish trick. What else can you expect if you are fighting a deadly war and everybody pretends, who's fighting? It's peace. It's a war, believe me."

The lawyer had risen when Yakov had limped into the room. This time there was no screen separating the prisoner from his visitor. Ostrovsky had at once cautioned him with a gesture, then whispered in his ear, "Speak quietly—to the floor. They say there's no guard outside the door but speak as if Grubeshov stands there if not the devil."

He was past sixty, a stocky man with a lined face and baldish head from which a few gray hairs rose like stubble. He had bent legs, wore two-toned button shoes, a black cravat and a short beard.

He had, when the prisoner appeared, stared at Yakov as though unable to believe this was the one. Finally he believed and his eyes changed from surprise to concern. He spoke in intense whispered Yiddish with more than one emotion. "I will introduce myself, Mr. Bok, Julius Ostrovsky of the Kiev bar. I'm glad I'm here at last but don't cheer yet, it's a long way to go. Anyway, some friends sent me."

"I'm thankful."

"You have friends though not all Jews, I'm sorry to say, are your friends. What I mean is that if a man hides his head in a bucket, whose friend is he? To my great regret some of our people shiver in every weather. We have organized a committee to help you but their caution is excessive. They're afraid to 'meddle' or there'll be another calamity. That's in itself a calamity. They shoot with popguns and run from the noise. Still, who has all friends?"

"Then who are my friends?"

"I am one and there are others. Take my word, you're not alone."

"Can you do anything for me? I'm sick of prison."

"What we can do we'll do. It's a long fight, I don't have to tell you, and the odds are against us. Still, anyway, calm, calm, calm. As the sages say, there are always two possibilities. One we know from too long experience; the other—the miracle—we will hope for. It's easy to hope, it's the waiting that spoils it. But two possibilities make the odds even. So enough philosophy. At this minute there's not much good news; finally we squeezed out an indictment, which means they will now have to schedule the case for trial, though when I leave to Rashi. But first, if you'll excuse me, I'll give you the bad news." Ostrovsky sighed. "I'm sorry that your father-in-law, Shmuel Rabinovitch, who I had the pleasure to meet and talk to last summer—a gifted man—is now, I'm sorry to tell you, dead from diabetes. This your wife wrote me in a letter."

"Ah," said Yakov.

Death had preceded itself. Poor Shmuel, the fixer thought, now I'll never see him again. That's what happens when you say goodbye to a friend and ride out into the world.

He covered his face with his hands and wept.

"He was a good man, he tried to educate me."

"The thing about life is how fast it goes," Ostrovsky said.

"Faster than that."

"You suffer for us all," the lawyer said huskily. "I would be honored to be in your place."

"It's without honor," Yakov said, wiping his eyes with his fingers, and rubbing his hands together. "It's a dirty suffering."

"You've got my respect."

"If you don't mind tell me how my case stands. Tell me the truth."

"The truth is that things are bad though how bad I don't know myself. The case is clear enough—it's a bad joke from top to bottom—but it's mixed up in the worst way with the political situation. Kiev, you understand, is a medieval city full of wild superstition and mysticism. It has always been the heart of Russian reaction. The Black Hundreds, may they sink into their graves, have aroused against you the most ignorant and brutal of the masses. They are deathly afraid of Jews and at the same time frighten them to death. This reveals to you something about the human condition. Rich or poor, those of our brethren who can run out of here are running. Some who can't are already mourning. They sniff at the air and it stinks of pogrom. What's going on, as I say, nobody can say precisely. There's on the one hand a rumor that everything that happens, including your indictment, is another delay, and your trial, if you'll excuse me for saying it, will never take place; but on the other hand we hear it might start right after the Duma elections in September. Yes or no, they have no case against you. The civilized world knows this, including the Pope and his cardinals. If Grubeshov 'proves' anything it will be by the lies of 'the experts.' But we have our experts against them, for instance a Russian professor of theology, and I've written to Pavlov, the Tsar's surgeon, to testify on the medical report of the boy's autopsy and he hasn't said no yet. Grubeshov knows who the real murderers are but he shuts both eyes and stares at you. He went to law school with my oldest son and was famous for his socks and vests. Now he's famous for his anti-Semitic socks and vests. Out of Marfa Golov, that piece of trash, he tries to make if not a new saint, at least a persecuted heroine. Her blind lover tried last week to take his life but thank God, he's still alive. Also a clever journalist—may the Lord make more like him!—Pitirim Mirsky, discovered recently that Zhenia's father left him a life insurance legacy of five hundred rubles that the two murderers coveted, got, and at once spent. Two hogs, as they say, are worse than one. Mirsky printed this last week in *Poslednie Novosti*, and for that the publisher was fined and the press shut down by the police for three months. They must now discontinue all items about Golov. This is black reaction, but I'm not here to frighten you. You have enough to worry about."

"What else can frighten me?"

"If you feel bad think of Dreyfus. He went through the same thing with the script in French. We're persecuted in the most civilized languages."

"I've thought of him. It doesn't help."

"He was in prison many years, much longer than you."

"So far."

Ostrovsky, nodding absently as he gazed at the door, softened his whisper. "We also have an affidavit from Sofya Shiskovsky. One night she went into the toilet in Marfa's house to relieve herself, and there in the bathtub lay the naked corpse covered with wounds. So she screamed and ran out of the house. Marfa, who had gone for a minute upstairs to get a letter to prove a lie, ran after her and caught her in the street. That one—a madwoman of the First Guild—threatened to murder the whole Shiskovsky family if they breathed a word to anybody. They were afraid for Vasya, so they packed the furniture and moved out. When we finally located them, in a log hut in a back street in Moscow, she threatened to kill herself if we interfered with her, but with luck we got at least a short affidavit. She wouldn't let us question Vasya but we will try to have them both in court when the trial starts, if they aren't by that time in Asia. So this is another reason why the prosecution drags its feet: they can't prove a ritual murder but they won't stop trying, and the longer they take the more dangerous the situation becomes. It's dangerous because it's irrational, complex, secret. And it grows more dangerous as they get more desperate."

"Then what will I do?" said Yakov in despair. "How much more can I stand if I'm already half dead?"

"Patience, calm, calm, calm," Ostrovsky counseled, clasping his hands and squeezing. Then he looked at the fixer in a new light and struck his head with his palm.

"For God's sake, why are we standing yet? Come sit down. Forgive me, I'm blind in both eyes."

They sat then on a narrow bench in the far corner of the room away from the door, the lawyer still whispering. "Your case is tied up with the frustrations of recent Russian history. The Russo-Japanese War, I don't have to tell you, was a terrible disaster but it brought on the Revolution of 1905, which was coming anyway. 'War,' as Marx says, 'is the locomotive of history.' This was good for Russia but bad for the Jews. The government, as usual, blamed us for their troubles and not more than one day after the Tsar's concessions pogroms started simultaneously in three hundred towns. Of course you know this, what Jew doesn't?"

"Tell me anyway, what harm can it do?"

"The Tsar was frightened by the rising agitation—strikes, riots, assassinations. The country was paralyzed. After the Winter Palace massacre he reluctantly gave out a ukase promising the basic freedoms. He granted a Constitution, the Imperial Duma was established, and for a short time it looked—for Russia, you understand—like the beginning of a liberal period. The Jews cried hurray for the Tsar and wished him luck. Imagine, in the first Duma we had twelve deputies! Right away they brought up the question of equal rights for all and the abolition of the Pale of Settlement. Like a new world, no?"

"Yes, but go on."

"I'll go on but what can I say? In a sick country every step to health is an insult to those who live on its sickness. The imperial absolutists, the rightist elements, warned the Tsar his crown was slipping. He was already regretting the concessions and began to try to cancel them. In other words, for ten minutes he put on the lights and what he saw frightened him so much, since then he has been putting them out one by one so nobody will notice. As much as he could he changed back to an autocratic regime. The reactionary groups—the Union of Russian People, the Society of the Double-headed Eagle, the Union of the Archangel Michael—oppose worker and peasant movements, liberalism, socialism, any kind of reform, which also meant, naturally, the common enemy, the Jews. At the thought of a constitutional monarch their bones rattled. Organized together, they became the Black Hundreds, which means in gangs of a hundred for what disgusting purposes I don't have to tell you. They gnaw like rats to destroy the independence of the courts, the liberal press, the prestige of the Duma. To distract popular attention from the breaches of the Russian Constitution they incite nationalism against non-Orthodox Russians. They persecute every minority—Poles, Finns, Germans, us—but especially us. Popular discontent they divert into anti-Semitic outbreaks. It's a simple solution to their problems. Also they enjoy themselves because with the government's help they murder Jews and it's good for business."

"I'm only one man, what do they want from me?"

"One man is all they need so long as they can hold him up as an example of Jewish bloodthirst and criminality. To prove a point it's best to have a victim. In 1905 and 1906 thousands of innocent people were butchered, property damage in the millions of rubles. These pogroms were planned in the office of the Minister of Interior. We know that the anti-Jewish proclamations were printed on Police Department presses. And there are rumors that the Tsar himself contributes from the royal treasury for anti-Semitic books and pamphlets. We got all we need to frighten us but we're also frightened by rumors."

"By the wind," said Yakov.

"If you're frightened everything frightens you," Ostrovsky said. "Anyway, it's a long story but I'm making it short. Now I come direct to your door. When Premier Stolypin, no friend of ours, wanted, before the election of the second Duma, to throw a few bones to the Jews, a few little rights to stop their big complaints, the reactionaries ran to the Tsar and right away he changed the Electoral Laws, taking away the vote from a large part of the population to reduce Jewish and liberal representation in the Duma and cut down opposition to the government. We now have maybe three deputies for three and a half million Jews and these too they want to get rid of. A year ago they assassinated one right in the street. But now I come to you. An atmosphere of hysteria developed all over the country. Still, there was some progress, don't ask me how, and the Imperial Duma was once more discussing whether, yes or no, to abolish the Pale of Jewish Settlement when right at this minute, when the Black Hundreds were frantic, one day a Christian boy was found dead in a cave and there appeared on the scene, Yakov Bok."

The fixer sat numbed. He waited for Ostrovsky to spit, but the lawyer sighed deeply and went on talking. "Where you came from nobody knew, or who you were, but you came just in time. I understand you came on a horse. When they saw you they pounced, and that's why we're sitting here now. But don't feel too bad, if it weren't you there'd be another in your place."

"Yes," said Yakov. "Somebody like me. I've thought it all out."

"So that's your bag of history," Ostrovsky said.

"In that case, what difference does it make if my trial comes or it doesn't?"

Ostrovsky got up, tiptoed to the door and abruptly opened it. Then he returned to the bench. "No one there but this way they'll know we're alert to them. I told you the worst," he said as he sat down, "now I'll tell you the best: You have a chance. What kind of chance? A chance. A chance is a chance, it's better than no chance. Anyway, hear me out so I can stop talking. First of all, not every Russian is your enemy. God forbid. The intelligentsia is disturbed by this case. Many luminaries of literature, science, and the professions have objected against the blood ritual slander. Not so long ago the Kharkov Medical Society passed a resolution protesting your imprisonment, and the next thing that happened the society was dissolved by the government authorities. I told you already about *Poslednie Novosti*. Other newspapers have been fined for their probing articles and editorials. I know members of the bar who openly say that Marfa Golov and her lover committed the murder. Some say she wrote the original letter to the Black Hundreds, accusing the Jews of the crime. My theory is they came to her and asked her to write such a letter. Anyway, an opposition exists, which is good and it's bad. Where there's opposition to reaction there's also repression; but better repression than public sanction of injustice. So a chance you've got."

"Not more?"

"More. Freedom exists in the cracks of the state. Even in Russia a little justice can be found. It's a strange world. On the one hand we have the strictest autocracy; on the other we are approaching anarchy; in between courts exist and justice is possible. The law lives in the minds of men. If a judge is honest the law is protected. If that's the case, so are you. Also a jury is a jury—human beings—they could free you in five minutes."

"Should I hope?" said the fixer.

"If it doesn't hurt, hope. Still, since I'm telling the truth let me tell it all. Once we're on trial some witnesses will lie because they're frightened, and others because they're liars. Also you can expect that the Minister of Justice will appoint a presiding judge who is favorable to the prosecution. If the verdict is guilty his career will advance. And we also suspect that intellectuals and liberals will be eliminated from the jury lists and there's nothing we can do about it. With those that are left we will have to contend. So if you must hope, hope. I'm sure Grubeshov isn't confident of his case. What's more important he's not confident of himself. He's ambitious but limited. In the end he will need better evidence than he has now. The trouble with resting your case on experts is that there are other experts. So I come back to the jury. In our favor is that although they may be ignorant peasants and shopkeepers, simple folk, as a rule they have little love for state officials, and when it comes to facts they can smell when they stink. For instance they know that Jewish roosters don't lay eggs. If Grubeshov strains he will make serious mistakes and your lawyer will know how to take advantage of them. He's an outstanding man from Moscow, Suslov-Smirnov, a Ukrainian by birth."

"Not you?" said Yakov in astonishment. "You aren't my lawyer?"

"I was," said Ostrovsky with an apologetic smile, "but not any more. Now I'm a witness."

"What kind of witness?"

"They accuse me of attempting to bribe Marfa Golov not to testify against you. Of course she swears to it. I talked to her, naturally, but the accusation is ridiculous, it's to keep me from defending you. I don't know if you've heard my name before, Mr. Bok? Probably not," he sighed, "but I have a little reputation in criminal cases. Still I don't want you to worry. Suslov-Smirnov I would use myself if I were in your place. He will be chief of your defense. He was in his youth anti-Semitic but he has now become a vigorous defender of the rights of Jews."

Yakov groaned. "Who needs a former anti-Semite?"

"You can take my word," Ostrovsky said quickly. "He is a brilliant lawyer, and his conversion is sincere. Next time I come I will bring him to you. Believe me, he will know how to deal with these people."

He glanced at his ticking watch, tucked it into his vest pocket, then hurried to the door and opened it. A guard with a rifle was standing there. Without surprise the lawyer shut the door and returned to the prisoner.

"I will speak what's on my mind," he said in Russian. "I say this against my will, Mr. Bok, and with a heavy heart. You have suffered much and I don't want to add to your burdens, but the prosecution is desperate and this makes me fear for your life. If you should die, naturally an unproved case will help the government more than a verdict against them, no matter how much they are suspected of or criticized for your death. I think you know what I mean. So all I will say to you is be careful. Don't allow yourself to be provoked. Remember—patience, calm, you have a few friends."

Yakov said he wanted to live.

"Please," said Ostrovsky.

4

He was not, on his return to the cell, locked in chains. They had been torn out of the wall and the holes cemented. The fixer, all but weightless, sat on the edge of the wooden bed, his head in rarefied air, his body roaring with excitement. He listened to the noise for half an hour before he knew he was listening to his swarming clanking thoughts. Shmuel was dead, let him rest in peace. He had deserved better than he had got. A lawyer, Ostrovsky, had been to see him. He had spoken of the trial; there was a chance. Another lawyer, a reformed Ukrainian anti-Semite, would defend him in court before a prejudiced judge and ignorant jury. But that was all in the future, when, nobody could say. Now he was at least no longer anonymous to all but his prosecutors and jailers. He was not unknown. There had blown up from somewhere a public opinion. Not every Russian believed him guilty. The fog was thinning a little. Newspapers were printing articles casting doubt on the accusation. Some lawyers were openly blaming Marfa Golov. A doctors' society had protested his imprisonment. He had become—who would have thought it?—a public person. Yakov laughed and wept a little. It was fantastic to believe. He tried to be hopeful but was immersed in fears of all there was still to live through.

"Why me?" he asked himself for the ten thousandth time. Why did it have to happen to a poor, half-ignorant fixer? Who needed this kind of education? Education he would have been satisfied to get from books. Each time he answered his question he answered it differently. He saw it as part personal fate—his various shortcomings and mistakes—but also as force of circumstance, though how you separated one from the other—if one really could—was beyond him. Who, for instance, *had* to go find Nikolai Maximovitch lying drunk in the snow and drag him home to start off an endless series of miserable events? Was that the word of God, inexorable Necessity? Go find your fate—try first the fat Russian with his face in the snow. Go be kind to an anti-Semite and suffer for it. And from him to his daughter with the crippled leg was only one crippled step, and then another into the brickyard. And a crippled hop into prison. If he had stayed in the shtetl it would never have happened. At least not this. Something else would have happened, better not think what.

Once you leave you're out in the open; it rains and snows. It snows history, which means what happens to somebody starts in a web of events outside the personal. It starts of course before he gets there. We're all in history, that's sure, but some are more than others, Jews more than some. If it snows not everybody is out in it getting wet. He had been doused. He had to his painful surprise, stepped into history more deeply than others—it had worked out so. Why he would never know. Because he had taken to reading Spinoza? An idea makes you adventurous? Maybe, who knows? Anyway, if he hadn't been Yakov Bok, a born Jew, he would not have been, to start with, an outlaw in the Lukianovsky when they were looking for one; he would never have been arrested. They might still be looking. It was, you could say, history's doing, it was full of all sorts of barriers and limitations, as though certain doors had been boarded up in a house and to get out you had to jump out of a window. If you jumped you might land on your head. In history, thicker at times than at others, too much happens. Ostrovsky had explained this to him. If conditions were ripe whatever was likely to happen was waiting for you to come along so it could happen. With less history around you might walk by or through it: it looked like rain but the sun was shining. In the snow he had once come upon Nikolai Maximovitch Lebedev wearing his Black Hundreds button. Nobody lived in Eden any more.

Yet though his young mother and father had remained all their poor lives in the shtetl, the historical evil had galloped in to murder them there. So the "open," he thought, was anywhere. In or out, it was history that counted—the world's bad memory. It remembered the wrong things. So for a Jew it was the same wherever he went, he carried a remembered pack on his back—a condition of servitude, diminished opportunity, vulnerability. No, there was no need to go to Kiev, or Moscow, or any place else. You could stay in the shtetl and trade in air or beans, dance at weddings or funerals, spend your life in the synagogue, die in bed and pretend you had died in peace, but a Jew wasn't free. Because the government destroyed his freedom by reducing his worth. Therefore wherever he was or went and whatever happened was perilous. A door swung open at his approach. A hand reached forth and plucked him in by his Jewish beard—Yakov Bok, a freethinking Jew in a brick factory in Kiev, yet any Jew, any plausible Jew—to be the Tsar's adversary and victim; chosen to murder the corpse His Majesty had furnished free; to be imprisoned, starved, degraded, chained like an animal to a wall although he was innocent. Why? because no Jew was innocent in a corrupt state, the most visible sign of its corruption its fear and hatred of those it persecuted. Ostrovsky had reminded him that there was much more wrong with Russia than its anti-Semitism. Those who persecute the innocent were themselves never free. Instead of satisfying him this thought filled him with rage.

It had happened—he was back to this again—because he was Yakov Bok and had an extraordinary amount to learn. He had learned, it wasn't easy; the experience was his; it was worse than that, it was he. He was the experience. It also meant that now he was somebody else than he had been, who would have thought it? So I learned a little, he thought, I learned this but what good will it do me? Will it open the prison doors? Will it allow me to go out and take up my poor life again? Will it free me a little once I am free? Or have I only learned to know what my condition is—that the ocean is salty as you are drowning, and though you knew it you are drowned? Still, it was better than not knowing. A man had to learn, it was his nature.

Being without chains goaded impatience, what could he do with himself? Time began to move again, like a locomotive with two cars, three cars, four cars, a cluster of days, then two weeks gone, and to his horror, another season. It was autumn and he trembled at the thought of winter. The cold thought hurt his head. Suslov-Smirnov, an excitable, loose-boned long man with thick-lensed eyeglasses on a thin nose, and a bushy head of blond hair, had come four times to ask questions and take voluminous notes on thin sheets of paper—Ostrovsky had been forbidden to return. The lawyer had embraced the prisoner and promised—"Although we are hindered by stupid officials dragging their feet"—to move with all possible dispatch. "But in the meantime you must be careful of every step you take. Walk, as they say, on eggs, Mr. Bok. On eggs." He nodded, winked with both eyes, and pressed four fingers to his lips.

"Do you know," Yakov said, "that they killed Bibikov?"

"We know," whispered Suslov-Smirnov, looking around in

fright, "but we can't prove it. Say nothing or you'll make your situation worse."

"I've already said it," the fixer said, "to Grubeshov."

Suslov-Smirnov wrote it down quickly, then erased it and left. He said he would return but didn't, and no one would tell the fixer why. Have I made still another mistake? Again the indictment withdrawn? Yakov slowly tore at his flesh with his nails. The rest of another month leaked by. He again kept count of the days with bits of paper torn from the toilet paper strips. He weighed, he thought, a ton, all grief. His little hope—the hope he had foolishly dared—flickered, waned, withered. His legs were swollen and his back teeth, loose. He was at the lowest ebb of his life when the warden appeared with an immaculate paper, saluted, and said his trial was about to begin.

5

All night the cell was crowded with prisoners who had lived and died there. They were broken-faced, greenish-gray men, with haunted eyes, scarred shaved heads and ragged bodies, crowding the cell. Many stared wordlessly at the fixer and he at them, their eyes lit with longing for life. If one disappeared two appeared in his place. So many prisoners, thought the prisoner, it's a country of prisoners. They've freed the serfs, or so they say, but not the innocent prisoners. He beheld long lines of them, gaunt-eyed men with starved mouths, lines stretching through the thick walls to impoverished cities, the vast empty steppe, great snowy virgin forests, to the shabby wooden work camps in Siberia. Trofim Kogin was among them. He had broken his leg and lay in the snow as the long lines slowly moved past him. He lay with his eyes shut and mouth twitching but did not call for help.

"Help!" cried Yakov in the dark.

This night before his trial, the fixer was oppressed by fear of death and though he was deathly sleepy he would not sleep. When his heavy eyes shut momentarily he saw someone standing over him with a knife raised to rip his throat. So the fixer forced himself to stay awake. He threw aside his blanket to make it too cold to sleep. Yakov pinched his arms and thighs.

If anyone attempted to sneak into the cell he would shout when the door opened. To cry out was his only defense. It might scare the assassins if they thought any of the prisoners in the cells down the corridor would hear, and guess the Jew was being murdered. If they heard, after a while it would get to the outside that the officials had assassinated him rather than bring him to trial.

The wind wailed mutely in the prison yard. His heart was like a rusted chain, his muscles taut, as though each had been bound with wire. Even in the cold air he sweated. Amid the darkly luminous prisoners he saw spies waiting to kill him. One was the gray-haired warden with a gleaming two-headed ax. He tried to hide his crossed eye behind his hand but it shone like a jewel through his fingers. The Deputy Warden, his fly open, held a black bullwhip behind his back. And though the Tsar wore a white mask over his face and a black on the back of his head, Yakov recognized him standing in the far corner of the cell, dropping green drops into a glass of hot milk.

"It will make you sleep, Yakov Shepsovitch."

"After you, Your Majesty."

The Tsar faded in the dark. The spies disappeared but the lines of prisoners were endless.

What's next, the fixer thought, and when will it happen? Will the trial begin, or will they call it off at the last minute? Suppose they withdraw the Act of Indictment in the morning, hoping I collapse or go insane before they give me another. Many men have lived in prison longer and some under worse conditions, but if I have to live another year in this cell I would rather die. Then the sad-eyed prisoners who crowded the cell began to disappear. First those who were standing around the wooden bed, then those squeezed together in the center, then those at the walls, and finally the long lines of sunken-faced men, moaning women, and ghostly children with glazed eyes in purple sockets, extending through the prison walls into the snowy distance.

"Are you Jews or Russians?" the fixer asked them.

"We are Russian prisoners."

"You look like Jews," he said.

Yakov fell asleep. Knowing he had, he frantically strove to awake, hearing himself sob as he slept, but it was growing lighter in the cell and he soon saw Bibikov sitting at a table in his white summer suit, stirring a spoonful of strawberry jelly in his tea.

"This would hardly be the time for them to kill you, Yakov Shepsovitch," he said. "Anyone would know it was a put-up job, and it would arouse an outcry. What you must watch out for is the sudden and unexpected peril, the apparently accidental. So sleep now, without fear for your life, and if you should ever manage to get out of prison, keep in mind that the purpose of freedom is to create it for others."

"Your honor," said Yakov, "I've had an extraordinary insight."

"You don't say? What is it?"

"Something in myself has changed. I'm not the same man I was. I fear less and hate more."

Before daylight Zhenia came to him with his punctured face and bleeding chest and begged for the return of his life. Yakov laid both hands on the boy and tried to raise him from the dead but it wouldn't work.

In the morning the fixer was still alive. He had wakened in astonishment, his mood mixed, anticipation with depression. It was the end of October, two and a half years after his arrest in Nikolai Maximovitch's brickyard. Kogin told him the date when he came in with the prisoner's breakfast. This morning the gruel was boiled rice in hot milk, eight ounces of black bread, a yellow piece of butter, and an enamel pot of sweet-smelling tea, with a chunk of lemon and two lumps of sugar. There was also a cucumber and a small onion to chew on to strengthen his teeth and reduce the swelling of his legs. Kogin wasn't feeling well. His hands trembled when he put down the food. He looked flushed and said he wanted to get home to bed but the warden had ordered him to stay on till the prisoner had left for the courthouse.

"Full security regulations, the warden said."

Yakov did not touch the food.

"You'd better eat it," Kogin said.

"I'm not hungry."

"Eat anyway, it'll be a long day in court."

"I'm too nervous. If I ate now I'd vomit."

Berezhinsky entered the cell. He seemed uneasy, not knowing whether to smile or mourn. He smiled uneasily.

"Well, your day has come. Here's the trial now."

"What about my clothes?" Yakov asked. "Will I have to wear the prison ones or can I have my own?"

He wondered whether they were going to hand him a silken caftan and a round Hasidic fur hat.

"You'll find out about that," said Berezhinsky.

Both guards accompanied the prisoner to the bathhouse. He undressed and was allowed to soap and wash himself from a bucket of warm water. The warmth of the water brought secret tears to his eyes. He washed slowly with handfuls of water from the bucket. He washed the smells and dirt away.

Yakov was given a comb and carefully combed his long hair and beard, but then the prison barber appeared and said he must shave his head.

"No," the fixer shouted. "Why should I look like a prisoner now when I didn't before?"

"Because you are a prisoner," said Berezhinsky. "The gate's not open yet."

"Why now and not before?"

"Orders," said the prison barber, "so sit still and keep your mouth shut."

"Why does he cut my hair?" Yakov, angered, asked Kogin. He felt, then, the pangs of hunger.

"Orders must be obeyed," said the guard. "It's to show you had no special privileges and were treated like the others."

"I was treated worse than the others."

"If you know all the answers, then don't ask any questions," Kogin said in irritation.

"That's right," said Berezhinsky. "Keep your mouth shut."

When the hair clipping was done, Kogin went out and returned with the fixer's own clothes and told him to put them on.

Yakov got dressed in the bathhouse. He blessed his clothes though they hung on his bony body loosely and limply. The baggy pants were held up by a thin cord. The dank sheepskin coat hung almost to his knees. But the boots, though stiff, were comfortable.

Back in the cell, strangely lit in the light of two lamps, Kogin said, "Listen, Bok, I advise you to eat. I give you my word there's nothing to be afraid of in that food. You better eat."

"That's right," said Berezhinsky. "Do what you're told."

"I don't want to eat," said the fixer, "I want to fast."

"What the hell for?" said Kogin.

"For God's world."

"I thought you didn't believe in God."

"I don't."

"The hell with you," said Kogin.

"Well, good luck and no hard feelings," Berezhinsky said uneasily. "Duty is duty. The prisoner's the prisoner, the guard's the guard."

From the window came the sound of a troop of horses clattering into the prison yard.

"It's the Cossacks," said Berezhinsky.

"Will I have to walk in the middle of the street?"

"You'll find that out. The warden's waiting so hurry up or it will go hard on you."

As Yakov came out of the cell an escort of six Cossack guards with crossed bandoleers were lined up in the corridor. The captain, a burly man with a black mustache, ordered the guard to surround the prisoner.

"Forward march," commanded the escort captain.

The Cossacks marched the prisoner along the corridor toward the warden's office. Though Yakov tried to straighten his leg he walked with a limp. He went as quickly as he could to keep up with the guard. Kogin and Berezhinsky remained behind.

In the warden's inner office the captain carefully searched the prisoner; he wrote out a receipt for him and handed it to the warden.

"Just a minute, young man," said the warden. "I want to have a word of my own with the prisoner."

The captain saluted. "We leave at 8 A.M., sir." He went to wait in the outer office.

The old man wiped the corners of his mouth with a handkerchief. His eye was tearing so he wiped that too. He took out his snuffbox, then put it away.

Yakov watched him nervously. If he withdraws the indictment now I'll choke him to death.

"Well, Bok," said Warden Grizitskoy, "if you had had the sense to follow the Prosecuting Attorney's advice you'd be a free man today and out of the country. As it is now, you'll probably be convicted on the evidence and will spend the rest of your natural life in the strictest confinement."

The fixer scratched his palms.

The warden got his glasses out of a drawer, adjusted them on his nose, and read aloud an item from a newspaper lying on his desk. It was about a tailor in Odessa, Markovitch, a Jew, the father of five children, accused by the police of murdering a nine-year-old boy in a waterfront street late at night. He had then carried the child's body to his tailor shop and drained the still-warm corpse of its lifeblood. The police, suspicious of the tailor, who walked alone in the streets at night, had discovered bloodstains on the floor and had at once arrested him.

The warden put down the newspaper and removed his glasses.

"I'll tell you this, Bok: if we don't convict one of you we'll convict the other. We'll teach you all a lesson."

The fixer remained mute.

The warden, his mouth wet with anger, threw open the door and signaled the escort captain.

But then the Deputy Warden entered from the hall. He came in in a hurry, paying no attention to the escort captain.

"Warden," he said, "I have here a telegram that forbids special privileges for the Jewish prisoner Bok just because he happens to be going on trial. He hasn't been searched this morning through no fault of mine. Please have him returned to his cell to be searched in the usual way."

A sick pressure burdened the fixer's chest.

"Why should I be searched now? What will you find if you search me? Only my miseries. This man doesn't know where to stop."

"I've already searched him," said the Cossack captain to the Deputy Warden. "The prisoner is now in my custody. I've given the warden my personal receipt."

"It's on my desk," said the warden.

The Deputy Warden drew a folded white paper out of his tunic pocket. "This telegram is from his Imperial Majesty in St. Petersburg. It orders us to search the Jew most carefully to prevent any possible dangerous incident."

"Why wasn't the telegram sent to me?" asked the warden.

"I notified you it might come," said the Deputy Warden.

"That's right," said the warden, flustered.

"Why should I be insulted again?" Yakov shouted, the blood

burning in his face. "The guards saw me naked in the bathhouse and watched me dress. Also this captain searched me a few minutes ago in front of the warden. Why should I be further humiliated on the day of my trial?"

The warden banged his fist on the desk. "That will do. Be still, I warn you."

"No one wants your opinion," said the black-mustached captain coldly. "Forward march. Back to the cell."

There's more to this than it says in the telegram, Yakov thought. If they're trying to provoke me I'd better be careful.

Sick to his soul, he was marched to the cell by the Cossack guard.

"Welcome home," Berezhinsky laughed.

Kogin stared at the fixer in frightened surprise.

"Hurry it up," said the Cossack captain to the Deputy Warden.

"Please, friend, don't tell me how to do my job and I won't tell you how to do yours," said the Deputy Warden, coldly. His boots smelled as though he had freshly stepped in excrement.

"Inside and undress," he ordered Yakov.

The prisoner, the Deputy Warden, and the two guards entered the cell, leaving the captain and the escort guard waiting in the corridor. The Deputy Warden slammed the cell door shut.

Inside the cell Kogin crossed himself.

Yakov slowly undressed, shivering. He stood there naked, except for his undershirt. I must be careful, he thought, or it will go hard on me. Ostrovsky warned me. Yet as he told himself this he felt his rage growing. The blood roared in his ears. It was as though he had dug a hole, then put the shovel aside but the hole was still growing. It grew into a grave. He imagined himself tearing the Deputy Warden's face apart and kicking him to death.

"Open your mouth," Berezhinsky ran a dirty finger under his tongue.

"Now spread your ass apart."

Kogin stared at the wall.

"Take off that stinking undershirt," ordered the Deputy Warden.

I must calm my anger, thought the fixer, seeing the world black. Instead, his anger grew.

"Why should I?" he shouted. "I have never taken it off before. Why should I take it off now? Why do you insult me?"

"Take it off before I tear it off."

Yakov felt the cell tremble and dip. I should have eaten, he thought. It was a mistake not to. He saw a bald-headed thin naked man in a freezing prison cell ripping off his undershirt and to his horror watched him fling it into the face of the Deputy Warden.

A solemn silence filled the cell.

Though his wet eyes were lit, murderous, the Deputy Warden spoke calmly. "I am within my rights to punish you for interfering with and insulting a prison official in the performance of his duty."

He drew his revolver.

My dirty luck. Yakov thought of the way his life had gone. Now Shmuel is dead and Raisl has nothing to eat. I've never been of use to anybody and I'll never be.

"Hold on a minute, your honor," said Kogin to the Deputy Warden. His deep voice broke. "I've listened to this man night after night, I know his sorrows. Enough is enough, and anyway it's time for his trial to begin."

"Get out of my way or I'll cite you for insubordination, you son-of-a-bitch."

Kogin pressed the muzzle of his revolver against the Deputy Warden's neck.

Berezhinsky reached for his gun but before he could draw, Kogin fired.

He fired at the ceiling and after a while dust drifted to the floor.

A whistle sounded shrilly in the corridor. The prison bell clanged. The iron cell door was slammed open and the white-faced captain and his Cossack guards rushed into the cell.

"I've given my personal receipt," he roared.

"My head aches," Kogin muttered. He sank to his knees with blood on his face. The Deputy Warden had shot him.

6

A church bell tolled.

A black bird flew out of the sky. Crow? Hawk? Or the black

egg of a black eagle falling towards the carriage? If it isn't that what is it? If it's a bomb, thought Yakov, what can I do? I'll duck, what else can I do? If it's a bomb why was I ever born?

The prisoner, watched in silence by a crowd of officials, guests, and the mounted Cossacks in the yard, had limped amid the guard from the prison door to the massive black armored carriage drawn by four thick-necked, heavy-rumped horses at the gate. On the driver's seat sat a hawk-eyed coachman in a long coat and visored cap, whip in his hand.

The fixer was boosted up the metal step by two Cossacks and locked in the large-wheeled coach by the Chief of Police and his assistant. Inside it was dark and musty. An unlit lamp hung in the corner; the windows were round and small. Yakov put his eye to one of them, saw nothing he wanted to see—Warden Grizitskoy in military cap and coat rubbing a bloodshot eye—and sat back in the gloom.

The coachman shouted to the horses; a whip snapped and the huge carriage with its escort of fur-capped, gray-coated Cossack riders, a platoon in front with glittering lances, another in the rear with swords unsheathed, lumbered through the gate and rattled out on the cobblestone street. The coach moved quickly up the street, turned a corner and then went along an avenue with fields on one side and occasional factories and houses on the other.

I'm off, thought the fixer, for better or worse, and if it's worse it'll be worse than it was.

He sat for a while shrunken in loneliness, then through a window saw a bird in the sky and watched with emotion until he could no longer see it. The weak sun stained the thin drifting clouds and for a minute snow flurried in different directions. In a wood not far from the road the oaks retained their bronze leaves but the large chestnut trees were black and barren. Yakov, seeing them in memory in full bloom, regretted the seasons he had missed and the years of his youth lost in prison.

Though still stunned by Kogin's death he felt, finally, the relief of motion, though to what fate who could say? Yet on the move at last to the courthouse, his trial about to take place, they said, a full three years from the time he had left the shtetl and ridden to Kiev. Then as they passed the brick wall of a factory, its chimneys pouring out coal smoke whipped by the wind into the sky, he caught a reflected glimpse of a faded shrunken Jew in the circle of window and hid from him, but could not, a minute later, from the memory of his gaunt face, its darkened stringy beard white around the bitter mouth, and though he would not weep for himself, his palms, when he rubbed his eyes, were wet.

At the factory gate five or six workers had turned to watch the procession; but when it had gone a verst into the business district, the fixer looked up in astonishment at the masses of people gathered on both sides of the street. Though it was early morning the crowds stretched along, five and six deep, laborers and civil servants on their way to work, shopkeepers, peasants in sheepskin coats, women in shawls and a few in hats, a scattering of military cadets and soldiers, and here and there a gray-robed monk or priest staring at the carriage. The trolleys were stopped, passengers rising from their seats to look out the windows as the Cossack riders and lumbering coach passed by. In the sidestreets the police held up carriages and motorcars, and bullock carts from the provinces, piled high with vegetables and grains, or loaded with cans of milk. Along the route to the courthouse mounted police were stationed at intervals to keep order. Yakov moved from one window to another to see the crowds.

"Yakov Bok!" he called out. "Yakov Bok!"

The Cossack riding on the left side of the carriage, a thick-shouldered man with overhanging brows and a mustache turning gray, gazed impassively ahead; but the rider cantering along on the door side, a youth of twenty or so on a gray mare, from time to time stole a glance at Yakov when he was staring out the window, as though trying to measure his guilt or innocence.

"Innocent!" the fixer cried out to him. "Innocent!" And though he had no reason to, he smiled a little at the Cossack for his youth and good looks, and for being, as such things go, a free man, give or take a little. The Cossack then rode forward as the mare, raising her tail, dropped a steaming load on the street at which a schoolboy pointed.

Amid the crowd were a few Jews watching with commiseration or fear. Most of the Russian faces were impassive, though some showed hostility and some loathing. A shopkeeper in a smock spat at the carriage. Two boys hooted. Some of the men in the crowd wore Black Hundreds buttons and when Yakov, out of one window then quickly the other, saw how many of them there were at this place, he grew apprehensive. Where there was one there were a hundred. A man with a strained face and deadly eyes threw his hand into the air as though it had caught on fire. The fixer's scrotum shrank painfully and he tore at his chest with his fingers as a black bird seemed to fly out of the white hand clawing the air.

Yakov frantically ducked. If this is my death I've endured for nothing.

"You might have waited a bit, Yakov Bok," the chairman of the jury said. "None of us are gentry or educated folk, but neither are we without a bit of experience in the world. A man learns to recognize the truth even if he doesn't always live by it. And there are times he does that if it suits his fancy. The officials may not want us to know what the truth is but it comes in, you might say, through the chinks in the walls. They may try to deceive us, as they do often enough, but we will sift the evidence and if the facts are not as they say, then let them look to their consciences."

"They have none."

"So much the worse for them, in that case. You aren't born human for nothing, I say."

"I'm innocent," said Yakov, "you can look at me and see. Look in my face and say whether a man like me, whatever else he might do, could kill a boy and drain the blood out of his body. If I have any humanity in my heart and you are men you must know it. Tell me do I look like a murderer?"

The chairman was about to say but a violent explosion rocked the coach.

Yakov waited for death. He wandered for a while in a cemetery reading the names on the tombstones. Then he ran from grave to grave, searching them frantically, one after another, but could not find his name. After a while he stopped looking. He had waited a long time but maybe he had longer to wait. If you were a certain type death stayed its distance. Your afflictions were from life—a poor living, mistakes with people, the blows of fate. You lived, you suffered, but you lived.

He heard screams, shouts, commotion, the frightened whinnying of horses. The carriage rattled and seemed to leap up, then struck the ground and stopped dead, shuddering, but remained upright. The stench of gunpowder bored through his nostrils. A door lock snapped and the door fell ajar. He felt an overwhelming hunger to be back home, to see Raisl and set things straight, to decide what to do. "Raisl," he said, "dress the boy and pack the few things we need, we'll have to hide." He was about to kick the door open but warned himself not to. Through the cracked right window he saw people on the run. A squad of Cossacks with lances raised galloped away from the carriage. A squad with uplifted sabers galloped towards it, risen in their saddles. The gray mare lay dead on the cobblestones. Three policemen were lifting the young Cossack rider. His foot had been torn off by the bomb. The boot had been blown away and his leg was shattered and bloody. As they carried him past the carriage his eyes opened and he looked in horror and anguish at Yakov as though to say, "What has my foot got to do with it?"

The fixer shrank from the sight. The Cossack had fainted but his torn leg shook, spattering blood on the policemen. Then a Cossack colonel galloped up to the carriage, holding a sword aloft, shouting to the coachman, "Go on, go on!" He dismounted and tried to slam the door shut but it wouldn't lock. "Go on, go on!" he shouted. The carriage rumbled on, the horses picked up speed and broke into a fast trot. The colonel, on a white horse, cantered along beside the coach in place of the wounded Cossack.

Yakov sat in the gloomy coach overcome by hatred so intense his chest heaved as though the carriage were airless. He saw himself, after a while, sitting at a table somewhere, opposite the Tsar, a lit candle between them, in a cell or cellar, whatever it was. Nicholas the Second, of medium height, with frank blue eyes and neatly trimmed beard a little too large for his face, sat there naked, holding in his hand a small silver ikon of the Virgin Mary. Though distraught and pale, afflicted with a bad cough he had recently developed, he spoke in a gentle voice and with moving eloquence.

"Though you have me at a disadvantage, Yakov Shepsovitch, I will speak the truth to you. It isn't only that the Jews are freemasons and revolutionaries who make a shambles of our laws and demoralize our police by systematic bribery for social exemptions—I can forgive that a bit but not the other things, in particular the terrible crime you are accused of, which is so repellent to me personally. I refer to the draining of his lifeblood out of Zhenia Golov's body. I don't know whether you are aware that my own child, the Tsarevitch Alexis, is a haemophiliac? The newspapers, out of courtesy to the royal family, and the Tsarina in particular, do not, of course, mention it. We are fortunate in having four healthy daughters, the princesses Olga, the studious one; Tatyana, the prettiest, and something of a coquette—I say this with amusement; Maria, shy and sweet-tempered; and Anastasya, the youngest and liveliest of them; but when after many prayers an heir to the throne was born at last—it pleased God to make this joy our greatest trial—his blood unfortunately was deficient in that substance which is necessary for coagulation and healing. A small cut, the most trivial, and he may bleed to death. We look after him, as you can expect, with the greatest care, on tenterhooks every minute because even a quite ordinary fall may mean extreme peril. Alexei's veins are fragile, brittle, and in the slightest mishap internal bleeding causes him unbearable pain and torment. My dear wife and I—and I may add, the girls—live through death with this poor child. Permit me to ask, Yakov Shepsovitch, are you a father?"

"With all my heart."

"Then you can imagine our anguish," sighed the sad-eyed Tsar.

His hands trembled a little as he lit a green-papered Turkish cigarette from an enameled box on the table. He offered the box to Yakov but the fixer shook his head.

"I never wanted the crown, it kept me from being my true self, but I was not permitted to refuse. To rule is to bear a heavy cross. I've made mistakes, but not, I assure you, out of malice to anyone. My nature is not resolute, not like my late father's—we lived in terror of him—but what can a man do beyond the best he can? One is born as he is born and that's all there is to it. I thank God for my good qualities. To tell you the truth, Yakov Shepsovitch, I don't like to dwell on these things. But I am—I can truthfully say—a kind person and love my people. Though the Jews cause me a great deal of trouble, and we must sometimes suppress them to maintain order, believe me, I wish them well. As for you, if you permit me, I consider you a decent but mistaken man—I insist on honesty—and I must ask you to take note of my obligations and burdens. After all, it isn't as though you yourself are unaware of what suffering is. Surely it has taught you the meaning of mercy?"

He was coughing insistently now and his voice, when he finished, was unsteady.

Yakov moved uneasily in his chair. "Excuse me, Your Majesty, but what suffering has taught me is the uselessness of suffering, if you don't mind me saying so. Anyway, there's enough of that to live with naturally without piling a mountain of injustice on top. Rachmones, we say in Hebrew—mercy, one oughtn't to forget it, but one must also think how oppressed, ignorant and miserable most of us are in this country, gentiles as well as Jews, under your government and ministers. What it amounts to, Little Father, is that whether you wanted it or not you had your chance; in fact many chances, but the best you could give us with all good intentions is the poorest and most reactionary state in Europe. In other words, you've made out of this country a valley of bones. You had your chances and pissed them away. There's no argument against that. It's not easy to twist events by the tail but you might have done something for a better life for us all—for the future of Russia, one might say, but you didn't."

The Tsar rose, his phallus meager, coughing still, disturbed and angered. "I'm only one man though ruler yet you blame me for our whole history."

"For what you don't know, Your Majesty, and what you haven't learned. Your poor boy is a haemophiliac, something missing in the blood. In you, in spite of certain sentimental feelings, it is missing somewhere else—the sort of insight, you might call it, that creates in a man charity, respect for the most miserable. You say you are kind and prove it with pogroms."

"As for those," said the Tsar, "don't blame me. Water can't be prevented from flowing. They are a genuine expression of the will of the people."

"Then in that case there's no more to say." On the table at

the fixer's hand lay a revolver. Yakov pushed a bullet into the rusty cylinder chamber.

The Tsar sat down, watching without apparent emotion, though his face had grown white and his beard darker. "I am the victim, the sufferer for my poor people. What will be will be." He stubbed out his cigarette in the candle saucer. The light flickered but burnt on.

"Don't expect me to beg."

"This is also for the prison, the poison, the six daily searches. It's for Bibikov and Kogin and for a lot more that I won't even mention."

Pointing the gun at the Tsar's heart (though Bibikov, flailing his white arms, cried no no no no), Yakov pressed the trigger. Nicholas, in the act of crossing himself, overturned his chair, and fell, to his surprise, to the floor, the stain spreading on his breast.

The horses clopped on over the cobblestones.

As for history, Yakov thought, there are ways to reverse it. What the Tsar deserves is a bullet in the gut. Better him than us.

The left rear wheel of the carriage seemed to be wobbling.

One thing I've learned, he thought, there's no such thing as an unpolitical man, especially a Jew. You can't be one without the other, that's clear enough. You can't sit still and see yourself destroyed.

Afterwards he thought, Where there's no fight for it there's no freedom. What is it Spinoza says? If the state acts in ways that are abhorrent to human nature it's the lesser evil to destroy it. Death to the anti-Semites! Long live revolution! Long live liberty!

The crowds lining both sides of the streets were dense again, packed tight between curb and housefront. There were faces at every window and people standing on rooftops along the way. Among those in the street were Jews of the Plossky District. Some, as the carriage clattered by and they glimpsed the fixer, were openly weeping, wringing their hands. One thinly bearded man clawed his face. One or two waved at Yakov. Some shouted his name.

Source of The Fixer (1966)

AFTER MY last novel I was sniffing for an idea in the direction of injustice on the American scene, partly for obvious reasons—this was a time of revolutionary advances in Negro rights—and because I became involved with this theme in a way that sets off my imagination in terms of art. I had hoped to portray an American experience, possibly concerned with a Negro protagonist, but that didn't work out into a usable plan for a long fiction. Searching in a similar direction, I thought of the Sacco and Vanzetti case, but after I had read a few books about them I realized that for me the legend was beyond further invention. And simply retelling their lives and history didn't interest me. By this time a theme, perhaps as a residue of what I had read, had materialized around a man (not necessarily a moral man) who is arrested for a crime he didn't commit and spends years in prison. The suffering and rage he undergoes cause him to examine his life and values. The story would be about what he becomes in prison: whatever else it had to be about it had to be about how the idea of freedom grows in the mind of a man subjected to a grave injustice.

I was now looking for a story that had happened in the past and perhaps would happen again. I wanted the historical tie-up so I could invent it into myth. In other words, I wanted to show how recurrent, almost without thought, almost ritualistic, some of our unfortunate historical experiences are. I considered basing a fiction on the life of Caryl Chessman, and then on the Dreyfus case, but for different reasons neither idea suited me. Then I remembered—I had never forgotten—the name of Mendel Beilis, whom my father had told me about when I was a boy; and I remember being moved and frightened by the story. Beilis, an office manager in a Kiev brick factory in tsarist times, was a Jew accused of committing a ritual murder; he was charged with killing a Christian boy and stealing his blood for the making of Passover matzos. This superstition, in an early form directed against the first Christians, was turned against the Jews and persisted in Europe throughout the Middle Ages. In modern times it was rife among many of the masses of prerevolutionary Russia; and even nowadays, from time to time, the accusation is revived in the Soviet Union.

Beilis, when arrested for killing a boy and hiding his body in a cave, was a man of thirty-nine. For almost two-and-a-half years he was kept in prison without an indictment. He suffered greatly but was finally brought to trial and acquitted. In *The Fixer* I use some of his experiences, though not, basically, the man, partly because his life came to less than he had paid for by his suffering and endurance, and because I had to have room to invent. To his trials in prison I added something of Dreyfus's and Vanzetti's, shaping the whole to suggest the quality of the afflictions of the Jews under Hitler. These I dumped on the head of poor Yakov Bok, thirty, the fixer, or handyman, of the novel, a poor man seeking a better future and at once falling into a trap. He comes to Kiev on his father-in-law's horse, saves an anti-Semite from suffocating in the snow, is rewarded with a job in a brickyard, and is there arrested for the murder of a twelve-year-old boy he had one day chased from the brick kilns. Yakov had a lot to learn and maybe he learned it. His experiences in prison lead to a change in him that is the drama of the book.

So a novel that began as an idea concerned with injustice in America today has become one set in Russia fifty years ago, dealing with anti-Semitism there. Injustice is injustice.

PICTURES OF FIDELMAN
AN EXHIBITION

For Victor and Iza

Not to understand. Yes, that was my whole occupation during those years—I can assure you, it was not an easy one.

R. M. RILKE

The intellect of man is forced to choose
Perfection of the life, or of the work . . .

W. B. YEATS

Both.

A. FIDELMAN

An Exhibition

1

FIDELMAN, A self-confessed failure as a painter, came to Italy to prepare a critical study of Giotto, the opening chapter of which he had carried across the ocean in a new pigskin leather brief case, now gripped in his perspiring hand. Also new were his gum-soled oxblood shoes, a tweed suit he had on despite the late-September sun slanting hot in the Roman sky, although there was a lighter one in his bag; and a dacron shirt and set of cotton-dacron underwear, good for quick and easy washing for the traveler. His suitcase, a bulky two-strapped affair which embarrassed him slightly, he had borrowed from his sister Bessie. He planned, if he had any funds left at the end of the year, to buy a new one in Florence. Although he had been in not much of a mood when he had left the U.S.A., Fidelman picked up in Naples, and at the moment, as he stood in front of the Rome railroad station, after twenty minutes still absorbed in his first sight of the Eternal City, he was conscious of a certain exaltation that devolved on him after he had discovered directly across the many-vehicled piazza stood the remains of the Baths of Diocletian. Fidelman remembered having read that Michelangelo had helped in converting the baths into a church and convent, the latter ultimately changed into the museum that presently was there. "Imagine," he muttered. "Imagine all that history."

In the midst of his imagining, Fidelman experienced the sensation of suddenly seeing himself as he was, to the pinpoint, outside and in, not without bittersweet pleasure; and as the well-known image of his face rose before him he was taken by the depth of pure feeling in his eyes, slightly magnified by glasses, and the sensitivity of his elongated nostrils and often tremulous lips, nose divided from lips by a mustache of recent vintage that looked, Fidelman thought, as if it had been sculptured there, adding to his dignified appearance although he was a little on the short side. Almost at the same moment, this unexpectedly intense sense of his being—it was more than appearance—faded, exaltation having gone where exaltation goes, and Fidelman became aware that there was an exterior source to the strange, almost tri-dimensional reflection of himself he had felt as well as seen. Behind him, a short distance to the right, he had noticed a stranger—give a skeleton a couple of pounds—loitering near a bronze statue on a stone pedestal of the heavy-dugged Etruscan wolf suckling the infants Romulus and Remus, the man contemplating Fidelman already acquisitively so as to suggest to the traveler that he had been mirrored (lock, stock, barrel) in the other's gaze for some time, perhaps since he had stepped off the train. Casually studying him though pretending no, Fidelman beheld a person of about his own height, oddly dressed in brown knickers and black knee-length woolen socks drawn up over slightly bowed, broomstick legs, these grounded in small porous pointed shoes. His yellowed shirt was open at the gaunt throat, both sleeves rolled up over skinny, hairy arms. The stranger's high forehead was bronzed, his black hair thick behind small ears, the dark close-shaven beard tight on the face; his experienced nose was weighted at the tip, and the soft brown eyes, above all, wanted. Though his expression suggested humility he all but licked his lips as he approached the ex-painter.

"Shalom," he greeted Fidelman.

"Shalom," the other hesitantly replied, uttering the word—so far as he recalled—for the first time in his life. My God, he thought, a handout for sure. My first hello in Rome and it has to be a schnorrer.

The stranger extended a smiling hand. "Susskind," he said, "Shimon Susskind."

"Arthur Fidelman." Transferring his brief case to under his left arm while standing astride the big suitcase he shook hands with Susskind. A blue-smocked porter came by, glanced at Fidelman's bag, looked at him, then walked away.

Whether he knew it or not Susskind was rubbing his palms contemplatively together.

"Parla italiano?"

"Not with ease, although I read it fluently. You might say I need the practice."

"Yiddish?"

"I express myself best in English."

"Let it be English then." Susskind spoke with a slight British intonation. "I knew you were Jewish," he said, "the minute my eyes saw you."

Fidelman chose to ignore the remark. "Where did you pick up your knowledge of English?"

"In Israel."

Israel interested Fidelman. "You live there?"

"Once, not now," Susskind answered vaguely. He seemed suddenly bored.

"How so?"

Susskind twitched a shoulder. "Too much heavy labor for a man of my modest health. Also I couldn't stand the suspense."

Fidelman nodded.

"Furthermore, the desert air makes me constipated. In Rome I am lighthearted."

"A Jewish refugee from Israel, no less," Fidelman said with good humor.

"I'm always running," Susskind answered mirthlessly. If he was lighthearted he had yet to show it.

"Where else from, if I may ask?"

"Where else but Germany, Hungary, Poland? Where not?"

"Ah, that's so long ago." Fidelman then noticed the gray in the man's hair. "Well, I'd better be going." He picked up his bag as two porters hovered uncertainly nearby.

But Susskind offered certain services. "You got a hotel?"

"All picked and reserved."

"How long are you staying?"

What business is it of his? However, Fidelman courteously replied, "Two weeks in Rome, the rest of the year in Florence, with a few side trips to Siena, Assisi, Padua and maybe also Venice."

"You wish a guide in Rome?"

"Are you a guide?"

"Why not?"

"No," said Fidelman. "I'll look as I go along to museums, libraries, et cetera."

This caught Susskind's attention. "What are you, a professor?"

Fidelman couldn't help blushing. "Not exactly, really just a student."

"From which institution?"

He coughed a little. "By that I mean professional student, you might say. Call me Trofimov, from Chekhov. If there's something to learn I want to learn it."

"You have some kind of a project?" the other persisted. "A grant?"

"No grant. My money is hard earned. I worked and saved a long time to take a year in Italy. I made certain sacrifices. As for a project, I'm writing on the painter Giotto. He was one of the most important—"

"You don't have to tell me about Giotto," Susskind interrupted with a little smile.

"You've studied his work?"

"Who doesn't know Giotto?"

"That's interesting to me," said Fidelman, secretly irritated. "How do you happen to know him?"

"How do you?"

"I've given a good deal of time and study to his work."

"So I know him too."

I'd better get this over with before it begins to amount up to something, Fidelman thought. He set down his bag and fished with a finger in his leather coin purse. The two porters watched with interest, one taking a sandwich out of his pocket, unwrapping the newspaper and beginning to eat.

"This is for yourself," Fidelman said.

Susskind hardly glanced at the coin as he let it drop into his pants pocket. The porters then left.

The refugee had an odd way of standing motionless, like a cigar store Indian about to burst into flight. "In your luggage," he said vaguely, "would you maybe have a suit you can't use? I could use a suit."

At last he comes to the point. Fidelman, though annoyed, controlled himself. "All I have is a change from the one you now see me wearing. Don't get the wrong idea about me, Mr. Susskind. I'm not rich. In fact I'm poor. Don't let a few new clothes deceive you. I owe my sister money for them."

Susskind glanced down at his shabby baggy knickers. "I haven't had a suit for years. The one I was wearing when I ran away from Germany, fell apart. One day I was walking around naked."

"Isn't there a welfare organization that could help you out—some group in the Jewish community, interested in refugees?"

"The Jewish organizations wish to give me what they wish, not what I wish," Susskind replied bitterly. "The only thing they offer me is a ticket back to Israel."

"Why don't you take it?"

"I told you already, here I feel free."

"Freedom is a relative term."

"Don't tell me about freedom."

He knows all about that too, Fidelman thought. "So you feel free," he said, "but how do you live?"

Susskind coughed, a brutal cough.

Fidelman was about to say something more on the subject of freedom but left it unsaid. Jesus, I'll be saddled with him all day if I don't watch out.

"I'd better be getting off to the hotel." He bent again for his bag.

Susskind touched him on the shoulder and when Fidelman exasperatedly straightened up, the half dollar he had given the man was staring him in the eye.

"On this we both lose money."

"How do you mean?"

"Today the lira sells six twenty-three on the dollar, but for specie they only give you five hundred."

"In that case give it here and I'll let you have a dollar." From his billfold Fidelman quickly extracted a crisp bill and handed it to the refugee.

"Not more?" Susskind sighed.

"Not more," the student answered emphatically.

"Maybe you would like to see Diocletian's bath? There are some enjoyable Roman coffins inside. I will guide you for another dollar."

"No, thanks." Fidelman said goodbye, and lifting the suitcase, lugged it to the curb. A porter appeared and the student, after some hesitation, let him carry it toward the line of small dark-green taxis on the piazza. The porter offered to carry the brief case too but Fidelman wouldn't part with it. He gave the cab driver the address of the hotel, and the taxi took off with a lurch. Fidelman at last relaxed. Susskind, he noticed, had disappeared. Gone with his breeze, he thought. But on the way to the hotel he had an uneasy feeling that the refugee, crouched low, might be clinging to the little tire on the back of the cab; however he didn't look out to see.

Fidelman had reserved a room in an inexpensive hotel not far from the station with its very convenient bus terminal. Then, as was his habit, he got himself quickly and tightly organized. He was always concerned with not wasting time, as if it were his only wealth—not true, of course, though Fidelman admitted he was an ambitious person—and he soon arranged a schedule that made the most of his working hours. Mornings he usually visited the Italian libraries, searching their catalogues and archives, read in poor light, and made profuse notes. He napped for an hour after lunch, then at four, when the churches and museums were re-opening, hurried off to them with lists of frescoes and paintings he must see. He was anxious to get to Florence, at the same time a little unhappy at all he would not have time to take in in Rome. Fidelman promised himself to return if he could afford it, perhaps in the spring, and look at everything he pleased.

After dark he managed to unwind himself and relax. He ate as the Romans did, late, enjoyed a half liter of white wine and smoked a cigarette. Afterward he liked to wander—especially in the old sections near the Tiber. He had read that here, under his feet, were the ruins of Ancient Rome. It was an inspiring business, he, Arthur Fidelman, after all, born a Bronx boy, walking around in all this history. History was mysterious, the remembrance of things unknown, in a way burdensome, in a way a sensuous experience. It uplifted and depressed, why he did not know except that it excited his thoughts more than he thought good for him. This kind of excitement was all right up to a point, perfect maybe for a creative artist, but less so for a critic. A critic ought to live on beans. He walked for miles along the winding Tiber, gazing at the star-strewn skies. Once, after a couple of days in the Vatican Museum, he saw flights of angels—gold, blue, white—intermingled in the sky. "My God, I got to stop using my eyes so much," Fidelman said to himself. But back in his room he sometimes wrote till morning.

Late one night, about a week after his arrival in Rome, as

Fidelman was writing a few notes on the Byzantine style mosaics he had seen during the day, there was a knock on the door, and though the student, immersed in his work, was not conscious he had said "Avanti," he must have, for the door opened, and instead of an angel, in came Susskind in his shirt and baggy knickers.

Fidelman, who had all but forgotten the refugee, certainly never thought of him, half rose in astonishment. "Susskind," he exclaimed, "how did you get in here?"

Susskind for a moment stood motionless, then answered with a weary smile, "I'll tell you the truth, I know the clerk."

"But how did you know where I live?"

"I saw you walking in the street so I followed you."

"You mean you saw me accidentally?"

"How else? Did you leave me your address?"

Fidelman resumed his seat. "What can I do for you, Susskind?" He spoke grimly.

The refugee cleared his throat. "Professor, the days are warm but the nights are cold. You see how I go around naked." He held forth bluish arms, goosefleshed. "I came to ask you to reconsider about giving away your old suit."

"And who says it's an old suit?" Fidelman's voice thickened.

"One suit is new, so the other's old."

"Not precisely. I am afraid I have no suit for you, Susskind. The one I presently have hanging in the closet is a little more than a year old and I can't afford to give it away. Besides, it's gabardine, more like a summer suit."

"On me it will be for all seasons."

After a moment's reflection, Fidelman drew out his billfold and counted four single dollars. These he handed to Susskind.

"Buy yourself a warm sweater."

Susskind also counted the money, bill for bill. "If four," he said, "then why not five?"

Fidelman flushed. The man's warped nerve. "Because I happen to have four available," he answered. "That's twenty-five hundred lire. You should be able to buy a warm sweater and have something left over besides."

"I need a suit," Susskind said. "The days are warm but the nights are cold." He rubbed his arms. "What else I need I won't say."

"At least roll down your sleeves if you're so cold."

"That won't help me."

"Listen, Susskind," Fidelman said gently, "I would gladly give you the suit if I could afford to, but I can't. I have barely enough money to squeeze out a year for myself here. I've already told you I am indebted to my sister. Why don't you try to get yourself a job somewhere, no matter how menial? I'm sure that in a short time you'll work yourself up into a decent position."

"A job, he says," Susskind muttered gloomily. "Do you know what it means to get a job in Italy? Who will give me a job?"

"Who gives anybody a job? They have to go out and get it."

"You don't understand, professor. I am an Israeli citizen and this means I can only work for an Israeli company. How many Israeli companies are there here?—maybe two, El Al and Zim, and even if they had a job, they wouldn't give it to me because I have lost my passport. I would be better off now if I were stateless. A stateless person shows his laissez-passer and sometimes he can find a small job."

"But if you lost your passport why didn't you put in for a duplicate?"

"I did but did they give it to me?"

"Why not?"

"Why not? They say I sold it."

"Had they reason to think so?"

"I swear to you somebody stole it."

"Under such circumstances," Fidelman asked, "how do you live?"

"How do I live?" He chomped with his teeth. "I eat air."

"Seriously?"

"Seriously—on air. I also peddle," he confessed, "but to peddle you need a license and that the Italians won't give me. When they caught me peddling I was interned for six months in a work camp."

"Didn't they attempt to deport you?"

"They did but I sold my mother's old wedding ring that I kept in my pocket so many years. The Italians are a humane people. They took the money and let me go but they told me not to peddle more."

"So what do you do now?"

"I peddle. What should I do, beg?—I peddle. But last spring I got sick and gave my little money away to the doctors. I still have a bad cough." He coughed fruitily. "Now I have no capital to buy stock with. Listen, professor, maybe we can go in partnership together? Lend me twenty thousand lire and I will buy ladies' nylon stockings. After I sell them I will return you your money."

"I have no funds to invest, Susskind."

"You will get it back, with interest."

"I honestly am sorry for you," Fidelman said, "but why don't you at least do something practical? Why don't you go to the Joint Distribution Committee, for instance, and ask them to assist you? That's their business."

"I already told you why. They wish me to go back, I wish to stay here."

"I still think going back would be the best thing for you."

"No," cried Susskind angrily.

"If that's your decision, freely made, then why pick on me? Am I responsible for you then, Susskind?"

"Who else?" Susskind loudly replied.

"Lower your voice, please, people are sleeping around here," said Fidelman, beginning to perspire. "Why should I be?"

"You know what responsibility means?"

"I think so."

"Then you are responsible. Because you are a man. Because you are a Jew, aren't you?"

"Yes, goddamn it, but I'm not the only one in the whole wide world. Without prejudice, I refuse the obligation. I am a single individual and can't take on everybody's personal burden. I have the weight of my own to contend with."

He reached for his billfold and plucked out another dollar.

"This makes five. It's more than I can afford but take it and after this please leave me alone. I have made my contribution."

Susskind stood there, oddly motionless, an impassioned statue, and for a moment Fidelman wondered if he would stay all night, but at last the refugee thrust forth a stiff arm, took the fifth dollar and departed.

Early the next morning Fidelman moved out of the hotel into another, less convenient for him, but far away from Shimon Susskind and his endless demands.

This was Tuesday. On Wednesday, after a busy morning in the library, Fidelman entered a nearby trattoria and ordered a plate of spaghetti with tomato sauce. He was reading his *Messaggero*, anticipating the coming of the food, for he was unusually hungry, when he sensed a presence at the table. He looked up, expecting the waiter, but beheld instead Susskind standing there, alas, unchanged.

Is there no escape from him? thought Fidelman, severely vexed. Is this why I came to Rome?

"Shalom, professor," Susskind said, keeping his eyes off the table. "I was passing and saw you sitting here alone, so I came in to say shalom."

"Susskind," Fidelman said in anger, "have you been following me again?"

"How could I follow you?" asked the astonished Susskind. "Do I know where you live now?"

Though Fidelman blushed a little, he told himself he owed nobody an explanation. So he had found out he had moved —good.

"My feet are tired. Can I sit five minutes?"

"Sit."

Susskind drew out a chair. The spaghetti arrived steaming hot. Fidelman sprinkled it with cheese and wound his fork into several tender strands. One of the strings of spaghetti seemed to stretch for miles, so he stopped at a certain point and swallowed the forkful. Having foolishly neglected to cut the long string he was left sucking it, seemingly endlessly. This embarrassed him.

Susskind watched with rapt attention.

Fidelman at last reached the end of the long spaghetto, patted his mouth with a large napkin, and paused in his eating.

"Would you care for a plateful?"

Susskind, eyes hungry, hesitated. "Thanks," he said.

"Thanks yes or thanks no?"

"Thanks no." The eyes looked away.

Fidelman resumed eating, carefully winding his fork; he had had not much practice with this sort of thing and was soon involved in the same dilemma with the spaghetti. Seeing Susskind still watching him, he soon became tense.

"We are not Italians, professor," the refugee said. "Cut it in small pieces with your knife. Then you will swallow it easier."

"I'll handle it as I please," Fidelman responded testily. "This is my business. You attend to yours."

"My business," Susskind sighed, "don't exist. This morning I had to let a wonderful chance get away from me. I had a chance to buy ladies' stockings at three hundred lire if I had money to buy half a gross. I could easily sell them for five hundred a pair. We would have made a nice profit."

"The news doesn't interest me."

"So if not ladies' stockings, I can also get sweaters, scarves, men's socks, also cheap leather goods, ceramics—whatever would interest you."

"What interests me is what you did with the money I gave you for a sweater."

"It's getting cold, professor," Susskind said worriedly. "Soon comes the November rains, and in winter the tramontana. I thought I ought to save your money to buy a couple of kilos of chestnuts and a bag of charcoal for my burner. If you sit all day on a busy street corner you can sometimes make a thousand lire. Italians like hot chestnuts. But if I do this I will need some warm clothes, maybe a suit."

"A suit," Fidelman remarked sarcastically, "why not an overcoat?"

"I have a coat, poor that it is, but now I need a suit. How can anybody come in company without a suit?"

Fidelman's hand trembled as he laid down his fork. "To my mind you are irresponsible and I won't be saddled with you. I have the right to choose my own problems and the right to my privacy."

"Don't get excited, professor, it's bad for your digestion. Eat in peace." Susskind got up and left the trattoria.

Fidelman hadn't the appetite to finish his spaghetti. He paid the bill, waited ten minutes, then departed, glancing around from time to time to see if he were being followed. He headed down the sloping street to a small piazza where he saw a couple of cabs. Not that he could afford one, but he wanted to make sure Susskind didn't tail him back to his new hotel. He would warn the clerk at the desk never to allow anybody of the refugee's name or description even to make inquiries about him.

Susskind, however, stepped out from behind a plashing fountain at the center of the little piazza. Modestly addressing the speechless Fidelman, he said, "I don't wish to take only, professor. If I had something to give you, I would gladly give it to you."

"Thanks," snapped Fidelman, "just give me some peace of mind."

"That you have to find yourself," Susskind answered.

In the taxi Fidelman decided to leave for Florence the next day, rather than at the end of the week, and once and for all be done with the pest.

That night, after returning to his room from an unpleasurable walk in the Trastevere—he had a headache from too much wine at supper—Fidelman found his door ajar and at once recalled that he had forgotten to lock it, although he had as usual left the key with the desk clerk. He was at first frightened, but when he tried the armadio in which he kept his clothes and suitcase, it was shut tight. Hastily unlocking it, he was relieved to see his blue gabardine suit—a one-button jacket affair, the trousers a little frayed on the cuffs but all in good shape and usable for years to come—hanging amid some shirts the maid had pressed for him; and when he examined the contents of the suitcase he found nothing missing, including, thank God, his passport and traveler's checks. Gazing around the room, Fidelman saw all in place. Satisfied, he picked up a book and read ten pages before he thought of his brief case. He jumped to his feet and began to search everywhere, remembering distinctly that it had been on the night table as he had lain on the bed that afternoon, rereading his chapter. He searched under the bed and behind the night table, then again throughout the room, even on top of and behind the armadio. Fidelman hopelessly opened every drawer, no matter how small, but found neither the brief case, nor, what was far worse, the chapter in it.

With a groan he sank down on the bed, insulting himself for not having made a copy of the manuscript, for he had more than once warned himself that something like this might happen to it. But he hadn't because there were some revisions he had contemplated making, and he had planned to retype the entire chapter before beginning the next. He thought now of complaining to the owner of the hotel, who lived on the floor below, but it was already past midnight and he realized nothing could be done until morning. Who could have taken it? The maid or hall porter? It seemed unlikely they would risk their jobs to steal a piece of leather goods that would bring them only a few thousand lire in a pawn shop. Possibly a sneak thief? He would ask tomorrow if other persons on the floor were missing something. He somehow doubted it. If a thief, he would then and there have ditched the chapter and stuffed the brief case with Fidelman's oxblood shoes, left by the bed, and the fifteen-dollar R. H. Macy sweater that lay in full view on the desk. But if not the maid or porter or a sneak thief, then who? Though Fidelman had not the slightest shred of evidence to support his suspicions he could think of only one person—Susskind. This thought stung him. But if Susskind, why? Out of pique, perhaps, that he had not been given the suit he had coveted, nor was able to pry it out of the armadio? Try as he would, Fidelman could think of no one else and no other reason. Somehow the peddler had followed him home (he had suspected their meeting at the fountain) and had got into his room while he was out to supper.

Fidelman's sleep that night was wretched. He dreamed of pursuing the refugee in the Jewish catacombs under the ancient Appian Way, threatening him a blow on the presumptuous head with a seven-flamed candelabrum he clutched in his hand; while Susskind, clever ghost, who knew the ins and outs of all the crypts and alleys, eluded him at every turn. Then Fidelman's candles all blew out, leaving him sightless and alone in the cemeterial dark; but when the student arose in the morning and wearily drew up the noisy blinds, the yellow Italian, somewhat shrunken, sun winked him cheerfully in both bleary eyes.

Fidelman postponed going to Florence. He reported his loss to the Questura, and though the police were polite and eager to help, they could do nothing for him. On the form on which the inspector noted the complaint, he listed the brief case as worth ten thousand lire, and for "valore del manoscritto" he drew a line. Fidelman, after giving the matter a good deal of thought, did not report Susskind, first, because he had absolutely no proof, for the desk clerk swore he had seen no stranger around in knickers; second, because he was afraid of the consequences for the refugee if he were written down "suspected thief" as well as "unlicensed peddler" and inveterate refugee. He tried instead to rewrite the chapter, which he felt sure he knew by heart, but when he sat down at the desk there were important thoughts, whole paragraphs, even pages that went blank in the mind. He considered sending to America for his notes for the chapter but they were in a barrel in his sister's attic in Levittown, among many notes for other projects. The thought of Bessie, a mother of five, poking around in his things, and the work entailed in sorting the cards, then getting them packaged and mailed to him across the ocean, wearied Fidelman unspeakably; he was certain she would send the wrong ones. He laid down his pen and went into the street, seeking Susskind. He searched for him in neighborhoods where he had seen him before, and though Fidelman spent hours looking, literally days, Susskind never appeared; or if he perhaps did, the sight of Fidelman caused him to vanish. And when the student inquired about him at the Israeli consulate, the clerk, a new man on the job, said he had no record of such a person or his lost passport; on the other hand, the refugee was known at the JDC, but by name and address only, an impossibility, Fidelman thought. They gave him a number to go to but the place had long since been torn down to make way for an apartment house.

Time went without work, without accomplishment. To put an end to this appalling waste Fidelman tried to force himself back into his routine research and picture viewing. He moved out of the hotel, which he now could not stand for the harm it had done him (leaving a telephone number and urging he be called if the slightest clue turned up), and he took a room in a small pensione near the Stazione and here had breakfast and supper rather than go out. He was much concerned with expenditures and carefully recorded them in a notebook he had acquired for the purpose. Nights, instead of wandering in the city, feasting himself on its beauty and mystery, he kept his eyes glued to paper, sitting steadfastly at his desk in an attempt to re-create his initial chapter, because he was lost without a beginning. He had tried writing the second chapter from notes in his possession but it had come to nothing. Always Fidelman needed something solid behind him before he could advance, some worthwhile accomplishment upon which to build another. He worked late but his mood, or inspiration, or whatever it was, had deserted him, leaving him with growing anxiety, almost disorientation; of not knowing—it seemed to him for the first time in months—what he must do next, a feeling that was torture. Therefore he again took up his search for the refugee. He thought now that once he had settled it, knew that the man had or hadn't stolen his chapter—whether he recovered it or not seemed at the moment immaterial—just the knowing of it would ease his mind and again he would feel like working, the crucial element.

Daily he combed the crowded streets, searching for Susskind wherever people peddled. On successive Sunday mornings he took the long ride to the Porta Portese market and hunted for hours among the piles of second-hand goods and junk lining the back streets, hoping his brief case would magically appear, though it never did. He visited the open market at Piazza Fontanella Borghese, and observed the ambulant vendors at Piazza Dante. He looked among fruit and vegetable stalls set up in the streets, whenever he chanced upon them, and dawdled on busy street corners after dark, among beggars and fly-by-night peddlers. After the first cold snap at the end of October, when the chestnut sellers appeared throughout the city, huddled over pails of glowing coals, he sought in their faces the missing Susskind. Where in all of modern and ancient Rome was he? The man lived in the open air—he had to appear somewhere. Sometimes when riding in a bus or tram, Fidelman thought he had glimpsed somebody in a crowd, dressed in the refugee's clothes, and he invariably got off to run after whoever it was—once a man standing in front of the Banco di Santo Spirito, gone when Fidelman breathlessly arrived; and another time he overtook a person in knickers but this one wore a monocle. Sir Ian Susskind?

In November it drearily rained. Fidelman wore a blue beret with his trench coat and a pair of black Italian shoes, smaller, despite their pointed toes, than his burly oxbloods which overheated his feet and whose color he detested. But instead of visiting museums he frequented movie houses, sitting in the cheapest seats and regretting the cost. He was, at odd hours in certain streets, several times solicited by prostitutes, some heartbreakingly pretty, one a slender, unhappy-looking girl with bags under her eyes whom he desired mightily, but Fidelman feared for his health. He had got to know the face of Rome and spoke Italian fairly fluently but his heart was burdened, and in his blood raged a murderous hatred of the bandy-legged refugee—although there were times when he thought he might be wrong—so Fidelman more than once cursed him to perdition.

One Friday night, as the first star glowed over the Tiber, Fidelman, walking aimlessly along the left riverbank, came upon a synagogue and wandered in among a crowd of Sephardim with Italianate faces. One by one they paused before a sink in an antechamber to dip their hands under a flowing faucet, then in the house of worship touched with loose fingers their brows, mouths, and breasts as they bowed to the Ark, Fidelman doing likewise. Where in the world am I? Three rabbis rose from a bench and the service began, a long prayer, sometimes chanted, sometimes accompanied by invisible organ music, but no Susskind anywhere. Fidelman sat at a desk-like pew in the last row where he could inspect the congregants yet keep an eye on the door. The synagogue was unheated and the cold rose like an exudation from the marble floor. The student's freezing nose burned like a lit candle. He got up to go but the beadle, a stout man in a high hat and short caftan, wearing a long thick silver chain around his neck, fixed the student with his powerful left eye.

"From New York?" he inquired, slowly approaching.

Half the congregation turned to see who.

"State, not city," answered Fidelman, nursing an active embarrassment for the attention he was attracting. Taking advantage of a pause, he whispered, "Do you happen to know a man named Susskind? He wears knickers."

"A relative?" The beadle gazed at him sadly.

"Not exactly."

"My own son—killed in the Ardeatine Caves." Tears stood forth in his eyes.

"Ah, for that I'm sorry."

But the beadle had exhausted the subject. He wiped his wet lids with pudgy fingers and the curious Sephardim turned back to their prayer books.

"Which Susskind?" the beadle wanted to know.

"Shimon."

He scratched his ear. "Look in the ghetto."

"I looked."

"Look again."

The beadle walked slowly away and Fidelman sneaked out.

The ghetto lay behind the synagogue for several crooked well-packed blocks, encompassing aristocratic palazzi ruined by age and unbearable numbers, their discolored façades strung with lines of withered wet wash, the fountains in the piazzas, dirt-laden, dry. And dark stone tenements, built partly on centuries-old ghetto walls, inclined towards one another across narrow, cobblestoned streets. In and among the impoverished houses were the wholesale establishments of wealthy Jews, dark holes ending in jeweled interiors, silks and silver of all colors. In the mazed streets wandered the present-day poor, Fidelman among them, oppressed by history although, he joked to himself, it added years to his life.

A white moon shone upon the ghetto, lighting it like dark day. Once he thought he saw a ghost he knew by sight, and hastily followed him through a thick stone passage to a blank wall where shone in white letters under a tiny electric bulb: VIETATO URINARE. Here was a smell but no Susskind.

For thirty lire the student bought a dwarfed blackened banana from a street vendor (not S) on a bicycle and stopped to eat. A crowd of ragazzi gathered to watch.

"Anybody here know Susskind, a refugee wearing knickers?" Fidelman announced, stooping to point with the banana where the pants went beneath the knees. He also made his legs a trifle bowed but nobody noticed.

There was no response until he had finished his fruit, then a thin-faced boy with brown liquescent eyes out of Murillo, piped: "He sometimes works in the Campo Verano, the Jewish section."

There too? thought Fidelman. "Works in the cemetery?" he inquired. "With a shovel?"

"He prays for the dead," the boy answered, "for a small fee."

Fidelman bought him a quick banana and the others dispersed.

In the cemetery, deserted on the Sabbath—he should have come Sunday—Fidelman went among the graves, reading legends on tombstones, many topped with small brass candelabra, whilst withered yellow chrysanthemums lay on the stone tablets of other graves, dropped stealthily, he imagined, on All Souls' Day—a festival in another part of the cemetery—by renegade sons and daughters unable to bear the sight of their dead bereft of flowers whilst the crypts of the goyim were lit and in bloom. Many were burial places, he read on the stained stones, of those who, for one reason or another, had died in the late large war. Among them was an empty place, it said on a marble slab lying on the ground, for "My beloved father/ Betrayed by the damned Fascists/ Murdered at Auschwitz by the barbarous Nazis/ *O Crimine Orribile.*"

—But no Susskind.

Three months had gone by since Fidelman's arrival in Rome. Should he, he many times asked himself, leave the city and this foolish search? Why not off to Florence, and there, amid the art splendors of the world, be inspired to resume his work? But the loss of his first chapter was like a spell cast over him. There were times he scorned it as a man-made thing, like all such, replaceable; other times he feared it wasn't the chapter per se, but that his volatile curiosity had become somehow entangled with Susskind's personality—Had he repaid generosity by stealing a man's life work? Was he so distorted? To satisfy himself, to know man, Fidelman had to know, though at what a cost in precious time and effort. Sometimes he smiled wryly at all this; ridiculous, the chapter grieved him for itself only—the precious thing he had created then lost—especially when he got to thinking of the long diligent labor, how painstakingly he had built each idea, how cleverly mastered problems of order, form, how impressive the finished product, Giotto reborn! It broke the heart. What else, if after months he was here, still seeking?

And Fidelman was unchangingly convinced that Susskind had taken it, or why would he still be hiding? He sighed much and gained weight. Mulling over his frustrated career, on the backs of envelopes containing unanswered letters from his sister Bessie he aimlessly sketched little angels flying. Once, studying his minuscule drawings, it occurred to him that he might someday return to painting but the thought was more painful than Fidelman could bear.

One bright morning in mid-December, after a good night's sleep, his first in weeks, he vowed he would have another look at the Navicella and then be off to Florence. Shortly before noon he visited the porch of St. Peter's, trying, from his remembrance of Giotto's sketch, to see the mosaic as it had been before its many restorations. He hazarded a note or two in shaky handwriting, then left the church and was walking down the sweeping flight of stairs, when he beheld at the bottom—his heart misgave him, was he still seeing pictures, a sneaky apostle added to the overloaded boatful?—ecco, Susskind! The refugee, in beret and long green G.I. raincoat, from under whose skirts showed his black-stockinged rooster's ankles—indicating knickers going on above though hidden—was selling black and white rosaries to all who would buy. He held several strands of beads in one hand, while in the palm of the other a few gilded medallions glinted in the winter sun. Despite his outer clothing, Susskind looked, it must be said, unchanged, not a pound more of meat or muscle, the face though aged, ageless. Gazing at him, the student ground his teeth in remembrance. He was tempted quickly to hide, and unobserved, observe the thief; but his impatience, after the long unhappy search, was too much for him. With controlled trepidation he approached Susskind on his left as the refugee was busily engaged on the right, urging a sale of beads upon a woman drenched in black.

"Beads, rosaries, say your prayers with holy beads."

"Greetings, Susskind," Fidelman said, coming shakily down the stairs, dissembling the Unified Man, all peace and contentment. "One looks for you everywhere and finds you here. Wie geht's?"

Susskind, though his eyes flickered, showed no surprise to speak of. For a moment his expression seemed to say he had no idea who was this, had forgotten Fidelman's existence, but then at last remembered—somebody long ago from another country, whom you smiled on, then forgot.

"Still here?" he perhaps ironically joked.

"Still." Fidelman was embarrassed at his voice slipping.

"Rome holds you?"

"Rome," faltered the student, "—the air." He breathed deep and exhaled with emotion.

Noticing the refugee was not truly attentive, his eyes roving upon potential customers, Fidelman, girding himself, remarked, "By the way, Susskind, you didn't happen to notice—did you?—the brief case I was carrying with me around the time we met in September?"

"Brief case—what kind?" This he said absently, his eyes on the church doors.

"Pigskin. I had in it—" here Fidelman's voice could be heard cracking, "—a chapter of a critical work on Giotto I was writing. You know, I'm sure, the Trecento painter?"

"Who doesn't know Giotto?"

"Do you happen to recall whether you saw, if, that is—" He stopped, at a loss for words other than accusatory.

"Excuse me—business." Susskind broke away and bounced up the steps two at a time. A man he approached shied away. He had beads, didn't need others.

Fidelman had followed the refugee. "Reward," he muttered up close to his ear. "Fifteen thousand for the chapter, and who has it can keep the brand-new brief case. That's his business, no questions asked. Fair enough?"

Susskind spied a lady tourist, including camera and guide book. "Beads—holy beads." He held up both handsful, but she was just a Lutheran passing through.

"Slow today," Susskind complained as they walked down the stairs, "but maybe it's the items. Everybody has the same. If I had some big ceramics of the Holy Mother, they go like hot cakes—a good investment for somebody with a little cash."

"Use the reward for that," Fidelman cagily whispered, "buy Holy Mothers."

If he heard, Susskind gave no sign. At the sight of a family of nine emerging from the main portal above, the refugee, calling addio over his shoulder, fairly flew up the steps. But Fidelman uttered no response. I'll get the rat yet. He went off to hide behind a high fountain in the square. But the flying spume raised by the wind wet him, so he retreated behind a massive column and peeked out at short intervals to keep the peddler in sight.

At two o'clock, when St. Peter's closed to visitors, Susskind dumped his goods into his raincoat pockets and locked up shop. Fidelman followed him all the way home, indeed the ghetto, although along a street he had not consciously been on before, which led into an alley where the refugee pulled open a left-handed door, and without transition, was "home." Fidelman, sneaking up close, caught a dim glimpse of an overgrown closet containing bed and table. He found no address on wall or door, nor, to his surprise, any door lock. This for a moment depressed him. It meant Susskind had nothing worth stealing. Of his own, that is. The student promised himself to return tomorrow, when the occupant was elsewhere.

Return he did, in the morning, while the entrepreneur was out selling religious articles, glanced around once and was quickly inside. He shivered—a pitch-black freezing cave. Fidelman scratched up a thick match and confirmed bed and table, also a rickety chair, but no heat or light except a drippy candle stub in a saucer on the table. He lit the yellow candle and searched all over the place. In the table drawer a few eating implements plus safety razor, though where he shaved was a mystery, probably a public toilet. On a shelf above the thin-blanketed bed stood half a flask of red wine, part of a package of spaghetti, and a hard panino. Also an unexpected little fish bowl with a bony goldfish swimming around in Arctic seas. The fish, reflecting the candle flame, gulped repeatedly, threshing its frigid tail as Fidelman watched. He loves pets, thought the student. Under the bed he found a chamber pot, but nowhere a brief case with a fine critical chapter in it. The place was not more than an ice-box someone probably had lent the refugee to come in out of the rain. Alas, Fidelman sighed. Back in the pensione, it took a hot water bottle two hours to thaw him out; but from the visit he never fully recovered.

In this latest dream of Fidelman's he was spending the day in a cemetery all crowded with tombstones, when up out of an empty grave rose this long-nosed brown shade, Virgilio Susskind, beckoning.

Fidelman hurried over.

"Have you read Tolstoy?"

"Sparingly."

"Why is art?" asked the shade, drifting off.

Fidelman, willy-nilly, followed, and the ghost, as it vanished, led him up steps going through the ghetto and into a marble synagogue.

The student, left alone, because he could not resist the impulse, lay down upon the stone floor, his shoulders keeping strangely warm as he stared at the sunlit vault above. The fresco therein revealed this saint in fading blue, the sky flowing from his head, handing an old knight in a thin red robe his gold cloak. Nearby stood a humble horse and two stone hills.

Giotto. San Francesco dona le vesti al cavaliere povero.

Fidelman awoke running. He stuffed his blue gabardine into a paper bag, caught a bus, and knocked early on Susskind's heavy portal.

"Avanti." The refugee, already garbed in beret and raincoat (probably his pajamas), was standing at the table, lighting the candle with a flaming sheet of paper. To Fidelman the paper looked the underside of a typewritten page. Despite himself the student recalled in letters of fire his entire chapter.

"Here, Susskind," he said in a trembling voice, offering the bundle, "I bring you my suit. Wear it in good health."

The refugee glanced at it without expression. "What do you wish for it?"

"Nothing at all." Fidelman laid the bag on the table, called goodbye and left.

He soon heard footsteps clattering after him across the cobblestones.

"Excuse me, I kept this under my mattress for you." Susskind thrust at him the pigskin brief case.

Fidelman savagely opened it, searching frantically in each compartment, but the bag was empty. The refugee was already in flight. With a bellow the student started after him. "You bastard, you burned my chapter!"

"Have mercy," cried Susskind, "I did you a favor."

"I'll do you one and cut your throat."

"The words were there but the spirit was missing."

In a towering rage Fidelman forced a burst of speed, but the refugee, light as the wind in his marvelous knickers, green coattails flying, rapidly gained ground.

The ghetto Jews, framed in amazement in their medieval windows, stared at the wild pursuit. But in the middle of it, Fidelman, stout and short of breath, moved by all he had lately learned, had a triumphant insight.

"Susskind, come back," he shouted, half sobbing. "The suit is yours. All is forgiven."

He came to a dead halt but the refugee ran on. When last seen he was still running.

2

MONTHS AFTER vainly seeking a studio on the Vie Margutta, del Babuino, della Croce, and elsewhere in that neighborhood, Arthur Fidelman settled for part of a crowded, windowy, attic-like atelier on a cobblestone street in the Trastevere, strung high with sheets and underwear. He had, a week before, in "personal notices" in the American language newspaper in Rome, read: "Studio to share, cheap, many advantages, etc., A. Oliovino," and after much serious anguish (the curt advertisement having recalled dreams he had dreamed were dead), many indecisions, enunciations and renunciations, Fidelman had, one very cold late-December morning, hurried to the address given, a worn four-story building with a yellowish façade stained brown along the edges. On the top floor, in a thickly cluttered artist's studio smelling aromatically of turpentine and oil paints, the inspiring sight of an easel lit in unwavering light from the three large windows setting the former art student on fire once more to paint, he had dealt not with a pittore, as expected, but with a pittrice, Annamaria Oliovino.

The pittrice, a thin, almost gaunt, high-voiced restless type, with short black uncombed hair, violet mouth, distracted eyes and a tense neck, a woman with narrow buttocks and piercing breasts, was in her way attractive if not in truth beautiful. She had on a thick black woolen sweater, eroded black velveteen culottes, black socks, and leather sandals spotted with drops of paint. Fidelman and she eyed each other stealthily and he realized at once she was, as a woman, indifferent to him or his type, who or which made no difference. But after ten minutes, despite the turmoil she exuded even as she dispassionately answered his hesitant questions, Fidelman, ever a sucker for strange beauty and all sorts of experiences, felt himself involved with and falling for her. Not my deep dish, he warned himself, aware of all the dangers to him and his renewed desire to create art; yet he was already half in love with her. It can't be, he thought in desperation; but it could. It had happened to him before. In her presence he tightly shut both eyes and wholeheartedly wished against what might be. Really he trembled, and though he labored to extricate his fate from hers, he was already a plucked bird, greased, and ready for frying. Fidelman loudly protested within—cried out severely against the weak self, called himself ferocious names but could do not much, a victim of his familiar response, a too passionate fondness for strangers. So Annamaria, who had advertised a twenty thousand lire monthly rental, in the end doubled the sum, and Fidelman paid through both nostrils, cash for first and last months (should he attempt to fly by night) plus a deposit of ten thousand for possible damages. An hour later he moved in with his imitation leather suitcase. This happened in the dead of winter. Below the cold sunlit windows stood two frozen umbrella pines and beyond, in the near distance, sparkled the icy Tiber.

The studio was well heated, Annamaria had insisted, but the cold leaked in through the wide windows. It was more a blast; the art student shivered but was kept warm by his hidden love for the pittrice. It took him most of a day to clear himself a space to work, about a third of the studio was as much as he could manage. He stacked her canvases five deep against her portion of the walls, curious to examine them, but Annamaria watched his every move (he noticed several self-portraits) although she was at the same time painting a monumental natura morta of a loaf of bread with two garlic bulbs ("Pane ed Agli"). He moved stacks of *Oggi*, piles of postcards and yellowed letters, and a bundle of calendars going back to many years ago; also a Perugina candy box full of broken pieces of Etruscan pottery, one of small sea shells, and a third of medallions of various saints and of the Virgin, which she warned him to handle with care. He had uncovered a sagging cot by a dripping stone sink in his corner of the studio and there he slept. She furnished an old chafing dish and a broken table, and he bought a few household things he needed. Annamaria rented the art student an easel for a thousand lire a month. Her quarters were private, a room at the other end of the studio whose door she kept locked, handing him the key when he had to use the toilet. The wall was thin and the instrument noisy. He could hear the whistle and rush of her water, and though he tried to be quiet, because of the plumbing the bowl was always brimful and the pour of his stream embarrassed him. At night, if there was need, although he was tempted to use the sink, he fished out the yellowed, sedimented pot under his bed; once or twice, as he was using it in the thick of night, he had the impression she was awake and listening.

They painted in their overcoats, Annamaria wearing a black babushka, Fidelman a green wool hat pulled down over his frozen ears. She kept a pan of hot coals at her feet and every so often lifted a sandaled foot to toast it. The marble floor of the studio was sheer thick ice; Fidelman wore two pairs of tennis socks his sister Bessie had recently sent him from the States. Annamaria, a leftie, painted with a smeared leather glove on her hand, and theoretically his easel had been arranged so that he couldn't see what she was doing but he often sneaked looks at her work. The pittrice, to his surprise, painted with flicks of her fingers and wrists, peering at her performance with almost shut eyes. He noticed she alternated still lifes with huge lyric abstractions—massive whorls of red and gold exploding, these built on, entwined with, and ultimately concealing a small religious cross, her first two brush strokes on every canvas. Once when Fidelman gathered the nerve to ask her why the cross, she answered it was the symbol that gave the painting its meaning.

"What meaning?"

"The meaning I want it to have."

He was eager to know more but she was impatient. "Eh," she shrugged, "who can explain art."

Though her responses to his various attempts to become better acquainted were as a rule curt, and her voluntary attention to him, shorter still—she was able, apparently, to pretend he wasn't there—Fidelman's feeling for Annamaria grew, and he was as unhappy in love as he had ever been.

But he was patient, a persistent virtue, served her often in various capacities, for instance carrying down four flights of stairs her two bags of garbage shortly after supper—the portinaia was crippled and the portiere never around—sweeping the studio clean each morning, even running to retrieve a brush or paint tube when she happened to drop one—offering any service any time, you name it. She accepted these small favors without giving them notice.

One morning after reading a many-paged letter she had just got in the mail, Annamaria was sad, sullen, unable to work; she paced around restlessly, it troubled him. But after feverishly painting a widening purple spiral that continued off the canvas, she regained a measure of repose. This heightened her beauty, lent it somehow a youthful quality it didn't ordinarily have—he guessed her to be no older than twenty-seven or -eight; so Fidelman, inspired by the change in her, hoping it might foretoken better luck for him, approached Annamaria, removed his hat and suggested since she went out infrequently why not lunch for a change at the trattoria at the corner, Guido's, where workmen assembled and the veal and white wine were delicious? She, to his surprise, after darting an uneasy glance out of the window at the tops of the motionless umbrella pines, abruptly assented. They ate well and conversed like human beings, although she mostly limited herself to answering his modest questions. She informed Fidelman she had come from Naples to Rome two years ago, although it seemed much longer, and he told her he was from the United States. Being so physically close to her, able to inhale the odor of her body—like salted flowers—and intimately eating together, excited Fidelman, and he sat very still, not to rock the boat and spill a drop of what was so precious to him. Annamaria ate hungrily, her eyes usually lowered. Once she looked at him with a shade of a smile and he felt beatitude; the art student contemplated many such meals though he could ill afford them, every cent he spent, saved and sent by Bessie.

After zuppa inglese and a peeled apple she patted her lips with a napkin, and still in good humor, suggested they take the bus to the Piazza del Popolo and visit some painter friends of hers.

"I'll introduce you to Alberto Moravia."

"With pleasure," Fidelman said.

But when they stepped into the street and were walking to the bus stop near the river a cold wind blew up and Annamaria turned pale.

"Something wrong?" Fidelman inquired.

"The East Wind." She spoke testily.

"What wind?"

"The Evil Eye," she said with irritation. "Malocchio."

He had heard something of the sort. They returned quickly to the studio, their heads lowered against the noisy wind, the pittrice from time to time furtively crossing herself. A black-habited old nun passed them at the trattoria corner, from whom Annamaria turned in torment, muttering "Jettatura! Porca miseria!" When they were upstairs in the studio she insisted Fidelman touch his testicles three times to undo or dispel who knew what witchcraft, and he modestly obliged. Her request had inflamed him, although he cautioned himself to remember, it was in purpose and essence theological.

Later she received a visitor, a man who came to see her on Monday and Friday afternoons after his work in a government bureau. Her visitors, always men, whispered with her a minute, then left restlessly; most of them, excepting also Giancarlo Balducci, a cross-eyed illustrator—Fidelman never saw again. But the one who came oftenest stayed longest, a solemn gray-haired gent, Augusto Ottogalli, with watery blue eyes and missing side teeth, old enough to be her father for sure. He wore a slanted black fedora and a shabby gray overcoat too large for him, greeted Fidelman vacantly and made him inordinately jealous. When Augusto arrived in the afternoon the pittrice usually dropped anything she was doing and they retired to her room, at once noisily locked and bolted. The art student wandered alone in the studio for dreadful hours. When Augusto ultimately emerged, looking disheveled, and if successful, defeated, Fidelman turned his back on him and the old man hastily let himself out of the door. After his visits, and only his, Annamaria did not appear in the studio for the rest of the day. Once when Fidelman knocked on her door to invite her out to supper, she said to use the pot because she had a headache and was sound asleep. On another occasion when Augusto was locked long in her room with her, after a tormenting two hours Fidelman tiptoed over and put his jealous ear to the door. All he could hear was the buzz and sigh of their whispering. Peeking through the keyhole he saw them both in their overcoats, sitting on her bed, Augusto clasping her hands, whispering passionately, his nose empurpled with emotion, Annamaria's white face averted. When the art student checked an hour later, they were still at it, the old man imploring, the pittrice weeping. The next time, Augusto came with a priest, a portly, heavy-breathing man with a doubtful face. But as soon as they appeared in the studio Annamaria, enraged to fury, despite the impassioned entreatments of Augusto, began to throw at them anything of hers or Fidelman's she could lay hands on.

"Bloodsuckers!" she shouted, "scorpions! parasites!" until they had hastily retreated. Yet when Augusto, worn and harried, returned alone, without complaint she retired to her room with him.

Fidelman's work, despite the effort and despair he gave it, was going poorly. Every time he looked at unpainted canvas he saw harlequins, whores, tragic kings, fragmented musicians, the sick and the dread. Still, tradition was tradition and what if he wanted to make more? Since he had always loved art history he considered embarking on a "Mother and Child," but was afraid her image would come out too much Bessie—after all, a dozen years between them. Or maybe a moving "Pietà," the dead son's body held like a broken wave in mama's frail arms? A curse on art history—he fought the fully prefigured picture though some of his former best paintings had jumped in every detail to the mind. Yet if so where's true engagement? Sometimes I'd like to forget every picture I've seen, Fidelman thought. Almost in panic he sketched in charcoal a coattailed "Figure of a Jew Fleeing" and quickly hid it away. After that, ideas, prefigured or not, were scarce. "Astonish me," he muttered, wondering whether to return to surrealism. He also considered a series of "Relations to Places and Space," hard-edge constructions in squares and circles, the pleasures of tri-dimensional geometry of linear abstraction, only he had little heart for it. The furthest abstraction, Fidelman thought, is the blank canvas. A moment later he said to himself, if painting shows who you are why should not painting? I mean I oughtn't to worry about that.

After the incident with the priest Annamaria was despondent for a week, stayed in her room sometimes bitterly crying, Fidelman often standing helplessly by her door. However, her unhappy mood was prelude to a burst of creativity by the pittrice. Works by the dozens leaped from her brush and stylus. She went on with her lyric abstractions based on the theme of a hidden cross and spent hours with a long black candle, burning holes in heavy white paper ("Buchi Spontanei"). Having mixed coffee grounds, sparkling bits of crushed mirror and ground sea shells, she blew the dust on mucilaged paper ("Velo nella Nebbia"). She composed collages of rags and toilet paper. After a dozen linear studies ("Linee Discendenti"), she experimented with gold leaf sprayed with umber, the whole while wet drawn in long undulations with a fine comb. She framed this in a black frame and hung it on end like a diamond ("Luce di Candela"). Annamaria worked intently, her brow furrowed, violet mouth tightly pursed, eyes lit, nostrils palpitating in creative excitement; and when she had temporarily run out of new ideas she did a mythological bull in red clay ("La Donna Toro"), afterwards returning to natura morta with bunches of bananas; then self-portraits.

The pittrice occasionally took time out to see what Fidelman was up to, although not much, and then editing his efforts. She changed lines and altered figures, or swabbed paint over whole compositions that didn't appeal to her. There was not much that did, but Fidelman was grateful for any attention she gave his work, and even kept at it to incite her criticism. He could feel his heartbeat in his teeth whenever she stood close to him modifying his work, he deeply breathing her intimate smell of sweating flowers. She wore perfume only when Augusto came and it disappointed Fidelman that the old man should evoke the use of bottled fragrance; yet he was cheered that her natural odor which he, so to say, got for free, was so much more exciting than the stuff she doused herself with for her decrepit Romeo. He had noticed she had a bit of soft belly but he loved the pliant roundness and often daydreamed of it. Thinking it might please her, for he pleased her rarely (he reveried how it would be once she understood the true depth of his love for her), the art student experimented with some of the things Annamaria had done—spontaneous holes, for instance, several studies of "Lines Ascending," and two lyrical abstract expressionistic pieces based on, interwoven with, and ultimately concealing a Star of David, although for these attempts he soon discovered he had earned, instead of her good will, an increased measure of scorn.

However, Annamaria continued to eat lunch with him at Guido's, and more often than not, supper, although she said practically nothing during meals and afterwards let her eye roam over the faces of the men at the other tables. But there were times after they had eaten when she would agree to go for a short walk with Fidelman, if there was no serious wind; and once in a while they entered a movie in the Trastevere, for she hated to cross any of the bridges of the Tiber, and then only in a bus, sitting stiffly, staring ahead. As they were once riding Fidelman seized the opportunity to hold her tense fist in his, but as soon as they were safely across the river she tore it out of his grasp. He was by now giving her presents—tubes of paints, the best brushes, a few yards of Belgian linen, which she accepted without comment; she also borrowed small sums from him, nothing startling—a hundred lire today, five hundred tomorrow. And she announced one morning that he would thereafter, since he used so much of both, have to pay additional for water and electricity—he already paid extra for the heatless heat. Fidelman, though always worried about money, assented. He would give his last lira to lie on her soft belly, but she offered niente, not so much as a caress; until one day he was permitted to look on as she sketched herself nude in his presence. Since it was bitter cold the pittrice did this in two stages. First she removed her sweater and brassiere, and viewing herself in a long faded mirror, quickly sketched the upper half of her body before it turned blue. He was dizzily enamored of her form and flesh. Hastily fastening the brassiere and pulling on her sweater, Annamaria stepped out of her sandals and peeled off her culottes, and white panties torn at the crotch, then drew the rest of herself down to her toes. The art student begged permission to sketch along with her but the pittrice denied it, so he had, as best one can, to commit to memory her lovely treasures—the hard, piercing breasts, narrow shapely buttocks, vine-hidden labia, the font and sweet beginning of time. After she had drawn herself and dressed, and when Augusto appeared and they had retired behind her bolted door, Fidelman sat motionless on his high stool before the glittering blue-skied windows, slowly turning to ice to faint strains of Bach.

The art student increased his services to Annamaria; her increase was scorn, or so it seemed. This severely bruised his spirit. What have I done to deserve such treatment? That I pay my plenty of rent on time? That I buy her all sorts of presents, not to mention two full meals a day? That I live in flaming hot and freezing cold? That I passionately adore each sweet-and-sour bit of her? He figured it bored her to see so much of him. For a week Fidelman disappeared during the day, sat in cold libraries or moved around in frosty museums. He tried painting after midnight and into the early morning hours but the pittrice found out and unscrewed the bulbs before she went to bed. "Don't waste my electricity, this isn't America." He screwed in a dim blue bulb and worked silently from I A.M. to five. At dawn he discovered he had painted a blue picture. Fidelman wandered in the streets of the city. At night he slept in the studio and could hear her sleeping in her room. She slept restlessly, dreamed badly, and often moaned. He dreamed he had three eyes and was missing an ear, or nose.

For two weeks he spoke to no one but a dumpy four-and-a-half foot female on the third floor, and to her usually to say no. Fidelman, having often heard the music of Bach drifting up from below, had tried to picture the lady piano player, imagining a quiet blonde with a slender body, a woman of grace and beauty. It had turned out to be Clelia Montemaggio, a middle-aged old maid music teacher, who sat at the old upright piano, her apartment door open to let out the cooking smells, particularly fried fish on Friday. Once when coming up from taking down the garbage, Fidelman had paused to listen to part of a partita at her door and she had lassoed him in for an espresso and pastry. He ate and listened to Bach, her plump bottom moving spryly on the bench as she played not badly.

"Lo spirito," she called to him raptly over her shoulder, "l'architettura!"

Fidelman nodded. Thereafter whenever she spied him in the hall she attempted to entice him with cream-filled pastries and J.S.B., whom she played apparently exclusively.

"Come een," she called in English, "I weel play for you. We weel talk. There is no use for too much solitude." But the art student, burdened by his, spurned hers.

Unable to work, he wandered in the streets in a desolate mood, his spirit dusty in a city of fountains and leaky water taps. Water, water everywhere, spouting, flowing, dripping, whispering secrets, love love love, but not for him. If Rome's so sexy, where's mine? Fidelman's Romeless Rome. It belonged least to those who yearned most for it. With slow steps he climbed the Pincio, if possible to raise his spirits gazing down at the rooftops of the city, spires, cupolas, towers, monuments, compounded history and past time. It was in sight, possessable, all but its elusive spirit; after so long he was still straniero. He was then struck by a thought: if you could paint this sight, give it its quality in yours, the spirit belonged to you. History become aesthetic! Fidelman's scalp thickened. A wild rush of things he might paint swept sweetly through him: saints in good and bad health, whole or maimed, in gold and red; nude gray rabbis at Auschwitz, black or white Negroes—what not when *any* color dripped from your brush? And if these, so also ANNAMARIA ES PULCHRA. He all but cheered. What more intimate possession of a woman! He would paint her, whether she permitted or not, posed or not—she was his to paint, he could with eyes shut. Maybe something will come, after all, of my love for her. His spirits elevated, Fidelman ran most of the way home.

It took him eight days, a labor of love. He tried her as nude and although able to imagine every inch of her, could not commit it to canvas. Then he suffered until it occurred to him to paint her as "Virgin with Child." The idea astonished and elated him. Fidelman went feverishly to work and caught an immediate likeness in paint. Annamaria, saintly beautiful, held in her arms the infant resembling his little nephew Georgie. The pittrice, aware, of course, of his continuous activity, cast curious glances his way, but Fidelman, painting in the corner by the stone sink, kept the easel turned away from her. She pretended unconcern. Done for the day he covered the painting and carefully guarded it. The art student was painting Annamaria in a passion of tenderness for the infant at her breast, her face responsive to its innocence. When, on the ninth day, in trepidation Fidelman revealed his work, the pittrice's eyes clouded and her underlip curled. He was about to grab the canvas and smash it up all over the place when her expression fell apart. The art student postponed all movement but trembling. She seemed at first appalled, a darkness descended on her, she was undone. She wailed wordlessly, then sobbed, "You have seen my soul." They embraced tempestuously, her breasts stabbing him, Annamaria bawling on his shoulder. Fidelman kissed her wet face and salted lips, she murmuring as he fooled with the hook of her brassiere under her sweater, "Aspetta, aspetta, caro, viene Augusto." He was mad with expectation and suspense.

Augusto, who usually arrived punctually at four, did not appear that Friday afternoon. Uneasy as the hour approached, Annamaria seemed relieved as the streets grew dark. She had worked badly after viewing Fidelman's painting, sighed frequently, gazed at him with sweet-sad smiles. At six she gave in to his urging and they retired to her room, his unframed "Virgin with Child" already hanging above her bed, replacing a gaunt self-portrait. He was curiously disappointed in the picture—surfacy thin—and made a mental note to borrow it back in the morning to work on it more. But the conception, at least, deserved the reward. Annamaria cooked supper. She cut his meat for him and fed him forkfuls. She peeled Fidelman's orange and stirred sugar in his coffee. Afterwards, at his nod, she locked and bolted the studio and bedroom doors and they undressed and slipped under her blankets. How good to be for a change on this side of the locked door, Fidelman thought, relaxing marvelously. Annamaria, however, seemed tensely alert to the noises of the old building, including a parrot screeching, some shouting kids running up the stairs, a soprano singing "Ritorna vincitor!" But she calmed down and hotly embraced Fidelman. In the middle of a passionate kiss the doorbell rang.

Annamaria stiffened in his arms. "Diavolo! Augusto!"

"He'll go away," Fidelman advised. "Both doors locked."

But she was at once out of bed, pulling on her culottes. "Get dressed," she said.

He hopped up and hastily got into his pants.

Annamaria unlocked and unbolted the inner door and then

the outer. It was the postman waiting to collect ten lire for an overweight letter from Naples.

After she had read the long letter and wiped away a tear they undressed and got back into bed.

"Who is he to you?" Fidelman asked.

"Who?"

"Augusto."

"An old friend. Like a father. We went through much together."

"Were you lovers?"

"Look, if you want me take me. If you like to ask questions go back to school."

He determined to mind his business.

"Warm me," Annamaria said, "I'm freezing."

Fidelman stroked her slowly. After ten minutes she said, "'Gioco di mano, gioco di villano.' Use your imagination."

He used his imagination and she responded with excitement. "Dolce tesoro," she whispered, flicking the tip of her tongue into his ear, then with little bites biting his ear lobe.

The doorbell rang loudly.

"For Christ's sake, don't answer," Fidelman groaned. He tried to hold her down but she was already up, hunting her robe.

"Put on your pants," she hissed.

He had thoughts of waiting for her in bed but it ended with his dressing fully. She sent him to the door. It was the crippled portinaia, the art student having neglected to take down the garbage.

Annamaria furiously got the two bags and handed them to her.

In bed she was so cold her teeth chattered.

Tense with desire Fidelman warmed her.

"Angelo mio," she murmured. "Amore, possess me."

He was about to when she kicked her legs together and hastily rose. "The cursed door again!"

Fidelman gnashed his teeth. "I heard nothing."

In her torn yellow silk robe she hurried to the front door, opened and shut it, quickly locked and bolted it, did the same in her room and slid into bed.

"You were right, it was nobody."

She embraced him, her hairy armpits perfumed. He responded with postponed passion.

"Enough of antipasto," Annamaria said. She reached for his member.

Overwrought, Fidelman, though fighting himself not to, spent himself in her hand. Although he mightily willed resurrection, his wilted flower bit the dust.

She furiously shoved him out of bed, into the studio, flinging his clothes after him.

"Pig, beast, onanist!"

At least she lets me love her. Daily Fidelman shopped, cooked, and cleaned for her. Every morning he took her shopping sack off the hook, went down to the street market and returned with the bag stuffed full of greens, pasta, eggs, meat, cheese, wine, bread. Annamaria insisted on three hearty meals a day although she had once told him she no longer enjoyed eating. Twice he had seen her throw up her supper. What she enjoyed he didn't know except it wasn't Fidelman. After he had served her at her table he was allowed to eat alone in the studio. At two every afternoon she took her siesta and though it was forbidden to make noise, he was allowed to wash the dishes, dust and clean her room, swab the toilet bowl. She called "Fatso" and in he trotted to get her anything she had run out of—drawing pencils, sanitary belt, safety pins. After she waked from her nap, rain or shine, please or no please, he was now compelled to leave the studio so she could work in peace and quiet. He wandered, in the tramontana, from one cold two-bit movie to another. At seven he was back to prepare her supper, and twice a week Augusto's, who sported a new black hat and spiffy overcoat, and pitied the art student with both wet blue eyes but wouldn't look at him. After supper, another load of dishes, the garbage downstairs, and when Fidelman returned, with or without Augusto Annamaria was already closeted behind her bolted door. He checked through the keyhole on Mondays and Fridays but she and the old gent were always fully clothed. Fidelman had more than once complained to her that his punishment exceeded his crime, but the pittrice said he was a type she would never have any use for. In fact he did not exist for her. Not existing how could he paint, although he told himself he must? He couldn't. He aimlessly froze wherever he went, a mean cold that seared his lungs though under his overcoat he wore a new thick sweater Bessie had knitted for him, and two woolen scarves around his neck. Since the night Annamaria had kicked him out of bed he had not been warm; yet he often dreamed of ultimate victory. Once when he was on his lonely way out of the house—a night she was giving a party for some painter friends, Fidelman, a drooping butt in the corner of his mouth, carrying the garbage bags, met Clelia Montemaggio coming up the stairs.

"You look like a frozen board," she said. "Come in and enjoy the warmth and a little Bach."

Unable to unfreeze enough to say no, he continued down with the garbage.

"Every man gets the woman he deserves," she called after him.

"Who got," Fidelman muttered. "Who gets."

He considered jumping into the Tiber but it was full of ice that winter.

One night at the end of February, Annamaria, to Fidelman's astonishment—it deeply affected him—said he might go with her to a party at Giancarlo Balducci's studio on the Via dell'Oca; she needed somebody to accompany her in the bus across the bridge and Augusto was flat on his back with the Asian flu. The party was lively—painters, sculptors, some writers, two diplomats, a prince and a visiting Hindu sociologist, their ladies and three hotsy-totsy, scantily dressed, unattached girls. One of them, a shapely beauty with orange hair, green eyes, and warm ways became interested in Fidelman, except that he was dazed by Annamaria, seeing her in a dress for the first time, a ravishing rich ruby-colored affair. The cross-eyed host had provided simply a huge cut-glass bowl of spiced mulled wine, and the guests dipped ceramic glasses into it and guzzled away. Everyone but the art student seemed to be enjoying himself. One or two of the men disappeared into other rooms with female friends or acquaintances and Annamaria, in a gay mood, did a fast shimmy to rhythmic handclapping. She was drinking steadily and when she wanted her glass filled, politely called him "Arturo." He began to have mild thoughts of possibly possessing her.

The party bloomed, at least forty, and turned wildish. Practical jokes were played. Fidelman discovered his left shoe had been smeared with mustard. Balducci's black cat mewed at a fat lady's behind, a slice of sausage pinned to her dress. Before midnight there were two fist fights, Fidelman enjoying both but not getting involved though once he was socked on the neck by a sculptor who had aimed at a painter. The girl with the orange hair, still interested in the art student, invited him to join her in Balducci's bedroom but he continued to be devoted to Annamaria, his eyes tied to her every move. He was jealous of the illustrator, who whenever near her nipped her bottom.

One of the sculptors, Orazio Pinello, a slender man with a darkish face, heavy black brows, and bleached blond hair, approached Fidelman. "Haven't we met before, caro?"

"Maybe," the art student said, perspiring lightly. "I'm Arthur Fidelman, an American painter."

"You don't say? Action painter?"

"Always active."

"I refer of course to Abstract Expressionism."

"Of course. Well, sort of. On and off."

"Haven't I seen some of your work around? Galleria Schneider? Some symmetric hard-edge biomorphic forms? Not bad as I remember."

Fidelman thanked him, in full blush.

"Who are you here with?" Orazio Pinello asked.

"Annamaria Oliovino."

"Her?" said the sculptor. "But she's a fake."

"Is she?" Fidelman said with a sigh.

"Have you looked at her work?"

"With one eye. Her art is bad but I find her irresistible."

"Peccato." The sculptor shrugged and drifted away.

A minute later there was another fist fight, during which the green-eyed orange head conked Fidelman with a Chinese vase. He went out cold and when he came to, Annamaria and Balducci were undressing him in the illustrator's bedroom. Fidelman experienced an almost overwhelming pleasure, then Balducci explained that the art student had been chosen to pose in the nude for drawings both he and the pittrice would do of him. He explained there had been a discussion as to which of them did male nudes best and they had decided to settle it in a short contest. Two easels had been wheeled to the center of the studio; a half hour was allotted to the contestants, and the guests would judge who had done the better job. Though he at first objected because it was a cold night, Fidelman nevertheless felt warmish from wine so he agreed to pose; besides he was proud of his muscles and maybe if she sketched him nude it might arouse her interest in a tussle later. And if he wasn't painting he was at least being painted.

So the pittrice and Giancarlo Balducci, in paint-smeared smocks, worked for thirty minutes by the clock, the whole party silently looking on, with the exception of the orange-haired tart, who sat in the corner eating a prosciutto sandwich. Annamaria, her brow furrowed, lips pursed, drew intensely with crayon; Balducci worked calmly in colored chalk. The guests were absorbed, although after ten minutes the Hindu went home. A journalist locked himself in the painter's bedroom with orange head and would not admit his wife who pounded furiously on the door. Fidelman, standing barefoot on a rubber bathmat, was eager to see what Annamaria was accomplishing but had to be patient. When the half hour was up he was permitted to look. Balducci had drawn a flock of green and black abstract testiculate circles. Fidelman shuddered. But Annamaria's drawing was representational, not Fidelman although of course inspired by him: A gigantic funereal phallus that resembled a broken-backed snake. The blond sculptor inspected it with half-closed eyes, then yawned and left. By now the party was over, the guests departed, lights out except for a few dripping white candles. Balducci was collecting his ceramic glasses and emptying ash trays, and Annamaria had thrown up. The art student afterwards heard her begging the illustrator to sleep with her but Balducci complained of fatigue.

"I will if he won't," Fidelman offered.

Annamaria, enraged, spat on her picture of his unhappy phallus.

"Don't dare come near me," she cried. "Malocchio! Jettatura!"

The next morning he awoke sneezing, a nasty cold. How can I go on? Annamaria, showing no signs of pity or remorse, continued shrilly to berate him. "You've brought me nothing but bad luck since you came here. I'm letting you stay because you pay well but I warn you to stay out of my sight."

"But how—" he asked hoarsely.

"That doesn't concern me."

"—how will I paint?"

"Who cares? Paint at night."

"Without light—"

"Paint in the dark. I'll give you a can of black paint."

"How can you be so cruel to a man who loves—"

"I'll scream," she said.

He left in anguish. Later while she was at her siesta he came back, got some of his things and tried to paint in the hall. No dice. Fidelman wandered in the rain. He sat for hours on the Spanish Steps. Then he returned to the house and went slowly up the stairs. The door was locked. "Annamaria," he hoarsely called. Nobody answered. In the street he stood at the river wall, watching the dome of St. Peter's in the distance. Maybe a potion, Fidelman thought, or an amulet? He doubted either would work. How do you go about hanging yourself? In the late afternoon he went back to the house—would say he was sick, needed rest, possibly a doctor. He felt feverish. She could hardly refuse.

But she did, although explaining she felt bad herself. He held onto the banister as he went downstairs. Clelia Montemaggio's door was open. Fidelman paused, then continued down but she had seen him. "Come een, come een."

He went reluctantly in. She fed him camomile tea and panettone. He ate in a wolfish hurry as she seated herself at the piano.

"No Bach, please, my head aches from various troubles."

"Where's your dignity?" she asked.

"Try Chopin, that's lighter."

"Respect yourself, please."

Fidelman removed his hat as she began to play a Bach prelude, her bottom rhythmic on the bench. Though his cold oppressed him and he could hardly breathe, tonight the spirit, the architecture, moved him. He felt his face to see if he were crying but only his nose was wet. On the top of the piano Clelia had placed a bowl of white carnations in full bloom.

Each white petal seemed a white flower. If I could paint those gorgeous flowers, Fidelman thought. If I could paint something. By Jesus, if I could paint myself, that'd show them! Astonished by the thought he ran out of the house.

The art student hastened to a costume shop and settled on a cassock and fuzzy black soupbowl biretta, envisaging another Rembrandt: "Portrait of the Artist as Priest." He hurried with his bulky package back to the house. Annamaria was handing the garbage to the portinaia as Fidelman thrust his way into the studio. He quickly changed into the priest's vestments. The pittrice came in wildly to tell him where he got off, but when she saw Fidelman already painting himself as priest, with a moan she rushed into her room. He worked with smoking intensity and in no time created an amazing likeness. Annamaria, after stealthily re-entering the studio, with heaving bosom and agitated eyes closely followed his progress. At last, with a cry she threw herself at his feet.

"Forgive me, Father, for I have sinned—"

Dripping brush in hand, he stared down at her. "Please, I—"

"Oh Father, if you knew what I've done. I've been a whore—"

After a moment's thought Fidelman said, "If so I absolve you."

"Not without penance. First listen to the rest. I've had no luck with men, they're all bastards. Or else I jinx them. If you want the truth I'm an Evil Eye myself. Anybody who loves me is cursed."

He listened in fascination.

"Augusto is really my uncle. After many others he became my lover. At least he's gentle. My father found out and swore he'd kill us both. That's when I left Naples. I was pregnant and scared to death. A sin can go too far. Augusto told me to have the baby and leave it at an orphanage, but the night it was born I was confused and threw it into the Tiber. I was afraid it was an idiot."

She was sobbing. He drew back.

"Wait," she wept. "The next time in bed Augusto was impotent. Since then he's been imploring me to confess so he can get back his powers. But every time I step into the confessional my tongue turns to bone. The priest can't tear a word out of me. That's how it's been all my life, don't ask me why because I don't know."

She grabbed his knees. “Help me, Father, for Christ’s sake.”

Fidelman, after a short tormented time, said in a quavering voice, “I forgive you, my child.”

“The penance,” she wailed, “first the penance.”

After reflecting, he replied, “Say one hundred times each, Our Father and Hail Mary.”

“More,” Annamaria wept. “More, more. Much more.”

Gripping his knees so hard they shook she burrowed her head into his black-buttoned lap. He felt the surprised beginnings of an erection.

“In that case,” Fidelman said, shuddering a little, “better undress.”

“Only,” Annamaria said, “if you keep your vestments on.”

“Not the cassock, too clumsy.”

“At least the biretta.”

He agreed to that.

Annamaria undressed in a swoop. Her body was extraordinarily lovely, the flesh glowing. In her bed they tightly embraced. She clasped his buttocks, he cupped hers. Pumping slowly he nailed her to her cross.

3

FIDELMAN LISTLESSLY doodles all over a sheet of yellow paper. Odd indecipherable designs, ink-spotted blotched words, esoteric ideographs, tormented figures in a steaming sulfurous lake, a stylish nude rising newborn out of cold water. Not bad at all though more mannequin than Knidean Aphrodite. Scarpio, sharp-nosed on the former art student's gaunt left, looking up from his cards, inspects her with his good eye.

"Not bad, who is she? One of the girls here?"

"Nobody I really know."

"You must be hard up."

"I always am."

"Quiet," rumbles Angelo, the padrone, on Fidelman's far right, his two-chinned face molded in lard. He flips the top card.

Scarpio turns up a deuce, making eight and a half and out. He curses his Sainted Mother, Angelo wheezing. Fidelman shows four and his last hundred lire. He picks a cautious ace and sighs. Angelo, with seven showing, chooses this passionate moment to relieve himself.

"Wait for me," he orders. "Watch the pot, Scarpio."

"Who's that hanging?" Scarpio points to a long-coated figure loosely dangling from a gallows rope amid Fidelman's other doodles.

Who but Susskind, surely. A dim figure out of the past.

"Just a friend. Nobody you know."

"It'd better not be."

Scarpio picks up the yellow paper for a closer squint.

"But whose head?" he asks with interest. A long-nosed severed head bounces down the steps of the guillotine platform.

A man's head or his sex, Fidelman wonders. In either case a terrible wound.

"Looks a little like mine. At least the long jaw."

Scarpio points to a street scene. In front of American Express here's this starving white Negro pursued by a hooting mob of cowboys on horses.

Embarrassed by the recent past Fidelman blushes.

Long past midnight. They sit motionless in Angelo's stuffy office, a small lit bulb glowing darkly over a square wooden table on which lie a pack of puffy cards, Fidelman's naked hundred lire note, and a green bottle of Munich beer that the padrone of the Hotel du Ville, Milano, swills from between hands and games. Scarpio, his major-domo and secretary-lover, sips an espresso. Fidelman only watches, being without privileges. Each night they play sette e mezzo, jeenrummy, or baccarat and Fidelman loses the day's earnings, the few meager tips he has garnered from the whores for little services rendered. Angelo says nothing and takes all.

Scarpio, snickering, understands the street scene. Fidelman, adrift penniless in the stony gray Milanese streets, had picked his first pocket. An American tourist staring into a store window. The Texan, feeling the tug, and missing his wallet, had bellowed murder. A carabiniere looked wildly at Fidelman, who broke into a run, another well-dressed carabiniere on a horse clattering after him down the street, waving his sword over his head. Angelo, cleaning his fingernails with his penknife in front of his hotel, saw Fidelman coming pell-mell and ducked him around a corner, through a cellar door, into the Hotel du Ville, a joint for prostitutes who split fees with the padrone for the use of a room.

Angelo registered the former art student, gave him a tiny dark room, and pointing a gun, relieved him of his passport and the contents of the Texan's wallet. He warned him that if he ratted to anybody, he would report him to the Questura where his brother presided, as a dangerous alien thief. The former art student, desperate to escape, needed money to travel, so he sneaked into Angelo's room one morning and from the strapped suitcase under the bed, extracted fistfuls of lire, stuffing all his pockets. Scarpio, happening in, caught him at it and held a dagger to Fidelman's ribs—who fruitlessly pleaded they could both make a living from the suitcase—until the padrone appeared.

"A hunchback is straight only in his grave."

Angelo slapped Fidelman's face first with one fat hand, then with the other, till it turned red and the tears flowed freely. He chained him to the bed in his room for a week. When Fidelman promised to behave he was released and appointed mastro delle latrine, having to clean thirty toilets daily with a stiff brush, for room and board. He also assisted Teresa, the asthmatic, hairy-legged chambermaid, and ran errands for the whores. The former art student hoped to escape but the portiere or his assistant was at the door twenty-four hours a day. And thanks to the card games and his impassioned gambling, Fidelman was without sufficient funds to go anywhere, if there was anywhere to go. And without passport, so he stayed put.

Scarpio secretly feels Fidelman's thigh.

"Let go or I'll tell the padrone."

Angelo returns and flips up a card. Queen. Seven and a half on the button. He pockets Fidelman's last hundred lire.

"Go to bed," says Angelo, "it's a long day tomorrow."

Fidelman climbs up to his room on the fifth floor and stares out the window into the dark street to see how far down is death. Too far, so he undresses for bed. He looks every night and sometimes during the day. Teresa, screaming, had once held onto his two legs as Fidelman dangled half out of the window until one of the girls' naked customers, a barrel-chested man, rushed into the room and dragged him back in.

Sometimes Fidelman weeps in his sleep.

He awakes, cringing. Angelo and Scarpio are in his room but nobody hits him.

"Search anywhere," Fidelman offers. "You won't find a thing except maybe half a stale pastry."

"Shut up," says Angelo. "We want to make a proposition."

Fidelman slowly sits up. Scarpio produces the yellow sheet of scribbled fantasies. "We notice you draw." He points a dirty fingernail at the nude figure.

"After a fashion. I doodle and see what happens."

"Could you copy a painting?"

"What sort of painting?"

"Just a nude. Tiziano's 'Venus of Urbino.' The one after Giorgione."

"Oh that one?" Fidelman thinks. "I doubt that I could."

"Any fool can."

"Shut up, Scarpio." Angelo sits his bulk at the foot of

Fidelman's narrow bed. Scarpio, with his good eye, moodily inspects the cheerless view from the window.

"On Isola Bella in Lago Maggiore, about an hour from here," Angelo says, "there's a small castello full of lousy paintings, except for one which is a genuine Tiziano, authenticated by three art experts, including a brother-in-law of mine. It's worth half a million dollars but the owner is richer than Olivetti and won't sell though an American museum has offered a fortune."

"Very interesting."

"Exactly. Anyway it's insured for at least $400,000. Of course if anyone stole it it would be impossible to sell."

"Then why bother?"

"Bother what?"

"Whatever it is," Fidelman says lamely.

"You'll learn more by listening. Suppose it was stolen and held for ransom?"

"Ransom?"

"Ransom," Scarpio says from the window.

"At least $300,000," says Angelo, "a bargain for the insurance company. They'd save a hundred thousand on the deal."

He outlines a plan. They had photographed the Titian on both sides from all angles and distances and had collected from various art books the best color plates. They also had the exact measurements of the canvas and every figure on it. If Fidelman could make a decent copy they would duplicate the frame and on a dark night sneak the reproduction into the castello gallery and exit with the original. The guards were stupid and the advantage of the plan—instead of slitting the canvas out of its frame—was that nobody would recognize the substitution for days, possibly longer. In the meantime they would row the picture across the lake and truck it out of the country; one had a better chance in France. Once the picture was securely hidden, Angelo back at the hotel, Scarpio would get in touch with the insurance company. Recognizing the brilliance of the execution, they would kick in at once with the ransom money.

"If you make a good copy you'll get yours," says Angelo.

"Mine? What would that be?" Fidelman asks.

"Your passport," Angelo answers cagily. "Plus two hundred American dollars and a quick goodbye."

"Five hundred dollars," says Fidelman.

"Scarpio," the padrone says patiently, "show him what you have in your pants."

Scarpio unbuttons his jacket and draws a mean-looking dagger from a sheath under his belt.

"Three fifty," Fidelman says. "I'll need plane fare."

"Three fifty," nods Angelo. "Payable when you deliver the finished reproduction."

"And you pay for all supplies?"

"All expenses within reason. But if you try any monkey tricks—snitch or double cross, you'll wake up with your head missing, or something worse."

"Tell me," Fidelman says after a minute of contemplation, "what if I turn down the proposition? I mean in a friendly way?"

Angelo rises sternly from the creaking bed. "Then you'll stay here for the rest of your life. When you leave you leave in a coffin, very cheap wood."

"I see."

"Then it's settled," says Angelo.

"Take the morning off," says Scarpio.

"Thanks."

The padrone glares. "First finish the toilet bowls."

Am I worthy? Can I do it? Do I dare? He has these and other doubts, feels melancholy, and wastes time.

Angelo one morning calls him into his office. "Have a Munich beer."

"No, thanks."

"Cordial?"

"Nothing now."

"What's the matter with you? You look as if you buried your mother."

Fidelman sets down his mop and pail and says nothing.

"Why don't you put those things away and get started?" the padrone asks. "I've had the portiere move six trunks and some broken furniture out of the storeroom where you have two big windows. Scarpio wheeled in an easel and he's bought you brushes, colors and anything else you need."

"It's west light, not very even."

Angelo shrugs. "It's the best I can do. This is our season and I can't spare any other rooms. If you'd rather work at night we can set up some lamps. It's a waste of electricity but I'll make that concession to your temperament if you work fast and produce the goods."

"What's more I don't know the first thing about forging paintings. All I might do is just about copy the picture."

"That's all we ask. Leave the technical business to us. First do a decent drawing. When you're ready to paint I'll get you a piece of sixteenth-century Belgian linen that's been scraped clean of a former picture. You prime it with white lead and when it's dry you sketch. Once you finish the nude, Scarpio and I will bake it, put in the cracks, and age them with soot. We'll even stipple in fly spots before we varnish and glue. We'll do what's necessary. There are books on this subject and Scarpio reads like a demon. It isn't as complicated as you think."

"What about the truth of the colors?"

"I'll mix them for you. I've made a life study of Tiziano's work."

Fidelman's eyes are still unhappy.

"What's eating you now?"

"It's stealing another painter's ideas and work."

The padrone wheezes. "Tiziano will forgive you. Didn't he steal the figure of the Urbino from Giorgione? Didn't Rubens steal the Andrian nude from Tiziano? Art steals and so does everybody. You stole a wallet and tried to steal my lire. What's the difference? It's the way of the world. We're only human."

"It's a sort of desecration."

"Everybody desecrates. We live off the dead and they live off us. Take for instance religion."

"I doubt I can do it without seeing the original," Fidelman says. "The color plates you gave me aren't true."

"Neither is the original any more. You don't think Rembrandt painted in those sfumato browns? As for painting the Venus, you'll have to do the job here. If you copied it in the castello gallery one of those cretin guards might remember your face and next thing you know you'd be in trouble. So would we, which we wouldn't want, naturally."

"I still ought to see it."

The padrone reluctantly consents to a one-day excursion to Isola Bella, assigning Scarpio to closely accompany the copyist.

On the vaporetto to the island, Scarpio, wearing dark glasses and a light straw hat, turns to Fidelman.

"In all confidence what do you think of Angelo?"

"He's all right I guess. Why?"

"Do you think he's handsome?"

"Maybe he was once."

"You have many fine insights," Scarpio says. He points in the distance where the long blue lake disappears amid towering Alps. "Locarno, sixty kilometers."

"Is that so?" With Switzerland so close freedom swells in Fidelman's heart but he does nothing about it. Scarpio clings to him as to a virgin cousin, and sixty kilometers is a long swim with a knife in your back.

"That's the castello over there," the major-domo says. "It looks like a joint."

The castello is pink on a high terraced hill amid tall trees in formal gardens. It is full of tourists and bad paintings. But in the last gallery, "infinite riches in a little room," hangs the "Venus of Urbino" alone.

What a miracle, Fidelman thinks.

The golden brown-haired Venus, a woman of the real world, lies on her couch in serene beauty, her hand lightly touching her intimate mystery, the other holding red flowers, her nude body her truest accomplishment.

"I'd have painted somebody in bed with her," Scarpio says.

"Shut up," says Fidelman.

Scarpio, hurt, leaves the gallery.

Fidelman, alone with Venus, worships the painting. What magnificent tones, what extraordinary flesh that turns the body into spirit.

While Scarpio is out talking to the guard, the copyist hastily sketches the Venus, and with a Leica Angelo has given him for the purpose, takes several new color shots.

Afterwards he approaches the picture and kisses the lady's hands, thighs, and breasts, but as he murmurs, "I love you," a guard strikes him hard on the head with both fists.

That night as they are returning on the rapido to Milano,

Scarpio falls asleep, snoring. He awakens in a hurry, tugging at his dagger, but Fidelman hasn't moved.

The copyist throws himself into his work with passion. He has swallowed lightning and hopes it will strike whatever he touches. Yet he has nagging doubts he can do the job right and fears he will never escape alive from the Hotel du Ville. He tries at once to paint the Titian directly on canvas but hurriedly scrapes it clean when he sees what a garish mess he has made. The Venus is insanely disproportionate and the maids in the background foreshortened into dwarfs. He then takes Angelo's advice and makes several drawings on paper to master the composition before committing it again to canvas.

Angelo and Scarpio come up every night and shake their heads over the drawings.

"Not even close," says the padrone.

"Far from it," says Scarpio.

"I'm trying," Fidelman says, anguished.

"Try harder," Angelo answers grimly.

Fidelman has a sudden insight. "What happened to the last guy who tried?"

"He's still floating," Scarpio says.

"I'll need some practice," the copyist coughs. "My vision seems tight and the arm tires easily. I'd better go back to exercises to loosen up."

"What kind of exercises?" Scarpio inquires.

"Nothing physical, just some warm-up nudes to get me going."

"Don't overdo it," Angelo says. "You've got about a month, not much more. There's an advantage to making the exchange of pictures during the tourist season."

"Only a month?"

The padrone nods.

"Maybe you'd better trace it," Scarpio suggests.

"No."

"I'll tell you what," says Angelo. "I could find you an old reclining nude you can paint over. You might get the form of this one by altering the form of another."

"It's not honest, I mean to myself."

Everyone titters.

"Well, it's your headache," says Angelo.

Fidelman, unwilling to ask what happens if he fails, after they leave, feverishly draws faster.

Things go badly for the copyist. Working all day and often into the very early morning hours, he tries everything he can think of. Since he always distorts the figure of Venus, though he carries it perfect in his mind, he goes back to a study of Greek statuary with ruler and compass to compute the mathematical proportions of the ideal nude. Scarpio accompanies him to one or two museums. Fidelman also works with the Vetruvian square in the circle, experiments with Dürer's intersecting circles and triangles, and studies Leonardo's schematic heads and bodies. Nothing doing. He draws paper dolls, not women, certainly not Venus. He draws girls who will not grow up. He then tries sketching every nude he can lay eyes on in the art books Scarpio brings him from the library; from the Esquiline goddess to "Les Demoiselles d'Avignon." Fidelman copies not badly many figures from classical statuary and modern painting; but when he returns to his Venus, with something of a laugh she eludes him. What am I, bewitched, the copyist asks himself, and if so by whom? It's only a copy job so what's taking so long? He can't even guess, until he happens to see a naked whore cross the hall to enter a friend's room. Maybe the ideal is cold and I like it hot? Nature over art? Inspiration—the live model? Fidelman knocks on the door and tries to persuade the girl to pose for him but she can't for economic reasons. Neither will any of the others—there are four girls in the room.

A red-head among them calls out to Fidelman, "Shame on you, Arturo, are you too good to bring up pizzas and coffee any more?"

"I'm busy on a job for Angelo. Painting a picture, that is. A business proposition."

Their laughter further depresses his spirits. No inspiration from whores. Maybe too many naked women around make it impossible to draw a nude. Still he'd better try a live model, having tried everything else and failed.

In desperation, on the verge of panic because time is going

so fast, he thinks of Teresa, the chambermaid. She is a poor specimen of feminine beauty but the imagination can enhance anything. Fidelman asks her to pose for him, and Teresa, after a shy laugh, consents.

"I will if you promise not to tell anybody."

Fidelman promises.

She undresses, a meager, bony girl, breathing heavily, and he draws her with flat chest, distended belly, thin hips and hairy legs, unable to alter a single detail. Van Eyck would have loved her. When Teresa sees the drawing she weeps profusely.

"I thought you would make me beautiful."

"I had that in mind."

"Then why didn't you?"

"It's hard to say," says Fidelman.

"I'm not in the least bit sexy," Teresa weeps.

Considering her body with half-closed eyes, Fidelman tells her to go borrow a long slip.

"Get one from one of the girls and I'll draw you sexy."

She returns in a frilly white slip and looks so attractive that instead of painting her, Fidelman, with a lump in his throat, gets her to lie down with him on a dusty mattress in the room. Clasping her slip-encased form, the copyist shuts both eyes and concentrates on his elusive Venus. He feels about to recapture a rapturous experience and is looking forward to it but at the last minute it turns into a limerick he didn't know he knew:

"Whilst Titian was mixing rose madder,
His model was crouched on a ladder;
Her position to Titian suggested coition,
So he stopped mixing madder and had'er."

Angelo, entering the storeroom just then, lets out a bellow. He fires Teresa on her naked knees pleading with him not to, and Fidelman has to go back to latrine duty the rest of the day.

"You might as well keep me doing this permanently," Fidelman, disheartened, tells the padrone in his office afterward. "I'll never finish that cursed picture."

"Why not? What's eating you? I've treated you like a son."

"I'm blocked, that's what."

"Get to work, you'll feel better."

"I just can't paint."

"For what reason?"

"I don't know."

"Because you've had it too good here." Angelo angrily strikes Fidelman across the face. When the copyist sobs, he boots him hard in the rear.

That night Fidelman goes on a hunger strike but the padrone, hearing of it, threatens force-feeding.

After midnight Fidelman steals some clothes from a sleeping whore, dresses quickly, ties on a kerchief, makes up his eyes and lips, and walks out the door past Scarpio sitting on a bar stool, enjoying the night breeze. Having gone a block, fearing he will be chased, Fidelman breaks into a high-heeled run but it's too late. Scarpio has recognized him in afterthought and yells for the portiere. Fidelman kicks off his slippers and runs furiously but the skirt impedes him. The major-domo and portiere catch up with him and drag him, kicking and struggling, back to the hotel. A carabiniere, hearing the commotion, appears on the scene, but seeing how Fidelman is dressed, will do nothing for him. In the cellar Angelo hits him with a short rubber hose until he collapses.

Fidelman lies in bed three days, refusing to eat or get up.

"What'll we do now?" Angelo, worried, whispers. "How about a fortune teller? Either that or let's bury him."

"Astrology is better," Scarpio says. "I'll check his planets. If that doesn't work we'll try psychology. He's a suggestible type."

"Well, make it fast."

Scarpio tries astrology but it doesn't work: a mix-up of Venus with Mars he can't explain; so the next morning he tries psychology. He comes into Fidelman's room with a thick book under his arm. The art copyist is still in bed, smoking a butt.

"Do you believe in psychoanalysis?"

"Sort of."

"Maybe we'd better try that. I'm here to help you. Don't get up."

Scarpio opens the book to its first chapter. "The thing to do is associate freely."

"What's the point of this?"

"It might loosen you up. Do you have any memories of your mother? For instance, did you ever see her naked?"

"She died young," Fidelman says, on the verge of tears. "I was raised by my sister Bessie."

"Go on, I'm listening," says Scarpio.

"I can't. My mind goes blank."

Scarpio turns to the next chapter, flips through several pages, then rises with a sigh.

"It might be a medical matter. Take a physic tonight."

"I already have."

The major-domo shrugs. "Life is complicated. Anyway, keep track of your dreams. Write them down as soon as you have them."

Fidelman puffs his butt.

That night he dreams of Bessie about to bathe. He is peeking at her through the bathroom keyhole as she prepares her bath. Openmouthed he watches her remove her robe and step into the tub. Her hefty well-proportioned body then is young and full in the right places; and in the dream Fidelman, then fourteen, looks at her with longing that amounts to anguish. The older Fidelman, the dreamer, considers doing a "La Baigneuse" right then and there, but when Bessie begins to soap herself with Ivory soap, the boy slips into her room, opens her poor purse, filches fifty cents for the movies, and goes on tiptoes down the stairs.

He is shutting the vestibule door with great relief when Arturo Fidelman awakes with a headache in Milano. As he scribbles down his dream he suddenly remembers what Angelo had said: "Everybody steals. We're all human."

A stupendous thought occurs to him: Suppose he personally steals the picture?

A marvelous idea all around. Fidelman heartily eats that morning's breakfast.

To steal the picture he had to paint one. Within another day the copyist successfully sketches Titian's painting and then begins to work in oils on an old piece of Flemish linen that Angelo had hastily supplied him with after seeing the successful drawing. Fidelman underpaints the canvas and after it is dry begins the figure of Venus as the conspirators look on sucking their breaths.

"Stay relaxed," begs Angelo, sweating. "Don't spoil it now.

Remember you're painting the appearance of a picture. The original has already been done. Give us a decent copy and we'll do the rest with chemistry."

"I'm worried about the brush strokes."

"Nobody will notice them. Just keep in your mind that Tiziano painted resolutely with few strokes, his brush loaded with color. In the end he would paint with his fingers. We don't ask for perfection, just a good copy."

He rubs his fat hands nervously.

But Fidelman paints as though he were painting the original. He works alone late at night, when the conspirators are snoring, and he paints with what is left of his heart. He has caught the figure of the Venus but when it comes to her flesh, her thighs and breasts, he thinks he will never make it. As he paints he seems to remember every nude that has ever been done, Fidelman satyr, with Silenus beard and goatlegs, piping and peeking at backside, frontside, or both, at the "Rokeby Venus," "Bathsheba," "Suzanna," "Venus Anadyomene," "Olympia"; at picnickers in dress or undress, bathers ditto, Vanitas or Truth, Niobe or Leda, in chase or embrace, hausfrau or whore, amorous ladies modest or brazen, single or in crowds at the Turkish bath, in every conceivable shape or position, while he sports and disports until a trio of maenads pull his tail and he gallops after them through the dusky woods. He is at the same time choked by remembered lust for all the women he had ever desired, from Bessie to Annamaria Oliovino, and for their garters, underpants, slips or half-slips, brassieres and stockings. Although thus tormented, Fidelman feels himself falling in love with the one he is painting, every inch of her, including the ring on her pinky, bracelet on arm, the flowers she touches with her fingers, and the bright green earring that dangles from her eatable ear. He would have prayed her alive if he weren't certain she would fall in love, not with her famished creator, but surely the first Apollo Belvedere she lays eyes on. Is there, Fidelman asks himself, a world where love endures and is always satisfying? He answers in the negative. Still she is his as he paints, so he goes on, planning never to finish, to be happy in loving her, thus forever happy.

But he finishes the picture on a Saturday night, Angelo's

gun pressed to his head. Then the Venus is taken from him and Scarpio and Angelo bake, smoke, stipple and varnish, stretch and frame Fidelman's masterwork as the artist lies on his bed in his room in a state of collapse.

"The Venus of Urbino, c'est moi."

"What about my three hundred and fifty?" Fidelman asks Angelo during a card game in the padrone's stuffy office several days later. After finishing the painting the copyist is again back on janitorial duty.

"You'll collect when we've got the Tiziano."

"What about my passport?"

"Give it to him, Scarpio."

Scarpio hands him the passport. Fidelman flips through the booklet and sees all the pages intact.

"If you skiddoo now," Angelo warns him, "you'll get spit."

"Who's skiddooing?"

"So the plan is this: You and Scarpio will row out to the castello after midnight. The caretaker is an old man and half deaf. You hang our picture and breeze off with the other."

"If you wish," Fidelman suggests, "I'll gladly do the job myself. Alone, that is."

"Why alone?" Scarpio asks suspiciously.

"Don't be foolish," Angelo says. "With the frame it weighs half a ton. Now listen to directions and don't give any. One reason I detest Americans is they never know their place."

Fidelman apologizes.

"I'll follow in the putt-putt and wait for you halfway between Isola Bella and Stresa in case we need a little extra speed at the last minute."

"Do you expect trouble?"

"Not a bit. If there's any trouble it'll be your fault. In that case watch out."

"Off with his head," says Scarpio. He plays a deuce and takes the pot.

Fidelman laughs politely.

The next night, Scarpio rows a huge weatherbeaten boat, both oars muffled. It is a moonless night with touches of Alpine lightning in the distant sky. Fidelman sits on the stern, holding with both hands and balancing against his knees, the large framed painting, heavily wrapped in monk's cloth and cellophane and tied around with rope.

At the island the major-domo docks the boat and secures it. Fidelman, peering around in the dark, tries to memorize where they are. They carry the picture up two hundred steps, both puffing when they get to the formal gardens on top.

The castello is black except for a square of yellow light from the caretaker's turret window high above. As Scarpio snaps the lock of an embossed heavy wooden door with a strip of celluloid, the yellow window slowly opens and an old man peers down. They freeze against the wall until the window is drawn shut.

"Fast," Scarpio hisses. "If anyone sees us they'll wake the whole island."

Pushing open the creaking door, they quickly carry the painting, growing heavier as they hurry, through an enormous room cluttered with cheap statuary, and by the light of the major-domo's flashlight, ascend a narrow flight of spiral stairs. They hasten in sneakers down a deep-shadowed, tapestried hall into the picture gallery, Fidelman stopping in his tracks when he beholds the Venus, the true and magnificent image of his counterfeit creation.

"Let's get to work." Scarpio quickly unknots the rope and they unwrap Fidelman's painting and lean it against the wall. They are taking down the Titian when footsteps sound unmistakably in the hall. Scarpio's flashlight goes out.

"Sh, it's the caretaker. If he comes in I'll have to conk him."

"That'll kill Angelo's plan—deceit, not force."

"I'll think of that when we're out of here."

They press their backs to the wall, Fidelman's clammy, as the old man's steps draw nearer. The copyist has anguished visions of losing the picture and makes helter-skelter plans somehow to reclaim it. Then the footsteps falter, come to a stop, and after a minute of intense hesitation, move in another direction. A door slams and the sound is gone.

It takes Fidelman several seconds to breathe. They wait in the dark without moving until Scarpio shines his light. Both Venuses are resting against the same wall. The major-domo closely inspects each canvas with one eye shut, then signals the painting on the left. "That's the one, let's wrap it up."

Fidelman breaks into profuse sweat.

"Are you crazy? That's mine. Don't you know a work of art when you see it?" He points to the other picture.

"Art?" says Scarpio, removing his hat and turning pale. "Are you sure?" He peers at the painting.

"Without a doubt."

"Don't try to confuse me." He taps the dagger under his coat.

"The lighter one is the Titian," Fidelman says through a hoarse throat. "You smoked mine a shade darker."

"I could have sworn yours was the lighter."

"No, Titian's. He used light varnishes. It's a historical fact."

"Of course." Scarpio mops his brow with a dirty handkerchief. "The trouble is with my eyes. One is in bad shape and I overuse the other."

"That's tough," clucks Fidelman.

"Anyway, hurry up. Angelo's waiting on the lake. Remember, if there's any mistake he'll cut your throat first."

They hang the darker painting on the wall, quickly wrap the lighter and hastily carry it through the long hall and down the stairs, Fidelman leading the way with Scarpio's light.

At the dock the major-domo nervously turns to Fidelman. "Are you absolutely sure we have the right one?"

"I give you my word."

"I accept it but under the circumstances I'd better have another look. Shine the light through your fingers."

Scarpio kneels to undo the wrapping once more, and Fidelman trembling, brings the flashlight down hard on his straw hat, the light shattering in his hand. The major-domo, pulling at his dagger, collapses.

Fidelman has trouble loading the painting into the rowboat but finally gets it in and settled, and quickly takes off. In ten minutes he had rowed out of sight of the dark castled island. Not long afterward he thinks he hears Angelo's putt-putt behind him. His heart beats erratically but the padrone does not appear. He rows hard as the waves deepen.

Locarno, sixty kilometers.

A wavering flash of lightning pierces the broken sky, lighting the agitated lake all the way to the Alps, as a dreadful thought assails Fidelman: had he the right painting? After a minute he pulls in his oars, listens once more for Angelo, and hearing nothing, steps to the stern of the rowboat, letting it drift as he frantically unwraps the Venus.

In the pitch black, on the lake's choppy waters, he sees she is indeed his, and by the light of numerous matches adores his handiwork.

4

FRAVAGED Florentine, grieving, kicked apart a trial canvas, copy of one he had been working on for years, his foot through the poor mother's mouth, destroyed the son's insipid puss, age about ten. It deserved death for not coming to life. He stomped on them both, but not of course on the photograph still tacked to the easel ledge, sent years ago by sister Bessie, together with her last meager check. "I found this old photo of you and Momma when you were a little boy. Thought you might like to have it, she's been dead these many years." Inch by enraged inch he rent the canvas, though cheap linen he could ill afford, and would gladly have cremated the remains if there were a place to. He swooped up the mess with both hands, grabbed some smeared drawings, ran down four rickety flights and dumped all in the bowels of a huge burlap rubbish bag in front of the scabby mustard-walled house on Via S. Agostino. Fabio, the embittered dropsical landlord, asleep on his feet, awoke and begged for a few lire back rent but F ignored him. Across the broad piazza, Santo Spirito, nobly proportioned, stared him in the bushy-mustached face, but he would not look back. His impulse was to take the nearest bridge and jump off into the Arno, flowing again in green full flood after a dry summer; instead, he slowly ascended the stairs, pelted by the landlord's fruity curses. Upstairs in his desolate studio, he sat on his bed and wept. Then he lay with his head at the foot of the bed and wept.

The painter blew his nose at the open window and gazed for a reflective hour at the Tuscan hills in September haze. Otherwise, sunlight on the terraced silver-trunked olive trees, and San Miniato, sparkling, framed in the distance by black cypresses. Make an interesting impressionist oil, green and gold mosaics and those black trees of death, but that's been done. Not to mention Van Gogh's tormented cypresses. That's my trouble, everything's been done or is otherwise out of style—cubism, surrealism, action painting. If I could only guess what's next. Below, a stunted umbrella pine with a headful of black and white chirping swallows grew in the landlord's narrow yard, over a dilapidated henhouse that smelled to heaven, except that up here the smell was sweetened by the odor of red roof tiles. A small dirty white rooster crowed shrilly, the shrimpy brown hens clucking as they ran in dusty circles around three lemon trees in tubs. F's studio was a small room with a curtained kitchen alcove—several shelves, a stove and sink—the old-fashioned walls painted with faded rustic dancers, nymphs and shepherds, and on the ceiling a large scalloped cornucopia full of cracked and faded fruit.

He looked until the last of morning was gone, then briskly combed his thick mustache, sat at the table and ate a hard anise biscuit as his eyes roamed over some quotations he had stenciled on the wall.

Constable: "Painting is for me another word for feeling."

Whistler: "A masterpiece is finished from the beginning."

Pollock: "What is it that escapes me? The human? That humanity is greater than art?"

Nietzsche: "Art is not an imitation of nature but its metaphysical supplement, raised up beside it in order to overcome it."

Picasso: "People seize on painting in order to cover up their nakedness."

Ah, if I had his genius.

Still, he felt better, picked up a fourteen-inch Madonna he had carved and sanded it busily. Then he painted green eyes, black hair, pink lips and a sky-blue cloak, and waited around smoking until the statuette had dried. He wrapped it in a sheet of newspaper, dropped the package into a string bag and went again downstairs, wearing sockless sandals, tight pants, and black beret. Sometimes he wore sunglasses.

At the corner he stepped into midstreet, repelled by the old crone's door, the fortune teller, the eighth of seven sisters to hear her talk, six thick hairs sprouting from the wart on her chin; in order not to sneak in and ask, for one hundred lire, "Tell me, signora, will I ever make it? Will I finish my five years' painting of Mother and Son? My sure masterpiece—I know it in my bones—if I ever get it done."

Her shrill sibylic reply made sense. "A good cook doesn't throw out yesterday's soup."

"But will it be as good, I mean? Very good, signora, maybe a masterwork?"

"Masters make masterworks."

"And what about my luck, when will it change from the usual?"

"When you do. Art is long, inspiration, short. Luck is fine, but don't stop breathing."

"Will I avoid an unhappy fate?"

"It all depends."

That or something like it for one hundred lire. No bargain.

F sighed. Still, it somehow encouraged.

A window shutter was drawn up with a clatter and a paper cone of garbage came flying out at him. He ducked as the oily bag split on the cobblestones behind him.

BEWARE OF FALLING MASONRY.

He turned the corner, barely avoiding three roaring Vespas.

Vita pericolosa. It had been a suffocating summer slowly deflated to cool autumn. He hurried, not to worry his hunger, past the fruit and vegetable stalls in the piazza, zigzagging through the Oltrarno streets as he approached Ponte Vecchio. Ah, the painter's eye! He enjoyed the narrow crowded noisy streets, the washing hung from windows. Tourists were all but gone, but the workshops were preparing for next year's migration, mechanics assembling picture frames, cutting leather, plastering tile mosaics; women plaiting straw. He sneezed passing through a tannery reek followed by hot stink of stable. Above the din of traffic an old forge rumbling. F hastened by a minuscule gallery where one of his action paintings had been hanging downside up for more than a year. He had made no protest, art lives on accidents.

At a small square, thick with stone benches where before the war there had been houses, the old and lame of the quarter sat amid beggars and berouged elderly whores, one nearby combing her reddish-gray locks. Another fed pigeons with a crust of bread they approached and pecked at. One, not so old, in a homely floppy velvet hat, he gazed at twice; in fact no more than a girl with a slender youthful body. He could stand a little sexual comfort but it cost too much. Holding the Madonna tightly to his chest, the painter hastened into the woodworker's shop.

Alberto Panenero, the proprietor, in a brown smock smeared with wood dust and shavings, scattered three apprentices with a hiss and came forward, bowing.

"Ah, maestro, another of your charming Madonnas, let's hope?"

F unwrapped the wooden statuette of the modest Madonna.

The proprietor held it up as he examined it. He called together the apprentices. "Look at the workmanship, you ignoramuses," then dismissed them with a hiss.

"Beautiful?" F said.

"Of course. With that subject who can miss?"

"And the price?"

"Eh. What can one do? As usual."

F's face fell an inch. "Is it fair to pay only five thousand lire for a statuette that takes two weeks' work and sells on Via Tornabuoni for fifteen thousand, even twenty if someone takes it to St. Peter's and gets it blessed by the Pope?"

Panenero shrugged. "Ah, maestro, the world has changed since the time of true craftsmen. You and I we're fighting a losing battle. As for the Madonnas, I now get most of the job turned out by machine. My apprentices cut in the face, add a few folds to the robe, daub on a bit of paint, and I swear to you it costs me one third of what I pay you and goes for the same price to the shops. Of course, they don't approach the quality of your product—I'm an honest man—but do you think the tourists care? What's more the shopkeepers are stingier than ever, and believe me they're stingy in Florence. If I ask for more they offer less. If they pay me seventy-five hundred for yours I'm in luck. With that price, how can I take care of rent and my other expenses? I pay the wages of two masters and a journeyman on my other products, the antique furniture and so forth. I also employ three apprentices who have to eat or they're too weak to fart. My own family, including a clubfoot son and three useless daughters, comes to six people. Eh, I don't have to tell you it's no picnic earning a living nowadays. Still, if you'll put a bambino in the poor Madonna's arms, I'll up you five hundred."

"I'll take the five thousand."

The proprietor counted it out in worn fifty- and one-hundred-lire notes.

"The trouble with you, maestro, is you're a perfectionist. How many are there nowadays?"

"I guess that's so," F sighed. "Don't think I haven't thought of selling the Madonnas to the tourists myself, but if I have to do that as well as make them where's my painting time coming from, I'd like to know?"

"I agree with you totally," Panenero said, "still, for a bachelor you're not doing too badly. I'm always surprised you look so skinny. It must be hereditary."

"Most of my earnings go for supplies. Everything's shot up so, oils, pigments, turpentine, everything. A tube of cadmium costs close to thirteen hundred lire, so I try to keep bright yellow, not to mention vermilion, out of my pictures. Last week I had to pass up a sable brush they ask three thousand for. A roll of cotton canvas costs over ten thousand. With such prices what's left for meat?"

"Too much meat is bad for the digestion. My wife's brother eats meat twice a day and has liver trouble. A dish of good spaghetti with cheese will fatten you up without interfering with your liver. Anyway how's the painting coming?"

"Don't ask me so I won't lie."

In the market close by, F pinched the tender parts of two Bosc pears and a Spanish melon. He looked into a basket of figs, examined some pumpkins on hooks, inspected a bleeding dead rabbit and told himself he must do a couple of still lifes. He settled for a long loaf of bread and two etti of tripe. He also bought a brown egg for breakfast, six Nazionale cigarettes and a quarter of a head of cabbage. In a fit of well-being he bought three wine-red dahlias, and the old woman who sold them to him out of her basket handed him a marigold, free. Shopping for food's a blessing, he thought, you get down to brass tacks. It makes a lot in life seem less important, for instance painting a masterwork. He felt he needn't paint for the rest of his life and nothing much lost; but then anxiety moved like a current through his belly as the thought threatened and he had all he could do not to break into a sweat, run back to the studio, set up his canvas and start hitting it with paint. I'm a time-ravaged man, horrible curse on an artist.

The young whore with the baggy hat saw the flowers amid

his bundles as he approached, and through her short veil smiled dimly up at him.

F, for no reason he could think of, gave her the marigold, and the girl—she was no more than eighteen—held the flower awkwardly.

"What's your price, if you don't mind me asking?"

"What are you, a painter or something?"

"That's right, how did you know?"

"I think I guessed. Maybe it's your clothes, or the flowers or something." She smiled absently, her eyes roaming the benches, her hard mouth tight. "To answer your question, two thousand lire."

He raised his beret and walked on.

"You can have me for five hundred," called an old whore from her bench. "What she hasn't heard of I've practiced all my life. I have no objection to odd requests."

But F was running. Got to get back to work. He crossed the street through a flood of Fiats, carts, Vespas, and rushed back to his studio.

Afterward he sat on his bed, hands clasped between knees, looking at the canvas and thinking of the young whore. Maybe it'd relax me so I can paint.

He counted what was left of his money, then hid the paper lire in a knotted sock in his bureau drawer. He removed the sock and hid it in the armadio on the hat rack. Then he locked the armadio and hid the key in the bureau drawer. He dropped the drawer key into a jar of cloudy turpentine, figuring who would want to wet his hand fishing for it.

Maybe she'd let me charge it and I could pay when I have more money? I could do two Madonnas sometime and pay her out of the ten thousand lire.

Then he thought, She seemed interested in me as an artist. Maybe she'd trade for a drawing.

He riffled through a pile of charcoal drawings and came on one of a heavy-bellied nude cutting her toenails, one chunky foot on a backless chair. F trotted to the benches in the market piazza where the girl sat with a crushed marigold in her hand.

"Would you mind having a drawing instead? One of my own, that is?"

"Instead of what?"

"Instead of cash because I'm short. It's just a thought I had."

It took her a minute to run it through her head. "All right, if that's what you want."

He unrolled the drawing and showed it to her.

"Oh, all right."

But then she flushed under her veil and gazed embarrassed at F.

"Anything wrong?"

Her eyes miserably searched the piazza.

"It's nothing," she said after a minute. "I'll take your drawing." Then seeing him studying her she laughed nervously and said, "I was looking for my cousin. He's supposed to meet me here. Well, if he comes let him wait, he's a pain in the ass anyway."

She rose from the bench and they went together toward Via S. Agostino.

Fabio, the landlord, took one look and called her puttana.

"That'll do from you," said F, sternly.

"Pay your rent instead of pissing away the money."

Her name, she told him as they were undressing in his studio, was Esmeralda.

His was Arturo.

The girl's hair, when she tossed off her baggy hat, was brown and full. She had black eyes like plum pits, a small mouth on the sad side, Modigliani neck, strong though not exactly white teeth and a pimply brow. She wore long imitation-pearl earrings and kept them on. Esmeralda unzipped her clothes and they were at once in bed. It wasn't bad though she apologized for her performance.

As they lay smoking in bed—he had given her one of his six cigarettes—Esmeralda said, "The one I was looking for isn't my cousin, he's my pimp or at least he was. If he's there waiting for me I hope it's a blizzard and he freezes to death."

They had an espresso together. She said she liked the studio and offered to stay.

He was momentarily panicked. "I wouldn't want it to interfere with my painting. I mean I'm devoted to that. Besides, this is a small place."

"I'm a small girl, I'll take care of your needs and won't interfere with your work."

He finally agreed.

Though he had qualms concerning her health, he let her stay yet felt reasonably contented.

"Il Signor Ludovico Belvedere," the landlord called up from the ground floor, "a gentleman on his way up the stairs to see you. If he buys one of your pictures, you won't have any excuse for not paying last month's rent, not to mention June or July."

If it was really a gentleman, F went in to wash his hands as the stranger slowly, stopping to breathe, wound his way up the stairs. The painter had hastily removed the canvas from the easel, hiding it in the kitchen alcove. He soaped his hands thickly, the smoke from the butt in his mouth drifting into a closed eye. F quickly dried himself with a dirty towel. It was, instead of a gentleman, Esmeralda's seedy cugino, the pimp, a thin man past fifty, tall, with pouched small eyes and a pencil-line mustache. His hands and feet were small, he wore loose squeaky shoes with gray spats. His clothes though neatly pressed had seen better days. He carried a malacca cane and sported a pearl-gray hat. There was about him, though he seemed to mask it, a quality of having experienced everything, if not more, that gave F the momentary shivers.

Bowing courteously and speaking as though among friends, he was not, he explained, in the best of moods—to say nothing of his health—after a week of running around desperately trying to locate Esmeralda. He explained they had had a misunderstanding over a few lire through an unfortunate error, no more than a mistake in addition—carrying a one instead of a seven. "These things happen to the best of mathematicians, but what can you do with someone who won't listen to reason? She slapped my face and ran off. Through a mutual acquaintance I made an appointment to explain the matter to her, with proof from my accounts, but though she gave her word she didn't appear. It doesn't speak well for her maturity."

He had learned later from a friend in the Santo Spirito quarter that she was at the moment living with the signore. Ludovico apologized for disturbing him, but F must understand he had come out of urgent necessity.

"Per piacere, signore, I request your good will. A great deal is at stake for four people. She can continue to serve you from time to time if that's what she wants; but I hear from your landlord that you're not exactly prosperous, and on the other hand she has to support herself and a starving father in Fiesole. I don't suppose she's told you about him but if it weren't for me personally, he'd be lying in a common grave this minute growing flowers on his chest. She must come back to work under my guidance and protection not only because it's mutually beneficial but because it's a matter of communal responsibility; not only hers for me now that I've had a most serious operation, or both of us for her starving father, but also in reference to my aged mother, a woman of eighty-three who is seriously in need of proper nursing care. I understand you're an American, signore. That's one thing but Italy is a poor country. Here each of us is responsible for the welfare of four or five others or we all go under."

He spoke calmly, philosophically, occasionally breathlessly, as if his recent operation now and then caught up with him. And his intense small eyes wandered in different directions as he talked, as though he suspected Esmeralda might be hiding.

F, after his first indignation, listened with interest although disappointed the man had not turned out to be a wealthy picture buyer.

"She's had it with whoring," he said.

"Signore," Ludovico answered with emotion, "it's important to understand. The girl owes me much. She was seventeen when I came across her, a peasant girl living a wretched existence. I'll spare you the details because they'd turn your stomach. She had chosen this profession, the most difficult of all as we both know, but lacked the ability to handle herself. I met her by accident and offered to help her although this sort of thing wasn't in my regular line of work. To make the story short, I devoted many hours to her education and found her a better clientele—to give you an example, recently one of her newest customers, a rich cripple she sees every week, offered to marry her, but I advised against it because he's a contadino. I also took measures to protect her health and well-being. I advised her to go for periodic medical examinations, scared off badly behaved customers with a toy pistol, and tried in every way to reduce indignities and hazards. Believe me, I am a protective person and gave her my sincere affection. I treat her as if she were my own daughter. She isn't by chance in the next room? Why doesn't she come out and talk frankly?"

He pointed with his cane at the alcove curtain.

"That's the kitchen," said F. "She's at the market."

Ludovico, bereft, blew on his fingers, his eyes momentarily glazed as his glance mechanically wandered around the room. He seemed then to come to and gazed at some of F's pictures with interest. In a moment his features were animated.

"Naturally, you're a painter! Pardon me for overlooking it, a worried man is half blind. Besides, somebody said you were an insurance agent."

"No, I'm a painter."

The pimp borrowed F's last cigarette, took a few puffs as he studied the pictures on the wall with tightened eyes, then put out the barely-used butt and pocketed it.

"It's a remarkable coincidence." He had once, it turned out, been a frame maker and later part-owner of a small art gallery on Via Strozzi, and he was of course familiar with painting and the painting market. But the gallery, because of the machinations of his thieving partner, had failed. He hadn't re-opened it for lack of capital. It was shortly afterward he had had to have a lung removed.

"That's why I didn't finish your cigarette."

Ludovico coughed badly—F believed him.

"In this condition, naturally, I find it difficult to make a living. Even frame making wears me out. That's why it's advantageous for me to work with Esmeralda."

"Anyway, you certainly have your nerve," the painter replied. "I'm not just referring to your coming up here and telling me what I ought to do vis-à-vis someone who happens to be here because she asked to be, but I mean actually living off the proceeds of a girl's body. All in all, it isn't much of a moral thing to do. Esmeralda might in some ways be indebted to you but she doesn't owe you her soul."

The pimp leaned with dignity on his cane.

"Since you bring up the word, signore, are you a moral man?"

"In my art I am."

Ludovico sighed. "Ah, maestro, who are we to talk of what we understand so badly? Morality has a thousand sources and endless means of expression. As for the soul, who understands its mechanism? Remember, the thief on the cross was the one who rose to heaven with Our Lord." He coughed at length. "Keep in mind that the girl of her free will chose her calling, not I. She was in it without finesse or proficiency, although she is of course adequate. Her advantage is her youth and a certain directness but she needs advice and managerial assistance. Have you seen the hat she wears? Twice I tried to burn it. Obviously she lacks taste. The same is true for her clothes but she's very stubborn to deal with. Still, I devote myself to her and manage to improve conditions, for which I receive a modest but necessary commission. Considering the circumstances, how can this be an evil thing? The basis of morality is recognizing one another's needs and cooperating. Mutual generosity is nothing to criticize other people for. After all, what did Jesus teach?"

Ludovico had removed his hat. He was bald with several gray hairs parted in the center.

He seemed, now, depressed. "You aren't in love with her, are you, maestro? If so, say the word and I disappear. Love is love, after all. I don't forget I'm an Italian."

F thought for a minute.

"Not as yet, I don't think."

"In that case I hope you will not interfere with her decision?"

"What decision do you have in mind?"

"As to what she will do after I speak to her."

"You mean if she decides to leave?"

"Exactly."

"That's up to her."

The pimp ran a relieved hand over his perspiring head and replaced his hat. "The relationship may be momentarily convenient, but for a painter who has his work to think of you'll be better off without her."

"I didn't say I wanted her to go," said F. "All I said was I wouldn't interfere with her decision."

Ludovico bowed. "Ah, you have the objectivity of a true artist."

On his way out, he tossed aside the alcove curtain with his cane and uncovered F's painting on the kitchen table.

He seemed at first unable to believe his eyes. Standing back, he had a better look. "Straordinario," he murmured, kissing his fingertips.

F snatched the canvas, blew off the dust and carefully tucked it behind his bureau.

"It's work in progress," he explained. "I don't like to show it yet."

"Obviously it will be a very fine painting, one sees that at a glance. What do you call it?"

"'Mother and Son.'"

"In spirit it's pure Picasso."

"Is it?"

"I refer to his remark: 'You paint not what you see but what you know is there.'"

"That's right," F said, his voice husky.

"We all have to learn from the masters. There's nothing wrong with trying to do better that which they do best themselves. Thus new masters are born."

"Thank you."

"When you finish let me know. I am acquainted with people who are interested in buying fine serious contemporary work. I could get you an excellent price, of course for the usual commission. Anyway, it looks as though you are about to give birth to a painting of extraordinary merit. Permit me to congratulate you on your talent."

F blushed radiantly.

Esmeralda returned.

Ludovico fell to his knees.

"Go fuck yourself," she said.

"Ah, signorina, my misfortune is your good luck. Your friend is a superb artist. You can take my word for it."

How do you paint a Kaddish?

Here's Momma sitting on the stoop in her cotton housedress, awkward at having her picture taken yet with a dim smile on the dry old snapshot turning yellow that Bessie sent me years ago. Here's the snap, here's the painting of the same idea, why can't I make one out of both? How do you make art of an old photo, so to say? A single of a double image, the one in and the one out?

The painting, 51 × 38, was encrusted in places (her hands and feet) (his face) almost a quarter of an inch thick with paint, layer on layer giving it history, another word for thick past in the paint itself. The mystery was why in the five years he had been at it, on and off because he had to hide it away when it got to be too much for him, he hadn't been able to finish it though most of it was done already, except Momma's face. Five years' work here, mostly as he had first painted it, though he often added dibs and dabs, touches of brush or palette knife on the dry forms. He had tried it every which way, with Momma alone, sitting or standing, with or without him; and with Bessie in or out, but never Poppa, that living ghost; and I've made her old and young, and sometimes resembling Annamaria Oliovino, or Teresa, the chambermaid in Milan; even a little like Susskind, when my memory gets mixed up, who was a man I met when I first came to Rome. Momma apart and him apart, and then trying to bring them together in the tightly woven paint so they would be eternally mother and son as well as unique forms on canvas. So beautifully complete the idea of them together that the viewer couldn't help but think no one has to do it again because it's been done by F and can't be done better; in truth, a masterwork. He had painted her sad and happy, tall, short, realistic, expressionistic, cubistic, surrealistic, even in action splotches of violet and brown. Also in black and white, stark like Kline or Motherwell. Once he had molded a figure in clay from the old photo and tried to copy it, but that didn't work either.

The faces were changed almost every day he painted, his as a young boy, hers as herself (long since departed); but now though for a year he had let the boy be, his face and all, he was still never satisfied with hers—something always missing—for very long after he had put it down; and he daily or nightly scraped it off (another lost face) with his rusty palette knife, and tried once again the next day; then scraped that face the same night or the day after; or let it harden in hope for two days and then frantically, before the paint stiffened, scraped that face off, too. All in all he had destroyed more than a thousand faces and conceived another thousand for a woman who could barely afford one; yet couldn't settle on her true face—at least true for art. What was true for Bessie's old photo was true enough—you can't beat Kodak, but reduced on canvas, too much omitted. He sometimes thought of tearing up the old snapshot so he would have only memory (of it?) to go by, but couldn't bring himself to destroy this last image of her. He was afraid to tear up the snap and went on painting the face on the dumpy body on the chair on the stoop, little F standing blandly by her side knowing she had died though pretending, at least in paint, that he didn't; then scraping it off as the rest of the painting slowly thickened into a frieze.

I've caught the boy, more or less, and sometimes I seem to have her for a few minutes, though not when I look at them together. I don't paint her face so that it holds him in her presence. It comes out at best like two portraits in space and time. Should I stand him on the left instead of right? I tried it once and it didn't work; now I have this hard-as-rock-quarter-of-an-inch investment in the way they are now, and if I scrap either of them (chisel? dynamite?), I might as well throw out the canvas. I might as well scrap what's left of my life if I have to start over again.

How do you invent whoever she was? I remember so little, her death, not even the dying, just the end mostly, after a sickness they easily cure nowadays with penicillin. I was about six or seven, or maybe ten, and as I remember, didn't cry at the funeral. For years that never bothered me much, but when Bessie sent me the snap and I began painting Momma's pictures, I guess it did. Maybe I held it against her, I mean dying; either that or I am by nature a non-mourner, born that way whether one wants it or not. The truth is I am afraid to paint, like I might find out something about myself.

I have not said Kaddish, though I could have looked up the words.

What if she were still a wandering figure among the stars, unable to find the Pearly Gates?

He hid the canvas and turned then to the statuette of the Madonna without child. Esmeralda liked to see the chips fly as the Holy Mother rose out of wood.

The girl had coffee with milk in the morning, slept on a borrowed cot in the kitchen alcove and stayed out of his way while he was painting. The back of the canvas was what she saw when she came into the studio each morning for a few lire to shop with. It was understood she was not to try to look as he painted. "Malocchio," he said, and she nodded and withdrew on tiptoe. Because he found it uncomfortable to work with someone around, after a few days he had thought of asking her to leave, but when he considered how young she was, hardly grown up, like a young child's big sister, he changed his mind. Only once she indirectly referred to the painting, asking what was the snapshot he pored over so much. "Mind your business," F said; she shrugged and withdrew. In the kitchen she was slowly reading a love serial in a movie magazine. She shopped, cooked, kept the studio clean, although she did not bathe as often as he. In the kitchen, as he painted, she mended his socks and underwear, and altered her dresses. She had not much clothing, a sweater and skirt and two trollop's dresses, from one of which she removed two silver roses, from the other some rows of purple sequins. She sewed up the necklines and lowered the hems. She owned a tight black sweater that looked good on her because of her healthy bosom, long neck, dark eyes; also a few pieces of patched underwear, nothing enticing but a red chemise, not bad but too red, some baubles of jewelry she had bought on the Ponte Vecchio, and a modest pair of house shoes. Her gold high heels she had wrapped in newspaper and put away. How long for does she think? F thought. And the girl was a talented cook. She fed him well, mostly on macaroni, green vegetables cooked in olive oil, and now and then some tripe or rabbit. She did very well with a few lire, and all in all two lived cheaper than one. She made no complaints, though she could be sullen when, lost in his work or worry, he paid scant attention to her for days. She obliged in bed when he wanted her, could be tender, and generally made herself useful. Esmeralda once suggested she would pose for him in the nude but F wouldn't hear of it. Heavy-armed and long-footed, at times she reminded him of Bessie as a girl, though they weren't really much alike.

One October morning F sprang out of bed, terribly inspired. Before breakfast he got the painting out of its hiding place to finish off once and for all, only to discover that Bessie's snapshot was gone from the easel ledge. He shook Esmeralda awake but she hadn't seen it. F rushed downstairs, dumped the garbage bag on the sidewalk and frantically searched amid the hard spaghetti strings and mushy melon rinds, as the landlord waving both arms threatened suit. No luck. Upstairs, he hunted through the studio from top to bottom, Esmeralda diligently assisting, but they found nothing. He spent a terrible morning, not a stroke painted.

"But why do you need a picture to paint from, it's all so ridiculous."

"Are you sure you didn't take it?"

"Why would I take it? It's not a picture of me."

"To teach me a lesson or something?"

"Don't be a fool," she said.

He trembled in rage and misery.

In his presence she searched through his chest of drawers—he had been through them a dozen times—and on top, under a book on Uccello he had been reading, discovered the lost snap.

F blushed.

"I forgive your dirty suspicions," she said, her eyes clouding.

"Not that I deserve it," he admitted.

After lunch she tried on the floppy hat she had worn when he met her, to see how she could alter it.

The sight of the velvet hat on her excited his eye. F had another inspiration.

"I'll paint you in it—at least a drawing."

"What for? You said it's ugly on me."

"It's unique is why. Many a master in the past was enticed by a hat to do a portrait of the face beneath. Rembrandt, for instance."

"Oh, all right," Esmeralda said. "It's immaterial to me. I thought you'd want to be getting back to your painting."

"The day's shot for that."

She agreed to pose. He did a quick charcoal for a warm-up that came out entrancing, especially the hat. He began then to sketch her in pencil, possibly for a painting.

As he was drawing, F asked, "How did you happen to fall into prosti—your former profession? What I mean is, was it Ludovico's doing?"

"Prosti—profession," she mimicked. "Once you've cackled, lay the egg."

"I was trying to be considerate."

"Try again. Keeping your mouth shut about certain things is a better consideration; still, if it's only your curiosity you're out to satisfy, I'll tell you why. Ludovico had nothing to do with it, at least then, although he was one of my earliest customers and still owes me money for services rendered, not to mention certain sums he stole outright. He's the only pure bastard I know, all the others have strains of decency, not that it makes much difference. Anyway, it was my own idea, if you want to know. Maybe I was working up to be an artist's mistress."

F, letting the sarcasm pass, continued to sketch her.

"One thing I'll tell you, it wasn't because of any starving father, if that's what he's told you. My father has a tiny farm in Fiesole, he stinks of manure and is incredibly stingy. All he's ever parted with is his virginity. He's got my mother and sister drudging for him and is sore as a castrated bull that I escaped. I ran away because I was sick to my teeth of being a slave. What's more, he wasn't above giving me a feel now and then when he had nothing better to do. Thanks to him I can barely read and write. I turned to whoring because I don't want to be a maid and I don't know anything else. A truck driver on the autostrada gave me the idea. But in spite of my profession I'm incredibly shy, that's why I let Ludovico pimp for me."

She asked if she could see the drawing of herself, and when she had, said, "What are you going to call it?"

He had thought, "Portrait of a Young Whore," but answered, "'Portrait of a Young Woman.' I might do an oil from it."

"It's immaterial to me," Esmeralda said, but she was pleased.

"The reason I stayed here is I thought you'd be kind to me. Besides, if a man is an artist I figured he must know about life. If he does maybe he can teach me something. So far all I've learned is you're like everybody else, shivering in your drawers. That's how it goes, when you think you have nothing there's somebody with less."

F made three more drawings on paper, with and without the hat, and one with the black hat and Esmeralda holding marigolds.

The next morning he carved half a wooden Madonna in a few

hours, and to celebrate, took Esmeralda to the Uffizi in the afternoon and explained some of the great works of art to her.

She didn't always understand his allusions but was grateful. "You're not so dumb," she said.

"One picks up things."

That evening they went to a movie and afterward stopped for a gelato in a café off the Piazza della Signoria. Men looked her over. F stared them down. She smiled at him tenderly. "You're a lot more relaxed when you're working on the Madonnas. When you're painting with that snapshot in front of you, you haven't the civility of a dog."

He admitted the truth of it.

She confessed she had stolen a long look at his painting when he was downstairs going through the garbage bag for the snap.

To his surprise he did not condemn her.

"What did you think of it?"

"Who is she, the one without the face?"

"My mother, she died young."

"What's the matter with the boy?"

"What do you mean?"

"He looks kind of sad."

"That's the way it's supposed to be. But I don't want to talk about it. That can ruin the painting."

"To me it's as though you were trying to paint yourself into your mother's arms."

He was momentarily stunned. "Do you think so?"

"It's obvious to me. A mother's a mother, a son's a son."

"True, but it might be like an attempt on my part to release her from the arms of death. But that sort of stuff doesn't matter much. It's first and foremost a painting, potentially a first-class work if I ever get it done. If I could complete it the way I sometimes see it in my mind's eye, I bet it could be something extraordinary. If a man does only one such painting in his lifetime, he can call himself a success. I sometimes think that if I could paint such a picture, much that was wrong in my life would rearrange itself and add up to more, if you know what I mean."

"In what way?"

"I could forgive myself for past errors."

"Not me," Esmeralda said. "I'd have to paint ten great pictures." She laughed at the thought.

As they were crossing the bridge, Esmeralda said, "You're really nutty. I don't see why a man would give up five years of his life just to paint one picture. If it was me I'd put it aside and do something I could sell."

"I do once in a while, like this portrait of you I'm working on now, but I always go back to 'Mother and Son.'"

"Why does everybody talk about art so much?" she asked. "Even Ludovico, when he's not adding up his accounts, he's talking about art."

"Art's what it must be, which is beauty, and more, which is mostly mystery. That's what people talk about."

"In this picture you're painting of me, what's the mystery?"

"The mystery is you've been captured, yet there's more—you've become art."

"You mean it's not me any more?"

"It never was. Art isn't life."

"Then the hell with it. If I have my choice I'll take life. If there's not that there's no art."

"Without art there's no life to speak of, at least for me. If I'm not an artist, then I'm nothing."

"My God, aren't you a man?"

"Not really, without art."

"Personally, I think you have a lot to learn."

"I'm learning," F sighed.

"What's so great about mystery?" she asked. "I don't like it. There's enough around without making more."

"Being involved in it."

"Explain that to me."

"It's complicated, but one thing would be that a man like me—you understand—is actually working in art. The idea came to me late, I wasted most of my youth. The mystery of art is that more is there than you put down and every stroke adds to it. You look at your painting and see this bull's eye staring at you though all you've painted is an old tree. It's also a mystery to me why I haven't been able to finish my best painting though I am dying to."

"If you ask me," Esmeralda said, "my idea of a mystery is

why I am in love with you, though it's clear to me you don't see me for dirt."

She burst into tears.

A week later Ludovico, come for a morning visit wearing new yellow gloves, saw the completed portrait of Esmeralda, 48 × 30, with black hat, long neck, and marigolds. He was bowled over.

"Fantastic. If you pay me half, I can get you a million lire for this work of art."

F agreed, so the pimp, crossing himself, left with the painting.

One afternoon when Esmeralda was out, Ludovico, breathing badly after four flights of stairs, appeared in the studio lugging a tape recorder he had borrowed for an interview with F.

"What for?"

"To keep a record for the future. I'll get it printed in *International Arts.* My cousin is assistant to the business manager. It will help you get a gallery for your first one-man show."

"Who needs a gallery if all I can show is unfinished canvases?"

"You'd better increase your output. Sit down here and talk into the microphone. I've turned it on. Don't worry about the machine, it won't crawl up your leg. Just relax and answer my questions candidly. Also don't waste time justifying yourself. Are you ready?"

"Yes."

LUD: Very well. Ludovico Belvedere speaking, interviewing the painter Fidelman. Tell me, Arturo, as an American what does painting mean to you?

F: It's my whole life.

LUD: What kind of person do you think an artist is when he's painting? Do you think he's a king or an emperor, or a seer or prophet?

F: I don't know for sure. I often feel like a constipated witch doctor.

LUD: Please talk with good sense. If you're going to be scatological I'll stop the machine.

F: I didn't mean anything bad.

LUD: As an American painter, what do you think of Jackson Pollock? Do you agree that he is a liberating influence?

F: I guess so. The truth is you have to liberate yourself.

LUD: We're talking about painting, not your personal psychology. Jackson Pollock, as any cultured person will tell you, has changed the course of modern painting. Don't think we don't know about him in this country, we're not exactly backward. We can all learn from him, including you. Do you agree that anyone who works in the modes of the past has only leavings to work with?

F: Only partly, the past is pretty rich.

LUD: I go now to the next question. Who is your favorite painter?

F: Ah—well, I don't think I have one, I have many.

LUD: If you think that's an advantage, you're wrong. There's no need of hubris. If an interviewer asked me that question, I would reply "Leonardo, Raphael, Michelangelo," or someone else but not the entire pantheon of painters.

F: I answered honestly.

LUD: Anyway, to go on, what is your avowed purpose in art?

F: To do the best I can. To do more than that. My momentary purpose is to create my uncreated masterpiece.

LUD: The one of your mother?

F: That's right, "Mother and Son."

LUD: But where is your originality? Why are you so concerned with subject matter?

F: I reject originality.

LUD: What's that? Please explain yourself.

F: Maybe I'm not ready, not just yet.

LUD: Mother of God! How old are you?

F: About forty. A little more.

LUD: But why are you so cautious and conservative? I'm fifty-two and have the mind of a youth. Tell me, what's your opinion of pop art? Think before you speak.

F: If it stays away from me, I'll stay away from it.

LUD: (garbled)

F: What did you say?

LUD: Please attend to the question at hand. I wish you would explain to me clearly why you paint.

F: With my paintings I try to stop the flow of time.

LUD: That's a ridiculous statement, but go on anyway.

F: I've said it.

LUD: Say it more comprehensibly. The public will read this.

F: Well, art is my means for understanding life and trying out certain assumptions I have. I make art, it makes me.

LUD: We have a proverb: "The bray of an ass can't be heard in heaven."

F: Frankly, I don't care for some of your remarks.

LUD: Are you saying the canvas is the alter ego of the artist's miserable self?

F: That's not what I said and I don't like what you're saying.

LUD: I'll try to be more respectful. Maestro, once you spoke to me of your art as moral. What did you mean by that?

F: It's just a thought I had, I guess. I suppose I mean that maybe a painting sort of gives value to a human being as he responds to it. You might say it enlarges his consciousness. If he feels beauty it makes him more than he was, it adds, you might say, to his humanity.

LUD: What do you mean "responds"? A man responds in rape, doesn't he? Doesn't that enlarge the consciousness, as you put it?

F: It's a different response. Rape isn't art.

LUD: An emotion is an emotion, no matter how it arises. In itself it is not moral or immoral. Suppose someone responds to the sunset on the Arno? Is that better or more moral than the response to the smell of a drowned corpse? What about bad art? Suppose the response is with more feeling than to a great painting—does that prove bad art is moral, as you call it?

F: I guess not. All right, maybe the painting itself doesn't have it, but putting it another way, maybe the artist does; that is he does when he's painting—creating form, order. Order protects us all, doesn't it?

LUD: Yes, the way a prison does. Remember, some of the biggest pricks, if you will excuse the use of this word, have been great painters. Does that necessarily make them moral men? Of course not. What if a painter kills his father and then paints a beautiful Ascension?

F: Maybe I'm not putting it exactly right. Maybe what I'm

trying to say is that I feel most moral when I'm painting, like being engaged with truth.

LUD: So now it's what you feel. I speak with respect, maestro, but you do nothing but assault me with garbage.

F: Look, Ludovico, I don't understand, if you don't mind my saying so, why you brought this machine up here if all you want to do is insult me. Now take it away, it's using up work-time.

LUD: I am not a servant, maestro. I may have been forced into menial work through circumstance, but Ludovico Belvedere has kept his dignity. Don't think that because you are an American you can go on trampling on the rights of Europeans. You have caused me unnecessary personal discomfort and sorrow by interfering in a business relationship between this unfortunate girl and myself, and the lives of four people have been seriously affected. You don't seem to realize the harm you are doing—

END OF INTERVIEW.

F had assaulted the tape recorder.

Each morning he awoke earlier to paint, waiting for dawn though the light from the streaked sky was, of course, impossible. He had lately been capable of very little patience with the necessities of daily life; to wash, dress, eat, even go to the toilet; and the matter became most inconvenient when his nervous impatience seeped into painting itself. It was a burdensome business to take the canvas out of its hiding place behind the armadio and arrange it on the easel, select and mix his paints, tack up the old snapshot (most unbearable) and begin work. He could have covered the canvas on the easel at night and left the snapshot tacked on permanently, but was obsessed to remove it each time after he put the paints away, soaked his brushes in turpentine, cleaned up. Formerly, just picking up a brush and standing in thought, or reverie, or sometimes blankly, before painting, would ease interior constrictions to the point where he could relax sufficiently to enjoy the work; and once he had painted for an hour, which sometimes came to no more than a stroke or two, he felt well enough to permit himself to eat half a roll and swallow an espresso Esmeralda had prepared, and afterward go with lit butt and magazine to the gabinetto. But now there were days he stood in terror before "Mother and Son" and shivered with every stroke he put down.

He painted out of anguish, a dark color. The canvas remained much the same, the boy as he had been, the fickle mother's face daily changing; daily he scraped it off as Esmeralda moaned in the kitchen; she knew the sound of palette knife on canvas. It was then it occurred to F to use the girl as a model for his mother. Though she was only eighteen, it might help to have a living model for Momma as a young woman though she was touching middle age when Bessie took the photo, and was of course another sort of person; still, such were the paradoxes of art. Esmeralda agreed and stripped herself to the skin, but the painter sternly ordered her to dress; it was her face he was painting. She did as he demanded and patiently posed, sweetly, absently, uncomplaining, for hours, as he, fighting against his need for privacy in the creative act, tried anew to invent the mother's face. I've done all I can with imagination, I mean on top of the snapshot. And though at the end of the day he scraped her face off as the model wept, F urged her to be calm because he now had a brand-new idea: to paint himself not with Momma any more but Bessie instead, "Brother and Sister." Esmeralda's face lit up because "then you'll stop using the snapshot." But F replied, "Not exactly," he still needed it to get the true relationship of them "in space as well as psychology."

As they were into the spaghetti at supper, the girl wanted to know if all artists had it so hard.

"How hard?"

"So that it takes them years to paint a picture?"

"Some do and some don't. What's on your mind?"

"Oh, I don't know," she said.

He slammed down his fork. "Are you doubting my talent, you whore?"

She got up and went into the gabinetto.

F lay on his bed, his face engulfed in a pillowful of black thoughts.

After a while Esmeralda came out and kissed his ear.

"I forgive you, tesoro, I want you to succeed."

"I will," he cried, springing up from the bed.

The next day he rigged up a young boy's costume—blouse and knee pants, and painted in it to get to the heart of bygone days, but that didn't work either so he went back to putting Esmeralda into the painting and scraping her face off each night.

To live, to paint, to live to paint he had to continue carving Madonnas; being impatient he made them more reluctantly. When Esmeralda pointed out they had some sauce but no spaghetti, in three days he hurried out a statuette then hurried it over to Panenero's shop. The woodworker unfortunately couldn't use it. "My apprentices," he shrugged, "are turning them out by the barrelful. Frankly, they model each stroke on yours and work fast. Eh, that's what happens to craft in these times. So the stuff piles up and the tourists won't be here till spring. It's a long time till the hackensacks and lederhosen come over the Alps, maestro. Still, because it's you and I admire your skill, I'll offer you two thousand lire, take it or leave it. This is my busy day."

F left without a word, in afterthought wondering whose yellow gloves he had seen lying on the counter. On his way along the riverbank he flung the Madonna into the Arno. She struck the green water with a golden splash, sank, then rose to the surface, and turning on her back, floated downstream, eyes to the blue sky.

He later carved two more Madonnas, finely wrought pieces, and peddled them himself to shops on the Vie Tornabuoni and della Vigna Nuova. No luck. The shelves were crammed full of religious figures, though one of the merchants offered him six thousand lire for a Marilyn Monroe, nude if possible.

"I have no skill for that sort of thing."

"What about John the Baptist in shaggy skins?"

"What about him?"

"I offer five thousand."

"I find him an uninteresting figure."

Esmeralda then tried selling the statuettes. F wouldn't let her offer them to Panenero, so the girl, holding a Holy Mother in each arm, stood in the Piazza del Duomo and finally sold one to a huge German priest for twelve hundred; and the other she gave to a widow in weeds at Santa Maria Novella for eight hundred lire. F, when he heard, ground his teeth, and though she pleaded with him to be reasonable, swore he would carve no more.

He worked at odd jobs, one in a laundry, that tired him so he couldn't paint at night. One morning he tried chalking blue-robed Madonnas with Child, after Raphael, on the sidewalks before the Baptistery, Santa Chiara, the Stazione Centrale, where he was almost arrested. Passers-by stopped to watch him work but moved on quickly when he passed the hat. A few tossed small coins upon the image of the Holy Mother and F collected them and went to the next spot. A brown-robed monk in sandals followed him.

"Why don't you look for productive work?"

"Advice is cheap."

"So is your art."

He went to the Cappella Brancacci and sat the rest of the day staring in the half dark at the Masaccio frescoes. Geniuses made masterworks. If you weren't greatly gifted the way was hard, a masterwork was a miracle. Still, somehow or other art abounded in miracles.

He borrowed a fishing pole from an artist neighbor and fished, amid a line of men with bent rods, off the Ponte Trinita. F tied the rod to a nail on the railing and paced back and forth, returning every few minutes to check his line as the float bobbed in the Arno. He caught nothing, but the old fisherman next to him, who had pulled in eight fish, gave him a one-eyed crippled eel. It was a cloudy November day, then rainy, patches of damp appearing on the studio ceiling. The cornucopia leaked. The house was cold, Fabio wouldn't turn on the heat till December. It was hard to get warm. But Esmeralda made a tasty crippled-eel soup. The next night she cooked a handful of borrowed polenta that popped in the pot as it boiled. For lunch the following day there was stale bread and half an onion apiece. But for Sunday supper she served boiled meat, green beans and a salad of beet leaves. He suspiciously asked how come, and she admitted she had borrowed a few hundred lire from Ludovico.

"How are we supposed to pay him back?"

"We won't, he owes me plenty."

"Don't borrow from him any more."

"I'm not afraid of him, he's afraid of me."

"I don't like him coming around. I'm at my most dishonest among dishonest men."

"Don't trust him, Arturo," she said, frightened. "He'd knife you if he could."

"He won't get the chance."

Afterward she asked, "Why don't you carve a Madonna or two? Two thousand lire now and then is nothing to spit at. Besides you do beautiful work in wood."

"Not for the price, it's not worth my time."

The landlord, wearing a woman's black shawl, entered without knocking, shouting for his rent.

"I'll get the municipality to throw you both out, the puttana and you. You're fouling up this house with your illicit activities. Your friend told me what goes on here. I have all the necessary information."

"You know where you can stick it," said F. "If we weren't here the flat would go to ruin. It was empty six years before I moved in, you'll never rent it if I move out."

"You're no Florentine," Fabio shouted. "You're not even an Italian."

F got himself a badly paid job as journeyman in a woodworking establishment, not Panenero's. He worked long hours turning out delicate tapered legs for antique tables and did no painting. In the street, going back and forth from work, he looked for coins people might have dropped. He switched off the light after Esmeralda had washed the supper dishes, watched carefully what she cooked, and ate, and doled out shopping money sparsely. Once she sold six inches of her hair to a man with a sack who had knocked on the door, so she could buy herself some warm underwear.

Finally she could stand it no longer. "What are you going to do?"

"What can I do that I haven't?"

"I don't know. Do you want me to go back to my work?"

"I never said so."

"If I don't you'll be like this forever. It's what you're like when you're not painting."

He remained mute.

"Why don't you speak?"

"What can I say?"

"You can say no."

"No," he said.

"It sounds like yes."

He went out for a long walk and for a while hung around the palazzo where Dostoevsky had written the last pages of *The Idiot*. It did no good. When he returned he said nothing to Esmeralda. In fact he did not feel too bad though he knew he ought to. In fact he had been thinking of asking her to go to work, whatever she might do. It's circumstances, he thought.

Esmeralda had got out her black hat, the two dresses, and her gold shoes. On the velvet hat she sewed the silver roses. She raised the hems of the dresses above her knees and unstitched the necklines to expose the rounded tops of her hard breasts. The purple sequins she threw into the garbage.

"Anyway, I'll need protection," she said.

"How do you mean?"

"You know what I mean. I don't want those bastards hurting me or not paying in full. It's blood money."

"I'll protect you," F said.

He wore dark glasses, a black velour hat pulled low over one eye and a brown overcoat with a ratty fur collar buttoned tight under the chin and extending to his ankles; he walked in white sneakers. He thought of growing a beard but gave that up. His bristly reddish mustache was thicker than it had ever been. And he carried a snappy cane with a slender sword inside.

They went together to the Piazza della Repubblica, almost merrily. "For art," she said, then after a moment, bitterly, "art, my ass."

She cursed him from the depth of her heart and then forgave him. "It's my nature," she said. "I can't bear a grudge."

He promised to marry her once he had finished the painting.

F paints all morning after Esmeralda has posed; she bathes, does her nails and toes and makes herself up with mascara. After a leisurely lunch they leave the house and go across the bridge to the Piazza della Repubblica. She sits on a bench with her legs crossed high, smoking; and F is at a bench nearby, sketching in a pad in which he sometimes finds himself drawing dirty pictures: men and women, women and women, men and men. But he doesn't consort with the other pimps who sit together playing cards; nor does Esmeralda talk with the other whores, they call her hoity-toity. When a man approaches to ask whether she happens to be free she nods, or looking at him through her short veil, says yes as though she could just as well have said no. She gets up, the other whores watching her with their eyes and mouths, and wanders with her client into one of the crooked side streets, to a tiny room they have rented close by so there's no waste of man-hours getting back to the piazza. The room has a bed, water bowl, chamber pot.

When Esmeralda rises from the bench, F slips his drawing pad into his coat pocket and leisurely follows them. Sometimes it is a beautiful late-fall afternoon and he takes deep breaths as he walks. On occasion he stops to pick up a pack of Nazionale, and if he's a little hungry, gulps an espresso and a bit of pastry. He then goes up the smelly stairs and waits outside the door, sketching little pictures in the dim electric glow, as Esmeralda performs; or files his fingernails. It takes fifteen or twenty minutes for the customer to come out. Some would like to stay longer but can't if they won't pay for it. As a rule there are no arguments. The man dresses and sometimes leaves a tip if it has been most enjoyable. Esmeralda is still dressing, bored with getting in and out of her clothes. Only once thus far has she had to call F in to deal with a runt who said it hadn't been any good so no sense paying.

F enters with the sword drawn out of his cane and points it at the man's hairy throat. "Pay," he says, "and beat it." The runt, gone two shades white, hurriedly leaves assisted by a boot in the pants. Esmeralda watches without expression. She hands F the money—usually two thousand lire, sometimes three; and if she can get it from a wealthy-type client, or an older man especially fond of eighteen-year-old girls, seven or eight thousand. That sum is rare. F counts the money—often in small bills—and slips it into his wallet, wrapping a fat rubber band around it. In the evening they go home together, Esmeralda doing her shopping on the way. They try not to work at night unless it's been a bad day. In that case they go out after supper, when the piazza is lit in neon signs and the bars and cafés are doing business; the competition is stiff—some very beautiful women in extraordinary clothes. F goes into the bars and seeks out men who seem to be alone. He asks them if they want a pretty girl, and if one shows interest, leads him to Esmeralda. When it's rainy or freezing cold, they stay in and play cards or listen to the radio. F has opened an account in the Banco di Santo Spirito so they can draw from it in the winter if Esmeralda is sick and can't work. They go to bed after midnight. The next morning F gets up early and paints. Esmeralda sleeps late.

One morning F paints with his dark glasses on, until she wakes up and screams at him.

Later, when she is out buying material for a dress, Ludovico strides into the studio, incensed. His usually pallid face is flushed. He shakes his malacca at F.

"Why wasn't I informed that she had gone back to work? I demand a commission. She took all her instruction from me!"

F is about to run him out of the room by the worn seat of his overcoat but then has this interesting thought: Ludovico could take her over while he stays home to paint all day, for which he would pay him eight percent of Esmeralda's earnings.

"Per cortesia," says the pimp haughtily. "At the very least twenty-five percent. I have many obligations and am a sick man besides."

"Eight is all we can afford, not a penny more."

Esmeralda returns with a package or two and when she comprehends what the argument is, swears she will quit rather than work with Ludovico.

"You can do your own whoring," she says to F. "I'll go back to Fiesole."

He tries to calm her. "It's just that he's so sick is the reason I thought I'd cut him in."

"Sick?"

"He's got one lung."

"He has three lungs and four balls."

F heaves the pimp down the stairs.

In the afternoon he sits on a bench not far from Esmeralda's in the Piazza della Repubblica, sketching himself on his drawing pad.

Esmeralda burned Bessie's old snapshot when F was in the toilet. "I'm getting old," she said, "where's my future?" F considered strangling her but couldn't bring himself to; besides, he hadn't been using the photo since having Esmeralda as model. Still, for a time he felt lost without it, the physical presence of the decaying snap his only visible link to Ma, Bessie, the past. Anyway, now that it was gone it was gone, a memory become intangible again. He painted with more fervor yet detachment; fervor to complete the work, detachment toward image, object, subject. Esmeralda left him to his devices, went off for most of the afternoon and handed him the lire, fewer than before, when she returned. He painted with new confidence, amusement, wonder. The subject had changed from "Mother and Son" to "Brother and Sister" (Esmeralda as Bessie), to let's face it, "Prostitute and Procurer." Though she no longer posed, he was becoming clearer in his inner eye as to what he wanted. Once he retained her face for a week before scraping it off. I'm getting there. And though he considered sandpapering his own face off and substituting Ludovico as pimp, the magnificent thing was that in the end he kept himself in. This is my most honest piece of work. Esmeralda was the now nineteen-year-old prostitute; and he, with a stroke here and there aging himself a bit, a fifteen-year-old procurer. This was the surprise that made the painting. And what it means, I suppose, is I am what I became from a young age. Then he thought, it has no meaning, a painting's a painting.

The picture completed itself. F was afraid to finish it: What would he do next and how long would that take? But the picture was, one day, done. It assumed a completion: This woman and man together, prostitute and procurer. She was a girl with fear in both black eyes, a vulnerable if stately neck, and a steely small mouth; he was a boy with tight insides, on the verge of crying. The presence of each protected the other. A Holy Sacrament. The form leaped to the eye. He had tormented, ecstatic, yet confused feelings, but at last felt triumphant—it was done! Though deeply drained, moved, he was satisfied, completed—ah, art!

He called Esmeralda to look at the painting. Her lips trembled, she lost color, turned away, finally she spoke. "For me it's me. You've caught me as I am, there's no doubt of it. The picture is a marvel." She wept as she gazed at it. "Now I can quit what I'm doing. Let's get married, Arturo."

Ludovico, limping a little in his squeaky shoes, came upstairs to beg their pardons, but when he saw the finished painting on the easel stood stiff in awe.

"I'm speechless," he said, "what more can I say?"

"Don't bother," said Esmeralda, "nobody wants your stinking opinion."

They opened a bottle of Soave and Esmeralda borrowed a pan and baked a loin of veal, to celebrate. Their artist neighbors came in, Citelli, an illustrator, and his dark meager wife; it was a festive occasion. F afterwards related the story of his life and they all listened, absorbed.

When the neighbors left and the three were alone, Ludovico objectively discussed his weak nature.

"Compared to some I've met in the streets of Florence, I'm not a bad person, but my trouble is I forgive myself too easily. That has its disadvantages because then there are no true barriers to a harmful act, if you understand my meaning. It's the easy way out, but what else can you do if you grew up with certain disadvantages? My father was criminally inclined and it's from him I inherited my worst tendencies. It's clear enough that goats don't have puppies. I'm vain, selfish, although not arrogant, and given almost exclusively to petty evil. Nothing serious but serious enough. Of course I've wanted to change my ways, but at my age what can one change? Can you change yourself, maestro? Yet I readily confess who I am and ask your pardon for any inconvenience I might have caused you in the past. Either of you."

"Drop dead," said Esmeralda.

"The man's sincere," F said, irritated. "There's no need to be so cruel."

"Come to bed, Arturo." She entered the gabinetto as Ludovico went on with his confession.

"To tell the truth, I am myself a failed artist, but at least I contribute to the creativity of others by offering fruitful suggestions, though you're free to do as you please. Anyway, your painting is a marvel. Of course it's Picassoid, but you've outdone him in some of his strategies."

F expressed thanks and gratitude.

"At first glance I thought that since the bodies of the two figures are so much more thickly painted than their faces, especially the girl's, this destroyed the unity of surface, but when I think of some of the impastos I've seen, and the more I study your painting, the more I feel that's not important."

"I don't think it'll bother anybody so long as it looks like a spontaneous act."

"True, and therefore my only criticism is that maybe the painting suffers from an excess of darkness. It needs more light. I'd say a soupçon of lemon and a little red, not more than a trace. But I leave it to you."

Esmeralda came out of the gabinetto in a red nightgown with a black lace bodice.

"Don't touch it," she warned. "You'll never make it better."

"How would you know?" F said.

"I have my eyes."

"Maybe she's right," Ludovico said, with a yawn. "Who knows with art? Well, I'm on my way. If you want to sell your painting for a handsome price, my advice is take it to a reliable dealer. There are one or two in the city whose names and addresses I'll bring you in the morning."

"Don't bother," Esmeralda said. "We don't need your assistance."

"I want to keep it around for a few days to look at," F confessed.

"As you please." Ludovico tipped his hat good night and left limping. F and Esmeralda went to bed together. Later she returned to her cot in the kitchen, took off her red nightgown and put on an old one of white muslin.

F for a while wondered what to paint next. Maybe sort of a portrait of Ludovico, his face reflected in a mirror, with two sets of aqueous sneaky eyes. He slept soundly but in the middle of the night awoke depressed. He went over his painting inch by inch and it seemed to him a disappointment. Where was Momma after all these years? He got up to look, and doing so, changed his mind; not bad at all, though Ludovico was right, the picture was dark and could stand a touch of light. He laid out his paints and brushes and began to work, almost at once achieving the effect he sought. And then he thought he would work a bit on the girl's face, no more than a stroke or two around the eyes and mouth, to make her expression truer to life. More the prostitute, himself a little older. When the sun blazed through both windows, he realized he had been working for hours. F put down his brush, washed up and returned for a look at the painting. Sickened to his gut, he saw what he felt: He had ruined it. It slowly drowned in his eyes.

Ludovico came in with a well-dressed paunchy friend, an art dealer. They looked at the picture and laughed.

Five long years down the drain. F squeezed a tube of black on the canvas and with a thick brush smeared it over both faces in all directions.

When Esmeralda pulled open the curtain and saw the mess, moaning, she came at him with the bread knife. "Murderer!"

F twisted it out of her grasp, and in anguish lifted the blade into his gut.

"This serves me right."

"A moral act," Ludovico agreed.

5

FIDELMAN PISSING in muddy water discovers water over his head. Modigliani wanders by searching by searchlight for his lost statues in Livorno canal. They told me to dump them in the canal, so I fucked them, I dumped them. Ne ha viste? Macchè. How come that light works underwater? Hashish. If we wake we drown, says Fidelman. *Chants de Maldoror.* His eyeless face drained of blood but not yellow light, Modi goes up canal as Fidelman drifts down.

Woodcut. Knight, Death and the Devil. Dürer.

Au fond il s'est suicidé. Anon.

Broken rusting balls of Venus. Ah, to sculpt a perfect hole, the volume and gravity constant. Invent space. Surround matter with hole rather than vice versa. That would have won me enduring fame and fortune and spared me all this wandering.

Cathedral of Erotic Misery. Schwitters.

Everybody says you're dead, otherwise why do you never write? Madonna Adoring the Child, Mater Dolorosa. Madonna della Peste. Long White Knights. Lives of the Saints. S. Sebastian, arrow collector, swimming in bloody sewer. Pictured transfixed with arrows. S. Denis, decapitated. Pictured holding his head. S. Agatha, breasts shorn clean, running enflamed. Painted carrying both bloody breasts in white salver. S. Stephen, crowned with rocks. Shown stoned. S. Lucy tearing out eyes for suitor smitten by same. Portrayed bearing two-eyed omelet on dish. S. Catherine, broken apart on spiked wheel. Pictured married to wheel. S. Laurence, roasted on slow grill. *I am roasted on one side. Now turn me over and eat.* Shown cooked but uneaten. S. Bartholomew, flayed alive. Standing with skin draped over skinned arm. S. Fima, eaten by rats. Pictured with happy young rat. S. Simon Zelotes, sawed in half. Shown with bleeding cross-cut saw. S. Genet in prison, pictured with boys. S. Fidel Uomo, stuffing his ass with flowers.

Still Life with Herrings. S. Soutine.

He divideth the gefilte fish and matzos.

Drawing. Flights of birds over dark woods, sparrows, finches, thrushes, white doves, martins, swallows, eagles. Birds with human faces crapping human on whom they crap.

Wood sculpture. Man holding sacrificial goat. Cubist goat with triangular titties. Goat eating hanged goat.

The Enigma of Isidor Ducasse. Man Ray.

In this time Fidelman, after making studies of the work of Donatello, in particular of the Annunciation carved in stone for the church of S. Croce, the S. George in armor, with all the beauty of youth and the courage of the knight, and the bald man known as Il Zuccone, from figures in the façade of Giotto's Campanile, about whom it was said the sculptor, addressing his creation, would cry out, Speak, Speak: In this time the American began to work in original images dug into the soil. To those who expressed astonishment regarding this extraordinary venture, Fidelman is said to have replied, Being a poor man I can neither purchase nor borrow hard or soft stone; therefore, since this is so, I create my figures as hollows in the earth. In sum, my material is the soil, my tools a pickax and shovel, my sculpture the act of digging rather than carving or assembling. However, the pleasure in creation is not less than that felt by Michelangelo.

After attempting first several huge ziggurats that because of the rains tumbled down like Towers of Babel, he began to work labyrinths and mazes dug in the earth and constructed in the form of jewels. Later he refined and simplified this method, building a succession of spontaneously placed holes, each a perfect square, which when seen together constituted a sculpture. These Fidelman exhibited throughout Italy in whatsoever place he came.

Having arrived in a city carrying his tools on his shoulder and a few possessions in a knotted bundle on his arm, the sculptor searched in the environs until he had come upon a small plot of land he could dig on without the formality of paying rent. Because this good fortune was not always possible, he was more than once rudely separated from his sculptures as they were in the act of being constructed, and by the tip of someone's boot, ejected from the property whereon he worked, the hollows then being filled in by the angry landowners. For this reason the sculptor often chose public places and dug in parks, or squares, if this were possible, which to do so he sometimes pretended, when questioned by officials of the police, that he was an underground repairman sent there by the Municipality. If he was disbelieved by these and dragged off to jail, he lay several days recuperating from the efforts of his labors, not unpleasantly. There are worse places than jails, Fidelman is said to have said, and once I am set free I shall begin my sculptures in another place. To sum up, he dug where he could, yet not far from the marketplace where many of the inhabitants of the city passed by daily, and where, if he was not unlucky, the soil was friable and not too hard with rock to be dug. This task he performed, as was his custom, quickly and expertly. Just as Giotto is said to have been able to draw a perfect free-hand circle, so could Fidelman dig a perfect square hole without measurement. He arranged the sculptures singly or in pairs according to the necessity of the Art. These were about a braccio in volume, sometimes two, or two-and-a-half if Fidelman was not too fatigued. The smaller sculpture took from two to three hours to construct, the larger perhaps five or six; and if the final grouping was to contain three pieces, this meant a long day, indeed, and possibly two, of continual digging. There were times when because of weariness Fidelman would have compromised for a single braccio piece; but in the end Art prevailed and he dug as he must to fulfill those forms that must be fulfilled.

After constructing his sculptures the artist, unwinding a canvas sign on stilts, advertised the exhibition. The admission requested was ten lire, which was paid to him in the roped-off entrance way, the artist standing with a container in his hand. Not many were enticed to visit the exhibition, especially when it snowed or rained, although Fidelman was heard to say that the weather did not the least harm to his sculptures, indeed, sometimes improved them by changing volume and texture as well as affecting other qualities. And it was as though nature, which until now was acted upon by the artist, now acted upon the Art itself, an unexpected but satisfying happening, since thus were changed the forms of a form. Even on the most crowded days when more than several persons came to view his holes in the earth, the sculptor earned a meager sum, not more than two or three hundred lire at most. He well understood that his bread derived from the curious among the inhabitants, rather than from the true lovers of Art, but for this phenomenon took no responsibility since it was his need to create and not be concerned with the commerce of Art. Those few who came to the exhibit, they viewed the sculptures at times in amazement and disbelief, whether at the perfect constructions or at their own stupidity, if indeed they believed they were stupid, is not known. Some of the viewers, after gazing steadfastly at the sculptures, were like sheep in their expression, as if wondering whether they had been deceived; some were stony faced, as if they knew they had been. But few complained aloud, being ashamed to admit their folly, if indeed it were folly. To the one or two who rudely questioned him, saying, Why do you pass off on us as sculpture an empty hole or two? the artist, with the greatest tact and courtesy, replied, It were well if you relaxed before my sculptures, if you mean to enjoy them, and yield yourself to the pleasure they evoke in the surprise of their forms. At these words he who had complained fell silent, not certain he had truly understood the significance of the work of Art he had seen. On occasion a visitor would speak to the artist to compliment him, which he received with gratitude. Eh, maestro, your sculptures touch my heart. I thank you from the bottom of my own, the artist is said to have replied, blowing his nose to hide the gratification that he felt.

There is a story told that in Naples in a small park near the broad avenue called Via Caracciolo, one day a young man waited until the remaining other visitor had left the exhibit so that he might speak to the sculptor. Maestro, said he most earnestly, it distresses me to do so, but I must pray you to return to me the ten lire I paid for admission to your exhibit. I have seen no more than two square holes in the ground and am much dissatisfied. The fault lies in you that you have seen only holes, Fidelman is said to have replied. I cannot, however, return the admission fee to you, for doing so might cause me to lose confidence in my work. Why do you refuse me my just request? said the poorly attired young man, whose dark eyes, although intense and comely, were mournful. I ask for my young babes. My wife gave me money so that I might buy bread for our supper, of which we have little. We are poor folk and I have no steady work. Yet when I observed the sign calling attention to your sculptures, which though I looked for them I could see none visible, I was moved by curiosity, an enduring weakness of mine and the cause of much of my misery. It came into my heart that I must see these sculptures, so I gave up the ten lire, I will confess, in fear and trepidation, hoping to be edified and benefited although fearful I would not be. I hoped that your sculptures, since they are described on the banner as new in the history of Art, might teach me what I myself must make in order that I may fulfill my desire to be great in Art; but all I can see are two large holes, the one dug deeper by about a braccio than the other. Holes are of no use to me, my life being full of them, so I beg you to return the lire that I may hasten to the baker's shop to buy the bread I was sent for.

After hearing him out, Fidelman is said to have answered, I do not as a rule explain my sculptures to the public, but since you are an attractive young man who has turned his thoughts to becoming an artist, I will say to you what your eyes have not seen, in order that you may be edified and benefited.

I hope that may be so, said the young man, although I doubt it.

Listen before you doubt. Primus, although the sculpture is more or less invisible it is sculpture nevertheless. Because you can't see it doesn't mean it isn't there. As for use or uselessness, rather think that that is Art which is made by the artist to be Art. Secundus, you must keep in mind that any sculpture is a form existing at a point radiating in all directions, therefore since it is dug into the Italian earth the sculpture vibrates overtones of Italy's Art, history, politics, religion; even nature as one experiences it in this country. There is also a metaphysic in relation of down to up, and vice versa, but I won't pursue that matter now. Suffice to say, my sculpture is not unrelated, though not necessarily purposefully, to its environment, whether seen or unseen. Tertius, in relation to the above, it is impossible to describe the range of choices, conscious or unconscious, that exist in the creation of a single sculptured hole. However, let it be understood that choice, as I use the word in this context, means artistic freedom, for I do not in advance choose the exact form and position of the hole; it chooses me.

The essential thing is to maintain contact with it as it is being achieved. If the artist loses contact with his hole, than which there is none like it in the universe; then the hole will not respond and the sculpture will fail. Thus I mean to show you that constructs of a sculpture which appear to be merely holes are, in truth, in the hands of the artist, elements of a conceptual work of Art.

You speak well, maestro, but I am dull-witted and find it difficult to comprehend such things. It would not surprise me that I forgot what you have so courteously explained before I arrive at the next piazza. May I not therefore have the ten lire back? I will be ever grateful to you.

Tough titty if you can't comprehend Art, Fidelman is said to have replied. Fuck off now.

The youth left, sighing, without his ten lire, nor with bread for his babes.

Not long after he had departed, as it grew dusk, the sculptor took down the banner of his exhibit and gathered his tools so that he might fill in the sculpture and leave for another city. As he was making these preparations a stranger appeared, wrapped in the folds of a heavy cloak, although winter still hid in its cave and the fields were ripe with grain. The stranger's nether limbs, clothed in coarse black stockings, were short and bowed, and his half-concealed visage, iron eyes in a leather face, caused the flesh on Fidelman's neck to prickle and thicken. But the stranger, averting his glance and speaking pleasantly, yet as though to his own hands, and in the accent of one from a foreign land, graciously prayed the sculptor for permission to view his sculpture, the effect of which he had heard was extraordinary. He explained he had been delayed on board ship and apologized for appearing so late in the day. Fidelman, having recovered somewhat from his surprise at the stranger's odd garments and countenance, is said to have replied it made no difference that he had come late so long as he paid the admission fee.

This the stranger did forthwith with a gold coin for which he neither asked nor received change. He glanced fleetingly at the sculpture and turned away as though dazzled, the which the sculptor is said to have wondered at.

But instead of departing the exhibit now that he had viewed

it, however hastily, the stranger tarried, his back to that place where the sculpture stood fixed in the earth, the red sun sinking at his shoulders. As though reflecting still upon that he had seen, he consumed an apple, the core of which he tossed over his left shoulder into one of the holes of the sculpture; an act that is said to have angered Fidelman although he refrained from complaint, it may be because he feared this stranger was an agent of the police, so it were better he said nothing.

If you'll excuse me, said the stranger at last, please explain to me what means these two holes that they have in them nothing but the dark inside?

The meaning lies in what they are as they seem to be, and the dark you note within, although I did not plan it so or put it there, may be thought of as an attribute of the aesthetic, Fidelman is said to have replied.

So what then did you put there?

To wit, the sculpture.

At that the stranger laughed, his laughter not unlike the bray of a goat. All I saw was nothing. To me, if you'll pardon me, is a hole nothing. This I will prove to you. If you will look in the small hole there is now there an apple core. If not for this would be empty the hole. If empty would be there nothing.

Emptiness is not nothing if it has form.

Form, if you will excuse me my expression, is not what is the whole of Art.

One might argue that, but neither is content if that's what you intend to imply. Form may be and often is the content of Art.

You don't say?

I do indeed.

The stranger spat on both of his hands and rubbed them together, a disagreeable odor rising from them.

In this case I will give you form.

Since the stranger stood now scarce visible in the dark, the sculptor began to be in great fear, his legs, in truth, trembling.

Who are you? Fidelman is said finally to have demanded.

I am also that youth that he is now dead in the Bay of Naples, that you would not give him back his poor ten lire so he could buy bread for his babies.

Are you not the devil? the sculptor is said to have cried out.

I am also him.

Quid ego feci?

This I will tell you. You have not yet learned what is the difference between something and nothing.

Bending for the shovel, the stranger smote the horrified Fidelman with its blade a resounding blow on the head, the sculptor toppling as though dead into the larger of the two holes he himself had dug. He-who-Fidelman-did-not-know then proceeded to shovel in earth until the sculpture and its creator were extinguished.

So it's a grave, the stranger is said to have muttered. So now we got form but we also got content.

Collage. The Flayed Ox. Rembrandt. Hanging Fowl. Soutine. Young Man with Death's Head. Van Leyden. Funeral at Ornans. Courbet. Bishop Eaten by Worms. Murillo. Last Supper, Last Judgment, Last Inning.

I paint with my prick. Renoir. I paint with my ulcer. Soutine. I paint with my paint. Fidelman.

One can study nature, dissect and analyze and balance it without making paintings. Bonnard.

Gouache. Unemployed Musician. Fiddleman.

Painting is nothing more than the art of expressing the invisible through the visible. Fromentin. Indefinite Divisibility. Tanguy. Definite Invisibility. Fidelman.

I'm making the last paintings which anyone can make. Reinhardt. I've made them. I like my paintings because anyone can do them. Warhol. Me too.

Erased de Kooning Drawing. Rauschenberg. Erased Rauschenberg. de Kooning. Lithograph. Eraser. Fidelman.

Modigliani climbs and falls. He tries to scale a brick wall with bleeding fingers, his eyes lit crystals of heroin, whisky, pain. He climbs and falls in silence.

My God, what's all that climbing and falling for?

For art, you cretin.

Thunder and lightning.

Portrait of an Old Jew Seated. Rembrandt. Portrait of an Old Jew in an Armchair. Rembrandt. It beats walking.

Then I dreamt that I woke suddenly, with an unspeakable shock, to the consciousness that someone was lying in bed beside me. I put my hand out and touched the soft naked shoulder of a woman; and a cold gentle little woman's voice said: I have not been in bed for a hundred years. Raverat. The Rat Killer. Rembrandt.

Elle m'a mordu aux couilles. Modigliani.

Mosaic. Piazza Amerina, Sicily. IVth Cent. A.D. All that remains after so long a time.

*

Susskind preacheth up on the mountain, a piece of green palm branch behind his head. (He has no halo, here the mosaic is broken.) Three small cactus plants groweth at his bare feet./ Tell the truth. Dont cheat. If its easy it dont mean its good. Be kind, specially to those that they got less than you. I want for everybody justice. Must also be charity. If you feel good give charity. If you feel bad give charity. Must also be mercy. Be nice, dont fight. Children, how can we live without mercy? If you have no mercy for me I shall not live. Love, mercy, charity. Its not so easy believe me.

*

At the bottom of the brown hill they stand there by the huge lichenous rock that riseth above them on the top of which is a broad tree with a twisted trunk./ Ah, Master, my eyes watereth. Thou speakest true. I love thy words. I love thee more than thy words. If I could paint thee with my paints, then would my heart soar to the Gates of Heaven. I will be forever thy disciple, no ifs or buts./ This is already iffed. If you will follow me, follow. If you will follow must be for Who I Am. Also please, no paints or paintings. Remember the Law, what it says. No graven images, which is profanation and idolatry. Nobody can paint Who I Am. Not on papyrus, or make me into an idol of wood, or stone, not even in the sand. Dont try, its a sin. Here is a parable: And the Lord called unto Moses and spoke to him, Moses, come thou on this mountain and I will show Myself so thou mayst see Me, and none but thee; and Moses answered: Lord, if I see Thee, then wilt Thou become as a graven image on mine eye and I be blind. Then spake the Lord, saying, Thou art my beloved Son, in whom I am well pleased, and for this there is no Promised Land./ Whats the parable of that? Its more a paradox, Id say./ If you dont know its not for you./ Tell me, Master, art thou the

Living God? Art thou at least the Son of God?/ So we will see, its not impossible./ Art thou the Redeemer?/ This could be also, Im not sure myself. Depends what happens./ Is thy fate ordained?/ I act like I Am. Who knows my fate? All I know is somebody will betray me. Dont ask how I know, I know. You dont but I do. This is the difference./ It is not I, Master, I will never betray thee. Cast me out now if thou believest I speak not the TRUTH./ What happens will happen. So give up your paints and your brushes and follow me where I go, and we will see what we will see. This we will see./ Master, tis as good as done.

*

Fidelman droppeth into the Dead Sea all his paints and brushes, except one. These dissolve in the salted sea. (A piece of the blue sea is faded.)

*

(In this picture) As Susskind preacheth to the multitude, on the shore of the green sea of Galilee where sail the little ships of the fisher men, as even the red fishes and the white fishes come to listen at the marge of the water, the black goats stand still on the hills, the painter, who hideth behind a palm tree, sketcheth with a coal on papyrus the face and figure of the Master./ If I could do a portrait of him as he is in this life I will be remembered forever in human history. Nobody can call that betrayal, I dont think, for its for the good of us all./ My child, why do you do that which I forbade you? Dont think I cant see you, I can. I wish I couldnt see what I see, but I can.

*

The painter kneeleth on his knees. (A few tesserae are missing from his face, including one of the eye, and a few black stones from his beard.)/ Master, forgive me. All I meant to do was preserve thy likeness for a future time. I guess it gotteth to be too much for me, the thought that I might. Forgive, forgive in thy mercy. Ill burn everything, I promise, papyrus, charcoal, a roll of canvas I have hid in my hut, also this last paint brush although a favorite of mine./ Listen to me, there are two horses, one brown, the other black. The brown obeys his master, the black does not. Which is the better horse?/ Both are the same./ How is this so?/ One obeys and the other does not, but they are both thoroughbreds./ You have an easy tongue. If I cant change you I must suffer my fate. This is a fact./ Master, have no further worries on that score, I am a changed man down to my toe nails, I give thee my word.

*

Fidelman speaketh to himself in a solitary place in Capernaum./ This talent it is death to hide lodged in me useless. How am I ever going to make a living or win my spurs? How can I compete in this world if both my hands are tied and my eyes blindfolded? Whats so moral about that? How is a man meant to fulfill himself if he isnt allowed to paint? Its graven image versus grave damages to myself and talent. Which harms the most there is no doubt. One can take just so much./ He gnasheth his teeth. He waileth to the sky. He teareth his cheeks and pulleth out the hairs of his head and beard. He butteth his skull against the crumbling brick wall. On this spot the wall is stained red with blood./ Satan saith Ha Ha.

*

As Susskind sat at meat he spoke thus. Verily I say, one of you who eats now at this table will betray me, dont ask who./ His followers blusheth. Their faces are in shades of pink. No one blusheth not. Fidelman blusheth red./ But if he knows, it cant be all that wrong to do it. What I mean is Im not doing it in any sneaky way, that is, for after all he knows./ He that has betrayed me once will betray me twice. He will betray me thrice./ Fidelman counteth on his fingers.

*

He is now in the abode of the high priest Caiaphas./ (Here the mosaic is almost all destroyed. Only the painter's short-fingered hand survives.) Fidelmans heavy hand is filled with thirty-nine pieces of silver.

*

The painter runneth out to buy paints, brushes, canvas.

*

On the Mount of Olives appeareth the painter amid a multitude with swords, staves, and lengths of lead pipe. Also come the chief priest, the chief of police, scribes, elders, the guards with dogs, the onlookers to look on. Fidelman goeth to the master and kisseth him full on the lips./ Twice, saith Susskind./ He wept.

*

He hath on his head a crown of rusty chain links. A guard smiteth his head and spitteth on his eye. In mockery they worship Susskind./ Its a hard life, he saith./ He draggeth the beam of the cross up a hill. Fidelman watcheth from behind a mask.

*

12 12 12 12 12 12 12 12 12 12 12 12 12 12 12 12 12 12 12 12
369 369 369 369 369 369 369 369 369 369 369 369 369 369
veyizmirveyizmirveyizmirveyizmirveyizmirveyizmirveyiz
12369123691236912369123691236912369123691236912369123691236

*

Fidelman painteth three canvases. The Crucifixion he painteth red on red. The Descent from the Cross he painteth white on white. For the Resurrection, on Easter morning, he leaveth the canvas blank.

*

P
t o tem
L
E
Suss
King

*

Je vous emmerde. Modigliani.

Oil on wood. Bottle fucking guitar? Bull impaled on pole? One-eyed carp stuffed in staring green bottle? Clown spooning dog dung out of sawdust? Staircase ascending a nude? Black-stockinged whore reading pornographic book by lamplight? Still life: three apple cores plus one long gray hair? Boy pissing on old man's shoe? The blue disease? Balding woman dyeing her hair? Buggers of Calais? Blood oozing from ceiling on foggy night?

Rembrandt was the first great master whose sitters sometimes dreaded seeing their portraits. Malraux. I is another. Rimbaud.

1. Watercolor. Tree growing in all directions. Nothing namable taxonomically speaking, like weeping willow with stiff spotted leaves, some rotted brown-green. Otherwise stylized apple-green-to-gold leaves. Not maple or sycamore same though resembling both, enlarged, painted to cover whole tree

from roots to topmost spotted leaf. The leaves are the tree. Branches like black veins, thins to thicks, visible behind or through leaves. No birds in tree, not rook or raven. Impression is of mystery. Nothing more is seen at first but if viewer keeps looking tree is cleverly a human face. Leaves and branches delineate strained features, also lonely hollow anguished eyes. What is this horror I am or represent? Painter can think of none, for portrait is of a child and he remembers happy childhood, or so it seems. Exactly what face has done, or where has been, or knows, or wants to know, or is or isn't experiencing, isn't visible, nor can be explained as tone, memory, feeling; or something that happened in later life that painter can't recall. Maybe it never happened. It's as though this face is hiding in a tree or pretending to be one while waiting for something to happen in life and that something when it happened was nothing. Nothing much. 2. Triptych. Woodcut. It's about forbidden love. In the first black-and-white panel this guy is taking his sister in her black-and-white bathrobe. She squirms but loves it. Can be done in white-and-black for contrast. Man Seducing Sister or Vice Versa. The second panel is about the shame of the first, where he takes to masturbating in the cellar. It's dark so you can't see much of his face but there's just enough light to see what he's up to. Man Spilling Seed on Damp Cellar Floor. Then here in this third panel, two men doing it, each with his three-fingered hand on the other's maulstick. This can be inked darkly because they wouldn't want to be seen. 3. Then having prepared it for painting he began to think what he would paint upon it that would frighten everyone that saw it, having the effect of the head of Medusa. So he brought for that purpose to his room, which no one entered but himself, lizards, grasshoppers, serpents, butterflies, locusts, bats, and other strange animals of the kind, and from them all he produced a great animal so horrible and fearful that it seemed to poison the air with its fiery breath. This he represented coming out of some dark rocks with venom issuing from its open jaws, fire from its eyes, and smoke from its nostrils, a monstrous and horrible thing indeed. Lives of the Painters: Leonardo. 4. Figure; wood, string, and found objects. Picasso.

Incisore. The cylinder, the sphere, the cone. Cézanne. The

impact of an acute angle of a triangle on a circle promises an effect no less powerful than the finger of God touching the finger of Adam in Michelangelo. Kandinsky.

Fidelman, etcher, left a single engraving of the series called A Painter's Progress. Originally there were six copper plates, drypoint, all with their prints destroyed, how or why is not known. Only a single imperfect artist's proof entitled "The Cave" survives. This etching represents a painter at work, resemblance to whom may easily be guessed. Each night, according to a tattered diary he had kept for a while, he entered the cave in question through a cellar he had the key to, when all the lights in the old clapboard house, several boards missing, were out, curtains thickly drawn over each narrow window. The painter in the etching worked all night, night after night, inch by slow inch covering the rough limestone surface of the voluminous cave at the end of a labyrinth under the cellar, with intricate designs of geometric figures; and he left before dawn, his coming and going unknown to his sister, who lived in the house alone. The walls and part of the roof of the huge cave that he had been decorating for years and years and estimated at least two more to go before his labors were ended, were painted in an extraordinary tapestry of simple figures in black, salmon, gold-yellow, sea-green and apricot, although the colors cannot of course be discerned in the three-toned engraving—a rich design of circles and triangles, discrete or interlocking, of salmon triangles encompassed within apricot circles, and sea-green circles within pale gold-yellow triangles, blown like masses of autumn leaves over the firmament of the cave.

The painter of the cave, wearing a leafy loincloth as he labored, varied the patterns of the geometric design. He was at that time of his life engaged in developing a more intricate conception of circles within circles of various hues and shades including copper red and light olive; and to extend his art further, of triangles within triangles within concentric circles. He drove himself at his work, intending when his labor was done to climb the dark stairs ascending to his sister's first floor and tell her what he had accomplished in the cave below. Bessie, long a widow, all her children married and scattered across the continent, her oldest daughter in Montreal, lived, except for occasional visitors, mostly the doctor, alone in the old frame house she had come to as a young bride, in Newark, New Jersey. She was at this time, ill and possibly dying. Nobody he could think of had told her artist-brother, but he figured he somehow knew. Call it intuition. It was his hope she would remain alive until he had completed his art work of the cave and she could at last see how it had turned out.

Bessie, he would say, I did this for you and you know why.

Fidelman worked by the light of a single dusty 100-watt bulb, the old-fashioned kind with a glass spicule at the bottom, dangling from a wire from the ceiling of the cave, that he had installed when he first came there to paint. For a long time he had distrusted the bulb because he had never had to replace it, and sometimes it glowed like a waning moon after he had switched it off, making him feel slightly uneasy and a little lumpy in the chest. He suspected a presence, immanent or otherwise, around; though who or why, and under what circumstances, he could not say. Nothing or nobody substantial. Anyway, he didn't care for the bulb. He knew why when it began, one night, to speak to him. How does a bulb speak? With the sound of light. Fidelman for a while did not respond, first because he couldn't, his throat constricted; and second, because he suspected this might be he talking to himself; yet when it spoke again, this time he answered.

Fidelman, said the voice of, or from within, the bulb, why are you here such a long time in this cave? Painting—this we know—but why do you paint so long a whole cave? What kind of business is this?

Leaving my mark is what. For the ages to see. This place will someday be crowded with visitors at a dollar a throw. Mark my words.

But why in this way if there are better?

What would you suggest, for instance?

Whatever I suggest is too late now, but why don't you go at least upstairs and say hello to your sister who hasn't seen you in years? Go before it is too late, because she is now dying.

Not quite just yet I can't go, said the painter. I can't until my work is finished because I want to show her what I've accomplished once it's done.

Go up to her now, this is the last chance. Your work in this cave will take years yet. Tell her at least hello. What have you got to lose? To her it will be a wonderful thing.

No, I can't. It's all too complicated. I can't go till I've finished the job. The truth is I hate the past. It caught me unawares. I'd rather not see her just yet. Maybe next week or so.

It's a short trip up the stairs to say hello to her. What can you lose if it's only fourteen steps and then you're there?

It's too complicated, like I said. I hate the past.

So why do you blame her for this?

I don't blame anybody at all. I just don't want to see her. At least not just yet.

If she dies she's dead. You can talk all you want then but she won't answer you.

It's no fault of mine if people die. There's nothing I can do about it.

Nobody is talking about fault or not fault. All we are talking about is to go upstairs.

I can't I told you, it's too complicated, I hate the past, it caught me unawares. If there's anything to blame I don't blame her. I just don't want to see her is all, at least not just yet until my work here is done.

Don't be so proud my friend. Pride ain't spinach. You can't eat it, so it won't make you grow. Remember what happened to the Greeks.

Praxiteles? He who first showed Aphrodite naked? Phidias, whose centaur's head is thought to be a self-portrait? Who have you got in mind?

No, the one that he tore out his eyes. Watch out for hubris. It's poison ivy. Trouble you got enough, you want also blisters? Also an electric bulb don't give so often advice so listen with care. When did you hear last that an electric bulb gave advice? Did I advise Napoleon? Did I advise Van Gogh? This is like a miracle, so why don't you take advantage and go upstairs?

Well, you've got a point there. There's some truth to it, I suppose. I might at that, come to think of it. As you say, it's not everybody who gets advice in this way. There's something Biblical about it, if I may say. Furthermore, I'm not getting any younger and I haven't seen Bessie in years. Plus I do owe her something, after all. Be my Virgil, which way to up the stairs?

I will show you which way but I can't go with you. Up to a point but not further if you know what I mean. A bulb is a bulb. Light I got but not feet. After all, this is the Universe, everything is laws.

Fidelman slowly climbs up the stone, then wooden, stairs, lit generously from bottom clear to top by the bulb, and opens the creaking door into a narrow corridor. He walks along it till he comes to a small room where Bessie is lying in a sagging double bed.

Hello, Bessie, I've been downstairs most of the time, but I came up to say hello.

Why are you so naked, Arthur? It's winter outside.

It's how I am nowadays.

Arthur, said Bessie, why did you stop writing for so long? Why didn't you answer my letters?

I guess I had nothing much to write. Nothing much has happened to me. There wasn't much to say.

Remember how Mama used to give us an apple to eat with a slice of bread?

I don't like to remember those things any more.

Anyway, thanks for coming up to see me, Arthur. It's a nice thing to do when a person is so alone. At least I know what you look like and where you are nowadays.

Bessie died and rose to heaven, holding in her heart her brother's hello.

Flights of circles, cones, triangles.

End of drypoint etching.

The ugly and plebeian face with which Rembrandt was ill-favored was accompanied by untidy and dirty clothes, since it was his custom, when working, to wipe his brushes on himself, and to do other things of a similar nature. Jakob Rosenberg.

If you're dead how do you go on living?

Natura morta: still life. Oil on paper.

6

VENICE, FLOATING city of green and golden canals. Fidelman floated too, from stem to stern. When the sirocco relentlessly blew in late autumn the island dipped on ancient creaking piles toward the outer isles, then gently tipped to the mainland against the backwash of oily waters. The ex-painter, often seasick in the municipal garbage boat, fished with a net out of the smelly canals, dead rats and lettuce leaves. He had come for the Biennale and stayed on.

November fog settled on the webbed-canaled and narrow-streeted city, obscuring campanile, church steeples, and the red-tiled roofs of houses tilted together from opposite sides of streets. Oars splashing, he skirted the mist-moving vaporetti, his shouts and curses opposing their horns and the tolling bellbuoys in the lagoon. For Fidelman no buoy bells tolled, no church bells either; he kept no track of tide or time. On All Souls' Day, unable to resist, he rowed after a black-and-silver funeral barge and cortège of draped mourning gondolas moving like silent arrows across the water to San Michele, gloomy cypressed isle of the dead; the corpse of a young girl in white laid stiff in a casket covered with wreaths of hothouse flowers guarded by wooden angels. She waits, whatever she waited for, or sought, or hungered for, no longer. Ah, i poveri morti, though that depends on how you look at it. He had looked too long.

Fidelman, December ferryman, ferried standing passengers, their heads in mist, to the opposite rainy shore of the Grand Canal. Whichever shore. The wet winter rain drummed on the crooked roofs of the façade-eroded palazzi standing in undulating slime-green algae; and upon moving clusters of black bobbing umbrellas in the dark streets and marketplaces. The ex-painter wandered wet-hatted, seeking in shop windows who knows what treat the tourists hadn't coveted and bought. Venice was full of goods he hungered for and detested. Yet he sought an object of art nobody would recognize but Fidelman.

In January the cold swollen tides of the Adriatic rose again over the Mole, swirling a meter deep on the Piazza and flooding the pavimento of San Marco. If you had to, you could swim to the altar. Gondolas stealthily glided over the Stones of Venice, wet Bride of the Sea, drowning greenly an inch or two annually as Fidelman, a cold fish in his thin pants, inch by inch also drowned, envisioning Tintoretto: "Venice Overwhelmed by Tidal Wave."

The rain blew away before the sunlit cold but not the pools and ponds, more than one campo alongside open water or canal, flooded. Fidelman staked a claim, having been fired from cross-canal transportation on the complaint of two patriotic gondoliers, and now did his ferrying piggyback for one hundred lire per person, skinny old men half-price if they didn't grip him too tightly around the neck. He had once read of a fiendish beggar who had strangled and drowned a good samaritan carrying him across a flooded brook. Fat people he served last, after he had ferried across the others on line, though they roundly berated him for prejudice, or offered twice the going rate. One aristocratic huge old dame with a voice that rose out of a tuba belabored him with her slender silk umbrella.

Fidelman waded in hip boots through high water glinting like shards of broken mirror in the freezing winter sunlight, and deposited his customers on dry ground whence they proceeded hurriedly along narrow streets and alleys. Occasionally while transporting a female he gave her a modified feel along the leg, which roused no response through winter clothing; still it was good for the morale. One attractive, long-nosed, almost oriental-eyed young Venetian woman who mounted his back, began at once to giggle, and laughed, unable to control it, mirthfully as he slowly sloshed across the pond. She sat on Fidelman, enjoying the ride, her rump bumping his, cheek pressed to his frozen ear, hugging him casually, a pair of shapely black-stockinged legs clasped in the crooks of his arms; and when he tenderly set her down, his penis erect, athrob, she kissed him affectionately and hastily went her way. As Fidelman watched she turned back, smiling sadly, as though they had once been lovers and the affair was ended. Then she waved goodbye and walked on. He wished she hadn't, for he was after a while in love with her.

When the water receded as the bora roared, drying the city, uncovering here and there a drowned cat, the winter light sprang up crystal clear as Fidelman, once more jobless, holding onto his hat—you can't chase them on the canals—sought his lady, to no avail. He searched from the Public Gardens to the Slaughter House and on both sides of the humpbacked Grand Canal. And he haunted the little square of blessed memory where he had once carried her across the wet water, chain smoking used butts from a pocketful in his overcoat as he watched a steam-breathed sweeper sweeping at the mud with a twig broom; but she never appeared. A few of his former clients passed by, all ignoring him but the large aristocratic lady, who called him a son-of-a-dog-in-heat. You can't win them all.

Afterwards, wandering along the Mercerie in the early evening, through a shop window hung with wires dripping strings of glass beads and trinkets, he had the sudden sense he had glimpsed her, saw himself reflected in her large dark eyes. If he was truly conscious she was standing behind a counter, this slim-bodied, slant-eyed, long-nosed, handsome Venetian, staring at him as though contemplating the mark of fate in the face of a stranger. Then taking another swift look and this time recognizing who he was she lifted a frightened hand to her bosom and turned abruptly away. He ducked close to the glass under the beads, pawing the window as though to see her better, but she was no longer there; the shop was empty. Fidelman flung away a good butt and entered. The shop was crowded, its shelves laden with glass knickknacks, baubles, Madonnas, medallions, crap for tourists, which proved nothing although he wondered if she had disappeared for reasons of taste.

Where the woman had been, now stood a nearsighted man past sixty, in a gray suit, with puffy brows and pot belly, who gazed at the former ferryman in surprise, if not distaste—as though he knew he was there for no good cause—yet courteously inquired if he could assist him. Fidelman, secretly shivering, modestly priced a vase or two, politely listened to the verdict, nodded, bowed, casting a wild look through the open door into the rear room where a corpulent glass blower sat at a table working with a small torch, in the process of creating a green glass snake; but no one else. After desperately trying to think what else to do, pretending to be thoughtfully counting the change in his pocket though they both knew he had none, then asking if he could use the gabinetto and being refused, Fidelman thanked the shopkeeper and left. He had visions of her disappearing in a mist. The next day, and every day for two weeks thereafter he passed the shop seven or eight times daily. The shopkeeper once in exasperation thrust his arm at him in an obscene gesture but otherwise paid no attention. Fidelman never saw his dream girl in the shop. He had doubts he ever had: trompe l'oeil, mirage, déjà vue, or something of the sort.

He then gave her up, no easy trick if you had nothing. Like blowing kisses or kissing blows. Eh, Fidelman, you old cocker, there was a time you would have held on longer. Onto what? I had nothing, I gave up nothing. Nothing from nothing equals nothing. Say more and it's confronting death. On the other hand spring came early that year: to his surprise flowers looking out of house windows. Young jewel-like leaves of myrtles and laurels rose above ancient brick walls in back alleys. Subtle pinks, apricots, lavenders streaked an underwater architecture of floating Gothic and Moorish palazzi. Mosaics glittered, golden and black, on the faces of churches. Sandali sailed under bridges, heaped high with eggplants, green peppers, mounds of string beans. The canals widened, golden light on green water, pure Canaletto all the way to the Rialto. A sense of sea enlivened the air, lagoon and Adriatic under high blue sky above the outer islands. Fantasticando: Eastern galleons, huge battletubs approaching with cannons booming, star and crescent billowing on red sails, from Byzantium of mosaic saints and dancing dolphins. Boom, tara, War! History, the Most Serene Venetian Republic, Othello singing Verdi as Desdemona tussles in the hay with Iago under a weeping-willow tree. Fidelman, golden-robed Doge of Venice, though maybe better not since they garroted, stabbed, poisoned half the poor bastards. The Doge is dead, long live the dog that did him in! Boom, tara, yay! Fidelman III, Crusader on horse, hacking at Saladin and a thousand infidels! Fidelman in the Accademia! Ah Bellini, Giorgione, Tiziano, carissimi! The ex-painter wiped a wet eyelid, felt better and decided he hadn't given her up after all. She is still present, lives in the mind. He kept an eye cocked for the sight of her, and with surprise, though not astonishment spied her in the glass trinket shop, which he now passed only once in a longing while. There she wasn't but if you looked again, she was.

Churchbells.

Cannon scattering pigeons in San Marco.

Gondolas lit with Japanese lanterns.

Holy Mother, you have sent your Blessed Daughter. His heart, if he had a bit left, missed six beats and flapped like a mass of furled banners. He tapped on the window and out she came.

They talked quickly, intensely, searching one another with six eyes. She spoke her name: Margherita Fassoli, that made it real, an immediate commitment. She was herself real at last, no longer wildgoose shade he chased in a maze of dead-end canals, under low arches, and in alleyways. Breathless, she had only a moment; her uncle out for an espresso forbade her to be friendly with strangers. She had been ill for weeks—niente, a persistent virus—was better now, had hoped he would come by. He did not say how often he had, fruitlessly.

"Fidelman," he told her. "Where can we go, I have no money?"

She seemed momentarily stunned, hadn't given it a thought; then confessed she was a married woman—he knew—her husband a glass blower who worked in Murano, Beppo Fassoli. If nothing else he treated her kindly. "He gets annoyed about the kids sometimes but otherwise he's considerate. I'm sure you'll like him, he's wise about life."

"I can't invite you to my dump, Margherita," Fidelman said. "All it is is a lousy rathole with a bed that would collapse with two in it. And nothing else but a wine bottle to piss in. Should you open the window you have no idea of the stench of the canal."

She was desolated, squeezed her hands white but could not offer her place. They had four rooms and two boys, Riccardo and Rodolfo, eight and ten, little terrors. That made her around thirty or so, not a bad age for a woman. She was simple, spontaneous, direct—had already taken his hard hand and pressed it to her bosom. Her nose and eyes, pure Venetian. Her glossy hair, parted in the center, was rolled in braided circles over the ears. Her eyes were beyond him: the depth, light in dark, quiet enduring sadness—who knows where or from what. Whoever she was she knew who.

Margherita was urging him to go before her uncle returned.

"I will if you say when I can see you."

She gazed at him hungrily, eating with mouth, eyes. "Do you really want to, caro? There are so many better-looking women around."

"Passionately. But it's now or never, I'm frankly famished. Another day of dreaming and I'm a dead man. The ghost gives up."

"Oh my God, what do you mean?"

"I mean living on dreams. Sleeping with them. I can't any more though I've accomplished nothing."

"Mio caro," she all but wept.

"Couldn't we go some place you know? I haven't a lousy lira to rent a room. Do you happen to have a friend with an apartment we could borrow?"

She reflected hopelessly. Though her eyes lit she shrugged her shoulders.

"Maybe. I'll have to ask. But stop shivering as though you were in heat and take your hand out of your pocket. It doesn't look nice."

"I won't apologize for my passion. I'm hard up, it's now or never."

She finally agreed, asked him to meet her at the campanile after work. She would beg off around three.

"The boys come home from school at six and I've got to be there or they'll wreck the furniture. Beppo doesn't control them well enough. Usually he's not home before eight."

"All we need is a good hour."

"There's no need to rush, caro."

They kissed in the street. A passing tourist snapped a picture. The uncle hurried towards them, nearsightedly seeing nothing. Margherita disappeared into the shop as Fidelman walked quickly away.

This time is different, this one loves me.

They met at the bell tower, a dozen clucking pigeons at their feet. Margherita was tired around the eyes, a smudge of darkness, but worked up a listless smile; he blamed it on her recent illness. On the walk across the neck of the city she became animated again, showed him where Tintoretto had lived, in a Moorish section with turbaned figures and kneeling camels sculptured on stone plaques on house walls. Her matchstick street, take a few steps you were out of it, led into Fondamenta Nuove. In fact from her door he could see the island cemetery, thick with graves, across the water. They entered an old building, scabby masonry showing thin orange bricks, four stories high, terrazzi at the top floor loaded with potted plants—this house separated from the one it leaned towards across the narrow way by two or three buttresses at rooftop. She walked up the stairs, Fidelman at her direction trailing by two flights. He heard her open three locks with a bunch of keys. She left the door ajar for him.

"I'll undress, you come in after I'm in bed," she said.

"Wouldn't you want me to undress you?"

"I'm a modest person. I can't help it, don't press me."

But Fidelman, after quickly counting to a hundred and fifty, walked in on her anyway. She was standing in the semi-dark, the blinds down, but he found the light and snapped it on.

"You couldn't wait," she said bitterly.

"Painters love nudes, also ex-painters."

She was patient as he looked her over: heavier in the haunch and breasts than he had imagined; these were strong binding garments she wore. Her shapely legs were veined, splotched purple here and there. Slim at the waist but the stomach streaked with lesions of her pregnancies. She was forty if she was a day.

"Well, caro, are you disenchanted?"

"No more than usual," Fidelman confessed. "Still, you're not bad-looking although you play yourself down."

"At my age there's no pretending I'm in the first flush of youth."

She unbraided her hair. They sank into a deep bed with high head- and foot-board and at once embraced.

"Why you're not hard at all," she said in surprise. He removed his member from her hand. "I'll get there myself, it won't take but a few minutes. Just act affectionate."

Her breasts were formless and he felt a roll of flesh above her hips. Fidelman snapped on the lamp. The same woman. He snapped it off.

"Do you mind if I get on top?" she asked. "It's hard to breathe since I had my illness."

"Be my guest."

They were tender to each other and both soon came, Margherita with vigor, making sounds of pleasure, Fidelman a while after in thoughtful silence. He fell asleep for a few minutes, had a quick dream which he couldn't recall. When he woke the blinds were up, Margherita filing her nails in bed. An old woman in a padded chair at the window was reading a folded newspaper.

The ex-painter sat up. "For Christ's sake, who is she?"

"Beppo's mother. She likes to read at that window. Don't worry, she won't say a thing. She's a deaf-mute in both ears."

"My God, she can write, can't she?"

"Don't get excited, she's not a suspicious type. I called a friend as you asked me to, but she couldn't accommodate us. I don't care for her sort anyway, she gives herself airs, so it's just as well. That's why I brought you here. Are you disappointed, amore mio?"

Beppo Fassoli, when Fidelman arrived one night famished for supper—he now supported himself by hawking corn for pigeons on the Piazza San Marco—gave his guest a glass rose with six red petals. The radio was blaring Cavaradossi singing, "L'arte nel suo mistero/ Le diverse bellezze insiem confonde—" but Beppo snapped it off impatiently.

"The red in this rose is Venetian red. It is made from twenty-four-carat gold mixed in the formula."

"Real gold? You don't say." The ex-painter, touched by the gift, was embarrassed at being given since he had already taken. "What do you make besides roses?"

The glass blower shrugged. "Fish, flasks of all sorts, the sentimental animals of Disney. Our craft has fallen to the level of the taste of the tourists."

"Eh," Fidelman agreed.

Margherita sat at the head of the table, ladling out plates of steaming ravioli to Rodolfo and Riccardo, quiet only while eating: otherwise slapping, kicking, shoving, incessantly testing each other's strength of arm, leg, lung. Beppo's old mother sat at the other end of the table attending her son at her right hand, Fidelman opposite him feeling terribly exposed. The deaf woman was up and down to supply the glass blower with ravioli, cheese, bread, white wine; she counted spoonfuls of sugar into his espresso, stirred the cup and sipped a taste before he drank. Beppo ate slowly, paying little attention to his wife. He never once addressed her, except to throw her a look, with drawn thick brows—his eyes were green—when the boys were getting restless. She shut them up with a hiss and a glare. In that case, concluded Fidelman, nobody's cuckolding anybody. Beppo moodily picked his teeth with a fork tine. Their eyes met across two empty ravioli plates and both gazed away.

Though short of inches, the glass blower was a strong, muscular, handsome type, thick-shouldered, hairy. He appeared younger than his wife but Fidelman knew he wasn't. Maybe she looked older because he looked younger, an easy way to slap her in the face. If he was slapping; Fidelman wasn't sure. Did Beppo suspect him of usurping his rights as husband? Had the old deaf mother spelled it out on paper; she did not, after all, see with her ears, suspicious or not. He worried but Margherita assured him it was a waste of time.

"He doesn't know, just keep calm."

"He won't find out? I'd hate to hurt him—or vice versa. Mightn't he guess, do you think?"

"It's not his nature. His mind is usually occupied with other matters. There are men of that sort."

"What occupies his mind?"

"Everything but me. On the other hand it's full of facts and fantasy. He also likes to live life. His father was the same but died young."

Beppo seemed to like the ex-painter's company. He liked, he said, the artistic viewpoint. Once he rowed Fidelman to Murano to see the glass factory where he worked, VETRERIE ARTISTICHE. While they were there he blew Fidelman a small bird and set it in the cooling oven. The next night he presented it to him at supper to the applause of all at the table. He also invited the guest to go rowing in the lagoon Sunday with him and the boys. Beppo fished and caught nothing. The ex-painter, never having caught anything in his life, would not fish; he had vague thoughts of sketching but hadn't brought along pad or pencil. Fidelman enjoyed watching the floating city from the water. Venice, sober, dark, sank in winter; rose, a magic island giving off light, in summer. They rowed behind the Giudecca, the boys diving naked off the boat, their young asses flashing in sunlight before they splashed into blue water.

"Bravi, ragazzi," Beppo cheered. "Bello! Bellissimo! Non è bello, Fidelman?"

"Beautiful," murmured Fidelman, without innocence. He was spending more and more time with the glass blower, though it wasn't exactly easy to be sleeping with a man's wife and being friends with him. Still, somebody else might have made an effort to dislike him. Fidelman now visited Margherita one or two afternoons a week, depending on circumstances and desire—mostly hers; he was experiencing the first long liaison of his life. And he stayed often for supper because Beppo made it a standing invitation.

"I'm ashamed to leech on you."

"What's an extra plate of macaroni?"

He thought of Margherita's sex as an extra plate of something.

After supper they left the kids and dishes to the women. Beppo knew the cafés and liked the one the gondoliers frequented in Calle degli Assassini—away from the tourists, who had their own way of drowning the city. They drank grappa, played cards, sang and told each other the day's adventures. When they were bored they watched television. The ex-painter, a butt in his mouth, liked to sketch the gondoliers in all poses and positions. When Beppo complimented him on one or two of the drawings, Fidelman confided to him the failures of his life in art. The glass blower listened at length with moody tender interest. It made Fidelman increasingly unhappy to be sleeping with Margherita and confessing irrelevancies to her husband; but the more he thought about it the more convinced he became that Beppo knew the situation and tolerated it. Is it because we're friends and he likes me? he asked himself, but then figured the man had a girl of his own somewhere, possibly Murano.

One day the glass blower confessed he slept with his wife on rare occasions, including her birthdays.

"Doesn't that make it hard all around?" the ex-painter asked thickly.

"Some things are harder than others."

Relieved of guilt, Fidelman all but embraced him.

That night, in a burst of inspiration and trust, he asked

Beppo to come to his room on Sunday morning to look at his paintings—the few that remained. He had destroyed most but had kept a dozen perhaps justificatory pictures, and a few pieces of sculpture.

"I'll give you a private exhibition." He did not ask himself why; he was afraid of the answer.

"Do you like art, Beppo?"

"I love art," said the glass blower. "It comes to me naturally."

"What does?"

"Love for art. I never studied it at school. My taste formed itself naturally."

"This isn't classic stuff, if you know what I mean. It's modernist and you mightn't care for it."

Beppo answered that he had attended the last five Biennali. "My spirit is modern," he said haughtily.

"I was only kidding," Fidelman answered lamely, but the truth of it was he was no longer eager to show the glass blower his work and didn't know how to withdraw with grace, without insulting him more than he already might have.

Sunday morning, in a panic at his folly, he ran to Beppo's flat to tell him not to come, but Margherita, half-dressed, said he had already left. She invited Fidelman to stay for a half hour, the boys were in church; but the ex-painter was running with all his might and beat Beppo to his house. He seriously considered flight, hiding, not answering the bell; then Beppo knocked and entered, wincing at the disorder.

Fidelman apologized: he had changed his mind. "If you didn't like my paintings it'd make me feel bad, especially since you're a dear friend."

"I understand, Arturo, but maybe it's better to show me your work anyway. Who knows, I might be genuinely enthusiastic. Besides, if we're friends, we're friends for good or bad, better or worse."

Fidelman, touched, confused, not at all sure he knew what he was doing, or why, lifted a canvas and placed it on the kitchen table, against the wall, facing a small round window.

"This, you'll notice, has been influenced by Barney Newman, if you know who he is. The broad lavender band bisecting the black field at dead center is obviously the vital element organizing the picture. At the same time it achieves, partly through color, a quality of linear universality, in my case horizontal whereas Newman does it vertically. Lately I've been sort of thinking maybe I could paint something more original based on a series of crisscrossing abstract canals."

Beppo nodded gravely. Leaning forward in somewhat the pose of Rodin's Thinker with a bit of belly, he sat on a half barrel Fidelman had in his room for want of a chair, his broad feet placed apart, his pants hiked up his hairy shins and calves, an unlit long cigar in his mouth. He gazed at the picture as if he were seeing it forever, with a shade of puzzlement and annoyance Fidelman noted and feared: half-stunned if it weren't concentration—and occasionally Beppo sighed. It occurred to the ex-painter that he looked in his handsome way much like his mother. Who is this man? he thought, and why am I breaking my heart for him: I mean do I have to show him my private work? Why the revelation? He had then and there an urge to paint Beppo to his core, so much like a seizure he thought of it as sexual, and to his surprise found himself desiring Margherita so strongly he had to restrain himself from rushing out to jump into bed with her.

My life will end in calamity, Fidelman thought. Everything is out of joint again and I'm not helping by showing these pictures. You can pull up nails and let the past loose once too often.

Reluctantly, as if he were lifting pure lead, he placed a framed painting on the table.

"This is a spray job, an undercoating of apple-green acrylic resin, then a haphazard haze of indigo, creating a mood and a half before I applied a reconciling rose in varying values and intensities. Note how the base colors, invading without being totally visible, infect the rose so that it's both present and you might say evanescing. It's hard to explain a picture of this sort because it's something more than merely a poem of color. We're dealing with certain kinds of essences. In a way this and the other picture I just showed you are related, the other stating the masculine principle, this obviously feminine. Frankly, the inspiration is Rothko but I learned a trick or two from some of the things I've seen in *Art News* done by my contemporaries."

His voice at this point cracked, but Beppo's expression was unchanged and he still said nothing.

A scow passing by in the canal below agitated gem-like reflections of sunlit water on the ceiling. Fidelman waited till the rumble of the boat had disappeared into the distance.

"This," he said wearily, "is an old sculpture I did years ago, 'Fragment of a Head'—marble."

Beppo, as though smiling, nodded.

A broken head he responds to. Jesus God, whatever led me to do this? It'll all end in disaster.

In quick succession he showed a surrealistic landscape based on a frottage of tree bark, an old still life with rotting flowers, an old madonna with old child, and an old sentimental self-portrait.

"These show me at various phases of development," Fidelman said, barely able to speak. "You needn't comment on each if you don't want to, though I would be interested in your overall impression."

Beppo sat silent, lighting his cigar.

"Here's a piece of pop sculpture, 'Soft Toilet Seat,' made out of vinylite. It was exhibited for two weeks in New York City. Originally I had a triptych of seats nailed on beaverboard more or less saying, 'Fuck all art, one must be free of the artistic alibi,' though I don't wholly subscribe to that. I can take just so much dada, so I cut it down to the single seat you see before you."

"Can you shit through it?" the glass blower ultimately asked.

"Art isn't life," Fidelman said. Then he said, "Don't be a wise guy, Beppo."

"Not that these things can't be done but you haven't done them. Your work lacks authority and originality. It lacks more than that, but I won't say what now. If you want my advice there's one thing I'd do with this stuff."

"Such as what?" said the ex-painter, fearing the worst.

"Burn them all."

"I thought you'd say that, you cruel fairy bastard."

Leaping up with Fidelman's kitchen knife in his hand, Beppo slashed the toilet seat and two paintings.

Fidelman interposed his body between the knife and the other canvases. "Have mercy!"

"Let me finish these off," the glass blower said hoarsely. "It's for your own sake. Show who's master of your fate—bad art or you."

Fidelman savagely struggled with him for the knife but at a crucial moment, as though a spinning color wheel had turned dead white, something failed in him and he relaxed his grip. Beppo quickly slashed up the other canvases. Afterwards they went downstairs and in a corner of the junk-filled vegetable patch next to the smelly back canal, burned everything, including the fragmented marble head, which Beppo had smashed against a rock.

"Don't waste your life doing what you can't do."

"Why shouldn't I keep trying?"

"After twenty years if the rooster hasn't crowed she should know she's a hen. Your painting will never pay back the part of your life you've given up for it."

"What about Van Gogh? He never sold a single painting in his lifetime."

"You're not Van Gogh. Besides he was crazy."

Fidelman left the garden in a stupor; he wandered a day, his eyes glazed in grief. On Tuesday, somewhat calmer through exhaustion, though the weight of his emptiness dragged like a dead dog chained around his neck, he presented himself to Margherita, who, with tears in her eyes, embraced him, knowing what had happened.

"Come, tesoro," she said, leading him to the marriage bed. "For our mutual relief, me from my life and you from art."

As they were in the midst of violent intercourse, Fidelman on top, Margherita more loving than ever, the bedroom door opened and he glimpsed a nude hairy body wearing a horn or carrying a weapon; before he could rise he felt Beppo land on him. Fidelman cried out, expecting death between the shoulders. Margherita, shoving herself up with a grunt, slipped out from under them and fled out of the room. Fidelman rolled to the right and left to be rid of his incubus, but Beppo had him tightly pinned, his nose to the bedboard, his ass in the air.

"Don't hurt me, Beppo, please, I have piles."

"It'll be a cool job, I'm wearing mentholated vaseline. You'll be surprised at the pleasure."

"Is your mother watching?"

"At her age she has no curiosity."

"I suppose I deserve this."

"Think of love," the glass blower murmured. "You've run from it all your life."

He stopped running.

Venice slowed down though it went on floating, its canals floating on Venice.

"Leonardo, Michelangelo," Fidelman murmured.

"If you can't invent art, invent life," Beppo advised him.

For good or ill Fidelman loved him; he could not help himself; he ought to have known. Beppo was handsome, hardworking, and loved to breathe; he smelled (and tasted) of oil and vinegar; he was, after all, a tender man and gentle lover. Fidelman had never in his life said "I love you" without reservation to anyone. He said it to Beppo. If that's the way it works, that's the way it works. Better love than no love. If you sneeze at life it backs off and instead of fruit you're holding a bone. If I'm a late bloomer at least I've bloomed in love.

"It's a good way to be," explained Beppo, "we're not like everybody else. I like it better with men because the company is more interesting and it's easier to be friends with somebody who speaks your language."

They were together as often as possible, everywhere except in Beppo's house. Fidelman had stopped going there.

"Naturally," said Beppo. "It wouldn't be discreet."

"What does Margherita say?"

"She's said it before, I don't listen."

"Will you stay married to her?"

"Of course. I've got two boys and an old mother to think of."

"I guess so," said Fidelman.

Yet he was for once in his life on the whole serene; discontented only during the day when they were on separate islands, Beppo in Murano, and Fidelman selling pigeon feed on the Piazza San Marco. He spent most of his time thinking of Beppo and the glass blower said he thought of him. They talked it over and one summer morning Fidelman gave up his bird-food business and went with Beppo to Murano. At 6 A.M. they met at the Fondamenta Nuove. They stepped into Beppo's rowboat, and each taking an oar, rowed past San

Michele towards Murano. The water was calm and it took no more than twenty minutes to reach the island. Beppo spoke quietly to the assistant manager of the glassworks and got him to put on his friend as an apprentice and part-time man of all work. He was the oldest of the apprentices, some of them kids, but he didn't mind because Beppo, who was teaching him the rites of love, also taught him to blow glass.

Working with the hot molten glass excited Fidelman sexually. He felt creative, his heart in his pants. "With pipe, tongs, shears, you can make a form or change it into its opposite," Beppo said. "For instance, with a snip or two of the scissors, if it suits you, you can change the male organ into the female." The glass blower laughed heartily. Fidelman doubted he would be so minded; the thought evoked pain. Still it helped you understand the possibilities of life. And amid the possibilities was working with glass as an art form, though for certain reasons he did not say so to Beppo, who all day long, his face wet, armpits sweated, at intervals swigging from a beer or water bottle, blew varieties of fish and Disney creatures served up to him by an assistant from a wood or steel mold, for further shaping and decoration. For a change of pace he blew wine goblets, slim-waisted vases, flasks of odd shapes and sizes.

Fidelman, among other things, loved dipping the tapered blowpipe into the flaming opening of the noisy furnace—like poking into the living substance of the sun for a puddle of flowing fire—Prometheus Fidelman—a viscous gob of sunflesh hanging from the pipe like a human organ: breast, kidney, stomach or phallus, cooling as it gaseously flamed, out of which if one were skilled enough, lucky, knew the right people, he would create glass objects of expected yet unexpected forms. He blew gently into the red-hot glowing mass a single soft bubble of breath—it made no difference if the blower had eaten garlic or flowers—a small inside hole without spittle or seeds, a teardrop, gut, uterus, which itself became its object of birth: a sculptured womb; shaped, elongated by pendulum swing of pipe, the living metal teased and shorn into shape by tongs and scissors. Give the bubble a mouth and it became beaker, ewer, vase, amphora or burial urn, anything the mouth foretold, or heart desired, or blower could blow. If you knew how, you could blow anything.

Not yet of course Fidelman although he was learning. As apprentice he blew as Beppo shaped; or delivered the master fresh fish, Birds of Paradise, woodland creatures that he or another assistant blew into pristine form in molds; he also applied stems to vessels blown by Beppo, the stem shaped by a flick or two of his tool. To permit him to open and work at the mouth of any kind of container, Fidelman aimed a red-hot cone of glass at the bubble's bottom, Beppo gripping the gob with his tongs and leading it to the point of attachment. With his shears he creased the neck of the bubble and with a tap detached it from the blowpipe; he left Fidelman holding the open-mouthed possibility: the open mouth. Every move they made was in essence sexual, a marvelous interaction because, among other things, it saved time and trouble: you worked and loved at once. When a glass object was completed, Fidelman hastily trotted to the cooling kiln in the rear with the thing on a wooden board, to stash away before it cracked. And he handed one tool or another to Beppo, who hardly looked at him during working hours, the assistant assisting for love's sake however he could. There were no spoken orders once you knew the process. He watched the glass blower and foresaw his needs, in essence a new experience for him. Otherwise he stood by, greedily watching the masters at other benches to absorb what they knew.

Impatient, agitated at times by all there was to learn, the variety of skills to master, Fidelman persuaded Beppo to stay on and teach him for an hour or two after the crowd of glass workers had gone home, the workshop talk and shouting silenced, five of the six furnace openings banked down, one blazing in a perpetual violet and lemon roar. He practiced then what he couldn't during the day, and though Beppo, eating an apple or smoking a butt, did not always encourage it, blew forms he had never blown before, or seen blown, evolving monstrosities of glass, so huge and complicated it took fifteen minutes to break their grip on the iron when he wanted to discard them. Many of Fidelman's creations cracked in mid-air, or against something on the workbench in a careless move. Those he completed intact stood (or fell) unbalanced, lopsided, malformed. But he worked for the first time in his life, instructed. Up to now he had taught himself and not got over it.

In the fall Margherita objected to the nightwork—it was

killing her husband. Beppo's complexion had turned pale, his eyes were bloodshot, the skin around them, dark and puffy. She was already half a widow, what more did they want? Abandoning the night sessions they came to work earlier, at half past four, leaving the Fondamenta bundled in overcoats against the stabbing wet cold, the fog cradled on the choppy water plopping against the boats at the dock, a star visible if they were lucky. They navigated by instinct—Beppo's—and made Murano usually on time, though once in a while they rowed in circles around the cemetery, lost in and breathing fog. "In the end we pay for everything," Beppo muttered. Suffering from loss of sleep he sometimes conked out at his work during the day, Fidelman having to wake him furtively; so in the end they decided that the apprentice himself would stay on alone nights, doing what he felt he had to do. Each assured the other it was for his benefit. "Though in a way it's mad," said the master to Fidelman; "the more you give up the more you undertake."

However it was arranged and settled with the assistant manager, who had been assured it was all for the good of the company. Because Beppo left in the rowboat, and the vaporetto, before it expired at midnight, was fantastically slow making its stations, Fidelman considered renting a second-hand rowboat for himself; but then the thought occurred that taking a small room in a house on Murano, maybe with a little garden, would make more sense—be cheaper in the long run, and he could spend more time in the factory. Beppo could stay over when he felt like it, and they would as usual be together on Sundays.

Fidelman located a tiny room on Campo S. Bernardo, from which he could see the airport on the mainland and Burano and Torcello. But Beppo, when he heard, was infuriated. "You have no consideration for others, it's plain to see."

After he had calmed down, he said, "Why are you so fanatic about this accursed glass? After all, it's only glass."

"Life is short if you don't hurry."

"A fanatic never knows when to stop. It's obvious you want to repeat your fate."

"What fate do you have in mind?"

"Yours."

The apprentice sighed but hurried. For months he tried everything he saw others doing: cut glass in diamond patterns, carved glass as gems, practiced diamond point and acid engraving, flash painting with stains, gold and silver leaf applied in reverse: gods and goddesses in classic poses pretending left is right. In the spring he hungered to be involved with modern forms. Fidelman envisioned glass sculptures, a difficult enterprise, deciding first to experiment with compositions of mixed colors ladled into and cast in molds. He invented objets trouvés—what better way to find what wasn't lost?—and worked with peacock's tails and Argus eyes in targets, casting concentric circles: amber/ lavender/ black/ green. He fabricated abstract stained-glass windows, created Op Art designs of mosaics, collages of broken glass, and spent hours dripping glass on hot glass in the manner of Pollock.

Beppo from time to time watched, picking his teeth with an old toothpick.

"You're doing the same things you did in your paintings, that's the lousy hair in the egg. It's easy to see, half a talent is worse than none."

His criticism upset Fidelman so badly that he did not appear in the factory for a week. Is he wrong or am I? He went back one night to see what he had done, and when he saw, chopped it up with a hammer. He decided again, as he had more than once in the past, that he had no true distinction as an artist and this time would try not to forget it.

Fidelman cut out night work and spent the time with Beppo in the city. The glass blower asked no questions and made no comments. He was once again very tender and after a while Fidelman's heart stopped being a brick and began breathing. They drank with the gondoliers on the Calle degli Assassini and stayed away from painters and sculptors.

One day when they met by accident on the Rialto, Margherita, her large eyes vague, hair plaited in circles over her ears, her arms around a grocery bundle, stopped Fidelman and begged him to leave Venice.

"Listen, Fidelman, we've been friends, let's stay friends. All I ask is that you leave Beppo and go some place else. After all, in the eyes of God he's my husband. Now, because of you he's rarely around and my family is a mess. The boys are always in trouble, his mother complains all day, and I'm at the end of my strength. Beppo may be a homo but he's a good provider and not a bad father when there are no men friends around to divert him from domestic life. The boys listen to his voice when they hear it. We have our little pleasures. He knows life and keeps me informed. Sometimes we visit friends, sometimes we go to a movie together and stop at a bar on our way home. In other words, things are better when he's around even though the sex is short. Occasionally he will throw me a lay if I suck him up good beforehand. It isn't a perfect life but I've learned to be satisfied, and was, more or less, before you came around. Since then, though there was some pleasure with you—I don't deny it—it ended quickly, and to tell the truth I'm worse off than I was before, so that's why I ask you to go."

In despair Fidelman rowed back to the factory and blew a huge glass bubble, larger and thicker than any he had blown before. He got it off the blowpipe with the help of an apprentice he had persuaded to stay over, and worked on its mouth in fear and doubtful confidence with tongs and a wet opening tool of smoking wood. Heating and reheating for several nights, he dipped, swung, lengthened, shaped, until the glass on his blowpipe turned out to be a capacious heavy red bowl, iron become ice. When he had cooled it without cracking he considered etching on it some scenes of Venice but decided no. The bowl was severe and graceful and sat solid, upright. It held the clear light and even seemed to listen. Fidelman polished it carefully, and when it was done, filled it with cold water and with a sigh dipped in his hands. He showed the bowl to Beppo, who said it was a good job, beautifully proportioned and reminding him of something the old Greeks had done. I kept my finger in art, Fidelman wept when he was alone. The next day, though they searched high and low with a crowd of apprentices, the bowl was missing and could not be found. Beppo suspected the assistant manager.

Before leaving Venice, Fidelman blew a slightly humpbacked green horse for Beppo, the color of his eyes. "Up yours," said the glass blower, grieving at the gray in Fidelman's hair. He sold the horse for a decent sum and gave Fidelman the lire. They kissed and parted.

Fidelman sailed from Venice on a Portuguese freighter.

In America he worked as a craftsman in glass and loved men and women.

TEN STORIES

Idiots First

THE THICK ticking of the tin clock stopped. Mendel, dozing in the dark, awoke in fright. The pain returned as he listened. He drew on his cold embittered clothing, and wasted minutes sitting at the edge of the bed.

"Isaac," he ultimately sighed.

In the kitchen, Isaac, his astonished mouth open, held six peanuts in his palm. He placed each on the table. "One . . . two . . . nine."

He gathered each peanut and appeared in the doorway. Mendel, in loose hat and long overcoat, still sat on the bed. Isaac watched with small eyes and ears, thick hair graying the sides of his head.

"Schlaf," he nasally said.

"No," muttered Mendel. As if stifling he rose. "Come, Isaac."

He wound his old watch though the sight of the stopped mechanism nauseated him.

Isaac wanted to hold it to his ear.

"No, it's late." Mendel put the watch carefully away. In the drawer he found the little paper bag of crumpled ones and fives and slipped it into his overcoat pocket. He helped Isaac on with his coat.

Isaac looked at one dark window, then at the other. Mendel stared at both blank windows.

They went slowly down the darkly lit stairs, Mendel first, Isaac watching the moving shadows on the wall. To one long shadow he offered a peanut.

"Hungrig."

In the vestibule the old man gazed through the thin glass. The November night was cold and bleak. Opening the door, he cautiously thrust his head out. Though he saw nothing he quickly shut the door.

"Ginzburg, that he came to see me yesterday," he whispered in Isaac's ear.

Isaac sucked air.

"You know who I mean?"

Isaac combed his chin with his fingers.

"That's the one, with the black whiskers. Don't talk to him or go with him if he asks you."

Isaac moaned.

"Young people he don't bother so much," Mendel said in afterthought.

It was suppertime and the street was empty, but the store windows dimly lit their way to the corner. They crossed the deserted street and went on. Isaac, with a happy cry, pointed to the three golden balls. Mendel smiled but was exhausted when they got to the pawnshop.

The pawnbroker, a red-bearded man with black horn-rimmed glasses, was eating a whitefish at the rear of the store. He craned his head, saw them, and settled back to sip his tea.

In five minutes he came forward, patting his shapeless lips with a large white handkerchief.

Mendel, breathing heavily, handed him the worn gold watch. The pawnbroker, raising his glasses, screwed in his eyepiece. He turned the watch over once. "Eight dollars."

The dying man wet his cracked lips. "I must have thirty-five."

"So go to Rothschild."

"Cost me myself sixty."

"In 1905." The pawnbroker handed back the watch. It had stopped ticking. Mendel wound it slowly. It ticked hollowly.

"Isaac must go to my uncle that he lives in California."

"It's a free country," said the pawnbroker.

Isaac, watching a banjo, snickered.

"What's the matter with him?" the pawnbroker asked.

"So let be eight dollars," muttered Mendel, "but where will I get the rest till tonight?"

"How much for my hat and coat?" he asked.

"No sale." The pawnbroker went behind the cage and wrote out a ticket. He locked the watch in a small drawer but Mendel still heard it ticking.

In the street he slipped the eight dollars into the paper bag, then searched in his pockets for a scrap of writing. Finding it, he strained to read the address by the light of the street lamp.

As they trudged to the subway, Mendel pointed to the sprinkled sky.

"Isaac, look how many stars are tonight."

"Eggs," said Isaac.

"First we will go to Mr. Fishbein, after we will eat."

They got off the train in upper Manhattan and had to walk several blocks before they located Fishbein's house.

"A regular palace," Mendel murmured, looking forward to a moment's warmth.

Isaac stared uneasily at the heavy door of the house.

Mendel rang. The servant, a man with long sideburns, came to the door and said Mr. and Mrs. Fishbein were dining and could see no one.

"He should eat in peace but we will wait till he finishes."

"Come back tomorrow morning. Tomorrow morning Mr. Fishbein will talk to you. He don't do business or charity at this time of the night."

"Charity I am not interested—"

"Come back tomorrow."

"Tell him it's life or death—"

"Whose life or death?"

"So if not his, then mine."

"Don't be such a big smart aleck."

"Look me in my face," said Mendel, "and tell me if I got time till tomorrow morning?"

The servant stared at him, then at Isaac, and reluctantly let them in.

The foyer was a vast high-ceilinged room with many oil paintings on the walls, voluminous silken draperies, a thick flowered rug on the floor, and a marble staircase.

Mr. Fishbein, a paunchy bald-headed man with hairy nostrils and small patent-leather feet, ran lightly down the stairs, a large napkin tucked under a tuxedo coat button. He stopped on the fifth step from the bottom and examined his visitors.

"Who comes on Friday night to a man that he has guests to spoil him his supper?"

"Excuse me that I bother you, Mr. Fishbein," Mendel said. "If I didn't come now I couldn't come tomorrow."

"Without more preliminaries, please state your business. I'm a hungry man."

"Hungrig," wailed Isaac.

Fishbein adjusted his pince-nez. "What's the matter with him?"

"This is my son Isaac. He is like this all his life."

Isaac mewled.

"I am sending him to California."

"Mr. Fishbein don't contribute to personal pleasure trips."

"I am a sick man and he must go tonight on the train to my Uncle Leo."

"I never give to unorganized charity," Fishbein said, "but if you are hungry I will invite you downstairs in my kitchen. We having tonight chicken with stuffed derma."

"All I ask is thirty-five dollars for the train to my uncle in California. I have already the rest."

"Who is your uncle? How old a man?"

"Eighty-one years, a long life to him."

Fishbein burst into laughter. "Eighty-one years and you are sending him this halfwit."

Mendel, flailing both arms, cried, "Please, without names."

Fishbein politely conceded.

"Where is open the door there we go in the house," the sick man said. "If you will kindly give me thirty-five dollars, God will bless you. What is thirty-five dollars to Mr. Fishbein? Nothing. To me, for my boy, is everything."

Fishbein drew himself up to his tallest height.

"Private contributions I don't make—only to institutions. This is my fixed policy."

Mendel sank to his creaking knees on the rug.

"Please, Mr. Fishbein, if not thirty-five, give maybe twenty."

"Levinson!" Fishbein angrily called.

The servant with the long sideburns appeared at the top of the stairs.

"Show this party where is the door—unless he wishes to partake food before leaving the premises."

"For what I got chicken won't cure it," Mendel said.

"This way if you please," said Levinson, descending.

Isaac assisted his father up.

"Take him to an institution," Fishbein advised over the marble balustrade. He ran quickly up the stairs and they were at once outside, buffeted by winds.

The walk to the subway was tedious. The wind blew mournfully. Mendel, breathless, glanced furtively at shadows. Isaac, clutching his peanuts in his frozen fist, clung to his father's side. They entered a small park to rest for a minute on a stone bench under a leafless two-branched tree. The thick right branch was raised, the thin left one hung down. A very pale moon rose slowly. So did a stranger as they approached the bench.

"Gut yuntif," he said hoarsely.

Mendel, drained of blood, waved his wasted arms. Isaac yowled sickly. Then a bell chimed and it was only ten. Mendel let out a piercing anguished cry as the bearded stranger disappeared into the bushes. A policeman came running and, though he beat the bushes with his nightstick, could turn up nothing. Mendel and Isaac hurried out of the little park. When Mendel glanced back the dead tree had its thin arm raised, the thick one down. He moaned.

They boarded a trolley, stopping at the home of a former friend, but he had died years ago. On the same block they went into a cafeteria and ordered two fried eggs for Isaac. The tables were crowded except where a heavyset man sat eating soup with kasha. After one look at him they left in haste, although Isaac wept.

Mendel had another address on a slip of paper but the house was too far away, in Queens, so they stood in a doorway shivering.

What can I do, he frantically thought, in one short hour?

He remembered the furniture in the house. It was junk but might bring a few dollars. "Come, Isaac." They went once more to the pawnbroker's to talk to him, but the shop was dark and an iron gate—rings and gold watches glinting through it—was drawn tight across his place of business.

They huddled behind a telephone pole, both freezing. Isaac whimpered.

"See the big moon, Isaac. The whole sky is white."

He pointed but Isaac wouldn't look.

Mendel dreamed for a minute of the sky lit up, long sheets of light in all directions. Under the sky, in California, sat Uncle Leo drinking tea with lemon. Mendel felt warm but woke up cold.

Across the street stood an ancient brick synagogue.

He pounded on the huge door but no one appeared. He waited till he had breath and desperately knocked again. At last there were footsteps within, and the synagogue door creaked open on its massive brass hinges.

A darkly dressed sexton, holding a dripping candle, glared at them.

"Who knocks this time of night with so much noise on the synagogue door?"

Mendel told the sexton his troubles. "Please, I would like to speak to the rabbi."

"The rabbi is an old man. He sleeps now. His wife won't let you see him. Go home and come back tomorrow."

"To tomorrow I said goodbye already. I am a dying man."

Though the sexton seemed doubtful he pointed to an old wooden house next door. "In there he lives." He disappeared into the synagogue with his lit candle casting shadows around him.

Mendel, with Isaac clutching his sleeve, went up the wooden steps and rang the bell. After five minutes a big-faced, gray-haired, bulky woman came out on the porch with a torn robe thrown over her nightdress. She emphatically said the rabbi was sleeping and could not be waked.

But as she was insisting, the rabbi himself tottered to the door. He listened a minute and said, "Who wants to see me let them come in."

They entered a cluttered room. The rabbi was an old skinny man with bent shoulders and a wisp of white beard. He wore a flannel nightgown and black skullcap; his feet were bare.

"Vey is mir," his wife muttered. "Put on shoes or tomorrow comes sure pneumonia." She was a woman with a big belly, years younger than her husband. Staring at Isaac, she turned away.

Mendel apologetically related his errand. "All I need is thirty-five dollars."

"Thirty-five?" said the rabbi's wife. "Why not thirty-five thousand? Who has so much money? My husband is a poor rabbi. The doctors take away every penny."

"Dear friend," said the rabbi, "if I had I would give you."

"I got already seventy," Mendel said, heavy-hearted. "All I need more is thirty-five."

"God will give you," said the rabbi.

"In the grave," said Mendel. "I need tonight. Come, Isaac."

"Wait," called the rabbi.

He hurried inside, came out with a fur-lined caftan, and handed it to Mendel.

"Yascha," shrieked his wife, "not your new coat!"

"I got my old one. Who needs two coats for one old body?"

"Yascha, I am screaming—"

"Who can go among poor people, tell me, in a new coat?"

"Yascha," she cried, "what can this man do with your coat? He needs tonight the money. The pawnbrokers are asleep."

"So let him wake them up."

"No." She grabbed the coat from Mendel.

He held onto a sleeve, wrestling her for the coat. Her I know, Mendel thought. "Shylock," he muttered. Her eyes glittered.

The rabbi groaned and tottered dizzily. His wife cried out as Mendel yanked the coat from her hands.

"Run," cried the rabbi.

"Run, Isaac."

They ran out of the house and down the steps.

"Stop, you thief," called the rabbi's wife.

The rabbi pressed both hands to his temples and fell to the floor. "Help!" his wife wept. "Heart attack! Help!"

But Mendel and Isaac ran through the streets with the rabbi's new fur-lined caftan. After them noiselessly ran Ginzburg.

It was very late when Mendel bought the train ticket in the only booth open.

There was no time to stop for a sandwich so Isaac ate his peanuts and they hurried to the train in the vast deserted station.

"So in the morning," Mendel gasped as they ran, "there comes a man that he sells sandwiches and coffee. Eat but get change. When reaches California the train, will be waiting for you on the station Uncle Leo. If you don't recognize him he will recognize you. Tell him I send best regards."

But when they arrived at the gate to the platform it was shut, the light out.

"Too late," said the uniformed ticket collector, a bulky, bearded man with hairy nostrils and a fishy smell.

He pointed to the station clock. "Already past twelve."

"But I see standing there still the train," Mendel said, hopping in his grief.

"It just left—in one more minute."

"A minute is enough. Just open the gate."

"Too late I told you."

Mendel socked his bony chest with both hands. "With my whole heart I beg you this little favor."

"Favors you had enough already. For you the train is gone. You shoulda been dead already at midnight. I told you that yesterday. This is the best I can do."

"Ginzburg!" Mendel shrank from him.

"Who else?" The voice was metallic, eyes glittered, the expression amused.

"For myself," the old man begged, "I don't ask a thing. But what will happen to my boy?"

Ginzburg shrugged slightly. "What will happen happens. This isn't my responsibility. I got enough to think about without worrying about somebody on one cylinder."

"What then is your responsibility?"

"To create conditions. To make happen what happens. I ain't in the anthropomorphic business."

"Whichever business you in, where is your pity?"

"This ain't my commodity. The law is the law."

"Which law is this?"

"The cosmic, universal law, goddamn it, the one I got to follow myself."

"What kind of a law is it?" cried Mendel. "For God's sake, don't you understand what I went through in my life with this poor boy? Look at him. For thirty-nine years, since the day he was born, I wait for him to grow up, but he don't. Do you understand what this means in a father's heart? Why don't you let him go to his uncle?" His voice had risen and he was shouting.

Isaac mewled loudly.

"Better calm down or you'll hurt somebody's feelings," Ginzburg said, with a wink toward Isaac.

"All my life," Mendel cried, his body trembling, "what did I have? I was poor. I suffered from my health. When I worked I worked too hard. When I didn't work was worse. My wife died a young woman. But I didn't ask from anybody nothing. Now I ask a small favor. Be so kind, Mr. Ginzburg."

The ticket collector was picking his teeth with a matchstick.

"You ain't the only one, my friend, some got it worse than you. That's how it goes."

"You dog you." Mendel lunged at Ginzburg's throat and began to choke. "You bastard, don't you understand what it means human?"

They struggled nose to nose. Ginzburg, though his astonished eyes bulged, began to laugh. "You pipsqueak nothing. I'll freeze you to pieces."

His eyes lit in rage, and Mendel felt an unbearable cold like an icy dagger invading his body, all of his parts shriveling.

Now I die without helping Isaac.

A crowd gathered. Isaac yelped in fright.

Clinging to Ginzburg in his last agony, Mendel saw reflected in the ticket collector's eyes the depth of his terror. Ginzburg, staring at himself in Mendel's eyes, saw mirrored in them the extent of his own awful wrath. He beheld a shimmering, starry, blinding light that produced darkness.

Ginzburg looked astounded. "Who, me?"

His grip on the squirming old man loosened, and Mendel, his heart barely beating, slumped to the ground.

"Go," Ginzburg muttered, "take him to the train."

"Let pass," he commanded a guard.

The crowd parted. Isaac helped his father up and they tottered down the steps to the platform where the train waited, lit and ready to go.

Mendel found Isaac a coach seat and hastily embraced him. "Help Uncle Leo, Isaakl. Also remember your father and mother."

"Be nice to him," he said to the conductor. "Show him where everything is."

He waited on the platform until the train began slowly to move. Isaac sat at the edge of his seat, his face strained in the direction of his journey. When the train was gone, Mendel ascended the stairs to see what had become of Ginzburg.

Suppose a Wedding

(A SCENE OF A PLAY)

MAURICE FEUER *is a retired sick Jewish actor trying to influence his daughter* ADELE *in her choice of a husband. She is engaged to* LEON SINGER, *a young sporting goods store owner from Newark.* FEUER *approves of* BEN GLICKMAN, *a poor beginning writer in the building—a tenement house off Second Avenue in Manhattan—who seems to share his values in life. At any rate* FEUER *likes him.* FLORENCE FEUER, *the actor's wife, once an actress now a beautician, who has also been around and garnered her kind of wisdom, is all for* LEON. *On a hot mid-August day* LEON *has driven in from New Jersey to surprise* ADELE, *when she arrives home from work, and take her to dinner. As the curtain rises,* LEON, *while waiting for her, is playing cards with the actor. Because of the heat the apartment door is open and people occasionally pass by in the hall.*

Leon. [quietly] Rummy. This one is mine. [He puts down his cards and begins to add up the score.]

Feuer. [Rising and pushing back his chair, the ACTOR removes his glasses, and without warning, declaims emotionally in Yiddish] My God, you're killing your poor father, this is what you're doing. For your whole life I worked bitter hard to take care of you the way a father should. To feed and clothe you. To give you the best kind of education. To teach you what's right. And so how do you pay me back? You pay me back by becoming a tramp. By living with a married man, a cheap, dirty person who has absolutely no respect for you. A bum who used you like dirt. Worse than dirt. And now when he doesn't want you any more and kicks you out of his bed, you come to me crying, begging I should take you back. My daughter, for what I went through with you, there's no more forgiveness. My heart is milked of tears. It's like a piece of rock. I don't want to see you again in my whole life. Go, but remember, you killed your father. [He hangs his head.]

Leon. [perplexed] What's that about?

Feuer. [assuming his identity as he puts on his glasses] Don't you understand Yiddish?

Leon. Only some of the words.

Feuer. Tst-tst. [sitting] It's from a play I once played in the Second Avenue Theater, "Sein Tochter's Geliebter." I was brilliant in this part—magnificent. All the critics raved about me even though the play was schmaltz. Even the *New York Times* sent somebody and he wrote in his review that Maurice Feuer is not only a wonderful actor, he is also a magician. What I could do with such a lousy play was unbelievable. I made it come to life. I made it believable.

[LEON begins to deal out a new hand as FEUER goes on]

Feuer. I also played in "Greener Felder," "Ghosts," "The Dybbuk," "The Cherry Orchard," "Naches fon Kinder," "Gott fon Nachoma," and "Yoshe Kalb." Schwartz played Reb Melech and I played Yoshe. I was brilliant—marvelous. The play ran three years in New York, and after we played in London, Paris, Prague and Warsaw. We also brought it for a season in South America and played it in Rio, then for sixteen weeks in Buenos Aires . . .

[Struck by a memory FEUER falls silent.]

Leon. It's your move.

[The ACTOR absently takes a card and without looking gets rid of another. LEON picks up a card, examines it carefully, then drops it among the discards.]

Leon. Your move.

[FEUER, coming back to life, looks at a card and places it on the discard pile.]

Feuer. This piece I recited to you is a father talking to his daughter. She took the wrong man and it ruined her life.

[LEON, examining his cards, has nothing to say.]

Feuer. [needling a little] You couldn't understand it?

Leon. Only partly. Still in all, when I had to I was able to give directions in Yiddish to an old baba with a wig who I met in downtown Newark, on how to get to Brooklyn, New York.

[As they talk they continue the rummy game.]

Feuer. Adele knows Yiddish perfect. She learned when she was a little girl. She used to write me letters in Yiddish—they were brilliant. She also had a wonderful handwriting.

Leon. Maybe she'll teach our kids.

[He is unaware of FEUER regarding him ironically.]

Feuer. [trying a new tack] Do you know something about Jewish history?

Leon. [amiably] Not very much. [afterthought] If you're worried about religion, don't worry. I was Bar Mitzvahed.

Feuer. I'm not worried about anything. Tell me, do you know any of the big Yiddish writers—Peretz, Sholem Aleichem, Asch?

Leon. I've heard about them.

Feuer. Do you read serious books?

Leon. Sure, I belong to the Book Find Club.

Feuer. Why don't you pick your own books? Why did you go to college for?

Leon. I mostly do. It's no harm to belong to a good book club, it saves you time. [looking at his wrist watch] What time is Adele due? It's getting late.

Feuer. Why didn't you telephone her so she would know you were coming? It's not expensive to telephone.

Leon. I thought I'd give her a surprise. My brother Mortie came into Newark this morning, and he did me the favor to take over the shop so I could get away early. We keep open Wednesday nights.

Feuer. [consulting an old pocket watch] She's late.

Leon. Rummy. I win again. [He shows his cards.]

Feuer. [hiding his annoyance] But my best roles were in Shakespeare—"Shylock, der Yid," "Hamlet, der Yeshiva Bucher" —I was wonderful in the kaddish scene for his father, the dead king. And I also played "Kaynig Lear und sein Tochter."

[Rising and again removing his glasses, he recites in English]:

"Down from the waist they are centaurs,
Though women all above;
But to the girdle do the gods inherit,
Beneath is all the fiends':
There's hell, there's darkness, there's the
Sulphurous pit,
Burning, scalding, stench, consumption. Fie, fie,
Fie, poh, poh. Give me an ounce of civet good
Apothecary, to sweeten my imagination."

[LEON, as though this were not news to him, finishes adding up the score. He shuffles the cards thoroughly as FEUER puts on his glasses, and sitting, regards him objectively.]

Leon. Another game? We're running even now, two and two. Almost the same points.

Feuer. The last one.

[LEON deals again and the game goes on.]

Feuer. [after playing a card, continuing to needle] Tell me, Leon, do you like tragedy?

Leon. Do I like it?

Feuer. Do you like to see a tragedy on the stage or read tragic books?

Leon. I can take it or leave it. Generally my nature is cheerful.

Feuer. [building] But you went to college. You're a good business man. Adele says you read the *New York Times* everyday. In other words you're an intelligent person. So answer me this question: Why do all the best writers and poets write tragedy? And why does every theater play such plays and all kinds of people pay their good money to see tragedies? Why is that?

Leon. To tell the truth, I never had occasion to give it much thought.

Feuer. [a touch of malice] Do me a favor, think about it now.

Leon. [wary] I'm not so sure I can tell you exactly but I suppose it's because a lot of life is like that. You realize what's what.

Feuer. What do you mean, "suppose"? Don't you know for sure? Think what we live through everyday—accidents, murders, sickness, disappointments. The thought of death alone is enough.

Leon. [subdued] I know what you mean.

Feuer. [sarcasm evident] You think you know. Do you really know the condition of human existence? Do you know what the universe means? I'm not talking about who's dead but also about millions of people—in the millions—who live for nothing. They have nothing but poverty, disease, suffering. Or they live in a prison like the Russians. Is this your idea of a good life for everybody?

[BEN GLICKMAN appears at the doorway, looks in hungrily, sees LEON and goes on his way upstairs. Neither of the card players has noticed him.]

Leon. I wouldn't say that.

Feuer. If you know, you know conditions and you got to do something about them. A man has to be interested to ask for change where it is necessary, to help which way he can.

Leon. I try to help. I give regularly to charity, including the United Jewish Appeal.

Feuer. This isn't enough.

Leon. What do you do?

Feuer. [laying down his cards; emotionally] What do I do? I suffer for those who suffer. My heart bleeds for all the injustice in this world.

[LEON is silently studying his cards.]

Feuer. [picking up his hand, speaking quietly though still with a purpose] Do you ever think what happens to you—inside your soul, when you see a tragic play, for instance Shakespeare?

Leon. [suddenly recalling] I feel a catharsis through pity and terror.

Feuer. [after a pause] Don't quote me your college books. A writer writes tragedy so people don't forget that they are human. He shows us the conditions that exist. He organizes for us the meaning of our lives so it is clear to our eyes. That's why he writes it, that's why we play it. My best roles were tragic roles. I enjoyed them the most though I was also marvelous in comedy. "Leid macht auch lachen."

[He laughs dramatically, then quietly draws a card and lays down his hand triumphantly.] Rummy!

Leon. You win. [He begins to tote up the score.] I guess I owe you exactly fifty-one cents. [Taking out his change purse he puts down two quarters and a penny and gently pushes the money towards FEUER's side of the table.]

Feuer. [casually; ignoring the money] So how is the baseball situation now, Leon?

Leon. [He bites.] I think the Yanks and Dodgers are leading as usual. [catching on] I'm afraid I'm not following the situation very closely, Mr. Feuer.

Feuer. If you don't follow it, what do you talk about to your sporting goods customers?

Leon. [patiently] Different things, though not necessarily sports. People are people—they talk about a lot of things. [He slides the three coins a bit farther forward.] You better put this away, Mr. Feuer.

Feuer. I'm not worried about the money. I play because I like to play. [A thought strikes him.] You know the story about the famous rabbi and the rich man? He was rich and a miser. The rabbi took him to the window and said, "What do you see, tell me?" The rich man looked and he said, "I see the street, what else should I see?" "What's in the street?" "What's in the street?" said the rich Jew, "people—they're walking in the street." Then the rabbi took him to a mirror in the room and he said, "What do you see now?" "What do I see now?" said the rich man. "Naturally I see myself, of course." "Aha," said the rabbi. "You'll notice in the window is glass, and there is also glass in the mirror. But the glass in the mirror has silver painted on the back, and once there's the silver you stop seeing everybody else and you only see yourself."

Leon. [still patient] The way I look at it is this. Rummy is a game of chance. If you play for cash the loser pays with cash and the winner accepts with good grace.

[Again he slides the coins towards FEUER.]

Feuer. [pushing them back] Please don't tell me about manners. About manners I knew before you were born.

Leon. Mr. Feuer, if you want to insult me, there are better ways.

Feuer. Why should I insult you?

Leon. Please don't think I am a dope. It's as plain as anyone's nose that you don't like me though I wish I knew why.

Feuer. I'll tell you why if you'll kindly tell me what you are living for? What is your philosophy of life?

Leon. I live because I'm alive.

Feuer. Good, but what do you *want* from your life? That's also important.

Leon. [beginning to show irritation] That's my business. Listen, Mr. Feuer, don't think I am so dense that I don't understand the reasons for this inquisition you gave me. You pretend you are cordial but it's for the purpose of needling me. I'm not so dense that I don't know what you're insinuating—that I'm not interested in the right things and also that I'm money conscious. But that's all a camouflage. You have some pretty strong prejudices and that's why you're annoyed that Adele is going to marry me.

Feuer. That's a father's privilege.

Leon. I guess you have no respect for your daughter's judgment.

Feuer. I have plenty of respect but she isn't your type. I don't say you're a bad person but you aren't the right man for her.

Leon. Who's the right man?

Feuer. More an artistic type. Like her own nature.

Leon. That's just what I figured you would say, and if you'll excuse me, it's a batty point of view. A man is a man, not a profession. I've worked darn hard all my life for everything I have. I got myself a decent education which I paid for myself, even if it isn't a B.A. education. No matter what you think, if you look around, the world doesn't run on art. What it runs on I'm not going to argue with you but I'll say this. At the least you ought to respect me if for no other reason, then because your daughter does. Just because I'm no longhair writer doesn't make me unworthy of her, or for that matter it doesn't make Adele unworthy of me. [rising] Someday I hope you'll wake up to the facts of life.

[FLORENCE FEUER appears on the stairs and momentarily pauses when she hears voices.]

Leon. People aren't the same as their businesses. I am not what I sell. And even if I happened to sell irradiated toilet seats, I still wouldn't worship them. I would use them for the purpose that they are intended.

[FLORENCE enters the apartment.]

Feuer. Whatever you sell or don't sell, if Adele marries somebody she don't love, she'll regret it.

Florence. [gasping] Feuer—for God's sake! Leon, don't believe him—

Leon. [to FLORENCE] Hello, Mrs. Feuer. When Adele comes home, tell her I'll be back to take her out to dinner.

[He leaves with dignity.]

[FLORENCE sits down in the chair LEON has just occupied

and slowly removes her shoes. For a minute she sits there not saying a word. The ACTOR is silent, too, then goes to the sink and pours himself a long glass of water. He stands there drinking thirstily.]

Florence. [with weary bitterness] What's the matter, Feuer, aren't you satisfied with all your miseries? What do you want from this poor girl's life? Do you hate her?

Feuer. [coolly] I'm doing her a favor.

Florence. To ruin her life?

Feuer. To save it. This boy means well but he's a first-class mediocrity. I'm convinced for sure now.

Florence. [wearily patient] Are you blind? Take your eyes in your hand and look again. How can you stay in the same room with Leon and not see what a fine person he is? The trouble is you're jealous.

Feuer. If I wasn't jealous of Maurice Schwartz why should I be jealous of Leon Singer?

Florence. Why did you insult him for nothing?

Feuer. Who insulted him?

Florence. You did. Why did he leave with his face so red?

Feuer. What am I, a diagnostician? All I asked him was a few honest questions. It's a father's privilege.

Florence. I can imagine what you asked him.

Feuer. I asked him what he lived for. I asked him what's his philosophy, if any. I have a right to know.

Florence. Why don't you ask yourself and leave him alone?

Feuer. I didn't ask him anything I don't ask myself.

Florence. Please leave him alone. Adele picked him, not you. She's marrying him, not you. Leave them alone before you start a calamity.

Feuer. My opinion is she don't love him.

Florence. Are you crazy? Who told you such a thing?

Feuer. She's not in love, she thinks she is.

Florence. What are you now, a fortune teller?—Miss Lonelyhearts? Have you loved so well that you know all about it?

Feuer. How well I loved *I* know. I also know her and I know she doesn't really love him.

Florence. And I know you encouraged this boy upstairs to come here on his night off. Don't think I don't know you asked her to go out with him.

Feuer. She didn't go because he didn't ask. But yesterday he called her to go for a walk tonight, and she said yes.

Florence. [rising] Oh my God. [She cracks her knuckles on her breasts.] Does Leon know?

Feuer. Who cares if he knows?

Florence. [angrily] Feuer, if you break up this engagement I will leave you. Cook your own vegetables.

[FEUER glares at her.]

Florence. You ought to be ashamed to do this to her. What can she get from a poor writer without a steady job—even without a college education that you talk so much about—who writes all day without success.

Feuer. First you learn your art, then you have success. Someday he'll be a first-class writer.

Florence. How do you know?

Feuer. He read me a story—it was brilliant.

Florence. One story don't mean a thing.

Feuer. One is all I need.

Florence. [intensely] What can a starving writer give her? A decent home? Can he afford to have children? Will he consider her first when she needs him, or his egotism? I want her to have a future, not a cold water flat with a poor man.

Feuer. Maybe he won't be rich but he'll have a rich life. With him she could have a real excitement in her life—not a middle-class existence where the real pleasure is to go shopping for something you don't need. Don't underestimate Ben Glickman. I talked to him many times and I know his nature. This is a passionate man—how many are left in the world? He doesn't tell me what he has suffered but I can see in his eyes. He knows what life means and he knows what's real. He'll be good for Adele. He will understand her and love her like she needs to be loved.

Florence. To me he looks sick, like a starved animal. And what are you talking about love when she doesn't even know him? What kind of foolishness is this? It's because you see yourself in him, that's who you see. You see another egoist.

Feuer. Who can talk to you? You're full of foolish anxieties you want to give me.

Florence. Who else can I give them to?

Feuer. This isn't talk, it's confusion.

Florence. You confuse her. Soon she won't know what she's doing. You confused me too.

Feuer. You confused yourself.

Florence. [angrily] Egoist! Egoist! You don't deserve to have such a son-in-law.

Feuer. [sarcastic] Did I deserve to have such a wife?

Florence. [rising] Never, you never deserved me.

[She picks up her shoes, drops them into the living room closet, and steps into slippers. Returning to the kitchen she opens the refrigerator door, takes out a few things, and begins wordlessly to prepare supper. FEUER is thumbing through a magazine she had brought home. After a minute FLORENCE goes to the hall door and quietly shuts it.]

Feuer. [without turning his head] Don't close the door, it's too hot.

Florence. [quietly] I want to talk to you one minute—private.

Feuer. Talk. But keep the door open. I'm suffocating.

Florence. Please, Feuer, stop exaggerating. Stop performing. You won't die. All I want to do is talk to you without the neighbors' ears in our door.

Feuer. [shouting] Leave the door open I told you.

Florence. [opening it] You make me sick!

Feuer. [rising to the occasion] You made me sick!

Florence. [though not wanting to, losing her temper] Blame yourself. You were sick to begin with from the day I met you. You spoiled my life.

Feuer. You spoiled it yourself.

Florence. [vehemently] No, you spoiled it. You don't know where to stop. Every time you stab yourself you stab me twice. I used to be a nice person but you spoiled my nature. You're impossible to live with and impossible to talk to. You don't even converse any more. When you open your mouth, right away you're yelling—it's always an argument.

Feuer. Who else is yelling if I may ask you?

Florence. You spoiled my character.

Feuer. I didn't interfere with existing conditions.

Florence. [on the verge of tears] You did, you did!

Feuer. If you believe this, you're lying to yourself.

Florence. You're the one who lied. You lied about the choristers you couldn't stay away from them, even with a wife and child. I gave you my love but you couldn't say no to the chorus girls. If one of them looked at you you turned into a rooster. You had no will.

Feuer. I have a *magnificent* will.

Florence. If her garter was loose you took off her stocking. If she took it off herself you helped her to take off the other.

Feuer. [bitterly] And which two-bit actors took off your stockings? And how many times in your married life?

Florence. You started the whole dirty business. *You* started it. I never wanted that kind of a life, it wasn't my nature.

Feuer. It went on for years.

Florence. You left me three times, once two whole years. Also many times you were on the road for months when I couldn't go. I was human. I made mistakes.

Feuer. You could've thought of your child instead of sending her from one place to another, in the hands of strangers who made her sick.

Florence. Feuer, for God's sake, I can't stand any more. Why didn't you take care of her? Because you weren't there. Because you were busy in bed with somebody else.

Feuer. [blazing] You son of a bitch!

[FLORENCE stares at him, then seems to crumple and slowly lowers herself into a chair. She puts her hands on the table, palms up, and lowering her head, sobs into them. She sobs with her whole body, a wailing weeping.]

[FEUER goes to the door and quietly shuts it. He attempts to approach her but can't. He goes to the sink for another glass of water but pours it out without drinking, staring vaguely out the window. Wandering to the mirror, he stands there looking at himself, not enjoying what he sees. Gradually FLORENCE stops crying, raises her head and sits quietly at the table, one hand shading her eyes. After a while she blows her nose, and wipes her eyes with a handkerchief. FEUER, after glaring at his image, in weariness lies down on the day bed.]

Florence. [very quietly] What's that smell?

Feuer. [wearily] Gas.

Florence. What kind of gas?

Feuer. Human gas. Whatever you smell you want immediate identification.

Florence. [after a while] Don't you feel well?

Feuer. Perfect.

Florence. [still quietly] Did you take your pills today?

Feuer. I took. [He jumps up from the bed and speaks suddenly, vehemently.] Florence, I'm sorry. In my heart I love you. My tongue is filthy but not my heart.

Florence. [after a pause] How can you love a son of a bitch?

Feuer. Don't poison me with my words. I have enough poison in me already. I say what I don't mean.

Florence. What do you mean?

Feuer. I say that too.

Florence. [still half stunned] How can anyone love a son of a bitch?

Feuer. [savagely striking his chest] *I* am the son of a bitch.

Florence. [musing] It's my fault. I shouldn't fight with you. I don't know why I do it. Maybe it's change of life. What am I changing? Where is my life? It's true, I neglected her, she's the one who suffered. I still feel terrible about those days. But you left me. I had to work. I was out all day. At night I was afraid to be alone. I began to look for company. I was ashamed to let her see me so I sent her away. There was nobody to send her to so I sent her to strangers.

Feuer. [unable to restrain it] To friends of your lovers. To their relatives too.

Florence. Have mercy on me, Feuer. My lovers I buried long ago. They're all dead. Don't dig them out of their graves. For what I did to my child I still suffer. You don't have to hurt me more. I know how to hurt myself. [She cries quietly.]

[The ACTOR approaches her chair and stands behind her.]

Feuer. I was a fool. I didn't know what I was doing. I didn't understand my own nature. I talked big but accomplished nothing. Even as an actor I wasn't one of the best. Thomashefsky, Jacob Adler, Schwartz—all were better than me. Their names are famous. Two years off the stage and my name is dead. This is what I deserve—I don't fool myself.

Florence. You were a good actor.

Feuer. I wasn't a good actor and I am not a good man.

[She rises and they embrace.]

Florence. I forgave you but you don't forgive me.

Feuer. I don't forgive myself.

Florence. [again remembering] Three times you left me.

Feuer. I always came back.

Florence. It took so long. I hurt her so much. [She wipes her eyes with her fingers.]

Feuer. Enough now. It was my fault too. I hurt her and I hurt you. Why did I hurt you?—because you were there to hurt. You were the only one [he pauses—there was another but he doesn't say so]—the only one who could stand me.

Florence. You try to be good.

Feuer. No.

Florence. Yes. [after a minute] Please do me a favor, Feuer, and I won't ask for anything else—let Leon alone. Let Adele alone. Let them find their life together. It's all I ask you. For her sake—or there will be terrible trouble.

[The door opens and ADELE enters, discovering them in each other's arms.]

Adele. [sadly] Ah, you've been fighting again. [She shuts the door.]

[FLORENCE goes to the sink, washes her eyes with cold water and dries them with a kitchen towel. FEUER, after kissing ADELE, goes to the bathroom.]

Adele. [putting her purse and a paper down on the table] What were you fighting about?

Florence. We weren't fighting. It was a disagreement. Leon was here.

Adele. Leon? When?

Florence. He came to surprise you. He wants you to eat dinner with him. Please, darling, go. He'll be right back in a few minutes.

Adele. Where is he now?

Florence. I don't know. I wasn't here. Papa told me. I think they were playing rummy and he said something to Leon.

Adele. Nasty?

Florence. Papa got sarcastic and Leon didn't like it. But he said he would come back soon.

Adele. I wasn't expecting him tonight.

Florence. It was a surprise.

Adele. I wish he had at least called me. I already promised Ben I would go for a walk with him tonight.

Florence. A walk is nothing.

Adele. I promised.

Florence. Adele, you're an engaged girl. Leon came all the way from Newark to take you to dinner. You ought to go.

Adele. Being engaged doesn't mean I'm not entitled to a free minute to myself.

Florence. Who said that? All I said was Leon was here. You can tell this boy upstairs you'll see him some other time.

Adele. He called me up and I said yes.

Florence. It isn't such a big promise.

Adele. I can't understand why Leon didn't call.

Florence. Call or not call, it's not nice to say no when he's already here. Adele, mamale, please see him tonight. I don't want you to walk with that boy. It's dangerous.

[She hadn't meant to say quite that.]

Adele. A walk isn't a wedding, Mama.

Florence. It could be worse than a wedding.

Adele. For God's sake, what do you mean?

Florence. [cracking her knuckles on her bosom] You can walk to your grave with a little walk.

[FEUER comes out of the bathroom, looks at himself earnestly in the mirror, mutters something derogatory, and enters the kitchen.]

Adele. Doesn't anyone trust me?

Feuer. I trust you.

Florence. [to ADELE] Is this what you want all your life? [indicating the apartment.]

Adele. I don't see the relationship.

Florence. [deeply troubled] For my sake don't go out with this writer. Don't make any more complications in your life. Life is complicated enough.

[There is a knock on the door.]

Florence. Come in.

[LEON enters, carrying a large bouquet of flowers.]

Florence. Leon!

Leon. Hello, everybody. [to ADELE] This is for you, honey.

Adele. Hello, darling.

[He hands her the flowers and they kiss.]

Leon. Hello, Mrs. Feuer. Good evening, Mr. Feuer.

[He bears no grudges.]

Feuer. Good evening.

[ADELE hands the bouquet to her mother, who hunts for something to put it into. While she is doing that, FEUER takes up his newspaper, excuses himself, and after drawing the curtain separating the rooms, sits on the day bed, reading. FLORENCE, disapproving the drawn curtain but glad to have FEUER out of the way, attends first to the flowers, then fixes her cold supper. LEON has seated himself at the table, and ADELE, after setting the vase of new flowers on the window sill, is sitting near him.]

Florence. Leon, would you like to eat with us? It's not much—just a salad with smoked white fish. Also a few potato pancakes, though not for Feuer—he can't eat them.

Leon. Thanks very much but I was thinking of asking Adele to go out and eat Chinese tonight.

[He looks at her.]

Adele. I'm sorry Leon, if I had known you were coming I would have said yes. That is if you had called before Ben asked me. He's that friend of Papa's who writes. You met him.

Leon. [disappointed] Couldn't you break it with him, honey?

Adele. [hesitantly] I'd rather not.

Leon. What's so special about this guy? I mean that you gave him the date? Is it because he's a writer?

Adele. [defensively] You said I could go out once in a while if I felt like it.

Leon. I said it and I stick by it. All I want to know is why you're going out with him?

Adele. I guess I have the feeling he's gone through a lot.

Florence. Everybody goes through a lot—

Adele. I like him, he's interesting. I like to talk to him.

Leon. I appreciate his problems but the fact of it is I've come all the way from Newark, New Jersey, to be with the girl I'm engaged to—

Florence. Mamale—

Adele. Please, Mama—

[FLORENCE removes her apron and retires behind the curtain. FEUER, who has been listening, raises his paper as she enters and pretends he's reading. FLORENCE, not sure she has made the right move, lights a cigarette and sits in the armchair, flipping through the pages of a magazine.]

Leon. [lowering his voice] Honey, I don't dig it. I thought you'd surely be happy to have this kind of a surprise from me.

Adele. [gently] I am. It's a nice surprise. But all I'm saying is I feel committed tonight. [aware of his concern] Don't worry, it's not serious. Don't make anything serious out of it. It's just that he's a lonely person, I guess. You feel that when you're with him.

Leon. I'm lonely too. Couldn't you postpone it till tomorrow night?

Adele. He's off tonight. Tomorrow he works.

Leon. Then till the next time he's off? I'll exchange him tonight for then. [again lowering his voice] You haven't forgotten our plan to spend a week in the country together in September?

Adele. [a little cold] I don't see what the relationship of this is with that.

Leon. Well, maybe there isn't but why don't you think it over? I mean about tonight.

Adele. I feel I ought to keep my word with him.

Leon. [edgy] What's the matter, Adele—you don't seem cordial at all. What is it, the atmosphere here?

Adele. If you don't like the atmosphere, why do you come here?

Leon. I don't want to fight with you.

Adele. I don't want to fight with you.

Leon. [after a minute] Maybe you're right. Give me a kiss and I'll call it quits.

Adele. I'll kiss you because I like you.

[They kiss.]

Adele. [gently] I'll postpone it with him if you really want me to.

Feuer. [from behind the curtain] Do what *you* want.

Florence. [hushed whisper] Please, for God's sake, Feuer.

Leon. [as though he had heard nothing] Let's make a compromise. What time is he showing up here?

Adele. I don't know, around eight, I suppose. He didn't say exactly.

Leon. All right, whatever time. [He looks at his wrist watch.] It's ten to six. We can still go out, have our Chinese meal and I'll have you back in the car at fifteen after eight. Then you can go for a short walk and when you come back I'll be waiting and we can drive down to Coney Island.

Adele. For the first suggestion, okay. I'll go to the Chinese restaurant with you. But I don't want to rush him, while we're walking, to get back for the drive. It's not that kind of date.

Leon. [annoyed] What kind of date is it?

Adele. A very innocent one.

[There's a knock on the door. ADELE gets up and opens it. Both FLORENCE and FEUER are attentive. BEN enters with a small bouquet of daffodils.]

Ben. Am I too early?

[No one answers as the curtain goes down.]

The Jewbird

THE WINDOW was open so the skinny bird flew in. Flappity-flap with its frazzled black wings. That's how it goes. It's open, you're in. Closed, you're out and that's your fate. The bird wearily flapped through the open kitchen window of Harry Cohen's top-floor apartment on First Avenue near the lower East River. On a rod on the wall hung an escaped canary cage, its door wide open, but this black-type longbeaked bird—its ruffled head and small dull eyes, crossed a little, making it look like a dissipated crow—landed if not smack on Cohen's thick lamb chop, at least on the table, close by. The frozen-foods salesman was sitting at supper with his wife and young son on a hot August evening a year ago. Cohen, a heavy man with hairy chest and beefy shorts; Edie, in skinny yellow shorts and red halter; and their ten-year-old Morris (after her father)—Maurie, they called him, a nice kid though not overly bright—were all in the city after two weeks out, because Cohen's mother was dying. They had been enjoying Kingston, New York, but drove back when Mama got sick in her flat in the Bronx.

"Right on the table," said Cohen, putting down his beer glass and swatting at the bird. "Son of a bitch."

"Harry, take care with your language," Edie said, looking at Maurie, who watched every move.

The bird cawed hoarsely and with a flap of its bedraggled wings—feathers tufted this way and that—rose heavily to the top of the open kitchen door, where it perched staring down.

"Gevalt, a pogrom!"

"It's a talking bird," said Edie in astonishment.

"In Jewish," said Maurie.

"Wise guy," muttered Cohen. He gnawed on his chop, then put down the bone. "So if you can talk, say what's your business. What do you want here?"

"If you can't spare a lamb chop," said the bird, "I'll settle for a piece of herring with a crust of bread. You can't live on your nerve forever."

"This ain't a restaurant," Cohen replied. "All I'm asking is what brings you to this address?"

"The window was open," the bird sighed; adding after a moment, "I'm running. I'm flying but I'm also running."

"From whom?" asked Edie with interest.

"Anti-Semeets."

"Anti-Semites?" they all said.

"That's from who."

"What kind of anti-Semites bother a bird?" Edie asked.

"Any kind," said the bird, "also including eagles, vultures, and hawks. And once in a while some crows will take your eyes out."

"But aren't you a crow?"

"Me? I'm a Jewbird."

Cohen laughed heartily. "What do you mean by that?"

The bird began dovening. He prayed without Book or tallith, but with passion. Edie bowed her head though not Cohen. And Maurie rocked back and forth with the prayers, looking up with one wide-open eye.

When the prayer was done Cohen remarked, "No hat, no phylacteries?"

"I'm an old radical."

"You're sure you're not some kind of a ghost or dybbuk?"

"Not a dybbuk," answered the bird, "though one of my relatives had such an experience once. It's all over now, thanks God. They freed her from a former lover, a crazy jealous man. She's now the mother of two wonderful children."

"Birds?" Cohen asked slyly.

"Why not?"

"What kind of birds?"

"Like me. Jewbirds."

Cohen tipped back in his chair and guffawed. "That's a big laugh. I heard of a Jewfish but not a Jewbird."

"We're once removed." The bird rested on one skinny leg, then on the other. "Please, could you spare maybe a piece of herring with a small crust of bread?"

Edie got up from the table.

"What are you doing?" Cohen asked her.

"I'll clear the dishes."

Cohen turned to the bird. "So what's your name, if you don't mind saying?"

"Call me Schwartz."

"He might be an old Jew changed into a bird by somebody," said Edie, removing a plate.

"Are you?" asked Harry, lighting a cigar.

"Who knows?" answered Schwartz. "Does God tell us everything?"

Maurie got up on his chair. "What kind of herring?" he asked the bird in excitement.

"Get down, Maurie, or you'll fall," ordered Cohen.

"If you haven't got matjes, I'll take schmaltz," said Schwartz.

"All we have is marinated, with slices of onion—in a jar," said Edie.

"If you'll open for me the jar I'll eat marinated. Do you have also, if you don't mind, a piece of rye bread—the spitz?"

Edie thought she had.

"Feed him out on the balcony," Cohen said. He spoke to the bird. "After that take off."

Schwartz closed both bird eyes. "I'm tired and it's a long way."

"Which direction are you headed, north or south?"

Schwartz, barely lifting his wings, shrugged.

"You don't know where you're going?"

"Where there's charity I'll go."

"Let him stay, Papa," said Maurie. "He's only a bird."

"So stay the night," Cohen said, "but not longer."

In the morning Cohen ordered the bird out of the house but Maurie cried, so Schwartz stayed for a while. Maurie was still on vacation from school and his friends were away. He was lonely and Edie enjoyed the fun he had playing with the bird.

"He's no trouble at all," she told Cohen, "and besides his appetite is very small."

"What'll you do when he makes dirty?"

"He flies across the street in a tree when he makes dirty, and if nobody passes below, who notices?"

"So all right," said Cohen, "but I'm dead set against it. I warn you he ain't gonna stay here long."

"What have you got against the poor bird?"

"Poor bird, my ass. He's a foxy bastard. He thinks he's a Jew."

"What difference does it make what he thinks?"

"A Jewbird, what a chutzpah. One false move and he's out on his drumsticks."

At Cohen's insistence Schwartz lived out on the balcony in a new wooden birdhouse Edie had bought him.

"With many thanks," said Schwartz, "though I would rather have a human roof over my head. You know how it is at my age. I like the warm, the windows, the smell of cooking. I would also be glad to see once in a while the *Jewish Morning Journal* and have now and then a schnapps because it helps my breathing, thanks God. But whatever you give me, you won't hear complaints."

However, when Cohen brought home a bird feeder full of dried corn, Schwartz said, "Impossible."

Cohen was annoyed. "What's the matter, crosseyes, is your life getting too good for you? Are you forgetting what it means to be migratory? I'll bet a helluva lot of crows you happen to be acquainted with, Jews or otherwise, would give their eyeteeth to eat this corn."

Schwartz did not answer. What can you say to a grubber yung?

"Not for my digestion," he later explained to Edie. "Cramps. Herring is better even if it makes you thirsty. At least rainwater don't cost anything." He laughed sadly in breathy caws.

And herring, thanks to Edie, who knew where to shop, was what Schwartz got, with an occasional piece of potato pancake, and even a bit of soupmeat when Cohen wasn't looking.

When school began in September, before Cohen would once again suggest giving the bird the boot, Edie prevailed on him to wait a little while until Maurie adjusted.

"To deprive him right now might hurt his school work, and you know what trouble we had last year."

"So okay, but sooner or later the bird goes. That I promise you."

Schwartz, though nobody had asked him, took on full responsibility for Maurie's performance in school. In return for favors granted, when he was let in for an hour or two at night, he spent most of his time overseeing the boy's lessons. He sat on top of the dresser near Maurie's desk as he laboriously wrote out his homework. Maurie was a restless type and Schwartz gently kept him to his studies. He also listened to him practice his screechy violin, taking a few minutes off now and then to rest his ears in the bathroom. And they afterwards played dominoes. The boy was an indifferent checkers player and it was impossible to teach him chess. When he was sick, Schwartz read him comic books though he personally disliked them. But Maurie's work improved in school and even his violin teacher admitted his playing was better. Edie gave Schwartz credit for these improvements though the bird pooh-poohed them.

Yet he was proud there was nothing lower than C minuses on Maurie's report card, and on Edie's insistence celebrated with a little schnapps.

"If he keeps up like this," Cohen said, "I'll get him in an Ivy League college for sure."

"Oh, I hope so," sighed Edie.

But Schwartz shook his head. "He's a good boy—you don't have to worry. He won't be a shicker or a wife beater, God forbid, but a scholar he'll never be, if you know what I mean, although maybe a good mechanic. It's no disgrace in these times."

"If I was you," Cohen said, angered, "I'd keep my big snoot out of other people's private business."

"Harry, please," said Edie.

"My goddamn patience is wearing out. That crosseyes butts into everything."

Though he wasn't exactly a welcome guest in the house, Schwartz gained a few ounces although he did not improve in appearance. He looked bedraggled as ever, his feathers unkempt, as though he had just flown out of a snowstorm. He spent, he admitted, little time taking care of himself. Too much to think about. "Also outside plumbing," he told Edie. Still there was more glow to his eyes so that though Cohen went on calling him crosseyes he said it less emphatically.

Liking his situation, Schwartz tried tactfully to stay out of Cohen's way, but one night when Edie was at the movies and Maurie was taking a hot shower, the frozen-foods salesman began a quarrel with the bird.

"For Christ sake, why don't you wash yourself sometimes? Why must you always stink like a dead fish?"

"Mr. Cohen, if you'll pardon me, if somebody eats garlic he will smell from garlic. I eat herring three times a day. Feed me flowers and I will smell like flowers."

"Who's obligated to feed you anything at all? You're lucky to get herring."

"Excuse me, I'm not complaining," said the bird. "You're complaining."

"What's more," said Cohen, "even from out on the balcony I can hear you snoring away like a pig. It keeps me awake nights."

"Snoring," said Schwartz, "isn't a crime, thanks God."

"All in all you are a goddamn pest and freeloader. Next thing you'll want to sleep in bed next to my wife."

"Mr. Cohen," said Schwartz, "on this rest assured. A bird is a bird."

"So you say, but how do I know you're a bird and not some kind of a goddamn devil?"

"If I was a devil you would know already. And I don't mean because your son's good marks."

"Shut up, you bastard bird," shouted Cohen.

"Grubber yung," cawed Schwartz, rising to the tips of his talons, his long wings outstretched.

Cohen was about to lunge for the bird's scrawny neck but Maurie came out of the bathroom, and for the rest of the evening until Schwartz's bedtime on the balcony, there was pretend peace.

But the quarrel had deeply disturbed Schwartz and he slept badly. His snoring woke him, and awake, he was fearful of what would become of him. Wanting to stay out of Cohen's way, he kept to the birdhouse as much as possible. Cramped by it, he paced back and forth on the balcony ledge, or sat on the birdhouse roof, staring into space. In the evenings, while overseeing Maurie's lessons, he often fell asleep. Awakening, he nervously hopped around exploring the four corners of the room. He spent much time in Maurie's closet, and carefully examined his bureau drawers when they were left open. And once when he found a large paper bag on the floor, Schwartz poked his way into it to investigate what possibilities were. The boy was amused to see the bird in the paper bag.

"He wants to build a nest," he said to his mother.

Edie, sensing Schwartz's unhappiness, spoke to him quietly.

"Maybe if you did some of the things my husband wants you, you would get along better with him."

"Give me a for instance," Schwartz said.

"Like take a bath, for instance."

"I'm too old for baths," said the bird. "My feathers fall out without baths."

"He says you have a bad smell."

"Everybody smells. Some people smell because of their thoughts or because who they are. My bad smell comes from the food I eat. What does his come from?"

"I better not ask him or it might make him mad," said Edie.

In late November Schwartz froze on the balcony in the fog and cold, and especially on rainy days he woke with stiff joints and could barely move his wings. Already he felt twinges of rheumatism. He would have liked to spend more time in the warm house, particularly when Maurie was in school and Cohen at work. But though Edie was goodhearted and might have sneaked him in in the morning, just to thaw out, he was afraid to ask her. In the meantime Cohen, who had been reading articles about the migration of birds, came out on the balcony one night after work when Edie was in the kitchen preparing pot roast, and peeking into the birdhouse, warned Schwartz to be on his way soon if he knew what was good for him. "Time to hit the flyways."

"Mr. Cohen, why do you hate me so much?" asked the bird. "What did I do to you?"

"Because you're an A-number-one troublemaker, that's why. What's more, whoever heard of a Jewbird? Now scat or it's open war."

But Schwartz stubbornly refused to depart so Cohen embarked on a campaign of harassing him, meanwhile hiding it from Edie and Maurie. Maurie hated violence and Cohen didn't want to leave a bad impression. He thought maybe if he played dirty tricks on the bird he would fly off without being physically kicked out. The vacation was over, let him make his easy living off the fat of somebody else's land. Cohen worried about the effect of the bird's departure on Maurie's schooling but decided to take the chance, first, because the boy now seemed to have the knack of studying—give the black bird-bastard credit—and second, because Schwartz was driving him bats by being there always, even in his dreams.

The frozen-foods salesman began his campaign against the bird by mixing watery cat food with the herring slices in Schwartz's dish. He also blew up and popped numerous paper bags outside the birdhouse as the bird slept, and when he had got Schwartz good and nervous, though not enough to leave, he brought a full-grown cat into the house, supposedly a gift for little Maurie, who had always wanted a pussy. The cat never stopped springing up at Schwartz whenever he saw him, one day managing to claw out several of his tail feathers. And even at lesson time, when the cat was usually excluded from Maurie's room, though somehow or other he quickly found his way in at the end of the lesson, Schwartz was desperately fearful of his life and flew from pinnacle to pinnacle—light fixture to clothes tree to door top—in order to elude the beast's wet jaws.

Once when the bird complained to Edie how hazardous his existence was, she said, "Be patient, Mr. Schwartz. When the cat gets to know you better he won't try to catch you any more."

"When he stops trying we will both be in Paradise," Schwartz answered. "Do me a favor and get rid of him. He makes my whole life worry. I'm losing feathers like a tree loses leaves."

"I'm awfully sorry but Maurie likes the pussy and sleeps with it."

What could Schwartz do? He worried but came to no decision, being afraid to leave. So he ate the herring garnished with cat food, tried hard not to hear the paper bags bursting like firecrackers outside the birdhouse at night, and lived terror-stricken, closer to the ceiling than the floor, as the cat, his tail flicking, endlessly watched him.

Weeks went by. Then on the day after Cohen's mother had died in her flat in the Bronx, when Maurie came home with a zero on an arithmetic test, Cohen, enraged, waited until Edie had taken the boy to his violin lesson, then openly attacked the bird. He chased him with a broom on the balcony and Schwartz frantically flew back and forth, finally escaping into his birdhouse. Cohen triumphantly reached in, and grabbing both skinny legs, dragged the bird out, cawing loudly, his wings wildly beating. He whirled the bird around and around his head. But Schwartz, as he moved in circles, managed to swoop down and catch Cohen's nose in his beak, and hung on for dear life. Cohen cried out in great pain, punched at the bird with his fist, and tugging at its legs with all his might, pulled his nose free. Again he swung the yawking Schwartz around until the bird grew dizzy, then with a furious heave, flung him into the night. Schwartz sank like a stone into the street. Cohen then tossed the birdhouse and feeder after him, listening at the ledge until they crashed on the sidewalk below. For a full hour, broom in hand, his heart palpitating and nose throbbing with pain, Cohen waited for Schwartz to return, but the brokenhearted bird didn't.

That's the end of that dirty bastard, the salesman thought and went in. Edie and Maurie had come home.

"Look," said Cohen, pointing to his bloody nose swollen three times its size, "what that sonofabitchy bird did. It's a permanent scar."

"Where is he now?" Edie asked, frightened.

"I threw him out and he flew away. Good riddance."

Nobody said no, though Edie touched a handkerchief to her eyes and Maurie rapidly tried the nine-times table and found he knew approximately half.

In the spring when the winter's snow had melted, the boy, moved by a memory, wandered in the neighborhood, looking for Schwartz. He found a dead black bird in a small lot by the river, his two wings broken, neck twisted, and both bird-eyes plucked clean.

"Who did it to you, Mr. Schwartz?" Maurie wept.

"Anti-Semeets," Edie said later.

Life Is Better than Death

SHE SEEMED to remember the man from the same day last year. He was standing at a nearby grave, occasionally turning to look around, while Etta, a rosary in her hand, prayed for the repose of the soul of her husband, Armando. Sometimes she prayed he would move over and let her lie down with him so her heart might be eased. It was the second of November, All Souls' Day in the cimitero Campo Verano, in Rome, and it had begun to drizzle after she had laid down the bouquet of yellow chrysanthemums on the grave Armando wouldn't have had if it wasn't for a generous uncle, a doctor in Perugia. Without this uncle Etta had no idea where Armando would be buried, certainly in a much less attractive grave, though she would have resisted his often expressed desire to be cremated.

Etta worked for meager wages in a draper's shop and Armando had left no insurance. The bright large yellow flowers, glowing in November gloom on the faded grass, moved her and tears gushed forth. Although she felt uncomfortably feverish when she cried like that, Etta was glad she had, because crying seemed to be the only thing that relieved her. She was thirty, dressed in full mourning. Her figure was slim, her moist brown eyes red-rimmed and darkly ringed, the skin pale and her features grown thin. Since the accidental death of Armando, a few months more than a year ago, she came almost daily during the long Roman afternoon to pray at his grave. She was devoted to his memory, ravaged within. Etta went to confession twice a week and took communion every Sunday. She lit candles for Armando at La Madonna Addolorata, and had a mass offered once a month, more often when she had a little extra money. Whenever she returned to the cold flat she still lived in and could not give up because it had once also been his, Etta thought of Armando, recalling him as he had looked ten years ago, not as when he had died. Invariably she felt an oppressive pang and ate very little.

It was raining quietly when she finished her rosary. Etta dropped the beads into her purse and opened a black umbrella.

The man from the other grave, wearing a darkish green hat and a tight black overcoat, had stopped a few feet behind her, cupping his small hands over a cigarette as he lit it. Seeing her turn from the grave he touched his hat. He was a short man with dark eyes and a barely visible mustache. He had meaty ears but was handsome.

"Your husband?" he asked respectfully, letting the smoke flow as he spoke, holding his cigarette cupped in his palm to keep it from getting wet.

She said it was.

He nodded in the direction of the grave where he had stood. "My wife. One day while I was on my job she was hurrying to meet a lover and was killed at once by a taxi in the Piazza Bologna." He spoke without bitterness, without apparent emotion, but his eyes were restless.

She noticed that he had put up his coat collar and was getting wet. Hesitantly she offered to share her umbrella with him on the way to the bus stop.

"Cesare Montaldo," he murmured, gravely accepting the umbrella and holding it high enough for both of them.

"Etta Oliva." She was in her high heels almost half a head taller than he.

They walked slowly along an avenue of damp cypresses to the gates of the cemetery, Etta keeping from him that she had been so deeply stricken by his story she could not get out even a sympathetic comment.

"Mourning is a hard business," Cesare said. "If people knew there'd be less death."

She sighed a slight smile.

Across the street from the bus stop was a bar with tables under a drawn awning. Cesare suggested coffee or perhaps an ice.

She thanked him and was about to refuse but his sad serious expression changed her mind and she went with him across the street. He guided her gently by the elbow, the other hand firmly holding the umbrella over them. She said she felt cold and they went inside.

He ordered an espresso but Etta settled for a piece of pastry which she politely picked at with her fork. Between puffs of a cigarette he talked about himself. His voice was low and he spoke well. He was a free-lance journalist, he said. Formerly he had worked in a government office but the work was boring so he had quit in disgust although he was in line for the directorship. "I would have directed the boredom." Now he was toying with the idea of going to America. He had a brother in Boston who wanted him to visit for several months and then decide whether he would emigrate permanently. The brother thought they could arrange that Cesare might come in through Canada. He had considered the idea but could not bring himself to break his ties with this kind of life for that. He seemed also to think that he would find it hard not to be able to go to his dead wife's grave when he was moved to do so. "You know how it is," he said, "with somebody you have once loved."

Etta felt for her handkerchief in her purse and touched her eyes.

"And you?" he asked sympathetically.

To her surprise she began to tell him her story. Though she had often related it to priests, she never had to anyone else, not even a friend. But she was telling it to a stranger because he seemed to be a man who would understand. And if later she regretted telling him, what difference would it make once he was gone?

She confessed she had prayed for her husband's death, and Cesare put down his coffee cup and sat with his cigarette between his lips, not puffing as she talked.

Armando, Etta said, had fallen in love with a cousin who had come during the summer from Perugia for a job in Rome. Her father had suggested that she live with them, and Armando and Etta, after talking it over, decided to let her stay for a while. They would save her rent to buy a secondhand television set so they could watch "Lascia o Raddoppia," the quiz program that everyone in Rome watched on Thursday nights, and that way save themselves the embarrassment of waiting for invitations and having to accept them from neighbors they didn't like. The cousin came, Laura Ansaldo, a big-boned pretty girl of eighteen with thick brown hair and large eyes. She slept on the sofa in the living room, was easy to get along with, and made herself helpful in the kitchen before and after supper. Etta had liked her until she noticed that Armando had gone mad over the girl. She then tried to get rid of Laura but Armando threatened he would leave if she bothered her. One day Etta had come home from work and found them naked in the marriage bed. She had screamed and wept. She called Laura a stinking whore and swore she would kill her if she didn't leave the house that minute. Armando was contrite. He promised he would send the girl back to Perugia, and the next day in the Stazione Termini had put her on the train. But the separation from her was more than he could bear. He grew nervous and miserable. Armando confessed himself one Saturday night, and for the first time in ten years took communion, but instead of calming down he desired the girl ever so much more strongly. After a week he told Etta that he was going to get his cousin and bring her back to Rome.

"If you bring that whore here," Etta shouted, "I'll pray to Christ that you drop dead before you get back."

"In that case," Armando said, "start praying."

When he left the house she fell on her knees and prayed for his death.

That night Armando went with a friend to get Laura. The friend had a truck and was going to Assisi. On the way back he would pick them up in Perugia and drive to Rome. They started out when it was still twilight but it soon grew dark. Armando drove for a while, then felt sleepy and crawled into the back of the truck. The Perugian hills were foggy after a hot September day and the truck hit a rock in the road with a hard bump. Armando, in deep sleep, rolled out of the open tailgate of the truck, hitting the road with head and shoulders, then rolling down the hill. He was dead before he stopped rolling. When she heard of this Etta fainted away and it was two days before she could speak. After that she had prayed for her own death, and often did.

Etta turned her back to the other tables, though they were empty, and wept openly and quietly.

After a while Cesare squashed his butt. "Calma, signora. If God had wanted your husband to live he would still be living. Prayers have little relevance to the situation. To my way of thinking the whole thing was no more than a coincidence. It's best not to go too far with religion or it becomes troublesome."

"A prayer is a prayer," she said. "I suffer for mine."

Cesare pursed his lips. "But who can judge these things? They're much more complicated than most of us know. In the case of my wife I didn't pray for her death but I confess I might have wished it. Am I in a better position than you?"

"My prayer was a sin. You don't have that on your mind. It's worse than what you just might have thought."

"That's only a technical thing, signora."

"If Armando had lived," she said after a minute, "he would have been twenty-nine next month. I am a year older. But my life is useless now. I wait to join him."

He shook his head, seemed moved, and ordered an espresso for her.

Though Etta had stopped crying, for the first time in months she felt substantially disburdened.

Cesare would put her on the bus; as they were crossing the street he suggested they might meet now and then since they had so much in common.

"I live like a nun," she said.

He lifted his hat. "Coraggio," and she smiled at him for his kindness.

When she returned home that night the anguish of life without Armando recommenced. She remembered him as he had been when he was courting her and felt uneasy for having talked about him to Cesare. And she vowed for herself continued prayers, rosaries, her own penitence to win him further indulgences in Purgatory.

Etta saw Cesare on a Sunday afternoon a week later. He had written her name in his little book and was able to locate her apartment in a house on the Via Nomentana through the help of a friend in the electric company.

When he knocked on her door she was surprised to see him, turned rather pale, though he hung back doubtfully. He said he had found out by accident where she lived and she asked for no details. Cesare had brought a small bunch of violets which she embarrassedly accepted and put in water.

"You're looking better, signora," he said.

"My mourning for Armando goes on," she answered with a sad smile.

"Moderazione," he counseled, flicking his meaty ear with his finger. "You're still a young woman, and at that not bad-looking. You ought to acknowledge it to yourself. There are certain advantages to self-belief."

Etta made coffee and Cesare insisted on going out for a half dozen pastries.

He said as they were eating that he was considering emigrating if nothing better turned up soon. After a pause he said he had decided he had given more than his share to the dead. "I've been faithful to her memory but I have to think of myself once in a while. There comes a time when one has to return to life. It's only natural. Where there's life there's life."

She lowered her eyes and sipped her coffee.

Cesare set down his cup and got up. He put on his coat and thanked her. As he was buttoning his overcoat he said he would drop by again when he was in the neighborhood. He had a journalist friend who lived close by.

"Don't forget I'm still in mourning," Etta said.

He looked up at her respectfully. "Who can forget that, signora? Who would want to so long as you mourn?"

She then felt uneasy.

"You know my story." She spoke as though she was explaining again.

"I know," he said, "that we were both betrayed. They died and we suffer. My wife ate flowers and I belch."

"They suffer too. If Armando must suffer, I don't want it to be about me. I want him to feel that I'm still married to him." Her eyes were moist again.

"He's dead, signora. The marriage is over," Cesare said. "There's no marriage without his presence unless you expect the Holy Ghost." He spoke dryly, adding quietly, "Your needs are different from a dead man's, you're a healthy woman. Let's face the facts."

"Not spiritually," she said quickly.

"Spiritually and physically, there's no love in death."

She blushed and spoke in excitement. "There's love for the dead. Let him feel that I'm paying for my sin at the same time he is for his. To help him into heaven I keep myself pure. Let him feel that."

Cesare nodded and left, but Etta, after he had gone, continued to be troubled. She felt uneasy, could not define her mood, and stayed longer than usual at Armando's grave when she went the next day. She promised herself not to see Cesare again. In the next weeks she became a little miserly.

The journalist returned one evening almost a month later and Etta stood at the door in a way that indicated he would not be asked in. She had seen herself doing this if he appeared. But Cesare, with his hat in his hand, suggested a short stroll. The suggestion seemed so modest that she agreed. They walked down the Via Nomentana, Etta wearing her highest heels, Cesare unself-consciously talking. He wore small patent-leather shoes and smoked as they strolled.

It was already early December, still late autumn rather than winter. A few leaves clung to a few trees and a warmish mist hung in the air. For a while Cesare talked of the political situation, but after an espresso in a bar on the Via Venti Settembre, as they were walking back he brought up the subject she had hoped to avoid. Cesare seemed suddenly to have lost his calm, unable to restrain what he had been planning to say. His voice was intense, his gestures impatient, his dark eyes restless. Although his outburst frightened her she could do nothing to prevent it.

"Signora," he said, "wherever your husband is you're not helping him by putting this penance on yourself. To help him, the best thing you can do is take up your normal life. Otherwise he will continue to suffer doubly, once for something he was guilty of, and the second time for the unfair burden your denial of life imposes on him."

"I am repenting my sins, not punishing him." She was too disturbed to say more, considered walking home wordless, then slamming the front door in his face; but she heard herself hastily saying, "If we became intimate it would be like adultery. We would be betraying the dead."

"Why is it you see everything in reverse?"

Cesare had stopped under a tree and almost jumped as he spoke. "They—*they* betrayed us. If you'll pardon me, signora, the truth is my wife was a pig. Your husband was a pig. We mourn because we hate them. Let's have the dignity to face the facts."

"No more," she moaned, hastily walking on. "Don't say anything else, I don't want to hear it."

"Etta," said Cesare passionately, walking after her, "this is my last word and then I'll nail my tongue to my jaw. Just remember this. If Our Lord Himself, this minute, let Armando rise from the dead to take up his life on earth, tonight—he would be lying in his cousin's bed."

She began to cry. Etta walked on, crying, realizing the truth of his remark. Cesare seemed to have said all he had wanted to, gently held her arm, breathing heavily as he escorted her back to her apartment. At the outer door, as she was trying to think how to get rid of him, how to end this, without waiting a minute he tipped his hat and walked off.

For more than a week Etta went through many torments. She felt a passionate desire to sleep with Cesare. Overnight her body became a torch. Her dreams were erotic. She saw Armando naked in bed with Laura, and in the same bed she saw herself with Cesare, clasping his body to hers. But she resisted—prayed, confessed her most lustful thoughts, and stayed for hours at Armando's grave to calm her mind.

Cesare knocked at her door one night, and because she was repelled when he suggested the marriage bed, went with him to his rooms. Though she felt guilty afterwards she continued to visit Armando's grave, though less frequently, and she didn't tell Cesare that she had been to the cemetery when she went to his flat afterwards. Nor did he ask her, nor talk about his wife or Armando.

At first her uneasiness was intense. Etta felt as though she had committed adultery against the memory of her husband, but when she told herself over and over—there was no husband, he was dead; there was no husband, she was alone—she began to believe it. There was no husband, there was only his memory. She was not committing adultery. She was a lonely woman and had a lover, a widower, a gentle and affectionate man.

One night as they were lying in bed she asked Cesare about the possibility of marriage and he said that love was more important. They both knew how marriage destroyed love.

And when, two months later, she found she was pregnant and hurried that morning to Cesare's rooms to tell him, the journalist, in his pajamas, calmed her. "Let's not regret human life."

"It's your child," said Etta.

"I'll acknowledge it as mine," Cesare said, and Etta went home disturbed but happy.

The next day, when she returned at her usual hour, after having told Armando at his grave that she was at last going to have a baby, Cesare was gone.

"Moved," the landlady said, with a poof of her hand, and she didn't know where.

Though Etta's heart hurt and she mourned the loss of Cesare, try as she would she could not, even with the life in her womb, escape thinking of herself as a confirmed sinner; and she never returned to the cemetery to stand again at Armando's grave.

Black Is My Favorite Color

CHARITY QUIETNESS sits in the toilet eating her two hard-boiled eggs while I'm having my ham sandwich and coffee in the kitchen. That's how it goes, only don't get the idea of ghettoes. If there's a ghetto I'm the one that's in it. She's my cleaning woman from Father Divine and comes in once a week to my small three-room apartment on my day off from the liquor store. "Peace," she says to me, "Father reached on down and took me right up in Heaven." She's a small person with a flat body, frizzy hair, and a quiet face that the light shines out of, and Mama had such eyes before she died. The first time Charity Quietness came in to clean, a little more than a year and a half, I made the mistake to ask her to sit down at the kitchen table with me and eat her lunch. I was still feeling not so hot after Ornita left, but I'm the kind of a man—Nat Lime, forty-four, a bachelor with a daily growing bald spot on the back of my head, and I could lose frankly fifteen pounds—who enjoys company so long as he has it. So she cooked up her two hard-boiled eggs and sat down and took a small bite out of one of them. But after a minute she stopped chewing and she got up and carried the eggs in a cup to the bathroom, and since then she eats there. I said to her more than once, "Okay, Charity Quietness, so have it your way, eat the eggs in the kitchen by yourself and I'll eat when you're done," but she smiles absentminded, and eats in the toilet. It's my fate with colored people.

Although black is still my favorite color you wouldn't know it from my luck except in short quantities, even though I do all right in the liquor store business in Harlem, on Eighth Avenue between 110th and 111th. I speak with respect. A large part of my life I've had dealings with Negro people, most on a business basis but sometimes for friendly reasons with genuine feeling on both sides. I'm drawn to them. At this time of my life I should have one or two good colored friends, but the fault isn't necessarily mine. If they knew what was in my heart toward them, but how can you tell that to anybody nowadays?

I've tried more than once but the language of the heart either is a dead language or else nobody understands it the way you speak it. Very few. What I'm saying is, personally for me there's only one human color and that's the color of blood. I like a black person if not because he's black, then because I'm white. It comes to the same thing. If I wasn't white my first choice would be black. I'm satisfied to be white because I have no other choice. Anyway, I got an eye for color. I appreciate. Who wants everybody to be the same? Maybe it's like some kind of a talent. Nat Lime might be a liquor dealer in Harlem, but once in the jungle in New Guinea in the Second World War, I got the idea, when I shot at a running Jap and missed him, that I had some kind of a talent, though maybe it's the kind where you have a good idea now and then, but in the end what do they come to? After all, it's a strange world.

Where Charity Quietness eats her eggs makes me think about Buster Wilson when we were both boys in the Williamsburg section of Brooklyn. There was this long block of rundown dirty frame houses in the middle of a not-so-hot white neighborhood full of pushcarts. The Negro houses looked to me like they had been born and died there, dead not long after the beginning of the world. I lived on the next street. My father was a cutter with arthritis in both hands, big red knuckles and fingers so swollen he didn't cut, and my mother was the one who went to work. She sold paper bags from a secondhand pushcart on Ellery Street. We didn't starve but nobody ate chicken unless we were sick, or the chicken was. This was my first acquaintance with a lot of black people and I used to poke around on their poor block. I think I thought, brother, if there can be like this, what can't there be? I mean I caught an early idea what life was about. Anyway, I met Buster Wilson there. He used to play marbles by himself. I sat on the curb across the street, watching him shoot one marble lefty and the other one righty. The hand that won picked up the marbles. It wasn't so much of a game but he didn't ask me to come over. My idea was to be friendly, only he never encouraged, he discouraged. Why did I pick him out for a friend? Maybe because I had no others then, we were new in the neighborhood, from Manhattan. Also I liked his type. Buster did everything alone. He was a skinny kid and his brothers' clothes hung on him like worn-out potato sacks. He was a beanpole boy, about twelve, and I was then ten. His arms and legs were burnt-out matchsticks. He always wore a brown wool sweater, one arm half unraveled, the other went down to the wrist. His long and narrow head had a white part cut straight in the short woolly hair, maybe with a ruler there, by his father, a barber but too drunk to stay a barber. In those days though I had little myself I was old enough to know who was better off, and the whole block of colored houses made me feel bad in the daylight. But I went there as much as I could because the street was full of life. In the night it looked different, it's hard to tell a cripple in the dark. Sometimes I was afraid to walk by the houses when they were dark and quiet. I was afraid there were people looking at me that I couldn't see. I liked it better when they had parties at night and everybody had a good time. The musicians played their banjos and saxophones and the houses shook with the music and laughing. The young girls, with their pretty dresses and ribbons in their hair, caught me in my throat when I saw them through the windows.

But with the parties came drinking and fights. Sundays were bad days after the Saturday night parties. I remember once that Buster's father, also long and loose, always wearing a dirty gray Homburg hat, chased another black man in the street with a half-inch chisel. The other one, maybe five feet high, lost his shoe and when they wrestled on the ground he was already bleeding through his suit, a thick red blood smearing the sidewalk. I was frightened by the blood and wanted to pour it back in the man who was bleeding from the chisel. On another time Buster's father was playing in a crap game with two big bouncy red dice, in the back of an alley between two middle houses. Then about six men started fist-fighting there, and they ran out of the alley and hit each other in the street. The neighbors, including children, came out and watched, everybody afraid but nobody moving to do anything. I saw the same thing near my store in Harlem, years later, a big crowd watching two men in the street, their breaths hanging in the air on a winter night, murdering each other with switch knives, but nobody moved to call a cop. I didn't either. Anyway, I was just a young kid but I still remember how the cops drove up in a police paddy wagon and broke up the fight by hitting everybody they could hit with big nightsticks. This was in the days before La Guardia. Most of the fighters were knocked out cold, only one or two got away. Buster's father started to run back in his house but a cop ran after him and cracked him on his Homburg hat with a club, right on the front porch. Then the Negro men were lifted up by the cops, one at the arms and the other at the feet, and they heaved them in the paddy wagon. Buster's father hit the back of the wagon and fell, with his nose spouting very red blood, on top of three other men. I personally couldn't stand it, I was scared of the human race so I ran home, but I remember Buster watching without any expression in his eyes. I stole an extra fifteen cents from my mother's pocketbook and I ran back and asked Buster if he wanted to go to the movies, I would pay. He said yes. This was the first time he talked to me.

So we went more than once to the movies. But we never got to be friends. Maybe because it was a one-way proposition—from me to him. Which includes my invitations to go with me, my (poor mother's) movie money, Hershey chocolate bars, watermelon slices, even my best Nick Carter and Merriwell books that I spent hours picking up in the junk shops, and that he never gave me back. Once, he let me go in his house to get a match so we could smoke some butts we found, but it smelled so heavy, so impossible, I died till I got out of there. What I saw in the way of furniture I won't mention—the best was falling apart in pieces. Maybe we went to the movies all together five or six matinees that spring and in the summertime, but when the shows were over he usually walked home by himself.

"Why don't you wait for me, Buster?" I said. "We're both going in the same direction."

But he was walking ahead and didn't hear me. Anyway he didn't answer.

One day when I wasn't expecting it he hit me in the teeth. I felt like crying but not because of the pain. I spit blood and said, "What did you hit me for? What did I do to you?"

"Because you a Jew bastard. Take your Jew movies and your Jew candy and shove them up your Jew ass."

And he ran away.

I thought to myself how was I to know he didn't like the movies. When I was a man I thought, you can't force it.

Years later, in the prime of my life, I met Mrs. Ornita Harris. She was standing by herself under an open umbrella at the bus stop, crosstown 110th, and I picked up her green glove that she had dropped on the wet sidewalk. It was in the end of November. Before I could ask her was it hers, she grabbed the glove out of my hand, closed her umbrella, and stepped in the bus. I got on right after her. I was annoyed so I said, "If you'll pardon me, Miss, there's no law that you have to say thanks, but at least don't make a criminal out of me."

"Well, I'm sorry," she said, "but I don't like white men trying to do me favors."

I tipped my hat and that was that. In ten minutes I got off the bus but she was already gone.

Who expected to see her again, but I did. She came into my store about a week later for a bottle of Scotch.

"I would offer you a discount," I told her, "but I know you don't like a certain kind of a favor and I'm not looking for a slap in the face."

Then she recognized me and got a little embarrassed.

"I'm sorry I misunderstood you that day."

"So mistakes happen."

The result was she took the discount. I gave her a dollar off.

She used to come in every two weeks for a fifth of Haig & Haig. Sometimes I waited on her, sometimes my helpers, Jimmy or Mason, also colored, but I said to give the discount. They both looked at me but I had nothing to be ashamed. In the spring when she came in we used to talk once in a while. She was a slim woman, dark, but not the most dark, about thirty years I would say, also well built, with a combination nice legs and a good-size bosom that I like. Her face was pretty, with big eyes and high cheekbones, but lips a little thick and nose a little broad. Sometimes she didn't feel like talking, she paid for the bottle, less discount, and walked out. Her eyes were tired and she didn't look to me like a happy woman.

I found out her husband was once a window cleaner on the big buildings, but one day his safety belt broke and he fell fifteen stories. After the funeral she got a job as a manicurist in a Times Square barber shop. I told her I was a bachelor and lived with my mother in a small three-room apartment on West Eighty-third near Broadway. My mother had cancer, and Ornita said she was very sorry.

One night in July we went out together. How that happened I'm still not so sure. I guess I asked her and she didn't say no. Where do you go out with a Negro woman? We went to the Village. We had a good dinner and walked in Washington Square Park. It was a hot night. Nobody was surprised when they saw us, nobody looked at us like we were against the law. If they looked maybe they saw my new lightweight suit that I bought yesterday and my shiny bald spot when we walked under a lamp, also how pretty she was for a man my type. We went in a movie on West Eighth Street. I didn't want to go in but she said she had heard about the picture. We went in like strangers and we came out like strangers. I wondered what was in her mind and I thought to myself, whatever is in there it's not a certain white man that I know. All night long we went together like we were chained. After the movie she wouldn't let me take her back to Harlem. When I put her in a taxi she asked me, "Why did we bother?"

For the steak, I thought of saying. Instead I said, "You're worth the bother."

"Thanks anyway."

Kiddo, I thought to myself after the taxi left, you just found out what's what, now the best thing is forget her.

It's easy to say. In August we went out the second time. That was the night she wore a purple dress and I thought to myself, my God, what colors. Who paints that picture paints a masterpiece. Everybody looked at us but I had pleasure. That night when she took off her dress it was in a furnished room I had the sense to rent a few days before. With my sick mother, I couldn't ask her to come to my apartment, and she didn't want me to go home with her where she lived with her brother's family on West 115th near Lenox Avenue. Under her purple dress she wore a black slip, and when she took that off she had white underwear. When she took off the white underwear she was black again. But I know where the next white was, if you want to call it white. And that was the night I think I fell in love with her, the first time in my life, though I have liked one or two nice girls I used to go with when I was a boy. It was a serious proposition. I'm the kind of a man when I think of love I'm thinking of marriage. I guess that's why I am a bachelor.

That same week I had a holdup in my place, two big men—both black—with revolvers. One got excited when I rang open the cash register so he could take the money, and he hit me over the ear with his gun. I stayed in the hospital a couple of weeks. Otherwise I was insured. Ornita came to see me. She sat on a chair without talking much. Finally I saw she was uncomfortable so I suggested she ought to go home.

"I'm sorry it happened," she said.

"Don't talk like it's your fault."

When I got out of the hospital my mother was dead. She was a wonderful person. My father died when I was thirteen and all by herself she kept the family alive and together. I sat shiva for a week and remembered how she sold paper bags on her pushcart. I remembered her life and what she tried to teach me. Nathan, she said, if you ever forget you are a Jew a goy will remind you. Mama, I said, rest in peace on this subject. But if I do something you don't like, remember, on earth it's harder than where you are. Then when my week of mourning was finished, one night I said, "Ornita, let's get married. We're both honest people and if you love me like I love you it won't be such a bad time. If you don't like New York I'll sell out here and we'll move some place else. Maybe to San Francisco where nobody knows us. I was there for a week in the Second War and I saw white and colored living together."

"Nat," she answered me, "I like you but I'd be afraid. My husband woulda killed me."

"Your husband is dead."

"Not in my memory."

"In that case I'll wait."

"Do you know what it'd be like—I mean the life we could expect?"

"Ornita," I said, "I'm the kind of a man, if he picks his own way of life he's satisfied."

"What about children? Were you looking forward to half-Jewish polka dots?"

"I was looking forward to children."

"I can't," she said.

Can't is can't. I saw she was afraid and the best thing was not to push. Sometimes when we met she was so nervous that whatever we did she couldn't enjoy it. At the same time I still thought I had a chance. We were together more and more. I got rid of my furnished room and she came to my apartment—I gave away Mama's bed and bought a new one. She stayed with me all day on Sundays. When she wasn't so nervous she was affectionate, and if I know what love is, I had it. We went out a couple of times a week, the same way—usually I met her in Times Square and sent her home in a taxi, but I talked more about marriage and she talked less against it. One night she told me she was still trying to convince herself but she was almost convinced. I took an inventory of my liquor stock so I could put the store up for sale.

Ornita knew what I was doing. One day she quit her job, the next she took it back. She also went away a week to visit her sister in Philadelphia for a little rest. She came back tired but said maybe. Maybe is maybe so I'll wait. The way she said it, it was closer to yes. That was the winter two years ago. When she was in Philadelphia I called up a friend of mine from the army, now a CPA, and told him I would appreciate an invitation for an evening. He knew why. His wife said yes right away. When Ornita came back we went there. The wife made a fine dinner. It wasn't a bad time and they told us to come again. Ornita had a few drinks. She looked relaxed, wonderful. Later, because of a twenty-four-hour taxi strike I had to take her home on the subway. When we got to the 116th Street station she told me to go back on the train, and she would walk the couple of blocks to her house. I didn't like a woman walking alone on the streets at that time of the night. She said she never had any trouble but I insisted nothing doing. I said I would walk to her stoop with her and when she went upstairs I would go to the subway.

On the way there, on 115th in the middle of the block before Lenox, we were stopped by three men—maybe they were boys. One had a black hat with a half-inch brim, one a green cloth hat, and the third wore a black leather cap. The green hat was wearing a short coat and the other two had long ones. It was under a streetlight but the leather cap snapped a six-inch switchblade open in the light.

"What you doin' with this white son of a bitch?" he said to Ornita.

"I'm minding my own business," she answered him, "and I wish you would too."

"Boys," I said, "we're all brothers. I'm a reliable merchant in the neighborhood. This young lady is my dear friend. We don't want any trouble. Please let us pass."

"You talk like a Jew landlord," said the green hat. "Fifty a week for a single room."

"No charge fo' the rats," said the half-inch brim.

"Believe me, I'm no landlord. My store is Nathan's Liquors between Hundred Tenth and Eleventh. I also have two colored clerks, Mason and Jimmy, and they will tell you I pay good wages as well as I give discounts to certain customers."

"Shut your mouth, Jewboy," said the leather cap, and he moved the knife back and forth in front of my coat button. "No more black pussy for you."

"Speak with respect about this lady, please."

I got slapped on my mouth.

"That ain't no lady," said the long face in the half-inch brim, "that's black pussy. She deserve to have evvy bit of her hair shave off. How you like to have evvy bit of your hair shave off, black pussy?"

"Please leave me and this gentleman alone or I'm gonna scream long and loud. That's my house three doors down."

They slapped her. I never heard such a scream. Like her husband was falling fifteen stories.

I hit the one that slapped her and the next I knew I was laying in the gutter with a pain in my head. I thought, goodbye, Nat, they'll stab me for sure, but all they did was take my wallet and run in three directions.

Ornita walked back with me to the subway and she wouldn't let me go home with her again.

"Just get home safely."

She looked terrible. Her face was gray and I still remembered her scream. It was a terrible winter night, very cold February, and it took me an hour and ten minutes to get home. I felt bad for leaving her but what could I do?

We had a date downtown the next night but she didn't show up, the first time.

In the morning I called her in her place of business.

"For God's sake, Ornita, if we got married and moved away we wouldn't have the kind of trouble that we had. We wouldn't come in that neighborhood any more."

"Yes, we would. I have family there and don't want to move anyplace else. The truth of it is I can't marry you, Nat. I got troubles enough of my own."

"I coulda sworn you love me."

"Maybe I do but I can't marry you."

"For God's sake, why?"

"I got enough trouble of my own."

I went that night in a cab to her brother's house to see her. He was a quiet man with a thin mustache. "She gone," he said, "left for a long visit to some close relatives in the South. She said to tell you she appreciate your intentions but didn't think it will work out."

"Thank you kindly," I said.

Don't ask me how I got home.

Once, on Eighth Avenue, a couple of blocks from my store, I saw a blind man with a white cane tapping on the sidewalk. I figured we were going in the same direction so I took his arm.

"I can tell you're white," he said.

A heavy colored woman with a full shopping bag rushed after us.

"Never mind," she said, "I know where he live."

She pushed me with her shoulder and I hurt my leg on the fire hydrant.

That's how it is. I give my heart and they kick me in my teeth.

"Charity Quietness—you hear me?—come out of that goddamn toilet!"

The German Refugee

Oskar Gassner sits in his cotton-mesh undershirt and summer bathrobe at the window of his stuffy, hot, dark hotel room on West Tenth Street as I cautiously knock. Outside, across the sky, a late-June green twilight fades in darkness. The refugee fumbles for the light and stares at me, hiding despair but not pain.

I was in those days a poor student and would brashly attempt to teach anybody anything for a buck an hour, although I have since learned better. Mostly I gave English lessons to recently arrived refugees. The college sent me, I had acquired a little experience. Already a few of my students were trying their broken English, theirs and mine, in the American marketplace. I was then just twenty, on my way into my senior year in college, a skinny, life-hungry kid, eating himself waiting for the next world war to start. It was a miserable cheat. Here I was panting to get going, and across the ocean Adolf Hitler, in black boots and a square mustache, was tearing up and spitting at all the flowers. Will I ever forget what went on with Danzig that summer?

Times were still hard from the Depression but I made a little living from the poor refugees. They were all over uptown Broadway in 1939. I had four I tutored—Karl Otto Alp, the former film star; Wolfgang Novak, once a brilliant economist; Friedrich Wilhelm Wolff, who had taught medieval history at Heidelberg; and after the night I met him in his disordered cheap hotel room, Oskar Gassner, the Berlin critic and journalist, at one time on the *Acht Uhr Abendblatt*. They were accomplished men. I had my nerve associating with them, but that's what a world crisis does for people, they get educated.

Oskar was maybe fifty, his thick hair turning gray. He had a big face and heavy hands. His shoulders sagged. His eyes, too, were heavy, a clouded blue; and as he stared at me after I had identified myself, doubt spread in them like underwater currents. It was as if, on seeing me, he had again been defeated. I had to wait until he came to. I stayed at the door in silence. In such cases I would rather be elsewhere, but I had to make a living. Finally he opened the door and I entered. Rather, he released it and I was in. "Bitte"—he offered me a seat and didn't know where to sit himself. He would attempt to say something and then stop, as though it could not possibly be said. The room was cluttered with clothing, boxes of books he had managed to get out of Germany, and some paintings. Oskar sat on a box and attempted to fan himself with his meaty hand. "Zis heat," he muttered, forcing his mind to the deed. "Impozzible. I do not know such heat." It was bad enough for me but terrible for him. He had difficulty breathing. He tried to speak, lifted a hand, and let it drop. He breathed as though he was fighting a war; and maybe he won because after ten minutes we sat and slowly talked.

Like most educated Germans Oskar had at one time studied English. Although he was certain he couldn't say a word he managed to put together a fairly decent, if sometimes comical English sentence. He misplaced consonants, mixed up nouns and verbs, and mangled idioms, yet we were able at once to communicate. We conversed in English, with an occasional assist by me in pidgin-German or Yiddish, what he called "Jiddish." He had been to America before, last year for a short visit. He had come a month before Kristallnacht, when the Nazis shattered the Jewish store windows and burnt all the synagogues, to see if he could find a job for himself; he had no relatives in America and getting a job would permit him quickly to enter the country. He had been promised something, not in journalism, but with the help of a foundation, as a lecturer. Then he returned to Berlin, and after a frightening delay of six months was permitted to emigrate. He had sold whatever he could, managed to get some paintings, gifts of Bauhaus friends, and some boxes of books out by bribing two Dutch border guards; he had said goodbye to his wife and left the accursed country. He gazed at me with cloudy eyes. "We parted amicably," he said in German, "my wife was gentile. Her mother was an appalling anti-Semite. They returned to live in Stettin." I asked no questions. Gentile is gentile, Germany is Germany.

His new job was in the Institute for Public Studies, in New York. He was to give a lecture a week in the fall term and during next spring, a course, in English translation, in "The Literature of the Weimar Republic." He had never taught before and was afraid to. He was in that way to be introduced to the public, but the thought of giving the lecture in English just about paralyzed him. He didn't see how he could do it. "How is it pozzible? I cannot say two words. I cannot pronounziate. I will make a fool of myself." His melancholy deepened. Already in the two months since his arrival, and a round of diminishingly expensive hotel rooms, he had had two English tutors, and I was the third. The others had given him up, he said, because his progress was so poor, and he thought he also depressed them. He asked me whether I felt I could do something for him, or should he go to a speech specialist, someone, say, who charged five dollars an hour, and beg his assistance? "You could try him," I said, "and then come back to me." In those days I figured what I knew, I knew. At that he managed a smile. Still, I wanted him to make up his mind or it would be no confidence down the line. He said, after a while, he would stay with me. If he went to the five-dollar professor it might help his tongue but not his appetite. He would have no money left to eat with. The Institute had paid him in advance for the summer, but it was only three hundred dollars and all he had.

He looked at me dully. "Ich weiss nicht, wie ich weiter machen soll."

I figured it was time to move past the first step. Either we did that quickly or it would be like drilling rock for a long time.

"Let's stand at the mirror," I said.

He rose with a sigh and stood there beside me, I thin, elongated, red-headed, praying for success, his and mine; Oskar uneasy, fearful, finding it hard to face either of us in the faded round glass above his dresser.

"Please," I said to him, "could you say 'right'?"

"Ghight," he gargled.

"No—right. You put your tongue here." I showed him where as he tensely watched the mirror. I tensely watched him. "The tip of it curls behind the ridge on top, like this."

He placed his tongue where I showed him.

"Please," I said, "now say right."

Oskar's tongue fluttered. "Rright."

"That's good. Now say 'treasure'—that's harder."

"Tgheasure."

"The tongue goes up in front, not in the back of the mouth. Look."

He tried, his brow wet, eyes straining, "Trreasure."

"That's it."

"A miracle," Oskar murmured.

I said if he had done that he could do the rest.

We went for a bus ride up Fifth Avenue and then walked for a while around Central Park Lake. He had put on his German hat, with its hatband bow at the back, a broad-lapeled wool suit, a necktie twice as wide as the one I was wearing, and walked with a small-footed waddle. The night wasn't bad, it had got a bit cooler. There were a few large stars in the sky and they made me sad.

"Do you sink I will succezz?"

"Why not?" I asked.

Later he bought me a bottle of beer.

To many of these people, articulate as they were, the great loss was the loss of language—that they could not say what was in them to say. You have some subtle thought and it comes out like a piece of broken bottle. They could, of course, manage to communicate, but just to communicate was frustrating. As Karl Otto Alp, the ex-film star who became a buyer for Macy's, put it years later, "I felt like a child, or worse, often like a moron. I am left with myself unexpressed. What I know, indeed, what I am, becomes to me a burden. My tongue hangs useless." The same with Oskar it figures. There was a terrible sense of useless tongue, and I think the reason for his trouble with his other tutors was that to keep from drowning in things unsaid he wanted to swallow the ocean in a gulp: today he would learn English and tomorrow wow them with an impeccable Fourth of July speech, followed by a successful lecture at the Institute for Public Studies.

We performed our lessons slowly, step by step, everything in its place. After Oskar moved to a two-room apartment in a house on West Eighty-fifth Street, near the Drive, we met three times a week at four-thirty, worked an hour and a half, then, since it was too hot to cook, had supper at the Seventy-second Street Automat and conversed on my time. The lessons we divided into three parts: diction exercises and reading aloud; then grammar, because Oskar felt the necessity of it, and composition correction; with conversation, as I said, thrown in at supper. So far as I could see he was coming along. None of these exercises was giving him as much trouble as they apparently had in the past. He seemed to be learning and his mood lightened. There were moments of elation as he heard his accent flying off. For instance when sink became think. He stopped calling himself "hopelezz," and I became his "bezt teacher," a little joke I liked.

Neither of us said much about the lecture he had to give early in October, and I kept my fingers crossed. It was somehow to come out of what we were doing daily, I think I felt, but exactly how, I had no idea; and to tell the truth, though I didn't say so to Oskar, the lecture frightened me. That and the ten more to follow during the fall term. Later, when I learned that he had been attempting, with the help of the dictionary, to write in English and had produced "a complete disahster," I suggested maybe he ought to stick to German and we could afterwards both try to put it into passable English. I was cheating when I said that because my German is meager, enough to read simple stuff but certainly not good enough for serious translation; anyway, the idea was to get Oskar into production and worry about translating later. He sweated with it, from enervating morning to exhausted night, but no matter what language he tried, though he had been a professional writer for a generation and knew his subject cold, the lecture refused to move past page one.

It was a sticky, hot July, and the heat didn't help at all.

I had met Oskar at the end of June, and by the seventeenth of July we were no longer doing lessons. They had foundered on the "impozzible" lecture. He had worked on it each day in frenzy and growing despair. After writing more than a hundred opening pages he furiously flung his pen against the wall, shouting he could not longer write in that filthy tongue. He cursed the German language. He hated the damned country and the damned people. After that, what was bad became worse. When he gave up attempting to write the lecture, he stopped making progress in English. He seemed to forget what he already knew. His tongue thickened and the accent returned in all its fruitiness. The little he had to say was in handcuffed and tortured English. The only German I heard him speak was in a whisper to himself. I doubt he knew he was talking it. That ended our formal work together, though I did drop in every other day or so to sit with him. For hours he sat motionless in a large green velour armchair, hot enough to broil in, and through tall windows stared at the colorless sky above Eighty-fifth Street with a wet depressed eye.

Then once he said to me, "If I do not this legture prepare, I will take my life."

"Let's begin, Oskar," I said. "You dictate and I'll write. The ideas count, not the spelling."

He didn't answer so I stopped talking.

He had plunged into an involved melancholy. We sat for hours, often in profound silence. This was alarming to me, though I had already had some experience with such depression. Wolfgang Novak, the economist, though English came more easily to him, was another. His problems arose mainly, I think, from physical illness. And he felt a greater sense of the lost country than Oskar. Sometimes in the early evening I persuaded Oskar to come with me for a short walk on the Drive. The tail end of sunsets over the Palisades seemed to appeal to him. At least he looked. He would put on full regalia—hat, suit coat, tie, no matter how hot or what I suggested—and we went slowly down the stairs, I wondering whether he would make it to the bottom.

We walked slowly uptown, stopping to sit on a bench and watch night rise above the Hudson. When we returned to his room, if I sensed he had loosened up a bit, we listened to music on the radio; but if I tried to sneak in a news broadcast, he said to me, "Please, I cannot more stand of world misery." I shut off the radio. He was right, it was a time of no good news. I squeezed my brain. What could I tell him? Was it good news to be alive? Who could argue the point? Sometimes I read aloud to him—I remember he liked the first part of *Life on the*

Mississippi. We still went to the Automat once or twice a week, he perhaps out of habit, because he didn't feel like going anywhere—I to get him out of his room. Oskar ate little, he toyed with a spoon. His eyes looked as though they had been squirted with a dark dye.

Once after a momentary cooling rainstorm we sat on newspapers on a wet bench overlooking the river and Oskar at last began to talk. In tormented English he conveyed his intense and everlasting hatred of the Nazis for destroying his career, uprooting his life, and flinging him like a piece of bleeding meat to the hawks. He cursed them thickly, the German nation, an inhuman, conscienceless, merciless people. "They are pigs mazquerading as peacogs," he said. "I feel certain that my wife, in her heart, was a Jew hater." It was a terrible bitterness, and eloquence beyond the words he spoke. He became silent again. I wanted to hear more about his wife but decided not to ask.

Afterwards in the dark, Oskar confessed that he had attempted suicide during his first week in America. He was living, at the end of May, in a small hotel, and had one night filled himself with barbiturates; but his phone had fallen off the table and the hotel operator had sent up the elevator boy, who found him unconscious and called the police. He was revived in the hospital.

"I did not mean to do it," he said, "it was a mistage."

"Don't ever think of it," I said, "it's total defeat."

"I don't," he said wearily, "because it is so arduouz to come bag to life."

"Please, for any reason whatever."

Afterwards when we were walking, he surprised me by saying, "Maybe we ought to try now the legture onze more."

We trudged back to the house and he sat at his hot desk, I trying to read as he slowly began to reconstruct the first page of his lecture. He wrote, of course, in German.

He got nowhere. We were back to sitting in silence in the heat. Sometimes, after a few minutes, I had to take off before his mood overcame mine. One afternoon I came unwillingly up the stairs—there were times I felt momentary surges of irritation with him—and was frightened to find Oskar's door ajar.

When I knocked no one answered. As I stood there, chilled down the spine, I realized I was thinking about the possibility of his attempting suicide again. "Oskar?" I went into the apartment, looked into both rooms and the bathroom, but he wasn't there. I thought he might have drifted out to get something from a store and took the opportunity to look quickly around. There was nothing startling in the medicine chest, no pills but aspirin, no iodine. Thinking, for some reason, of a gun, I searched his desk drawer. In it I found a thin-paper airmail letter from Germany. Even if I had wanted to, I couldn't read the handwriting, but as I held it in my hand I did make out a sentence: "Ich bin dir siebenundzwanzig Jahre treu gewesen." There was no gun in the drawer. I shut it and stopped looking. It had occurred to me if you want to kill yourself all you need is a straight pin. When Oskar returned he said he had been sitting in the public library, unable to read.

Now we are once more enacting the changeless scene, curtain rising on two speechless characters in a furnished apartment, I in a straight-back chair, Oskar in the velour armchair that smothered rather than supported him, his flesh gray, the big gray face unfocused, sagging. I reached over to switch on the radio but he barely looked at me in a way that begged no. I then got up to leave but Oskar, clearing his throat, thickly asked me to stay. I stayed, thinking, was there more to this than I could see into? His problems, God knows, were real enough, but could there be something more than a refugee's displacement, alienation, financial insecurity, being in a strange land without friends or a speakable tongue? My speculation was the old one: not all drown in this ocean, why does he? After a while I shaped the thought and asked him was there something below the surface, invisible? I was full of this thing from college, and wondered if there mightn't be some unknown quantity in his depression that a psychiatrist maybe might help him with, enough to get him started on his lecture.

He meditated on this and after a few minutes haltingly said he had been psychoanalyzed in Vienna as a young man. "Just the jusual drek," he said, "fears and fantazies that afterwaards no longer bothered me."

"They don't now?"

"Not."

"You've written many articles and lectures before," I said. "What I can't understand, though I know how hard the situation is, is why you can never get past page one."

He half lifted his hand. "It is a paralyzis of my will. The whole legture is clear in my mind, but the minute I write down a single word—or in English or in German—I have a terrible fear I will not be able to write the negst. As though someone has thrown a stone at a window and the whole house—the whole idea zmashes. This repeats, until I am dezperate."

He said the fear grew as he worked that he would die before he completed the lecture, or if not that, he would write it so disgracefully he would wish for death. The fear immobilized him.

"I have lozt faith. I do not—not longer possezz my former value of myself. In my life there has been too much illusion."

I tried to believe what I was saying: "Have confidence, the feeling will pass."

"Confidenze I have not. For this and alzo whatever elze I have lozt I thank the Nazis."

It was by then mid-August and things were growing steadily worse wherever one looked. The Poles were mobilizing for war. Oskar hardly moved. I was full of worries though I pretended calm weather.

He sat in his massive armchair, breathing like a wounded animal.

"Who can write aboud Walt Whitman in such terrible times?"

"Why don't you change the subject?"

"It mages no differenze what is the subject. It is all uzelezz."

I came every day, as a friend, neglecting my other students and therefore my livelihood. I had a panicky feeling that if things went on as they were going they would end in Oskar's suicide; and I felt a frenzied desire to prevent that. What's more, I was sometimes afraid I was myself becoming melancholy, a new talent, call it, of taking less pleasure in my little pleasures. And the heat continued, oppressive, relentless. We thought of escape into the country, but neither of us had the money. One day I bought Oskar a secondhand electric fan—wondering why we hadn't thought of that before—and he sat in the breeze for hours each day, until after a week, shortly after the Soviet-Nazi non-aggression pact was signed, the motor gave out. He could not sleep at night and sat at his desk with a wet towel on his head, still attempting to write the lecture. He wrote reams on a treadmill, it came out nothing. When he slept in exhaustion he had fantastic frightening dreams of the Nazis inflicting torture, sometimes forcing him to look upon the corpses of those they had slain. In one dream he told me about he had gone back to Germany to visit his wife. She wasn't home and he had been directed to a cemetery. There, though the tombstone read another name, her blood seeped out of the earth above her shallow grave. He groaned aloud at the memory.

Afterwards he told me something about her. They had met as students, lived together, and were married at twenty-three. It wasn't a very happy marriage. She had turned into a sickly woman, unable to have children. "Something was wrong with her interior strugture."

Though I asked no questions, Oskar said, "I offered her to come with me here, but she refused this."

"For what reason?"

"She did not think I wished her to come."

"Did you?" I asked.

"Not," he said.

He explained he had lived with her for almost twenty-seven years under difficult circumstances. She had been ambivalent about their Jewish friends and his relatives, though outwardly she seemed not a prejudiced person. But her mother was always a dreadful anti-Semite.

"I have nothing to blame myzelf," Oskar said.

He took to his bed. I took to the New York Public Library. I read some of the German poets he was trying to write about, in English translation. Then I read *Leaves of Grass* and wrote down what I thought one or two of them had got from Whitman. One day, toward the end of August, I brought Oskar what I had written. It was in good part guessing, but my idea wasn't to do the lecture for him. He lay on his back, motionless, and listened sadly to what I had written. Then he said, no, it wasn't the love of death they had got from Whitman—that ran through German poetry—but it was most of all his feeling for Brudermensch, his humanity.

"But this does not grow long on German earth," he said, "and is soon deztroyed."

I said I was sorry I had got it wrong, but he thanked me anyway.

I left, defeated, and as I was going down the stairs, heard the sound of sobbing. I will quit this, I thought, it has got to be too much for me. I can't drown with him.

I stayed home the next day, tasting a new kind of private misery too old for somebody my age, but that same night Oskar called me on the phone, blessing me wildly for having read those notes to him. He had got up to write me a letter to say what I had missed, and it ended in his having written half the lecture. He had slept all day and tonight intended to finish it up.

"I thank you," he said, "for much, alzo including your faith in me."

"Thank God," I said, not telling him I had just about lost it.

Oskar completed his lecture—wrote and rewrote it—during the first week in September. The Nazis had invaded Poland, and though we were greatly troubled, there was some sense of release; maybe the brave Poles would beat them. It took another week to translate the lecture, but here we had the assistance of Friedrich Wilhelm Wolff, the historian, a gentle, erudite man, who liked translating and promised his help with future lectures. We then had about two weeks to work on Oskar's delivery. The weather had changed, and so, slowly, had he. He had awakened from defeat, battered, after a wearying battle. He had lost close to twenty pounds. His complexion was still gray; when I looked at his face I expected to see scars, but it had lost its flabby unfocused quality. His blue eyes had returned to life and he walked with quick steps, as though to pick up a few for all the steps he hadn't taken during those long hot days he had lain in his room.

We went back to our former routine, meeting three late afternoons a week for diction, grammar, and the other exercises. I taught him the phonetic alphabet and transcribed lists of words he was mispronouncing. He worked many hours trying to fit each sound in place, holding a matchstick between his teeth to keep his jaws apart as he exercised his tongue. All this can be a dreadfully boring business unless you think you have a future. Looking at him, I realized what's meant when somebody is called "another man."

The lecture, which I now knew by heart, went off well. The director of the Institute had invited a number of prominent people. Oskar was the first refugee they had employed, and there was a move to make the public cognizant of what was then a new ingredient in American life. Two reporters had come with a lady photographer. The auditorium of the Institute was crowded. I sat in the last row, promising to put up my hand if he couldn't be heard, but it wasn't necessary. Oskar, in a blue suit, his hair cut, was of course nervous, but you couldn't see it unless you studied him. When he stepped up to the lectern, spread out his manuscript, and spoke his first English sentence in public, my heart hesitated; only he and I, of everybody there, had any idea of the anguish he had been through. His enunciation wasn't at all bad—a few *s*'s for *th*'s, and he once said bag for back, but otherwise he did all right. He read poetry well—in both languages—and though Walt Whitman, in his mouth, sounded a little as though he had come to the shores of Long Island as a German immigrant, still the poetry read as poetry:

And I know the Spirit of God is the brother of my own,
And that all the men ever born are also my brothers,
  and the women my sisters and lovers,
And that the kelson of creation is love . . .

Oskar read it as though he believed it. Warsaw had fallen, but the verses were somehow protective. I sat back conscious of two things: how easy it is to hide the deepest wounds; and the pride I felt in the job I had done.

Two days later I came up the stairs into Oskar's apartment to find a crowd there. The refugee, his face beet-red, lips bluish, a trace of froth in the corners of his mouth, lay on the floor in his limp pajamas, two firemen on their knees working over him with an inhalator. The windows were open and the air stank.

A policeman asked me who I was and I couldn't answer.

"No, oh no."

I said no but it was unchangeably yes. He had taken his life—gas—I hadn't even thought of the stove in the kitchen.

"Why?" I asked myself. "Why did he do it?" Maybe it was the fate of Poland on top of everything else, but the only answer anyone could come up with was Oskar's scribbled note that he wasn't well, and had left Martin Goldberg all his possessions. I am Martin Goldberg.

I was sick for a week, had no desire either to inherit or investigate, but I thought I ought to look through his things before the court impounded them, so I spent a morning sitting in the depths of Oskar's armchair, trying to read his correspondence. I had found in the top drawer a thin packet of letters from his wife and an airmail letter of recent date from his mother-in-law.

She writes in a tight script it takes me hours to decipher, that her daughter, after Oskar abandons her, against her own mother's fervent pleas and anguish, is converted to Judaism by a vengeful rabbi. One night the Brown Shirts appear, and though the mother wildly waves her bronze crucifix in their faces, they drag Frau Gassner, together with the other Jews, out of the apartment house, and transport them in lorries to a small border town in conquered Poland. There, it is rumored, she is shot in the head and topples into an open ditch with the naked Jewish men, their wives and children, some Polish soldiers, and a handful of gypsies.

A Choice of Profession

CRONIN, AFTER discovering that his wife, Marge, had been two-timing him with a friend, suffered months of crisis. He had loved Marge and jealousy lingered unbearably. He lived through an anguish of degrading emotions, and a few months after his divorce, left a well-paying job in Chicago to take up teaching. He had always wanted to teach. Cronin taught composition and survey of literature in a small college town in Northern California, and after an initially exhilarating period, began to find it a bore. This caused him worry because he hoped to be at peace in the profession. He wasn't sure whether it was true boredom or simply not knowing whether he wanted to teach the rest of his life. He was bored mostly outside the classroom—the endless grading of papers and bookkeeping chores; and for a man of his type, Cronin felt, he had too much to read. He also felt he had been asking from teaching more than he was entitled to. He had always thought of teaching as something religious and perhaps still did. It had to do with giving oneself to others, a way of being he hadn't achieved in his marriage. Cronin, a tall, bulky-shouldered man with sensitive eyes, and a full brown mustache, smoked too much. His trousers were usually smeared with cigarette ashes he brushed off his thighs; and lately, after a period of forbearance, he had begun to drink. Apart from students there were few women around who weren't married, and he was alone too often. Though at the beginning he was invited to faculty parties, he wanted nothing to do with the wives of his colleagues.

The fall wore away. Cronin remained aimlessly in town during the winter vacation. In the spring term a new student, an older girl, appeared in his literature class. Unlike most of the other girls, she wore bright attractive dresses and high heels. She wore her light hair in a bun from which strands slipped but she was otherwise feminine and neat, a mature woman, he realized. Although she wasn't really pretty, her face was open and attractive. Cronin wondered at her experienced eyes and deep-breasted figure. She had slender shoulders and fairly heavy but shapely legs. He thought at first she might be a faculty wife but she was without their combination of articulateness and timidity; he didn't think she was married. He also liked the way she listened to him in class. Many of the students, when he lectured or read poetry, looked sleepy, stupefied, or exalted, but she listened down to bedrock, as if she were expecting a message or had got it. Cronin noticed that the others in the class might listen to the poetry but she also listened to Cronin. Her name, not very charming, was Mary Lou Miller. He could tell she regarded him as a man, and after so long a dry, almost perilous season, he responded to her as a woman. Though Cronin wasn't planning to become involved with a student, he had at times considered taking up with one but resisted it on principle. He wanted to be protected in love by certain rules, but loving a student meant no rules to begin with.

He continued to be interested in her and she occasionally would wait at his desk after class and walk with him in the direction of his office. He often thought she had something personal to say to him, but when she spoke it was usually to say that one or another poem had moved her; her taste, he thought, was a little too inclusive. Mary Lou rarely recited in class. He found her a bit boring when they talked for more than five minutes, but that secretly pleased him because the attraction to her was quite strong and this was a form of insurance. One morning, during a free hour, he went to the registrar's office on some pretext or other, and looked up her records. Cronin was surprised to discover she was twenty-four and only a first-year student. He, though he sometimes felt forty, was twenty-nine. Because they were so close in age, as well as for other reasons, he decided to ask her out. That same afternoon Mary Lou knocked on his office door and came in to see him about a quiz he had just returned. She had got a low C and it worried her. Cronin lit her cigarette and noticed that she watched him intently, his eyes, mustache, hands, as he explained what she might have written on her paper. They were sitting within a foot of one another, and when she raised both arms to fix her bun, the imprint of her large nipples on her dress caught his attention. It was during this talk in the office that he suggested they go for a drive one evening at the end of the week. Mary Lou agreed, saying maybe they could stop off somewhere for a drink, and Cronin, momentarily hesitating, said he thought they might. All the while they had been talking she was looking at him from some inner place in herself, and he had the feeling he had been appraising her superficially.

On the ride that night Mary Lou sat close to Cronin. She had at first sat at the door but soon her warm side was pressed to his though he had not seen her move. They had started at sunset and for an hour the sky was light. The Northern California winter, though colder than he had anticipated, was mild compared to a winter in Chicago, but Cronin was glad to be in touch with spring. He liked the lengthening days, and tonight it was a relief to be with a woman once more. The car passed through a number of neon-lit mountain towns neither of them had been in before, and Cronin noticed that every motel flashed vacancy signs. Part of his good mood was an awareness of the approach of a new season, and part, that he had thought it over and decided there was nothing to worry about. She was a woman, no eighteen-year-old kid he would be taking advantage of. Nor was he married and about to commit adultery. He felt a sincere interest in her.

It was a pleasant evening drive in early March and on their way back they stopped off at a bar in Red Bluff, about forty miles from the college, where it was unlikely anyone they knew would see them. The waiter brought drinks and when Mary Lou had finished hers she excused herself, went to the ladies' room, and upon returning, asked for another on the rocks. She had on a bright blue dress, rather short, and wore no stockings. During the week she used no lip rouge or nail polish; tonight she had both on and Cronin thought he liked her better without them. She smiled at him, her face, after she had had two, flushed. In repose her smile settled into the tail end of bitterness, an expression touched with cynicism, and he wondered about her. They had talked about themselves on the ride, she less than he, Cronin reticently. She had been brought up on a farm in Idaho. He had spent most of his life in Evanston, Illinois, where his grandfather, an evangelical minister, had lived and preached. Cronin's father had died when Cronin was fourteen. Mary Lou told him she had once been married and was now divorced. He had guessed something of the sort and at that point admitted he had been divorced himself. He could feel his leg touching hers under the table and realized it was her doing. Cronin, pretty much contented, had had one drink to her two, and he was nursing his first when she asked for a third. She had become quiet but when their eyes met she smiled again.

"Do you mind if I call you Mary Louise?" Cronin asked her.

"You can if you want to," she said, "but my real name is Mary Lou. That's on my birth certificate."

He asked her how long she had been married before her divorce.

"Oh, just about three years. One that I didn't live with him. How about yourself?"

"Two," said Cronin.

She drank from her glass. He liked the fact that she was satisfied with a few biographical details. A fuller exchange of information could come later.

He lit a cigarette, only his second since they had come in, whereas she squashed one butt to light another. He wondered why she was nervous.

"Happy?" Cronin asked.

"I'm okay, thanks." She crushed a newly lit cigarette, thought about it and lit another.

She seemed about to say something, paused, and said, "How long have you been teaching, if you don't mind me asking you?"

Cronin wondered what was on her mind. "Not so long," he answered. "This is only my first year."

"You sure put a lot in it."

He could feel the calf of her leg pressed warmly against his; yet she was momentarily inattentive, vaguely looking around at the people in the bar.

"How about you?" he asked.

"In what ways?"

"How is it you started college so comparatively late?"

She finished her drink. "I never wanted to go when I graduated high school. Instead I worked a couple of years, then I joined the Wacs." She fell silent.

He asked if she wanted him to order another drink.

"Not right away." Mary Lou's eyes focused on his face. "First I want to tell you something about myself. Do you want to hear it?"

"Yes, if you want to tell me."

"It's about my life," Mary Lou said. "When I was in the Wacs I met this guy, Ray A. Miller, a T-5 from Providence, Rhode Island, and we got hitched in secret in Las Vegas. He was a first-class prick."

Cronin gazed at her, wondering if she had had one too many. He considered suggesting they leave now but Mary Lou, sitting there solidly, smoking the last cigarette in her pack, told Cronin what she had started out to.

"I call him that word because that's what he was. He married me just to live easy off me. He talked me into doing what he wanted, and I was too goddamn stupid to say no, because at that time I loved him. After we left the service he set me up in this flea-bitten three-room apartment in San Francisco, where I was a call girl. He took the dough and I got the shit."

"Call girl?" Cronin almost groaned.

"A whore, if you want me to say it."

Cronin was overwhelmed. He felt a momentary constricting fright and a strange uneasy jealousy, followed by a sense of disappointment and unexpected loss.

"I'm sorry," he said. Her leg was tense against his but he let his stay though it seemed to him it trembled. His cigarette ash broke, and while brushing it off his thigh, Cronin managed to withdraw his leg from hers. Her face was impassive.

Mary Lou slowly fixed her bun, removing a large number of hairpins and placing them thickly back again.

"I suppose you have a bad opinion of me now?" she said to Cronin, after she had fixed her hair.

He said he had no opinion at all, though he knew he had. "I'm just sorry it happened."

She looked at him intently. "One thing I want you to know is I don't have that kind of a life any more. I'm not interested in it. I'm interested in taking it as it comes or goes but not for money any more. That won't happen to me again."

Cronin said he was surprised it ever had.

"It was just a job I had to do," Mary Lou explained. "That's how I thought about it. I kept on it because I was afraid Ray would walk out on me. He always knew what he wanted but I didn't. He was a strong type and I wasn't."

"Did he walk out?"

She nodded. "We were having fights about what to do with the dough. He said he was going to start some kind of a business but he never did."

"That's when you quit?"

She lowered her eyes. "Not all at once. I stayed for a while to get some money to go to college with. I didn't stay long and I haven't got enough, so I have to work in the cafeteria."

"When did you finally quit?"

"In three months, when I got arrested."

He asked about that.

"My apartment was raided by two San Francisco bulls. But it was my first offense so the judge paroled me. I'm paroled now and for one more year."

"I guess you've been through the mill," Cronin said, toying with his glass.

"I sure have," said Mary Lou, "but I'm not the same person I once was. I learned a lot."

"Would you care for a last drink before we leave?" he asked. "It's getting late. We've got an hour's drive."

"No, but thanks anyway."

"I'll just have a last drink."

The waiter brought Cronin a Scotch.

"Tell me why you told me this," he asked Mary Lou after he had drunk from his glass.

"I don't know for sure," she said. "Some of it is because I like you. I like the way you teach in your class. That's why I got the idea of telling you."

"But why, specifically?"

"Because everything's different now."

"The past doesn't bother you?"

"Not much. I wanted to tell you before this but I couldn't do it in your office without a drink to start me off."

"Do you want me to do anything for you?" Cronin asked her.

"For instance, what?" said Mary Lou.

"If you want to talk to anybody about yourself I could get you the name of a psychiatrist."

"Thanks," she said. "I don't need one. The guy I talk to about myself will have to do it for nothing, for kicks."

She asked Cronin for one of his cigarettes and smoked while he finished his drink.

As they were getting ready to leave, Mary Lou said, "The way I figure, it wasn't all my fault but it's dead and gone now. I got the right to think of the future."

"You have," said Cronin.

On the ride home he felt more objective and not unsympathetic to the girl, yet he was still disappointed, and from time to time, irritated with himself.

"Anyway," Cronin told her, "you can work for a better way of life now."

"That's why I want an education for," Mary Lou said.

2.

It took Cronin a surprisingly long time to get over having been let down by Mary Lou. He had built her up in his mind as a woman he might want to spend some time with, and the surprise of her revelation, and his disillusionment, lingered so long he felt unsettled. "What's this, Marge all over again?" He didn't want any more of that, and not from this girl. He saw her in class, as usual, three times a week. She seemed to listen with the same interest, maybe less interested, but she didn't approach him and no longer waited at his desk to walk with him to his office. Cronin understood that to mean he was to make the next move now that he knew, but he didn't make it. What could he say to her—that he wished he didn't know? Or now that he knew, sometimes when he glanced at her in class he pictured her being paid off by the last guy she had slept with. She was in his thoughts much of the time. He wondered what would have happened that night they were out if she hadn't made that confession. Could he have guessed from the way she performed in bed that she had been a professional? He continued to think of having her and sometimes the thought was so wearing he avoided looking at her in class. He found his desire hard to bear but after a month it wore down. She seemed not very interesting to him then, and he was often aware how hard her expression was. He felt sorry for her and occasionally smiled, and once in a while she seemed cynically to smile back.

Cronin had made friends with a painter, George Getz, an assistant professor in the art department, an active, prematurely bald man, with whom he went on sketching trips, usually on Saturday or Sunday afternoon. George sketched or did water colors as Cronin looked on or sat against a tree, smoking. Sometimes he wandered along streams and in the woods. When the painter, married from youth and the father of three girls, was tied down during the weekend, Cronin drove off by himself or tried walking alone, though generally he cared little for walking in town, and wasn't sure which direction to go next. One fine Sunday in April, when George was busy with his family, Cronin started on a walk but it soon began to seem like work so he returned to his apartment and sat on the bed. Wanting company he searched in his mind for who, and after some doubts looked up Mary Lou Miller's number and dialed it. He wasn't sure why he had, though he knew it bothered him a little. "Hello there," she said. She had hesitated on hearing his voice but seemed cordial enough. Cronin wondered about a drive and she said she wouldn't mind. He called for her in his car. She looked a little distant when she came out and he was surprised at how attractive. He noticed she seemed to be prettier on warm days.

"How are things with you?" Cronin asked as he held the door open for her.

"All right, I guess. How are they with you?"

"Fine," Cronin said.

"How's the teaching?"

"Fine. I'm enjoying it more than I was."

Not much more but it was too much trouble to explain why.

She seemed at ease. They drove towards the mountains along some of the side roads he had explored with George, until they came to a long blue lake shaped like a bird in flight. Cronin parked the car and they went through a scattering of pine trees, down to the water. At his suggestion they walked part of the way around the lake, and back. It took more than an hour and Mary Lou said she hadn't walked that much in years.

"Life's pleasures are cheap," Cronin said.

"No, they're not," said Mary Lou.

He let it pass. They had said nothing about last time, there was nothing to say really. The beauty of the day had lightened Cronin's mood—he remembered having dreamed of Marge last night and had awakened uneasy. But Mary Lou's company, he admitted to himself, had made the walk around the lake enjoyable. She was wearing a yellow cotton dress that showed her figure off, and her hair, to the large thick knot on her neck, was for once neatly arranged. She was rather quiet, as though a word too much might defeat her, but once she loosened up they talked amiably. She seemed to Cronin, as he sat by her side gazing at the lake, no more nor less than any woman he had known. The way he presently saw it was that she was entitled to her mistakes. He was to his. Yet though he tried to forget what she had told him, the fact that she had been a whore kept nagging him. She had known many men, how large a crowd they would make following her now, he was afraid to guess. He had never known anyone like her, and that he was with her now struck him as somewhat strange. But Cronin thought what an unusual thing present time was. In the present a person is what she is becoming and not what she was. She was this heavy-but-shapely-legged girl in a yellow dress, sitting by his side as though she belonged there. Cronin thought this was an interesting lesson for him. The past interfered if you let it. People feared it because they thought it predicted the future. It didn't if you realized how much life changed, and concentrated on what it had changed to, and lived that. He began again to think of the possibility of friendship with Mary Lou.

She got up, brushing pine needles off her dress. "It's hot," she said. "Would you mind if I peeled and went in for a dip?"

"Go ahead," said Cronin.

"Why don't you come in yourself?" she asked. "You could keep your shorts on and later get dry in the sun."

"No, I don't think so," he said, "I'm not much of a swimmer."

"Neither am I," Mary Lou said, "but I like the water."

She unzipped her dress and pulled it over her head. Then she kicked off her shoes, stepped out of a half slip and removed her white underwear. He enjoyed the fullness of her form, the beauty of her breasts. Mary Lou walked into the water, shivered, and began to swim. Cronin sat watching her, one arm around his knees as he smoked. After swimming a while, Mary Lou, her flesh lit in the sunlight, came out of the water, drew on her underpants, then let the sun dry her as she redid her damp hair. He was moved by her wet body after bathing.

When she had dressed, Cronin suggested they have dinner together and Mary Lou agreed. "But first you come up to my joint for a drink. I want to show you how I fixed it up."

He said he would like to.

On their ride back she was talkative. She told Cronin about her life as a child. Her father had been a small wheat farmer in Idaho. She had one married sister and two married brothers. She said the oldest brother was a big bastard.

"He's pretty rich by now," she said, "and he talks a lot about God's grace but in his heart he is a bastard. When I was thirteen one day he grabbed me in the barn and laid me though I didn't want to."

"Oh, Christ," said Cronin. "You committed incest?"

"It all happened when I was a kid."

"Why don't you keep these things to yourself?" Cronin said. "What makes you think I want to hear them?"

"I guess I felt I trusted you."

"Well, don't trust me," he shouted.

He drove to her house and let her off at the curb. Then he drove away.

The next morning Mary Lou did not appear in Cronin's class, and a few days later her drop-slip came through.

3.

A week had gone by when Cronin one day saw her walking with George Getz, and his heart was flooded with jealous misery. He thought he was rid of his desire for the girl; but seeing her walking at the painter's side, talking animatedly, George interested, Mary Lou good to look at in a white summer dress and doing very well, thanks, without Cronin, awoke in him a sense of loss and jealousy. He thought he might be in love with her. Cronin watched them go up the stairs of the art building, and though he had no good reason to, pictured them in each other's arms, naked on George's studio couch. The effect was frightening.

My God, thought Cronin, here I am thinking of her with the same miserable feelings I had about Marge. I can't go through that again.

He fought to put her out of his mind—the insistent suspicion of an affair between her and the painter—but his memory of her body at the lake, and imagining the experience she had had with men, what she would do with George, for instance, and might have done with Cronin if they had become lovers, made things worse. Thinking of her experiences was like trying to stop the pain of a particular wound by stabbing yourself elsewhere. His only relief was to get drunk but when that wore off the anguish was worse.

One morning he was so desperately jealous—the most useless of emotions, and especially useless in a situation where the girl really meant little to him, almost nothing, and the past, despite all his theorizing and good intentions, much too much—that he waited for them for hours, in the foyer of the school of architecture across the street from the art building. Cronin did not at first know why he was waiting but that he had to, perhaps to satisfy himself they were or weren't having an affair. He saw neither of them then, but on the next afternoon he followed the painter at a distance to Mary Lou's apartment. Cronin saw him go in shortly before five P.M., and was still unhappily waiting under a tree across the street, several houses down, when George came out at half-past ten. Cronin was wakeful all night.

Terrified that this should mean so much to him, he tried to work out some means of relief. Should he telephone the girl and ask her back into his class so that they could once more be on good terms? Or if that meant trouble with the registrar's office, couldn't he just call and apologize for acting as he had, then offer to resume their friendship? Or could he scare George away by telling him about her past?

The painter was a family man, a careful sort, and Cronin felt sure he would end it with Mary Lou if he thought anyone suspected he was involved with her; he wanted to go on feeding his three girls. But telling him about her seemed such a stinking thing to do that Cronin couldn't face it. Still, things were so bad he finally decided to speak to George. He felt that if he could be sure the painter wasn't being intimate with her, his jealousy would die out and the girl fade in his thoughts.

He waited till George invited him on another sketching afternoon, and was glad to have the chance to bring it up then, rather than to have to seek the painter out in his office or studio. They were at the edge of the woods, George at work on a water color, when Cronin spoke of the girl and asked whether George knew that Mary Lou had once been a prostitute in San Francisco for a couple of years.

George wiped his brush with a rag, then asked Cronin where he had got his information.

Cronin said he had got it from her. "She was married to someone who set her up professionally and cut in on the take. After he left her she quit."

"What a son of a bitch," said George. He worked for a while, then turned to Cronin and asked, "Why do you tell me about it?"

"I thought you ought to know."

"Why ought I?"

"Isn't she a student of yours?"

"No, she isn't. She came to my office and offered to model for me. It's hard to get girls to pose in the nude around here so I said yes. That's all there is between us."

He seemed embarrassed.

Cronin looked away. "I didn't think there was anything between you. I just thought you would want to know, if she was your student. I didn't know she wasn't."

"Well," said George, "I know now, but I still intend to use her as a model."

"I don't see why not."

"Thanks for telling me, though," George said. "I've sometimes felt there's a bit of the slut in her. It wouldn't pay to get involved."

Cronin, feeling some repulsion for himself, then said, "To tell the truth, George, I'm not entirely innocent in this. I've wanted to take the girl to bed."

"Have you?"

"No."

"I almost did," George said.

Though Cronin wasn't sure the painter had or hadn't, he was certain he wouldn't dare be intimate with her now. When he got home he felt relief, mingled with shame that had him talking to himself, but he slept better that night.

4.

A few nights later Mary Lou rang Cronin's door bell, walked up the stairs, and when she was admitted into his apartment, said she wanted to talk to him. Cronin, reading in pajamas and robe, offered her a Scotch but she refused. Her face was pale, her expression embittered. She was wearing Levi's and a baggy sweater; the hair spilled out of her bun.

"Look," Mary Lou said to Cronin, "I didn't come here for any favors, but did you say anything to Professor Getz about me? I mean what I told you about San Francisco?"

"Did he say I had?" Cronin asked.

"No, but we were being friendly and then he changed to me. I figure somebody must have told him something, and I thought nobody knew anything but you, so you must've told him."

Cronin admitted it. "I thought he ought to know, considering the circumstances."

"Such as what?" she asked sullenly.

He hesitated. "He's a married man with three kids. There could be serious trouble."

"That's his goddamn business."

He admitted that too. "I'm sorry, Mary Lou. All I can say is that my life has been confused and complicated lately."

"What about mine?" She was sitting in a chair, then turned her head and wept.

Cronin poured her a drink but Mary Lou wouldn't take it.

"The reason I told you those things is because I thought you were a guy I could trust and be friends with. Instead it was the opposite. I'm sorry what I told you got you so bothered, but there's a lot worse than that, and one thing I want you to know is it doesn't bother me any more. I made my peace with my life."

"I haven't," said Cronin.

"I don't want to hear about it," said Mary Lou, and though he asked her to stay she left.

Afterwards he thought, She has learned something from her experience that I haven't learned from mine. And he felt sorry for Mary Lou, for the way he had treated her. It's not easy to be moral, Cronin thought. He decided, before he went to bed, not to come back to this college in the fall, to quit teaching.

On Commencement Day, Cronin met Mary Lou in the street, in her yellow dress, and they stopped to talk. She had put on weight but wasn't looking well, and as they talked her stomach rumbled. In embarrassment she covered her abdomen.

"It's from studying," she said. "I got awfully worried about my finals. The doctor in the infirmary said to watch out or I might wind up with an ulcer."

Cronin also advised her to take care. "Your health comes first."

They said goodby. He never saw her again but a year later, in Chicago, he had a card from her. She wrote she was still at college, majoring in education, and hoped someday to teach.

Man in the Drawer

A SOFT shalom I thought I heard but considering the Slavic cast of the driver's face it seemed unlikely. He had been eyeing me in his rearview mirror since I had stepped into the taxi and, to tell the truth, I had momentary apprehensions. I'm forty-seven and have recently lost weight but not, I confess, nervousness. It's my American clothes, I thought at first. One is a recognizable stranger. Unless he had been tailing me to begin with, but how could that be if it was a passing cab I had hailed myself?

The taxi driver sat in his shirt sleeves on a cool June day, not more than 50° Fahrenheit. He was a man in his thirties who looked as if what he ate didn't fully feed him—in afterthought a discontented type, his face on the tired side, not bad-looking—now that I'd studied him a little, though the head seemed pressed a bit flat by somebody's heavy hand even though protected by a mat of healthy hair. His face, as I said, veered toward Slavic: broad cheekbones, small firm chin, but he sported a longish nose and a distinctive larynx on a slender hairy neck; a mixed type, it appeared. At any rate, the shalom had seemed to alter his appearance, even the probing eyes. He was dissatisfied for certain this fine June day—his job, fate, appearance—whatever. And a sort of indigenous sadness hung on or around him, coming God knows from where; nor did he seem to mind if who he was, was immediately apparent; not everybody could do that or wanted to. This one showed himself as is. Not too prosperous, I would say, yet no underground man. He sat firm in his seat, all of him driving, a touch frantically. I have an experienced eye for details.

"Israeli?" he asked in a whisper.

"Amerikansky." I know no Russian, just a few polite words.

He dug into his shirt pocket for a thin pack of cigarettes and swung his arm over the seat, the Volga swerving to avoid a truck making a turn.

"Take care!"

I was thrown sideways—no apologies. Extracting a Bulgarian cigarette I wasn't eager to smoke—too strong—I handed him his pack. I was considering offering my prosperous American cigarettes in return but didn't want to affront him.

"Feliks Levitansky," he said. "How do you do? I am taxi driver." His accent was strong, verging on fruity, but redeemed by fluency of tongue.

"Ah, you speak English? I sort of thought so."

"My profession is translator—English, French." He shrugged sideways.

"Howard Harvitz is my name. I'm here for a short vacation, about three weeks. My wife died not so long ago, and I'm traveling partly to relieve my mind."

My voice caught, but then I went on to say that if I could manage to dig up some material for a magazine article or two, so much the better.

In sympathy Levitansky raised both hands from the wheel.

"Watch out, for God's sake!"

"Horovitz?" he asked.

I spelled it for him. "Frankly, it was Harris after I entered college but I changed it back recently. My father had it legally done after I graduated from high school. He was a doctor, a practical sort."

"You don't look to me Jewish."

"If not why did you say shalom?"

"Sometimes you say." After a minute he asked, "For which reason?"

"For which reason what?"

"Why you changed back your name?"

"I had a crisis in my life."

"Existential? Economic?"

"To tell the truth I changed it back after my wife died."

"What is the significance?"

"The significance is I am closer to myself."

The driver popped a match with his thumbnail and lit his cigarette.

"I am marginal Jew," he said, "although my father—Avrahm Isaakovich Levitansky—was Jewish. Because my mother was gentile woman I was given choice, but she insisted me to register for internal passport with notation of Jewish nationality in respect for my father. I did so."

"You don't say!"

"My father died in my childhood. I was rised—raised?—to respect Jewish people and religion, but I went my own way. I am atheist. This is almost inevitable."

"You mean Soviet life?"

Levitansky smoked without replying as I grew embarrassed by my question. I looked around to see if I knew where we were. In afterthought he asked, "To which destination?"

I said, still on the former subject, that I had been not much a Jew myself. "My mother and father were totally assimilated."

"By their choice?"

"Of course by their choice."

"Do you wish," he then asked, "to visit Central Synagogue on Arkhipova Street? Very interesting experience."

"Not just now," I said, "but take me to the Chekhov Museum on Sadovaya Kudrinskaya."

At that the driver, sighing, seemed to take heart.

Rose, I said to myself.

I blew my nose. After her death I had planned to visit the Soviet Union but couldn't get myself to move. I'm a slow man after a blow, though I confess I've never been one for making his mind up in a hurry about important things. Eight months later, when I was more or less packing, I felt that some of the relief I was looking for derived, in addition to what was still on my mind, from the necessity of making an unexpected serious personal decision. Out of loneliness I had begun to see my former wife, Lillian, in the spring; and before long, since she had remained unmarried and attractive, to my surprise there was some hesitant talk of remarriage; these things slip from one sentence to another before you know it. If we did get married we could turn the Russian trip into a sort of honeymoon—I won't say second because we hadn't had much of a first. In the end, since our lives had been so frankly complicated—hard on each other—I found it hard to make up my mind, though Lillian, I give her credit, seemed to be willing to take the chance. My feelings were so difficult to assess I decided to decide nothing for sure. Lillian, who is a forthright type with a mind like a lawyer's, asked me if I was cooling to the idea, and I told her that since the death of my wife I had been examining my life and needed more time to see where I stood. "Still?" she said, meaning the self-searching, and implying forever. All I could answer was "Still," and then in anger, "Forever." I warned myself: Beware of further complicated entanglements.

Well, that almost killed it. It wasn't a particularly happy evening, though it had its moments. I had once been very much in love with Lillian. I figured then that a change of scene for me, maybe a month abroad, might be helpful. I had for a long time wanted to visit the U.S.S.R., and taking the time to be alone and, I hoped, at ease to think things through, might give the trip additional value.

So I was surprised, once my visa was granted—though not too surprised—that my anticipation was by now blunted and I was experiencing some uneasiness. I blamed it on a dread of traveling that sometimes hits me before I move. Will I get there? Will the plane be hijacked? Maybe a war breaks out and I'm surrounded by artillery. To be frank, though I've resisted the idea, I consider myself an anxious man, which, when I try to explain it to myself, means being this minute halfway into the next. I sit still in a hurry, worry uselessly about the future, and carry the burden of an overripe conscience.

I realized that what troubled me most about going into Soviet Russia were those stories in the papers of some tourist or casual traveler in this or that Soviet city who is, without warning, grabbed by the secret police on charges of "spying," "illegal economic activity," "hooliganism," or whatnot. This poor guy, like somebody from Sudbury, Mass., is held incommunicado until he confesses, and is then sentenced to a prison camp in the wilds of Siberia. After I got my visa I sometimes had fantasies of a stranger shoving a fat envelope of papers into my hand, and then arresting me as I was stupidly reading them—of course for spying. What would I do in that case? I think I would pitch the envelope into the street, shouting, "Don't pull that one on me, I can't read Russian," and walk away with whatever dignity I had, hoping that would freeze them in their tracks. A man in danger, if he's walking away from it, seems indifferent, innocent. At least to himself; then in my mind I hear footsteps coming after me, and since my reveries tend to be rational, two husky KGB men grab me, shove my arms up my back, and make the arrest. Not for littering the streets, as I hope might be the case, but for "attempting to dispose of certain incriminating documents," a fact it's hard to deny.

I see H. Harvitz yelling, squirming, kicking right and left, till his mouth is shut by somebody's stinking palm and he is dragged by force—not to mention a blackjack whack on the skull—into the inevitable black Zis I've read about and see on movie screens.

The cold war is a frightening business. I've sometimes wished spying had reached such a pitch of perfection that both the U.S.S.R. and the U.S.A. knew everything there is to know about the other, and having sensibly exchanged this information by trading computers that keep facts up to date, let each other alone thereafter. That ruins the spying business; there's that much more sanity in the world, and for a man like me the thought of a trip to the Soviet Union is pure pleasure.

Right away at the Kiev airport I had a sort of scare, after flying in from Paris on a mid-June afternoon. A customs official confiscated from my suitcase five copies of *Visible Secrets*, a poetry anthology for high school students I had edited some years ago, which I had brought along to give away to Russians I met who might be interested in American poetry. I was asked to sign a document the official had written out in Cyrillic, except that *Visible Secrets* was printed in English, "secrets" underlined. The uniformed customs officer, a heavyset man with a layer of limp hair on a smallish head, red stars on his shoulders, said that the paper I was required to sign stated I understood it was not permitted to bring five copies of a foreign book into the Soviet Union; but I would get my property back at the Moscow airport when I left the country. I worried that I oughtn't to sign but was urged to by my Intourist guide, a bleached blonde with wobbly heels whose looks and good humor kept me calm, though my clothes were frankly steaming. She said it was a matter of no great consequence and advised me to write my signature quickly, because it was delaying our departure to the Dniepro Hotel.

At that point I asked what would happen if I parted with the books, no longer claimed them as my property. The Intouristka inquired of the customs man, who answered calmly, earnestly, and at great length.

"He says," she said, "that the Soviet Union will not take away from a foreign visitor his legal property."

Since I had only four days in the city and time was going faster than usual, I reluctantly signed the paper plus four carbons—one for each book—or five mysterious government departments?—and was given a copy which I filed in my billfold.

Despite this incident—it had its comic quality—my stay in Kiev, in spite of the loneliness I usually experience my first few days in a strange city, went quickly and interestingly. In the mornings I was driven around in a private car on guided tours of the hilly, broad-avenued, green-leaved city, whose colors were reminiscent of a subdued Rome. But in the afternoons I wandered around alone. I would start by taking a bus or streetcar, riding a few kilometers, then getting off to walk in this or that neighborhood. Once I strayed into a peasants' market where collective farmers and country folk in beards and boots out of a nineteenth-century Russian novel sold their produce to city people. I thought I must write about this to Rose—I meant of course Lillian. Another time, in a deserted street when I happened to think of the customs receipt in my billfold, I turned in my tracks to see if I was being followed. I wasn't but enjoyed the adventure.

An experience I liked less was getting lost one late afternoon several kilometers above a boathouse on the Dnieper. I was walking along the riverbank liking the boats and island beaches and, before I knew it, had come a good distance from the hotel and was eager to get back because I was hungry. I didn't feel like retracing my route on foot—much too much tourism in three days—so I thought of a cab, and since none was around, maybe an autobus that might be going in the general direction I had come from. I tried approaching a few passers-by whom I addressed in English or pidgin-German, and occasionally trying "Pardonnez-moi"; but the effect was apparently to embarrass them. One young woman ran a few awkward steps from me before she began to walk again.

Though frustrated, irritated, I spoke to two men passing by, one of whom, the minute he heard my first few words, walked on quickly, his eyes aimed straight ahead, the other indicating by gestures he was deaf and dumb. On impulse I tried him in halting Yiddish that my grandfather had taught me when I was a child, and was then directed, in an undertone in the same language, to a nearby bus stop.

As I was unlocking the door to my room, thinking this was a story I would be telling friends all winter, my phone was ringing. It was a woman's voice. I understood "Gospodin Garvitz" and one or two other words as she spoke at length in musical Russian. Her voice had the lilt of a singer's. Though I couldn't get the gist of her remarks, I had this sudden vivid reverie, you might call it, of me walking with a pretty Russian girl in a white birchwood near Yasnaya Polyana, and coming out of the trees, sincerely talking, into a meadow that sloped to the water; then rowing her around in a small lovely lake. It was a peaceful business. I even had thoughts: Wouldn't it be something if I got myself engaged to a Russian girl? That was the general picture, but when the caller was done talking, whatever I had to say I said in English and she slowly hung up.

After breakfast the next morning, she, or somebody who sounded like her—I was aware of the contralto quality—called again.

"If you understand English," I said, "or maybe a little German or French—even Yiddish if you happen to know it—we'd get along fine. But not in Russian, I'm sorry to say. Nyet Russki. I'd be glad to meet you for lunch or whatever you like; so if you get the drift of my remarks why don't you say da? Then dial the English interpreter on extension 37. She could explain to me what's what and we can meet at your convenience."

I had the impression she was listening with both ears, but after a while the phone hung silent in my hand. I wondered where she had got my name, and was someone testing me to find out whether I did or didn't speak Russian. I honestly did not.

Afterwards I wrote a short letter to Lillian, telling her I would be leaving for Moscow via Aeroflot, tomorrow at 4 P.M., and I intended to stay there for two weeks, with a break of maybe three or four days in Leningrad, at the Astoria Hotel. I wrote down the exact dates and later airmailed the letter in a street box some distance from the hotel, whatever good that did. I hoped Lillian would get it in time to reach me by return mail before I left the Soviet Union. To tell the truth I was uneasy all day.

But by the next morning my mood had shifted, and as I was standing at the railing in a park above the Dnieper, looking at the buildings going up across the river in what had once been steppeland, I experienced a curious sense of relief. The vast construction I beheld—it was as though two or three scattered small cities were rising out of the earth—astonished me. This sort of thing was going on all over Russia—halfway around the world—and when I considered what it meant in terms of sheer labor, capital goods, plain morale, I was then and there convinced that the Soviet Union would never willingly provoke a war, nuclear or otherwise, with the United States. Neither would America, in its right mind, with the Soviet Union.

For the first time since I had come to Russia I felt secure and safe, and I enjoyed there, at the breezy railing above the Dnieper, a rare few minutes of euphoria.

Why is it that the most interesting architecture is from Czarist times? I asked myself, and if I'm not mistaken Levitansky quivered, no doubt coincidental. Unless I had spoken aloud to myself, which I sometimes do; I decided I hadn't. We were on our way to the museum, hitting a fast eighty kilometers, because traffic was sparse.

"What do you think of my country, the Union of Soviet Socialist Republics?" the driver inquired, turning his head to see where I was.

"I would appreciate it if you kept your eyes on the road."

"Don't be nervous, I drive now for years."

Then I answered that I was impressed by much I had seen. Obviously it was a great country.

Levitansky's round face appeared in the mirror smiling pleasantly, his teeth eroded. The smile seemed to have come from within the mouth. Now that he had revealed his half-Jewish antecedents I had the impression he looked more Jewish than Slavic, and more dissatisfied than I had previously thought. That I got from the restless eyes.

"Also our system—Communism?"

I answered carefully, not wanting to give offense. "I'll be honest with you. I've seen some unusual things—even inspiring—but my personal taste is for a lot more individual freedom than people seem to have here. America has its serious faults, God knows, but at least we're privileged to criticize—if you know what I mean. My father used to say, 'You can't beat the Bill of Rights.' It's an open society, which means freedom of choice, at least in theory."

"Communism is altogether better political system," Levitansky replied candidly, "although it is not in present stage totally realized. In present stage"—he swallowed, reflected, did not finish the thought. Instead he said, "Our Revolution was magnificent and holy event. I love early Soviet history, excitement of Communist idealism, and magnificent victory over bourgeois and imperialist forces. Overnight was lifted up—uplifted—the whole suffering masses. Pasternak called this 'splendid surgery.' Evgeny Zamyatin—maybe you know his books?—spoke thus: 'The Revolution consumes the earth with fire, but then is born a new life.' Many of our poets said similar things."

I didn't argue, each to his own revolution.

"You told before," said Levitansky, glancing at me again in the mirror, "that you wish to write articles about your visit. Political or not political?"

"What I have in mind is something on the literary museums of Moscow for an American travel magazine. That's the sort of thing I do. I'm a free-lance writer." I laughed apologetically. It's strange how stresses shift when you're in another country.

Levitansky politely joined in the laugh, stopping in midcourse. "I wish to be certain, what is free-lance writer?"

I told him. "I also edit a bit. I've done anthologies of poetry and essays, both for high school kids."

"We have here free-lance. I am writer also," Levitansky said solemnly.

"You don't say? You mean as translator?"

"Translation is my profession but I am also original writer."

"Then you do three things to earn a living—write, translate, and drive this cab?"

"The taxi is not my true work."

"Are you translating anything in particular now?"

The driver cleared his throat. "In present time I have no translation project."

"What sort of thing do you write?"

"I write stories."

"Is that so? What kind, if I might ask?"

"I will tell you what kind—little ones—short stories, imagined from life."

"Have you published any?"

He seemed about to turn around to look me in the eye but reached instead into his shirt pocket. I offered my American pack. He shook out a cigarette and lit it, exhaling slowly.

"A few pieces although not recently. To tell the truth"—he sighed—"I write presently for the drawer. You know this expression? Like Isaac Babel, 'I am master of the genre of silence.'"

"I've heard it," I said, not knowing what else to say.

"The mice should read and criticize," Levitansky said bitterly. "This what they don't eat and make their drops—droppings—on. It is perfect criticism."

"I'm sorry about that."

"We arrive now to Chekhov Museum."

I leaned forward to pay him and made the impulsive mistake of adding a one-ruble tip. His face flared. "I am Soviet citizen." He forcibly returned the ruble.

"Call it a thoughtless error," I apologized. "No harm meant."

"Hiroshima! Nagasaki!" he taunted as the Volga took off in a burst of smoke. "Aggressor against the suffering poor people of Vietnam!"

"That's none of my doing," I called after him.

An hour and a half later, after I had signed the guest book and was leaving the museum, I saw a man standing, smoking, under a linden tree across the street. Nearby was a parked taxi. We stared at each other—I wasn't certain at first who it was, but Levitansky nodded amiably to me, calling "Welcome! Welcome!" He waved an arm, smiling open-mouthed. He had combed his thick hair and was wearing a loose dark suit coat over a tieless white shirt, and baggy pants. His socks, striped red-white-and-blue, you could see through his sandals.

I am forgiven, I thought. "Welcome to you," I said, crossing the street.

"How did you enjoy Chekhov Museum?"

"I did indeed. I've made a lot of notes. You know what they

have there? They have one of his black fedoras, also his pince-nez that you see in pictures of him. Awfully moving."

Levitansky wiped an eye—to my surprise. He seemed not quite the same man, modified. It's funny, you hear a few personal facts from a stranger and he changes as he speaks. The taxi driver is now a writer, even if part-time. Anyway, that's my dominant impression.

"Excuse me my former anger," Levitansky explained. "Now is not for me the best of times. 'It was the best of times, it was the worst of times,'" he said, smiling sadly.

"So long as you pardon my unintentional blunder. Are you perhaps free to drive me to the Metropole, or are you here by coincidence?"

I looked around to see if anyone was coming out of the museum.

"If you wish to engage me I will drive you, but at first I wish to show you something—how do you say?—of interest."

He reached through the open front window of the taxi and brought forth a flat package wrapped in brown paper tied with red string.

"Stories which I wrote."

"I don't read Russian," I said.

"My wife has translated some of them. She is not by her profession a translator, although her English is advanced and sensitive. She had been for two years in England for Soviet Purchasing Commission. We became acquainted in university. I prefer not to translate my stories because I do not translate so well Russian into English, although I do it beautifully the opposite. Also I will not force myself—it is like self-imitation. Perhaps the stories appear a little awkward in English—also my wife admits this—but you can read and form opinion."

Though he offered the package hesitantly, he offered it as if it was a bouquet of spring flowers. Can it be some sort of trick? I asked myself. Are they testing me because I signed that damned document in the Kiev airport, five copies no less?

Levitansky seemed to know my thought. "It is purely stories."

He bit the string in two, and laying the package on the fender of the Volga, unpeeled the wrapping. There were the stories, clipped separately, typed on long sheets of thin blue paper. I took one Levitansky handed me and scanned the top page—it seemed a story—then I flipped through the other pages and handed the manuscript back. "I'm not much a critic of stories."

"I don't seek critic. I seek for reader with literary experience and taste. If you have redacted books of poems and also essays, you will be able to judge literary quality of my stories. Please, I request you will read them."

After a long minute I heard myself say, "Well, I might at that." I didn't recognize the voice and wasn't sure why I had said what I had. You might say I spoke apart from myself, with reluctance that either he wasn't aware of or chose to ignore.

"If you respect—if you approve my stories, perhaps you will be able to arrange for publication in Paris or either London?" His larynx wobbled.

I stared at the man. "I don't happen to be going to Paris, and I'll be in London only between planes to the U.S.A."

"In this event, perhaps you will show to your publisher, and he will publish my work in America?" Levitansky was now visibly uneasy.

"In America?" I said, raising my voice in disbelief.

For the first time he gazed around before replying.

"If you will be so kind to show them to publisher of your books—he is reliable publisher?—perhaps he will wish to bring out volume of my stories? I will make contract whatever he will like. Money, if I could get, is not an idea."

"Whatever volume are you talking about?"

He said that from thirty stories he had written he had chosen eighteen, of which these were a sample. "Unfortunately more are not now translated. My wife is biochemist assistant and works long hours in laboratory. I am sure your publisher will enjoy to read these. It will depend on your opinion."

Either this man has a fantastic imagination, or he's out of his right mind. "I wouldn't want to get myself involved in smuggling a Russian manuscript out of Russia."

"I have informed you that my manuscript is of made-up stories."

"That may be but it's still a chancy enterprise. I'd be taking chances I have no desire to take, to be frank."

"At least if you will read," he sighed.

I took the stories again and thumbed slowly through each. What I was looking for I couldn't say: maybe a booby trap? Should I or shouldn't I? Why should I?

He handed me the wrapping paper and I rolled up the stories in it. The quicker I read them, the quicker I've read them. I stepped into the cab.

"As I said, I'm at the Metropole. Come by tonight about nine o'clock and I'll give you my opinion for what it's worth. But I'm afraid I'll have to limit it to that, Mr. Levitansky, without further obligation or expectations, or it's no deal. My room number is 538."

"Tonight?—so soon?" he said, scratching both palms. "You must read with care so you will realize the art."

"Tomorrow night, then, same time. I'd rather not have them in my room longer than that."

Levitansky agreed. Whistling through eroded teeth, he drove me carefully to the Metropole.

That night, sipping vodka from a drinking glass, I read Levitansky's stories. They were simply and strongly written—I had almost expected it—and not badly translated; in fact the translation read much better than I had been led to think, although there were of course some gaffes—odd constructions, ill-fitting stiff words, some indicated by question marks and taken, I suppose, from a thesaurus. And the stories, short tales dealing—somewhat to my surprise—mostly with Moscow Jews, were good, artistically done, really moving. The situations they revealed weren't exactly news to me: I'm a careful reader of the *Times.* But the stories weren't written to complain. What they had to say was achieved as form, no telling the dancer from the dance. I poured myself another glass of the potato potion—I was beginning to feel high, occasionally wondering why I was putting so much away—relaxing, I guess. I then reread the stories with admiration for Levitansky. I had the feeling he was no ordinary man. I felt excited, then depressed, as if I had been let in on a secret I didn't want to know.

It's a hard life here for a fiction writer, I thought.

Afterwards, having the stories around made me uneasy. In one of them a Russian writer burns his stories in the kitchen sink. Obviously nobody had burned these. I thought to myself, if I'm caught with them in my possession, considering what they indicate about conditions here, there's no question I'll be up to my hips in trouble. I wish I had insisted that Levitansky come back for them tonight.

There was a solid rap on the door. I felt I had risen a few inches out of my chair. It was, after a while, only Levitansky.

"Out of the question," I said, thrusting the stories at him. "Absolutely out of the question!"

The next night we sat facing each other over glasses of cognac in the writer's small, book-crowded study. He was dignified, at first haughty, wounded, hardly masking his impatience. I wasn't myself exactly comfortable.

I had come out of courtesy and other considerations, I guess; principally a dissatisfaction I couldn't define.

Levitansky, the taxi driver rattling around in his Volga-Pegasus, amateur trying to palm off a half-ass ms., had faded in my mind, and I saw him now as a serious Soviet writer with publishing problems. There are many others. What can I do for him? I thought. Why should I?

"I didn't express what I really felt last night," I apologized. "You caught me by surprise, I'm sorry to say."

Levitansky was scratching each hand with the blunt fingers of the other. "How did you acquire my address?"

I reached into my pocket for a wad of folded brown wrapping paper. "It's on this—Novo Ostapovskaya Street, 488, Flat 59. I took a cab."

"I had forgotten this."

Maybe, I thought.

Still, I had practically had to put my foot in the door to get in. Levitansky's wife had answered my uncertain knock, her eyes immediately worried, an expression I took to be the one she lived with. The eyes, astonished to behold a stranger, became outright uneasy once I inquired in English for her husband. I felt, as in Kiev, that my native tongue had become my enemy.

"Have you not the wrong apartment?"

"I hope not. Not if Gospodin Levitansky lives here. I came to see him about his—ah—manuscript."

Her eyes darkened as her face paled. Ten seconds later I was in the flat, the door locked behind me.

"Levitansky!" she summoned him. It had a reluctant quality: Come but don't come.

He appeared in apparently the same shirt, pants, tricolor socks. There was at first pretend-boredom in a tense, tired face. He could not, however, conceal excitement, his lit eyes roving over my face.

"Oh ho," Levitansky said.

My God, I thought, has he been expecting me?

"I came to talk to you for a few minutes, if you don't mind," I said. "I want to say what I think of the stories you kindly let me read."

He curtly spoke in Russian to his wife and she snapped an answer back. "I wish to introduce my wife, Irina Filipovna Levitansky, biochemist. She is patient although not a saint."

She smiled tentatively, an attractive woman about twenty-eight, a little on the hefty side, in house slippers and plain dress. The edge of her slip hung below her skirt.

There was a touch of British in her accent. "I am pleased to be acquainted." If so one hardly noticed. She stepped into black pumps and slipped a bracelet on her wrist, a lit cigarette dangling from the corner of her mouth. Her legs and arms were shapely, her brown hair cut short. I had the impression of tight lips in a pale face.

"I will go to Kovalevsky, next door," she said.

"Not on my account, I hope? All I have to say—"

"Our neighbors in the next flat." Levitansky grimaced. "Also thin walls." He knocked a knuckle on a hollow wall.

I indicated my dismay.

"Please, not long," Irina said, "because I am afraid."

Surely not of me? Agent Howard Harvitz, C.I.A.—a comical thought.

Their small square living room wasn't unattractive but Levitansky signaled the study inside. He offered sweet cognac in whiskey tumblers, then sat facing me at the edge of his chair, repressed energy all but visible. I had the momentary sense his chair was about to move, fly off.

If it does he flies alone.

"What I came to say," I told him, "is that I like your stories and am sorry I didn't say so last night. I like the primary, close-to-the-bone quality of the writing. The stories impress me as strong if simply wrought; I appreciate your feeling for people and at the same time the objectivity with which you render them. It's sort of Chekhovian in quality, but more compressed, sinewy, direct, if you know what I mean. For instance, that story about the old father coming to see his son who ducks out on him. I can't comment on your style, having only read the stories in translation."

"Chekhovian," Levitansky admitted, smiling through his worn teeth, "is fine compliment. Mayakovsky, our early Soviet poet, described him 'the strong and gay artist of the world.' I wish it was possible for Levitansky to be so gay in life and art." He seemed to be staring at the drawn shade in the room, though maybe no place in particular, then said, perhaps heartening himself, "In Russian is magnificent my style—precise, economy, including wit. The style may be difficult to translate in English because is less rich language."

"I've heard that said. In fairness I should add I have some reservations about the stories, yet who hasn't on any given piece of imaginative work?"

"I have myself reservations."

The admission made, I skipped the criticism. I had been wondering about a picture on his bookcase and then asked who it was. "It's a face I've seen before. The eyes are poetic, you might say."

"So is the voice. This is picture of Boris Pasternak as young man. On the wall yonder is Mayakovsky. He was also remarkable poet, wild, joyful, neurasthenic, a lover of the Revolution. He spoke: 'This is *my* Revolution.' To him was it 'a holy washerwoman who cleaned off all the filth from the earth.' Unfortunately he was later disillusioned and also shot himself."

"I have read that."

"He wrote: 'I wish to be understood by my country—but if no, I will fly through Russia like a slanting rainstorm.'"

"Have you by chance read *Dr. Zhivago*?"

"I have read," the writer sighed, and then began to declaim in Russian—I guessed some lines from a poem.

"It is to Marina Tsvetayeva, Soviet poetess, good friend of Pasternak." Levitansky fiddled with the pack of cigarettes on the table. "The end of her life was unfortunate."

"Is there no picture of Osip Mandelstam?" I hesitated as I spoke the name.

He reacted as though he had just met me. "You know Mandelstam?"

"Just a few poems in an anthology."

"Our best poet—he is holy—gone with so many others. My wife does not hang his photograph."

"I guess why I really came," I said after a minute, "is I wanted to express my sympathy and respect."

Levitansky popped a match with his thumbnail. His hand trembled as he shook the flame out without lighting the cigarette.

Embarrassed for him, I pretended to be looking elsewhere. "It's a small room. Does your son sleep here?"

"Don't confuse my story of writer, which you have read, with life of author. My wife and I are married eight years, but without children."

"Might I ask whether the experience you describe in that same story—the interview with the editor—was true?"

"Not true although truth," the writer said impatiently. "I write from imagination. I am not interested to repeat contents of diaries or total memory."

"On that I go along."

"Also, which is not in story, I have submitted to Soviet journals sketches and tales many many times but only few have been published, although not my best. Some people, but only few, know my work through samizdat, which is passing from one to another the manuscript."

"Did you submit any of the Jewish stories?"

"Please, stories are stories, they have not nationality."

"I mean by that those about Jews."

"Some I have submitted but they were not accepted."

I said, "After reading the stories you gave me, I wondered how it is you write so well about Jews? You call yourself marginal—that was your word—yet you write with authority. Not that one can't, I suppose, but it's surprising when one does."

"Imagination makes authority. When I write about Jews comes out stories, so I write about Jews. Is not important that I am half-Jew. What is important is observation, feeling, also art. In the past I have observed my Jewish father. Also I study, sometimes, Jews in the synagogue. I sit on the bench for strangers. The gabbai watches me with dark eyes and I watch him. But whatever I write, whether is about Jews, Galicians, or Georgians, must be work of invention, or for me it does not live."

"I'm not much of a synagogue-goer myself," I told him, "but I like to drop in once in a while to be refreshed by the language and images of a time and place where God was. That may be strange because I had no religious education to speak of."

"I am atheist."

"I understand what you mean by imagination—as for instance that prayer-shawl story. But am I right"—I lowered my voice—"that you are saying something about the condition of Jews in this country?"

"I do not make propaganda," Levitansky said sternly. "I am not Israeli spokesman. I am Soviet artist."

"I didn't mean you weren't but there's a strong sympathy for Jews, and ideas are born in life. One senses an awareness of injustice."

"Whatever is the injustice, the product must be art."

"Well, I respect your philosophy."

"Please do not respect so much," the writer said irritably. "We have in this country a quotation: 'It is impossible to make out of apology a fur coat.' The idea is similar. I appreciate your respect but need now practical assistance.

"Listen at first to me," Levitansky went on, slapping the table with his palm. "I am in desperate situation. I have written for years but little is published. In the past, one, two editors who were friends told me, private, that my stories are excellent but I violate social realism. This what you call objectivity they called it excessive naturalism and sentiment. It is hard to listen to such nonsense. They advise me swim but not to use my legs. They have warned me; also they have made excuses for me which I do not like them. Even they say I am crazy, although I explained them I submit my stories *because* Soviet Union is great country. A great country does not fear what artist writes. A great country breathes into its lungs work of writers, painters, musicians, and becomes more strong. That I told to them but they replied I am not sufficient realist. This is the reason I am not invited to be member of Writers' Union. Without this is impossible to publish." He smiled sourly. "They have demanded me to stop submitting to journals my work, so I have stopped."

"I'm sorry about that," I said. "I don't myself believe any good comes from exiling poets."

"I cannot continue any more in this fashion," Levitansky said, laying his hand on his heart. "I feel I am locked in drawer with my stories. Now I must get out or I suffocate. It becomes for me each day more difficult to write. It is not easy to request a stranger for such important personal favor. My wife advised me not. She is angry, also frightened, but it is impossible to go on in this way. I know in my bones I am important Soviet writer. I must have audience. I wish to see my books to be read by Soviet people. I wish to have in minds different than my own and my wife acknowledgment of my art. I wish them to know my work is related to Russian writers of the past as well as modern. I am in tradition of Chekhov, Gorky, Isaac Babel. I know if book of my stories will be published, it will make for me favorable reputation. This is reason why you must help me—it is necessary for my interior liberty."

His confession came in an agitated burst. I use the word advisedly because that's partly what upset me. I have never cared for confessions such as are meant to involve unwilling people in others' personal problems. Russians are past masters of the art—you can see it in their novels.

"I appreciate the honor of your request," I said, "but all I am is a passing tourist. That's a pretty tenuous relationship between us."

"I do not ask tourist—I ask human being—man," Levitansky said passionately. "Also you are free-lance writer. You know now what I am and what is on my heart. You sit in my house. Who else can I ask? I would prefer to publish in Europe my stories, maybe with Mondadori or Einaudi in Italy, but if this is impossible to you I will publish in America. Someday my work will be read in my own country, maybe after I am dead. This is terrible irony but my generation lives on such ironies. Since I am not now ambitious to die it will be great relief to me to know that at least in one language is alive my art. Mandelstam wrote: 'I will be enclosed in some alien speech.' Better so than nothing."

"You say I know who you are, but do you know who I am?" I asked him. "I'm a plain person, not very imaginative, though I don't write a bad article. My whole life, for some reason, has been without much real adventure, except I was divorced once and remarried happily to a woman whose death I am still mourning. Now I'm here more or less on a vacation, not to jeopardize myself by taking chances of an unknown sort. What's more—and this is the main thing I came to tell you—I wouldn't at all be surprised if I am already under suspicion and would do you more harm than good."

I told Levitansky about the airport incident in Kiev. "I signed a document I couldn't even read, which was a foolish thing to do."

"In Kiev this happened?"

"That's right."

He laughed dismally. "It would not happen to you if you entered through Moscow. In the Ukraine—what is your word?—they are rubes, country people."

"That might be—nevertheless I signed the paper."

"Do you have copy?"

"Not with me. In my desk drawer in the hotel."

"I am certain this is receipt for your books which officials will return to you when you depart from Soviet Union."

"That's what I'd be afraid of."

"Why afraid?" he asked. "Are you afraid to receive back umbrella which you have lost?"

"I'd be afraid one thing might lead to another—more questions, other searches. It would be stupid to have your manuscript in my suitcase, in Russian, no less, that I can't even read. Suppose they accuse me of being some kind of courier transferring stolen documents?"

The thought raised me to my feet. I realized the tension in the room was thick as steam, mostly mine.

Levitansky rose, embittered. "There is no question of spying. I do not think I have presented myself as traitor to my country."

"I didn't say anything of the sort. All I'm saying is I don't want to get into trouble with the Soviet authorities. Nobody can blame me for that. In other words the enterprise isn't for me."

"I have made at one time inquirings," Levitansky insisted. "You will have nothing to fear for tourist who has been a few weeks in U.S.S.R. under guidance of Intourist, and does not speak Russian. They sometimes ask questions to political people, also bourgeois journalists who have made bad impression. I would deliver to you the manuscript in the last instant. It is typed on less than one hundred fifty sheets thin paper and will make small package, weightless. If it should look to you like trouble, you can leave it in dustbin. My name will not be anywhere and if they find it and track—trace to me the stories, I will answer I threw them out myself. They won't believe this, but what other can I say? It will make no difference anyway. If I stop my writing I may as well be dead. No harm will come to you."

"I'd rather not, if you don't mind."

With what I guess was a curse of despair, Levitansky reached for the portrait on his bookcase and flung it against the wall. Pasternak struck Mayakovsky, splattering him with glass, shattering himself, and both pictures crashed to the floor.

"Free-lance writer," he shouted, "go to hell to America! Tell to Negroes about Bill of Rights! Tell them they are free although you keep them slaves! Talk to sacrificed Vietnamese people that you respect them!"

Irina Filipovna entered the room on the run. "Feliks," she entreated, "Kovalevsky hears every word!

"Please," she begged me, "please go away. Leave poor Levitansky alone. I beg you from my miserable heart."

I left in a hurry. The next day I flew to Leningrad.

Three days later, after a tense visit to Leningrad, I was sitting loosely in a beat-up taxi with a cheerful Intouristka, a half hour after my arrival at the Moscow airport. We were driving to the Ukraine Hotel, where I was assigned for my remaining days in the Soviet Union. I would have preferred the Metropole again because it is so conveniently located and I was used to it, but on second thought, better some place where a certain party wouldn't know I lived. The Volga we were riding in seemed somehow familiar, but if so it was safely in the hands of a small stranger with a large wool cap, a man wearing sunglasses, who paid me no particular attention.

I had had a rather special several minutes in Leningrad on my first day. On a white summer's evening, shortly after I had unpacked in my room at the Astoria, I discovered the Winter Palace and Hermitage after a walk along Nevsky Prospekt.

Chancing on Palace Square, vast, deserted at the moment, I felt an unexpected intense emotion thinking of the revolutionary events that had occurred on this spot. My God, I thought, why should I feel myself part of Russian history? It's a contagious business, what happens to men. On the Palace Bridge I gazed at the ice-blue Neva, in the distance the golden steeple of the cathedral built by Peter the Great gleaming under masses of wind-driven clouds in patches of green sky. It's the Soviet Union but it's still Russia.

The next day I woke up anxious. In the street I was approached twice by strangers speaking English; I think my suede shoes attracted them. The first, tight-eyed and badly dressed, wanted to sell me blackmarket rubles. "Nyet," I said, tipping my straw hat and hurrying on. The second, a tall, bearded boy of about nineteen, with a left-sided tuft longer than the right, wearing a home-knitted green pullover, offered to buy jazz records, "youth clothes," and American cigarettes. "Sorry, nothing for sale." I escaped him too, except that green sweater followed me for a kilometer along one of the canals. I broke into a run. When I looked back he had disappeared. I slept badly—it stayed light too long past midnight; and in the morning inquired about the possibility of an immediate flight to Helsinki. I was informed I couldn't book one for a week. I decided to return to Moscow a day before I had planned to, mostly to see what they had in the Dostoevsky Museum.

I had been thinking about Levitansky. How much of a writer was he really? I had read three of eighteen stories he wanted to publish. Suppose he had showed me the best and the others were mediocre or thereabouts? Was it worth taking a chance for that kind of book? I thought, the best thing for my peace of mind is to forget the guy. Before checking out of the Astoria I received a chatty letter from Lillian, forwarded from Moscow, apparently not in response to my recent one to her but written earlier. Should I marry her? Did I dare? The phone rang piercingly, but when I picked up the receiver no one answered. On the plane to Moscow I had visions of a crash; there must be many nobody ever reads of.

In my room on the twelfth floor of the Ukraine I relaxed in a green plastic-covered armchair. There was also a single low bed and a utilitarian pinewood desk, an apple-green telephone plunked on it for instant use. I'll be home in a week, I thought. Now I'd better shave and see if anything is left in the way of a concert or opera ticket for tonight. I'm in a mood for music.

The electric plug in the bathroom didn't work, so I put away my shaver and was lathering up when I jumped to a single explosive knock on the door. I opened it slowly and there stood Levitansky with a brown paper packet in his hand.

Is this son of a bitch out to compromise me?

"How did you happen to find out where I was only twenty minutes after I got back, Mr. Levitansky?"

"How I found you?" the writer shrugged. He seemed deathly tired, the face longer, leaner, resembling a hungry fox on his last unsteady legs, but still in business.

"My brother-in-law was chauffeur for you from the airport. He heard the girl inquire your name. We have spoke of you. Dmitri—this is my wife's brother—informed me you have registered at the Ukraine. I inquired downstairs your room number and it was granted to me."

"However it happened," I said firmly, "I want you to know I haven't changed my mind. I don't want to get more involved. I thought it all through while I was in Leningrad and that's my decision."

"I may come in?"

"Please, but for obvious reasons I'd appreciate a short visit."

Levitansky sat, thin knees pressed together in the armchair, his parcel awkwardly on his lap. If he was happy he had found me, it did nothing for his expression.

I finished shaving, put on a fresh white shirt, and sat down on the bed. "Sorry I have nothing to offer in the way of an aperitif but I could call downstairs?"

Levitansky twiddled his fingers no. He was dressed without change down to his socks. Did his wife wash out the same pair each night, or were all his socks tricolored?

"To speak frankly," I said, "I have to protest this constant tension you've whipped up in and around me. Nobody in his right mind can expect a complete stranger visiting the Soviet Union to pull his chestnuts out of the fire. It's your country that's hindering you as a writer, not me or the United States of America. Since you live here what can you do but live with it?"

"I love my country," Levitansky said.

"Nobody denies it. That holds for me, though love for country—let's face it—is a mixed bag. Nationality isn't soul as I'm sure you agree. But what I'm also saying is there are things about his country one might not like that he has to make his peace with. I'm assuming you're not thinking of counter-revolution. So if you're up against a wall you can't climb, or dig under, or outflank, at least stop banging your head against it, not to mention mine. Do what you can. It's amazing, for instance, what can be said in a fairy tale."

"I have written already my fairy tales," he said moodily. "Now is the time for truth without disguises. I will make my peace to this point where it interferes with my interior liberty; and then I must stop to make my peace. My brother-in-law has also told to me, 'You must write acceptable stories, others can do it, so why cannot you?' And I have answered to him, 'Yes, but must be acceptable to *me*!' "

"In that case, aren't you up against the impossible? If you permit me to say it, are those Jews in your stories, if they can't have their matzos and prayer books, any freer in their religious lives than you are as a writer? What I mean is, one has to face up to the nature of his society."

"I have faced up. Do you face up to yours?" he asked with a flash of scorn.

"My own problem is not that I can't express myself but that I don't. In my own mind Vietnam is a demoralizing mistake, yet I've never really opposed it except to sign petitions and vote for congressmen who say they're against the war. My first wife used to criticize me. She said I wrote the wrong things and was involved in everything but useful action. My second wife knew it but made me think she didn't. Maybe I'm just waking up to the fact that the U.S. government has for years been mucking up my self-respect."

Levitansky's larynx moved up like a flag on a pole, then sank.

He tried again, saying, "The Soviet Union preservates for us the great victories of our Revolution. Because of this I have remained for years at peace with the State. Communism is still to me inspirational ideal although this historical period is spoiled by leaders with impoverished view of humanity. They have pissed on Revolution."

"Stalin?"

"Him especially, but also others. Even so I have obeyed Party directives, and when I could not longer obey I wrote for drawer. I said to myself, 'Levitansky, history changes every minute and also Communism will change.' I believed if the State restricts two, three generations of artists, what is this against development of true socialist society—maybe best society of world history? So what does it mean if some of us are sacrificed to Party purpose? The aesthetic mode is not in necessity greater than politics—than needs of Revolution. Then in fifty years more will be secure the State, and all Soviet artists will say whatever they wish. This is what I tried to think, but do not longer think so. I do not believe more in partiinost, which is guided thought, an expression which is to me ridiculous. I do not think Revolution is fulfilled in country of unpublished novelists, poets, playwriters, who hide in drawers whole libraries of literature that will never be printed or if so, it will be printed after they stink in their graves. I think now the State will never be secure—never! It is not in the nature of politics, or human condition, to be finished with Revolution. Evgeny Zamyatin told: 'There is no final revolution. Revolutions are infinite!'"

"I guess that's along my own line of thinking," I said, hoping for reasons of personal safety to forestall Levitansky's ultimate confession—which he, with brooding eyes, was already relentlessly making—lest in the end it imprison me in his will and history.

"I have learned from writing my stories," the writer was saying, "that imagination is enemy of the State. I have learned from my writing that I am not free man. I ask for your help, not to harm my country, which still has magnificent socialistic possibilities, but in order to help me escape its worst errors. I do not wish to defame Russia. My purpose in my work is to show its true heart. So have done our writers from Pushkin to Pasternak and also, in his own way, Solzhenitsyn. If you believe in democratic humanism you must help artist to be free. Is not true?"

I got up, I think to shake myself out of his question. "What exactly is my responsibility to you, Levitansky?" I tried to contain the exasperation I felt.

"We are members of mankind. If I am drowning you must assist to save me."

"In unknown waters if I can't swim?"

"If not, throw to me rope."

"I'm a visitor here. I've told you I may be suspect. For all I know you yourself might be a Soviet agent out to get me, or the room may be bugged, and then where are we? Mr. Levitansky, please, I don't want to hear or argue any more. I'll just plead personal inability and ask you to leave."

"Bugged?"

"By a listening device planted in this room."

Levitansky turned gray. He sat a moment in meditation, then rose wearily from the chair.

"I withdraw now request for your assistance. I accept your word that you are not capable. I do not wish to make criticism of you. All I wish to say, Gospodin Garvitz, is it requires more to change a man's character than to change his name."

Levitansky left the room, leaving in his wake faint fumes of cognac. He had also passed gas.

"Come back!" I called, not too loudly, but if he heard through the door he didn't answer. Good riddance, I thought. Not that I don't sympathize with him but look what he's done to *my* interior liberty. Who has to come thousands of miles to Russia to get entangled in this kind of mess? It's a helluva way to spend a vacation.

The writer had gone but not his sneaky manuscript. It was lying on my bed.

"That's his baby, not mine." Angered, I knotted my tie and slipped on my coat, then via the English-language number, called for a cab.

A half hour later I was in the taxi, riding back and forth along Novo Ostapovskaya Street until I spotted the apartment house I thought it might be. It wasn't, it was another like it. I paid the driver and walked till I thought I had located it. After going up the stairs I was sure I had. When I knocked on Levitansky's door, the writer, looking older, distant—as if he'd been away on a trip and had just returned; or maybe simply interrupted at his work, his thoughts still in his words on the page, his pen in hand—stared at me. Very blankly.

"Levitansky, my heart breaks for you, I swear, but I am not, at this time of my life, considering my condition and recent experiences, in much of a mood to embark on a dangerous adventure. Please accept deepest regrets."

I thrust the manuscript into his hand and went down the stairs. Hurrying out of the building, I was, to my horror, unable to avoid Irina Levitansky coming in. Her eyes lit in fright as she recognized me an instant before I hit her full force and sent her sprawling along the walk.

"Oh, my God, what have I done? I beg your pardon!" I helped the dazed, hurt woman to her feet, brushed off her soiled skirt, and futilely, her pink blouse, split and torn on her lacerated arm and shoulder. I stopped dead when I felt myself experiencing erotic sensation.

Irina Filipovna held a handkerchief to her bloody nostril and wept a little. We sat on a stone bench, a girl of ten and her little brother watching us. Irina said something to them in Russian and they moved off.

"I was frightened of you also as you are of us," she said. "I trust you now because Levitansky does. But I will not urge you to take the manuscript. The responsibility is for you to decide."

"It's not a responsibility I want."

She said as though to herself, "Maybe I will leave Levitansky. He is wretched so much it is no longer a marriage. He drinks. Also he does not earn a living. My brother Dmitri allows him to drive the taxi two, three hours of the day, to my brother's disadvantage. Except for a ruble or two from this, I support him. Levitansky does not longer receive translation commissions. Also a neighbor in the house—I am sure Kovalevsky—has denounced him to the police for delinquency and parasitism. There will be a hearing. Levitansky says he will burn his manuscripts."

I said I had just returned the package of stories.

"He will not," she said. "But even if he burns, he will write more. If they take him away in prison he will write on toilet paper. When he comes out, he will write on newspaper margins. He sits this minute at his table. He is a magnificent writer. I cannot ask him not to write, but now I must decide if this is the condition I wish for myself for the rest of my life."

Irina sat in silence, an attractive woman with shapely legs

and feet, in a soiled skirt and torn blouse. I left her on the stone bench, her handkerchief squeezed in her fist.

That night—July 2, I was leaving the Soviet Union on the fifth—I experienced massive self-doubt. If I'm a coward why has it taken me so long to discover it? Where does anxiety end and cowardice begin? Feelings get mixed, sure enough, but not all cowards are anxious men and not all anxious men are cowards. Many "sensitive" (Rose's word), tense, even frightened human beings did in fear what had to be done, the fear calling up effort when it's time to fight or jump off a rooftop into a river. There comes a time in a man's life when to get where he has to—if there are no doors or windows—he walks through a wall.

On the other hand, suppose one is courageous in a hopeless cause—you concentrate on courage but not enough on horse sense? To get to the point of the problem endlessly on my mind, how do I finally decide it's a sensible and worthwhile thing to smuggle out Levitansky's manuscript, given my reasonable doubts of the ultimate worth of the operation? Granted, as I now grant, he's trustworthy and his wife is that and more; still, does it pay a man like me to run the risk?

If six thousand Soviet writers can't do very much to squeeze out another drop of freedom as artists, who am I to fight their battle—H. Harvitz, knight-of-the-free-lance from Manhattan? How far do you go, granted all men, including Communists, are created free and equal and justice is for all? How far do you go for art, if you're for Yeats, Matisse, and Ludwig van Beethoven? Not to mention Tolstoy and Dostoevsky. So far as to get yourself intentionally involved: the HH Ms. Smuggling Service? Will the President and State Department send up three cheers for my contribution to the cause of artistic social justice? And suppose it amounts to no more than a gaffe in the end?— What will I prove if I sneak out Levitansky's manuscript and all it turns out to be is just another passable book of stories?

That's how I argued with myself on more than one occasion, but soon I argued myself into solid indecision. What it boils down to, I'd say, is he expects me to help him because I'm an American. That's quite a nerve.

Two nights later—odd not to have the Fourth of July on

July 4 (I was listening for firecrackers)—a quiet light-lemon summer's evening in Moscow, after two monotonously uneasy days, though I was still writing museum notes, for relief I took myself off to the Bolshoi to hear *Tosca*. It was sung in Russian by a busty lady and a handsome Slavic tenor, but the Italian plot was unchanged, and in the end Scarpia, who had promised "death" by fake bullets, gave in sneaky exchange a fusillade of hot lead; another artist bit the dust and Floria Tosca learned the hard way that love wasn't what she had thought.

Next to me sat another full-breasted woman, this one a lovely Russian of maybe thirty in a white dress that fitted a well-formed figure, her blond hair piled in a birdlike mass on her splendid head. Lillian could look like that though not Rose. This woman—sitting alone, it turned out—spoke flawless English in a mezzo-soprano with a slight accent.

During the first intermission she asked in friendly fashion, managing to seem detached but interested: "Are you American? Or perhaps Swedish?"

"Not Swedish. American is correct. How did you happen to guess?"

"I noticed, if it does not bother you that I say it," she remarked with a charming laugh, "a certain self-satisfaction."

"You got the wrong party."

When she opened her purse a fragrance of springtime burst forth—fresh flowers; the warmth of her body rose to my nostrils. I was moved by memories of the hungers of youth—dreams, longing.

During intermission she touched my arm and said in a low voice, "May I ask a favor? Do you depart soon from the Soviet Union?"

"In fact tomorrow."

"How fortunate for me. Would it offer too much difficulty to mail, wherever you are going, an airmail letter addressed to my husband, who is presently in Paris? Our airmail service takes two weeks to arrive in the West. I shall be grateful."

I glanced at the envelope addressed half in French, half in Cyrillic, and said I wouldn't mind. But during the next act sweat grew active on my body, and at the end of the opera, after Tosca's shriek of death, I handed the letter back to the not wholly surprised lady, saying I was sorry. I had the feeling

I had heard her voice before. I hurried back to the hotel, determined not to leave my room for any reason other than breakfast; then out and into the wide blue sky.

I later fell asleep over a book and a bottle of sweetish warm beer a waiter had brought up, pretending to myself I was relaxed though I was concerned with worried thoughts of the departure and flight home; and when I awoke, three minutes on my wristwatch later, it seemed to me I had made the acquaintance of some new nightmares. I was momentarily panicked by the idea that someone had planted a letter on me, and I searched through the pockets of my two suits. Nyet. Then I recalled that in one of my dreams a drawer in a table I was sitting at had slowly come open, and Feliks Levitansky, a dwarf who lived in it along with a few friendly mice, managed to scale the wooden wall on the comb he used as a ladder, and to hop from the drawer ledge to the top of the table. He leered in my face, shook his Lilliputian fist, and shouted in high-pitched but (to me) understandable Russian, "Atombombnik! You massacred innocent Japanese people! Amerikansky bastards!"

"That's unfair," I cried out. "I was no more than a kid in college."

That's a sad dream, I thought.

Afterwards this occurred to me: Suppose what happened to Levitansky happens to me. Suppose America gets caught up in a war with China in some semi-reluctant stupid way, and to make fast hash of it—despite my frantic loud protestations: mostly I wave my arms and shout obscenities—we spatter them, before they can get going, with a few dozen H-bombs, boiling up a thick atomic soup of about two hundred million Orientals—blood, gristle, marrow, and lots of floating Chinese eyeballs. We win the war because the Soviets hadn't been able to make up their minds whom to shoot their missiles at first. And suppose after this unheard-of slaughter, about ten million Americans, in self-revulsion, head for the borders to flee the country. To stop the loss of wealth, the refugees are intercepted by the army in tanks and turned back. Harvitz hides in his room with shades drawn, writing in a fury of protest an epic poem condemning the mass butchery by America. What nation, Asiatic or other, is next? Nobody in the States wants to publish the poem because it might start riots and another flight of refugees to Canada and Mexico; then one day there's a knock on the door, and it isn't the F.B.I. but a bearded Levitansky, in better times a Soviet tourist, a modern, not medieval, Communist. He kindly offers to sneak the manuscript of the poem out for publication in the Soviet Union.

Why? Harvitz suspiciously asks.

Why not? To give the book its liberty.

I awoke after a restless night. I had been instructed by Intourist to be in the lobby with my baggage two hours before flight time, at 11 A.M. I was shaved and dressed by six, and at seven had breakfast—I was very hungry—of yogurt, sausage, and scrambled eggs in the twelfth-floor buffet. I went out to hunt for a taxi. They were hard to come by at this hour, but I finally located one near the American Embassy, not far from the hotel. Speaking my usual mixture of primitive German and French, I persuaded the driver by first suggesting, then slipping him an acceptable two rubles, to take me to Levitansky's house and wait a few minutes till I came out. Going hastily up the stairs, I knocked on his door, apologizing when he opened it, to the half-pajamaed, iron-faced writer, for waking him this early in the day. Without peace of mind or certainty of purpose I asked him whether he still wanted me to smuggle out his manuscript of stories. I got for my trouble the door slammed in my face.

A half hour later I had everything packed and was locking the suitcase. A knock on the door—half a rap, you might call it. For the suitcase, I thought. I was momentarily startled by the sight of a small man in a thick cap wearing a long trench coat. He winked, and against the will I winked back. I had recognized Levitansky's brother-in-law Dmitri, the taxi driver. He slid in, unbuttoned his coat, and brought forth the wrapped manuscript. Holding a finger to his lips, he handed it to me before I could say I was no longer interested.

"Levitansky changed his mind?"

"Not changed mind," he whispered. "Was afraid your voice to be heard by Kovalevsky."

"I'm sorry, I should have thought of that."

"Levitansky say not write to him," the brother-in-law said in a low tone. "When is published book, please to send to him copy of *Das Kapital.* He will understand message."

I reluctantly agreed.

The brother-in-law, a short shapeless figure with sad eyes, winked again, shook hands with a steamy palm, and slipped out of my room.

I unlocked my suitcase and laid the manuscript on top of my shirts. Then I unpacked half the contents and slipped the manuscript into a folder containing my notes on literary museums and a few letters from Lillian. I then and there decided that if I got back to the States, the next time I saw her I would ask her to marry me. The phone was ringing as I left the room.

On my way to the airport, alone in a taxi—no Intourist girl accompanied me—I felt, on and off, nauseated. If it's not the sausage and yogurt it must just be ordinary fear. Still, if Levitansky has the courage to send these stories out, the least I can do is give him a hand. When one thinks of it it's little enough he does for human freedom during the course of his life. At the airport if I can dig up a Bromo or its Russian equivalent I know I'll feel better.

The driver was observing me in the mirror, a stern man with the head of a scholar, impassively smoking.

"Le jour fait beau," I said.

He pointed with an upraised finger to a sign in English at one side of the road to the airport:

"Long live peace in the world!"

"Peace with freedom." I smiled at the thought of somebody, not Howard Harvitz, painting that in red on the Soviet sign.

We drove on, I foreseeing my exit from the Soviet Union. I had made discreet inquiries from time to time and an Intourist girl in Leningrad had told me I had first to show my papers at the passport-control desk, turn in all my rubles—a serious offense to walk off with any—and then check luggage; no inspection, she swore. And that was that. Unless, of course, the official at the passport desk found my name on a list and said I had to go to the customs office for a package. In that case—if nobody said so I wouldn't remind him—I would go get my books. I figured I wouldn't open the package, just tear off a bit of the wrapping, if they were wrapped, as though to make sure they were the books I expected, and then saunter away with the package under my arm.

I had heard that a KGB man was stationed at the ramp as

one boarded a plane. He asked for your passport, checked the picture, threw you a stare through dark lenses and, if there was no serious lack of resemblance, tore out your expired visa, pocketed it, and let you embark.

In ten minutes you were aloft, seat belts fastened in three languages, watching the plane banking west. Maybe if I looked hard I might see in the distance Feliks Levitansky on the roof waving his red-white-and-blue socks on a bamboo pole. Then the plane leveled off, and we were above the clouds, flying westward. And that's what I would be doing for five or six hours unless the pilot received radio instructions to turn back; or maybe land in Czechoslovakia or East Germany, where two big-hatted detectives boarded the plane. By an act of imagination and will I made it some other passenger they were arresting. I got the plane into the air again and we flew on without incident until we touched down in free London.

As the taxi approached the Moscow airport, fingering my ticket and gripping my suitcase handle, I wished for courage equal to Levitansky's when they discovered he was the author of a book of stories I had managed to get published, and his trial and suffering began.

Levitansky's first story, translated by his wife, Irina Filipovna, was about an old man, a widower of seventy-eight, who hoped to have matzos for Passover.

Last year he had got his quota. They had been baked in the State bakery and sold in the State stores; but this year the State bakeries were not permitted to bake them. The officials said the machines had broken down but who believed them?

The old man went to the rabbi, an older man with a tormented beard, and asked him where he could get matzos. He feared that he mightn't have them this year.

"So do I," confessed the old rabbi. He said he had been told to tell his congregants to buy flour and bake them at home. The State stores would sell them the flour.

"What good is that for me?" asked the widower. He reminded the rabbi that he had no home to speak of, a single small room with a one-burner electric stove. His wife had died two years ago. His only living child, a married daughter, was with her husband in Birobijan. His other relatives—the few who were left after the German invasion—two female cousins his age—lived in Odessa; and he himself, even if he could find an oven, did not know how to bake matzos. And if he couldn't what should he do?

The rabbi then promised he would try to get the widower a kilo or two of matzos, and the old man, rejoicing, blessed him.

He waited anxiously a month but the rabbi never mentioned the matzos. Maybe he had forgotten. After all he was an old man burdened with worries, and the widower did not want to press him. However, Passover was coming on wings, so he must do something. A week before the Holy Days he hurried to the rabbi's flat and spoke to him there.

"Rabbi," he begged, "you promised me a kilo or two of matzos. What happened to them?"

"I know I promised," said the rabbi, "but I'm no longer sure to whom. It's easy to promise." He dabbed at his face with a damp handkerchief. "I was warned I could be arrested on charges of profiteering in the production and sale of matzos. I was told it could happen even if I were to give them away for nothing. It's a new crime they've invented. Still, take them anyway. If they arrest me, I'm an old man, and how long can an old man live in Lubyanka? Not so long, thank God. Here, I'll give you a small pack but you must tell no one where you got the matzos."

"May the Lord eternally bless you, rabbi. As for dying in prison, rather let it happen to our enemies."

The rabbi went to his closet and got out a small pack of matzos, already wrapped and tied with knotted twine. When the widower offered in a whisper to pay him, at least the cost of the flour, the rabbi wouldn't hear of it. "God provides," he said, "although at times with difficulty." He said there was hardly enough for all who wanted matzos, so he must take what he got and be thankful.

"I will eat less," said the old man. "I will count mouthfuls. I will save the last matzo to look at and kiss if there isn't enough to last me. He will understand."

Overjoyed to have even a few matzos, he rode home on the trolley car and there met another Jew, a man with a withered hand. They conversed in Yiddish in low tones. The stranger had glanced at the almost square package, then at the widower, and had hoarsely whispered, "Matzos?" The widower, tears starting in his eyes, nodded. "With God's grace." "Where did you get them?" "God provides." "So if He provides let Him provide me," the stranger brooded. "I'm not so lucky. I was hoping for a package from relatives in Cleveland, America. They wrote they would send me a large pack of the finest matzos, but when I inquire of the authorities they say no matzos have arrived. You know when they will get here?" he muttered. "After Passover by a month or two, and what good will they be then?"

The widower nodded sadly. The stranger wiped his eyes with his good hand and after a short while left the trolley amid a number of people getting off. He had not bothered to say goodbye, and neither had the widower, not to remind him of his own good fortune. But when the time came for the old man to leave the trolley he glanced down between his feet where he had placed the package of matzos, and nothing was there. His feet were there. The old man felt harrowed, as though someone had ripped a large nail up his spine. He searched frantically throughout that car, going a long way past his stop, querying every passenger, the woman conductor, the motorman, but they all swore they had not seen his matzos.

Then it occurred to him that the stranger with the withered hand had stolen them.

The widower in his misery asked himself, Would a Jew have robbed another of his precious matzos? It didn't seem possible, but it was.

As for me I haven't even a matzo to look at now. If I could steal any, whether from Jew or Russian, I would steal them. He thought he would steal them even from the old rabbi.

The widower went home without his matzos and had none for Passover.

The story called "Tallith" concerned a youth of seventeen, beardless but for some stray hairs on his chin, who had come from Kirov to the steps of the synagogue on Arkhipova Street in Moscow. He had brought with him a capacious prayer shawl, a white garment of luminous beauty, which he offered for sale to a cluster of Jews of various sorts and sizes—curious, apprehensive, greedy at the sight of the shawl—for fifteen rubles. Most of them avoided the youth, particularly the older Jews, despite the fact that some of the more devout among them were worried about their prayer shawls, eroded on their shoulders after years of daily use, which they could not replace. "It's the informers among us who have put him up to this," they whispered among themselves, "so they will have someone to inform on."

Still, in spite of the warnings of their elders, several of the younger men examined the tallith and admired it. "Where did you get such a fine prayer shawl?" the youth was asked. "It was my father's who recently died," he said. "It was given to him by a rich Jew he had once befriended." "Then why don't you keep it for yourself, you're a Jew, aren't you?" "Yes," said the youth, not the least embarrassed, "but I am going to Bratsk as a komsomol volunteer and I need a few rubles to get married. Besides I'm a confirmed atheist."

One young man with fat unshaven cheeks, who admired the deeply white shawl, its white glowing in whiteness, with its long silk fringes, whispered to the youth he might consider buying it for five rubles. But he was overheard by the gabbai, the lay leader of the congregation, who raised his cane and shouted at the whisperer, "Hooligan, if you buy that shawl, beware it doesn't become your shroud." The Jew with the unshaven cheeks retreated.

"Don't strike him," cried the frightened rabbi, who had come out of the synagogue and saw the gabbai with his cane upraised. He urged the congregants to begin prayers at once. To the youth he said, "Please go away from here, we are burdened with enough trouble. It is forbidden for anyone to sell religious articles. Do you want us to be accused of criminal economic activity? Do you want the doors of the shul to be shut forever? So do us and yourself a mitzvah and go away."

The congregants moved inside. The youth was left standing alone on the steps; but then the gabbai came out of the door, a man with a deformed spine and a wad of cotton stuck in a leaking ear.

"Look here," he said. "I know you stole it. Still, after all is said and done, a tallith is a tallith and God asks no questions of His worshippers. I offer eight rubles for it, take it or leave it. Talk fast before the services end and the others come out."

"Make it ten and it's yours," said the youth. The gabbai gazed at him shrewdly. "Eight is all I have, but wait here and I'll borrow two rubles from my brother-in-law."

The youth waited patiently. Dusk was heavy. In a few minutes a black car drove up, stopped in front of the synagogue, and two policemen got out. The youth realized that the gabbai had informed on him. Not knowing what else to do he hastily draped the prayer shawl over his head and began loudly to pray. He prayed a passionate kaddish. The police hesitated to approach him while he was praying, and they stood at the bottom of the steps waiting for him to be done. The congregants came out and could not believe their ears. No one imagined the youth could pray so fervently. What moved them was the tone, the wail and passion of a man truly praying. Perhaps his father had indeed recently died. All listened attentively, and many wished he would pray forever, for they knew that as soon as he stopped he would be seized and thrown into prison.

It has grown dark. A moon hovers behind murky clouds over the synagogue steeple. The youth's voice is heard in prayer. The congregants are huddled in the dark street, listening. Both police agents are still there, although they cannot be seen. Neither can the youth. All that can be seen is the white shawl luminously praying.

The last of the stories translated by Irina Filipovna was about a writer of mixed parentage, a Russian father and Jewish mother, who had secretly been writing stories for years. He had from a young age wanted to write but had at first not had the courage—it seemed like such a merciless undertaking—so he had gone into translation instead; and then when he had, one day, started to write seriously and exultantly, after a while he found to his surprise that many of his stories—about half—were of Jews.

For a half-Jew that's a reasonable proportion, he thought. The others were about Russians who sometimes resembled members of his father's family. "It's good to have such different sources for ideas," he told his wife. "This way I can cover a varied range of experiences in life."

After several years of work he had submitted a selection of his stories to a trusted friend of university days, Viktor Zverkov, an editor of the Progress Publishing House; and the writer appeared at his office one morning after receiving a hastily scribbled cryptic note from his friend, to discuss his work with him. Zverkov, a troubled man to begin with—he told everyone his wife did not respect him—jumped up from his chair and turned the key in the door, his ear pressed a minute at the crack. He then went quickly to his desk and withdrew the manuscript from a drawer he first had to unlock with a key he kept in his pocket. He was a heavy-set man with a flushed complexion, stained teeth, and a hoarse voice; and he handled the writer's manuscript with unease, as if it might leap up and wound him in the face.

"Please, Tolya," he whispered breathily, bringing his head close to the writer's, "you must take these awful stories away at once."

"What's the matter with you? Why are you shaking so?" said the writer.

"Don't pretend to be naïve. I am frankly amazed that you are submitting such unorthodox material for publication. My opinion as an editor is that they are of doubtful literary merit—I won't say devoid of it, Tolya, I have to be honest—but as stories they are a frightful affront to our society. I can't understand why you should take it on yourself to write about Jews. What do you know about them? Your culture is not the least Jewish, it's Soviet Russian. The whole business smacks of hypocrisy—of anti-Semitism."

He got up to shut the window and peered into a closet before sitting down.

"Are you out of your mind, Viktor?" said the writer. "My stories are in no sense anti-Semitic. One would have to read them standing on his head to make that judgment."

"There can be only one logical interpretation," the editor argued. "According to my most lenient analysis, which is favorable to you as a person—of let's call it decent intent—the stories fly in the face of socialist realism and reveal a dangerous inclination—perhaps even a stronger word should be used—to anti-Soviet sentiment. Maybe you're not entirely aware of this—I know how a story can pull a writer by the nose. As an editor I have to be sensitive to such things. I know, Tolya, from our conversations that you are a sincere believer in socialism; I won't accuse you of being defamatory to the Soviet system, but others may. In fact, I know they will. If one of the editors of *Oktyabr* was to read your stories, believe me, your career would explode in a mess. You seem not to have a normal awareness of what self-preservation is, and what's appallingly worse, you're not above entangling innocent bystanders in your fate. If these stories were mine, I assure you I would never have brought them to you. I urge you to destroy them at once before they destroy you."

He drank thirstily from a glass of water on his desk.

"That's the last thing I would do," answered the writer in anger. "These stories, if not in tone or subject matter, are written in the spirit of our early Soviet writers—the joyous spirits of the years just after the Revolution."

"I think you know what happened to many of those 'joyous spirits.'"

The writer for a moment stared at him. "Well, then, what of those stories that are not about the experience of Jews? Some are pieces about homely aspects of Russian life. What I hoped is that you might personally recommend one or two such stories to *Novy Mir* or *Yunost.* They are innocuous sketches and well written."

"Not the one about the two prostitutes," said the editor. "That contains hidden social criticism, and is adversely naturalistic."

"A prostitute lives a social life."

"That may be but I can't recommend it for publication. I must advise you, Tolya, if you expect to receive further commissions for translations from us, you must immediately rid yourself of this whole manuscript so as to avoid the possibility of serious consequences both to yourself and family, and to the publishing house that has employed you so faithfully and generously in the past."

"Since you didn't write the stories yourself, you needn't be afraid, Viktor Alexandrovich," the writer said ironically.

"I am not a coward, if that's what you're hinting, Anatoly Borisovich, but if a wild locomotive is running loose on the rails, I know which way to jump."

The writer hastily gathered up his manuscript, stuffed the papers into his leather case, and returned home by bus. His wife was still away at work. He took out the stories and, after reading through one, burned it, page by page, in the kitchen sink.

His nine-year-old son, returning from school, said, "Papa, what are you burning in the sink? That's no place for a fire."

"I'm burning my talent," said the writer. He said, "And my integrity, and my heritage."

My Son the Murderer

HE WAKES feeling his father is in the hallway, listening. He listens to him sleep and dream. Listening to him get up and fumble for his pants. He won't put on his shoes. To him not going to the kitchen to eat. Staring with shut eyes in the mirror. Sitting an hour on the toilet. Flipping the pages of a book he can't read. To his anguish, loneliness. The father stands in the hall. The son hears him listen.

My son the stranger, he won't tell me anything.

I open the door and see my father in the hall. Why are you standing there, why don't you go to work?

On account of I took my vacation in the winter instead of the summer like I usually do.

What the hell for if you spend it in this dark smelly hallway, watching my every move? Guessing what you can't see. Why are you always spying on me?

My father goes to the bedroom and after a while sneaks out in the hallway again, listening.

I hear him sometimes in his room but he don't talk to me and I don't know what's what. It's a terrible feeling for a father. Maybe someday he will write me a letter, My dear father . . .

My dear son Harry, open up your door. My son the prisoner.

My wife leaves in the morning to stay with my married daughter, who is expecting her fourth child. The mother cooks and cleans for her and takes care of the three children. My daughter is having a bad pregnancy, with high blood pressure, and lays in bed most of the time. This is what the doctor advised her. My wife is gone all day. She worries something is wrong with Harry. Since he graduated college last summer he is alone, nervous, in his own thoughts. If you talk to him, half the time he yells if he answers you. He reads the papers, smokes, he stays in his room. Or once in a while he goes for a walk in the street.

How was the walk, Harry?

A walk.

My wife advised him to go look for work, and a couple of

times he went, but when he got some kind of an offer he didn't take the job.

It's not that I don't want to work. It's that I feel bad.

So why do you feel bad?

I feel what I feel. I feel what is.

Is it your health, sonny? Maybe you ought to go to a doctor?

I asked you not to call me by that name any more. It's not my health. Whatever it is I don't want to talk about it. The work wasn't the kind I want.

So take something temporary in the meantime, my wife said to him.

He starts to yell. Everything's temporary. Why should I add more to what's temporary? My gut feels temporary. The goddamn world is temporary. On top of that I don't want temporary work. I want the opposite of temporary, but where is it? Where do you find it?

My father listens in the kitchen.

My temporary son.

She says I'll feel better if I work. I say I won't. I'm twenty-two since December, a college graduate, and you know where you can stick that. At night I watch the news programs. I watch the war from day to day. It's a big burning war on a small screen. It rains bombs and the flames roar higher. Sometimes I lean over and touch the war with the flat of my hand. I wait for my hand to die.

My son with the dead hand.

I expect to be drafted any day but it doesn't bother me the way it used to. I won't go. I'll go to Canada or somewhere I can go.

The way he is frightens my wife and she is glad to go to my daughter's house early in the morning to take care of the three children. I stay with him in the house but he don't talk to me.

You ought to call up Harry and talk to him, my wife says to my daughter.

I will sometime but don't forget there's nine years' difference between our ages. I think he thinks of me as another mother around and one is enough. I used to like him when he was a little boy but now it's hard to deal with a person who won't reciprocate to you.

She's got high blood pressure. I think she's afraid to call.

I took two weeks off from my work. I'm a clerk at the stamp window in the post office. I told the superintendent I wasn't feeling so good, which is no lie, and he said I should take sick leave. I said I wasn't that sick, I only needed a little vacation. But I told my friend Moe Berkman I was staying out because Harry has me worried.

I understand what you mean, Leo. I got my own worries and anxieties about my kids. If you got two girls growing up you got hostages to fortune. Still in all we got to live. Why don't you come to poker on this Friday night? We got a nice game going. Don't deprive yourself of a good form of relaxation.

I'll see how I feel by Friday how everything is coming along. I can't promise you.

Try to come. These things, if you give them time, all will pass away. If it looks better to you, come on over. Even if it don't look so good, come on over anyway because it might relieve your tension and worry that you're under. It's not so good for your heart at your age if you carry that much worry around.

It's the worst kind of worry. If I worry about myself I know what the worry is. What I mean, there's no mystery. I can say to myself, Leo you're a big fool, stop worrying about nothing—over what, a few bucks? Over my health that has always stood up pretty good although I have my ups and downs? Over that I'm now close to sixty and not getting any younger? Everybody that don't die by age fifty-nine gets to be sixty. You can't beat time when it runs along with you. But if the worry is about somebody else, that's the worst kind. That's the real worry because if he won't tell you, you can't get inside of the other person and find out why. You don't know where's the switch to turn off. All you do is worry more.

So I wait out in the hall.

Harry, don't worry so much about the war.

Please don't tell me what to worry about or what not to worry about.

Harry, your father loves you. When you were a little boy,

every night when I came home you used to run to me. I picked you up and lifted you up to the ceiling. You liked to touch it with your small hand.

I don't want to hear about that any more. It's the very thing I don't want to hear. I don't want to hear about when I was a child.

Harry, we live like strangers. All I'm saying is I remember better days. I remember when we weren't afraid to show we loved each other.

He says nothing.

Let me cook you an egg.

An egg is the last thing in the world I want.

So what do you want?

He put his coat on. He pulled his hat off the clothes tree and went down into the street.

Harry walked along Ocean Parkway in his long overcoat and creased brown hat. His father was following him and it filled him with rage.

He walked at a fast pace up the broad avenue. In the old days there was a bridle path at the side of the walk where the concrete bicycle path is now. And there were fewer trees, their black branches cutting the sunless sky. At the corner of Avenue X, just about where you can smell Coney Island, he crossed the street and began to walk home. He pretended not to see his father cross over, though he was infuriated. The father crossed over and followed his son home. When he got to the house he figured Harry was upstairs already. He was in his room with the door shut. Whatever he did in his room he was already doing.

Leo took out his small key and opened the mailbox. There were three letters. He looked to see if one of them was, by any chance, from his son to him. My dear father, let me explain myself. The reason I act as I do . . . There was no such letter. One of the letters was from the Post Office Clerks Benevolent Society, which he slipped into his coat pocket. The other two letters were for Harry. One was from the draft board. He brought it up to his son's room, knocked on the door, and waited.

He waited for a while.

To the boy's grunt he said, There is a draft-board letter here for you. He turned the knob and entered the room. His son was lying on his bed with his eyes shut.

Leave it on the table.

Do you want me to open it for you, Harry?

No, I don't want you to open it. Leave it on the table. I know what's in it.

Did you write them another letter?

That's my goddamn business.

The father left it on the table.

The other letter to his son he took into the kitchen, shut the door, and boiled up some water in a pot. He thought he would read it quickly and seal it carefully with a little paste, then go downstairs and put it back in the mailbox. His wife would take it out with her key when she returned from their daughter's house and bring it up to Harry.

The father read the letter. It was a short letter from a girl. The girl said Harry had borrowed two of her books more than six months ago and since she valued them highly she would like him to send them back to her. Could he do that as soon as possible so that she wouldn't have to write again?

As Leo was reading the girl's letter Harry came into the kitchen and when he saw the surprised and guilty look on his father's face, he tore the letter out of his hands.

I ought to murder you the way you spy on me.

Leo turned away, looking out of the small kitchen window into the dark apartment-house courtyard. His face burned, he felt sick.

Harry read the letter at a glance and tore it up. He then tore up the envelope marked personal.

If you do this again don't be surprised if I kill you. I'm sick of you spying on me.

Harry, you are talking to your father.

He left the house.

Leo went into his room and looked around. He looked in the dresser drawers and found nothing unusual. On the desk by the window was a paper Harry had written on. It said: Dear Edith, why don't you go fuck yourself? If you write me another stupid letter I'll murder you.

The father got his hat and coat and left the house. He ran

slowly for a while, running then walking until he saw Harry on the other side of the street. He followed him, half a block behind.

He followed Harry to Coney Island Avenue and was in time to see him board a trolleybus going to the Island. Leo had to wait for the next one. He thought of taking a taxi and following the trolleybus, but no taxi came by. The next bus came fifteen minutes later and he took it all the way to the Island. It was February and Coney Island was wet, cold, and deserted. There were few cars on Surf Avenue and few people on the streets. It felt like snow. Leo walked on the boardwalk amid snow flurries, looking for his son. The gray sunless beaches were empty. The hot-dog stands, shooting galleries, and bathhouses were shuttered up. The gunmetal ocean, moving like melted lead, looked freezing. A wind blew in off the water and worked its way into his clothes so that he shivered as he walked. The wind white-capped the leaden waves and the slow surf broke on the empty beaches with a quiet roar.

He walked in the blow almost to Sea Gate, searching for his son, and then walked back again. On his way toward Brighton Beach he saw a man on the shore standing in the foaming surf. Leo hurried down the boardwalk stairs and onto the ribbed-sand beach. The man on the roaring shore was Harry, standing in water to the tops of his shoes.

Leo ran to his son. Harry, it was a mistake, excuse me, I'm sorry I opened your letter.

Harry did not move. He stood in the water, his eyes on the swelling leaden waves.

Harry, I'm frightened. Tell me what's the matter. My son, have mercy on me.

I'm frightened of the world, Harry thought. It fills me with fright.

He said nothing.

A blast of wind lifted his father's hat and carried it away over the beach. It looked as though it was going to be blown into the surf, but then the wind blew it toward the boardwalk, rolling like a wheel along the wet sand. Leo chased after his hat. He chased it one way, then another, then toward the water. The wind blew the hat against his legs and he caught it. By now he was crying. Breathless, he wiped his eyes with icy fingers and returned to his son at the edge of the water.

He is a lonely man. This is the type he is. He will always be lonely.

My son who made himself into a lonely man.

Harry, what can I say to you? All I can say to you is who says life is easy? Since when? It wasn't for me and it isn't for you. It's life, that's the way it is—what more can I say? But if a person don't want to live what can he do if he's dead? Nothing is nothing, it's better to live.

Come home, Harry, he said. It's cold here. You'll catch a cold with your feet in the water.

Harry stood motionless in the water and after a while his father left. As he was leaving, the wind plucked his hat off his head and sent it rolling along the shore. He watched it go.

My father listens in the hallway. He follows me in the street. We meet at the edge of the water.

He runs after his hat.

My son stands with his feet in the ocean.

An Exorcism

FOGEL, A writer, had had another letter from Gary Simson, the would-be writer, a request as usual. He wrote fiction but hadn't jelled. Fogel, out of respect, saved letters from writers but was tempted not to include Simson although he had begun to publish. I am not his mentor, though he calls himself my student. If so what have I taught him? In the end he placed the letter in his files. I have his others, he thought.

Eli Fogel was a better than ordinary writer but not especially "successful." He disliked the word. His productivity was limited by his pace which, for reasons of having to breathe hard to enjoy life, was slow. Two and a half books in fifteen years, the half a paperback of undistinguished verse. My limp is symbolic, he thought. His leg had been injured in a bicycle accident as a youth, though with the built-up shoe the limp was less noticeable than when he hobbled around barefoot. He limped for his lacks. Fogel, for instance, regretted never having married, blaming this on his devotion to work. It's not that it has to be one or the other, but for me it's one or none. He was, mildly, a monomaniac. That simplified life but reduced it—what else? Still, he did not pity himself. It amused Fogel rather than not that the protagonists of his two published novels were married men with families, their wounds deriving from sources other than hurt members and primal loneliness. Imagination saves me, he thought.

Both his novels had received praise, though not much else; and Fogel had for the past six years labored on a third, about half completed. Since he declined to write reviews, lecture, or teach regularly, he ran into money problems. Fortunately he had from his father a small inheritance that came to five thousand annually, a shrinking sum in an inflated world; so Fogel reluctantly accepted summer-school invitations, or taught, somewhat on the prickly side, at writers' conferences, one or two a summer. With what he had he made do.

It was at one of these conferences in Buffalo, in June, and at another in mid-August of the same summer, on the campus of a small college in the White Mountains, that the writer had met, and later renewed a friendship with, Gary Simson, then less than half Fogel's age; a friendship of sorts, mild, fallible, but for a while satisfying; that is to say, possessing some of the attributes and possibilities of friendship.

Gary, a slight glaze in his eyes as he listened to Fogel talk about writing, wanted, he seriously confessed with a worried brow, "more than anything," even "desperately," to be a writer—the desperation inciting goose bumps on Fogel's flesh, putting him off for a full fifteen minutes. He sat in depressed silence in his office as the youth fidgeted. "What's the rush?" the writer ultimately asked. "I've got to get there," the youth replied. "Get where?" "I want to be a good writer someday, Mr. Fogel." "It's a long haul, my boy," Eli Fogel said. "Make a friend of time. And steer clear of desperation. Desperate people tend to be bad writers, increasing desperation." He laughed a little, not unkindly. Gary sat nodding as though he had learned the lesson of his life. He was twenty-two, a curly-haired senior in college, with a broad fleshy face and frame. On his appearance at the Buffalo conference he wore a full reddish mustache drooping down the sides of his thick-lipped mouth. He shaved it off on meeting Fogel and then grew it again later in the summer. He was six feet tall and his height and breadth made him look older than he was, if not wiser. For a while after his talk with Fogel he pretended to be more casual about his work, one who skirted excess and got it right. He pretended to be Fogel a bit, amusing Fogel. He had never had a disciple before and felt affection for the boy. Gary livened things up for the writer. One could see him in the distance, coming with his yellow guitar. He strummed without distinction but sang fairly well, a tenor aspiring, related to art. "Sing me 'Ochi Chernye,' Gary," Fogel said, and the youth obliged as the older man became pleasantly melancholic, thinking what if he'd had a son. Touch a hand to a guitar and Fogel had a wet eye. And Gary offered services as well as devoted attention: got books Fogel needed from the library; drove him into town when he had errands to do; could be depended on to retrieve forgotten lecture notes in his room—as if it were in compensation, though Fogel required none, for the privilege of sitting at his feet and plying him with questions about the art of fiction. Fogel, touched by his amiability, all he had yet to learn, by his own knowledge of the sadnesses of a writer's life, invited him, usually with one or another of his friends, to his room for a drink before dinner. Gary brought along a thick notebook to jot down Fogel's table talk. He showed him the first sentence he had copied down: "Imagination is not necessarily Id," causing the writer when he read it to laugh uncomfortably. Gary laughed too. Fogel thought the note taking silly but didn't object when Gary scribbled down long passages, although he doubted he had wisdom of any serious sort to offer. He was wiser in his work—one would be who revised often enough. He wished Gary would go to his books for answers to some of the questions he asked and stop treating poor Fogel like a guru.

"You can't dissect a writer to learn what writing is or entails. One learns from experience, or should. I can't teach anyone to be a writer, Gary—I've said that in my lectures. All I do here is talk about some things I've learned and hope somebody talented is listening. I always regret coming to these conferences."

"You can give insights, can't you?"

"Insights you can get from your mother."

"More specifically, if I might ask, what do you think of my writing thus far, sir?"

Fogel reflected. "Promise you have—that's all I can say now, but keep working."

"What should I work most for?"

"Search possibility in and out and beyond the fact. I have the impression when I read your stories—the two in Buffalo and the one you've given me here—that you remember or research too much. Memory is an ingredient, Gary, not the whole stew; and don't make the error some do of living life as though it were a future fiction. Invent, my boy."

"I'll certainly try, Mr. Fogel." He seemed worried.

Fogel lectured four mornings a week at eight-thirty so he could spend the rest of the day at work. His large bright room in a guest house close to a pine grove, whose fragrance he breathed as he wrote on a cracked table by a curtained window, was comfortable even on hot afternoons. He worked every day, half day on Sundays, quitting as a rule around four; then soaked in a smallish stained tub, dressed leisurely, whistling through his teeth, in a white flannel suit fifteen years in service, and waited, holding a book before his nose, for someone to come for a drink. During the last week of the White Mountain conference he saw Gary each night. Sometimes they drove to a movie in town, or walked after supper along a path by a stream, the youth stopping to jot down in his notebook sentences given off by Fogel, chaff as well as grain. They went on until the mosquitoes thickened or Fogel's limp began to limp. He wore a Panama hat, slightly yellowed, and white shoes he whitened daily, one with a higher heel than the other. Fogel's pouched dark eyes, even as he spoke animatedly, were contemplative, and he listened with care to Gary though he didn't always hear. In the last year or two he had lost weight and his white suit hung on his shoulders. He looked small by Gary's side, although he was shorter by only three inches. And once the youth, in a burst of vitality or affection, his one imaginative act of the summer, lifted Fogel at the hips and held him breathless in the air. The writer gazed into Gary's gold-flecked eyes; that he found them doorless to the self filled him with remorse.

Or Gary drove them in his noisy Peugeot to a small piano-playing bar by a crossroads several miles the other side of town, sometimes in the company of one or two students, occasionally a colleague but usually students; and this made it a fuller pleasure because Fogel enjoyed being with women. Gary, who had a talent for acquiring pretty girls, one night brought along one of the loveliest Fogel had ever seen. The girl, about twenty-five, with streaked dyed-blond and dark hair wore a red dress on her long-waisted body, the breasts ample, loose, her buttocks shapely, sweet. A rare find indeed; but the youth, senseless, sullen, or stoned, gave her scant attention. He glanced at her once in a while as if trying to remember where he had met her. Sad-eyed, she drank Scotch on the rocks, gnawing her lip as she watched his eyes roving over the dancers on the floor. Too bad she doesn't know how much I appreciate her, Fogel mused.

Where does he get so many attractive girls—he had been

equally effective in Buffalo—and why doesn't he bring the same one two nights running? This blessed creature in red would last me half a lifetime. The youth's taste in women could not be faulted—but he seemed, after a short time, unmoved by them and yawned openly, although it was rumored he enjoyed an active heterosexual life. He has so many and goes through them so quickly—where does he think one learns longing? Where does poetry come from? She's too good for him, he thought, not knowing exactly why, unless she was good for *him*. Ah youth, ah summer. Once again he seriously considered the possibility of marriage. After all, how old is forty-six—not, in any case, *old*. A good twenty-five or thirty years to go, enough to raise a family.

On what?

For his companion Fogel had asked along a schoolteacher from his class, a Miss Rudel from Manhattan, unmarried but not lacking a sense of humor; nor did she take her dabbling in fiction seriously, a pleasant change from the desperate ladies who haunted the conference. But he looked her over and found her wanting, then found himself wanting.

Perhaps because the evening had acquired a sexual tone he remembered Lucy Matthews, a desperate writer presently attending his lectures. About a week ago, after going through a shoe box full of exasperating stories she had left with him, representing the past year's work, he had told her bluntly, "Miss Matthews, let's not pretend that writing is a substitute for talent." And when she quietly gasped, cracking the knuckles of one hand, then of the other, he went on: "If you are out to save your soul, there are better ways."

The lady gazed bleakly at Fogel; a slim woman with fair figure, tense neck, and anxious eyes.

"But, Mr. Fogel, how does one go about finding out the extent of her talent? Some of my former professors told me I write capable stories, yet you seem to think I'm hopeless." Tears brimmed in her eyes.

Fogel was about to soften his judgment but warned himself it would be less than honest to encourage her. She was from Cedar Falls and this was her fourth conference of the summer. He vowed again to give them up forever.

Lucy Matthews plucked a Kleenex out of her handbag and

quietly cried, waiting for perhaps a good word, but the writer, sitting in silence, had none to offer. She got up and hurriedly left the office.

But at ten o'clock that night, dressed in a taffeta party dress, her hair brushed into a bright sheen, briskly perfumed, Lucy tapped on Fogel's house door. Accepting his surprised invitation to enter, after three silent sips of bourbon and water, she lifted her noisy dress over her head and stood there naked.

"Mr. Fogel," she whispered passionately, "you aren't afraid to tell the truth. Your work represents art. I feel that if I could hold you in my arms I would be close to both—art and truth."

"It just isn't so," Fogel replied as he fought off the feeling that he had stepped into a Sherwood Anderson story. "I would like to sleep with you, frankly, but not for the reasons stated. If you had said, 'Fogel, you may be an odd duck but you've aroused me tonight and I would gladly go to bed with you'—could you say that?"

"If you prefer fellation—" Lucy whispered tensely.

"Thank you kindly," he said with tenderness, "I prefer the embrace of a woman. Would you care to answer my question?"

Shivering around the shoulders, Lucy Matthews came to her finest moment at writing conferences.

"I can't truly say so."

"Ah, too bad," Fogel sighed. "Anyway, I'm privileged you saw fit to undress in my presence."

She slipped on the dress at her feet and departed. Fogel especially regretted the loss because the only woman he had slept with that summer, a young chambermaid in a Buffalo hotel he had stayed at in June, had hurt him dreadfully.

"Are you dreaming about something, Mr. Fogel?" Gary asked.

"Only vaguely," Fogel replied.

"An idea for a story, I bet?"

"It may come to that."

When the conference ended, Gary, waiting outside the lecture barn to take Fogel to the train, asked him, "Will I ever be a good writer, do you think, Mr. Fogel?"

"It depends on commitment. You'll have to prove yourself."

"I will if you have faith in me."

"Even if I have no faith in you. Who is Eli Fogel, after all, but a man trying to make his own way through the woods."

Fogel smiled at the youth and, though not knowing exactly why, felt he had to say, "One must grow spirit, Gary."

The youth blinked in the strong sunlight.

"I'm glad we're both writers, Mr. Fogel."

The next spring, a wet springtime, Fogel, wandering in a damp hat and coat in the periodical room of the New York Public Library, without forethought plucked off the shelf a college magazine and came upon Gary Simson in the table of contents, as the author of a story called "Travails of a Writer." He was surprised because they were in correspondence and Gary hadn't told him he had published his first story. Maybe it wasn't such a good one? Reading it quickly Fogel found it wasn't; but that wasn't why Gary hadn't mentioned it. The reason depressed him.

The story concerned a Mr. L. E. Vogel, a sarcastic, self-centered, although not thoroughly bad-natured middle-aged writer with a clubfoot, who wore in summertime a white suit, the pants of which dripped over his heels, an old-fashioned straw hat, and the same yellow knitted necktie, day after day. He was a short man with a loud laugh that embarrassed him, and he walked a good deal though he limped. One summer he had taught at a writers' conference in Syracuse, New York. There the writer had fallen for a college girl chambermaid at the hotel he had lived in during his two weeks of lecturing. She had slept with him for kicks after learning he had published two novels. Once was enough for her, but Vogel, having tasted young flesh, was hooked hard. He fell in love with the girl, constantly sought her presence—a blond tease of twenty—with solemn offers of marriage, until she became sick of him. To get him off her back she arranged with a boyfriend to enter his room with a passkey and give him a bad time. Vogel, soaking in his afternoon tub, heard someone shout, "Fire, everybody out!" He climbed out of the bath, was grabbed by the arm and shoved into the hall by the boyfriend, who pulled the door shut after him and disappeared down the stairs. The naked writer wandered like a half-drowned animal in the huge hotel hall, knocking at doors that were slammed in his face, until he found an elderly lady who handed him a blanket to cover himself and phoned the manager for a key to his room. Vogel, heartbroken that the girl had done this to him—he understood at once she had contrived the plot and for what reason—packed and left Syracuse a full week before the conference had ended.

"Poor Vogel swore off love to keep on writing."

End of "Travails of a Writer."

Arriving home, Eli Fogel dashed a white pitcher of daffodils to the kitchen floor, and kicked with his bad leg at the shards and flowers.

"Swine! Have I taught you nothing?"

Incensed, humiliated to the hilt (the story revived the memory; he suffered from both), Fogel, in a rare rage, cursed out Gary, wished on him a terrifying punishment. But reason prevailed and he wrote him, instead, a scalding letter.

Where had he got the story? Probably it was rife as gossip. He pictured the girl and her friend regaling all who would hear, screaming over the part where the hairy-chested satyr wanders in a wet daze in the hotel hallway. Gary might easily have heard it from them or friends of theirs. Or perhaps he had slept with the girl and she had confided it directly. Good God, had *he* put her up to it? No, probably not.

Why, then, had he written it? Why hadn't he spared Fogel this mortification, though it was obvious he had not expected him to find the story and read it? That wasn't the point; the point was he had not refrained—out of friendship—from writing it. So much for friendship. He detested the thought that the boy had sucked up to him all summer to collect facts for the piece. Or possibly he had heard the story and been tempted by it, Fogel hoped, *after* the White Mountain conference. He had probably harbored the "idea" during the summer but did not decide to write it until he got back to San Francisco, where he went to college. All he had to do was salt the anecdote with some details of appearance, a few mannerisms, and the tale was as good as written, acceptable at once for publication in the college quarterly. Maybe Gary had thought of it as a sort of homage: this good writer I know portrayed as human being. He hadn't been able to resist. After a summer of too much talk of writing he had felt the necessity of having something immediately in print, no matter what. He had got it down on paper almost wholly as received. It invented nothing, in essence a memoir once removed.

When he felt he had regained objectivity, Fogel sat at his desk facing the landlady's garden behind the house and, dipping his fountain pen into black ink, began a letter to Gary: "I congratulate you on the publication of your first story although I cannot rejoice in it."

He tore that up and on another sheet wrote:

> Your story, as is, signified little and one wonders why it was written. Perhaps it represents the desperate act of one determined to break into print without the patience, the art—ultimately—to transmute a piece of gossip into a fiction; and in the process, incidentally, betraying a friend. If this poor thing indicates the force and depth of your imagination, I suggest you give up writing.
>
> L. E. Vogel, indeed! Yours truly, Eli Fogel.
>
> P.S. Look up "travail." It's an experience not easy to come by.

After sealing the letter he didn't send it. We all have our hang-ups, Fogel thought. Besides, life isn't that long. He tore it up and sent a Picasso postcard instead, a woman with six faces sitting on a chamber pot.

> Dear Gary, I read your story in *SF Unicorn*. I wish I could say it was a good story, but it isn't, not so good as the ones I read last summer that you couldn't get published. I wish I had had your opportunity to write about L. E. Vogel; I would have done him justice.

He received, airmail, a four-page, single-spaced letter from Gary.

> To tell the honest truth I *was* kind of anxious about my writing. I couldn't finish a story for months after the W. M. conference, and without doubt took the easy way out. All I can say is I hope you will forgive and forget. Once I reread the story in the *Unicorn* I prayed that you wouldn't see it. If I have hurt our friendship, which I truly hope I haven't, I am willing to try to do better if you have the patience. I would like to be a better friend.
>
> Also I recently read in an article about Thomas Wolfe that

> he said it was all right to write about other people you might know, but it's wrong to include their address and phone number. As you know, Mr. Fogel, I have a lot to learn about writing, that's for sure. As for what you could have done with the same material, please don't compare your magnificent powers with my poor ones.
>
> I enclose a picture of my latest bride as well as one of myself.

In the envelope was an underexposed snapshot of a long-haired brunette in briefest bikini, sitting on a blanket by Gary's yellow guitar, on a California beach. Resting back on her arms, she stared distantly, certainly not happily, at the birdie; lost, as it were, to time and tide. She looked worn, cheerless, as though she had been had, and was, in her own mind, past having. She seemed to understand what she had experienced. She was, for Fogel, so true, lovely, possible, present, so beautifully formed, that he thought of her as a work of art and audibly sighed.

Gary, the hero himself of the other, overexposed colored snap, probably taken by the discontented lady herself, wore white bathing trunks, prominent genitals, and a handsome sunburned body; spare, dark, leaner than he was when Fogel had seen him last. His eyes staring blankly at the camera contradicted the smile on his face. Perhaps he was not looking at the unhappy lady but through her. The youth darkened in bright sunlight as the beholder beheld, or was Fogel prejudiced?

On the back of his picture Gary had scrawled, "You may not recognize me so well. I've changed, I've lost weight."

"What do you mean 'bride'?" Fogel wrote in the postscript of his reply forgiving Gary. He had urged patience in writing. "If you push time, time pushes you. One has less control."

"Not in the married sense," Gary explained when he appeared in person in Fogel's flat, in dungaree jacket and field boots, wearing a six-day growth of beard after driving practically nonstop across the country in a new secondhand station wagon, during the winter recess. He had brought his guitar and played "Ochi Chornye" for Fogel.

They were at first stiff with each other. Fogel, despite goodwill, felt distaste for the youth, but by degrees relented and they talked exhaustively. The older man had, more than once, to set aside the image of himself dripping along the hotel hallway before he could renew affection for Gary. The guitar helped. His singing sometimes brought tears to the eyes. Ah, the human voice, nothing like it for celebrating or lamenting life. I must have misjudged his capacity to relate, or else he does it better. And why should I bear him a grudge for his errors, considering those I make myself?

It was therefore freer talk than they had engaged in last summer, as though between equals, about many more interesting matters than when Gary was hastily taking it down to preserve for humanity. Yet as they conversed, particularly when Fogel spoke of writing, the youth's fingers twitched as though he were recording the older man's remarks in an invisible notebook, causing him later to say, "Don't worry if you can't remember word for word, Gary. Have you read Proust? Even when he remembers he invents."

"Not as of yet, but he's on my list."

There was still something naïve about him, though he was bright enough and gave the impression that he had experienced more than one ordinarily would have at his age. Possibly this was an effect of the size of his corpus, plenty of room to stuff in experience. Fogel was at the point of asking what women meant to him, but it was a foolish question so he refrained; Gary was young, let him find his way. Fogel would not want to be that young again.

The youth remained for three days in the small guest room in Fogel's rent-controlled flat in the three-story brick house on West Ninth Street. Gary one night invited over some friends, Fogel adding two or three former students, including Miss Rudel. A noisy crowded party flowered, especially pleasurable to Fogel when Gary sang, strumming his guitar, and a young man with a thin beard and hair to his shoulders accompanied him on a recorder. Marvelous combinations, inventions, the new youth dreamed up. The guests played records they had brought along and danced. A girl who smelled heavily of pot, dancing barefoot, kissed Fogel and drew him into the circle of her gyrations. The steps weren't so hard, he decided, really they were no steps, so he pulled off his shoes and danced in his black socks, his limp as though choreographed in. At any rate, no one seemed to notice and Fogel had an enjoyable time. He again felt grateful to the youth for lifting him, almost against his will, out of his solitude.

On the morning he left, Gary, bathed, shaved, fragrantly lotioned, in white T-shirt and clean cords, tossed a duffel bag into the station wagon and stood talking on the lowest stoop step with Fogel, who had come out to see him off. The writer sensed Gary was leading up to something, although he was ostensibly saying goodbye. After some introductory noises the youth apologized for bringing "this" up but he had a request to make, if Fogel didn't mind. Fogel, after momentary hesitation, didn't mind. Gary said he was applying for admission to one or two writing centers in universities on the West Coast and he sort of hoped Fogel would write him a letter of recommendation. Maybe two.

"I don't see why not."

"Hey thanks, Mr. Fogel, and I don't want to bug you but I hope you won't mind if I put your name down as a reference on other applications now and then?"

"What for, Gary? Remember, I'm a working writer." He felt momentarily uneasy, as though he were being asked to extend credit beyond credit earned.

"I promise I'll keep it to the barest minimum. Just if I apply for a fellowship to help me out financially, or something like that."

"That seems all right. I'll consider each request on its merits."

"That's exactly what I want you to do, Mr. Fogel."

Before the youth drove off, Fogel was moved to ask him why he wanted to be a writer.

"To express myself as I am and also create art," Gary quickly replied. "To convey my experience so that I become part of my readers' experience, so, as you might say, neither of us is alone."

Fogel nodded.

"Why are you writing?"

"Because it's in me to write. Because I can't not write." Fogel laughed embarrassedly.

"That doesn't contradict what I said."

"I wouldn't want to contradict it." He did not say Gary remembered his summer notes perhaps better than he knew.

The youth thrust forth his hand impulsively. "I'm grateful for your friendship as well as hospitality, Mr. Fogel."

"Call me Eli if you like."

"I'll certainly try," Gary said huskily.

Several months later he wrote from the Coast: "Is morality a necessary part of fiction? I mean, does it have to be? A girl I go with here said it does. I would like to have your opinion. Fondly, Gary."

"It is as it becomes aesthetic," Fogel replied, wondering if the girl was the brunette in the bikini. "Another way to put it is that nothing that is art is merely moral."

"I guess what I meant to ask," Gary wrote, "is does the artist *have* to be moral?"

"Neither the artist nor his work."

"Thanks for being so frank, Mr. Fogel."

In rereading these letters before filing them, Fogel noticed that Gary always addressed him by his last name.

Better that way.

In two years Fogel lost four pounds and wrote seventy more pages of his novel. He had hoped to write one hundred and fifty pages but had slowed down. Perfection comes hard to an imperfectionist. He had visions of himself dying before the book was completed. It was a terrible thought: Fogel seated at the table, staring at his manuscript, pen in hand, the page ending in a blot. He had been blocked several months last fall and winter but slowly wrote himself out of it. Afterward he loved the world a bit better.

He hadn't seen Gary during this time, though they still corresponded. Fogel left his letters lying around unopened for months before answering them. The youth had written in November that he was driving East before Christmas and could he call on Fogel? He had answered better not until the writing was going well once more. Gary then wrote, "We must have some kind of mutual ESP, because the same thing has happened to me. I mean it's mostly because I have been uptight about future worries after I get my M.F.A. in June, especially money worries. Otherwise I've had two stories published, as you know, in the last year." (Both troubled Fogel: unrisen loaves. Gary said they had been "definitely invented." One was about a sex-starved man and the other about a sex-starved woman.) "And I've been thinking ahead because I want to get to work on a novel and wonder if you would like to recommend me to the MacDowell Colony for a six months' stay so I can get started on it?"

Fogel wrote: "Gary, I've recommended you for everything in sight because I thought you ought to have a chance to prove yourself. But I'd be less than honest if I didn't admit I've been doing it uneasily the last one or two times because there's such a thing as overextending goodwill. I'll think it over if you can send me something really good in the way of a fiction, either a new story or chapter or two of your novel."

He got in reply, hastily, Gary. The youth appeared several days later, as Fogel was in the street on his way to the liquor store on the corner. He heard the bleat of a horn, a dark green microbus drew up to the curb, and Gary Simson hopped out of the door and pumped the writer's hand.

"I have this new story for you." He held up a black dispatch case.

Though he smiled broadly he looked as though he hadn't slept for a week. His face was worn, eyes hardened, as if something in his nature had deepened. He was on the verge of desperate, Fogel thought.

"I'm sorry I couldn't warn you but I came up from the Coast suddenly, and as you know, you have no phone." He paused, suffering his usual opening stiffness although Fogel returned his smile.

"Have you had supper, Gary?"

"Not as of yet."

"We'll go upstairs and have a bit."

"Fantastic," Gary said. "And it's a pleasure to see you after all this time gone. You're looking swell but a little thin and pasty-faced."

"Vicissitudes, Gary. Not to mention endless labor, which is the only way I seem able to survive. One ought to be careful how he creates his life's order."

He was about to suggest calling a few people for a party but thought it premature.

They ate a simple meal. Fogel cooked a tasty soufflé. There was salad, Italian bread, and wine. Both ate hungrily and smoked Gary's cigars over coffee.

In Fogel's study the youth snapped open the dispatch case lock he had been fiddling with—too bad it wasn't the guitar—and they were at once alertly attentive to each other. Fogel detected an odor of sweat and Gary proved it by wiping his face, then twice around the flushed neck with his handkerchief.

"This is the first draft of a story I did the other day, my first in months. As I wrote you in my letter, I just wasn't making the scene for a while. I got the idea for this story the night before last. I was planning to drop in on you yesterday but instead spent the day on twenty cups of coffee in this girl's room while she was out working, and finally knocked off the story. It feels good to me. Would you care to hear it, Mr. Fogel?"

"A first draft?" asked Fogel in disappointment. "Why don't you finish it and let me read it then?"

"I would certainly do that if the closing date for my application wasn't hitting me in the eye this coming Monday. I'd really like to work on it another week at the very least, and the only reason I suggest reading it to you now is so you will have a quick idea of the merits of what I've done with it so far."

"Well, then let me read it myself," Fogel said. "I get more out of it that way."

"My typing isn't so hot, as you well know, and it'll be hard for you to make out the corrections in my lousy handwriting. I'd better read it to you."

Fogel nodded, removing his shoes to ease his feet. So did Gary. He sat cross-legged on the couch in tennis socks, holding his papers. Fogel, rocking slowly in his rocker, gazed melancholically at the pile of his own manuscript on the writing table. Remembering his youthful aspirations, the writer wanted Gary's story to be good.

The youth brushed his lips with a wet thumb. "I haven't got a sure title yet but I was thinking of calling it 'Three Go Down.'" He began to read and Fogel's rocker stopped creaking.

The narrator of the story was George, a graduate student at Stanford who had driven to New York and, having nothing to do one spring day, had looked up Connie, who had been in love with him last summer. She lived in the West Village, in an apartment with two friends, Grace and Buffy, pretty girls; and soon George, while eating with them, on learning that none of the girls was going out that night, had decided to sleep with each of them, one after the other. He wanted it to be a test of himself. Connie, he figured, he had been in before and knew the way back. Grace was uneasy when he looked her over, which he thought of as an advantage. Buffy, the best looking of the lot, seemed a cool drink of water, aloof or pretending it, maybe impossible, but he wouldn't think of her as yet. It was a long night and there was no hurry.

George invited Connie for a walk and later bought her a drink in a bar on Sullivan Street. While they were at the bar he told her he hadn't forgotten last summer in Bloomington, Indiana. Connie called him a shit for bringing it up. George, after saying nothing, said it had been one of the best summers of his life. He then became deeply silent. They had a second drink and in the street she softened to him and walked close by his side.

It was a warm airy evening and they wandered in the Village streets. George said it was his impression that Buffy was a pothead, but Connie said it was ridiculous, Buffy was the really stable one of them. She worked for a youth opportunity program as secretary in charge of anything. Her father had been killed in the Korean War and she was devoted to her widowed mother and two younger sisters in Spokane.

"What about Grace?"

Connie admitted that Buffy had a lot more patience with Grace than she had. Grace's problems, though she didn't say what they were, were more than Connie cared to contend with. "Even when she has a good time she comes home in a funk and pulls out some more of her eyelashes, one by one, while sitting at the mirror."

After a while George told Connie that he had loved her last summer but hadn't been willing to admit it to himself. His father had been hooked into an early marriage and he didn't want that to happen to him; the old man had regretted it all his life. Connie again called him a shit but let him kiss her when he wanted to.

When she said she would sleep with him George said there was a mattress in his bus and why bother going upstairs? Connie laughed and said she had never made love in a microbus but was willing to try if he parked in a quiet, private place.

In the bus he gave it to her the way he remembered she liked it.

Connie went to bed with a headache. She had said he could stay in the living room till morning and no later. "That's our rule and Buffy doesn't like it if we break it." George sat on the sofa, reading a magazine for a while, then looked into Grace's room. Her door was open and he went in without knocking. Most of Grace's eyelashes were gone. She wore a terry-cloth robe and said she didn't mind talking to George so long as he kept his machismo in his pants. She wasn't careful with her robe and he saw her large bruised breasts through the nightgown.

That's her bag, George thought.

He started talking sex with her and told her about some girlfriends he had in California who had given it to him in various interesting ways. She listened with slack mouth and uneasy eyes while drying her hair with a large towel.

George asked her where the gin was, he would make the drinks. She said she didn't want a drink. He asked her if she wanted to split a joint.

"I'm not interested," Grace said.

"What interests you?" George said.

"I'll bet you slept with Connie."

"Why don't you ask her?"

He then said he knew what interested her. George got up, and though she grabbed his hands, he freed one, forced her chin up, and French-kissed her. She shoved him away, her robe falling open. George, pretending he was a prizefighter, went into a crouch, ducked, then feinted with his left. With his right hand he grabbed her breast and twisted hard. Grace gasped and was about to cry. Instead, after wavering hesitations, searching his face, she swung to him, her eyes unfocused, grinning. When they kissed she bit his lip. George punched her between the legs. Grace came close again with a quiet moan. He began to pull off her robe but she caught his hands, then shut the door.

"Not here," Grace whispered.

"Put on your dress and meet me downstairs."

She came down in a green dress, wearing nothing underneath but her bruises. Grace stepped into the bus. "I love you," she said.

George handed her his belt and said she could hit him a few whacks but not too hard.

Buffy had been reading in bed. She said come in when he knocked but, seeing who it was, drew up her legs and asked him not to since it was late and she had to go to work in the morning. George offered her one of the joints he had got from Grace but Buffy said to cool it. He asked her if she would mind talking for a few minutes, then he'd go. She said she would mind. George then told her he was leaving for the war in the morning.

She asked him why was that, they were sending few draftees in.

"My draft board was saving me up. They were sore at all the postponements I had requested."

"Why don't you refuse to serve?"

He said he had been a physical coward all his life and it was time to get over it. She called it a useless, unjust war, but George said you only died once. He offered her the joint again and she lit up. Buffy smoked for a few minutes, then said it wasn't turning her on.

"Nor me either," George admitted. "Why don't you get dressed and come out for a walk? It's a nice night."

When she asked him hadn't he done enough walking with Connie and Grace, he told her she was the one who really aroused him.

"Before I left I wanted to tell you."

"I must be five years older than you."

"That doesn't change my feelings."

"What malarkey," she said.

George said goodbye. He thanked her for the supper and for talking to him. "See you after the war."

"Connie said you were staying here tonight."

He said he would be sleeping in his bus downstairs. He had to be at Fort Dix at seven, and before that had to deliver the bus to a friend who would drive him to Jersey, then keep it for him while he was away. He was leaving at 5:00 A.M., and no sense waking everybody in the house.

"Are you afraid of death?" Buffy asked him.

"Who wouldn't be?"

He shut her door and went down the stairs. In the bus George, plugging in the shaver, began to shave for the morning. There was a tap on the door. It was Buffy in skirt and sweater, ready for a walk. Her hair in a coil at the neck fell over her right breast. She wore a golden bracelet high up on her left arm.

When they returned it was still a warm breezy night. After talking quietly awhile they entered the microbus. George plowed her three times and the third time she finally came.

As they lay on the narrow mattress, smoking, she asked him whether he had also had Connie and Grace that night, and George admitted it.

"Three go down."

That was the story.

What have I fostered? Fogel thought.

"Ah," said the writer, his bad leg trembling. He stepped into his slippers to pour himself a drink and was angered by the empty bourbon bottle. He drank a long unsatisfactory glass of water.

Gary had finished strong and was at the edge of the couch, his feet turned inward. He was observing his tennis socks, occasionally darting glances at Fogel.

"You like?" he finally had to ask. "I don't mind if you slog it to me so long as it's the truth."

"I guess Connie's right in characterizing George as a shit?"

"Up to a point, an anti-hero is an anti-hero," George explained defensively. "What the story means is that's how the crow flies, or words of that effect. In other words, c'est la vie. But how do you like it is what I want to know."

Fogel sat motionless in his rocker.

"I wish you were more than a walking tape recorder of your personal experiences, Gary."

He did not accuse him of having lived the experience to record it, though the thought was distastefully on his mind.

Gary laced up his shoes, a glaze of annoyance in his eyes.

"I don't see what's so bad about that. You yourself once said that story material has no pedigree of any kind. You told me it depends on what the writer does with it."

"That's right," said Fogel. "To be honest, I would have to say that, all in all, this story seems an improvement over your last two. It's a compelling narrative."

"Well, that's a lot better, Mr. Fogel."

"As for the recommendation, I want to think about it. I'm not sure."

Gary rose, waving both arms. "Jesus, Mr. Fogel, give me a

break. What am I going to live on for the next year? I have no father who left *me* a trust fund of five thousand bucks a year as you told me your father did for you."

"You have me there," said Fogel, rising from the rocker. "I've got to have a drink. I was on my way to the liquor store when you drove up."

Gary offered to go for the bottle but Fogel wouldn't hear of it.

The writer limped down the stairs in his slippers. At the curb stood the green bus. The sight of it nauseated him.

He's no friend of mine.

He went to the corner and on an impulse returned to the bus to try the door handle. The door was open. The back seats had been removed and on the floor lay a battered pink-and-gray thin-striped mattress.

In the liquor store Fogel bought a fifth of bourbon. Stepping into Gary's bus he pulled the door shut. The curtains were drawn. He did not flick on the light.

As he opened the whiskey bottle, Fogel, as though surprised by what he was about to do, told himself, "I have the better imagination."

On his knees, using a small silver penknife he kept to sharpen pencils, the writer thoroughly slashed the mattress and sloshed whiskey over it. He lit the soaked cotton batting with several matches. The mattress stank as it burned with a blue flame.

Fogel then went upstairs and told Gary he had entered his story to give it a more judicious ending.

After the firemen had extinguished the blaze and the youth had driven off in his smoky bus, the writer took his letters out of the folder in his files and tore them up.

He got one last communication from Gary, enclosing a magazine with the published "Three Go Down" much as he had written it in the first draft. Amid the pages he had inserted some leaves of poison ivy.

CHRONOLOGY

NOTE ON THE TEXTS

NOTES

Chronology

1914 Bernard Malamud born April 26 in Brooklyn, New York, the first child of Max (Mendel) Malamud and Bertha (Brucha) Fidelman. (Max, born 1885, a poor, uneducated grocer, had come to America in 1905 from a Jewish shtetl near Kamianets-Podilsky in Ukraine, then part of the Russian Empire, fleeing from pogroms and the threat of conscription to join two of his brothers who had established themselves in Brooklyn. Born to a somewhat better-off family, the daughter of a *shochet* [a ritual slaughterer of meat], Bertha, born 1888, left Kamianets-Podilskyi in 1909 to join her brother in America, and married Max the following year. They lived first on Flushing Avenue, then above and behind a series of unsuccessful grocery stores in the Brooklyn neighborhoods of Williamsburg and Flatbush. A son had been delivered stillborn in 1912.)

1917 Brother Eugene born in May. Family believes that damage to mother's left leg was due to the birth of one of her sons; during his boyhood Malamud would feel guilty about causing the injury. Mother is increasingly depressed, reclusive, and overweight, and probably suffers from schizophrenia. Yiddish is the primary language spoken at home, with occasional Russian.

1919 With a partner, father buys grocery on 15th Avenue in the Borough Park section of Brooklyn, the largest and fanciest of his stores, but is forced to sell within a year after partner takes off with the money that had been invested. Malamud enters kindergarten and his English rapidly improves.

1920–23 Attends elementary school on Cortelyou Road in Brooklyn where he first finds access to books; reads *Robinson Crusoe*, *A Tale of Two Cities*, and *Treasure Island*, as well as dime novels and Horatio Alger's boys' adventure books. At home, would listen through living room window to piano-playing across the street: "I was moved by the music being played by someone in one of the houses nearby, perhaps a girl my age, and was hungry to hear more of it." Enrolls in the third grade at P.S. 181, an outstanding new school with a middle-class and largely Jewish student body, to which Malamud traveled via trolley five miles every day on his own. Thrives and is challenged at the school, which he will recall as being "the most important school in my life," and displays a talent for telling and writing stories. Avidly goes to the movies and is enchanted by silent films. Catches pneumonia at age nine and is close to being pronounced dead when an injection of digitalis restores his heartbeat; in celebration of his recovery, father buys him *The Book of Knowledge*, a twenty-volume children's encyclopedia.

1924–26 After several of his grocery ventures have failed, father settles in to operating a German-style delicatessen at 1111 Gravesend Avenue (now McDonald Avenue), so called for its proximity to Washington Cemetery. Brother Eugene shows early signs of lifelong mental illness, and Malamud, sometimes reluctantly, takes a parental role toward him, especially during Eugene's unhappy experience at school, where he is mocked and bullied.

1927 Turns thirteen but is not given a bar mitzvah ceremony. Returns from school one afternoon to find his mother on the kitchen floor after she had swallowed a can of disinfectant in a suicide attempt. She is committed to Kings County Hospital; father manages to pay for her to be sent to a private mental hospital in Queens. Malamud works part-time in father's store.

1928 Enters Erasmus Hall High School in Flatbush, where he will edit the school magazine and act in the school's theater group.

1929 Mother dies in May in mental hospital; Malamud is not told the cause of death but in later years he will suspect suicide. His last view of mother was her waving through the window of the institution.

1931 Father marries Liza (Elizabeth) Merov. "Neither of the boys had any affection for their step-mother," Malamud would recall in 1951. The grocery store remains barely profitable: "It was not very good anywhere until the Depression, then it was bad."

1932–35 Wins Richard Young prize in 1932 for autobiographical essay "Life—From Behind a Counter," finishing second in the national Scholastic Awards. After graduating from Erasmus Hall, enters City College in Manhattan. Is praised by his professor Theodore Goodman for his stories, including an early version of "The Bill," which is later included in *The Magic Barrel.* Works part-time, including summers, at hotels in the Catskills.

1936–37 Graduates from City College with a B.A. in 1936. Works for $4.50 a day as teacher-in-training in New York public schools, but over the next two years twice fails teaching exams to become a permanent substitute teacher, first because of oversimplifying his writing style, then apparently because of his slight lisp. Takes out government loan to pay for graduate study in English at Columbia University.

1938–39 Works sporadically, taking odd jobs in factories and department stores and tutoring German-Jewish refugees in English (which will provide subject matter for story "The German Refugee," first published in 1963). Passes civil service examinations that lead to work as postal clerk and letter carrier. Receives first temporary teaching position as a substitute at Lafayette High School in Brooklyn in 1939.

1940 Accepts job as a clerk for U.S. Census Bureau in Washington, D.C., and is soon promoted; writes at his office in afternoons after his work is finished. Begins to submit short sketches of real life to the *Washington Post*, and for the first time is paid for his writing when several are published in column "The Post Impressionist" (including "The Refugee," "Sunday in the Park," "The People's Gallery," "Vacancy"). Writes story "Armistice." Returns to Brooklyn to teach at his former school, Erasmus Hall High, at evening classes there and at other New York City schools, while writing short stories during the day.

1942 Works on long autobiographical novel, "The Light Sleeper," about a young man's loneliness and despair. At a party in February, meets Ann deChiara (b. 1917), from New Rochelle, New York, of Italian immigrant parentage, who had graduated from Cornell University three years earlier with a degree in French; they soon become romantically involved, though during their long courtship Malamud worries about how he can combine marriage with a writer's life. Is exempted from military service as a result of stomach condition and teaching profession, though Eugene was called up for active service over four years, mainly in the Pacific, until discharged as a result of battle fatigue. Malamud moves out of family home to lodgings in

Flatbush. Receives M.A. from Columbia after submitting thesis, "Thomas Hardy's Reputation as Poet in American Periodicals." Writes story "Spring Rain." Continues teaching in the evening, though he also works for a short time in a war materials factory. Briefly consults a psychiatrist.

1943–44 Writes posthumously published story "The Grocery Store" in 1943, the year his short stories are first published: "Benefit Performance" in *Threshold* (February); "The Place is Different Now," a forerunner of *The Assistant*, in *American Prefaces* (Spring); "Steady Customer" in *New Threshold* (August); and "The Literary Life of Laban Goldman" in *Assembly* (November).

1945 Marries Ann on November 6 in a civil ceremony at the New York Society for Ethical Culture. Is estranged from father because he has married a Gentile woman; Ann's father also refuses to receive them in his house for more than two years. Moves from Brooklyn to 1 King Street in Greenwich Village.

1947 On the basis of his published work, receives invitation to spend summer working on his novel at Yaddo artists' colony at Saratoga Springs, New York, but is unable to accept for family and economic reasons; Ann, who had worked for the advertising agency Young & Rubicam, is now pregnant with their first child, and will no longer be contributing to the family finances. Birth of son, Paul Francis, in October, which brings about reconciliation with father.

1948 At Malamud's urging, Eugene undergoes psychoanalytic treatment for anxiety, depression, and paranoia and visits the Malamuds weekly, struggling with employment while still living with father and stepmother. Malamud completes "The Light Sleeper" and his agent, Diarmuid Russell of Russell & Volkening, begins sending it to prospective publishers. Teaches evening classes at Harlem Evening High School, but to support his family must now also teach during the day at Chelsea Vocational High School.

1949 In response to the opportunities offered by the G.I. Bill, Ann types more than two hundred standard letters for Malamud in application for posts in the teaching of literature. One of the few replies is from Oregon State College in Corvallis, Oregon, a state-endowed institution of six thousand students providing practical education in agriculture in particular, with the liberal arts constituting merely "the Lower Division." Appointed in July, he is allowed to teach freshman composition but not literature because he lacks a Ph.D. Moves family to Oregon, where the landscape is a revelation to him. Teaches three days a week for an initial annual salary of $3,600; spends the other four days writing.

1950 Works on a novel combining baseball and myth that would become *The Natural.* Publishes "The Cost of Living," story about a struggling grocery store in Brooklyn, in *Harper's Bazaar* in March and sends copy to his father. Publishes "The Prison" in *Commentary* (September) and "The First Seven Years" in *Partisan Review* (September–October); these stories are admired by Harcourt, Brace and Company editor Robert Giroux, who writes Malamud to show interest in publishing a novel and a collection of short stories.

1951 Publishes "The Death of Me" in *World Review* (April), and "The Bill" and "An Apology" in *Commentary* (April and November). Burns manuscript of "A Light Sleeper" after it has been rejected by numerous publishers: "My only triumph was in completing it after so many years of toil." Completes *The Natural* in October, having worked through only two main drafts, fewer than those of his later, more continuously laborious process of revision. Writes on October 15 to brother Eugene, who is increasingly delusional, paranoid, and suicidal, that he felt he had to leave New York "to be an effective man, to provide for my family and do my work—the writing I had to do. . . . That this should hurt you was, as you describe it, a bad break." Eugene is committed in early November to Kings County Hospital, the facility where their mother had been taken after her suicide attempt in 1927; he is transferred to Kings Park State Hospital and then to Kings Park Veterans' Memorial Hospital on Long Island, where he is diagnosed as schizophrenic.

1952 Malamud receives telegram from Giroux on January 7 that *The Natural* has been accepted by Harcourt, Brace and Company. Daughter Janna Ellen born January 19. To congratulate the family father sends $350 toward the purchase of a washing machine; not long afterward, in March, he suffers a heart attack, though at first he tells

Malamud that he is taking bed rest merely because of a cold. Eugene is declared an incompetent person by order of the New York Supreme Court in May. Malamud takes train cross-country to see his father and visit Eugene in hospital in June. Publishes "The Loan" in July in *Commentary.* Eugene is allowed home in July; hereafter he writes to his brother weekly or fortnightly for twenty years and just as regularly Malamud replies. Under the editorship of Giroux, *The Natural*, dedicated to Malamud's father, is published in July to mixed reviews. In the summer, Malamud begins novel "The Broken Snow," later "The Man Nobody Could Lift," about a schizophrenic. Earns $1,225 in income from royalties, rising to $2,700 the following year.

1953 Publishes "The Girl of My Dreams" in *American Mercury* in January. Submits draft of "The Man Nobody Could Lift" to Giroux, who in November advises against publication on grounds of overall quality (the first chapter will be published posthumously in 1997 as "A Confession of Murder" in *The Complete Stories of Bernard Malamud*, edited by Giroux).

1954 Father dies of a heart attack in March. In April, Malamud begins a novel about a Brooklyn grocery store, with working title "The Apprentice," that will become *The Assistant.* Receives promotion to assistant professor at Oregon State and is allowed to teach literature. Publishes "The Magic Barrel" in *Partisan Review* in November.

1955 Continues working steadily on *The Assistant*; as with all of his subsequent novels, the manuscript goes through multiple drafts and repetitions since revision was for Malamud the essential life of a writer: "I have succeeded in afterthought. I connect revisions with reformation." Thinks of himself as one of what William James called "twice-born souls" who struggle to establish themselves from a poor start through second chances: "Some are born whole; others must seek this blessed state in a struggle to achieve order. That is no loss to speak of; ultimately such seeking becomes the subject matter of fiction." Publishes under pen name Peter Lumm a children's novel, *Kim of Korea*, coauthored with Faith Norris, a colleague at Oregon State who wrote the first, main version that was then revised by Malamud. Publishes "The Mourners" in *Discovery*

(January) and "The Angel Levine" in *Commentary* (December). Having lived in rented houses since arriving in Oregon, buys house at 445 North 31st Street in Corvallis. Critic Leslie Fiedler publishes a brief appreciative essay on *The Natural* in *Folio*, which he sends to Malamud: "I shan't forget," Malamud would later write, "that he appreciated the quality of my imaginative writing before anyone else wrote about it."

1956 Under contract to Harcourt, Brace, submits *The Assistant* in spring but it is rejected, as it would be by Viking. Sends manuscript to Robert Giroux (now at Farrar, Straus & Cudahy), who is shocked by Harcourt's rejection. Receives $4,000 *Partisan Review*–Rockefeller Foundation fellowship in fiction and obtains sabbatical from Oregon State; takes family to live and write in Rome from autumn until the following summer. Departs by ship from New York in late August, and receives word on transatlantic crossing from Giroux that Farrar, Straus & Cudahy will publish *The Assistant*. Arrives in Rome, and the family settles into a two-bedroom apartment near Piazza Bologna: "Italy unrolled like a foreign film; what was going on before my eyes seemed close to unreality." Publishes "A Summer's Reading" in *The New Yorker* (September 22) and "Take Pity" in *America* (September 25).

1957 Travels throughout Italy and visits Austria and France. Makes final revisions to page proofs of *The Assistant*, which is published in April by Farrar, Straus & Cudahy to favorable reviews. Writes posthumously published story "The Elevator." Returns with family to the United States in the summer. In December, begins writing *A New Life*, novel loosely based on his experience at Oregon State. Earns $6,500 this year, including $2,800 in royalties.

1958 Publishes "The Last Mohican" in *Partisan Review* (Spring) and "Behold the Key" in *Commentary* (May), both included in *The Magic Barrel*, collection of thirteen short stories dedicated to Eugene and published by Farrar, Straus & Cudahy in May. Receives Rosenthal Foundation Award from the National Institute of Arts and Letters and the Daroff Memorial Fiction Award of the Jewish Book Council of America for *The Assistant*. Spends two months at Yaddo on a summer fellowship, working on *A New Life*. Promoted to associate professor at Oregon State "through his distinction as a writer," he no longer has to teach freshman composition and can focus his teaching on literature and creative writing instead.

1959 Publishes "The Maid's Shoes" in *Partisan Review* (Winter). Wins National Book Award for *The Magic Barrel.* Receives Ford Foundation grant of $15,000 providing two years' time to devote himself to his writing; refuses invitation to teach at Harvard because it would violate the terms of the award.

1960–61 Works steadily on *A New Life* throughout 1960 and completes the novel early the following year. Eugene is again hospitalized, as suicidal, in Brooklyn State Hospital, from early 1961 to August. Malamud teaches creative writing in summer school at Harvard. Largely through the initiative of the poet Howard Nemerov, obtains teaching post in Division of Language and Literature at Bennington College in Bennington, Vermont, a progressive liberal arts college for women (until 1969, when it becomes coeducational), at a salary of around $8,000. Arrives with family in Bennington in September. Publishes *A New Life* with Farrar, Straus & Cudahy in October. Publishes "Idiots First" in *Commentary* in December.

1962 Publishes "Still Life" in *Partisan Review* (Winter). Searching for the subject of his next novel, spends several months reading about social injustice in the United States.

1963 Publishes "Suppose a Wedding" in *New Statesman* (February 8), "The Jewbird" and "Black Is My Favorite Color" in *Reporter* (April 11 and July 18), "Life Is Better than Death" in *Esquire* (May), "Naked Nude" in *Playboy* (August), "The German Refugee" in *The Saturday Evening Post* (September 14), and "A Choice of Profession" in *Commentary* (September); these are among the twelve stories he collects in *Idiots First*, published by Farrar, Straus & Company in the fall. Travels to England and Italy. In the fall, begins *The Fixer*, novel about anti-Semitism drawing on the Dreyfus affair and the case of Mendel Beilis, a Jew arrested in Kiev in 1911 on false charges of having committed a ritual murder of a Christian boy.

1964 Is elected in February as a member of the National Institute of Arts and Letters.

1965 Completes first draft of *The Fixer.* In summer, travels in Spain, France, and, to research *The Fixer*, the Soviet Union.

1966 Completes *The Fixer* in early spring after more laborious revising than ever before: "The book nearly killed me." Moves to Cambridge, Massachusetts, for two years after being named visiting lecturer in the English Department at Harvard.

1967 Wins both National Book Award and Pulitzer Prize for *The Fixer*. Is elected member of American Academy of Arts and Sciences. *A Malamud Reader*, anthology with an introduction by Philip Rahv, is published by Farrar, Straus & Giroux. Malamud makes $230,000 in gross income, compared to $20,000 per year in the early 1960s.

1968 Visits Israel in March. Returns to Bennington after Harvard position ends. Buys 1930s colonial-style house on two-and-a-half acres at 11 Catamount Lane, Old Bennington, at cost of $35,000. Publishes "A Pimp's Revenge" in *Playboy* (September), "My Son the Murderer" in *Esquire* (November), "An Exorcism" in *Harper's* (December), and both "Man in the Drawer" and "Pictures of the Artist" (later "Pictures of Fidelman") in *The Atlantic* (April and December). Refuses offer to travel to the set of the film adaptation of *The Fixer* in Hungary, partly because the filmmakers tell him they do not wish to make the movie too Jewish; released in December, the film (directed by John Frankenheimer and starring Alan Bates) makes him more financially secure, earning him around $200,000.

1969 Begins novel *The Tenants*, set against the background of race relations in the 1960s. Publishes with Farrar, Straus & Giroux *Pictures of Fidelman: An Exhibition*: inspired by his stay in Italy, it is a picaresque novel in six linked stories, including one previously published in *The Magic Barrel* and two in *Idiots First*. Receives O. Henry Prize for "Man in the Drawer," story inspired by his trip to the Soviet Union. Writes screenplay for *The Assistant* but option not taken up. Rents apartment in Manhattan; the Malamuds will increasingly spend the fall and winter in New York City. Begins giving his papers to the Library of Congress.

1970 Begins writing in notebooks labeled "The Juggler," working title for the novel that will become *Dubin's Lives*. Film adaptation *The Angel Levine*, directed by Ján Kadár and starring Zero Mostel and Harry Belafonte, is released in July.

1971 *The Tenants* is published in the fall by Farrar, Straus &

Giroux. Malamud travels with Ann in the fall to London, where they live for five months.

1972 Purchases two-bedroom apartment in Lincoln Towers complex on Manhattan's Upper West Side. Publishes "God's Wrath" and "Talking Horse" in *The Atlantic* (February and April), "The Letter" in *Esquire* (August), and "The Silver Crown" in *Playboy* (December).

1973 Begins writing "The Juggler" in February: the first draft, instead of taking the usual one year, takes three. Settles for $39,000 in reluctant lawsuit with Elliott Gould and associates over bankruptcy in relation to proposed filming of *A New Life*. Publishes "Notes from a Lady at a Dinner Party" in *Harper's* (February), "In Retirement" in *The Atlantic* (March), and "Rembrandt's Hat" in *The New Yorker* (March), all of which are collected in a volume of eight short stories, *Rembrandt's Hat*, published by Farrar, Straus & Giroux in March. Eugene Malamud dies of heart attack, October 30, aged 55: he had carried on living above his father's old store, with stepmother Liza until her death in 1967 and thereafter alone. Malamud wrote the funeral eulogy ("He was a wounded man trying to keep going") but did not deliver it in person because he is admitted to hospital on October 31, with suspected heart problems of his own.

1974 Is interviewed by his friend Daniel Stern for *The Paris Review*'s "Writers at Work" series.

1976 Marriage of daughter Janna to David Smith. Writes in notebook on 21 October "[Saul] Bellow gets Nobel Prize, I win $24.25 in poker."

1977 In February, receives annual B'nai B'rith Jewish Heritage Award. Publishes excerpts from forthcoming *Dubin's Lives* in *The New Yorker* (April 18 and 25) and *Playboy* (December).

1978 Publishes excerpt from *Dubin's Lives* in *The Atlantic* (January). Completes *Dubin's Lives* in August. Makes visit with Ann to Hungary, arranged by translator and scholar Tamas Ungvari. Signs five hundred copies of *The Fixer* for Hungarian admirers; the Hungarian reception of the novel now gives him back his belief in that book.

1979 Publishes *Dubin's Lives* with a first printing of fifty thousand copies from Farrar, Straus & Giroux, his largest ever, and an advance of $150,000. Begins two-year term as president of PEN American Center, concerning himself in particular with writers' freedom throughout the world, the state of the publishing industry, and the provision of books within prisons in the United States.

1980 Publishes "A Wig" in *The Atlantic* (January). Begins novel *God's Grace*. Receives the Governor's Award for Excellence in the Arts from the Vermont Council on the Arts.

1981 Receives Brandeis Creative Arts Award. Awarded one-year fellowship of the Center for Advanced Study in the Behavioral Sciences at Stanford University; arrives with Ann in California in September. Increasingly concerned about his history of angina, decides on three-vessel coronary bypass operation at Stanford, requiring two weeks' hospitalization and two months' convalescence, to be delayed until following year so he can finish *God's Grace*.

1982 Completes *God's Grace*, published in the summer by Farrar, Straus & Giroux. Undergoes bypass surgery on March 10 and suffers a stroke on the operating table. When coming round, he is asked his name and age, and replies "William Dubin, 57." He is 68 and the name he gives is that of the biographer protagonist of *Dubin's Lives*. By December, though he has recovered many of his functions, including use of his right arm, he experiences difficulty in reading, handwriting, memory, and spatial awareness. He has to relearn much vocabulary and reports feeling "diminished," registering an increased inability in social life to get people involved with him. His ability to write creatively is thereafter impaired.

1983 In May, receives Gold Medal for Fiction from American Academy and Institute of Arts and Letters. Publishes "The Model" in *The Atlantic* (August), the only new story to be included in *The Stories of Bernard Malamud*, his selection of his shorter fiction, which is brought out by Farrar, Straus & Giroux in the fall.

1984 Publishes brief stories "Alma Redeemed" in *Commentary* (July), and "In Kew Gardens" in *Partisan Review* (Fall–Winter), on Alma Mahler and Virginia Woolf, respectively, written as if through the interests of Dubin, his fictional biographer. Film of *The Natural*, starring Robert Redford, earns him $125,000, but he does not admire the adaptation, particularly the changed, more optimistic ending.

Determined to write a new novel, he struggles to begin draft of *The People*, about a Jewish peddler who becomes chief of an American Indian tribe in the Pacific Northwest. Concerned about future, has worth of his total estate estimated at about $1,200,000. Prepares memoir "Long Work, Short Life," delivered at Bennington College in the Ben Belitt memorial lectureship series, October 13.

1985 Publishes "Zora's Noise" in *GQ* (January) and "A Lost Grave" in *Esquire* (May). Wins Premio Mondello, Italian literary prize. Struggling still to write *The People* (which was posthumously published in draft state by the estate with most of his uncollected stories in 1989), he reads opening chapters in July to Philip Roth, who later wrote: "He wanted to be told that what he had painfully composed while enduring all his burdens was something more than he himself must have known it to be in his heart."

1986 Dies of heart attack, March 18, in apartment in Lincoln Towers. Last note to self, found by his son Paul on writing desk, repeats four times "Don't be fragile." Is cremated; ashes buried in Mount Auburn Cemetery, Cambridge, Massachusetts.

Note on the Texts

This volume contains Bernard Malamud's novels *A New Life* (1961), *The Fixer* (1966), and *Pictures of Fidelman* (1969), along with ten stories first published from 1961 to 1968.

In 1957, Malamud wrote to his editor Robert Giroux about his plans for a "seventy-five to one hundred thousand word novel whose title may be *The Easterner* or *The Fanatic*." Malamud described his protagonist as being "a New Yorker of thirty, possibly Jewish, possibly an ex-Catholic, a man with a religious bent, who, after a period of unhappiness, perhaps even drunkenness, accepts a position to teach in a small college in the Northwest." Ideas that would find their way into this novel, eventually called *A New Life*, had been recorded in entries in a notebook labeled "Story Ideas—Oregon," which Malamud used from 1948 to 1956. Malamud began writing the novel in December 1957 and continued steadily over the next three years, aided by uninterrupted time to write at the Yaddo artists' colony in Saratoga Springs, New York, during the summer of 1958, and a two-year Ford Foundation grant. *A New Life* was published by Farrar, Straus & Cudahy in New York in October 1961. It was also published that year by Eyre and Spottiswoode in London. The text printed here is taken from the 1961 Farrar, Straus & Cudahy edition of *A New Life*.

After *A New Life* was published, Malamud decided that his next novel would address themes of social injustice, and he spent several months in 1962 researching possible subjects. Planning at first to write about an American event, Malamud chose instead to set his novel in Czarist Russia and to draw significantly on the case of Mendel Beilis, a Jew falsely charged with the ritual murder of a Christian boy and arrested in Kiev in 1911. Malamud wrote *The Fixer* from the fall of 1963 to the spring of 1966; he conducted research during a visit to the Soviet Union in 1965. Even for Malamud, who extensively revised drafts of his novels, the process of writing *The Fixer* was laborious. "It wore me out," he told *Newsweek*, "but I wouldn't let go of it—and that proved to me at last that I'm a professional." The novel was published in 1966 by Farrar, Straus & Giroux in New York and Eyre and Spottiswoode in London. This volume prints the text of the 1966 Farrar, Straus & Giroux edition of *The Fixer*. The text of "Source of *The Fixer*," written in 1966, is taken from *Talking Horse: Bernard Malamud on Life and Work*, eds. Alan Cheuse and Nicholas Delbanco (New York: Columbia University Press, 1996).

Malamud's episodic novel *Pictures of Fidelman* has its origins in the story "The Last Mohican" (published in *Partisan Review*, Spring 1958), which was also included in his story collection *The Magic Barrel* (1958). When he wrote a second story about the artist Arthur Fidelman in Italy, "Still Life" (published in *Partisan Review*, Winter 1962), he began to conceive of his protagonist's adventures as forming a loose but unified work. He published three more Fidelman tales as freestanding short stories in periodicals: "Naked Nude" in *Playboy*, August 1963; "A Pimp's Revenge" in *Playboy*, September 1968; and "Pictures of the Artist" (as "Pictures of Fidelman") in *The Atlantic*, December 1968. "Still Life" and "Naked Nude" were also collected in *Idiots First* (1963). The book's final chapter, "Glass Blower of Venice," was published for the first time when *Pictures of Fidelman* was brought out in April 1969 by Farrar, Straus & Giroux. An English edition was also published in 1969 by Eyre and Spottiswoode. The 1969 Farrar, Straus & Giroux edition of *Pictures of Fidelman* contains the text printed here.

All the stories in the section "Ten Stories" were first published in periodicals, and all but one, "An Apology," were collected in either *Idiots First* (1963) or *Rembrandt's Hat* (1973). Seven stories were later included in *The Stories of Bernard Malamud* (1983) and contain mostly light revisions by Malamud. These changes are almost always sentence-level revisions that correct errors, improve occasionally awkward phrasing, add a clarifying detail, or eliminate verbal redundancy. Two deleted passages from "Man in the Drawer," exceptional because of their length, are printed in this volume's notes.

Listed below are the sources and other information about the publication history of the stories, keyed to the following abbreviations:

IF *Idiots First*. New York: Farrar, Straus & Company, 1963.
RH *Rembrandt's Hat*. New York: Farrar, Straus & Giroux, 1973.
SBM *The Stories of Bernard Malamud*. New York: Farrar, Straus & Giroux, 1983.
TP *The People and Uncollected Stories*. Ed. Robert Giroux. New York: Farrar, Straus & Giroux, 1989.

Idiots First. *SBM*. First published in *Commentary*, December 1961. Included in *IF*.

Suppose a Wedding. *IF*. First published in *New Statesman*, February 8, 1963.

The Jewbird. *SBM*. First published in *Reporter*, April 11, 1963. Included in *IF*.

Life Is Better than Death. *SBM*. First published in *Esquire*, May 1963. Included in *IF*.

Black Is My Favorite Color. *SBM.* First published in *Reporter*, July 18, 1963. Included in *IF.*
The German Refugee. *SBM.* First published in *The Saturday Evening Post*, September 14, 1963. Included in *IF.*
A Choice of Profession. *IF.* First published in *Commentary*, September 1963.
Man in the Drawer. *SBM.* First published in *The Atlantic*, April 1968. Included in *RH.*
My Son the Murderer. *SBM.* First published in *Esquire*, November 1968. Included in *RH.*
An Exorcism. *TP.* First published in *Harper's*, December 1968.

This volume presents the texts of the original printings chosen for inclusion here, but it does not attempt to reproduce nontextual features of their typographic design. The texts are presented without change, except for the correction of typographical errors. Spelling, punctuation, and capitalization are often expressive features and are not altered, even when inconsistent or irregular. The following is a list of typographical errors corrected, cited by page and line number: 23.26, "papa"; 24.9, was) but; 25.23, Gettsyburg; 40.39, book store; 46.30, retangular; 55.19, lumbermill; 55.34, levis (and *passim*); 56.17, add—my dissertation, are; 58.15, radical?'; 58.22, Gilleys"; 59.14, 'Sad; 59.14, things.'; 68.34, a inch; 68.36, broken; 76.25, goddam (and *passim*); 84.9, everyman's; 85.5, course was; 93.29, week-end; 100.35, 'Tis; 109.13, birds nests; 118.26, everyone; 118.26, freshman (and *passim*); 122.37, side the; 123.7, manchiego; 123.24, principle; 145.39, Mrs. Beatty; 148.28, her.; 149.25, present "— to; 151.22, *Readers Guide*; 170.30, Camelias; 172.28, presently was,; 174.8, Bullocks.; 189.13, the block.; 193.29, what had it; 198.22, Aeropagitica; 200.34, Chekov; 201.9, himself.; 202.15, use to; 212.1, heart easing; 212.13, to river,; 212.40, heavy hearted; 227.10, Gilleys?"; 228.9, Lover's Lane; 228.12, voice.; 231.24, self-frustation; 233.1, Moby Dick; 253.3, afficionado; 254.30, lasted; and; 259.35, trouble maker; 264.9, politics).; 265.37, papa."; 269.39, the President; 274.33–34, possibilties; 293.17, vize; 298.35, you? She; 307.22, unforseen; 312.16, you—during; 312.16, which, as; 327.30, "common"; 337.15, awhile; 338.19, Gentiles; 348.13, was spiritual; 353.30–31, righteousness sake; 363.25, or nine; 365.4, stupefied.; 393.34, Colonal; 400.26, Petropavelsky (and *passim*); 415.36, Bodyanksy; 426.19, This, perfidy,; 444.9–10, Raisl Shmuel's; 451.9, Warden," we; 467.20, "Mama-Papa,"; 478.6, haleh (and passim); 501.5, Podovoloshchisk; 506.10, of lame,; 520.23, seige; 527.37, he slay; 545.37, bedbench; 548.24, everyday; 556.12, tsadik; 556.23, shirt" had; 557.27, there's no; 562.3, it's peace; 573.26, improverished; 596.7, infant; 613.35, Wie gehts?"; 620.30, response; 628.32, "Ritorna, vincitor!"; 631.22–23, Via dell' Oca;; 637.13–14, fat right; 655.36, my sure; 657.39, one hundred-lire; 669.30, right."; 672.9, asked, "Even; 675.28, suppose the; 691.27, Carracciola,; 696.7, long a time. [no section break]; 706.35, black-stocking legs; 707.29, knicknacks; 709.32, the canal.; 749.19, [Cracking; 755.26, papa,"; 777.24, someplace; 796.20, eighteen year old; 799.26, scotch (and *passim*); 814.15, wouldn't it; 825.37, Writers Union; 856.31, Chornye.

Notes

In the notes below, the reference numbers denote page and line of this volume (the line count includes chapter headings). Biblical quotations are keyed to the King James Version. Quotations from Shakespeare are keyed to *The Riverside Shakespeare*, ed. G. Blakemore Evans (Boston: Houghton Mifflin, 1974). For more biographical information than is contained in the Chronology, see *Talking Horse: Bernard Malamud on Life and Work*, eds. Alan Cheuse and Nicholas Delbanco (New York: Columbia University Press, 1996); Philip Davis, *Bernard Malamud: A Writer's Life* (Oxford: Oxford University Press, 2007); *Conversations with Bernard Malamud*, ed. Lawrence Lasher (Jackson: University Press of Mississippi, 1991); and Janna Malamud Smith, *My Father Is a Book: A Memoir of Bernard Malamud* (Boston: Houghton Mifflin, 2006).

A NEW LIFE

3.1–3 Lo, levin . . . ULYSSES] From episode 14 ("Oxen of the Sun") of *Ulysses* (1922) by Irish novelist James Joyce (1882–1941).

10.1–2 peak load of veterans] Reference to the effect of the G.I. Bill, officially called the Servicemen's Readjustment Act (1944), which guaranteed veterans access to higher education and provided tuition funding.

15.9 Howells] American novelist and critic William Dean Howells (1837–1920).

15.12 *PMLA*] *Proceedings of the Modern Language Association*, academic journal published since 1884.

29.27–28 Smith brothers . . . box] The bearded faces of the brothers William Wallace Smith (1830–1913) and Andrew Smith (1836–1895) graced the packaging of their Smith Brothers' Cough Drops, first sold in boxes in 1872.

32.5 Izaak Walton] English writer (1593–1683), author of *The Compleat Angler* (1676), a celebration of fishing.

38.38 when Henry Wallace . . . president] Formerly vice-president under Franklin D. Roosevelt (1941–45), Henry Wallace (1888–1965) ran for president as the Progressive Party candidate in the 1948 election.

40.29 Moscow Trials, Lenin and Trotsky, the Lysenko theory] Public show trials were held in Moscow in August 1936, January 1937, and March 1938, during which prominent Soviet Communists were falsely accused of conspiring with the exiled Leon Trotsky (1879–1940) to overthrow Josef Stalin and his regime. Among those executed on charges of treason were Grigory Zinoviev (1883–1936), Lev Kamenev (1883–1936), and Nikolai Bukharin (1888–1938). Trotsky, a revolutionary theorist and politician who played a major role along with Lenin in the Bolshevik seizure of power in 1917, was exiled by Stalin and assassinated in Mexico City by an agent of the Soviet secret police (NKVD) on August 20, 1940. Agronomist Trofim Lysenko (1898–1976), director of the Institute of Genetics of the Soviet Academy of Science from 1940 to 1965, was a proponent of the inheritance of acquired characteristics and denied the validity of Mendelian genetics.

43.5 fellow-traveling] Term used to describe those who sympathized with communism but were not members of the Communist Party.

44.5–6 I am not now . . . Communist Party] In the late 1940s public employees in many states, including university professors, were required to sign a loyalty oath affirming that they were not members of the Communist Party; similar statements were elicited from some of those called to testify before congressional investigating committees in the 1940s and 1950s.

52.24 "To change . . . Montaigne] Cf. "Of Repentance," in *Essays,* bk. 3 (1595), by French writer Michel de Montaigne (1533–1592): "I may presently change, not only by chance, but by intention" ("Je pourrai tantôt changer, non de fortune seulement, mais aussi d'intention").

52.24–25 "Important principles . . . Lincoln] From Lincoln's last public address, delivered from a balcony at the White House on April 11, 1865.

53.38–40 Herefords . . . Angus] Breeds of cattle.

56.17–18 as long in the making . . . born] In *Tristram Shandy* (1759–67), novel by the Anglo-Irish novelist and clergyman Laurence Sterne (1713–1768), Tristram deals at great length with the pre-natal period of his life.

56.18–19 Uncle Toby . . . Namur.] Tristram Shandy's uncle, one of the major characters in Sterne's novel, suffered a wound to his groin during the English siege of Namur in the Spanish Netherlands during the War of the Grand Alliance (1689–97).

56.25–27 such a building . . . Adam.] *Tristram Shandy*, bk. 4, ch. 32.

56.32 sad vicissitude of things] Sterne, *Sermons* (1767), no. 16: "The Character of Shimei."

57.21–22 They order . . . France.] Cf. the first line of Sterne's *A Sentimental Journey Through France and Italy* (1768): "They order, said I, this matter better in France."

63.15–16 William James . . . Bred.'] The speech on college education by American philosopher and psychologist William James (1842–1910) was delivered at Radcliffe College on November 7, 1907.

67.17 Had not Concord been for Thoreau] American writer Henry David

Thoreau (1817–1862) was born and spent most of his life in Concord, Massachusetts, including the two-year period of living in solitude that was the basis for *Walden* (1854).

77.3 Et tu, Brute] Latin: You too, Brutus? Purported words of Julius Caesar (100–44 B.C.E.) after being stabbed by conspirators, spoken to his friend Brutus (85–42 B.C.E.). See Shakespeare, *Julius Caesar* (1599), III.i.77.

80.21–22 Labor . . . of life] *Tristram Shandy*, bk. 5, ch. 3.

82.12 *Piers Plowman*] *The Vision of Piers Plowman* (c. 1367–70, c. 1377–79, c. 1385–86), long poem in alliterative verse by the English poet William Langland (c. 1330–c. 1400).

88.10 Piper Cubs] Small, lightweight single-engine aircraft built in various models from 1937 to 1983.

88.18 five percenters] Influence peddlers in Washington, so called for the commission taken when government contracts were awarded to private businesses, the subject of an inquiry in 1949 by the investigative subcommittee of the Senate Committee on Expenditures in the Executive Departments.

88.18–19 Ben Hogan's . . . June] Champion American golfer Ben Hogan (1912–1997) was injured in a near-fatal automobile accident in February 1949 but returned to professional golf the following year and won the U.S. Open in June 1950.

90.1 Chinooks] Fish from a large and highly prized species of salmon, also known as king salmon.

100.35–36 'Tis known . . . bad] *Tristram Shandy*, bk. 1, ch. 17.

106.4 Thackeray on him] In *The English Humourists of the Eighteenth Century* (1851), lecture series by English novelist William Makepeace Thackeray (1811–1863).

109.18–19 pathetic fallacy] The attribution of human emotion to the natural world. The term was coined by English critic John Ruskin (1819–1900) in *Modern Painters*, vol. 3 (1856).

114.18–20 "The Eve of St. Agnes" . . . Wall"] Poem (1820) by English poet John Keats (1795–1821); "Flower in the Crannied Wall" by Alfred, Lord Tennyson (1809–1892), dates from 1869.

116.24 Hardy] English novelist and poet Thomas Hardy (1840–1928), author of *Under the Greenwood Tree* (1872), *Far from the Madding Crowd* (1874), and *The Return of the Native* (1878).

122.21–22 Faust, or Gatsby; . . . his balls] Faust is the scholar in German legend who makes a pact with the Devil to win knowledge and seduce the young maiden Gretchen; the most renowned version of the story is the drama (1808, 1832) by Johann Wolfgang von Goethe (1749–1832). *The Great Gatsby*

(1925), novel by American writer F. Scott Fitzgerald (1896–1940), concerns the protagonist's yearning for his lost love, Daisy. St. Anthony (c. 251–356) was beset by temptations in the deserts of Egypt, the subject of numerous paintings and a work (1874) by French writer Gustave Flaubert (1821–1880); the reference to castration may be to the self-mutilation of another important figure in early Christianity, Origen (c. 185–c. 254).

127.33–34 "Alps on Alps arise"] From "An Essay on Criticism" (1711), poem by English poet Alexander Pope (1688–1744).

134.6 Cortez—Balboa, that is] In his poem "On First Looking into Chapman's Homer" (1817), John Keats incorrectly credited Spanish explorer and conquistador Hernán Cortés (c. 1485–1547) as being the first European to see the Pacific from the New World, instead of Vasco Núñez de Balboa (c. 1475–1519), who did so on the isthmus of Panama in 1513.

146.16 *The Woodlanders*] Novel (1887) by Thomas Hardy.

147.16 fourth Isaiah] The book of Isaiah is thought to be a compilation from three different periods (Proto-, Deutero-, and Trito-Isaiah), as though by three different prophets.

149.13 fishy in Denmark] See Shakespeare, *Hamlet* (1600–1601), I.iv.72: "Something is rotten in the state of Denmark."

149.27 John Stuart Mill] English philosopher and political economist (1806–1873), author of *On Liberty* (1859).

151.12–13 *Reader's Digest . . . Home*] General-interest monthly magazines: *Reader's Digest*, founded 1922; *Coronet*, 1936–71; *The American Home*, specializing in home and gardens, 1928–77.

171.1–2 new birth in freedom] Cf. Abraham Lincoln's Gettysburg Address (1863): "that this nation, under God, shall have a new birth of freedom."

172.29–30 Natty Bumppo . . . BAR] Natty Bumppo, hero of James Fenimore Cooper's series of five Leatherstocking novels (1823–41), who grew up among Delaware Indians; according to legend, American woodsman Daniel Boone (1734–1820) could wrestle and kill bears.

182.10 My young love's rip'ning breasts] Cf. Keats, "Bright Star" (1819): "Pillowed upon my fair love's ripening breast. . . ."

186.23–24 I'll never let you go, Mr. Micawber] In *David Copperfield* (1850), novel by Charles Dickens (1812–1870), Mrs. Micawber frequently repeats her determination never to desert her impecunious husband.

198.22 *Areopagitica*] Prose tract (1644) of the English poet John Milton (1608–1674) written in defense of unlicensed printing.

200.4 goniff] Yiddish: thief.

200.11–12 Alger Hiss and Whittaker Chambers] Alger Hiss (1904–1996) held several positions in the administration of Franklin D. Roosevelt and worked for the State Department from 1936 to 1947. He was accused in 1948 by Whittaker Chambers (1901–1961), a former Communist, of having been a Soviet intelligence agent. Hiss was convicted of perjury in 1950 after he denied Chambers's charges before a federal grand jury and served forty-four months of a five-year sentence. Although Hiss maintained for the remainder of his life that the charges against him were false, documents made public in the 1990s, including deciphered Soviet cables, strongly indicate that he served as a Soviet intelligence agent.

200.33–34 was striving . . . himself] See the letter (January 7, 1889) of the Russian playwright and short story writer Anton Chekhov (1860–1904) to his friend and publisher A. S. Suvorin, in which he sketches out a story about a "young man" who "squeezes the serf out of himself, drop by drop, and how, upon waking one beautiful morning, he no longer feels a serf's blood running through his veins, but the real blood of a man."

201.7 R. Chase] American critic and professor Richard Volney Chase (1914–1962), author of *Herman Melville: A Critical Study* (1949).

203.4–8 'Whoever would be . . . your mind.'] From "Self-Reliance" (1841), essay by American philosopher Ralph Waldo Emerson (1803–1882).

213.31–33 Arthur Dimmesdale Levin . . . chest] In *The Scarlet Letter* (1850), novel by Nathaniel Hawthorne (1804–1864), Hester Prynne becomes pregnant as a result of her affair with Reverend Arthur Dimmesdale. Refusing to reveal the identity of her lover, she is made to wear the scarlet letter "A" on her clothing. Dimmesdale conceals his part in the affair for most of the novel.

218.37–39 'Tis the rising . . . Franklin.] See *Notes of Debates in the Federal Convention of 1787* by James Madison (1751–1836), on the signing of the Constitution on September 17, 1787: "Whilst the last members were signing it Doctr. FRANKLIN looking towards the Presidents Chair, at the back of which a rising sun happened to be painted, observed to a few members near him, that Painters had found it difficult to distinguish in their art a rising from a setting sun. I have said he, often and often in the course of the Session, and the vicissitudes of my hopes and fears as to its issue, looked at that behind the President without being able to tell whether it was rising or setting: But now at length I have the happiness to know that it is a rising and not a setting Sun."

222.12–13 Which way . . . Hell.] Spoken by Satan in Milton's *Paradise Lost* (1667), bk. 4, l. 75.

223.2–4 A grief . . . tear.] From "Dejection: An Ode" (1802), st. 2, by English poet Samuel Taylor Coleridge (1772–1834).

232.8–9 Love alters not . . . of doom.] From Shakespeare, sonnet 116.

232.22–23 But tasks in hours . . . fulfill'd.] From "Morality" (1852), st. 1, by English poet and critic Matthew Arnold (1822–1888).

234.29 Time's winged chariot] From "To His Coy Mistress" (c. 1651), l. 22, by English poet Andrew Marvell (1621–1678).

237.26–27 Man . . . world!] Cf. Shakespeare, *Hamlet*, II.ii.307, referring to man as "the beauty of the world."

238.3 Sweet are the uses of humility] Cf. Shakespeare, *As You Like It* (1599), II.i.12: "Sweet are the uses of adversity."

238.12–13 "God's handkerchief," Whitman called it] See "Song of Myself" (1855), 6, by American poet Walt Whitman (1819–1892), where grass is called "the handkerchief of the Lord."

240.2–3 Mill: "Men are . . . manufacturers] From John Stuart Mill's inaugural address (1867) as rector of the University of St. Andrews in Scotland.

254.11–13 George Santayana . . . and enthusiastic.] From *Character and Opinion in the United States* (1934) by American philosopher and essayist George Santayana (1863–1952).

261.25–26 Pandora's horrors] In Greek mythology Pandora, the first mortal woman, opened a large jar full of the evils of the world.

264.11 Savonarola] Girolamo Savonarola (1452–1498), Florentine monk, reformer, and moral scourge.

265.24 Shot . . . fell—] The opening of "The Arrow and the Song" (1845) by American poet Henry Wadsworth Longfellow (1807–1882).

265.28 All . . . fate—] The first line of Longfellow's "The Builders," written in 1846.

276.2 Bunyanseed] Amalgam of the names of the legendary American frontiersmen Paul Bunyan and Johnny Appleseed.

276.2–3 Fautor et Cultor Bonorum] Latin: protector and friend of the forces of good, from *Ab Urbe Condita Libri* 9.46.13, by the Roman historian Livy (59 B.C.E.– 17 C.E.).

277.8–12 There is a natural aristocracy . . . *society.*] From a letter (October 28, 1813) from Thomas Jefferson (1743–1826) to John Adams (1735–1826).

277.36–37 power . . . Acton] "Power tends to corrupt and absolute power corrupts absolutely": from a letter (April 3, 1887) from the English Catholic philosopher and historian of science John Emmerich Edward Dalberg-Acton, 1st Baron Acton (1834–1902), to Mandell Creighton.

278.6 three cars in every garage] A reference to the 1928 Republican campaign slogan "A Chicken in Every Pot, A Car in Every Garage."

278.40–279.1 the more he took a liking to it.] Sterne, *Tristram Shandy*, bk. 2, ch. 3.

285.15 Chingachgook] Mohican chief in James Fenimore Cooper's Leatherstocking novels (see note 172.29–30).

291.34 The time is out of joint] Shakespeare, *Hamlet* I.v.188.

292.6 QUO VADIS] Latin: Whither are you going? According to Christian tradition, recorded in the apocryphal Acts of Peter, as Peter is fleeing Rome these are the words he speaks to an apparition of Jesus, who replies that he is going to Rome to be crucified again.

293.37 Thought is . . . flesh.] From Hardy, *The Return of the Native*, bk. 2, ch. 6.

302.7 Levin, poor man's Parnell] Irish nationalist leader Charles Stewart Parnell (1846–1891) was ousted from his leadership of the Irish Parliamentary Party in the wake of public revelations about his extramarital affair with Katherine O'Shea.

319.1–2 A penny saved . . . earned.] Traditional adage that has often been attributed to Benjamin Franklin.

319.4 God tempers . . . lamb.] French proverb quoted in Sterne, *A Sentimental Journey.*

THE FIXER

323.1–2 Irrational . . . YEATS] From "The Gyres" (1938), l. 4, by Irish poet William Butler Yeats (1865–1939).

323.3–8 O yonge Hugh . . . CHAUCER] From the final stanza of Chaucer's "The Prioress's Tale" (c. 1387). In 1255, in Lincoln, England, the corpse of an eight-year-old boy named Hugh (later known as Little Saint Hugh) was found in a well. A local Jew was accused of murdering him, confessed under torture, and was executed. Nearly one hundred Jews were then arrested in the belief that the boy had been tortured and crucified in an act of ritual murder, and eighteen were hanged for their purported involvement in the crime.

325.5 Vey iz mir] Yiddish: Woe is me.

325.17–18 *Kievlyanin*] A Kiev newspaper.

325.27 Black Hundreds] Extremist supporters of the Romanov dynasty in Russia, notorious for their nationalism, xenophobia, and anti-Semitism.

327.32 Nogid] Yiddish: wealthy man.

328.1 treyf] Yiddish: non-kosher food.

331.11 the legal ten] According to Jewish law, a married man could take a second wife if there were no children after ten years of marriage with his first wife.

331.24 Khmelnitsky] Ukrainian Cossack leader Bohdan Chmielnitzski (c. 1595–1657), at whose instigation tens of thousands of Jews were massacred in 1648 and 1649.

331.31 white nights] Period around the summer solstice of late sunsets and early sunrises in the higher latitudes of the Northern Hemisphere, when it is never fully dark.

331.40 the Pale] Area in the Russian Empire where Jews were allowed permanent residency, established in 1791 by Catherine the Great (1729–1796).

332.1 The Tsar] Nicholas II (1868–1918), emperor of Russia, 1894–1917.

332.2 Stolypin] Petr Arkadevich Stolypin (1862–1911), chairman of the Council of Ministers, 1906–11, who proposed an ambitious policy of land reform.

333.39 shnorrer] Yiddish: beggar, scrounger.

336.7 phylacteries] Tefillin, two small black leather boxes containing scrolls of sacred verses from the Torah and wrapped around the left arm and forehead by Jewish men when they recite their morning prayers.

336.17 meshummed] Hebrew: apostate (literally "destroyed one").

336.25 shul] Yiddish: synagogue.

336.25 the Podol] Area in the center of Kiev, the city's original craft and commercial district.

336.26 Blessed are . . . God.] Jeremiah 17:7.

336.27 Socialist Bund] Bundism (Unionism) was a Jewish secular socialist movement founded in 1897.

336.38 Eighteen Blessings] The Shemoneh Esrei or Amidah, a central prayer in Jewish worship, comprising praise, petition, and gratitude.

342.24 Lilith, Queen of Evil Spirits] In kabbalistic literature and Jewish legend, a demon who had been Adam's wife before Eve. After abandoning Adam, she mated with Asmodeus, king of the demons, and other evil spirits. She and her many offspring, the lilin, were believed to prey on children.

344.16–17 Pan whosis, Pani whatsis.] Polish honorifics for men and women, respectively.

344.37 Zhid] Derogatory term for Jew.

346.5–6 the Jerusalem of Russia] So called in particular because of the Monastery of the Caves (Pechersk Lavra), a pilgrimage site where many Eastern Orthodox saints were buried.

347.13 Lavra catacombs] The network of underground caves at the Monastery of the Caves.

347.22 St. Andrew] A patron saint of Russia.

352.16–17 lost a son at Port Arthur] Port in Manchuria, site of a surprise Japanese attack on the Russian fleet, February 8, 1904, the inaugural event of the Russo-Japanese War. The port was later besieged for more than six months, ending in its surrender to the Japanese on January 2, 1905.

353.19–20 Blessed are . . . of heaven.] From Jesus' Sermon on the Mount,

Matthew 5–7; along with the biblical quotations that follow at 353.27–28 and 353.30–31, part of the teachings known as the Beatitudes.

357.1 *Pagliacci*] *I Pagliacci* ("The Clowns," 1892), opera by Italian composer Ruggero Leoncavallo (1857–1919).

360.32–33 Romanov Jubilee] The celebrations planned for 1913 to commemorate the three-hundredth anniversary of the first Romanov czar.

364.17 Hasidim] Members of a branch of Judaism emphasizing mysticism and spiritual enthusiasm, and opposing itself to what was regarded as overly legalistic Talmudic teaching. It was founded in the Polish-Lithuanian Commonwealth by Israel ben Eliezer (c. 1700–1760), known as the Baal Shem Tov (Master of the Good Name).

370.18 Rasputin and the Empress] Grigori Rasputin (1872–1916), mystic and counselor to the imperial family. He exercised particular influence over Czarina Alexandra Fyodorovna (1872–1918) because of his purported powers to heal her son Alexei, who suffered from hemophilia.

370.29 revolt . . . Decembrists] An uprising of Russian military officers in December 1825 against the ascension of Nicholas I (1796–1855) was quickly suppressed and its leaders were executed or exiled to Siberia.

371.27–28 torn to pieces . . . him] Dutch republican statesman Johan de Witt (1625–1672) was falsely accused of collaboration with the enemy during the invasion of the Dutch Republic by Louis XIV. Johan and his brother were beaten to death by an angry mob.

373.16 Gevalt!] Yiddish expression of surprise and dismay.

400.13 Seymists] Jewish Socialist Workers Party (whose first letters spell out "SERP," meaning "sickle" in Russian), founded in 1905.

400.13 Volkspartei] "People's Party" ("Evreiskaia Narodnaia Partiia," "Jewish People's Party" in Russian), socialist Jewish political party that first published its platform in 1907.

401.26 Misnogid] Misnagid, a rationalist Jew and an opponent of Hasidism.

402.15 tzadikim] Name given to the righteous individuals and spiritual masters who maintain Jewish ethical justice in the world.

402.17 'pidion,' which is a fee of some sort] Pidyon, Hebrew for "redemption"; term used most notably in the "Pidyon ha-Ben," a ceremony to redeem and bless a firstborn son through the bestowal of silver coins.

402.27 afikomen] A piece of unleavened bread set aside to be the last piece of food eaten at the Passover feast.

403.16 matzo shmuro] Literally "guarded matzo," unleavened bread whose ingredients are strictly supervised to ensure they are kosher when eaten during Passover.

407.28 the poor sick boy] See note 370.18.

426.39 destruction of their Temple] In Jerusalem in 70 C.E.

427.3 Maimonides] Moses Maimonides (1135–1204), Jewish philosopher, author of *Guide for the Perplexed.*

428.11 Polovostian raids] The Cumans (Polovtsy), a nomadic warrior people, plundered the Monastery of the Caves (see note 346.5–6; called "Pechera Monastery" at 428.13) in 1096.

428.13 Kherson] City in southern Ukraine.

449.11 Pinsk] Town in present-day Belarus that long had a large Jewish population.

458.25 ukase] Proclamation, decree, edict.

458.31 Emancipation] In 1861, serfs in Russia were freed by decree of Czar Alexander II (1818–1881).

458.37–39 certain Roman Catholic Popes . . . forgotten] Pope Innocent IV (c. 1195–1254; ruled 1243–54); Gregory X (c. 1210–1276; ruled 1271–76); Paul III (1468–1549; ruled 1534–49); and Cardinal Giovanni Ganganelli (1769–1774), later Clement XIV, appointed to investigate blood libel by Benedict XIV (1675–1758; ruled 1740–58).

460.8 prohibitions in Leviticus] See Leviticus 7:26, 17:10–16.

460.12–13 allow King David . . . to Him] See 1 Chronicles 22:8, 28:3.

487.6–7 Peretz . . . Aleichem] I. L. Peretz (1852–1915), Yiddish poet, essayist, and playwright, born in Poland. Shalom Aleichem, pen name (meaning "peace be unto you," a Hebrew greeting) of Yiddish writer and humorist Sholem Rabinovitch (1859–1916), from Ukraine.

487.22–488.13 Behold . . . consumed.] The fragments are from Psalms 7:14–15, 6:6, 102:3–4, 35:11, 31:13, 10:12, 10:15, 18:9, 18:14, 18:37. Malamud tends to quote from the New American Standard Bible.

496.17 Sh'ma . . . is one!] First line of the prayer recited twice daily, in the morning and in the evening, and often uttered in the face of death.

505.10–12 Therefore you shall . . . eyes.] Deuteronomy 11:18.

507.8–14 Truly, truly . . . in him.] John 6:53–56.

507.36–37 Which of you . . . believe me?] John 8:46.

508.1–2 But it is easier . . . become void.] Luke 16:17.

508.7–9 Judge not . . . you get.] Matthew 7:1.

514.20–515.4 And let her put away . . . now.] Hosea 2:2–7. According to Hosea 1:2–3, Hosea married the prostitute Gomer at God's command, because the people of Israel had "committed great whoredom, departing from the Lord."

522.5 Tsarina Elizabeth Petrovna] Russian empress (1709–1762; ruled 1741–62).

522.6–8 Jews were expelled . . . 1742] Several imperial edicts ordering the expulsion of Jews from the Ukrainian territory known as Little Russia were issued from 1721 to 1742. Enforcement of the 1742 decree resulted in the deportation of about six hundred Jews to Poland.

524.14 erev shabos] Sabbath eve: Friday night.

526.26–27 When prayers go up blessings descend.] Yiddish proverb.

527.37 Though he slay me . . . Him.] Job 13:15.

552.38–39 melamed] Hebrew: teacher.

559.40 Kishinev massacres] Government supported anti-Jewish pogroms in 1903 in Chişinău (now the capital of Moldova) in Russia. Accounts of the massacres were reported throughout the world.

564.19 *Poslednie Novosti*] Liberal newspaper ("The Latest News").

564.25 Dreyfus] French-Jewish artillery officer Alfred Dreyfus (1859–1935), who in October 1894 was wrongfully arrested on charges of treason and sentenced to life imprisonment. The intense controversy that followed resulted in the case being reopened, and in September 1899 Dreyfus was pardoned by President Emile Loubet. He was fully exonerated by a military commission on July 12, 1906, and one week later publicly decorated with the Légion d'Honneur.

565.24 as Marx says] The source of the quotation is not Marx but, in a slightly different form ("wars have always been powerful locomotives of world history"), the German Marxist Karl Kautsky (1854–1938), in "War and Revolution" (1912).

589.10 Sacco and Vanzetti case] Nicola Sacco (1891–1927) and Bartolomeo Vanzetti (1888–1927) were anarchist Italian immigrants convicted of murder and armed robbery in 1920 and executed in 1927 despite international protests that their guilt had not been proven.

589.26 Caryl Chessman] Caryl Chessman (1921–1960) was convicted in 1948 on seventeen counts of robbery, kidnapping, and rape, and after a series of appeals and stays was executed at San Quentin Prison on May 2, 1960. (At the time, kidnapping with bodily harm was a capital offense in California.) He wrote four books while in prison, and his case became an international cause célèbre for anti–death penalty advocates.

PICTURES OF FIDELMAN

595.20 Baths of Diocletian] Luxurious public baths begun during the reign (284–305) of the emperor Diocletian (245–c. 313) and completed in 306.

596.7–8 Etruscan wolf . . . Remus] Romulus and Remus, the brothers who according to legend were the founders of Rome, were found and suckled by a she-wolf, after being abandoned to die as newborn infants. The Capitoline Wolf is a bronze statue, first said to be of Etruscan origin by the art historian Johann Joachim Winkelmann (1717–1768); recent radiocarbon tests have supported the hypothesis that it is in fact a medieval sculpture.

598.3 Trofimov, from Chekhov] Peter Trofimov is the poorly dressed perennial student in Chekhov's play *The Cherry Orchard* (1904).

602.15 El Al and Zim] Israeli airline and shipping service, respectively.

603.12 Joint Distribution Committee] Worldwide American Jewish humanitarian aid organization.

605.17 tramontana] A winter wind that blows over the Alps and Apennines to the western coast of Italy.

606.19 armadio] Italian: armoire.

607.25 Jewish catacombs] The Vigna Randanini catacombs, underground Jewish burial complex along the ancient Appian Way.

610.38 Ardeatine Caves] Mass murder on March 24, 1944, of 335 Italian men and boys, including 77 Jews, by the SS as a reprisal for a Partisan attack on one of their police units that killed 33 men.

611.27 VIETATO URINARE] Italian: urination forbidden.

611.36 Murillo] Bartolomé Esteban Murillo (1617–1682), Spanish painter who specialized in religious subjects.

613.9 Navicella] Early-fourteenth-century mosaic attributed to Italian artist Giotto (c. 1266–1337) in St. Peter's Basilica in Vatican City, showing St. Peter with Christ walking on the Sea of Galilee.

613.34–35 Wie gehts?] German: How goes it?

614.15 Trecento] Italian: fourteenth century.

615.37 shade, Virgilio] Reference to Roman poet Virgil (70–19 B.C.E.), whom Dante made his protagonist's ghostly guide in his *Divine Comedy*.

616.1–3 Tolstoy . . . "Why Is Art?"] Russian writer Leo Tolstoy (1828–1910) published *What is Art?* in 1896.

616.13 San Francesco . . . povero.] Italian: St. Francis giving his cloak to the poor knight, reference to Giotto's fresco *St. Francis Giving His Cloak to a Poor Man* (1296–99), in the Upper Church of San Francesco, Assisi.

618.19 pittore . . . pittrice] Italian: painter (masculine and feminine forms).

619.25–26 natura morta] Italian: still life.

619.27 *Oggi*] Popular Italian weekly magazine ("Today").

620.37–38 portinaia . . . portiere] Italian: caretaker (feminine and masculine forms).

621.32 Piazza del Popolo] Large square in Rome.

622.7 Jettatura!] The casting of an evil eye. "Porca miseria" (622.7–8) is the bitch (literally, female pig) misery.

624.5 Buchi Spontanei] Italian: spontaneous holes.

624.7 mucilaged] Paper treated with a thick gluey substance produced by plants, here used to create a sort of veil of mist.

624.7–8 Velo nella Nebbia] Italian: veil in the mist.

624.9 Linee Discendenti] Italian: lines descending.

624.12–13 Luce di candela] Italian: candlelight.

624.16–17 La Donna Toro] Italian: the bull woman.

627.14 straniero] Italian: a foreigner.

627.21 ES PULCHRA] Latin: is beautiful.

628.10–11 Aspetta, aspetta, caro, viene Augusto.] Italian: Wait, wait, dear, Augusto is coming.

628.32 "Ritorna vincitor!"] Aria ("Return a conqueror!") from *Aida* (1871), opera by Italian composer Giuseppe Verdi (1813–1901).

629.16 Gioco . . . villano.] Italian: it's not nice to use your hands.

629.18 Dolce tesoro] Italian: sweet treasure.

632.18–20 Action painter . . . Abstract Expressionism] "Action painting" was a term coined by American art critic Harold Rosenberg (1906–1978) in 1952 to describe the work of postwar American Abstract Expressionist artists, in particular Jackson Pollock (1912–1956) and Willem de Kooning (1904–1997).

632.32 Peccato] Italian: a pity.

637.6 Knidean Aphrodite] Monumental statue of the nude Aphrodite at Cnidus (an ancient Greek settlement in modern-day Turkey) by the fourth-century B.C.E. sculptor Praxiteles.

638.9 sette e mezzo] Italian card game ("seven and a half") similar to blackjack.

638.17 carabiniere] Policeman.

638.28 the Questura] Police headquarters.

639.36–37 Tiziano's 'Venus of Urbino' . . . Giorgione] Oil painting (1538) of a reclining nude woman by the Italian painter Titian (c. 1490–1576), a pose based on *Sleeping Venus* (c. 1507–1510), by Italian painter Giorgione (c. 1477–1510), completed by Titian.

640.7 Olivetti] Italian industrialist Adriano Olivetti (1901–1960), who greatly expanded the typewriter company founded by his father.

642.25–26 Didn't Rubens steal . . . Tiziano?] Titian's painting *The Bacchanal at Andros* (1523–26) was freely copied by Flemish artist Peter Paul Rubens (1577–1640) in the mid-1630s.

642.35 sfumato browns] A subtle gradation of brown tones, without sharp edges.

643.20 infinite riches in a little room] From the play *The Jew of Malta* (c. 1592), I.i.37, by English playwright and poet Christopher Marlowe (1564–1593).

645.12–14 Vetruvian square . . . and bodies.] Exercises in proportion involving Leonardo da Vinci's (1452–1519) geometrical representation of the human body c. 1490 after the first-century B.C.E. Roman architect Vitruvius, and the similar work of German artist Albrecht Dürer (1471–1528).

645.18 Esquiline goddess] Roman statue of a nude Venus (c. 50 C.E.) found on the Esquiline Hill in Rome in 1874.

645.18 Les demoiselles d'Avignon] Painting (1907) of five nude prostitutes by Spanish artist Pablo Picasso, a breakthrough in Cubist painting.

646.9 Van Eyck] Jan Van Eyck (1395–1441), Flemish painter.

648.19–20 "La Baigneuse"] French for female bather, a frequent subject in nineteenth- and twentieth-century painting.

649.16 Silenus] An aged satyr in Greek mythology, a drunken follower of Dionysus.

649.17 "Rokeby Venus"] Painting of a nude (1647–51) by Spanish artist Diego Velázquez (1599–1660).

649.18 "Bathsheba," "Suzanna"] Female subjects in painting drawn from Hebrew scripture, often shown nude or partially dressed; among the best-known versions of both subjects are paintings by Dutch artist Rembrandt van Rijn (1606–1669).

649.18 "Venus Anadyomene," "Olympia"] *Venus Rising from the Sea* (1520), nude by Titian; *Olympia* (1863), nude by French painter Édouard Manet (1832–1883).

649.19 Vanitas] Latin: vanity. A subgenre of seventeenth-century Dutch still-life painting, depicting skulls and other signs of human mortality.

649.20 Niobe or Leda, in chase or embrace] In Greek art, the sorrows of Niobe over the loss of her children was a subject often shown on Attic vases; Michelangelo, Leonardo, and other artists painted depictions of the story in which the mortal Leda, wife of King Tyndareus of Sparta, is seduced or raped by Zeus in the form of a swan.

649.34 Apollo Belvedere] Marble statue of the Greek god, thought to be a second-century Roman copy after a lost Greek bronze. In the eighteenth and nineteenth centuries it was held up as an aesthetic ideal.

655.15 Constable . . . feeling.] See the letter (October 23, 1821) to the Reverend John Fisher by the English landscape painter John Constable (1776–1837): "Painting is but another word for feeling."

655.16 Whistler . . . beginning.] See *The Gentle Art of Making Enemies* (1892) by American artist James Abbott McNeill Whistler (1834–1903): "The work of the master reeks not of the sweat of the brow—suggests no effort and is finished from the beginning."

655.19–20 Nietzsche . . . overcome it.] From *The Birth of Tragedy* (1872) by German philosopher Friedrich Nietzsche (1844–1900).

655.21–22 Picasso . . . nakedness.] Remark recorded in Christian Zervos, "Conversation with Picasso" (1935).

666.25 Kline or Motherwell] American abstract artists Franz Kline (1910–1962) and Robert Motherwell (1915–1991).

669.16 Uccello] Paolo Uccello (1397–1475), Florentine painter.

671.1 Uffizi] Art museum in Florence.

677.1 gabinetto] Italian: lavatory.

679.16 Masaccio] The frescoes by Masaccio (1401–1428) in the Brancacci Chapel of the Santa Maria del Carmine church in Florence include *The Expulsion from the Garden of Eden.*

681.5–6 the palazzo . . . *The Idiot*] Russian novelist Fyodor Dostoevsky (1821–1881) completed his novel *The Idiot* in Florence in January 1869.

682.14 Nazionale] Italian brand of king-size cigarettes.

688.3–4 Modigliani . . . Livorno canal.] Italian Jewish artist Amedeo Modigliani (1884–1920), born and raised in Livorno, was said to have reacted to negative criticism of his sculptures by throwing them in a rage into one of the city's canals.

688.5–6 Ne ha viste? Macchè] Italian: Any sight of them? Not a bit.

688.7 we wake we drown] Cf. the final line of "The Love Song of J. Alfred Prufrock" (1915), poem by American poet T. S. Eliot (1888–1965): "Till human voices wake us, and we drown."

688.7 *Chants de Maldoror*] Prose poem (1868–70) by the French writer Comte de Lautréamont, pseudonym of Isidore Lucien Ducasse (1846–1870), much admired by Modigliani and later the Surrealists.

688.10 Knight, Death and the Devil] Large engraving (1513) by Dürer showing a knight defying death through his faith.

688.11 *Au fond il s'est suicidé*] French: In essence he killed himself.

688.16 Cathedral of Erotic Misery] Early title of the sculptural installation *Merzbau* (c. 1923–37) by German artist Kurt Schwitters (1887–1948), constructed over many years in the artist's studio in Hanover. The installation was a kind of three-dimensional collage, with stalactite-like columns and cave-like recesses in which Schwitters placed small objects he had come upon or that put him in mind of friends.

688.18–32 Madonna adoring . . . crosscut saw.] Fidelman is thinking of the traditional iconography used in paintings of Christian saints and martyrs in medieval and Renaissance art.

688.32 S. Genet in prison . . . boys.] French poet, essayist, and novelist Jean Genet (1910–1986) wrote candidly of his homosexuality and life as a hustler in autobiographical novels such as *The Miracle of the Rose* (1946) and *The Thief's Journal* (1949) and was the subject of Jean-Paul Sartre's *Saint Genet: Actor and Martyr* (1952).

688.34 Still Life with Herrings] Painting (1916) by French Jewish artist Chaim Soutine (1893–1943).

689.6 The Enigma of Isidore Ducasse] The title of the art-object created and photographed by American artist Man Ray (born Emmanuel Radnitzky, 1890–1976) in 1920, a sewing machine wrapped in an army blanket. In *Les Chants de Maldoror*, Lautréamont (see second note 688.7) had used as a simile for beauty "the fortuitous encounter of a sewing machine and an umbrella on a dissecting table."

689.11 Il Zuccone] Lo Zuccone (literally "pumpkinhead"), nickname for marble statue (1423–25) of the prophet Habukkuk, depicted bald, made by Italian painter and sculptor Donatello (1386–1466) for the Campanile (bell tower) of Florence Cathedral designed by Giotto.

689.23–24 because of the rains . . . of Babel] See Genesis 11; the account of God destroying the overweening tower by wind comes from legends such as those recorded in Josephus, *Antiquities of the Jews* (c. 94 C.E.) by the Jewish Roman historian Josephus Flavius (37– c. 100 C.E.).

690.17 braccio] Italian for "arm," a varying unit of measure used in the Renaissance.

695.3 *Quid ego feci?*] Latin: What have I done?

695.14–16 The Flayed . . . Ornans. Courbet.] The paintings *Slaughtered Ox* (1655) by Rembrandt, which inspired an homage by Soutine (c. 1925), and Soutine's *Hanging Fowl* (1925); the engraving (1519) of a young man holding a skull by Dutch artist Lucas van Leyden (1494–1533); the painting *The Burial at Ornans* (1849–50) by French artist Gustave Courbet (1819–1877).

695.16 Bishop Eaten by Worms. Murillo] *Finis gloriae mundi* ("The End of Worldly Glory," 1672), painting of a dead bishop and other corpses by Spanish artist Juan de Valdés Leal (1622–1690) in the Hospital of Charity, Seville; his friend Murillo is reported to have told him, "You have to hold your nose to look at this."

695.18 I paint with my prick.] Pierre-Auguste Renoir (1841–1919), French Impressionist painter, as quoted in Jean Renoir's biography *Renoir, My Father* (1958); Albert André's *Renoir* (1919) records the artist as saying, "It's with my brush that I make love."

695.18 ulcer. Soutine] Soutine died of a perforated ulcer in 1943.

695.21 Bonnard] Pierre Bonnard (1867–1947), French painter, member of the avant-garde artists' group known as the Nabis.

695.23–24 Painting is nothing more . . . Fromentin] From *The Masters of Past Time* (1876) by French painter and writer Eugène Fromentin (1820–1876).

695.24 Indefinite Divisibility] Painting (1942) by French Surrealist artist Yves Tanguy (1900–1955).

695.26–27 I'm making . . . Reinhardt] Quoted in the catalogue for the 1966 exhibition of the American abstract painter Ad Reinhardt (1913–1967) at the Jewish Museum, New York.

695.29 de Kooning . . . Rauschenberg] In 1953 American artist Robert Rauschenberg (1925–2008) erased a drawing by his friend Willem de Kooning and exhibited it as a new work of his own.

695.37 Portrait of an Old Jew Seated. Rembrandt.] Rembrandt's paintings of this subject date from 1645 to 1660.

695.39–696.3 Then I dreamt . . . Raverat] A quotation from *Period Piece: A Cambridge Childhood* (1952), a memoir by the English wood engraver Gwen Raverat (1885–1957).

696.3–4 The Rat Killer] *The Rat-Catcher*, etching (1632) by Rembrandt.

696.5 *Elle m'a mordu aux couilles*] French: She bit me in the balls! So said Modigliani of the English writer Beatrice Hastings (born Emily Haigh, 1879–1943), with whom he began an affair in 1914. The incident is cited in Pierre Sichel's 1967 biography of Modigliani.

696.6 Mosaic. Piazza Armerina, Sicily] Located near the town of Piazza Armerina in central Sicily, the palatial Villa Romana del Casale (early fourth century) contains an extensive collection of well-preserved Roman mosaics.

697.6–7 It is not I . . . betray thee.] See Judas's denial that he will betray Jesus, Matthew 26:25.

698.4–5 Capernaum] Town where Jesus taught and performed miracles.

698.16–23 Susskind sat at meat . . . thrice] Following the events of the Last Supper, Matthew 26:21–23.

698.24 high priest Caiaphas] Jewish high priest appointed by the Romans to try Jesus.

698.29 Mount of Olives] Where Jesus preached, stood when he wept over Jerusalem, and returned on the night of his betrayal (Matthew 26:30).

698.33 kisseth him full on the lips] As Judas did to Jesus, identifying him to the soldiers who would arrest him, in Matthew 26:48–50.

699.1–2 a crown . . . and spitteth] See Matthew 27:29–30.

699.20 *Je vous emmerde*] French: Screw you.

699.27 Staircase ascending a nude] Play on the title of *Nude Descending a Staircase, No. 2* (1912), painting by French artist Marcel Duchamp (1887–1968).

699.27 Buggers of Calais] Play on the title of *The Burghers of Calais* (1888), monumental sculpture group by French sculptor Auguste Rodin (1840–1917) depicting the six men who offered themselves up for execution if the English would lift their siege of Calais during the Hundred Years' War.

699.29–30 Rembrandt . . . Malraux] From *The Voices of Silence* (1951) by French novelist and cultural critic André Malraux (1901–1976).

699.30–31 I is another. Rimbaud] From two letters of French poet Arthur Rimbaud (1854–1891): to Georges Izambard, May 13, 1871, and to Paul Demeny, May 15, 1871.

700.29–30 effect of the head of Medusa] In Greek mythology, Medusa was a Gorgon who would turn to stone anyone who looked at her directly.

700.37–38 Lives of the Painters] Collection of artists' biographies by Italian painter Giorgio Vasari (1511–1574) published in 1550.

700.40 Incisore] Italian: engraver.

700.40 The cylinder . . . Cézanne] See the letter (April 15, 1904) of French artist Paul Cézanne to Émile Bernard: "Treat nature by the cylinder, the sphere, the cone, everything in perspective!"

700.40–701.3 The impact . . . Kandinsky] From *Cahiers d'Art* 6 (1931) by Russian artist Wassily Kandinsky (1866–1944), referring to Michelangelo's depiction of God's creation of Adam in the Sistine Chapel.

703.25 Praxiteles . . . Aphrodite naked] See note 637.6.

703.25–26 Phidias, whose centaur] Greek sculptor, painter, and architect (490–430 B.C.E.) who sculpted a centaur for the Parthenon.

704.28–31 The ugly and plebeian face . . . Rosenberg] Characterization of Rembrandt by the Florentine writer Filippo Baldinucci (1624–1697), quoted in *Rembrandt* (1948) by German-born art historian Jakob Rosenberg (1893–1980).

705.19 San Michele] Cemetery island in the Venetian lagoon.

706.4–5 Stones of Venice] Reference to three-volume study (1851–53) of Venetian art and architecture by English art critic John Ruskin (1819–1900).

706.7 Tintoretto] Venetian artist Jacopo Tintoretto (1518–1594).

708.26 Canaletto] Italian artist (1697–1768) who specialized in landscapes of Venice.

708.32 Othello singing Verdi] The Italian composer Giuseppe Verdi (1813–1901) made an opera out of Shakespeare's play in 1897.

708.34 Doge] Title of the chief magistrate and leader of the Venetian Republic from the seventh to the eighteenth centuries.

708.37–38 Crusader . . . Saladin] The military victories in the Middle East of Saladin (c. 1138–1193), first sultan of Egypt and Syria, led to the launching of the Third Crusade, 1189–92.

708.39 Bellini] Venetian painter Giovanni Bellini (1430–1516).

708.39 carissimi] Italian: dear.

712.21–22 Cavaradossi singing . . . confonde] In *Tosca* (1900), opera by Italian composer Giacomo Puccini (1858–1924), the painter Mario Cavaradossi sings an aria, "Recondita Armonia" ("Strange Harmony"), that compares the portrait of the blonde Mary Magdalene he is painting with his dark-haired beloved Tosca: "Art with its many mysteries, blends all together such different beauties."

715.37–38 Barney Newman] Barnett Newman (1905–1970), American abstract painter.

716.36 Rothko] Mark Rothko (1903–1970), Russian-born American abstract artist.

723.7 objets trouvés] French: found objects.

723.9 Argus eyes] In Greek mythology, Argus is an all-seeing giant watchman with one hundred eyes.

723.11 Op Art] Style of art that employs visual illusions, which came to prominence in the 1960s.

TEN STORIES

731.9 Gut yuntif] Yiddish greeting, literally "Good (religious) holiday."

737.5 "Sein Tochter's Geliebter"] Yiddish: "His Daughter's Beloved."

737.13–15 "Greener Felder," . . . "Yoshe Kalb."] Plays: *Green Fields* (1916), love story by Yiddish dramatist and novelist Peretz Hirschbein (1880–1948); *Ghosts* (1882) by Norwegian playwright Henrik Ibsen (1828–1906); *The Dybbuk* by Russian Jewish playwright S. Ansky (pseudonym of Shloyme-Zanvl

Rappoport, 1863–1920), first performed posthumously in 1920; *The Cherry Orchard* (1904) by Chekhov; *Naches fon Kinder* ("Happiness from Children"); *Gott fon Nachoma* (1910), translated as *The God of Vengeance*, by Polish-born American writer Sholem Asch (1880–1957); *Yoshe Kalb* (1933), stage adaptation of novel (1932) by Polish-born American novelist I. J. Singer (1893–1944).

738.27–40 Shakespeare . . . imagination.] Feuer cites his roles as "Shylock, the Jew," "Hamlet, the Yeshiva Boy," and "King Lear and his Daughters," then quotes *King Lear* (1603–6), IV.vi.124–31.

740.9 United Jewish Appeal] Jewish philanthropic organization founded in 1939 to raise funds to aid Jews in Europe and Palestine.

740.20–21 catharsis through pity and terror] Central concept in Aristotle's theory of tragedy in his *Poetics* (c. 335 B.C.E.).

740.28 Leid macht auch lachen] Yiddish saying: Sorrow also makes for laughter.

743.16 Maurice Schwartz] Prominent Russian-born actor (1889–1960) and founder of the Yiddish Art Theatre in 1918.

747.32–33 Thomashefsky, Jacob Adler] Boris Thomashefsky (1866–1939), actor, director, and producer, who founded the National Theater in New York in 1912; Jacob Adler (1853–1926), perhaps best known for his leading role in Jacob Gordin's *The Yiddish King Lear* (1892) and as Shylock in Yiddish version of *The Merchant of Venice.*

754.23 dybbuk] Malicious spirit of the dead who takes possession of a living person.

757.20 shicker] Yiddish: drunkard.

758.22 Grubber yung] Yiddish: uncouth young man.

764.32 Lascia o Raddoppia] "Lascia o raddoppia?" ("Leave It or Double It?"), Italian quiz show, 1955–59, derived from the American program *The $64,000 Question.*

774.2–3 days before La Guardia] Fiorello La Guardia (1882–1947), progressive Republican mayor of New York, 1934–45.

774.21–22 Nick Carter and Merriwell books] Dime-novel detective Nick Carter first appeared in *The Old Detective's Pupil* (1886) and was then featured in his own magazine, *Nick Carter Weekly*; many of his adventures were first-person narratives published under the pseudonym Nick Carter. Frank Merriwell was a fictional schoolboy sports star created by Burt L. Standish (pseudonym of Gilbert Patten, 1866–1945), featured in more than two hundred books.

781.28 *Acht Uhr Abendblatt*] Berlin newspaper ("The Eight P.M. Evening Paper").

782.23 Kristallnacht] Nazi pogrom of November 9–10, 1938, "Crystal

Night," so called for the broken glass of Jewish-owned shops, in which ninety-one German Jews were killed.

783.24–25 Ich weiss nicht . . . soll.] German: I don't know what more I should do.

786.40–787.1 *Life on the Mississipi*] Memoir (1883) by Mark Twain (pseudonym of Samuel Clemens, 1835–1910).

788.12–13 Ich bin . . . gewesen.] German: I have been faithful to you for twenty-seven years.

790.3 after the Soviet-Nazi non-aggression pact was signed] In Moscow on August 23, 1939.

790.34 *Leaves of Grass*] Collection of poems by the American poet Walt Whitman (1819–1892), first published in 1855 and expanded throughout Whitman's lifetime.

792.25–28 *And I know . . . love*] From Whitman, "Song of Myself," sec. 5, in *Leaves of Grass*. Whitman's poem reads "a kelson" rather than "the kelson."

793.18 Brown Shirts] The Sturmabteilung (SA), a Nazi paramilitary organization whose members were often called "brown shirts" because of the color of their uniforms.

808.10 hailed myself?] The version of "Man in the Drawer" from *The Stories of Bernard Malamud* (1983), which is the text printed here, contains among its revisions to the story as it appeared in *Rembrandt's Hat* (1973) two uncharacteristically long deleted passages. The text of the story in *Rembrandt's Hat* contains the following paragraphs after ". . . hailed myself?":

> He had picked me up in his noisy Volga of ancient vintage on the Lenin Hills, where I had been wandering all afternoon in and around Moscow University. Finally I'd had enough of sightseeing, and when I saw the cab, hallooed and waved both arms. The driver, cruising in a hurry, had stopped, you might say, on a kopek, as though I were someone he was dying to give a ride to; maybe somebody he had mistaken for a friend. Considering my recent experiences in Kiev, a friend was someone I wouldn't mind being mistaken for.
>
> From the moment we met, our eyes were caught in a developing recognition although we were complete strangers. I knew nobody in Moscow except an Intourist girl or two. In the mottled mirror his face seemed mildly distorted—badly reflected; but not the eyes, small, canny, curious—they probed, tugged, doubted, seemed to beg to know: give him a word and he'd be grateful, though why and for what cause he didn't say. Then, as if the whole thing wearied him insufferably, he pretended no further interest.
>
> Serves him right, I thought, but it wouldn't hurt if he paid a little attention to the road now and then or we'll never get where we're going, wherever that is. I realized I hadn't said because I wasn't sure

myself—anywhere but back to the Metropole just yet. It was one of those days I couldn't stand a hotel room.

"Shalom!" he said finally out loud.

"Shalom to you." So it was what I had heard, who would have thought so? We both relaxed, looking at opposite sides of the street.

810.14–15 Chekhov Museum] Chekhov's house in Moscow was turned into a museum in 1954.

814.7 Gospodin] Respectful form of address, equivalent to "Mister."

814.12 Yasnaya Polyana] Rural estate of Leo Tolstoy.

816.13 Pasternak called this 'splendid surgery.'] Said of the Bolshevik revolution by the eponymous protagonist of *Doctor Zhivago* (1957), novel by Russian novelist and poet Boris Pasternak (1890–1960).

816.14–16 Evgeny Zamyatin . . . a new life.] From "On Literature, Revolution, Entropy, and Other Matters" (1923) by Russian writer Evgeny Zamyatin (1884–1937), best known as the author of the dystopian novel *We* (1920–21).

817.10–11 Isaac Babel . . . genre of silence.] Remark made at the First Congress of Soviet Writers in 1934 by Russian Jewish short story writer Isaac Babel (1894–1940), an ironic defense of his modest output at the time.

818.9–10 It was the best . . . times] The opening words of Charles Dickens's novel *A Tale of Two Cities* (1859).

823.8 Mayakovsky] Vladimir Mayakovsky (1893–1930), Russian poet, playwright, and actor.

823.36–38 Marina Tsvetayeva . . . end of her life] Russian poet, playwright, and essayist (1892–1941) who lived in exile, 1922–39, mostly in Paris; after her return to the Soviet Union her husband was executed and her daughter Alya imprisoned. Evacuated to a small town outside Moscow during the Nazi invasion, she was suspected of being a spy and otherwise harassed. Unable to support herself or her teenaged son, she committed suicide by hanging on August 31, 1941.

823.39–824.4 Osip Mandelstam . . . gone with so many others.] Russian Jewish poet Osip Mandelstam (1891–1938) was sentenced to five years' forced labor for counterrevolutionary activity in 1938. He died in the Vtoraya Rechka transit camp near Vladivostok while en route to the Kolyma labor camps in northeastern Siberia.

826.14 Gorky] Maxim Gorky (1868–1936), Russian writer and playwright.

826.30 Mondadori or Einaudi] Distinguished Italian publishing houses.

829.25 Dostoevsky Museum] Conversion of the apartment in Moscow where Dostoevsky lived until he was sixteen.

832.34–35 Pushkin . . . Solzhenitsyn] Alexander Pushkin (1799–1837),

Russian Romantic poet; Alexander Solzhenitsyn (1918–2008), Russian novelist and dissident.

836.4 Bolshoi] Moscow's Bolshoi Theatre for opera and ballet.

840.22 Levitansky's first story] The text of "Man in the Drawer" in *Rembrandt's Hat* contains a different first story (the "story about the old father coming to see his son who ducks out on him" mentioned at 823.4–5), omitted from the version in *The Stories of Bernard Malamud*:

> Levitansky's first story of the four in English was about an old father, a pensioner, who was not feeling well and wanted his son, with whom he had had continuous strong disagreements, and whom he hadn't seen in eight months, to know. He decided to pay him a short visit. Since the son had moved from his flat to a larger one and had not forwarded his address, the father went to call on him at work. The son was an official of some sort with an office in a new State building. The father had never been there although he knew where it was because a neighbor on a walk with him had pointed it out.
>
> The pensioner sat in a chair in his son's large outer office, waiting for him to be free for a few minutes. "Yuri," he thought he would say, "all I want to tell you is that I'm not up to my usual self. My breath is short and I have pains in my chest. In fact, I'm not well. After all, we're father and son and you ought to know the state of my health, seeing it's not so good and your mother is dead."
>
> The son's assistant secretary, a modern girl in a short tight skirt, said he was attending an important administrative conference.
>
> "A conference is a conference," the father said. He wouldn't want to interfere with it and didn't mind waiting although he was still having nauseating twinges of pain.
>
> The father waited patiently in the chair for several hours; and though he had a few times risen and urgently spoken to the assistant secretary, he was, by the end of the day, still unable to see his son. The girl, putting on her pink hat, advised the old man that the official had already left the building. He hadn't been able to see his father because he had unexpectedly been called away on an important State matter.
>
> "Go home and he will telephone you in the morning."
>
> "I have no telephone," said the old pensioner impatiently. "He knows that."
>
> The assistant secretary; the private secretary, an older woman from the inside office; and later the caretaker of the building, all tried to persuade the father to go home, but he wouldn't leave.
>
> The private secretary said her husband was expecting her and she could stay no longer. After a while the assistant secretary with the pink hat also left. The caretaker, a man with wet eyes and a ragged mustache, tried to persuade the old man to leave. "What sort of foolishness is it to wait all night in a pitch-dark building? You'll frighten

yourself out of your wits, not to speak of other discomforts you're bound to suffer."

"No," said the sick father, "I will wait. When my son comes in tomorrow morning I'll tell him something he hasn't learned yet. I'll tell him what he does to me his children will do to him."

The caretaker departed. The old man was left alone waiting for his son to appear in the morning.

"I'll report him to the Party," he muttered.

841.22 Lubyanka] The headquarters in Moscow of Soviet state security, 1918–91, with an adjoining prison.

842.33 Tallith] Prayer shawl for Jewish males.

843.15 komsomol] Soviet Communist Party youth organization.

843.32 mitzvah] Hebrew: a moral deed, an act of kindness, here a favor.

844.9 kaddish] Jewish prayer of mourning.

846.3 *Oktyabr*] Soviet Yiddish newspaper ("October") published in Minsk.

846.21 *Novy Mir* or *Yunost*] Russian literary magazines ("New World" and "Youth").

856.31 Ochi Chernye] "Dark Eyes," Russian song (1884) with lyrics (1843) by Ukrainian poet Yevhen Hrebinka (1812–1848).

860.13 stepped into a Sherwood Anderson story] American novelist and short story writer Sherwood Anderson (1876–1941), author of *Winesburg, Ohio* (1919), with its tales of lonely aspiration.

867.39 the MacDowell Colony] Artists' colony in Peterborough, New Hampshire.

This book is set in 10 point ITC Galliard Pro, a face designed for digital composition by Matthew Carter and based on the sixteenth-century face Granjon. The paper is acid-free lightweight opaque and meets the requirements for permanence of the American National Standards Institute. The binding material is Brillianta, a woven rayon cloth made by Van Heek–Scholco Textielfabrieken, Holland. Composition by Dedicated Book Services. Printing and binding by Edwards Brothers Malloy, Ann Arbor. Designed by Bruce Campbell.